SWEET ROMANCE

SWEET ROMANCE

AN ANTHOLOGY

ELANA JOHNSON   MERRI MAYWETHER

LILY ALEXANDER   ELLE BOTZ   MAGGIE DALLEN

E.J. DEAN   MEREDITH DEICHLER

FRIEDA J DOWNING   LAUREN ELIZABETH

KRISTEN ETHRIDGE   KERRY EVELYN

PENELOPE FREED   K. A. GANDY

JENNA HENDRICKS   CHELLE HONIKER

DANIELLE KEIL   LYZ KELLEY

RANDILEIGH KENNEDY   D.E. MALONE

JO NOELLE   LYNETTE PAUL   RACHEL RADNER

RONNIE ROBERTS   KARI SHUEY

CARINA TAYLOR   CALLIE TIMMINS

CRAIG MARTELLE, INC

Craig Martelle, Inc

PO Box 10235

Fairbanks, AK 99710

First Edition, December 2020

ISBN (Print) 978-1-953062-06-2

❀ Created with Vellum

~

Curators

Lasairiona McMaster
Erika Everest
Merri Maywether
Jenna Hendricks

~

Beta Readers

Alice Briggs
Tamara Carr
Glenda Hislop
Paula Hurdle
AM Scott
Fleur Wilkinson

~

CONTENTS

FOREWORD

CRAIG MARTELLE

The foundation of love is found in sweet romance, when the greatest joy is in two on the journey to become one.

I include romance in all my books because I think a good romance is critical to all great tales. My stories aren't in that genre, but I have been blessed by getting to learn a great number of compelling authors who do.

I want to thank the curation team of Lasairiona McMaster, Erika Everest, Merri Maywether, and Jenna Hendricks for their work in bringing this anthology to fruition. It takes a love of the genre and desire to help their fellow authors. What you see in this volume of Sweet Romance are the stories that passed over a number of hurdles and crawled through broken glass to get to the end. It wasn't an easy process, but isn't love worth it?

That's what these stories are about, taking a chance when an opportunity arises, oftimes when you least expect it, and working to make the best of it.

When reality and tales mesh. Sweet Romance. The rose petals are softest when stroked away from the thorns. Take care and feel the love.

The authors included in this volume spin their tales to make you cry in joy, feel what needs to be felt, cheer for the happy couple when all is said and done.

What more is there to say? You didn't pick this book up to listen to me pontificate. You got it to read new and original material from Elana, Merri, and more. So many more. Get a glass of wine and get comfortable. Let the stories take you away.

This is a 20Booksto50k® initiative on behalf of all our members as we teach the business of being a professional author, because we believe a rising tide lifts all boats.

Peace, fellow humans.

Craig Martelle

December 2020

HAPPY BIRTHDAY, VICTOR SANDBERG

MERRI MAYWETHER

It's Victor's birthday. Two things happen at the exact same moment. Mayra buries the lifelong crush she has had on Victor. Victor decides only one present matters—Mayra's heart.

1

———

*I*f Mayra Redman ever saw Victor Sandberg again, it would be too soon. She didn't care about his gorgeous eyes; the ones that peered into her soul when their gaze met. He followed it with an awkward smile. The one that started with a curve on his lips' left side and crawled like a ladybug on a summer day to reveal a sweet expression that said, "You know I'll make it up to you one day." Mayra swooned briefly. She didn't care about that either. There was no way Victor could dig himself out of this ditch. She was done with him.

Her hickory brown eyes that usually held the spark of laughter burned, threatening to release tears. Through a jaw tightened in frustration, Mayra grumbled. "I will not talk to you ever again, Victor Sandberg." She added her best death glare for emphasis because she was not being melodramatic. She was d-o-n-e, done.

To preserve some of her dignity, she pulled at the bottom of her favorite white blouse soaked with the cherry cola that Victor spilled down the front of it. The cherry cola she had made for his birthday party. The same cherry cola that she had invested days of her life making so his day would be special.

Bacchus had wine. Venus had an apple. Mayra had cherries she picked with her own hands and made into a syrup in an act of adoration for Victor. When she pitted the cherries, she imagined this would be the recipe that caught Victor's attention. Of course, he'd take one sip and declare his appreciation of Mayra. After all, who else would take extraordinary measures to make him happy?

As she stood in her mother's kitchen stirring the pot, Mayra felt the burning in her chest. A still small voice within her said *this year would be different*. Victor would come to his senses and see what Mayra had known since they were seven. Victor and Mayra were destined to be together.

In light of the new circumstance, Mayra suspected the steam from the syrup had made her delusional.

The signs pointed toward their history repeating itself. Mayra had tried to do something to impress Victor, and he had used it as material to antagonize her. This time he approached her with a red solo cup full of the soda in his hand. "This is pure sugar," he taunted. "What are you trying to do? Give a man diabetes?" A brief sting from the cold drink sliding down her chest ended the conversation.

Victor had had the decency to lose his smile.

Mayra hadn't caught the full expression because of the burning sensation on her chest. She peeked inside her shirt and pulled out the ice cube that was lodged in her bra cup.

With the sugar from the cherry syrup crystallizing on her chest by the seconds, Mayra glanced down to assess the damage. The reddish-brown splat extended from chin to waist. Her favorite shirt was probably ruined, and all of Ashbrook could see the silhouette of her lace padded bra.

Mayra gasped her dismay, pursed her lips, and began the march to her pickup. It was a long one, too. Her course took her through the picnic tables she decorated with blue gingham tablecloths. Then she walked through the maze of multi-colored, fabric chairs that waited for people with burgers to relax. She resisted the urge to kick Victor's chair with the Sandberg Farm emblem on the back. Just in case it was his sister's chair. There was no point in being rude to an innocent bystander.

With every landmark she passed, up to the fallen logs used to separate the parking lot from the picnic area, Mayra hoped to the good Lord, she had the foresight to pack another shirt in her duffle bag. If he were especially merciful, it would coordinate with her red Converse All-Stars and red bandana she folded into a headband.

The laughter had left Victor's eyes and been replaced with concern. He walked backward while trying to stay one step ahead of Mayra. "Where are you going?"

"I'm not speaking to you," Mayra grumbled. Half of her hoped he would fall over backward so he could share in her embarrassment. If it happened in a mud puddle, it would be that much better. The logical side of her knew better than to ask the cosmos for anything like that. It would work against her because then she'd feel bad for Victor and fall into the dance they'd been in for years—the one where Victor did something stupid, and with the help of friends or family, earned his way back into Mayra's good graces.

Earlier in the day, Mayra prayed for a sign. She did it looking for one that proved they belonged together. Sadness touched the tip of her anger. The signs were there. Even if they weren't the ones she wanted.

John Mayfield hurried to Mayra's side. He handed his red Ashbrook Eagles microfiber towel to Mayra and defended her honor.

He yelled, "Give it a rest, man." It was a half-hearted defense, but it was more than Victor had ever done for her.

John's kindness soothed Mayra's bruised ego, but not enough for her to forgive Victor. She had waited for twenty-five years of her life for Victor to get a clue. Her mother said love would come when Mayra least expected it.

The odds of Victor fulfilling years of unrequited love were leaning toward it not happening. Ever.

Mayra glared at Victor as she dabbed at her shirt to clean the mess.

John had gone out of his way to try to help her; the least she could do was show him, and Victor, she appreciated the effort. With each tap, the truth rushed to the front of Mayra's mind, bringing with it the burning urge to cry. No, she would not give Victor Sandberg the dignity of seeing he could bring her to tears. John had been kinder to her in five minutes than Victor had been in their entire life. She was sure her anger had exaggerated the statistics, but not by that much.

What was it about Victor that had her heart atwitter for all those years? Sure, he was cute, but a bevy of attractive men lived in Ashbrook.

John interrupted the stream of thoughts that were getting her nowhere. "I liked the soda."

Mayra offered John a wilted smile to show her appreciation for his efforts, for the compliment, and for his chivalry. "This is a lost cause. It's probably best if I went home."

John was a nice enough guy. His sweet, intense brown eyes seemed to always ask for approval. He looked like he could knock down a building with one shoulder shove. Yet, everyone knew by the kind tone in John's voice that he couldn't hurt a fly.

"We haven't eaten yet," John rushed his words. "You're not going to let one mishap ruin your fun? Are you?"

The man was kind but blind. Mayra wrinkled her brow as she started to wonder. Maybe when men reached a certain level of attractiveness, they lost their sense of what made a woman happy?

Mayra was one breath away from committing to her conclusion when John added, "How about this? I have an extra shirt you can borrow."

"That's sweet, but I couldn't inconvenience you like that." The party wasn't fun anymore. Besides, the quicker Mayra created distance between herself and Victor, the easier it would be for her to lay her foolish crush to rest.

"Let's look at it a different way. This is an opportunity. They just started making root beer at the Yard House. I could take you there on a date, and you could compare their mix with yours." His clenched jaw said he expected rejection, but he had to ask, anyway.

"I don't know what to say." Mayra flushed. The Yard House was the safe first date eatery in town. People started at one table. Invariably, they migrated from table to table to catch up on the local gossip. Mayra and John being there together would add to the talk, but they'd never be left alone long enough for things to get too awkward.

John tipped on the back of his heels and steadied himself while regarding Mayra with a cautious expression. "This is the part where you say, thank you, and noon tomorrow would be perfect."

The heat rose in Mayra's cheeks. She had spent her life wishing Victor would see something special in her. It never occurred to Mayra that someone else might want her companionship. "I guess it's a date."

John grinned and bounced on his toes. "Let's get you that shirt." His extended elbow welcomed Mayra to walk alongside him. She slipped her hand in the crook. When they touched, it felt more like she was walking with her favorite uncle than a beau, but that didn't matter. They enjoyed each other's company, and it was more interest than Victor had shown her.

"I'm going to interrupt for a minute." Victor tapped on Mayra's arm and pushed between John and her until he was positioned in the middle of them. Then he wrapped his arms around both of their shoulders like they were buddies walking after a game. "I don't mean to put a damper on your fun."

"Then go away. I'm not talking to you anyway," Mayra squirmed to escape Victor's hold, but the weight of his presence pulled her into his side where she found she fit perfectly. Like John's touch, it expressed that he wanted her companionship. If she hadn't known it was Victor holding her, Mayra would have interpreted the gesture as territorial.

"This is my birthday party." Victor's gaze alternated between Mayra and John. His reminder was quickly followed with, "Mayra, hear me out. We've been friends long enough to know you won't stay angry with me."

He turned to face John. "This is how things work themselves out between Mayra and me. I do something stupid. Like try to compliment Mayra, but say it wrong. Then she gets angry with me." He gestured with his head, "Like she is now. Then we have some time apart. She cools down, and I figure out a way to atone for my mistake and return to her good graces."

Victor's cousin Eric joined, making the cozy group of three into an awkward quad. "We're in the middle of the seventh inning." He pointed at Victor and John. "You two need to come back to the game."

Eric and Victor were cousins but looked and behaved more like twins. Both bore the typical Sandberg frames: lean waist, sturdy shoulders, and eyes that were so captivating people stared the first time they saw Victor and Eric together. They also possessed the gift of communicating with each other without saying a word.

Mayra stopped short, jarring the motion of the group. The part of her that had grown up with Victor and Eric knew what was coming. She wanted to stamp her foot at them. She settled for crossing her arms in front of her chest. The feeling of stickiness against her shirt added to her resolve. "Can you please go away?"

When their eyes connected, and both nodded subtly, Mayra's heart dropped to somewhere below her knees. Her request to have some time with John to explore the possibilities of a future would be denied.

Eric's voice was patronizingly agreeable when he said, "Yes, Victor, it is your birthday. But we need to be considerate. After all, Mayra organized this shindig." He looked at John when he said, "Because we've known each other since before any of us could walk." His attention returned to Victor. "Mayra deserves to have some fun too."

Victor nodded to say he agreed with Eric's conclusion. He brightened like a light bulb and spoke to John. "We're not doing anything at noon tomorrow."

It was a lie. A whopper, too. Mayra's father told her that he was going to the Sandberg farm to help them maintain their equipment. She took in a large gulp of air. Fearing she'd say something to fuel the Sandberg cousins' antagonism, Mayra held the rebuttal in her throat.

John's face wrinkled at the odd turn of events. Mayra searched the area for reinforcements. Her best friends, Amanda and Gina, were never too far away. They'd have a solution to her dilemma.

She was not disappointed. Gina's wavy hair caught the wind, making it easier for Mayra to find her weaving between the pickups parked on the edge of the park. When Gina was a short distance away from Mayra and the men, she held a t-shirt and baby wipes in her hand. Gina and Mayra had many chats over the years about the Sandberg cousins. While Gina agreed they were handsome, she held the opinion that Eric and Victor were best appreciated at arm's length.

Her approach seemed to work. Gina was Eric's kryptonite. All Gina had to do was look at Eric.

Within seconds it was like a thundercloud had formed over Eric's head, and he gestured with his thumb toward the game and jogged away.

"Gina!" Victor called out his greeting like she was a long-lost friend who returned from a journey.

Gina froze in place. Her face begged to be released from the mess she knew she couldn't avoid.

Victor sidestepped away from the conversation, pulling John by the arm to follow him. "We're all going out for root beer tomorrow. You in?"

A stream of fireworks erupted in Mayra's mind. With it, she lost the words to respond. Victor pulled a "toll fee" on her. The toll fee stemmed from a variation of the London Bridge game they played in elementary school. Instead of getting locked in and rocked, a captured person could pay a toll to break free. The toll was doing whatever the kids who played the part of the bridge arms requested as payment. Usually, it was simple stuff. Let a person cut in line or run around the playground. In this instance, Victor had locked in Mayra, who would be given the freedom of a date with John Mayfield. That was if John and Mayra paid the toll of changing their excursion to a group outing.

Mayra's insides burned. Victor didn't want to have anything to do with Mayra, but he wouldn't let anyone else close to her too. Why had life chosen her to bear the burden of Victor Sanberg's shenanigans?

The guys returned to their game. Mayra escaped to her pickup to change into the shirt Gina loaned her. In the silence, she took a few breaths telling herself, "This too shall pass." How had yet to be seen, but it had to happen. A man only had so much tenacity. Victor had to have reached the end of his.

2

In theory, wearing Gina's t-shirt seemed like a good idea. Mayra's well-endowed chest strained against the confines of the fabric, stretching the image of the state of Montana.

Mayra resigned herself to the outcome. She'd simply tell her friends the day was a lost cause. It was better if she begged forgiveness for leaving them with the cleanup and went home. Except, Gina wasn't waiting alone for her at the tailgate of the pickup. None other than Mr. Ruin Mayra's day was there with her. His eyes bugged out, and Gina slapped him on the arm.

"I'm going home." Mayra spun around and headed back toward her vehicle.

"Wait, I have a shirt. You can wear it." Victor didn't give Mayra time to deny his offer. He jogged to his pickup, which was parked two spaces away from hers. "I always keep an extra. You never know when you're going to have to stop and help someone fix a flat." He pulled it out and waved it in the air like it was a victory flag.

Everyone knew "the someone" was his sister Kate. She'd been widowed young, and Victor stepped in to help her whenever he could.

"It's okay." The events of the day had defeated Mayra.

"I may not always be right. But when I am, I stick to it. What I said about us earlier is the Lord's honest truth. For as long as we've known each other, I've always tried to right my wrongs." Victor held the shirt out for Mayra to step into. "If I hadn't tripped, you wouldn't be in this mess in the first place."

Except, there was a time Victor hadn't righted a wrong between them. Shortly after he had returned to Ashbrook from college, Victor and Mayra had a discussion that became the harbinger of the rest of their adult life. They were at Mayra's annual star gazing party. All the friends had piled into pickups and parked at the edge of her father's land in a circle. The headlights faced outward, and the tailgates held thermoses full of spiked cocoa and baked goods. The people who had cleaner pickup beds loaded them with blankets for everyone to sit comfortably. Victor and Mayra had sat together in the back of his pickup. He asked her about inviting a girl to the barn dance. Mayra remembered thinking to herself, *Oh my, this is really happening.*

His voice had a sweet boyishness when he asked, "If I were to ask a woman out on a date, what kind of flowers should I give her?"

"Both of us know you can be irresistible when you want something. Just ask her." Mayra squeezed her arms against her body to prepare herself for the invitation.

"I will." Victor leaned his head against the pickup. Mayra observed the outline of his face. She wondered if the brim of his hat inclined toward the sky affected his view of the cosmos. Victor pointed toward something in the distance. "There's a meteor."

The request to go to the dance never materialized, and Mayra's enthusiasm leaked into the chilly evening air. Still the optimist, she silently reasoned why Victor hadn't ask her to the dance. Maybe he thought he was right and would approach her with flowers.

Little by little, people populated the back of Victor's pickup. It was the newest and largest, so it was bound to happen.

Weeks later, Mayra heard through the grapevine that Victor had invited a woman from Great Falls to the dance. Mayra wound up going with Gina and Amanda and hanging out with friends from Amanda's job.

Shortly after that, Victor started blowing it a lot with Mayra. He was curt with her or avoided her. Secretly she wondered if it was because she gave him bad advice. Time passed, and they fell into the rhythm of a quirky friendship.

Mayra was prepared to lie to Victor. To say his attempt at atonement had absolved him from hurting her feelings. To say she was tired. She didn't want to be in love with him anymore.

Victor's jaw tightened, and his right eyebrow stiffened into a straight line. "You were going to wear John's shirt. Why won't you wear mine?" His eyes dared Mayra to deny him.

This was a new look for Victor. Mayra shuddered at the thought of going against him. While they had bickered over the years, she had never outright challenged Victor. The expression on his face said it wasn't the right time to try. Mayra hated herself for bending, but what else could she do? "If you insist. Thank you."

"I insist." He slid the sleeve up her right arm and then halfway up the left. Mayra caught herself relishing in the combination of fabric softener and Victor's subtle scent. Her heart trembled, and Mayra's body warmed from the vulnerability that struck her.

When the shirt was on Mayra's shoulders, Victor stepped away to give her room to button it. His tender smile offered assurance that she was safe from further antagonism. His eyes expressed a hope that he had earned Mayra's forgiveness.

Mayra couldn't help it. The butterflies in her stomach danced. Of course, she'd forgive Victor. His earlier assessment of the dance of offense and forgiveness was their truth.

She also noticed that his voice had softened when he said, "I can get it back from you tomorrow." A quick nod affirmed his statement, and he backed away to return to the game.

The absence of Victor's presence cleared Mayra's head. She watched after him, murmuring, "What was that about?"

"I believe your date with John was Victor's wake-up call." Gina's hazel eyes glinted with amusement.

Mayra's first thought was that Gina was a beautiful soul, and she was glad to be her friend. When Mayra gave up, Gina fanned the embers of Mayra's secret wish. But Mayra had been burned too many times to dare to hope for the possibility of her friend's suggestion. "I don't know what to think anymore."

Their canvas shoes crunched on the wood chipped pathway back to the picnic grounds. "What if the syrup settled and his cup had a higher syrup to soda ratio than the rest of us." Lord love Gina. Her persistence picked up where Mayra's patience lagged.

Gina's suggestion wasn't that too far-fetched. That and Mayra needed a cool drink. It wouldn't hurt to test what remained. When they reached the table, they found the three-gallon drink dispenser was empty. There wasn't a drop of the homemade soda to be found, yet the ice chests were full of the canned soda they purchased from the store.

"What happened to the cherry cola?" Mayra called out to her friend Amanda, who was at the grill flipping the burgers.

A burger sizzled, and Amanda stepped away from the stream of smoke that plumed over the grill. She rubbed at her eyes with the back of her hand. "Talk to Victor. He probably drank one gallon by himself. If he isn't careful about that sweet tooth, he's going to get diabetes. I told him as much." The sizzle of a burger that fell into the flames pulled Amanda's attention away from the conversation.

"Can I say I told you so, now, or do I have to wait until after you mail out the wedding invitations?" Gina's smirk held the enthusiasm of a friend who knew a secret.

"But he." Mayra was at a loss.

Gina finished Mayra's sentence, "Acts like he doesn't care. When he gives you attention, he's a nuisance."

"Are we talking about Victor?" Amanda sprayed the fire with a squirt bottle. "Don't forget, sticks his foot in his mouth."

"You're the one who's been saying love happens when you least expect it. Maybe life opened Victor's eyes to the gift he had in front of him for his thirty-third birthday." Gina's cat that ate the canary grin pressed on Mayra's insistence that she get over Victor. It was too late. What was done was done. She made a promise to get over him. With time and space, it would happen. It had to happen for Mayra to preserve her sense of sanity.

When looking at the big picture, Mayra knew Victor was a good person. She saw it when he was with his family. Victor was a warm, kind man. She saw what kind of husband he would be when he stepped in and helped his widowed sister, Kate, raise her daughter.

Victor also defended what he loved fiercely. Mayra had seen it when some guys from a cutting crew tried to pick up on Kate for a fling. In the discomfort of her soda-stained shirt, Mayra took a good look and decided whoever married Victor would be a lucky woman. She sighed for what could have been and what would never be but felt a little better about the matter.

Hoots and hollers from the softball field pried through Mayra's sadness. "Oh, someone got a home run." She cupped her hand over her eyes to shield them from the sun to catch Victor circling around third base and heading for home. He stutter-stepped over the dusty-white diamond. When he stopped completely, his eyes flicked toward Mayra briefly. Like the other people around the picnic tables, she clapped before returning to set up the eating area.

Victor's teammates circled around him, and they celebrated his home run with high fives. His focus was back on the game. Mayra noticed the change in her reaction to Victor. She was happy for Victor because he was happy. But her heart lacked the desire to share the moment with him. That was when she knew her love for Victor Sandberg had changed.

3

Mayra decorated the tables with crafts inspired by her Pinterest board. She used burlap ribbon and spray paint to repurpose tin cans into cutlery and condiment containers. Mason jars filled with marbles and pretty rocks mixed between them were meant to be conversation starters. People disbursed the salads and desserts they contributed to the party on the tables, making it easier to go back for seconds. Then they arranged their lawn chairs in a circle where all of them could be together.

Mayra waited for people to choose chairs. When she saw the space beside John, she took it. Within minutes, Victor approached with a chair in one hand and his plate in the other. He positioned his chair next to Mayra. "I picked up an extra cookie. You can have it if you want it."

"I'm good, thank you." She showed him the slice of birthday cake on her plate.

Victor set his cookie on the side of his plate and said, "You know I'm going to make you change your mind." Then he took a bite of his burger.

John wiped his mouth with the back of his hand and muttered, "I need to make sure and tell Amanda these burgers are good." He leaned behind Mayra to talk to Victor, "She cooks almost as good as my mom."

Mayra silently bemoaned her fate. She had the luck of attracting Ashbrook's least likely to get married.

Victor leaned behind Mayra to talk to John. "You think these are good? Wait until you get a taste of Mayra's sliders. She uses–" He paused for a moment, then addressed Mayra. "What do you use on your sliders?"

"Worcestershire sauce." She forced a polite grin.

"Are you sure about that?" Victor eyed her suspiciously.

"Why would I be uncertain about what I use on my burgers?"

"Because you might be trying to trick me." Victor averted his attention to John. "You know, Mayra can be quite the joker."

It aggravated Mayra that Victor talked about her like they were best friends.

"Really?" John asked.

Knowing it was better to stay out of the conversation, Mayra chomped on a pickle. She found the sour taste suited her temperament.

"Nah, I'm joking," Victor answered. "I'm the prankster, and Mayra puts up with my shenanigans. She's done it for years. I hope she knows I appreciate how patient she has been with me over the years." He added, "If I didn't know any better, I'd say she was in love with me."

Mayra choked when he said it with the confidence that accompanied ignorance.

John patted Mayra on the back, and Victor eyed her suspiciously. When Mayra's throat cleared, she squeaked out, "My food went down the wrong pipe."

From that point forward, things just got worse. Mayra got into an argument with Victor over picking up the trash. When Mayra insisted it was her job to clean up and take care of things because it was his birthday, Victor mumbled loud enough for only Mayra to hear, "You'd think wearing my shirt would change her attitude."

She unbuttoned the top two buttons and said, "Well, take back your shirt."

"Put it back on. You don't want God and the world to see your goodies."

"Maybe, I do!" Mayra didn't, but she had it with Victor.

"You two need a time out," Eric barked.

"I'm going home. I hope you had a happy birthday, Victor." Mayra had reached the edge of the picnic area when she remembered she needed to bring home her jugs and dishes. She cast her eyes toward the sky and circled back.

Mayra was beyond humiliated and frustrated by Victor's antagonism. If that wasn't bad enough, thanks to Victor's innuendos, John had probably given up on her. Not that it mattered. Going out with John had lost its luster.

Mayra plastered on a grin that admitted the situation was beyond awkward and stacked the plastic bins on top of her red and white rolling ice chest. Victor's glare added to her discomfort.

Amanda and Gina came up alongside her. "We'll help you load the car."

By the time they reached Mayra's pickup, she was practically in tears. "This has been the worst day ever. I don't know what has got into Victor."

"I'll tell you," Amanda softly cajoled. "The man just realized you have goodies."

"And he doesn't want John anywhere near them," Gina said it like she was giving a biology lesson.

Mayra sniffled, "Well, I can share my goodies with whomever I please." Even though she had no intention of doing so.

"Mayra, we've grown up watching you pine for Victor. Why the change?" Amanda asked.

"You've always been there for Victor. Give him time to prove he'll be there for you," Gina suggested. "I bet you he will prove that you were right to be patient."

Victor jogged toward Mayra's pickup and stopped directly in front of her. "Before you go, I wanted to say thank you." He pulled her in for a hug. "I couldn't have had a better birthday."

Thanks to her friends' intervention on Victor's behalf, Mayra's indignation mellowed to confusion. She sputtered her disbelief in the compliment, "You said I tried to give you diabetes."

"Because I probably drank a gallon of the cherry cola." A flush of color ran through Victor's cheeks. Mayra got the impression that he figured out she was more upset about the poorly delivered compliment —not the soda spill. "I was going to tell you how much I drank. But that never happened because I tripped and—well, you know the rest of the story."

Mayra looked at the blue sky above them and then the trees around them. Everything seemed to be the same. Yet, when her gaze returned to Victor, she sensed things were different. The what or how had yet to be determined.

4

———————

John called Mayra to meet him earlier than the expected time. He explained the change saying, "I want to talk to you without an audience."

When Mayra walked through the doors, she noticed how anticipation within her matched the atmosphere of the warehouse-style eatery. One of the attendants wiped the plexiglass walls separating the bowling alley from the general eating area. Ping-pong paddles laid on the tables waiting for patrons to challenge each other. A couple of guys who had come home from college played the corn hole game lined on the outer wall. It seemed everyone was waiting for something to happen.

Her eyes finally fell on John, who sat in padded outdoor furniture with two glasses on the table beside him. When he saw Mayra, he rose to greet her. He looked handsome in his jeans that seemed to fit perfectly. His tucked in turquoise, plaid shirt pulled against the large silver belt buckle.

John's tentative smile softened Mayra's heart. It didn't pound in her chest the way it did when she saw Victor, but it had warmed when she saw him. The man she saw the day prior was dusty, sweaty, and wore loose-fitting basketball shorts with a sleeveless t-shirt. Mayra complimented the change. "You sure do clean up nice."

A flush ran through John's face, and his pursed lips tightened his face but failed at hiding the effect of Mayra's compliment. "Thank you."

"You look a lot better without soda on your clothes." Mayra laughed at his attempt at a joke, while her insides cringed. She had spent the morning curling the ends of her bobbed, brown hair. Trying a different approach toward men, she wore her favorite pastel pink, eyelet tank top so she'd look more feminine. Maybe if men saw the softer side of her, they'd treat her accordingly. Apparently, she had too lofty a goal.

John guided her to the table, and he handed Mayra one of the two drinks. "Thank you for coming here today." His voice sounded more like a business meeting than a quick get to know you before their friends arrived discussion.

Mayra sipped the homemade root beer. The deep, sweet taste was a little strong for her likes, but she appreciated the smooth texture of the beverage. "Thank you for buying my soda."

They sat in silence. Mayra could tell by the searching expression, John wanted to say something but didn't quite know how. She waited for him. He waited for her. Just as she was prepared to say something, John spoke. "I don't know what got into me yesterday."

"What do you mean?" Mayra was at a loss. It was Victor who was the pain. John had come to her rescue.

"I mean. I shouldn't have interfered with whatever it is you and Victor have going."

"There's nothing going on between Victor and me." Mayra's ability to dismiss her feelings for Victor brought her a more profound sense of clarity. For years she was like a puppy waiting for Victor to drop some cookie crumbles from the table. The soda fiasco was her writing on the wall. Mayra wanted more than crumbs. She wanted a full dose of a man's love. The kind of love where he'd go to any measure to show her she was valued. Not that she would ask, but it would feel good knowing that he would do it. Her tone was bittersweet. "Victor and I have been together for as long as I can remember." She quickly inserted, "as friends."

John's eyes said he'd listen, but he probably wouldn't believe her.

She recalled the aggravation from the birthday party and added, "Friends that need a break from each other."

"Look, Mayra, I think you're nice. But your—friend is more than I want to deal with." John gently set his root beer glass on the table.

Not only had Victor cast Mayra aside for years; he added insult to injury by taking an active role in ruining her future. She forced a smile to contain her disappointment. "I'm sorry you feel that way, but I understand."

Mayra tipped her root beer glass toward John. "Thank you for your honesty. I appreciate it."

John cast a tentative glance toward the door. "On that note, I think I'll head out before your friends arrive."

So there Mayra sat with two half glasses of root beer and her thoughts. She rehearsed the scene. When her friends arrived, they'd think she was stood up.

For years Mayra had pined after Victor. When she pinned her hopes on the glimmer of possibility, Victor threw her way; she was disappointed. John had done the same thing. He threw out a line. After he caught her, he threw her back in the water.

Mayra's heart hitched in her chest. What would her friends say? Would Victor return to his old ways? The humiliation was more than she wanted to bear. Mayra texted her friends to notify them that the date was canceled and gave them back the rest of their weekend.

5

____

The chain of events over the past two days boggled Mayra's mind. What could have happened to cause the disruption? There wasn't a full moon, nor solar flare, nor any other cosmic phenomenon to change the atmosphere around her.

On the dirt road, in the middle of farmland full of ripening barley, it clicked. It had to be the cherry syrup. Mayra wished it would bring her love, and John asked her out for the date. In the absence of the syrup, his affection waned.

With a resolute tone, Mayra looked at herself in the rear-view mirror. "The recipe goes in the burn barrel as soon as I go home." Her steering wheel pulled to the left as the back of her pickup wobbled. Mayra slowed and pulled to the side of the road.

Over the years, Mayra had seen her father's face turn red when he was thrown unexpected problems that would take time to resolve. Shortly after, his whitening hair would float away from his temples. Then came the warnings from her mother. The tender pleading. "Jack, your blood pressure." Her father's eyebrows rose and hid in the bill of his cap. He'd heave an exhalation, and his natural coloring slowly returned.

Mayra felt the heat and channeled her mother's patience. A flat tire was no big deal. She surveyed the area. Even the birds were quiet on the lazy summer day. It was obvious; nobody would drive by anytime soon. While she hadn't had to deal with a flat tire on her own, Mayra decided this was a manageable problem. Her father had taught her to change a tire as a teenager. This had to be a sign. The gradual incline out of her run on misfortune gave her hope.

She fit the tire wrench on the nut, flexed, and motioned to turn. Her muscles screamed in protest. Still, the nut didn't budge. Mayra added some weight to the motion but yielded the same result. "We can do this. Lefty loosey, righty tighty." Who we was, remained to be seen. Saying it smoothed the choking feeling of being alone.

Mayra wiped her brow. And tried again, and again.

Defeated, she did what any independent farm girl would do. She called her father.

He sympathized immediately. "Aw, honey. I fastened the nuts with an air compressor. There's no way you could get those off yourself." Her father's explanation bolstered Mayra's mood slightly. "Hold tight. Help will be there in fifteen minutes."

So Mayra sat on her bumper and waited. The breeze blowing through the barley gave off a sweetness. In spite of the circumstances, Mayra cherished the moment. In the quiet, the sense that everything would work out the way it was supposed to settled in Mayra's heart of hearts. Then she saw her life with clarity. Her love for Victor would never wane. Love wasn't easily killed. But it did change, and she felt the angst soften. One day, her feelings would be the material of stories Mayra would tell her granddaughters when they thought they were in love.

Some movement off in the distance caught Mayra's attention. She tilted her head for a closer inspection, to discover her problems were about to compound. A skunk waddled her way with the confidence of a woman on her way to a Sunday picnic.

Something broke in Mayra. Embodying the fierceness of a Baptist preacher at a tent revival, she bellowed, "Not today, devil." For added impact, Mayra took off her shoe and hurled it. It went pretty far, considering the trajectory was against the wind. Her pink sneaker landed after a couple of bounces in the middle of the gap between Mayra and her newest enemy. The skunk froze, raised its tail, and a cloud of dust expressed its opinion on the matter.

The thrill of victory was short. Mayra realized she'd have to traverse the road less one shoe to retrieve the one she tossed. She yelled, "I'm not afraid of a little discomfort," and started to cry.

"Is everything okay?"

Mayra froze. She hadn't heard the pickup come from behind her. She looked at the sky as if to ask the Good Lord why he sent, of all people, Victor Sandberg, in her least finest hour. She whimpered, "Just go away, please," and turned to look at the deflated tire.

The pickup door creaked, and Mayra heard the crunch of Victor's boots on the ground. Just thinking about what he might say to her increased the flow of tears.

She sniffled and wiped her tears away with the back of her hand. "You don't have to stop. My dad should be here any minute."

"He called me to come out."

"What?" Mayra pivoted to face Victor.

Victor nudged his head toward the bed of his pickup. "I was at the house when you called your dad. I told him I'd be glad to take care of you." He paused and wiggled his fingers to invite Mayra to close the gap between them. "You need to come on in for a hug."

The events of the past twenty-four hours broke Mayra. She didn't care anymore about her promise never to speak to Victor. She curled into his chest and inhaled his scent. He smelled clean and citrusy with a strong waft of masculinity.

Mayra's heart settled, and she understood how her father could calm down after her mother said a short phrase. Comfort from love minimized life's hardships. She croaked, "Thank you. I feel better," and braced herself for the emptiness she'd feel when she stepped away from Victor.

Victor gave her a little squeeze before releasing his hold on her. "Let's get you taken care of."

He sauntered to the pickup, pulled out the tools, and had the tire changed in ten minutes. Mayra then helped him store the tools in the metal toolbox affixed to the bed.

When he turned the lock securing the tools, Mayra sheepishly offered her appreciation. "Thank you. I'm sorry you had to go out of your way to help me."

Victor's lip quirked into that crooked grin that melted her heart every time. "I had planned to spend the afternoon with you anyway."

She left the "and our friends" unspoken. Mayra looked down at the ground to hide her embarrassment. "I'm not joining you for root beer." She winced under her discomfort. John's rebuff corroborated the reason behind Victor's distance over the years. There was something about Mayra that chased men away.

"After you left yesterday, John and I had a talk."

"You did?" Mayra's heart lurched. Was it possible what her friends said about Victor's feelings were true? Or was this another incidence where Victor tormented her because she was an easy target?

"A good thing was right in front of me." Victor shook his head like he almost couldn't believe it himself. "I didn't see it until John almost took it away from me."

It was too good to be true. Mayra was sure she was dreaming or was delirious from the stress. "Are you sure you're okay?"

Then Victor leaned in and kissed Mayra square on the lips.

He stepped away, leaving Mayra standing there with her fingers pressed against the tingle. "I'm doing this wrong. Wait here for just one second."

Victor hurried to his pickup and returned with a vase full of daisies. "I remember you saying one time that these were your favorite."

Mayra searched her memory for the conversation. Victor filled in the blank. "One time, you and Kate were talking about what a man would have to do to impress you. You said roses were too easy." The gold around the outer edges of Victor's eyes intensified, giving Mayra the impression he wanted her to understand deeply. "And that any man who was serious about winning your heart would go the extra measure. You've been going above and beyond for years, but it really hit me when I drank your soda yesterday."

He shook his head at all that had gone wrong. He didn't need to say anything. Mayra was there living it with him. She took Victor's hand in hers, squeezed it, and wagged her brows playfully. "If you really care about me, you'll walk with me to go get my shoe."

Both looked down at her one socked foot. Then they cast their attention to the lone shoe in the middle of the road. Mayra explained, "I threw it at the skunk."

"You wait here. I'll get it. Then we're going on a date like a real couple." Victor jogged to the shoe, picked it up and waved it at Mayra like he was her knight in shining armor.

Mayra held her hand to her heart and basked in the unexpected turn of events. Victor hadn't said one contrary thing to her. He made his intention clear when he said they were going on a date like a real couple. The stars had aligned. Mayra could feel it in the deepest places within her. She and Victor Sandberg were meant to be together. Mayra swooned and decided then and there that she'd make Victor Sandberg cherry cola for their first wedding anniversary.

AUTHOR'S NOTE

Hi, this is Merri. I hope Mayra and Victor's beginnings brought you a smile. This is where I'll share that they were inspired by some of the first friends I made when my husband brought me to live in his childhood home in Montana. I'd also like to let you in on a little secret. There's more. Victor and Mayra's wedding is in the last half of *The Chance to Win Her Heart*. Without giving too much away, I'll tell you Gina's life is about to be turned upside-down. So the novel actually has two happily ever afters.

Make sure to get your copy of the story and see how it all plays out.

ABOUT THE AUTHOR

Over twenty years ago, Merri Maywether went on a date with a very sweet man from Montana. Three weeks later they were engaged and they have lived happily ever after. They live on the family farm in small-town Montana. When she isn't writing stories, she can be found in the elementary school library or middle school writing classroom.

Looking for more stories about life in small-town Montana? Sign up to receive her newsletter

https://sendfox.com/smalltownstories

ONLY PRETENDING

KARI SHUEY

You can't pretend forever.

1

Peyton ducked below the window of the swinging kitchen door and spun, the plate of chocolate-covered strawberries still in her hand from the refreshment table. The kitchen staff stared at her with wide, unblinking eyes. Smiling, Peyton stepped aside to allow a caterer to pass.

Heat crawled up her neck. She couldn't hide forever. Eventually, her ex would find out she came to the wedding dateless. Peyton peered out the small square window. Where was the man who broke her heart?

The bimbo draped on Isaac's arm was a slap in the face. He'd broken up with Peyton just over a month ago.

Something landed on her shoulder. Peyton yelped, dropping the strawberries. Dang it! Those were her favorite. She whirled to stare into the most gorgeous deep blue eyes she'd ever seen.

The warmth in her face grew, and she ducked to clean the mess. Peyton rose and stepped to the side, but the tall man with olive skin and chocolate hair moved with her.

She pushed a strand of raven hair behind her ear. "Sorry, I'll stay out of the way."

He shook his head, a crooked smile on his face. "I'm sorry, you can't be here. This room is for caterers only. You need to leave."

Peyton's brows rose. "I can't stay for even a few minutes? There's a guy out there—"

He shifted and stared through the pane. "Is he bothering you?" The words came out in more of a growl as his features tightened.

"It's my ex." She clenched her jaw. He didn't need her life story.

The man's gaze met hers. "Oh... Unfortunately, you still have to leave."

Peyton's shoulders slumped. "Okay. Is there another exit I could take?"

"Sorry." He pursed his lips. "Don't you have a wingman or something?"

She sighed. "Nope."

The man took a deep breath and untied the apron. "I guess we have no choice. We'll have to go together."

Peyton's eyes widened and her mouth dropped open. "What? No, you don't have to—"

The man tossed his apron and nodded to another caterer. "You got this?" He tugged the empty plate from her hands and placed it on a nearby counter.

The caterer nodded. The man grabbed Peyton's hand, pulled it beneath his arm, and shouldered through the swinging door.

Peyton shuffled beside him into the glistening lights of the ballroom. The chandeliers winked at her as if they had a tantalizing secret. Isaac mingled on the other side of the room, his date hanging on his arm. Peyton's stomach roiled as the stranger led her closer.

Isaac's eyes flicked to her, and a greasy smile crossed her ex's face. "Peyton, I didn't think you were going to make it."

Peyton gritted her teeth. "Ashley's my best friend, Isaac. Of course I wouldn't miss this."

Isaac's gaze flitted from her to the man at her side, who stood a head taller than he was.

The stranger held out his hand. "Isaac, I've heard *so much* about you. I'm Kurt."

Isaac looked Kurt up and down, his lips pressed into a thin line. "That's funny. I haven't heard *anything* about you."

Kurt released Peyton's hand and wrapped his arm around her

shoulders. "That doesn't surprise me. We haven't officially set a date. I'm just glad she said yes."

Peyton stiffened. *What?* She fought the urge to push Kurt away. The muscles it took to keep a straight face weakened in their resolve. Forcing a smile, she rested her head against Kurt's shoulder and laid a hand on his chest.

Kurt squeezed her and chuckled. "When you know, you know. Isn't that right, sugar?"

She cringed. "Right."

Isaac's scowl almost made the knot in her chest worth it.

"Congratulations!" A shrill voice broke the staring contest.

Peyton jumped and stared at the platinum blonde woman in the skin-tight dress. The woman released Isaac and threw her arms around Peyton, the odor of her perfume burning Peyton's nostrils.

"Thanks." Peyton coughed, waiting for the woman to release her.

The woman pulled back and beamed. "I keep hinting to this one we should get hitched, but he likes to take it slow." She jerked a thumb at Isaac. His face turned purple.

A genuine grin touched Peyton's lips. "I'm sure you'll wear him down eventually."

Kurt's warm hand slipped around her waist, and he tugged her close. "I hate to break up this little reunion, but we only have a few hours before the party tonight. Peyton and I want to do some sightseeing first."

He pressed a kiss to her temple, flooding her whole body with a wave of warmth. She glanced up at his face, Isaac forgotten. A small part of her wondered what it would be like if this was real.

He led her out of the banquet hall, his chin dimpling as he tossed a smile over his shoulder. "Well, *that* was fun."

Her sanity returning, Peyton launched herself away from him and whirled. She glowered. "What was that?"

Kurt stepped toward her, his arm ready to capture her waist again. She backed away, and her heel caught on the commercial-grade carpet.

He grabbed her upper arms. "Whoa, are you okay? We should find someplace a bit more quiet if you want this to work. Isaac could come out any second."

"If I want *what* to work?" She yanked her arms from his grasp and laced her fingers behind her neck. "I don't even know who you are." She froze, and her gaze shot to his. "You're not a murderer, are you?"

He tossed his head back and laughed. "No, I'm not a murderer. Come on, let's get out of here."

"What? *Absolutely not.* I'm not going anywhere with you. You're crazy." She held up her hands between them.

"Come on, sugar, it'll be fun."

Peyton pointed a finger in his face. "Don't you dare call me that." Crossing her arms, she scooted farther away. "I'm grateful you got me out of there and all, but I'm not going to pretend I'm married to a guy I've never met."

"Engaged."

"Whatever. I'm still not doing it."

His blue eyes crinkled at the edges, and the dimple in his chin became more pronounced. "Why not? It won't hurt anything. We're only pretending."

Peyton's eyes narrowed.

He leaned against the wall beside her. "The way I see it, this whole thing is a win-win. You get even with your ex, and I get to enjoy the company of a beautiful woman."

Her mouth dropped open. "You didn't just say that." Who was this guy? "People don't go around pretending to be involved with complete strangers and calling them *sugar.*"

Kurt cocked his head to the side. "Where's your sense of adventure, Peyton? It's only for a few days, and then we'll never see each other again."

2

Kurt grinned. Peyton didn't recognize him. This whole thing got better and better. Her green eyes flicked to meet his before dropping to the ground. She twisted her sandaled toe into the carpet and chewed on her lower lip.

She was caving. All she needed was one more little push, and he'd get the chance to fix his biggest regret.

Kurt shoved his hands into his pockets and shrugged. "I'm sure Isaac would love to know you lied to him about this whole thing."

Peyton's head shot up, and her brows lowered over her fiery eyes. "*I* lied? Oh no you don't. If Isaac finds out about this farce, you're taking full credit."

He smirked.

"What's so funny? You made up a story that's going to destroy my life. You *knew* I didn't want anything to do with him, and—" She threw her hands into the air and paced in front of the open banquet room door. "Isaac is the epitome of everything that is wrong with my life, and you just gave him the ammunition to..."

Great, Isaac was headed their way across the banquet hall. His focus was on the girl beside him. Kurt held up a finger, but Peyton wouldn't stop her adorable tirade. His eyes shifted to the oncoming missile. Isaac would ruin everything. Kurt could apologize later—but he wasn't really sorry for what he was about to do.

He closed the distance between them and snaked an arm around her waist. He covered her quiet yelp with a firm kiss. With his free arm, he grasped the back of her neck and pulled her closer.

Peyton's hands pushed against his chest. He pulled away long enough to murmur, "Isaac's coming."

She stiffened, then relaxed, draping her arms over his shoulders. She lifted and twisted her head, giving him access to her neck. Kurt pressed kisses along her jaw. Her perfume invigorated him. The scent of honey mingled with something floral made the growing knot in his stomach tighten.

Someone cleared their throat.

Kurt lifted his gaze to Isaac. As if born for the stage, Peyton jumped and released Kurt. She faced the source of the interruption, a quiet giggle escaping her throat. Kurt slipped his arms around Peyton's waist. She leaned against him, and another thrill rippled through him. He smiled and rested his chin on her shoulder.

Isaac and his date walked by, and Peyton wiggled her fingers at them. The couple turned the corner. The moment they were out of sight, the magic vanished.

Peyton whirled, brows low, and shoved his shoulder. "You have to stop making decisions like that! It was highly inappropriate." Her cheeks reddened. She pressed a delicate hand against her flushed skin and broke eye contact.

However inappropriate, it was worth it. His whole body hummed with an energy he hadn't experienced in years. His gaze trailed down the simple sundress that hugged her curves perfectly. Isaac had been a fool for letting her slip through his fingers. Ashley had told Kurt plenty about Peyton, and so far he hadn't been disappointed in the slightest.

Kurt returned his attention to her face. Shoot, had she noticed him staring? When she lifted her eyes from the floor to his face, relief doused the anxiety.

The corners of her lips quirked up, and she rubbed her left arm. "But it was kinda nice to see him so angry."

An older couple exited the hall, and she stepped aside to lean against the textured cream-colored walls. She bit down on her lip again. The movement drew his focus, and the passionate desire returned with force. He should be nibbling on those soft pink lips.

"I can't believe I'm even considering this."

Kurt straightened. She was?

Peyton closed her eyes and dropped her head against the wall behind her. "Fine. You win."

His lips twitched. He couldn't give away how much he wanted this. She'd think he was insane. If she knew what he'd done to make this happen, she would never speak to him again.

Raising an eyebrow at her, he rubbed the scruff along his jaw. "Are you sure you're not the winner here?"

Peyton rolled her eyes and straightened, pushing away from the wall. "I never asked for your help. You got us into this mess, and you get to make sure it doesn't blow up in our faces. If it means I don't have to deal with Isaac for the next two days, I'll play your little game."

Kurt rubbed his hands together. "Then let's have some fun."

Peyton blew out an exaggerated sigh. "If you say so."

3

———————

Nausea flooded her stomach—or was it butterflies from that kiss? The kiss was short-lived, but her lips tingled with the memory. Isaac had never kissed her with that kind of passion. This Kurt guy was an amazing actor.

When he lit a trail of flames along her neck... Goosebumps raised the hairs along her arms. Peyton rubbed them feverishly.

Kurt glanced in her direction. "You cold?"

His smooth voice exacerbated the problem.

"It's the air conditioning." What a stupid lie. He would see right through that. She waited for him to make a snarky comment, but he didn't.

They crossed the marble tile in the foyer and passed through the sliding doors. Humid heat enveloped them. Great, by evening her hair would be a mess. Not a cute beach wave mess, but the frizzy Weird Al kind, one where he stuck his finger in a socket.

She dragged her palms over her scalp. Why hadn't she thought to bring an elastic? Oh well, it wasn't like Kurt was her real boyfriend. She could be herself without worrying she was making a bad impression. He'd already seen her anxiety in the kitchen and her angry outbursts. If that didn't make him run for the hills, nothing would.

A smile crossed her face unbidden. She'd never been in a relationship where she didn't constantly fret over what the guy thought. Makeup, nice clothes, and perfect personality had been the priority.

Peyton tossed a glance at Kurt. It would have been nice to meet him under different circumstances. If she had met him back home, she might have flirted a little and showed him she was a catch.

Truth be told, she would never entertain something real with a guy like him. She didn't like long-distance relationships. Even more important was her unwillingness to unload all her personal baggage on a guy who just wanted to have fun.

She clasped her hands behind her back. None of it mattered now. She was a mess, he knew it, and that simple fact lightened the load on her shoulders more than anything else could.

Peyton shuffled to a stop. Where were they? She scanned the street. Tourists ambled down the sidewalk, ducking into unfamiliar store fronts. She didn't recognize the hotel beside her.

Kurt continued a few paces before he turned. "Is everything okay?"

Peyton shook her head. "No."

"No?"

She folded her arms. "Pretending we're engaged at the wedding events is one thing, but leaving the hotel to wander all over the island is another ballgame. We need to go back."

His brows pinched together. "Why?"

Her forehead creased. "Do I have to spell it out for you?"

His mouth spread into a soft smile. "Maybe you do."

She groaned. "I. Don't. Know. You. I can't say for certain you're not going to throw me in the back of some van and do who knows what."

Kurt swaggered toward her. Her heart skipped a beat. She wouldn't show fear. She'd agreed to this whole charade, but she refused to let him intimidate her.

He reached into his pocket, and she flinched. Great. Apparently, her body hadn't gotten the memo.

He had the gall to chuckle as he pulled out his wallet. Using his finger and thumb, he pulled something out of the faded leather pockets. He offered her a card between two fingers.

"Here. If something happens to you, you have my ID."

Peyton stared at the offering and wrinkled her nose. "What am I supposed to do with that?"

Kurt shrugged. "I don't work at the hotel. I'm a caterer, but I'm based in Idaho."

Her brows shot up as she wrapped her fingers around the card. "You're lying."

He returned the wallet to his pocket. "I'm doing the happy couple a favor." He tilted his head at the card in her hand. "If something happens to that ID, I can't get home."

Peyton stared at the ID. Sure enough, Kurt Michaels lived in Boise, Idaho. She glanced at him and tucked a damp piece of hair behind her ear. They lived about twenty minutes from one another.

Flutters erupted in her chest, and she shoved them down. Just because he lived close didn't mean it would work out. She squeezed her eyes shut. Her heart had a mind of its own. No matter how much it wanted this, she would put her foot down.

Dumb, dumb, dumb. She shook her head and held the card out to him. "Not good enough. You could still do something to me if you wanted it back."

He leaned closer so his mouth was right by her ear. The hairs stood on the back of her neck as his breath whispered against her skin.

"Sugar, if I wanted to do something to you, I would have already." Kurt pulled back and flashed her a smile. "I'll be a perfect gentleman."

She snorted. Like when he pulled her into that toe-curling kiss without permission. Cheeks warming, she squinted at him and tilted her head to the side. "The bride and groom really know you?"

Kurt let out a long breath between pursed lips. "Yes." He pulled out his phone and swiped his finger across the screen. The screen reflected the sun as he passed the device to her. Ashley's name headed the top, and beneath it was the correct number.

Peyton lifted her eyes to his, then dropped them to the phone. She clicked the number and typed in the message bar. After clicking send, she handed it back to him.

Kurt: I kidnapped Peyton. If she doesn't make it back by the rehearsal dinner, call the cops.

His eyes trailed over the message, and he laughed. "You're smarter than you look." The phone beeped, and Kurt glanced down at it.

She leaned forward. "What did she say?"

He pressed the phone against his chest and turned. "Hang out with me today, and I'll show you."

Peyton folded her arms. "Fine. What did you have in mind?"

He shoved the phone into his pocket and grabbed her hand. "We have just enough time to make it to our appointment."

"We have an appointment?" She stumbled after him. Had Kurt planned on kidnapping someone at the wedding from the beginning? A small part hoped he'd planned to take her, but that wasn't possible. They'd never met.

Kurt dragged her down one street after another until they arrived at a bus stop. Puffing with exertion, he shot her a look out of the corner of his eye.

Peyton bent over, placing her hands on her knees and breathing heavily. "I don't think I've run like that since high school. You didn't answer my question."

"Technically, it's my appointment, but you get to come along."

The bus arrived. A sign in front flashed the destination.

She widened her eyes. "We're going to the airport?"

He offered her that heart-melting smile. "Yep. You're gonna love this."

On the bus, Peyton fiddled with her purse as she sat beside Kurt. He kept throwing things at her she wasn't prepared for. What was his deal? They had to be back to the hotel for the rehearsal dinner in a few hours. Why on earth would they need to go to the airport?

She chewed her lower lip. It would be okay. Ashley knew where she was, and she wouldn't have had Kurt cater her wedding if she didn't trust him. This would be fine.

Kurt wrapped his arm around Peyton's shoulders, and she jumped. He moved closer. "Don't worry. We're not going far. I'll have you back in one piece. Scout's honor."

The nod she attempted to give him did nothing to assuage her anxiety. They arrived at the airport, and once again, Kurt grabbed her hand. This time, they walked rather than ran through the terminals.

People rushed to make their flights, but time seemed to stand still as Kurt laced his fingers between hers. His warm hand squeezed hers, the firm grasp somehow comforting.

They turned down a less-busy hallway, and Kurt led her straight to a counter. A sign on the desk read, "Isle Sights: 45-Minute Helicopter Tour."

Peyton sucked in a breath and stared at Kurt as he spoke with the attendant behind the counter. The attendant handed them their tickets and motioned them to take a seat.

She whirled on him as soon as the attendant was no longer within hearing distance. "Who *are* you, really?"

Kurt laughed. "I'm a guy from Idaho who wants to have some fun at a destination wedding."

She folded her arms. "I don't believe you for a second."

He shrugged. "You don't have to believe me. You just have to come along for the ride."

4

———

*K*urt was pushing it. He wouldn't get away with this for long. Eventually, Peyton would figure out who he was. He just hoped she'd be willing to throw caution to the wind for the next few hours.

One day was all he had, and he intended her to fall for him by the end of it.

He laced his fingers between hers again. Her bright eyes met his, and she didn't pull away. Progress. Her full lips tugged to the sides, a pretty pink color dusting her cheeks. He lifted her hand to his lips and pressed a soft kiss to her velvet skin.

"Have you ever ridden in a helicopter?"

Peyton shook her head. "You?"

"A few times. But not here."

Her eyes narrowed, but she didn't say anything. Someone at the gate called his name, and they stood. Peyton's hand tightened around his as they approached the helicopter. Her hair whipped around her face, and the wind tugged at her dress. She let out a laugh that got lost in the gust, tugging her dress down with her free hand.

Once they were inside the aircraft, the pilot handed them headgear. Peyton donned her helmet and secured her seatbelt, a wide smile on her flushed face.

"I can't believe I'm actually doing this." Her voice came through the speaker.

"Me neither."

The pilot went over the rules, reminding them to stay strapped in due to their doorless request. Peyton's eyes widened even more, and as the helicopter lifted off the ground, she snatched Kurt's hand. He squeezed it before extracting his own and placing his arm around her shoulders. He offered his other hand as they rose higher into the sky.

She let out a little squeal and turned to stare at the shrinking island below them. They tilted, and a gasp escaped her lips.

Bursts of color from the natural flora dotted the vibrant greens and blues. They flew over Diamond Head, and the pilot recited facts about the once-erupting volcano. Next, they dipped close to Sacred Falls. The roar of the water crashing against the rocks as it tumbled to the pool below couldn't compare to the thunder of Kurt's heart as Peyton met his gaze, her eyes full of wonder and light. Even if nothing came from this little adventure, seeing Peyton like this made it worth it.

The tour ended with a fly-by of the beaches before the pilot headed toward the airport again. As the helicopter landed, Peyton pulled her hand from his and removed her helmet. Kurt removed his as well and hopped from the aircraft. He held out his hand. She looked at it, then accepted.

Peyton climbed down beside him, stumbled on her heels, and crashed into his chest. Kurt wrapped his arms around her waist, steadying her. She lifted her face, her bright green eyes flashing with something he couldn't read.

His focus shifted to her full pink lips. Would she hate him for kissing her without an excuse this time? Kurt's jaw tightened. Too soon. She needed to trust him more before he could attempt that.

The jarring whoosh of the helicopter blades sliced through his thoughts. He released her and stepped back. Grasping her hand, he tugged her toward the airport. He wanted to take her one more place before the rehearsal dinner.

"That was amazing." She rested her head on his shoulder. "I've never been that close to a waterfall."

Kurt's heart stuttered. His plan was working. He could practically see her defenses weakening every second they spent together. He set his cheek against the top of her head. "I'm glad you agreed to come."

"Me too." Her quiet voice sent chills rippling along his nerves. "You know, I didn't even want to come to the wedding. I thought I couldn't show my face after—" She shut her mouth and lifted her head. "I came to support Ashley. This is her special day, and I wasn't going to be the one to ruin it."

"I'm sure she appreciates that." Kurt gave her a half smile.

A tinkling laugh bubbled from her chest. "Oh, I don't think it really matters. She could have replaced me with anyone."

Kurt pulled Peyton to a stop and stood in front of her. "No. If I know Ashley like I think I do, it wouldn't have been the same without you. I think it took courage, sacrifice, and love for you to come here, even though you have to deal with he who shall not be named."

Her nose wrinkled, and she tipped her head to the side. "You're really something, you know that, Kurt?"

He blew on his fingers and rubbed them against his Polo shirt. "Well, I try."

She slugged him in the shoulder. "And humble too."

Kurt rubbed his shoulder with mock agony. "Ow."

Peyton rolled her eyes, but her grin grew. "Where to now?"

"Let's take a walk."

She gathered her hair with both hands and twisted it over her shoulder. "Sure. That sounds nice."

They took another bus ride toward their hotel. From there, they wandered through throngs of tourists to the beach. Kurt bought her a pineapple sorbet and grabbed a snow cone for himself before they reached the edges of the sand. The sun had lowered in the sky, and the rehearsal dinner was in a little over an hour.

The sky filled with bright crimson, scarlet, and orange hues as it met the ocean at the horizon. Occasionally, a breeze picked up Peyton's brown hair and played with it.

She kept shooting Kurt glances as she enjoyed her treat.

He smirked. "Well, go on."

"What?"

"You want to say something."

Peyton squinted. "You said you were a caterer?"

He nodded.

"You must be some hotshot to be willing to do this wedding."

Kurt laughed. "How do you figure?"

"Aren't you losing money coming here? The airfare alone..." Her eyes widened, and she flushed. "It's really none of my business. You said you were doing them a favor, so I assumed—"

He shoved his napkin in his pocket and shrugged. "Don't worry about it. I wouldn't say I'm a hotshot, but yeah, this gig isn't making any money." That didn't mean it wasn't worth it.

"How do you know Ashley?"

Kurt rubbed the back of his neck and stared at the waves lapping against the shoreline. "We go way back."

Her small pink tongue licked a drip that had escaped down the side of her cone. She peeked at him. "That's weird."

"What is?"

"I've known Ashley since college, but we've never met."

He bit back a smile. It wasn't for lack of trying. "Well, we've met now."

She returned his smile with one of her own. "Yes, we have." She nibbled off an edge of her sugar cone, and they continued down the beach. "It's too bad we hadn't met sooner. You could have saved me from the mistake that was the last three years of my life."

Kurt's heart flip-flopped. He shoved his hands in his pockets and kept his gaze straight ahead. He couldn't change the past, no matter how much he wanted to. All that mattered was moving forward. He opened his mouth. Maybe she'd be willing to spend more time together when they reached stateside.

She grinned and glanced away. "Kurt?"

He froze.

"Thanks for pretending with me today. This has been... nice."

With those few words, his hopes crumbled, but he forced a smile and nodded. "Yeah. It has been nice."

5

————

More than nice, spending time with Kurt had been fireworks. Between the butterflies and sparks lighting every nerve ending, Peyton wanted more. She met Kurt's eyes and, for what seemed like the hundredth time, wished he'd kiss her again like he had outside of the banquet hall. But everything fizzled. This was all pretend. Hadn't he insisted as much to get her out of the hotel?

Kurt's smile appeared, that adorable dimple indenting right below his full lips—lips she wanted pressed against her own. Peyton let out a deep sigh. She shouldn't show him how he affected her. He'd just laugh. Her stomach soured. Sure, Kurt seemed perfect on the surface, but she knew nothing about him. Time to focus on the ruse—make Isaac believe they were happy and in love. Then they'd go their separate ways.

With a toss of her head, she motioned to him. "You coming? If we don't leave now, we're going to be late."

He nodded. As he came up beside her, he brought his arm around her waist and pulled her to him. The knots in Peyton's stomach tightened. Every nerve ending along her body awakened at his nearness.

It was only pretend. She couldn't start falling for him.

Too late.

The aroma of cinnamon and apple pastries filled her senses, and she took a deep breath. No man should ever smell that good. "Do you have to help in the kitchen?" It would be best if she put some distance between them.

"Nope. One of the perks of being in charge."

He winked at her, which released another swarm of nerves. Shoot, shoot, shoot, shoot. Her stupid heart and its inability to keep a level head.

They made it to the hotel with minutes to spare. The wedding party stood outside the banquet hall, the wedding director shouting instructions. A bridesmaid grabbed Peyton's arm and dragged her to her place. A tall blond man smiled at her.

"You must be Ashley's friend, Peyton."

She swallowed and forced a smile. Her eyes left his face long enough to see Kurt duck into the banquet hall. Why was he frowning?

"I'm Taylor." He held out his arm. "I guess I'm escorting you in."

Peyton slipped her hand into the crook of his arm. "Nice to meet you."

"I've known Mason since we were in preschool…"

It would have been nicer to have Kurt escort her. She rolled her eyes. Whoever heard of a caterer being part of the wedding party? She craned her neck to look through the door. When this practice was over, she'd ask him what was so upsetting. Isaac wasn't around, so it wasn't him.

Peyton scrunched her lips to the side. She hadn't said something wrong, had she? No. They'd both been happy when they arrived at the hotel.

"How long have you known Ashley?" Taylor prodded her arm.

She jumped. "Hmm?"

Taylor smirked. "I'm sorry, was I boring you?"

Peyton patted his forearm. "Oh, no. I'm so sorry. I'm a little out of it tonight. I've known Ashley since—"

"It's your turn. Go!" a female voice hissed.

Peyton glanced over her shoulder at a redhead, who glared at her.

Taylor hunched his shoulders and mouthed the word "sorry." They picked up their steps and entered the banquet hall. Music echoed through the room, which had been transformed from an eating area to something resembling a chapel.

"Wow," Peyton whispered. "This is amazing."

Taylor ducked his head beside hers. "Yeah. They've been setting up all afternoon."

Peyton's eyes landed on Kurt as she passed him. His frown had deepened, and he slouched in a chair. When his eyes met hers, he straightened slightly, smiled, and gave a goofy wave. What was wrong?

When they arrived at the front of the room, Peyton parted from Taylor and found her place on the bride's side. She kept her eyes on the floor. *Don't look at him. If you do, you're a goner. You're already a goner.*

Peyton lifted her eyes and met Kurt's steady gaze. Why did life have to be so unfair? He made a face at her. A giggle erupted from her lips, and her hand flew to her mouth. The red-head shot her a death stare, causing Peyton's giggle to morph into a snort.

Flames filled her cheeks, and she scowled at Kurt. *Not funny.*

Yeah, it is.

The bridal chorus filled the air, and everyone turned to stare as Ashley paced down the aisle in her blouse and capris. The biggest smile lit her face, her focus on Mason, who stood at the front of the room.

What would it be like to have that? Peyton's eyes flitted to Kurt, and her chest tightened. He wasn't staring at Ashley. He was staring at her. Those deep blue eyes locked her in place. She couldn't breathe. The room, the people, even the music fell away, and all she could hear was her own breathing and the beat of her heart. Kurt blinked, and one corner of his lips lifted.

She broke eye contact and pulled a stray hair behind her ear. This was going too far. Her heart couldn't take it. He was toying with her like they were toying with Isaac. Enough was enough.

The bride and groom went over a brief ceremony. The wedding director told everyone to leave the way they came in. Taylor met her in the aisle and held out his arm, the smile on his face wide. Peyton grabbed his arm, and they headed toward the exit.

The second she was out of there, she would go to her room and not come out until the actual wedding. Isaac could spread all the lies he wanted. She wasn't going to pretend anymore.

6

───────

Something had changed. She wouldn't look at him. Kurt's grip tightened on the back of his chair as he turned to watch her and that guy retreat to the hall. He had to go after her before she slipped through his fingers. They'd go to dinner still, right? That was the big perk for those participating in the rehearsal.

His fingers white, Kurt allowed Ashley and Mason to get to the door before he launched out of his chair and hurried down the aisle. He knocked over a chair, sending it clattering to the floor.

A few gasps erupted. He didn't stop. Someone else would pick it up. Seeing Peyton was more important.

Kurt burst into the hallway. Where was she? His eyes raked over the occupants, but his dark-haired beauty was nowhere to be seen. She'd taken off. His breaths came faster. What happened? They were doing okay. Her statement about pretending had sliced through him like a dagger through a tapestry, but she was still smiling and enjoying herself.

He dug his hands through his hair and spun around. His eyes landed on his cousin, and he stalked toward her. He grabbed her upper arm and turned her to face him. "Where is she staying?"

Ashley's eyes widened. "Easy, Kurt. Who are you talking about?" Her gaze roved through the crowd, and a knowing smile covered her face. "How was your date?" Mason stood beside her, a slow grin replacing his concern as well.

"You can give me the third degree later. Tell me what room she's staying in."

Ashley shrugged. "I don't know. Everyone made their own reservations."

Kurt placed his hands on both her shoulders. "You have to find out. Something's wrong."

Her brows pinched. "What happened?"

"I'm not sure. One second she was having fun, playing along, and the next she wouldn't even look at me."

"Kurt! You haven't told her?" Ashley placed her hands on her hips. "Shame on you."

He laced his fingers behind his neck and threw his head back. "I know. Just help me find her, and I'll tell her everything."

Ashley shook her head. "I swear, if this goes south and she doesn't forgive me—"

Kurt groaned. "I'll tell her it was all my idea. Happy?"

She sighed. "One sec." Ashley pulled out her phone and sent a message.

Ashley: You took off. Is everything ok? You coming to dinner? Want me to bring you something?

"If she doesn't answer, there's nothing I can do. I don't think the hotel will tell me where she's staying."

Kurt folded his arms and tapped his foot.

Mason wrapped his arm around Ashley's shoulder. "Besides, you'll see her tomorrow. It's not like she's going to fly home and miss the main event."

Ashley's phone beeped. She swiped the screen and held it out for Kurt to see.

Peyton: Sorry, not feeling well. You don't have to do that. It's your night.

Kurt snatched the phone from her hand.

"Hey!" Ashley lunged forward, but he turned, and her hand missed. A small sound signaled when the message sent.

Ashley: It's not a problem. What's your rm number?

He handed the phone to her, a smug smile on his face.

She stuck out her tongue at him. "You twerp." Her phone beeped. Ashley's mouth twitched. "You're a lucky twerp, though."

Kurt's eyes widened. "Did she tell you?"

Ashley held the phone to her chest. "I'm only giving this to you on one condition."

"Fine, whatever."

"Double dates."

Kurt rolled his eyes and held out his palm, curling his fingers twice. "Tell me."

"She's in room 214."

He took off toward the elevator. The closer he got to her floor, the harder his heart beat against his ribs. He'd let her get away once. He wouldn't let it happen again.

7

Peyton smacked her palm against her forehead. She'd let herself get sucked into another mistake, all because of a pair of dark blue eyes. Why did she continue to torture herself?

Tomorrow she'd have to tell Kurt thanks, but she wouldn't be pretending. Let Isaac humiliate her. She wasn't going to get pulled deeper into something that would never be.

She should have told him after the rehearsal. Running away only complicated things more. He probably thought she was a lunatic. Peyton continued pacing the hotel room and fought the emotion that threatened to escape.

No. Tears were not allowed to make an appearance. She'd gotten herself into this mess, and she could deal with the consequences. She slouched onto the edge of the bed. How mortifying.

Three firm knocks hit her door. She lifted her head. Ashley wouldn't be done with dinner this early. Peyton dragged herself from the bed, across the room, and to the door. Lifting herself onto her toes, she peered out the spy hole.

Her hand flew to her mouth, and she ducked, sliding down the door to land on the floor. How had Kurt found her room? She wrapped her arms around her legs. Answering would be bad. No, she'd keep quiet. He'd go away eventually, right?

"Peyton, I know you're in there. Ashley gave me your room number."

Traitor.

She clambered to her feet and peered through the small hole. His palm rested on the door jamb as he leaned against it. A couple walked past the door, and he nodded to them.

When they were out of sight, he turned to the door again. "I'm not leaving until you let me in."

Peyton pressed her forehead to the cool surface and groaned. Time to face the music like she should have when she saw Isaac. Her hand wrapped around the handle, and she pulled the door open. She stepped into the hall, the door clicking behind her.

Kurt lifted his head, a crooked grin on his face. "Hey, sugar."

Her heart flipped, and she dug her nails into her palms. This was all for show. "You don't have to call me that. I haven't seen Isaac since the banquet. I don't know why we've been pretending all day. It's not like Isaac has spies following us."

His brows pushed together. "Peyton, I haven't been pretending."

Her mouth went dry. She swallowed, but the lump in her throat wouldn't move. "You're not?"

Kurt shook his head. "I've been in love with you from the moment I saw you. Today has only solidified it."

A laugh burst from her lips. "What? Since lunch time?"

His hand fell to his side. "For over three years."

Her mouth dropped open.

Kurt folded his arms. "Remember when Ashley wanted to set you up with her cousin?"

Peyton lowered her eyes to the ground momentarily before raising them. "The one who just got out of culinary school…"

He nodded. "The plan was to meet at that party. But Isaac got to you first." His steely gaze never wavered. "Ashley pointed you out, and from that moment I was smitten. I grabbed some drinks, but when I turned around, you were gone."

"You couldn't have known you loved me."

Kurt shrugged. "You're probably right. But after spending time with you today, I realize why I couldn't get you out of my head."

She wrung her hands. What was she supposed to say to that?

Shaking his head, he pulled out his phone. "I have proof." His finger slid across the screen then tapped. He offered it to her, a half-smile pulling at his lips. "I said I'd show you."

Kurt: I kidnapped Peyton. If she doesn't make it back by the rehearsal dinner, call the cops.

Ashley: Lol. I'm happy for you. You're really perfect for each other. Have fun.

He moved closer. She stepped back, but the door behind her prevented her from putting any distance between them. Blood rushed in her ears and heat trailed up her neck, spreading across her face.

"Every time I saw you with that jerk, I rationalized he must be making you happy. I'm not the type to break anyone up."

She shook her head. Her tongue felt swollen. "No, because I would have noticed you."

His smile and dimple appeared on his face. He scrubbed at the facial hair on his jaw. "I've only recently grown this out. It's not a surprise you didn't recognize me." His features became serious again. "Peyton, when I heard you'd split up with Isaac, I knew it was my chance."

"So why didn't you just ask me out?" Her heart thundered.

He lifted her chin with his finger. "Would you have gone out with me if I admitted to all of this?"

She pressed her lips into a firm line. Not likely.

"And I wasn't about to become your rebound guy. I wanted us to enjoy the day without the added stress of a 'first date.'"

"Oh." She breathed the word as his face continued to get closer.

"Sugar, I want you to know I don't expect you to believe me right away. I'll even give you space when we get back to the states. But I'm not leaving here without showing you what could be."

"Okay." Her chest heaved with each breath.

"You deserve to be treated right by someone who loves you for who you are. No more pretending, Peyton." Kurt cupped her face between his palms and brushed his lips against hers.

Sparks exploded behind her eyes. She brought up her hands behind his neck and tugged him closer. One of his arms wrapped around her waist, and his touch ignited flames that ran along every part of her body.

His kisses dropped to her jaw and trailed down her neck. Peyton wove her fingers through his hair and tugged, bringing his face up so he would meet her gaze. His navy eyes burned with a desire that mirrored her own.

Kurt's voice turned husky. "You can't tell me you don't feel it too."

He was right.

"All I'm asking is that we stop pretending. Give me a chance to make you happy."

She shook her head. "I can't be engaged to someone I barely know. Not past tomorrow anyway."

He let out a laugh. "I wouldn't expect you to. Just until Isaac leaves you alone."

Peyton smiled despite herself. "Okay."

Kurt's brows lifted. "Really?"

She shrugged. "I've been happier today than I have for the past three years. If you could wait for me for three years, it's the least I could do."

EPILOGUE
ONE YEAR LATER

Kurt fiddled with the cardboard box. His clammy palms would give him away if he wasn't careful. He shifted his weight from one foot to the other as he stood beneath the large oak tree outside Peyton's duplex.

A breeze blew through the leaves, calming his nerves. He shouldn't be nervous. They'd been in this position before. Except it wasn't the same. This time she would have a say.

The door opened, and she hurried down the steps. "Sorry I'm late. You ready?" She hugged him.

Kurt grinned and pressed a kiss to her lips. "We both know I'm patient."

"You're never going to let me live that down, are you?"

He wrapped his free arm around her waist. "Never."

She eyed the box in his hand. "Whatcha got there?"

Kurt glanced down at the box. "I made you something special at the restaurant."

Her eyes widened, and the corners of her mouth lifted. "Really?"

"Really."

Peyton took the box from his trembling fingers, and he shoved his hand in his pocket. Carefully, she opened the box. "Chocolate covered strawberries?"

"Only the best for you, sugar." He nodded to the box. "Try the middle one first. I did something special to it."

She lifted a brow and used a finger and thumb to pluck it from the box. Bringing the berry to her lips, she bit into the fruit. She jumped as a drip of red juice trailed down her chin. "Mmm. It's delicious, but I can't tell what you did to it."

He nodded to it. "Look again."

Peyton lifted the berry to examine it, then froze. A glint of silver peeked from the fruit. Her eyes shot to meet his. "Kurt," she whispered.

Kurt lowered to one knee, took the box from her hand, and placed it on the ground. Capturing her left hand in his, he willed his thundering heart to slow. "I want to be with you forever, Peyton." A smile spread across his face. "No more pretending."

She nodded, a tear slipping down her cheek as her smile mirrored his. "No more pretending."

ABOUT THE AUTHOR

Kari Shuey grew up in Utah but currently lives with her pack of hooligans in Idaho. She loves writing all things romance and suspense but has recently dipped her toe into paranormal mysteries. When she's not staying up until three in the morning creating worlds for the characters who won't leave her alone, she enjoys baking, drawing, reading, and movie night. Enjoy her current freebie by signing up for her newsletter below. You can follow her on Amazon, GoodReads, and BookBub.

https://www.karishuey.com

Sign up for her current freebie here: https://sendfox.com/lp/mp5jxd

SECRET DATE WITH A BILLIONAIRE

KRISTEN ETHRIDGE

Billionaire Luke Freiling can solve any cybersecurity challenge in front of him. But when Killian Cordan's life falls apart, the biggest challenge will be getting her niece back home while keeping his heart secure around the woman he's had a secret crush on for years.

1

----

*C*rying?

There was no crying in cybersecurity.

Well, at least not on his watch. Luke Freiling took his role as the Chief Product Officer of CyberCay Security Partners very seriously. As the world's largest firm dedicated to safeguarding technology, every employee at CyberCay believed in the company's mission to always be aware.

He'd been at this work for so long—literally since he and his four best friends took a coding class as freshmen in high school—that this inner vigilance remained on, even when he wasn't surveying the latest cyber threat intelligence and innovating technology to stop black-hat hackers and cybercrime around the world.

He liked to think that the strategies and solutions CyberCay put in place for clients made the bad guys cry. But he wasn't used to hearing the sounds of crying in his own office.

Luke left his office and followed the sound of sobs down the hall. It sounded like Killian Cordan. He'd know the sound of her anywhere. Always had.

He hesitated as he came close to the break room. Whatever was happening seemed to be coming from the general direction of the office refrigerator.

He really wanted to make a joke to himself that Killian was probably cleaning out the back of the fridge and found someone's sub sandwich from last month. Or an old bottle of chocolate milk from one of Ben's workouts—Luke's brother swore by the drink as the key to post-workout success.

The sounds coming from the break room, however, were anything but sweet. And they weren't a joke.

All of a sudden, he hesitated, pulling back a half-step from the doorway to the break room. If pressed to describe it, Luke would have to call this a wail. It wasn't just a choke. It wasn't even a sob.

This was *emotion*, so real he could feel it here in the hall, pushing him back to a safe spot beyond the door. It tapped him on the shoulder and told him to get back. It reminded him that Luke Freiling and crying women did not mix.

Luke Freiling and women didn't mix, period, actually. In the Freiling family, Ben did the wining and dining. As twins, they had a lot in common. But not in this particular area.

He wished Ben had been the one to work after hours tonight. He would have handled this so much better. Luke felt his mouth begin to go dry. He was at a loss. If he backed away, no one would know. Everyone else in the CyberCay office had left at least two hours ago. In fact, he'd thought he was the only one remaining in the corporate compound on the small Texas Gulf Coast island of Provident Cay. So, there was no way Killian expected anyone to come in and help solve whatever problem she was facing.

But...it was Killian in there, heartbroken.

The same Killian who greeted him every morning with the wide smile that always made him wish he was as much of a morning person as she was.

The same Killian who saved his bacon every year when he got too caught up in work and forgot to order his mom's birthday flowers.

The same Killian who would have walked in the break room for him, if the tables had been turned.

Luke raised his hand and knocked on the frame surrounding the break room door. He heard Killian's breath catch in her throat.

Great, he'd scared her. Now she would be upset *and* frightened. He wasn't helping the situation by being half in, half out.

He stepped into the room and saw Killian's moss-green eyes wet with tears and wide with fear. Streaks of red rimmed her eyelids. She'd clearly been crying for a while.

"You should go, Luke. I really don't want anyone to see me like this." Her words held no trace of the sunshine she'd showed that morning when she told Luke hello.

He closed his eyes. "So...I won't look."

Yeah, Ben would have totally handled that better. Too late now. At least Killian had long known he was just a nerd at heart.

She snuffed back a sniffle. "You look ridiculous."

"Probably so. Thank goodness we're the only ones here." He opened his eyes and hoped his smile came across as sincere.

"Yeah." Killian swiped at one lower eye lid with the edge of her palm.

Luke waded in. "Can I help?"

Killian blinked back a wave of fresh tears. "It's Emma," she said softly. "Davin's filed for an emergency custody petition."

That little girl meant the world to Killian. Now he understood the heartwrenching wail completely. He stopped a foot or so in front of Killian. "Where is she now?"

Killian hung her head. "With him. She went yesterday after school to stay with him through the weekend. What if he finds some way to not give her back?"

Luke could have closed the space between them with half a step. He could have taken her in his arms and let her know it would be okay.

But he didn't.

Because this was Killian. He'd loved her forever, but he knew she deserved better than the little he had to give.

"That's not going to happen. Not on my watch."

He was a security expert. He could at least promise her that much. It was the only promise he knew he could keep.

2

Today just wouldn't quit. Killian should have known when the ferry to Provident Cay hit a freighter ship wake this morning and knocked her mocha frap out of her hand and onto the deck that nothing good could come from this day. Even then, the weekend couldn't come soon enough. Then, she'd gotten the call from her lawyer.

She'd spent two hours on a knife's edge, trying to hold in all the emotions. She stuffed them all down like crumpled wrapping paper in a trash bag after Christmas morning.

She knew she couldn't afford to let anyone see her break down. She needed this job—now more than ever. The lawyer bills that were about to come would be way out of her league.

But Emma was worth it.

Emma was worth anything and everything.

Even having Luke Freiling walk in and observe the worst breakdown of her life.

She wanted to believe that Luke could make everything better—he saved the day for customers all the time. But this situation was not a cybersecurity breach.

Killian shook her head and blew out a deep breath. She didn't know what to say or to do.

"Come on, let's go." Luke tugged at her hand. Somehow, just the simple feeling of his fingers squeezing gently as they wrapped around her palm made her feel less alone.

"Go where?"

Luke began to walk out of the breakroom. Killian followed, knowing she couldn't stay by the beat-up office fridge any longer. "The Seahorse. We're going to get a pizza. Then we're going to figure this out."

Killian shook her head again, this time in disbelief. "The Seahorse? Pizza? How is pizza going to help?"

Luke came to an abrupt stop outside of his office door. He turned on the heel of his Olukai flip-flops and looked her squarely in the eye. "I have no idea. But we're going to find out. Together." He let go of her hand and reached for the doorknob. "And I do know for a fact that no good decisions can be made when you're hungry."

Killian stood motionless in the hallway and reminded herself to think about Emma—not Luke's eyes. But when he looked at her just now, they were filled with the same kindness she remembered from high school, when it seemed like Luke was the only person who didn't care that her dad had lost their home in a bankruptcy and her whole family had to move to one of the cheapest apartments in the worst part of Port Provident. It was the same mixture of concern and thoughtfulness she remembered when he took both of her hands in his at her sister's funeral, then raised them to his lips for a wordless kiss that spoke only of true, deep friendship.

And today, with Emma's very life on the line, Luke Freiling proved that even though he was a billionaire known the world over, a cybersecurity whizkid sought out by household names and brands everywhere, he was still the same person he'd always been.

She needed to trust him.

Emma needed her to trust him.

Maybe he didn't have a plan beyond pizza, but he was smart. Smarter than anyone she'd ever known in her life—and she desperately needed some smart ideas right now because her brain was completely fried tonight.

And Luke was loyal. He'd always been there, and Killian realized she couldn't say the same about most people in her life.

She needed Emma back and safe.

But for right now, Killian knew she needed Luke beside her too.

KILLIAN KEPT her hand snug inside Luke's as they walked out of the CyberCay office. Luke wasn't stupid. He knew she was simply holding on for her emotional life, trying to stay above the waves that threatened to take her down today.

But for just one moment, he stopped himself from listening to the voice of reason in his head. He'd talked himself out of reaching for her hand a hundred times.

But this evening, he wasn't saying a word.

The sound of their footsteps on the metal walkway attracted notice. "Hey, boss. I was just about to wrap up for the night. Thought everyone was gone."

A cool fall breeze whipped around the dock. "Just the two of us left."

Danny Betancourt stopped winding a rope on the boat. A second later, his glance flickered downward—then stopped with laser-like precision.

Luke straightened his fingers and let Killian's hand brush gently down each digit as they lost the connection. Danny was a good guy, and even if idle gossip got out, it wouldn't hurt Luke's reputation.

But Killian? It certainly wouldn't help her. Port Provident was a good town, but it was a small town. And some things you just couldn't live down in a small town. Having a fling with the boss would count as one of them. And he simply wouldn't do that to Killian.

Especially not now, when he knew she'd be in for the fight of her life to keep Emma.

Killian would need the support of friends, acquaintances, and even total strangers in the days ahead.

And as always, he would be there for Killian.

Even if he had to do it from afar—as always.

3

He'd dropped her hand the minute Danny Betancourt cast a glance their way.

Now, he asked for the booth all the way in the back corner of The Seahorse.

Killian should have known. Ever since she'd come to work at Cyber Cay, she felt a distance between her and Luke that could have stretched across Texas, from Port Provident to El Paso. He was never not friendly, not helpful, not warmly professional. Actually, he was the perfect boss.

But she missed the old Luke. The Luke who used to check up on her. The Luke who could make her laugh. The Luke who made her feel like she could do anything.

She needed that Luke desperately right now. She needed someone who cared. Someone who would be in her corner. Someone who could think of a solution she couldn't.

But this dimly lit back corner seemed to say it all. Killian put her elbow on the edge of the table and rested her chin in her palm as she studied the menu.

"I sent a couple of texts while we were on Danny's boat. I hope that's okay."

Killian looked up at the sound of Luke's voice. He was as serious as a CEO in a board room. Her heart dropped a bit, even though she knew Luke wouldn't put her private life on blast...

"I was hoping to keep this as quiet as possible, Luke."

He signaled the waitress across the room. "I know, but if you do things the same way you've always done them, it's simply not going to work."

Her spine stiffened and stacked up, one vertebra atop the next. "Are you saying I've been doing this wrong? Luke, I've done everything I've known to do since Emma came to live with me. I have done everything the right way."

"That's the problem." Luke left no room for argument. "Davin Letzger is scum. You think he's out there, worried about doing things the right way?"

A few years ago, in the heat of the first battle for Emma, Davin had punched her once, square in the chest. Suddenly, Killian felt that breathless feeling again. The same wave of shock and bile hit behind her breastbone and rose up into her throat.

She never thought Luke would make her feel sick to her stomach.

But she couldn't deny all the cluttered feelings and emotions now swirling, like a switch had been flipped and everything had gone into overdrive.

Emotion began to turn liquid in the corners of her eyes. No. She would not cry again in front of Luke. She would not let him see her as anything less than the formidable opponent Killian knew she had to be to make it through and get a victory for Emma. Thankfully, the waitress came over to take their drink order at just that moment, buying Killian some time to collect herself.

"A large sweet tea for you, right, Killian?" Luke rattled off the drink order Killian had faithfully given at every restaurant since high school. She nodded affirmatively, confirming his order on her behalf, then took a deep breath as the blonde teenager walked off toward the kitchen.

She took a deep breath. "So, who did you tell?"

"Josh Styles. I trust Josh. You need legal advice. You're a good person, but Davin isn't. You can't keep trying to handle this on your own."

Josh Styles was one of the five CyberCay partners and served as the Chief Administrative Officer. "But he's not a family law specialist, Luke.

He's your corporate lawyer. And I can't afford him—or any family law specialist, for that matter. I appreciate everything you do for me at work. I am paid fairly for what I do, but I don't have some high-powered position with a high-powered paycheck."

"I do."

He laid his hand on the table, palm up, inviting Killian to reciprocate. She couldn't hear that short phrase without thinking of all the times she'd daydreamed about saying those very words to Luke and having him say them back to her.

She'd just thought it would happen in a church. Not in the back-corner booth at a pizza joint.

Of course, if Killian was honest with herself, the reason it stayed a daydream is because she never let her guard down. She was too afraid of ruining her friendship with Luke Freiling to ever tell him the truth.

But now, she had to let her guard down. She had to be honest with Luke.

She had to do it for Emma.

"You're right, Luke." She laid her hand lightly on top of his. The tip of each finger pulsed with the beat of her heart and tiny sparks of electricity. "I need help. But can we keep this between us—and I guess Josh? I've raised Emma without help. It's hard for me to accept charity. I'll pay you back."

He placed his other hand on top of hers, cradling it like a pillow.

"This isn't charity, Killian. This is a lifelong friendship between you and me. Friends help each other. Friends care. We'll keep it a secret, not because you should be ashamed to accept what I'm offering—but because your best weapon is the element of surprise. I don't want Davin to know what's coming."

Killian smiled for the first time since her phone rang earlier today. She didn't know what was coming either, but she knew Luke.

And for right now, trusting in him would be enough.

4

———————

*L*uke's phone continued to ping with text after text. As Luke had expected, Josh took this one to heart. The CyberCay team was like a family. They'd started something small and seen it grow exponentially. But Luke and the rest of the leadership team took great pride in the fact that even though their name was known around the world by the most powerful people in business and government and high tech, the firm still had small-town—or, more specifically, small-island—roots.

The whole team would be on Killian's side. And Emma's.

But for now, the time wasn't right to blow this one wide open. Luke had made that clear to Josh.

That wasn't all, however. He'd seen the look on Danny's face at the dock. People would draw their own conclusions about why Killian, someone who had lost everything growing up—then lost even more a few years ago with her sister's death—would be with him. They'd question her motives and draw their own conclusions. Killian had been labeled a lot of things over the years, and Luke wouldn't let words like "gold digger" and the like be added to the list.

"I don't think I can go in, Luke." Killian's voice had hardly any breath behind the words. Luke could tell a lump had formed in her throat. "Emma should be in her room. She should be here with me. I don't even know if I can go to sleep, thinking about what people Davin has her around tonight. Did she get dinner? Did she watch a cartoon? Did she get tucked in? Is she safe?"

Killian turned her head, and her eyes pleaded with him. Luke could see the avalanche of thoughts coming and felt powerless to stop them from playing in her mind like some kind of cruel loop.

He took a step and closed the distance between them on the small step in front of Killian's apartment. Reaching out, he slid his hands on either side of her head, threading his fingers through the chocolate silk of her shoulder-length hair. And without a word, he made up for fifteen years of complicated history between them.

Leaning down, he put his mouth squarely on Killian's. He didn't know about the swirling thoughts in her mind, but every jumbled thought of his own hit pause.

This felt right.

That was all he knew. Usually driven by data and evidence, one simple feeling was all he needed to know right now.

A second passed, then Killian leaned in and extended the kiss. She knew it too.

Then she leaned back on her heel, pulling them both out of the moment.

"Luke." She looked toward the lone lightbulb in the apartment complex parking lot. "No one saw us, did they?"

He dropped his hands to his sides, knowing he'd never forget the feel of her hair as it slid between each knuckle. Giving a cursory look over his shoulder, he felt a defeated breath pause, then tighten, at the top of his chest. He hadn't imagined the slide of her lips as she deepened the kiss—but maybe he'd imagined what that signaled to her.

"No. There's no one out tonight." Luke knew it was time for him to return to Provident Cay. He needed to put some distance and a tiny saltwater channel between them. "You should probably go in, Killian. Lock the door behind you and make sure you stay safe," he said.

On the surface, his words sounded like standard concern for her well-being.

In reality though, they covered up the fact that he couldn't forget that he'd never been able to tell Killian how he truly felt about her.

Killian was safe from prying eyes.

But Luke wasn't safe from a heart that had enough of denying how it felt about the girl he'd loved since the moment he realized what love actually meant. He'd do anything to take care of Killian—except tell her the real reason why.

❧

A SWIFT KNOCKING at the door served as Killian's alarm clock Saturday morning. She didn't want to wake up. She wanted to stay wrapped in her dream—a dream where her mother was still alive, her father still ran his business, and her sister had never met Davin.

Of course, if that dream was reality, that would mean Killian wouldn't have Emma.

Getting up to answer the door seemed preferable to letting that thought seep into her heart and mind. Killian looked through the peephole inserted in the metal apartment door. It was Josh Styles. Slowly, she slid the chain and undid both deadbolts in the door, then opened it a crack. "Josh?"

"Hey, Killian. I'm glad you're here. I've been working on some things and I was hoping you could confirm a few details for me. Can I come in?"

Killian nodded, half-surprised to see Josh and a manila folder stuffed with papers standing on her doorstep. But Luke made a call. And things always happened when Luke made calls.

Josh stepped in quickly, and Killian closed the door behind him, flipping both deadbolts again out of habit. Josh walked straight to the card table that made up the furniture set in her dining room. He pulled some papers out of the folder. "Does any of this mean anything to you?"

"That's Yolo." Killian tapped the paper at the right, which featured a grainy photo of a large man with a beard. "Davin used to work for him. He came to Carliann's funeral with the others who made a scene over Emma."

A shudder crossed Killian's shoulders. That was the worst week of her life, but this week was quickly giving it a run for its money.

"So they were connected at the time?"

"Oh yes—still are, as far as I know. I mean, obviously, Yolo isn't his real name, but I don't know what it is. Everyone in that circle has a street nickname of some kind. I'm sorry I'm not more help."

He picked up the folder and gave a half-smile. "Don't be, Killian. We just have to find the right breadcrumbs and put them all together. I don't want to get your hopes up, so give me a few more days before I explain. But we need to find out more about Yolo. You've confirmed he has a close relationship with Davin." He walked back across the living room and toward the door. "And one more thing, you need to stay safe. I'm not sure it's safe here."

Killian's heart began to toss out extra beats. She couldn't hear herself think over the roar of blood pressure ringing in her ears. "Josh... Emma. Is she safe?"

Killian couldn't get any other words out. Liquid fear began to pulse in her veins. She could see tiny goosebumps prickling the skin of her forearms.

"I think so. I'm just not certain you are."

A knock sounded at the door. Killian grabbed the edge of the plastic chair to her left for stability. Josh took two quiet steps and angled his head to see out the peephole, then unlocked the deadbolts.

Luke walked into the apartment and a wave of claustrophobia crashed over Killian. Suddenly, her already-too-tiny-but-all-she-could-afford apartment felt like a cage. "You were right, Josh. Davin doesn't have much creativity in his passwords. Ben just found a way into the Garden Grove Nursery website—he's doing forensics now. Kyle left early this morning for deep sea fishing out on the boat, but I called him and he's coming back to the Cay. I caught Grant in Verbier—he was out on the slopes, but he's coming back into his chalet, then will log on and coordinate with Ben."

"But that's everyone. Every exec at CyberCay." Killian knew how stupid she sounded, but she couldn't believe what she was hearing. "This is like a major incident for a huge client."

Luke's moss-green eyes locked with Killian's and never wavered. "This is bigger than any client. This is family. You are family."

The sun peeked through cracks in the closed-up mini-blinds hanging on the front windows to the apartment. For the first time in the long hours since she'd gotten the call, Killian allowed herself to think about hope. Hope that she'd have Emma back.

But something else tugged at her heart.

She remembered all the times she'd shared a pizza with Luke after school. She remembered the time he mentioned they needed an organized receptionist to be the public face of CyberCay and he couldn't think of anyone better than her. She remembered how he'd held her hands at Carliann's funeral, just simply remaining quietly by her side during the hardest day of her life.

She remembered how once upon a time, back in those school days when their crowd of friends had been inseparable, she daydreamed about being Mrs. Luke Freiling—and about starting a family of their own together. And then life—and death—and loss had gotten in the way.

But then she remembered him walking her to the door last night and kissing her just like she'd always dreamed he would. She remembered rising up on her tiptoes to get closer to him. She remembered savoring the scent of cedar and pine in his cologne. She remembered thinking that kiss was everything she'd dreamed it would be.

And then Killian stopped herself. She forced herself to remember that in her experience, dreams rarely came true.

It would be easier that way.

5

"*H*op on," Luke said to Killian as they walked up to his pride and joy, a Ducati Multistrada V4, in the CyberCay parking lot. It had taken some convincing to get her to come with him and stay at his house back on Provident Cay, but until Josh could confirm additional police surveillance of Killian's apartment, it simply wasn't an option for her to remain by herself, unprotected.

"That looks unsafe."

Luke shrugged. "Sometimes the best things in life are."

Killian's laugh came out loudly, almost a half-cackle. "You were president of the high school chess club, Luke."

"I took risks." He pulled a helmet out of the private lockbox he'd had installed next to his front-row parking space. "That didn't sound convincing at all, did it?"

She shook her head and grinned. "Not a bit. I was there for every one of your matches, in case you've forgotten."

"I haven't." He handed her the smaller of the two helmets in the box. "I want to take a risk right now, if you really want to know."

She rested the helmet on the seat of the Ducati. "I do. We've been friends for years. You're helping me with Emma. I hope you know you can always be honest with me. What's on your mind?"

"You. You're on my mind."

She didn't move. Didn't give him a sign.

Then she bit her lip. It was her nervous energy tell. Luke had seen it a hundred times before.

"I can tell you want to say something—but I know you're having trouble putting together the words, Killian. So you don't have to say anything. Just hear me out, okay?"

She nodded, although it looked like she was holding her breath as she did so.

"I kissed you last night." Luke put it all out there, studying her face for any changes as his words crossed her ears. "But I think you kissed me back."

Her head bobbed again; this time, the motion came up a little shorter than before. But Luke saw it, and it spurred more words to come out of him. "I made a mistake."

Before he could say the rest of his sentence, Killian's eyes went wide. He'd said the wrong thing. Again. This was why he'd never told her about his true feelings. He always got it wrong.

But he didn't have time to think this one through or plan or strategize. He just had to fix it.

With a single step, he closed the gap between them, wrapped his arms around her shoulders, and leaned his lips against hers. Luke was through talking. Killian was too, opening her mouth and taking the kiss deeper than any hesitation that had hovered between them only seconds before.

He loved it.

And Luke knew he loved Killian. Always had. Always would.

She pulled back a little. Luke felt a tiny breeze kick up from the waves just a few feet away.

"Make a mistake again," Killian whispered.

Luke laughed, then pulled her against him, taking things faster than the Ducati beside them could ever hope to go.

ONCE THEY ARRIVED at Luke's house, he made a quick call to the housekeeper. Killian didn't hear what was said, but within minutes of arriving, a hot bath had been drawn in the guest suite, complete with crests of white, floating bubbles piled on top of the water. Killian looked out the floor-to-ceiling windows. The sun shimmered in the sky, casting glittery sparkles of gold at the crest of each bobbing wave that surrounded Provident Cay.

Killian took a deep breath, trying to absorb the tranquility of her surroundings. It felt so strange to be in a place like this, staring at waves and bubble baths—like she was on vacation—while Emma's situation remained so precarious.

A knock sounded at the door to the guest suite. "Killian? You in there?"

"Sure, Luke. Come on in. I'm just looking at the waves."

"There's never a bad view at this house, that's the truth." Luke stood in the doorway.

Killian felt her heart get lighter looking at his sheepish half smile. He'd always had the best shy smile. In the office, she always forced her gaze down when she saw it, thinking it wasn't a good thing to think about your boss' smile.

But here, now...they just seemed like old friends. And old friends could appreciate each other's best qualities, right? She answered her own question with a quiet 'yes' in her mind.

"Everyone told me this lot wouldn't work for what I wanted it to do. I told you I took risks sometimes."

The words fell heavy on Killian. "Is it a risk—me being here?"

Luke leaned up against the doorframe. His t-shirt with the logo of a local fishing company stretched across his shoulders. "Davin's crew won't find you here. And if they do, I have a security system that cost me almost a million dollars. They can't get in here."

Killian crossed her arms over her chest, trying to give herself a boost of courage to tell him what was in her mind and on her heart. She didn't want to be silent with Luke anymore. "Not Davin. What if people at work find out? I'm the administrative assistant sitting at the front desk. You're the Chief Product Officer. We work with great people, but they're all human. There will be gossip. I'm just tired of gossip about me, Luke. My mother died. My father went bankrupt. My sister was murdered, and it's never been solved. I'm raising my niece and in a custody battle with my sister's ex-boyfriend—and he has no problem telling people I live paycheck to paycheck. There are so many stories about me. I just can't take being the secretary dating the boss, too."

Dating. She said they were dating. She wished she could read Luke's mind right now. Did he catch that slip? Did he think she was crazy? Or worse...did he think she was wrong?

Luke swiftly crossed the room. He reached out and tucked flyaway hairs behind her ear. The whole tilt of her crazy world seemed to straighten out the minute he came near.

"I understand why the thought of that hurts, Killian. Okay, we'll keep this quiet for a while. I don't care if we go on secret dates, just as long as we can go on dates." Luke leaned close and whispered next to her cheek. "I don't care if we kiss in secret, just as long as I don't have to stop kissing you."

Killian lifted her arms and rested them on Luke's chiseled shoulders, then turned her face up to his. "You don't."

6

Meet me on the dock at seven o'clock. Wear something fancy.

Killian ran her finger down the side of the heavy card stock that had been slid under the door to the guest suite. She already knew Luke preferred using old-school fountain pens, but the boldness of the slick, dark ink against the thick creaminess of the almost fluffy paper made her smile. This note looked special.

It *was* special.

She didn't know what Luke had planned, but clearly he was up to something. Killian also wanted to laugh at his instruction to "wear something fancy." She'd brought two pairs of jeans, three t-shirts, a set of pajamas, some bras and underwear, and one scuffed-up pair of tennis shoes. Everything she had with her was about one step away from a date with a dumpster.

Her stay with Luke, however, did not resemble a dumpster. During the last two days, he had given Killian regular updates on what the CyberCay team was doing to safeguard Emma. Josh had connected with a friend at the Port Provident Police Department. Two officers went to Davin's to perform a welfare check, which set Killian's mind much more at ease. She would never be truly comforted until she could hug Emma tightly and take her home, but just knowing she had not been harmed did slow Killian's over-active imagination.

Additionally, the CyberCay executive team had all put their hands on the keyboards around the world and began to turn the full force of their cybersecurity investigation skills on Davin and his business dealings. Luke gave Killian a status report almost hourly, and his words and progress made Killian begin to believe Emma would be back under her roof soon.

This roof currently over her head was a long way from her battered, old apartment in Port Provident's Eastland neighborhood. She didn't hear any sirens whizzing down the streets. No one yelled in the parking lot below. There were books in the nightstand, a jetted bathtub, a shower with a river rock floor, and fluffy white towels in the bathroom —and above all, a view like a postcard from every angle.

The beach house on the edge of this private island owned by a group of friends she'd known her entire life felt like a hotel in many ways.

But every time Luke found Killian to give her an update on the fight for Emma, it felt like home.

She hoped one day she could provide Emma with a place even one-tenth as lovely as Luke's house. Emma deserved a pool and a big kitchen and reliable air conditioning. She deserved so much more than what Killian could offer right now. She had almost finished paying off the debt that had landed on her doorstep over the years through her family tragedies. After she got out from under payment after payment after payment, she would start taking classes again at Provident College and earn her degree.

Killian had a plan to set an example for Emma and to make her proud.

But for now, her only focus had to be getting Emma back for good.

And then...maybe she could take a little bit of time to focus on Luke Freiling. As long as she was putting together a list of dreams she now believed she could make into reality, Luke needed to be on it.

Killian looked at the clock. She had about thirty minutes left to get ready. Fortunately, it would only take about three-and-a-half minutes to get her jeans on and choose her so-called fanciest t-shirt. She opened the closet, then stopped and stared. More than thirty hangers hung on the first bar in the spacious area. Touching a sleeve on a silky blouse, Killian drifted her fingers down to a large tag attached to the seam.

Boutique Providentique. Port Provident's most exclusive women's clothing store—a small, select boutique that stocked clothes mostly from Parisian shops, as well as exclusive New York labels and unique pieces from around the world—also known as the place where Killian felt too broke to even window shop.

A note was perched on top of the end of the closet rod. Killian took it down and opened it.

I wasn't sure how much you could fit in the backpack you brought, so I made a few calls and sent Lena to the island at lunch to pick up a few things. I hope you like them. Pick your favorite for dinner tonight. Surprise me.

Surprise him? Killian didn't see how anyone could be more surprised than she was right now. She gave one last glance to her faded jeans on a far hanger, before plucking a sleeveless dress with a plunging V neckline and a crimson tie at the waist. The label was written in French, and Killian wished she could read the language so she could savor every little bit of this moment. She slid her feet into a pair of strappy silver high heels and smiled.

Luke had taken her to Paris, and she hadn't even left the guest suite yet. She had been dreaming a lot this afternoon, but something told her that whatever reality Luke had planned for tonight would be better than anything she could come up with in her mind.

7

_L_uke looked at his watch at least fourteen times in seven seconds. He wouldn't necessarily classify himself as nervous. Just anxious.

He faced some of the world's most dangerous and well-known cybercriminals day in and day out. But they didn't make him nervous. In fact, trying to outsmart them every time he walked in the door at CyberCay made him a little cocky, if he was being honest. He knew he was good at what he did.

But he didn't know if he'd be a good boyfriend. Sure, he'd dated over the years, but nothing ever got serious. He never let it. Because in the back of his mind, he knew no woman could ever measure up to Killian and the easy comfort he had always felt in her presence. The guys at CyberCay were his lifelong best friends.

But Killian...she was his confidante, his biggest cheerleader, and the one person he never wanted to let down.

He knew he loved her. He had always known that. But he'd never known quite how to tell her.

Tonight, that would all change.

He looked up at the moon, rising larger than life and orange above the horizon line between the water and infinity, and said a silent prayer asking for guidance. _Let me know what to say,_ he breathed silently, hoping that God and his heart and his mind would all meet up in the middle and make tonight work out for the best.

Luke looked up at the sound of tapping on the wooden dock. Killian's shoes were making all the noise, but the way her curves filled out the short, navy blue dress with the deeply cut neckline got all the attention.

"It's taking everything I have not to let my jaw drop to the sand at the bottom of the Gulf of Mexico, Killian. You look amazing."

She smiled and did a little twirl. *Yeah, her curves looked just as good from every angle.*

"Well, the Paris fashion and makeup fairy apparently visited today. How did you pull it off, Luke?"

He smiled, her clear happiness stoking the fire inside of him. "I made a few calls, and I made you go to the pool with a really long book. Plus, Lena's awesome. You've been so worried. I just wanted you to have something nice. I also had Lena pick up some new things for Emma. I told you that we could date in secret—but I didn't want it to feel any less special."

He held out his hand and helped her onto the boat.

"How big is this thing? This isn't the boat you had last summer."

"No, it's not. I got the itch at Christmas and ordered a new one. It was just delivered about six weeks ago. It's a 60-foot Cantius."

"It's bigger than my apartment, Luke." She quickly walked down the stairs to see what all the offshore yacht had to offer.

He laughed at her observation. "You're probably right. It certainly has more bedrooms."

"How many?" She shot her question back as she looked at what Lena had prepared and left warming in the galley kitchen.

"Three."

Killian rolled her eyes. "Great. Totally outmatched by a boat."

"You can stay here anytime you want."

She opened the door to the master stateroom, complete with a king-sized bed and a table and chairs. Killian looked around, then quickly flopped on the edge of the bed. "Can I stay forever?"

Luke would have said yes and gotten down on one knee right then —he knew that in the center of his soul—but now was not the time.

"Let's take these plates and go up to the bow lounge at the front. I have it set up for us to eat there. I brought Danny Betancourt to captain tonight so we could talk. I have news."

Instantly, Killian's whole face changed. She went from sassy and confident to nervous and pleading. Her love and fear for Emma was written into every contour of her expression. She picked up her plate and walked quietly to the front of the boat, barely nodding as they passed Danny.

Once she sat down and the boat began to move to open water, Luke poured a glass of wine, a 2014 Stag's Leap Cask 23 Cabernet Sauvignon. He took a sip to brace himself before he laid everything out. He could taste the full body of the blackberry in the wine and he hoped that Killian liked both the wine and the news he was about to tell her.

"Ben was able to put together a few clues about Davin by poking around on the Garden Grove website. He had a hunch about what some of these coded things meant, so Josh went back to his friends at PPPD. The cybercrime division there got the access they needed. While they were working, Grant took some of the breadcrumbs Ben uncovered and went out to the Dark Web and found that Davin's running a drug ring under the cover of his legal business. That's where Yolo comes in. Grant also found files on the dark web that clearly showed your sister knew what was going on and was about to go to the police. They turned on her."

The moonlight above made the instant pallor in Killian's face even more noticeable. She rolled the wine glass between her hands. "Oh, Carliann. Somehow, I always knew that's what happened. So, what does this mean, Luke?"

"It means we're headed to get Emma. A warrant has been issued for Davin's arrest—and Yolo's too. The Coast Guard is seizing the boat with the drugs on it right now before it makes it to port. Davin thinks he's meeting the boat at Pier 47. He will meet Port Provident PD there instead. Detective Rigo Vasquez already has Emma with him and he's bringing her to Pier 19 for us to pick her up. There is no more visitation with Davin—unless Emma visits him in jail. It's over. Forever."

"Forever?" Now the moonlight showed tears flowing down Killian's cheeks. Luke placed his wine glass on the table and plucked Killian's away too. He reached out, wiping away the streaks of saline with his thumb. "You did this for me. And for Emma."

Taking both of her hands, Luke lifted each one to his lips and gave each a slow kiss, one after the other, then laid them in Killian's lap.

"I told you we were family. I love you, Killian Cordan. I always have. Maybe I haven't ever known how to tell you until this moment, but I hope that I will always show that with my actions—now and forever."

"Forever." She reached up, cupping his face with her hands, then leaning so close he could practically taste the wine she'd sipped. "That's how long I've loved you too. And that's how long I'll love you from this day forward."

EPILOGUE

"*E*mma! Come to up to the bow lounge!" Luke called for the feisty girl who couldn't get enough of being out on the water in the eleven months since she was reunited with her aunt on the yacht that had been renamed *Emma Mae*.

"Okay—we're all here. Now what is it? I thought we were going to swim." Killian adjusted Emma's goggles over the bridge of her nose.

"Well, it's definitely time we take the plunge—together. As a family." Luke pulled open the Velcro that sealed the pocket on the side of his swim trunks and stuck his hand inside.

Killian craned her head to the side, trying to figure out what Luke was doing. They'd come out as a couple about six months ago and instead of talking in the office, as Killian had feared, their co-workers teamed up to play good-natured tricks on the couple as a sort of form of approval. A group of Luke's team had been on the boat with them earlier, and Killian wondered if someone had pulled another prank, like putting itching powder in Luke's shorts or something.

Luke dropped to one knee in front of Killian and Emma and held up two rings—one larger, with a marquise-cut diamond that put out more sparkle than the sun—and one smaller, with a heart-shaped ruby attached at the center.

"We started our journey together a long time ago, and since the night we brought Emma back home for good, we've journeyed together all over the Gulf of Mexico and the Caribbean here on the *Emma Mae*. We were afraid to mess up our friendship for so long—but Emma brought us together, made us see that there's nothing more important than a family that will always be there. There was a time when I thought I'd never have the courage to tell you how I felt, Killian—but now I can't tell you enough. The only thing left to say is will you marry me, Killian? Can I be your dad, Emma?"

Killian closed her eyes and felt the seabreeze brush across her face. It seemed as though her father, her mother, and her sister were there in spirit, making sure she knew their joy.

"If you're not gonna answer, Koko, I will. I'll marry you, Luke...I mean, Dad." Emma took the ring out of Luke's hand, and Killian couldn't contain her laughter.

"I'm not sure that's how it works, sweetie," Killian said, holding out her left hand for the ring of her own. She felt like her smile might outshine the diamond. "But I will. Yes, Luke, I'll marry you."

Luke slid the ring onto her fourth finger. "We're together. As a family—no more secrets. Forever."

ABOUT THE AUTHOR

Kristen Ethridge writes Sweet Escape Romance—stories with hope, heart, and happily-ever-after for publishers like Harlequin's Love Inspired line, Hallmark Publishing, and Laurel Lock Publishing. She's a Romance Writers of America Golden Heart Award nominee and both an Amazon Christian Fiction and Inspirational Romance #1 Best-Selling Author.

You can find Kristen in her native habitat—a Texas patio—where she is likely to be savoring the joy of a crispy taco and a glass of iced tea. She's almost convinced her family that it's normal to talk to imaginary people, as long as she puts it in a book. Find all of Kristen's books and get a reader-exclusive sweet escape romance as her gift to you when you sign up for Kristen's newsletter at www.kristenethridge.com.

I'M NOT SUPPOSED TO BE HERE

PENELOPE FREED

Can she heal her broken body while he mends her shattered soul?

1

LESLIE

"I don't think I can do it, N-Noémie." I trip over her name. Noémie Dubois hasn't been my teacher since I was a teenager, but even after years as a professional ballerina it's hard not to call my first ballet teacher anything other than Madame Dubois, especially by her first name.

"Yes you can, *cheri*," Noémie says, sadly. "Ballet is in your soul, you can't just give that up."

"I can barely walk Noémie, how on earth do you expect me to teach?" Excruciating spasms run through my spine and left leg, nearly knocking me off my feet as I stand next to her. The empty dance studio beckons me, tempting me inside. I grew up in this room. These four walls saw so many of my firsts—my first class at the age of 3, first time en pointe, my first love.

Now I'm back, broken and broken-hearted.

"Leslie, you have a gift, it would be a shame to let it wither and die." Noémie keeps at me, her lilting French accent softening her words.

"Just, let me think about it, okay?" I want so desperately to accept her generous offer but I'm terrified. "I don't want to let you down," I add, looking up at her. "What if I can't do it?"

"My darling Leslie, you won't know until you try. Let's see what your handsome therapist says next week. First heal your body, then we work on your soul."

Limping slowly back to my car, the aluminum cane I'd recently graduated to adds an arrhythmic beat to my steps. Just driving here was an accomplishment. Mike, my physical therapist, only cleared me for driving at today's appointment. The last two steps to my car send stabbing pains through my leg, gritting my teeth I barely make it before they give out.

The cane isn't the only new hardware I'm sporting since my accident. I hate that phrase, "my accident." It sounds like somehow it was my fault. It had been a glorious spring afternoon when I'd stepped off the sidewalk in front of Lincoln Center, the stage I'd dreamed of performing on since I was eight years old, when a motorcycle came flying up Columbus Ave and straight into me.

I'd woken up in the hospital to the worst news a dancer can hear—pelvis fractured, left femur shattered, left knee unrecognizable, with several dislocated ribs and a concussion to boot. I'd stopped listening after I heard the words "possible multiple surgery's" fall from the doctor's lips. Fixing me required a metal plate, rod, and several pins holding me together. Learning to walk again was my physical therapist's goal—no one mentioned ever dancing again.

When I was able to manage the cross-country flight, Mom helped me pack up my adorable west-side apartment and I came home. Here I was, the great Leslie Parker, up-and-coming-ballet-superstar, the youngest woman to be promoted to the rank of principal at the world-renowned Classical Ballet Company, back home in Camarillo, CA, barely able to walk.

I drive home slowly, partly because of the pain and partly because I don't want to go home yet, where the only things waiting for me are more pitying looks from my mom and a laptop overflowing with emails from well-meaning friends and family. Some offering sympathy, some offering advice, some full of thinly-disguised digs over who's taken my spot in the dressing room back at CBC. The only people I have any desire to see these days are my mom, Madam Dubois and Mike. Mike, the only one who doesn't treat me like I'm broken.

As a kid I'd vowed to do whatever it took to accomplish my dream of being a ballerina at the most prestigious ballet company in the country. I'd given up boyfriends, high school dances, and summers with my friends. Hell, I gave up carbs. I'd given up so much, only for it to be taken away from me in an instant.

I slam my hand into the steering wheel, once again overwhelmed at the unfairness of it all. Noémie is nuts, my body can barely handle driving to the studio and back, how would I ever manage to teach an entire ballet class?

2

MIKE

"Come on Leslie, last one. This time I mean it." That feisty little ballerina gives me the stink eye, exhales, adjusts the weights in her hands, and slowly bends her knees, staring me down the whole time.

"Hold it at the bottom for three, two, one. And up, nice and slow," I chant, careful not to be too nice. Three months ago, we'd ended our first session with her in my face yelling at me for being too soft, declaring if I wasn't going to challenge her, she would do it at home, herself.

Pretty sure I fell in love with her right then—her face flushed and sweaty, long chestnut hair in a messy ponytail down her back, wincing at each step it took her to point an accusing finger in my face. She looked so fragile, even skinnier up close than the photos my niece had excitedly shown me when I told her about my new patient, but the fire in her honey-colored eyes flashed a warning not to underestimate her.

Every session since, every Monday, Wednesday and Friday, all summer long, she's shown up ready to challenge herself, and me. Graduating from a wheelchair to a walker and now a cane, Leslie Parker is five feet, three inches of pure determination.

Her grunt as she finishes the last squat drags my thoughts back to the present. "That last one was tough Mike," she admits, surprising me.

"Leslie Parker, are you actually admitting that you can't do something?" I eye her from head to toe, noticing the slight lean to her right to take weight off her bad leg. My professional perusal doesn't stop me from admiring how attractive she is. Especially now she's starting to put a hint of muscle on, losing some of the gauntness she'd had at our first session. Or maybe it's just that the dark circles under her eyes have started to disappear.

"I never said I couldn't do it. I said it was tough," she corrects me, dropping the weights into my outstretched hand.

"You're the toughest fairy doll I've ever seen." Turning to put the weights away, I'm grateful for a chance to collect my thoughts. "Any plans for the weekend?"

"I think I'm going to hang out at my old dance studio for a little while tomorrow. Madame Dubois asked me to come watch a rehearsal. Other than that, I'll be doing the same thing I do every night."

"What? Try to take over the world?" I tease, hoping to get a smile out of her.

Leslie snorts a laugh just as she takes a sip of water. I watch in horror as she chokes and coughs, sending her leg into spasm. Diving across the room to catch her as her bad leg collapses underneath her sends us both tumbling to the floor in a painful heap.

"You okay?" Gently, I pick her up off the floor, worried at the meek way she's letting me help her instead of insisting she can do it herself. I steady her on her feet, cupping her elbows as she finds her balance. I don't want to let go yet. My heart pounds in my chest, whether from nerves at the question I bite back, or because seeing her fall reminds me of how far from recovered she really is. For a moment we just stand there, staring at each other. From my vantage point above her, I can see her breath pick up. Opening my mouth to ask her to dinner, she shakes her head and pats my chest.

"I'm fine, I'm okay," she brushes me off, leaning on the patient table to my right, determined to stand on her own two feet. Literally. "And no, not taking over the world. Just trying to get through the days."

"I would ask you to promise me you'll take it easy tonight, but I don't know that I trust you." Ever since her first appointment, Leslie's gotten deeper and deeper under my skin. This tough as nails ballerina who showed up at my practice broken and crushed, but determined to piece herself back together. Before she can protest, I plow on. "Do you want to hang out tonight? Maybe get dinner and catch a movie? I need to keep an eye on you after that fall."

Lelise stares up at me, blinking. "Like... a date?"

"Technically, you're my patient, so no. Do you want it to be?" I can't help asking, not wanting to spook her but also dying to know her answer.

"I—I..." My eyes are glued to her full lips as she nervously pulls the bottom one between her teeth. "I don't know?"

"Well, good thing it's not a date then." I add a wink for good measure. "Just pizza and a movie. As friends."

Leslie's eyes wander over my face for a long moment, studying me. For a tiny thing she commands the room, demanding my attention without saying a word. I couldn't move if I tried, I'm frozen, waiting for her to deem me worthy.

With a nod and a smile like the sun, she pats my chest once more. "Okay. You can pick me up at seven. My physical therapist doesn't want me driving too much yet." Did she just flirt with me? Before I can formulate a response, Leslie grins, grabs her cane and slowly limps out the door.

3

LESLIE

*A*t seven on the dot I open the front door and there is Mike, towering over me with that smile. I assumed his smile only made me forget my own name when we were in a therapy session, because that smile meant progress and progress is the goal. Guess I was wrong. That honest smile, paired with his square jaw and those shoulders, draws me to him before my brain reminds me to be careful of my step. My foot catches on the door jam, sending me flying right into Mike's arms with a gasp of pain. Being Mike, he doesn't just reach out to steady me, no, he has an arm behind my back and the other one scooping behind my knees to cradle me against him before I can do more than exhale. That was smoother than my most well-rehearsed pas de deux—if he had been my partner on stage, I would have been the envy of the rest of the girls. Looking at his face this close, I would probably be the envy of all the girls anyway. It should be illegal for your physical therapist to be this attractive.

"You ok?" For half a second, I just want to stay here, letting someone else be strong for me. My head is millimeters from resting against his chest before my brain catches up to the situation.

"Yeah. Yes. I'm fine," The words come out breathless, probably because my heart is racing. "You can put me down now."

99

His dark eyes regard me thoughtfully for a moment before turning playful. "Maybe I don't want to?"

My cheeks go bright pink, breaking the spell I was threatening to fall under. "I can walk Mike. Put me down." I glare, just to emphasize my point. Laughing, he gently sets me on my feet.

I reach back for my cane and purse, awkwardly juggling both before Mike takes them from me so I can lock the door. He hands me back my purse but offers me his elbow instead of my cane. "Shall we?"

The teasing, funny, Mike that I know from PT is on full display as we eat our pizza, as promised. What I only discover now, seeing him relaxed and unfettered by our patient-doctor relationship, is the fierce but subtle way he looks out for me. Tucking me into his side as we navigate the restaurant and the narrow seats of the movie theater so I don't have to struggle with my cane. The way he guides me to our seats for the showing of *Singing in the Rain* he surprised me with, before going to get popcorn and drinks, knowing my body needed a break without me having to admit it. This man. How can I resist him?

It's late by the time Mike pulls up to my house. "How are you feeling?" he asks, a hint of Therapist Mike in his tone. I lean back against the seat, not ready to leave him yet.

"Almost normal." I'm surprised at my own honesty. "You make me feel like my old self. Like I'm alive again, not just surviving the day." If I'm going to be honest, I might as well be truly honest.

"Leslie," his voice cracks and I smile, glad I'm not the only one feeling flustered. He clears his throat and tries again. "Leslie, I feel like I've known you my whole life. Or like my life only began the day I met you." His hand slips up to gently cup my cheek and I melt into it. "I don't know what your future is going to bring, but I know I desperately want to be part of it."

I'm speechless, words half-forming and flitting away before I can make sense of anything but the feeling of his hand on my cheek, the constant dull throbbing of my body forgotten.

"Right now, recovery is your focus, but one day it won't be. Eventually we aren't going to be in such a committed *professional* relationship." His grin dissolves the thick tension building between us. "What other kind of committed relationship we have at that point is up for discussion."

Before I can formulate a response he's out of the car and crossing to my door. The butterflies in my stomach keep me silent as he walks me to my front door. My key is in the lock before I finally can speak.

"Thank you for tonight. See you Monday?" Mike nods, holding my eyes with his for a long moment. For an instant I think he might lean down and kiss me. I want him to.

Instead, he wraps me up in his arms, his chin resting on top of my head. I hold him tight, allowing myself a moment of respite from being strong. And then he's gone, with a hoarse "Goodnight, Leslie," and the ghost of a kiss to the top of my head.

Floating, I slip inside, softly closing the door as he drives away. The last time I felt this happy I was standing on stage, listening to the applause of an adoring audience, sweaty and out of breath. I'm not sweaty now, but I'm just as out of breath.

WALKING into the studio two hours ago, the girls stared at me in awe, nervously glancing at each other. I'm sure they've grown up hearing stories about my time here. Several magazine articles about my career are framed on the walls. I suppose when I was last here as a student these girls would have been around seven or eight years old, maybe younger. Knowing myself, I would have been far too self-important to notice them at the time. It's a strange sensation to know that these girls not only knew who I was when I was "Leslie Parker, star ballerina" but they also remember when I was just plain old "Leslie Parker, aspiring dancer." It's humbling and uncomfortable.

And now? I ache.

My leg aches, my back aches, my hip aches, and my soul aches. I'm stiff from sitting in a plastic chair for hours, my cane tucked underneath it, out of the way.

My light-heartedness from last night is impossible to hold on to sitting here. Worse than the pain in my body are the jabs to my soul, watching these beautiful, whole, girls do what now I can only dream about. I want to get up and help the sixteen-year-old in front of me nail the difficult footwork she's struggling with. I'm longing to get up and do it myself.

"Leslie, dear, do you have anything to add?" Noémie says suddenly, startling me from my thoughts. "Or perhaps, if you feel up to it," she adds quietly, "you could take Jenny and Shelley to work on their solos?"

I swallow, unsure of how to answer. What if my legs won't hold me? How can I help them when I can't even walk? Noémie sees my hesitation, guessing, "Or perhaps I'll take them in the other room and you can watch these girls run through Waltz of the Flowers?"

My hesitation irks me. In my PT sessions I can put on the tough, 'don't tell me I can't do something,' attitude I developed in my years in New York, none of this timidity. Maybe it's because Mike doesn't see me as broken or maybe it's because I won't allow that motorcycle to take any more from me. Swallowing my fears, I nod. "Sure, I'll do my best."

Noémie rounds up the girls she needs, leaving behind a dozen teenagers, staring at me, waiting for direction. Taking a deep breath, I settle into the character I've played a thousand times.

"Ok girls, let's do this." My voice rings out with far more confidence than I feel and the girls scramble to find their starting positions. Nodding my head at the girl standing ready at the stereo, I brace my heart against the expected pain, and let the familiar delicate notes wash over me.

4

MIKE

"How was the rest of your weekend?" I ask as Leslie maneuvers onto the table, chin resting on her hands. She groans as I dig my fingers into the flesh of her hip. The muscles in her hip tense hard before eventually relaxing. She makes the same face every time—eyes closed, bottom lip caught between her teeth, slowly and deliberately breathing in and out through her nose. It makes me smile every time. The fact that she has to work so hard to relax reveals how much pain she's really in, and how determined she is to not let it show.

"You never answered my question, Fairy Doll." Tapping her hip and stepping back, she turns over onto her back, eyes fixed on the ceiling, a hint of pink at the tips of her ears.

"It was fine. How was yours?" I take hold of her uninjured right leg, one hand behind her knee, the other wrapped around her ankle. She's so slim my fingers overlap, and I wouldn't consider myself a giant. Just your slightly-taller-than-average guy. My American dad was kind enough to give me enough towering Viking genes to counteract my Japanese mother's tiny frame.

"Oh, you know, it was pretty low key. Went for a drive up the coast, enjoyed the sunshine." I lift her leg, pressing it up towards her chest. Her good leg has retained a surprising amount of flexibility, although not as much as she would like. In our first session I had bent it to a ninety-degree angle, like I normally would, but when it wouldn't go much farther, the frustration in her eyes had me mentally vowing to do whatever it took to help her. "How did it go at the studio on Saturday?"

The smile drops from her face at my words. Immediately, I want to take them back, kicking myself for bringing up the sensitive subject. Of course it was hard for her to watch those girls dancing, how could it not? She hasn't outright flirted with me this whole session, but she smiled and laughed on our non-date, the most relaxed I'd ever seen her. I wish I could find the words that would bring her back there.

She shrugs and I pause, waiting for her to say something else. When she doesn't, I release her leg and walk around the table to manipulate the other. Gently, I lift this one the same as the other. Her sharp inhalation when I take it just to ninety degrees is the only indication it hurts. Glancing at her face reveals silent tears rolling down her temples. Instinct has me lowering her leg and pulling her to sit up on the table, the need to gather her up in my arms more than I can resist, no matter how much I know I should.

Leslie's arms snake around my waist, holding me tight, like I'm the life-preserver keeping her afloat in the ocean of her grief. I don't hear them at first, but I feel the shaking of her shoulders as she fights the sobs muffled against my chest. All I can do is stand here holding her against me. Subconsciously, I cradle the back of her head with one hand, the other slowly rubbing up and down her back, my lips dancing above the crown of her head.

"It's okay, Leslie. I got you,' I whisper over and over, grateful there's no witnesses to her break down, the clinic empty this early in the morning. Another shuddering sob shakes her, buckling her leg. Scooping her up in my arms, I no longer care about anything other than taking care of this amazing woman who refuses to be weak, and sit on the nearest rolling stool. She tries to curl up in my lap but her leg and hip won't cooperate, instead dangling awkwardly at my side.

"I'm... I'm," Her words are strangled by sobs she can't seem to stop.

"Shhhhh, it's okay. I got you. Whatever you need. No apologies necessary."

"I didn't..." I feel her take a shaky breath against my chest and try to sit up.

"Nu-uh, nope." I squeeze her tight against me. "Just rest for a second. I'm here, just let me hold you."

Going limp against me, her sobs quiet. I reach over to the nearest table, snagging a box of tissues, which I drop in her lap. "You wanna talk about it?"

"Yes. No. I don't know." Her voice is so soft I almost have to hold my breath to hear her over the pounding of my own heart.

"Did I hurt you?" I'm pretty sure the answer is no, but I need to be sure.

"Oh! No. I mean, I had a twinge but it wasn't that."

"Is this about visiting the studio over the weekend?"

She inhales slowly, stalling. "Probably. I just keep saying to myself, 'I'm not supposed to be here,' and then I look around and I'm still here. This wasn't supposed to be my life, you know?" She goes quiet for a moment, then, her voice so small I can barely hear it. "I actually really enjoyed helping the kids. It felt so good to be doing something. But I don't know if I liked doing it because I'm bored out of my mind, because Noémie asked me to, or because I miss dancing and this is the closest I'll ever get again."

"My niece, Nadia, dances there, she was one of those flower girls you were teaching," I admit. "We had family dinner on Sunday and she couldn't stop talking about you. Whatever you said to those kids left an impression."

Leslie sits up, eyes searching my face. "Really?"

I grin. "Pretty sure she went home and wrote down every word you said in her diary and sleeps with it under her pillow." I'm rewarded with one of Leslie's infectious laughs. "You ready to get back to work, slacker?" I tease for good measure. As much as I want to wrap her up in bubble wrap so she never hurts again, I know that this was just a moment of vulnerability. I'm so grateful that she allowed herself to be weak with me, even if it's just for a moment.

Gently, I steady her as she gets her feet underneath her and stands. "Am I allowed to try the treadmill today?" She asks, eyeing it.

"If you do everything else without saying it's too easy, I'll let you try for five minutes. But you have to promise to be careful and go slowly." Her grin is like sunshine peeking through storm clouds.

Yup, I'm a goner for this woman.

5

———

LESLIE

"*B*onjour, *cheri!*" Noémie waves me over to her table in the coffee shop. I stop at the counter to order a salad and a cappuccino before making my way over to join her. "Come, come. I want to hear what your handsome doctor said."

Hearing my old teacher talk about Mike that way has my ears burning. Are you ever old enough not to be embarrassed discussing your love life with a teacher? "He's my physical therapist, not my doctor, Noémie."

Noémie waves my words away with a mischievous grin. "Handsome doctor rolls off the tongue so much better, no?"

"Well, you may have a point there." I grin.

"First, I want to know what he said about your recovery, then I want to know about everything else," she says saluting me with her cappuccino.

Squirming under her scrutiny I decide to start with the easier topic. "Mike says I'm doing well. We're cutting back my PT to twice a week and I'm allowed to start doing some things on my own at home, as long as I promise not to overdo it."

"This is good news, yes? Although maybe not so good if you see him less often?"

I can't help smiling at that. "It's good and bad. Good that I'm getting stronger. I walked on the treadmill without my cane for eight whole minutes last week." It was supposed to only be five, but Mike was distracted by the phone ringing so I kept going until he came back and told me off for it. "But yeah, I'll miss seeing him three days a week."

I'm saved from elaborating by the arrival of our salads. Not that Noémie lets that deter her for digging for more.

"You like him, no? Do not tell me he is just a friend, *cheri*... I know you better than that." Noémie points her fork at me, smiling.

"I do like him. He's the only person who doesn't treat me like I'm made of glass." Noémie opens her mouth to protest and I quickly back-track. "You don't now, but you did when I first came home."

Noémie regards me for a moment. "Leslie, *ma cheri*, it broke my heart to see you when you first came home. You were *le papillon*, a butterfly, that had been crushed. You needed time to grow strong again."

"Strong? Noémie, I still need a cane." Bless her for thinking I'm tougher than I am, but she has to know I'm still not ready for this.

"No, no. *Cheri*, you are so much stronger than you think." She taps her head, then her heart. She's not talking about my physical strength. "I've known you a long time. Always, when you face defeat, you need time to lick your wounds, but then you come back stronger, better."

I don't know what to say, so I take a bite of my salad instead. Noémie eyes me, knowing exactly what I'm doing. "He doesn't treat you as frag-ile, and he's handsome. What is there to be unsure about?"

Swallowing, the words spill out before I can change my mind. "Because I really, really like him. It snuck up on me while I was busy piecing myself back together. If I start dating him Noémie... I think he's it for me."

"And why is that bad?"

"Because it means staying here. Giving up on the chance of anything else."

Sadness fills Noémie's eyes as understanding dawns on her. "You would have to admit that dancing professionally is truly over for you."

Those are the words I can't bring myself to say. If I'm not a dancer, what am I? I can't stop the tears that spill over and drip down my cheeks. I haven't admitted to anyone, not even myself, that I would never dance again. That some small kernel of hope, hope that I would defy the odds and make a full recovery, lives deep down inside me.

"Oh, *ma cheri*," Noémie takes my hand across the table, squeezing reassuringly. "Your heart loves them both but you think you can only have one or the other." That's it exactly. The tears flow harder and I grab a napkin to dab my eyes. "My dear, I'm going to tell you something you don't want to hear. You're right. You cannot have both."

I'm stunned at her words. Noémie gives me a sad smile before continuing. "You cannot have both at the same time. But, *cheri*, you already had one. You had a career that people will be envious of for decades to come."

"But I wasn't ready for it to be over," I protest.

"No dancer is ever ready for it to be over. We never know which is going to be the last time we step on stage. But there is life after, I promise. Teaching, sharing what you know, can start to fill the hole it leaves behind. If you let it. This doctor of yours sounds special, don't give up the chance of an amazing future because you can't let go of who you used to be."

"I don't know if I can."

"Come to the studio on Wednesday at five o'clock. I have someone I want you to meet."

"Girls, this is Ms. Parker, she is going to watch our class today."

In unison, tiny voices chorus, "Hello Ms. Parker," accompanied by wobbly curtsey's. The class of six-year-old girls are curious about me, a few of them eyeing my cane tucked beneath my chair, but after a brief survey they turn their attention back to Noémie.

Noémie starts the class off by warming the girls up, skipping and galloping around the room. Most of them are uncoordinated, except for two girls who stand out—a pretty blonde and a serious redhead. The red-head has the most exquisite legs and feet, maybe even nicer than mine, concentrating on everything Madam says. The little blonde appears to be her good friend, standing close to her. I catch her doing a few extra twirls, but when it's time to work she gets to it, often the first to volunteer to try something.

Near the end of class, Noémie is teaching them a new step, a tricky little jump from one foot to the other. I notice the red head looking anxious and defeated as she struggles with the step, her blonde friend unsuccessfully trying to help. I glance up at Noémie and see her helping a few of the other girls on the other side of the studio. I catch her eye and nod my head toward the two girls.

"Girls," I call out softly, catching their attention. "Would you like some help?" I wave them over to my chair since I can't go to them. "Remind me of your names?" I ask as they stand in front of me, smiling.

"I'm Olivia, that's Hannah," the blonde answers for both of them. Hannah just smiles shyly at me. I smile back and start breaking down the step for them the same way I watched Noémie do it. Demonstrating it with my hands instead of my feet feels like cheating, but it doesn't stop them from understanding me. It takes a few minutes, but eventually it clicks for them and they each show me the step with newfound confidence. Olivia throws her arms around my neck before running away to join the rest of the class.

Hannah eyes me for a moment, a timid smile on her face. Then she drops into a little curtsy with a whispered "thank you," and runs off to join her friend. A little bubble of happiness bursts through me at seeing them do it easily now. It doesn't take away any of the pain of losing my ability to dance, but it floats up right alongside it, protecting me from the sharp edges of my grief. Funny, now that I've noticed it, I can feel other little bubbles of happiness joining it. Going out with Mike last weekend, good days in PT, spending time with my mom. Noémie was right, I can find happiness again, if I let myself.

For the first time since the accident I feel like there are still things to look forward to after all. After the class, I hide in Noémie's office to make a few phone calls.

6

MIKE

I spot her leaving the studio right away. The slight hiccupping step that I know so intimately, her chestnut hair gleaming in the setting sun.

"Bye Uncle Mike," Nadia's kiss on my cheek pulls me from my observation. Grabbing her bag, she slides out, closing the door behind her. "Hi Ms. Parker!" she calls before disappearing inside.

Rolling down my window, I call out to Leslie's retreating back. "Hey, can I buy you a coffee?" I park my car without giving her a chance to say no and jog to her side.

"Are you stalking me now? I just saw you this morning." Teasing. Teasing is a good sign, especially considering how quiet she was in our session this morning. I couldn't bring myself to pry, worried I was the cause. I can work with teasing.

"Nope, I give Nadia a ride every Wednesday. But I'm glad I ran into you." I offer her my elbow, reaching to take the cane from her so she can use me for support instead.

Her honey eyes are playful as she quips, "I don't know... My physical therapist might get mad at me for not using my cane."

"I think he'd be okay with it." I fire back, failing to hide my grin at our banter. Steering her into the coffee shop next door to the studio, I settle her at a table before going to order. While I wait at the counter for our drinks, a prickle up the back of my neck, like I'm being watched, takes me by surprise. A quick glance over my shoulder and I lock eyes with Leslie. Was she? Slowly, she bites her bottom lip, deliberately dropping her eyes from my face. Oh. Yeah. She did.

"Order for Mike!"

Grinning, I turn around and grab our drinks. Her obvious appreciation for my jeans sparking new confidence after how upset she's been. Do I pause to let her look a little longer? Maybe.

Dropping into the seat opposite Leslie, I hand over her drink. "So, what did Madam have you doing today?"

"She tricked me," Leslie's laugh washes over me like afternoon sun. "Told me she had someone she wanted me to meet. Turns out it was ten twirly six-year-olds." She gets a faraway look in her eye, but I don't interrupt. "There were these two girls in the class. Hannah and Olivia. They remind me so much of myself. Both are really talented and eager to learn. I'm pretty sure Noémie purposefully ambushed me with them to tempt me into accepting her offer."

"What offer?"

"A job offer. I mean, she offered me a job teaching at the studio when I'm ready. Not until I get clearance from you or Dr. Rose." She added hastily. "I don't know if I want to take it. I don't know what my plans are for..."

The excitement fades from her eyes as her voice trails off. Slowly, I reach across the table, curling my fingers around hers. "I'm not going to tell you what to do, not that you'd listen to me anyways, but I need you to know that whatever you decide, I just want you to be happy."

"Do you think I can be happy? Here, I mean?" She grasps my hand, hard.

"If you stay?" Her ponytail bounces with her vigorous nod. "I think you can be happy anywhere, but yes, I think you could be happy here. If you let yourself."

Leslie is silent for a few moments. Her thumb rubs small circles against mine, she's probably not even aware she's doing it but it's all I can think about.

"What about the job? Do you think I could teach one day? In your professional opinion," the last sentence is delivered with a smile, breaking the heavy atmosphere between us.

"I think you should consider it."

"You don't think it will be too much for me?" Studying her face, I think a tiny part of her wants me to say yes. But I'm not willing to give her permission to take the easy way out. I know Leslie well enough that not only will she regret it one day, but she'll probably never forgive me for it either, and I'm not willing to risk losing her over this. So I pull my hand free of hers, leaning both elbows on the table so I can look deep into her eyes.

"Fairy Doll, I can't tell you if it's going to be too hard for you mentally, but I can tell you that you're making really good progress physically. You don't need to make any decisions today but I can tell you what I know. You're a fighter. You may look like a fragile butterfly, but underneath you are titanium steel. This isn't going to break you."

"I've been putting off thinking about what happens next for as long as possible, but I'm going to have to face it sooner or later." Her voice is so quiet I have to lean close to hear it. "If I was being completely honest, I would tell you that I'm as fragile as everyone thinks I am. All I want to do is hide away. No one really understands how much work recovery is."

Not giving me a chance to interrupt, she goes on. "Everyone keeps telling me how brave I am, how they're so proud of how well I'm doing." Leslie's voice grows strong as she speaks. I want to sit back and bask in the glory of her. She has no idea how amazing she is. "I want to scream that I'm not brave, I'm not doing well. I'm so tired of pretending, of working so hard just to feel halfway normal. But I'm not dead and that's good enough for now." I fight the tears I can feel building in my eyes and the lump in my throat damming up the words I can't say yet. I love her.

Reaching across the table I take her hand, drawing her eyes to mine. "Hey. I know how hard it is. I see you. I have so much respect for how hard you've worked to get where you are. And we're not done yet, not by a long shot. We may never get you back on stage at Lincoln Center, but I am here for you, every step of the way. Literally."

"Are you saying that as my physical therapist, or as my friend?"

"Leslie Parker, let me be very clear. You are so deep under my skin that I don't know where I end and you begin. I am saying this as the man who wants to be there to cheer you on for every milestone you achieve and pick you up after every fall."

She's silent for a long moment, long enough for panic to start spreading through me, was it too much? Does she not feel that same way I do?

"Mike?"

"Yeah?"

"You're fired."

The panic I was fighting down explodes through my gut. No. This can't be happening, I can't lose her. I'll take it back, anything to keep her, even if it makes our therapy sessions torture, I can't lose her. "What? Why?"

Smiling, Leslie stands up, holding out a hand. "I'm firing you. There's something more important I need you for. Now, will you help me to my car? Preferably without the 'picking me up after I fall' part."

I'm frozen to my chair. "What are you saying, Fairy Doll?"

"I'm saying that maybe I can't live without your terrible jokes and ugly mug. I'm saying that even though I don't know what the future is going to bring, I think I'd like it if you were with me when it comes." The smile she gives me is so full of light, so free and easy, I feel like I'm meeting her for the very first time. *This* is how I want to see her smile every day, no hint of pain in her eyes. Just joy.

EPILOGUE

MIKE

"*Merci*," Noémie murmurs as we watch Leslie wrap her arms around Hannah and Olivia, "you saved her. I was afraid she would never come back to life after the accident, but you did it."

I shake my head, never taking my eyes off the incredible woman I'm lucky enough to love. "She did it. You're the one who gave her a purpose, showed her how to channel her passion in a new direction." Parents, dancers and stage crew bustle around us, cleaning up the mess left backstage after the year end recital. Noémie and I are packing up props and abandoned costumes while Leslie wisely chose not to argue with me about it. She's busy chatting away to the moms of the Dynamic Duo, as I've dubbed them, smiling and laughing. Her pride in these dancers is infectious.

Leslie dove head first into helping Noémie run the studio, taking on paperwork and administrative tasks while observing classes every chance she can, eager to learn from Noémie. I still see her at my clinic a couple days a week, from across the room while she works with my colleague. I can't say I regret her firing me as her therapist.

Not when it means I get to love her every day. Hopefully for the rest of my life.

Noémie pats my cheek. "True, she saved herself. But we each gave her a reason to fight for it. Come, I shall take advantage of those muscles of yours. Let's finish up." Dutifully, I follow her around the theater, carrying boxes and bins of who knows what. In the nine months since Leslie dragged me into this world, I've learned it's better not to ask.

Finally, it's just the three of us and the crew left, the bright lights of the theater turning off one by one until there's only the single ghost light left to stand center stage. Leslie leans against me, her head nestled against my shoulder. "This is my favorite part," she whispers. Does she notice the way she's subtly swaying, as if dancing to music only she can hear?

"It's magical, Fairy Doll." My voice is soft, afraid to disturb the spell that weaves around us. Silently, Noémie touches my shoulder and tiptoes away with a smile, the only person privy to my plan. I let Leslie's sway push us from side to side for a moment, knowing she's lost in her mind, reliving the countless stages she's danced on. Gently, I slide my arms around her waist, letting her lean back against my chest as we continue to sway. "If you told me a year ago I'd be standing on a stage, dancing with the love of my life and feeling nothing but joy I'd have laughed in your face."

Leslie turns to look up at my face, sliding her hands around my neck, smiling. "This isn't really dancing, you know."

"It isn't?" Before she can argue with me again, I sweep her up in my arms and spin slowly. Laughing, Leslie leans back in my arms, trusting me to hold her, one arm wrapped around my shoulders, the other sweeping open, as if she's sharing the joy she feels with the world. After a couple of rotations, I slow to a stop, not letting her go.

Those honey eyes study me, utterly trusting, vulnerable in a way only a few will ever have the privilege of seeing. Her hand rests against my cheek as I drown in her. "I love you." I'll never be able to tell her enough.

"I love you too." Her lips are soft and sweet as she presses them to mine, her tiny sigh music to my ears. "You're my favorite pas de deux partner. Most of them would have put me down by now."

"I'm never letting you go."

"You have to put me down eventually, you know."

"Do I? I distinctly remember you telling me that the best pas de deux partners make sure that their lady never falls. Maybe I want to be better than the best?"

"You're already the best thing that's ever happened to me." Her words are teasing but her voice is gentle, reverent. Slowly, I set her back on her feet, making sure she's steady before I let go and drop to one knee. Her eyes go wide as I dig in my pocket for the little box I put there this morning.

"Leslie," my voice cracks, just like on our first date, and I fight the lump in my throat at the reminder of how far we've come. She's already crying and laughing though her tears as I struggle to speak. "You are the most amazing person I have ever met. I hate that you lost your childhood dream and went through so much pain, but every day I wake up grateful that I met you, that I was allowed to have some small part of helping you build a new life. To help you find a new dream." The next words get stuck in my throat as my eyes fill.

"I want to be the last partner you ever dance with. Will you let me stay by your side for the rest of our lives? Build a new life, a new dream —together? Will you marry me?" I open the box, revealing the ring Noémie helped me pick out a few months ago. A solitaire encircled by smaller stones, a ballerina setting, perfect for my Leslie.

"Oh Mike." Tears run down her cheeks, but joy shines in her eyes as she stretches one hand towards me. "Being with you is better than anything I could have dreamed of. Yes, yes, of course I will!"

The ring slides easily onto her finger, as easily as I sweep her up in my arms, kissing, laughing, crying, knowing we're both exactly where we're supposed to be.

ABOUT THE AUTHOR

Penelope Freed lives in the Pacific Northwest where you can find her learning how to drive in the rain, walking her dog and making a mess in the kitchen. Her husband and daughter think she's a little bit bonkers and really hate it when she dances embarrassingly in public. Which she does, often.

After a lifetime in the ballet world, Penelope decided to start writing down the stories in her head instead of narrating her ballet classes with them—her former students are very thankful for this decision. Now, Penelope writes stories about dreamers, just like she is, who are willing to do whatever it takes to make those dreams come true.

If you want to keep up with Penelope, sign up for her newsletter here https://sendfox.com/penelopefreedbooks

Hannah and Olivia's story continues in the On Pointe series with special appearances by Leslie and Mike. Book 1, *Toe to Toe*, releases Feb 5, 2020, free to read in Kindle Unlimited! Available here https://books2read.com/u/bw7yJo.

WOUNDED HEARTS RANCH

JENNA HENDRICKS

Jerod's war wounds are more than skin deep. Will he allow Dana to get close enough to heal his wounded heart?

1

Jerod Stevens stood tall and proud as he watched his new sign, Crooked Arrow Ranch, be raised onto its post. He'd only owned the place for a few months, but he'd jumped out of the shoot faster than a raging bull trying to buck its rider in less than seven seconds. In fact, his ranch wasn't ready for anyone when his first seven residents joined him right before Christmas.

They had lost their housing when a fire ravaged the building. When the Home for a Warrior coordinator called Jerod, he was more than willing to change his Christmas plans and help out with a place to stay for Christmas. Turned out to be a lot more fun than he'd thought possible. Sure, there were some sour faces when he met them at the airport, but all in all they had a great time. Especially when he pulled out the Frenchtown Roasting Company's coffee and pastries. But what really put a smile on his new residents' faces was the Christmas breakfast—cinnamon rolls that curled the toes. They were so sweet, yet perfectly doughy.

Jerod was in love.

Not with a woman, although a certain barista at the coffee shop was quite beautiful. He was in love with the pastries. He had decided to make it a weekly tradition, and so every Sunday morning a tray of cinnamon rolls along with a vat of that week's special roast coffee waited for him at the Frenchtown Roasting Company.

A screeching sound brought him out of his reverie, and he looked around for what had made the noise that caused him to duck and cover behind the signage truck without even realizing what he had done. The noise, high-pitched and sounding like an RPG, caused his heart to race and sweat to form on his brow even though snow covered the ground and it couldn't be any warmer than thirty degrees out.

When the crunch of metal on metal hit his ears, he straightened up and ran to the two trucks. As he ran, his feet slipped and slid across the icy road. Of course, he should have realized that the road was going to be icy. Yesterday the sun came out for a few hours and melted away patches of snow. Then last night it got below freezing, and the mercury hadn't risen much since. Jerod put his arms out to balance himself as he continued forward.

The guys working on his sign followed him.

When Jerod arrived at the old red truck, he saw a young woman at the steering wheel, not moving. Her head was down on the steering wheel, as it was too old to have airbags. "Miss, can you hear me?" He pulled open the door with ease. While she had hit someone head-on, her old truck was like a tank—solid, and could take a beating without much damage.

When she still didn't move, he touched her shoulder and felt the cold permeating her being. For a moment he wondered if she was still alive. Then she stirred and moaned.

"Oohh." The woman's voice was low, and she sounded like she was going to be in a lot of pain. When she sat up, she almost slumped forward again. Her hand went to her head. "What happened?"

Jerod saw the blood flowing down her face and he pulled out his cell phone to call for help. "It's alright. Help is on its way."

When she turned her green eyes on him, he sucked in a breath. "Dana?"

She looked at him and smiled a lazy smile as her eyes glazed over. Her hand reached up and cupped his cheek. "Handsome cowboy," she said before her eyes fluttered closed and she slumped forward again.

Jerod acted quickly; his hands shot out to catch her before her head hit the old steering wheel, again. He noticed she wasn't wearing a seatbelt, and then realized the truck wasn't outfitted with any because of its age. "Dana? Are you alright?" He wasn't a medic, but he did have some medical training thanks to his many years in the Army. His Special Forces training also afforded him an extra training session. He checked her pulse. Not as strong as he would like, but it was there. She would be alright as long as the ambulance arrived soon.

When he heard the commotion from the other truck, he knew the sign installation guys were helping the other party, so he wasn't worried about them. Instead, he thought back to when he first met Dana and almost smiled.

It was last year and he had come to town to look at ranches. The McMasters were selling so they could retire to Florida. Jerod was tired and hungry when he arrived in Frenchtown, Montana on a hot summer day. He went to the only coffee shop in town hoping to get his favorite drink. There was only one barista on duty; she was tall with long auburn hair that curled down her back in a ponytail with just a few wisps over her shoulder.

There wasn't anyone else working the store, and there was a line out the door. Jerod shook his head and stood in line thinking they must have some great coffee if everyone was waiting so long in the afternoon heat for it.

When it was finally his turn, he walked up to the register and noticed the pretty woman with amazing green eyes.

"What can I get for you?" she asked in a monotone voice.

Jerod could tell she was overworked. So he asked, "What's everyone been in line for?"

She looked him in the eyes for the first time and hers opened wide. "Ah," she gulped. "We have a new cold coffee drink. Have you heard of cold brew?"

A slow smile spread across his face. "Why, yes I have. I'll take your largest one with cream and extra ice." He looked over at the pastry counter. "Do you have any sandwiches?"

The guy behind him laughed. "Mister, this isn't Starbucks. We have coffee and pastries here. If you want a sandwich, you'll have to head over to the diner or the Sip 'n' Go for a premade sandwich." He lowered his voice. "But I wouldn't recommend them for sandwiches. Lord only knows how long they've been in the fridge."

Jerod chuckled. "Thanks. I think I'll take the coffee and then head over to the diner for an actual meal."

"Good idea," the man behind him said.

Jerod noticed the nametag on the pretty barista and smiled at her. "Thanks, Dana."

She furrowed her brow and stared at him questioningly.

He pointed to her chest. "Nametag."

She snort-laughed and her cheeks reddened almost instantly. "Oh."

Jerod smiled when he thought back to that day. He had hoped he would one day get a chance to talk to her again, but since he'd been back in Frenchtown he hadn't seen the woman. This was the last way he wanted to meet her again.

The whirring sound of the sirens pierced his ears, and he flinched. This time, he caught himself before he freaked out and tried to hide. "It's only the ambulance," he told himself three times before he could breathe normally again.

An EMT rushed to his side and asked him about the accident as he began to check the woman for vitals and see if she could be moved safely.

"I don't really know what happened. I was watching the sign guys at my ranch." He pointed to the entrance to his ranch, which was only about two hundred feet away. "I was standing to the side, watching them install my new sign, when I heard screeching tires and then a crash of metal on metal." He shivered with the memory of the sounds. "Then I ran over and found Dana slumped over her steering wheel. I think she was unconscious."

"Did she wake up while you were here?" The EMT pulled Dana's eyelids back and checked her pupils.

"Yes, she did. But I don't know how coherent she was." Jerod explained how she passed out again and he tried to keep her from falling forward. He kept the bit about her calling him handsome to himself.

"Can you help me to get her out safely?" The EMT looked at Jerod and then at his gurney.

"Sure." Jerod pulled over the gurney and locked it in place.

The two men pulled Dana out of her truck and laid her out on the gurney. Once she was buckled in, the EMT put a blood pressure cuff on and checked her vitals. He called it in to the hospital, and Jerod helped him get her inside his ambulance.

The other EMT came over and reported what he'd found at the other truck. Turned out, they had seatbelts and airbags. Both of the passengers had a few bumps but otherwise felt fine. They were going to follow up with their doctor.

"Oh, where are you taking Dana?" Jerod asked just as the ambulance driver began to close his door.

"You know the patient?" the driver asked.

"Yes, well, sorta. She's the barista in town." He shrugged.

The driver chuckled. "Yeah, she is." He closed the door and they took off without saying where they were going.

"Good morning, Jerod. How goes the ranch?" Anise Banning asked as Jerod walked into the coffee shop the day after his sign was installed.

"Fine, thanks. How's Dana? Any word yet?" Jerod had worried about her all night long. He even prayed for her safety, something he didn't do much of lately. At least not since that day when he lost all of his team.

"How'd you know?" Anise shook her head. "Never mind, the Meddling Moms strike again."

"Actually, the accident happened right outside my ranch. I was there." He winced when he thought back to that sound. He hadn't slept well that night, mostly because of the recurring nightmares. This time, they featured Dana. Even though Dana hadn't been in Kandahar with Jerod and his Special Forces team, she was in his nightmares. Every time he closed his eyes, she was the one he'd witnessed dying from the roadside bomb. He had to keep telling himself that she was fine, and she was never in Afghanistan. As far as he knew, she hadn't even been in the Army.

"Oh, I'm sorry you had to see that." Anise winced and then went to the pastry case. "How about a huckleberry crumble? It's our featured pastry today. And of course your regular coffee."

"Thanks, but I'll stick with the cinnamon rolls, if you don't mind. And any word on Dana would be much appreciated." Jerod was a creature of habit. Once he found something he liked, he stuck with it. Not to mention, his residents at the ranch really loved the cinnamon rolls as well.

As Anise worked to complete his regular order, she filled him in on her condition. "She's going to be fine. They kept her overnight for observation since she was unconscious when the EMTs picked her up."

"So, she woke up?" Jerod had been worried about her and hoped it was nothing more than a concussion. He had seen plenty of those in his time.

"Yes, on the way to the hospital. And I spoke with her this morning. She's going to be just fine. Sore as heck, but she'll be back at work later this week, once she sees the doctor and gets released." Anise handed him his order and took his payment.

"Thanks, Anise. I appreciate it." He picked up his coffee and took a long drink.

"Should I give her a message?" The barista gave him a cheeky smile.

Jerod's mind went blank. "Ah." He had no idea what to say. "That's alright. I'm sure I'll see her later in the week. Thanks." He grabbed his boxed of cinnamon rolls and his carafe of hot coffee and left.

2

Dana Baker was sick and tired of being in the hospital, and it hadn't even been a full day yet. She didn't get much sleep, what with the nurses coming in at all hours of the night taking her vitals and checking that she was alright. It was a miracle she only had a concussion. The accident wasn't bad, but her old truck should have had at least seatbelts installed a long time ago. She'd asked her dad to do it years ago, but he never got around to it. He'd said that if the truck had survived that long without seatbelts, it didn't need them. She wondered what he'd say now.

A recurring memory kept flooding her thoughts. She never slept long enough for dreams, but each time she awoke, a handsome face flashed through her head and asked if she was alright. Something in the back of her mind told her it wasn't a dream, but reality. However, she couldn't remember his name. And she didn't think she knew him, but he seemed to know her.

"Dana." The doctor smiled and looked at her chart. "I don't want you doing anything for the next five days except rest. Do you understand?"

"Yes, as long as I can go home now."

He released her to her father and she went home for much needed rest.

Since she couldn't do anything, she used her time wisely, thinking about the cowboy with the chocolate-brown eyes who came to her rescue. At least, she thought he was the one who'd helped her. The doctor told her the cowboy who owned the ranch she'd crashed in front of was the one who helped her, but her memory was still hazy. All she could think of was the dreamy face of a man with a prominent chin, brown eyes she could easily get lost in, and wavy brown hair that needed a trim.

A fuzzy feeling entered her belly the more she thought of the image that seemed to be just out of her reach. All she could remember was the face of the man. Not his name, or what he was wearing, or anything really. Which was what made her think that maybe it *was* all just a dream.

∼

ONE WEEK AFTER HER ACCIDENT, Dana Baker was back at work and glad for it.

The bell above the door at the Frenchtown Roasting Company jingled, and Dana pasted on a smile that felt almost real before she looked up.

Shock shot through her like a bolt of lightning.

It couldn't be.

The man who'd just walked in through the front door of the coffee shop was the cowboy from her dreams, or was it her fantasies? She still wasn't sure which it was. But never in a million years did she think he really existed. At least, not the way she'd pictured him this past week.

"Dana! It's good to see you walking around, and back at work." Jerod smiled from ear to ear as he stepped toward her.

She took a step back.

He furrowed his brow. "Don't you remember me?"

She shook her head and put a hand to her stomach. She wasn't sure if that was butterflies running rampant or if she was going to be sick.

"I'm Jerod Stevens. I own the Crooked Arrow Ranch." He waited as he watched her face.

Something about the ranch name clicked, and she started to remember more about the accident. "You're the one who called 911."

"That's right, I am." He gave her a tentative smile and waited for her to respond.

Thoughts and memories mixed around her mind. She put a hand to her head and rubbed her temple. "It's coming back to me."

"Hey, don't stress. It's okay if you don't remember me, you were pretty out of it."

All of a sudden, her eyes popped open as wide as saucers. Then she mumbled, "Handsome cowboy."

Jerod watched as Dana's cheeks reddened and she put her hands on her face. He waved a hand in front of him. "Don't worry about it. You hit your head, hard."

She looked down and dreaded having to help him every time he came into the shop. "I don't think I'm feeling so well." Again, she put a hand to her head and rubbed. She was most definitely going to be sick.

Lottie Keith, owner of the coffee shop, walked up. "Why don't you go in the back and sit down? It's your break time, anyway." She smiled at her employee. Once Dana was gone, she turned back to Jerod. "Sorry about that. What can I get you?"

"Actually, I came in to check on Dana. I've been worried about her all week." Jerod put his hands in his front jeans pockets and rocked back and forth. He hoped he hadn't made things worse for the beautiful girl.

"Today's her first day back. It's going to take her a few days to get back into the swing of things, but she's fine. Thank you for your concern, Jerod." Lottie narrowed her eyes. "It *was* you, wasn't it?"

"Me?" he asked, not understanding.

"You're the one who rescued her."

He chuckled. "Well, I don't know about all that. But I was the one who called the ambulance." It wasn't like he had done much. He wasn't the one who rushed her to the hospital.

Lottie smiled. "Thank you. Coffee and a pastry on me today for your help."

3

———

The next few days were busy on the ranch. Jerod had two new residents joining him. With nine wounded warriors on the ranch, he was more than swamped. He got up when the rooster crowed and made sure the rest of the house was up, too. They went out as a team and fed the animals. Half of his barn was stocked with retired horses that just needed a good place to graze in their old age.

"Sam, help me out here." Jerod led the man with a prosthetic arm to the bales of hay stacked in the corner.

"What can I do?" The injured man still sounded angry. He had been with Jerod since Christmas and had already learned how to heave the bales of hay around. But for some reason, Sam still acted as though he couldn't do anything.

"Just like yesterday, you can move this here bale of hay out to the front of the barn and help fill the stalls with fresh hay after the guys rake out the old hay." It seemed that every day Jerod had to explain to the former soldier how to do the same tasks. It was almost as though he had no short-term memory, but Jerod knew better. The man was still too angry at the world to *want* to do anything. At least until it came to riding.

They had six mares as gentle as babies. The men all took turns riding them, and it seemed to help calm them down. Jerod also had some Jersey cows they milked every day. Three of his residents seemed to enjoy the milking process, and one of them, Mike, was quite good at churning fresh butter.

～

LATER THAT DAY, Jerod went into town to get some supplies. He happened to be walking by the Frenchtown Roasting Company when he noticed that Dana was working. That made twice in one week he'd seen her in the afternoon. Did that mean she only worked the later shift? Was that why he'd not seen her since coming back to town? He normally went into town early in the mornings. Maybe he would have to change up his schedule if it meant he'd see those pretty green eyes on a regular basis.

He turned back and decided to head in for some coffee. *Why not*, he thought. It was the afternoon, and he could use a pick-me-up. "Howdy, Dana," he greeted when he stepped up to the counter.

Her eyes widened, and she stammered, "Jer... Jerod. It's nice to see you."

He chuckled. "I see you remember me now." Jerod winked and enjoyed seeing her cheeks turn pink.

"Ahh, sorry about that. And thank you for calling the ambulance. I do appreciate your help." Dana touched her warm cheeks.

"Think nothing of it. I'm just glad you're alright." He looked her up and down. "Any lingering issues?"

She shook her head. "A few headaches here and there, but nothing major. The doc's given me the all-clear."

"I'm truly glad to hear that." Jerod smiled his pearly whites and placed his order, a cold brew with cream and extra ice. He didn't care that it was still just hovering above freezing. Spring was in the air, and he was ready to embrace it.

In fact, he was ready for even more. "Say, how about I take you to dinner on Friday? We could head over to Missoula and try out that Italian restaurant everyone's been talking about." He held his breath as he watched her face change.

～

Since her accident, Dana had been taking more chances than usual. She had begun wearing a little bit of makeup to work. Just that day she had worn her nice jeans. She had been trying to look nice for something. Or was it some*one*? Was her subconscious making this extra effort for a particular cowboy who filled his button-down, checked shirts too well?

Earlier that day, Anise had suggested that she date again. Dana hadn't been on a date in over a year, not since her lousy ex-boyfriend dumped her for his hairstylist. She should have known any man who used a high-end hairstylist and had more mani-pedis than the average woman wouldn't make for a good boyfriend. He was a player through and through. She hadn't believed the rumors, but now she wished she had.

However, now she wondered over everything she'd done the past few days and guessed it was all leading up to this. Wasn't it?

Just the day before, Lottie had commented on her choice of shirt and hairstyle. She had said something to effect of, "Boy howdy! Someone's out to catch herself a cowboy." Then she winked.

Dana was confused by the comment yesterday, but today? Was this what she was trying extra hard for? Or was Jerod just the lucky guy who happened to ask her out first?

Deciding that today was the day she would get back on that horse, she said yes.

"I'll pick you up at five-thirty. Will that be enough time after you get off work?" Jerod tipped his hat and took the drink Dana had offered to him.

"I don't work on Friday. So that'll work." She smiled, and the butterflies returned full force. Dana prayed she wouldn't end up getting sick in front of this sexy cowboy.

Dana watched the handsome cowboy saunter out the door. "What have I gotten myself into?"

Lottie came over. "Did you just say yes to a date?"

Dana leaned back against the counter and stared off into space. "I think I did." She turned toward Lottie. "Didn't I?"

Her boss laughed. "Yes, girl, you did. Something about you has changed since your accident, and I for one love it."

"I don't know. He's the guy I told you about last year. The cowboy that I said came in and was too cute for this one-horse town." Dana had thought about Jerod a lot since she'd first met him. Never did she think he'd ask her out. "It's not a pity date, is it?"

"Not even. Didn't you notice the way he looked at you?" Lottie waggled her brows and chuckled. "I think he's really into you."

Dana shook her head. "But, he's just so handsome." She waved a hand over herself. "And I'm, well, just plain."

Lottie turned her employee around and directed her to a mirror. "Look at that beautiful face. Even with the remnants of the bruise from your accident, you're gorgeous." She pulled on the ponytail. "And your hair. Dana, men love long, thick hair like yours. Trust me, he's into you."

Hope began to fill her heart as she thought about the man she had said yes to.

4

———————

Friday came, and Jerod wondered what had gotten into him. He'd never before asked a woman out so soon. There was just something about Dana that spoke to him. He had gone into town two more times that week and looked for her through the window of the coffee shop. He didn't go in, but he couldn't help himself. Her beautiful smile when she helped a customer sent a pang through his chest. He just *had* to get to know her better.

Jerod walked into the living room to get his keys and instantly regretted it.

Whistles and catcalls met him.

Sam, still mad at the world, looked him up and down. "The love of a good woman can ease a lot of hurts." He turned and walked out of the room, leaving Jerod standing there open-mouthed.

"What?" Jerod didn't know what to say to that cryptic revelation.

"Aren't you going to be late, lover boy?" Mike called out.

When Jerod looked at his watch, it was all he could do to keep from spitting out an expletive. His cuss jar was already overflowing from all of the guys not working hard enough at cleaning up their language. He didn't need to add any more money to it.

He yelled out over his shoulder as he left the ranch, "Don't wait up for me."

Jerod pulled up to the driveway of the Baker ranch and was only one minute late. He'd call that on time. Before he opened the door, he took a deep breath and exhaled it slowly. This was his first date since coming home. Shoot, it was his first date in almost three years. Being in the sandpit didn't exactly give him many opportunities to date. Sure, there were female soldiers, but he never wanted to date while he was deployed. He didn't think it was smart to let a woman into his heart when he needed to be one hundred percent on target. A woman would have only distracted him from his mission.

But now? He knew he could do this. When he looked into Dana's emerald pools, he knew he could do this.

The ranch was moving along better than he thought possible. He had already received one grant from the VA to help him hire a counselor who specialized in PTSD, and he had applied for another grant that would allow him to buy more horses and even some cattle to help the soldiers learn a new trade. One that would not only allow them to earn a living once they were ready to move on, but would also help them deal with the emotional impact of their new reality.

Before he left Walter Reed and was discharged after surviving the explosion, he'd done his research. Horses and other ranch animals helped some soldiers work through their demons. His plan was to help others, like him, who'd survived war only to come home and find themselves fighting another war. One that no one could see.

The counselors called it survivor's guilt along with post-traumatic stress disorder (PTSD). But Jerod called it surviving. Not a single person he'd met who'd survived came out unscathed. It was the part of war no one really spoke much about.

His goal was to change that. He wanted to help those like him, and those who had a worse experience, to come home and learn how to deal with who they had become.

Anyone who worked his ranch would have experienced war, or would at the very least be trained to help those who had. Like the counselor who would be joining his ranch that summer.

Jerod stopped mid-thought and got his mind back on what he was there for. Dana had come outside before he stepped up on the porch. She was stunning, with black jeans, black boots, and an emerald-green, button-up blouse that matched her eyes. His mouth opened, and he couldn't think. He stood there staring at the most beautiful woman he'd ever seen.

He blinked and licked his lips. "You look unbelievable."

Dana's cheeks turned pink when she checked him out. He remembered that he had worn his dark-blue pair of Wranglers with deep-tan cowboy boots and a green-and-black checked, button-up shirt.

He also had his hair cut earlier that day. It bugged him that his brown hair curled around the top edges of his shirt collar.

"Thank you." She motioned to him. "You don't look so bad yourself, cowboy."

He tipped his hat. "Thank ya, ma'am." Then he grinned wide and went up to her. When he offered her his elbow, she wrapped her arm around his.

Jerod was glad he'd made reservations for the Italian restaurant. The place was packed. He'd heard about it from Lottie Keith and her boyfriend, Cove Hamilton. The two of them seemed to come to this restaurant a lot. Or at least, they talked about it often. He'd wanted to try it, and was very happy when Dana agreed to join him.

The place was romantic; the lighting was low, there were candles on each tabletop, and the tables for two had high-backed booths to give them more privacy. While he could hear other patrons mumbling, he couldn't make out any conversations, even when he tried. "Have you ever been here?"

Dana looked around with wide eyes. "No, I haven't. But I've heard the food is to die for. Apparently the chef is some famous woman from Italy."

"Seriously? We're going to eat food from a real Italian chef? In Missoula, Montana?" Jerod would have never though it possible. Their little piece of the world was so remote, he doubted anyone in Italy had even heard of Montana—well, except for maybe Glacier National Park. Surely people around the world knew about their little park.

Dana nodded. "Yup, and I can't wait."

Conversation flowed smoothly for the next hour as they took their time enjoying the pasta and handcrafted sauces made from recipes created in Italy and perfected over generations. After they shared an out-of-this-world chocolate cannoli, they finally left the restaurant.

Jerod was feeling bold and took Dana's hand as they strolled outside.

"What do you say to a short walk before heading back?" Jerod wasn't ready for the night to end. He wanted to spend more time talking to the woman he was finally starting to get to know. Their conversations had effortlessly flowed from one topic to the next, and he knew they had a special connection already.

Maybe it was because he was the one who'd opened her truck door after her accident, even though she barely remembered him, or maybe there was something to the old adage of love at first sight. Either way, he wanted to explore whatever this was between them.

"I'd like that." She gave him a shy sideways smile and squeezed his hand.

It was close to eleven at night when he finally took her home. They both felt like popsicles when they got back into Jerod's truck. When his heater finally kicked in, he felt as though he was a fudge bar that had been left on the kitchen counter and all of his worries were slowly melting away. Once he was warm enough, he took off his gloves and reached for Dana's hand. She too had taken her gloves off.

Their fingers found each other easily in the dark of the cab, and he gave her hand a little squeeze. Everything was perfect. She was perfect. The night was perfect. Even the food was perfect. He wouldn't have changed one single thing.

That was until he ran over something on the road and his tire popped. In his head, he was transported back to Kandahar and his squad. They were driving down a dark road very different from the one he was on now. But instead of a simple flat tire, he was being fired upon by rocket-propelled grenades and a bomb went off on the side of the road, exploding the truck in front of him. The one carrying the bulk of their ammunition.

His Humvee hit a smoldering wreck of another Humvee and it flipped on its side. He had ended up on the bottom side of the truck, which was what saved him in the end.

Later, when he awoke in the German hospital, he learned that a drone came in and took care of the enemy for him, or he would never have survived what they still had planned. However, he was the only one who survived.

For weeks, Jerod thought those who died that day had it the best. He had wished he'd never survived only to live through the attack over and over again. Like tonight.

He couldn't see anything through the smoke in front of them, and he sat there in the truck rigid, unmoving.

Dana called out, "Jerod! Jerod! Wake up."

When he heard her voice the images began to shift, and what he thought was the bombing in Afghanistan morphed into the highway between Missoula and Frenchtown, Montana.

Thankfully, his foot had come off the gas pedal and they were slowing. But the truck was heading toward the side of the road. If he didn't act soon, they'd crash into the side of the mountain they were driving through.

5

Dana couldn't believe her luck. She'd gone twenty-five years and only recently had she been in a car accident. Now, not two weeks later, she was in her second one. Only this one could be avoided if she acted fast.

When Jerod froze at the wheel with a look of terror stuck on his face, she knew something was wrong. When he didn't respond to her calls, she knew she had to act. Dana leaned over and turned the steering wheel away from the edge of the highway. If she could keep the truck moving along the road, it would eventually slow on its own and they could come to a safe stop.

"Jerod, I need your help." She tried once more to get him to come out of whatever fugue state he was in. She'd read about this sort of thing. Soldiers who experienced something traumatic during their time in service would be just like everyone else until a noise took them back to the war. Usually, it was a car backfiring. His truck didn't do that. But the sound of a tire blowing could emulate the sound of an attack. Even she had flinched when it first happened.

There weren't any other cars around. Maybe she should take her seatbelt off and try to scooch over and put her foot on the brake. But she didn't want to take a chance that she'd be in another accident without a seatbelt on. But what choice did she have if Jerod wouldn't come out of it?

She tried once more. "Jerod, I need you. Wake up."

∼

HE BLINKED and looked around as though he had just woken from a long nap. "What?" His instincts kicked in, and he took the wheel back from Dana and slowly stopped the truck. Once they were safely to the side of the road, he looked at Dana. "Are you alright?"

Tears pricked the backs of her eyes. "Yes, I'm fine. But what about you?"

He sighed heavily and leaned his head on the steering wheel. "I'm fine."

"That wasn't fine." Dana put a hand on his shoulder.

Every fiber of his being screamed to push her away, except for one little thought niggling at the back of his mind—*the love of a good woman can erase a lot of hurts.*

When Sam told him that, Jerod had no idea the impact it would have on him that night. Still, he knew he could have killed Dana, could have killed them both. Even though he had wished for death for weeks after the attack, he no longer wanted to die. God had given him the will to live again. And now he had a new mission. One to help his fellow brothers and sisters in arms to get through their own nightmares so they could live again. A woman had no place in his heart while he was on a mission.

"I'll be fine. I'm sorry. I'll change the flat." Jerod got out, thankful he always kept a full-size spare for his truck.

Dana stood outside, watching as Jerod went to work.

Once he was done with the task at hand, he jumped back into his truck and stared out the front window. "Let's get you home where it's safe and warm." While Jerod had thought he was ready for this next normal part of life, he wasn't. Tonight was proof enough.

"Wait, what?" Dana stared at him. "Talk to me, Jerod. Let me be here for you."

He shook his head.

When they pulled up outside of her house, Jerod turned off his ignition and turned to Dana. Taking a moment to pull his thoughts together, he ran a hand through his hair. "I'm really sorry about how the night ended. I hope I didn't put you through any trauma."

～

THE ALMOST-ACCIDENT HADN'T BOTHERED her, not really. But what she felt happening between them now might bring about trauma. She had thought everything was going good. Better than good. Finally, she had found a man who seemed to respect her and was easy to talk to. She was also wildly attracted to him, although she wished he would have let his brown hair continue to curl over the top of his collar.

One of her secret desires this week was to run her fingers through his curly hair. But since he'd cut it, that wasn't going to happen. Although, if he was taking this conversation where she feared, it wouldn't have happened even if he didn't get his hair cut.

"No," she whispered. "No trauma." Dana wanted to say more, but was afraid she was the one overreacting here. Maybe he was just shaken up and everything would be fine once he calmed down.

Jerod grasped the steering wheel with his left hand. "I don't think we should see each other again."

"What?" Dana gasped. That was a bit too direct for her liking. She thought he could have at least softened the blow a little bit. But no, he seemed to want to get this over with lickety-split and leave her in the dust.

"I almost hurt you tonight." He shook his head and sat up straight. "If you hadn't brought me out of my stupor, I would have most likely killed us both, or at the very least seriously injured you."

Dana cut him off. "But you didn't. We're both fine. Nothing happened."

"But something did happen. We can't ignore how I reacted to a simple tire blow-out." He took a calming breath. "I'm sorry, but I'm not ready for this. Not yet."

"What about what I want? What if I'm willing to give it a try?" She smirked. "What if I drove for the next date?"

His stern expression softened. "But what happens when you can't drive? Or what if I attack you?"

"Have you done that before?" She had heard about men attacking their wives and girlfriends, thinking they were the enemy, but she didn't think Jerod would do that.

"No, but you're the first woman I've been out with since I came back stateside." Jerod ran a hand down his face.

"Look, I wasn't too sure about this to begin with, but after my accident and after how well dinner went, I think we should try it. You only live once, right?" Dana twisted in the seat to face him more directly, then took his hand and held it.

He squeezed her hand. "You may be right, but I'd never be able to live with myself if I hurt you."

She bit her lower lip and her nostrils flared. "What if making this decision without my input hurts me?"

"You know what I mean."

She shook her head. "I think you're wrong. But if this is what you want, I can't force you to care for me." Dana got out of the truck and walked straight inside her house without looking back.

Jerod sighed and started his truck. "Lord, am I making the right decision?"

6

———

"So, how'd the date go?" Lottie asked the second Dana walked through the door the next afternoon.

She pursed her lips and gave her boss a hard look. "I don't wanna talk about it."

"Oh, that bad? I'm sorry." Lottie pulled out her last hot chocolate bomb and set it inside a cup, then poured steaming-hot milk over it. "Here, you need this more than I do."

Dana looked inside the cup and watched as the chocolate bomb melted and the tiny marshmallows spread out along with some flecks of gold and peppermint candies. She smiled. "You always know what a person needs, don't you?"

Lottie shrugged. "I try."

On her break that afternoon, Dana was sitting in the back room and thinking about the night before.

Cove Hamilton came in and saw her sitting there. "Hey, why such a long face?"

She looked up at the handsome rodeo star who was dating her boss and rolled her eyes. "Men, pft."

"Ah, I see." Cove sat down across from her. "Maybe a man's perspective could help?" He arched a brow.

Dana rubbed her face and figured why not. She wasn't getting anywhere. Maybe a man's perspective would help her understand what was going on with Jerod.

Once Dana finished explaining the situation, Cove took a moment to think it over. "Do you care for this guy?"

She nodded. Dana didn't understand how she could have come to care for him so quickly, but she did. She didn't know if he was *the one*, but she did know that if she didn't try, she'd regret it forever. She had seen how Cove went after Lottie and won her heart. No one thought Lottie would ever date anyone again after she lost her husband. They had really inspired her. And Cove showed her that you shouldn't give up just because there's an obstacle in the way.

"Then go see him. I can tell you one thing for sure: all men have a knee-jerk reaction to protect the women in their life. It's very possible that Jerod did just that last night. And today he might be regretting what he said." Cove stood up and smiled. "Go get your man."

Lottie walked in. "I agree, but you might want to wait until your shift is over."

Dana couldn't help the chuckle that escaped.

WHEN SHE FOUND herself outside the front door of the Crooked Arrow Ranch, an hour after her shift ended, she paused before knocking. What was she going to say? She couldn't demand that they go out again. But maybe, just maybe she could try being his friend.

Before she could get up the courage to knock, the front door opened. A gruff man with a shaggy beard and a prosthetic left arm grunted. "Wha'd ya want?"

"Uh, hi. I'm Dana Baker, and I'd like to speak with Jerod." She had seen his truck in the drive, so she assumed he was home.

The man's face softened, and a semi-smile appeared. "Come on in. I'll let the dunderhead know you're here."

"Uh, okay." Dana raised her brows but didn't bother asking what he meant by *dunderhead*.

She took a seat in the clean but spartan living room on the only sofa they had.

After a few minutes, a surprised voice sent goosebumps down her spine. "Dana? What are you doing here?"

She stood up and turned around to look at him. Jerod was a mess. Not dirty, but his hair was mussed and his clothes were wrinkled, almost like he'd slept in them. "I thought I'd come by and check on you. See how you're doing."

"Well, go on. Tell her you made a mistake." The bearded man pushed Jerod into the room.

Jerod turned around and gave his friend a stern look. Then he looked back at Dana. "Dana, this here is Sam. Ignore him. I do most days."

Dana chuckled. "Hi Sam, nice to meet you."

He grunted and turned around to leave them alone.

"Well"—Dana's brows lifted—"I guess he's not one for chit-chat."

Jerod chuckled. "Nope."

"So, can we chat?" she asked.

He shrugged.

Dana sat back down on the sofa, and Jerod joined her.

Before she could say anything, Jerod spoke up. "I'm sorry about last night. I was rude and way too brusque with you."

She winced and nodded.

"I was also wrong," he added.

Dana held her breath, waiting for what he was going to say.

Jerod rubbed the stubble on his face and let out a breath. "I know better than to make rash decisions in the heat of the moment." He looked her in the eyes.

Dana's heart melted when she saw the pain in his eyes.

"I thought for sure I'd get you hurt by my actions." He gave her a sardonic smile. "Or inactions, as it were."

She reached out and put a hand on his, but she stayed quiet, letting him speak.

"I do want to make a go of this, but I'm worried about your safety." He waited for her to respond.

"I know." Dana nodded. "Cove told me that men think it's their responsibility to take care of the women in their lives. And I get that. But, I'm a grown woman. You need to let me say if I think it's too dangerous for me."

Jerod inhaled and slowly exhaled. "What do you think? Can you give this broken-down soldier another chance?"

Dana's face softened, and she scooted closer to Jerod. "Of course I can. On one condition."

"What's that?"

"You don't make major decisions for us without my input." Dana raised a brow and waited.

A slow smile crept across his face. "Deal."

Jerod leaned in slowly, giving Dana a chance to back away.

When she didn't, his lips met hers in a soft exploration.

She wrapped her arms around his neck, and he pulled her closer and deepened the kiss.

"It's about dang time," Sam said, and laughed.

The two broke apart and smiled at each other.

"Together?" Jerod asked.

"Together."

EPILOGUE

Six months later, Jerod was all smiles as he prepared a special steak dinner for Dana. The residents of the Crooked Arrow Ranch had all gone out for the night, knowing what Jerod had planned.

When dinner was over they lingered over dessert, sipping sweet tea. The purples, oranges, and reds of a Big Sky sunset almost brought tears to Dana's eyes.

"Hey, what's wrong?" Jerod asked.

She shook her head. "Nothing. This night is perfect. The sunsets here always fill me with emotion. That's all."

"Dana, you're more beautiful than any sunset, or sunrise. I've been all over the world and never found anyone like you."

Tears pooled in the corners of Dana's eyes.

Jerod got down on one knee. "I love you and couldn't imagine life without you. Will you do me the honor of being my wife for as long as we both shall live?" He pulled out a little red box with a sparkling diamond ring in the center.

As tears ran down Dana's cheeks, she smiled from ear to ear. "Of course I will. I love you, too."

They both stood and kissed as the last rays of sunshine melted what was once two wounded hearts, now coming together as one.

ABOUT THE AUTHOR

Jenna Hendricks writes Clean & Wholesome Contemporary Romance with Christian values. She loves to write about the cowboys she wishes she would one day meet. But is happy to wait on God's timing. Until then, she enjoys listening to audiobooks, eating chocolate, traveling the world, and spending time with her extended family. You can get a free eBook, discover her recipes, and see pictures of the places she visits by joining her newsletter or reading her books.

https://landing.mailerlite.com/webforms/landing/a5g5h3

https://www.amazon.com/Jenna-Hendricks/e/B083G6WQR7

CIDER SUGAR

LILY ALEXANDER

Can a craving for a sweet treat lead to an unexpected love match?

1

———

SHAW

*S*ome girls require champagne or fancy chocolates to celebrate special occasions.

Me? I just wanted a donut.

Not just any donut though—oh, no.

I wanted at least a dozen tiny pillowy rings of spiced apple cider flavored perfection, dusted in copious amounts of cinnamon sugar and served up in a very classy white paper bag.

My whole heart belonged to Mr. Pfeffernuss, the man who had been making cider donuts in the park every single autumn since I was a child. He was eighty if he was a day, but he still rolled the same traveling cart into the grass and fried that fluffy, delicious dough every year like the sweet, feisty little confection master he was.

I adored him.

Oh yes, I was going to get my celebratory treat.

I was feeling particularly good about the outcome of the Fall Festival this year. My modest little craft booth had managed to pull down a windfall of orders for my custom wreath and flower arrangement bundles, and it was the push I needed to finally—*finally*—get an actual storefront for my handmade gifts business.

The icing on the cake would be a pumpkin spice latte to go with them. My sister and I had a yearly tradition for the drinks, and we'd started this year with a bang. I was pretty sure it had been the combination of cider donuts and coffee that had pushed her over the edge and convinced her to agree to help me assemble the floral arrangements. Well, that and my shameless begging.

Even though it was officially a few weeks into fall, summer hadn't gotten the message that it was time to pack it in for the year. The California sun was bright and brutal when I stepped out of my apartment. Despite a bit of cool ocean breeze, I was starting to sweat by the time I finished up the short jog to the park.

Smile already a mile wide, I approached the familiar cart, amused as always by the whimsical cider jug, donut, and happy apple cartoons painted on the side.

"Good morning, Mr. P! How's the oil this morn—" I stopped mid-stride; thoughts completely arrested by the man in the black apron behind the counter.

He was tall. Gorgeous. Biceps for days and the beginnings of a sun-streaked top knot under his hairnet.

Very much *not* my octogenarian friend.

A pair of devastating blue eyes met mine and a generous mouth with a perfect cupid's bow tipped into a slight smile.

"Who the heck are you?" My mouth wasn't always my best asset.

Thankfully, he wasn't offended by my brash greeting. A chuckle burst from his chest and something strange happened in mine when he spoke.

"Good morning. Can I help you?"

"Where's Mr. Pfeffernuss? Is he okay?"

Never once did his gloved hands stop moving. They dunked and dusted donuts in a mountain of cinnamon sugar, piling the finished ones high. Without a pause, he then expertly arranged them into neat dozens across a sheet tray and slid it into the countertop display.

"Pops? He's great, I'm just helping out. I'm Neil."

"Oh. I'm so glad to hear that! I've never seen anyone but him here and I thought—" I didn't want to even say the words lest they manifest into something real. "I'm Shaw." I stupidly stuck a hand out. "Shawna, actually, but I prefer Shaw. Sorry." He paused awkwardly, gloved hands in front of him. I retracted my arm, my face glowing hot with my blush.

"Can I get you something, Shaw?" Amused, he raised an eyebrow as he assessed me.

"Um, yes. I'd love a fancy dozen, rolls and holes please."

The amused smile widened. Seeing it in all its glory was quite an experience.

"You got it." He filled a white paper bag with my order and handed it over. "You order like a pro. I'm guessing you come here often?"

I tipped my head to the side as I paid with what I knew to be the exact change for my order. "Now there's a classic line. Mr. P would be proud."

His bright eyes widened and he gave a startled laugh. "I didn't mean—"

Waving my hand—the one without donuts in it—I reassured him, "I know. It was just funny the way you said it. And I do. Come here often. This little cart has been my favorite part of fall for a long, long time. I come to get my fix and visit with Mr. P as much as I can."

He briefly crossed his arms over his broad chest, looking proud. "I'll be sure to tell Pops you said so."

I nodded and stepped back, oddly disappointed that our brief interaction was over. "Oh, he knows. He flirts with me shamelessly every time I stop by."

"That I definitely believe." He smiled again and busied himself with wiping down the tiny counter.

"Will he be back soon?" My question had a double motive, and while I thought I was being clever, he seemed to pick up on that immediately.

Neil grinned, one sandy eyebrow lifting. "We're not sure. He's okay, just not as young as he used to be. The festival took a lot out of him this year. Not to worry, though; I'll be here if he's not. You know—to be sure you can get your fix." He winked at me, and it took everything I had not to sigh like some smitten teenager. It was truly ridiculous.

I kinda loved it.

The blush in my cheeks had to be the color of Port by then. "Fantastic. Well, I'll see you around then."

"Have a great day, Shaw."

"You too, Neil."

Thankfully I managed not to trip over myself or anybody else as I backed away from the counter and headed toward my other favorite seasonal installation: the coffee cart.

Hands full of treats, I sought out my favorite wooden picnic table, one of a handful shaded by the wide branches of assorted maple and oak trees. Some leaves had just started to yellow out, but I knew in a few short weeks they would be blazing red and orange. I could hardly stand to wait for the change. It was the absolute best time of year, and it never lasted long enough.

Watching people in the park was usually a favorite pastime of mine, but my eyes kept wandering back to the donut cart. People playing frisbee with their adorable dogs or watching toddlers waddle and then fall onto their well-padded bottoms usually kept me entertained, but today my attention was elsewhere.

I watched as Neil handed out bags and paper-boat-fuls of donuts to eager and happy patrons. He was as enthusiastic as I'd ever seen Mr. Pfeffernuss. It gave me a second-hand smile just to watch, and not just because he was ridiculously handsome and his voice, even from a distance, did interesting things to my blood pressure.

I knew that before I managed to consume the entire bag of sugary goodness, I needed to force myself to get up and head home. I had some full-time adulting to do and the sugar definitely helped prepare me for visiting properties with my realtor and hitting up the bank.

I had a few important banking transactions to make—namely a large deposit for my sister, who had been vital in helping me get through the orders for the festival.

My twin never hesitated to tell me no when I asked for help if she couldn't or didn't want to, but this had been one occasion I *really* needed her to say yes. Putting together five hundred flower arrangements had been an enormous favor to ask, even at a hundred bucks a pop in revenue split between us. They weren't terribly complicated—just some cute little pumpkin baskets with flowers and some garnish—but the timeline had been short. Even with a few bumps in the process, she had pulled it off flawlessly. I was so grateful, there wasn't even a word to adequately express it. She *was* now dating the floral supplier's delivery guy, which definitely counted in my favor as I was technically the reason they met. I still hoped the money—which was going to help her get into partial ownership of the pub she worked at—was sufficient to show my appreciation.

Formulating a plan for the rest of my busy day, I tore my eyes away from the man inside the cart and started my walk home, already plotting a reason for another donut fix.

2

NEIL

I hadn't been at all prepared for the number of customers the cart got my first day on the job.

Pops had always loved that particular location, but I could never figure out why . . . until I ran it by myself all day.

Families, older couples, one particularly stunning blonde—there was no shortage of joyous, hungry patrons who all wanted heaps of my grandfather's signature cider donuts. The thing that most surprised me was that it was happening after the Fall Festival. I hadn't expected any kind of significant traffic based on Pops's previous year's sales records.

To be fair, I wasn't sure he was very consistent about keeping track and nothing was digital. I might have been better off looking into his supply purchases, but they, too, were paper and ink in a ledger.

After having seen what a single day was like running the business, I was proud of what he'd built and felt a bit bad that he couldn't be there himself to see his devoted fans.

Shaw in particular had been a bright spot I hadn't been expecting. The idea that she had a long-standing banter with my Pops made me smile. I wasn't at all surprised really; he was a life-long flirt and she was a lovely target for his charm. They seemed well-matched for playful, verbal sparring matches.

The idea of verbally sparring with her myself had my blood heated, but unless donuts were part of her morning routine, I wasn't counting on ever seeing her again. That thought pulled my mouth into a frown and I shook my head to clear it away, thankful that my hair was finally free from the itchy hairnet.

My body was sore in places I hadn't expected from hustling dough and sugar all day long. I hadn't been quite so excited about a hot shower, a meal, and some sleep since practicing twice a day for surfing competitions.

"Hey, Pops!" I announced myself as I entered my grandfather's house from the back door as was the rule for anyone not trying to sell vacuums or share religion. "I've got an unmarked bag with your name on it."

I made my way through the dimly lit kitchen into the bright, cozy living room. My Pops was posted up in his ancient, dark leather recliner like the king of his castle, remote in hand and feet elevated.

"Ah, Neil, my boy. Is it money?" He greeted me with a smile, gesturing to the paper bag in my hands.

"Nah, I left the money with the bank already. This is just donuts."

His smile widened which made his eyes crinkle even more. I'd gotten my sparkly blues from him.

"Hand 'em over. I need to be sure you aren't slinging inferior product while I'm taking my *rest*." He emphasized the last word like it was a swear.

I perched myself on the edge of his faded blue sofa, lacing my fingers together. I knew the donuts were fine; they were his exact recipe, tried and true, and something I could probably make in my sleep. I had plenty of ideas on changing things up a bit but wasn't quite sure how to broach the subject with him. The very last thing I wanted to do was make him feel like I was insulting the legacy he'd built.

His mouth worked as he sampled a ring, his eyes examining the miniature-sized donuts like they were fine gems. He turned them this way and that, making the sugar glint in the light from his lamp.

"You did good, young man." He finally nodded, winking at me. "Not that I had any doubt."

"Thanks, Pops. You feeling okay today?"

He grumbled a bit and shifted in his chair. "As good as I ever did.

You kids worry too much. I could have run the fryer today, same as always."

I raised an eyebrow and met his eye. "Pops, you know the doctor said that wasn't a good idea. If you want to be in fighting shape for the rest of the season, you need to conserve your energy."

He huffed, plunking another donut into his mouth before crumpling up the top of the bag and setting the leftovers on his little side table. "Isn't a single thing wrong with me that some honest work wouldn't cure."

We'd had this discussion before, multiple times. I understood he was frustrated, and I didn't blame him one bit. In thirty years, he'd never missed a single day behind the counter. Unfortunately, at eighty-two, his blood pressure wasn't maintaining on its own and the medication they'd started him on was only doing so much to help. Too much time on his feet left him weak, and after the weekend of the Fall Festival, he'd fainted in his kitchen.

Thankfully, he had helpful neighbors plus family checking in on him frequently. I hated to think what might have happened otherwise.

"I know Pops, but I'd rather have you there at your best. I'll need all the help I can get if today was any indication."

That comment both settled and distracted him.

"Yeah? Good day was it?" His smile was bright as he relaxed into his chair once more.

"Oh, yeah. We were jumping today, and it was just a regular Monday. Is that normal?"

He considered, rubbing his chin with his fingertips before answering. "Well, you saw the records. Every year's a bit different but being that we're past the festival, that's a bit unusual, I suppose."

"I'm going to need to be sure I stretch a bit more before going in tomorrow. I'm sore already and we went through a ton more dough than I'd planned for."

My grandad laughed, and it was one of the best sounds I'd heard all day. As if conjured by the positive emotions, I could hear the echoes of Shaw's teasing in my head. I felt an odd, tightening sensation in my chest.

"I thought you were a hotshot, professional surfer dude? Are you getting out of shape?"

"Probably. It's been a couple of years, Pops." I missed it, desperately, but at least I was still near the ocean. Finding a direction for my life after my injury was still a work in progress, but it seemed fried dough was in my blood.

Changing the subject, I said, "One of your regulars stopped by. She was worried about you."

He grinned. "Oh yeah? Which one? I've got groupies, you know."

I barked a laugh. "Oh, I know, old man. I found that out *quick* today. Her name was Shaw. Asked how the oil was and said your cart was her favorite part of fall."

My grandad's features relaxed as he smiled wide. "Shawna Connelly. Oh, yes. She's a picture, isn't she? Just a lovely young woman. Been coming to see me for a fancy dozen since she was just a little bit of a thing." He tilted his head. "Feisty that one. Got a dark-haired twin too, Shannon. Both of 'em pretty as can be. You manage to keep her around for a conversation?"

I shook my head, chuckling at my match-making grandad. "No, not really. We had a brief interlude over her bag of donuts and questions about you and then she left me for the coffee guy."

He laughed at my retelling of events, shaking his head. "Well, that's your loss, my boy. If you're lucky she'll be back by soon. She can't get enough of my sugary 'nuts."

Choking on a laugh, I said, "Pops. I'm *begging* you. Stop saying that."

My grandad rolled with laughter, going so far as to slap his knee at his joke. "You kids today—so uptight."

"If you say so, old man."

Once he quit laughing, we fell into a lull and I watched a few minutes of his favorite game show with him before getting to my feet to head home.

"You need anything else, Pops? I need a shower and some quality time with my sheets."

"Yeah, you do," he teased, nose wrinkled up in mock disgust before he tossed me another wink. "No thanks, I'm fine."

I leaned in and gave him a hug, noticing, and not for the first time, that his skin was thin like crepe paper and he wasn't quite as broad through the shoulders as he had been.

"Love you, Pops. Stay out of trouble, okay? See you tomorrow?"

"I'll do my best." I was nearly out of the room when he stopped me. "Neil?"

I turned around. "Yeah?"

"If you're going to try to get that Connelly girl, you may need to do something special." I waited, his gaze serious and penetrating as he spoke. My heart sped up as he continued, "I know you've been playing with my recipe for years now, son. No time like the present to start seeing if those changes are exactly what the business needs to survive the next thirty years, yeah? Assuming you want to take it over, that is."

I was stymied and could only blink for a moment. "Yes, sir," was the only response that came to my lips as a thousand thoughts buzzed around my head. That he knew shouldn't have surprised me, but his astute assessment of the entire situation was a shock.

He nodded once, seemingly quite pleased with himself, and settled back down into his chair. "I expect some samples of the new version tomorrow. And if I guess what you changed, I get to come with you on Friday."

My lips tipped up as I pulled myself together, getting ready to leave. "You drive a hard bargain. You're on, old-timer."

His amused chuckle followed me out the door, my recipe changes for the next day already decided by the time I got into my car.

3

SHAW

The whole week had been a flurry of activity and decision-making. I was well and truly exhausted by all of it.

I'd found a very promising location for my shop, but they expected more than I wanted to part with for the monthly lease and the space was larger than I'd need. It also had a very small, commercial kitchen, which I had no use for. There was one other property that was a very distant, second-place choice. I had some serious thinking to do—thinking that I would prefer to do with snacks.

The fact that I might see Neil again was certainly a consideration, but I was arguing with myself about how much to deny I was thinking about him. The real answer was quite a lot, which was very weird for me. I wasn't like this with men. I didn't do the swoon and stalk thing. I didn't even really date because my life was too busy and I felt bad not being able to give a potential relationship any attention. If I was being honest, Mr. Pfeffernuss had gotten more flirting out of me than anyone else ever had.

That was actually kind of sad.

Frowning, I tied my shoelaces and headed out the door, attempting to earn a few extra bites by jogging the half mile or so from my door to the park.

The breeze was cooler than it had been earlier in the week, which lifted my spirits a bit. By the time I got within visual distance of the cart, my frown had fully turned upside-down. I was even happier to find that there wasn't much of a line and that both Mr. P and Neil were crammed into the small space behind the counter.

"Good Morning, Mr. P! How's the oil this morning?" I couldn't help but smile wider as his face lit up when he spotted me.

"Well, good morning to you, young lady! The oil's popping just right, thanks for asking. I hear you met my grandson the other day?"

I glanced at Neil, who was smirking but plainly used to his grandfather's antics.

"Good morning, Shaw," he said, that rumbly voice making my pulse race a bit.

"Good morning, Neil," I returned the greeting, and the dimple in his left cheek deepened a bit. "I sure did, Mr. P. I was very surprised and a bit worried to find you missing, but he took good care of me."

"Glad to hear that." Mr. Pfeffernuss turned a playfully critical eye toward his grandson, but Neil just smiled and shook his head, busily turning a fresh batch of doughnuts in the vat of hot oil with what looked like long chopsticks. "What can we get for you today?"

"My usual, Mr. P. I'm glad to see you back." I tossed him a wink as I unzipped the small cross-body pouch I carried when I jogged, reaching for the cash inside.

"On the house today, young lady."

"You sure, Mr. P? I don't mind at all—"

"Your money's no good here." He shook his head.

"Well, thanks very much." I really did adore this sweet, old man.

"My pleasure."

He handed me the warm bag and I struggled to find something to say so that I could prolong the interaction. Nobody was waiting behind me in line, so I didn't have to rush and I wasn't ready to say goodbye to either of them just yet.

"Will you be back full time then?" I tried to disguise the disappointment in my tone. I loved Mr. Pfeffernuss, but I wanted to see more of Neil.

The older man grumbled under his breath. "I hope to be."

Neil turned, dipping and tossing the hot donuts into the bowl mounded with cinnamon sugar. He met my eye and I swallowed, feeling completely pinned by his gaze.

"Pops loves to work, but we're trying to talk him into retirement."

"Nonsense." Mr. P, who was never short with anyone, grunted in frustration at Neil.

As a distraction from the touchy topic, I reached into my bag and sampled one of the small rings. As always, the sugar and spice were a delight on my tongue, but today there was something new. The apple flavor was much more intense and there was an addition to the spices.

"You changed something." I blurted, my eyes darting between them as I finished chewing. I hadn't meant for my tone to be accusatory, but it had definitely come out that way.

Mr. P's agitation abruptly changed to amusement, and he started laughing. His eyes danced as he pointed a finger at his grandson. "You see? I told you someone would notice." He turned his attention back to me. "What do you taste, little lady?"

Neil looked torn between embarrassment and pride. I had no doubt that he had been responsible for the updates to Mr. P's recipe, but he didn't stop moving or speak until the batch he was sugaring was loaded into the display case.

"Pops is only here with me because he figured out my secret ingredients. He made a bet with me, and won." Neil smiled as he removed his sugar-coated gloves and leaned his elbows on the slightly elevated countertop to look down at me. "Do you like them?"

I nodded, reaching for another sample. "They're delicious. I think . . ." I thoughtfully chewed, starting to close my eyes so I could focus.

"Wait!" Pops exclaimed. "What's the wager?"

My eyes opened wide again and I stopped chewing.

"Wager?" Neil glanced at his grandfather, amused.

"What does she get if she guesses?"

"I don't need a prize—"

Mr. Pfeffernuss snapped his fingers. "I got it. If she guesses, you owe her dinner."

Neil choked out a laugh and I exhaled strongly enough that cinnamon and something hotter burned in my sinuses.

"Pops, you can't do things like that—"

"Sure, I can. What do you say, Ms. Connelly? He's a handsome young man, is he not? Retired professional surfer and current cider donut aficionado. He's fit and employed! You think him buying you dinner could be a winning situation?" The clever old man winked at me.

"What about you, Mr. P? You know you're the reason I come around so often for a treat." I winked back for good measure.

He snorted and laughed heartily at me. "We both know that's only half true, but I appreciate it, young lady. What do you say, is it a bet?"

Heart thumping, I met Neil's eye briefly and he shrugged one shoulder.

"As long as Neil's game. I don't want to be anyone's pity date."

Mr. Pfeffernuss gasped as if scandalized. "Never, my dear. Isn't that right, Neil?"

Neil watched me carefully, his sincerity coming through the azure depths of his gaze. "Absolutely. It would be my pleasure."

Satisfied, Mr. P clapped his hands. "All right then. So, go ahead, young lady. Tell us what you taste."

"Well, the apple flavor is much more intense. Sweeter, too. And there's something else in the sugar . . ." I focused, trying to determine what the slight heat on my tongue was from. "Ginger? And maybe nutmeg or cloves?"

Neil was staring at me with such intensity my heart started to pound. Mr. Pfeffernuss on the other hand was chuckling, and it quickly turned into a rolling laugh.

"Pretty close."

"Pretty close? You owe the girl dinner, son. The only thing she didn't guess was cardamom, and honestly, who would guess that? Well done, young lady, well done." He exited the cart through the small door on the side and started a slow walk in the direction of the coffee cart, clapping me on the shoulder on his way past. "I had a feeling you would nail that. Good for you! I'm going to take a little break, but it sure was nice to see you."

"You too Mr. P. I'll see you soon?" Still hooting, he was shaking his head as he ambled away. I turned my attention to Neil. "So . . . dinner?"

He looked a bit surprised. "You really want to go with me? You don't have to, you know. Pops likes to make trouble where he can—"

"I'd love to. Meet me at O'Malley's? Eight tonight?"

Neil smiled at me, nodding. "All right. It's a date."

"I'll see you later, then. They're fantastic, by the way. Whatever you changed, keep doing it."

If I wasn't mistaken—and I'd bet good money I wasn't—Neil blushed as he thanked me.

The redness in his cheeks and the slight twitch to his biceps as he twisted a rag in his hands as I started to leave was the best compliment I'd gotten in months.

4

—————

NEIL

That clever old man set me up.

And it worked.

Then, he'd just walked off into the horizon cackling.

I wanted to be mad about it, but I wasn't. Not even a little bit. His clever push had landed me a date with Shaw, and I was looking forward to it more than I cared to admit. I'd thought my day had been made just by seeing her again, but Pops went and pushed all the boundaries and made things infinitely better.

After Shaw left, we'd had a burst of customers all at once and it took me longer than it should have to realize that Pops hadn't come back to the cart. Panic started to set in as I glanced frantically around the park, but to my relief I found him lounging at one of the picnic tables with a cup of coffee, just looking around with a smile on his face.

I threw the "be right back" sign up on the counter, pulled off my gloves and hairnet, and jogged over to where he was sitting.

"You said you were taking a break, but I honestly didn't believe you." I slid onto the bench across from him.

"I was just admiring the view," he said, peacefully gazing around the park at the assorted groupings of families, couples, and people out enjoying the beautiful day. His tone was such that worry spiked in my veins.

"You all right, Pops?"

"I'm fine." He smiled at me. "You look good in there, son."

Pride overrode the worry, but only momentarily. "Thanks, Pops. What's going on?"

He shook his head gently. "I know I've been giving you all hell about retirement, but I was in that cart today for a total of two and a half hours, and I needed to sit here for thirty minutes just to feel like myself again." His eyes came up from the coffee cup and met mine. "I hate it."

I knew how he felt. After I got hurt during my last competition, nothing worked quite right between me and the waves. Sometimes just getting up on the board took everything I had.

"You had an amazing run, Pops. Thirty years just with the cart. That doesn't include all the amazing things you did at the café, or with Nana before she passed. You deserve to take a break."

He nodded, fidgeting with his cup. "I just worry that resting will tell my body I don't need it to work anymore."

I tried to be reassuring. "You've got plenty of gardening to do, right? Plus, whatever happens to the business, we'll need your final approval on things."

My grandad turned a smile my way. "You going to take over for me, kid?"

The proposition was incredibly tempting. It was something that had been tossed around a few times, but never seriously. Now . . . I wanted it. It felt like the right fit for me. And he was offering it to me if I wanted to take it.

"Is that what *you* want, Pops?"

A silver eyebrow lifted over a very intelligent blue eye. "I think you know I do. But I also think maybe . . . it should be more than just the cart now. That was just a fun seasonal thing, a good cash injection to keep the cafe running all those years. Not that you'd have to get rid of it —of course not. You could keep the old girl for nostalgia and special events. But I think you might want more than a rickety festival cart with a fryer and a sink."

His perception was pretty uncanny. I'd never told anyone that if I decided to take over when he retired, I'd want to make changes to the recipe and transition it to a full-time business. I thought it made sense, especially with the traffic we'd been getting, but I'd never actually breathed a word of that plan out loud.

"You might be right."

He turned his head my direction and let out that rolling laugh that made me smile. "'Might,' he says." He shook his head and carefully got to his feet. "Come on, young man. Let's go finish our donut slinging so you can get ready for your date." I joined him, matching his pace as we walked back to the cart where a couple of families were patiently waiting off to the side. "You're welcome, by the way." He winked at me.

I shook my head, and he just laughed that much harder.

I HADN'T BEEN to O'Malley's before, but I was well aware of the place. An old Irish pub, it was frequently on the "best places to eat" lists, and the patio was a big draw—especially this time of year.

I spotted Shaw at one of the tables outside, chatting with a waitress who looked shockingly like her, just with dark hair instead of blonde.

I waved in greeting and was able to bypass the actual entrance as the waitress—Shannon I was guessing based on what Pops had told me —opened a gate in the iron fencing that surrounded the patio.

"Come on in. Can I get you something to drink? I can recommend the chocolate stout. It's from a local micro-brewery."

"Sounds great, thanks."

Shannon nodded, and winked at her sister before disappearing into the bar.

Shaw stood, leaning in for a brief hug in greeting. Unsure of the protocol, I awkwardly kissed her cheek.

"You look good out of your apron," she said, expression quickly morphing to shock. "I didn't mean—"

Laughing, I shook my head. "Well, I guess we're even now. I know what you mean. I appreciate the compliment, and you look lovely as well."

The blush in her cheeks made my pulse spike a bit.

"Thanks. Was Mr. P okay working the rest of the day?"

I nodded, glancing down at the menu. "He took breaks when he needed to, but I think he might be about ready to hang up the apron for good."

Shaw gasped. "Oh, no! That's too bad. I'll miss everything about that cart if he does. But I understand—he's no spring chicken. He deserves to enjoy some retirement if that's what he wants."

I met her eyes and saw true sorrow there. "He suggested I take it over."

Surprise and cautious excitement danced in the blue depths. "Are you considering it?"

"I am."

"How wonderful. I bet he'll love that."

Her smile sent an irrational tingle through my chest. Making her happy made me happy. I'd felt that sensation briefly with some of the women I'd dated, but never with this kind of intensity. I wondered what it was about this woman that had me reacting in such a way.

"I'd probably want some kind of permanent location, though, so I've got some thinking to do." When I looked up from the menu again, I found her staring blankly at me. "Everything okay?"

"Yes. Totally fine." She looked down and fidgeted a bit. "I can recommend the shepherd's pie or the fish and chips. Honestly, everything here is good."

Shannon dropped off the drinks just then. "Need another minute?" she asked.

"I'm ready. Do you need time, Neil?"

I shook my head. "You had me at fish and chips."

Shannon smiled. "Good choice. You want your usual?" she asked Shaw.

"Is Liam cooking?"

Shannon shook her head. "No, it's James tonight."

Shaw's lip curled up and I found it oddly endearing. "Yeah, I guess."

"Sounds good." She didn't keep a notepad or pen but I trusted her. "Fish and chips and shepherd's pie. Anything else?"

When we didn't have anything else to request, she left us and Shaw turned to me, expression serious.

"Listen, I know we don't know each other very well, but I was looking at locations for my gift shop and there was a property with a small commercial kitchen in it. If I end up taking that one, and you're still interested in going permanent . . ." she hesitated, her normal confidence a bit shaken. She seemed uncomfortable as she picked at the label on her beer, but continued. "Anyway, it might be an option."

"Definitely an option worth considering. Where is it?"

Shaw gave me the rundown of where the building was and what it had to offer. The more she spoke, the more enamored I became with her and the suggestion she'd made. Her excitement over getting her business started was endearing. I could relate, and having someone to compare notes with while I embarked on a similar endeavor was comforting.

Even after the food came, she was full of gesturing, description and enthusiasm. We ate, talked and laughed. It was by far the best date I'd been on in a long, long time.

"I'm sorry. I completely dominated that whole conversation, didn't I?" She looked abashed as she sipped on the remainder of her drink, Shannon having already cleared our dishes away.

"It's all right. I rather enjoyed myself."

"You did?" She looked at me, disbelief in her eyes. "Thank God."

I couldn't help but laugh. She was adorable and had no idea how taken by her I was.

"I know we're not even done here quite yet, but could I take you out again, Shaw?"

She beamed. "I would enjoy that, very much."

I tipped my glass her direction before finishing the contents in agreement.

Parking around the pub was limited, and we'd both parked down the street in a public lot that also had access to the beach. After I paid the bill, we ambled down the strip together in the balmy evening, Shaw pulling a sweater tight over her shoulders against the chill.

"Are you working tomorrow?" she asked.

"Why, you already need a fix?"

"Maybe."

"I am."

"Maybe I'll come by and see you, then."

The very idea made my heart thump, and I realized that meant I already had it bad for this girl.

All too soon we were in the parking lot, and Shaw was unlocking the door to her car.

"Thanks again. I had a great time."

"Me too. I . . ." I hesitated, suddenly awkward and unsure of myself.

"If you want to kiss me, all you have to do is ask, Neil."

This girl. Her mouth was quite possibly going to end me in more ways than one.

Grinning, I obliged her. "May I kiss you, Shaw?"

"You'd better."

I smiled and tried to memorize the look on her face just then, the brightness of her eyes and the tilt of her lips. She had a freckle under her left eye and the tiniest scar along the bridge of her nose.

She was gorgeous.

I lowered my face to hers and her lush mouth responded with enthusiasm. Her arms lifted and her hands linked behind my neck. As I fell deeper into the kiss, I drifted my thumb along her jawline, reveling in the way her lips moved against mine. She left me breathless in the best possible way.

She was everything I didn't realize I was missing.

I owed Pops *big* for his match-making tactics.

5
____

SHAW

My jogging route just happened to take me through the park the next morning. And the one after that. Everything about Neil had me intrigued and feeling genuinely happy. I didn't want to be overly enthusiastic and say we were dating, but we were definitely seeing one another. Often.

We squeezed in a handful of dinners, some long conversations, and even an evening at the beach over the next couple of weeks.

Neil told me all about the abrupt end to his career as a professional surfer and I commiserated with my failed career as . . . anything. Ever. If nothing else, that earned me a sweet kiss of sympathy and a laugh.

It was true though—the shop was my one big dream, and I was so close to getting it I could hardly stand myself.

Neil also decided if I was going to come by every single morning, I was going to be his official taste-tester, and I was one hundred percent on board with that.

He started to let me inside the cart with him the second week, and walked me through the process during lulls between customers. I wasn't complaining one bit, because that put me in extremely close proximity to him out of necessity and allowed me access to all the donuts I could handle. There was no downside.

"Pops always used apple cider vinegar in his dough."

"The tang," I interjected and he smiled at me. My body appreciated it in so many ways. That dimple of his was deadly.

"Exactly. I went in a different direction, though. I'm using boiled apple cider." Neil showed me a massive glass jar full of what looked like dark honey. There were clear crystals all around the inside rim of the jar, shimmering in the light as he moved it.

"How do you make that?"

He was in his element and his enthusiasm was contagious. I wondered if this is how he'd felt on our date when I couldn't stop over-sharing about my shop. He maneuvered his body around me gracefully as he started a batch of dough in the limited space. Any effort I made to get out of the way seemed to make things worse, so I just stood still.

"You start with a couple gallons of cider and boil them low for about half a day. You end up with this molasses-like syrup with super concentrated flavor."

He gestured for me to sample from a small puddle with my finger-tip. It was an explosion of sweet apple and I could see why he wanted to make the switch.

After a quick pause to serve customers, he walked me through the rest of the dough process, then the sugar. His update was to add apple pie spice instead of just cinnamon, and I heartily approved. The dimension of taste with the changes was out of this world.

"They're perfect," I mumbled over a bite.

"Think so?"

I nodded. Neil was full of energy, bouncing on the balls of his feet. He swooped down and planted a brief kiss on my lips in his excitement. I stood up on my tip-toes to return the favor and we shared a sweet apple cider kiss in the tiny cart.

"Are you still looking at that building?" he asked, in a low voice, our faces close. His nearness and question both made my heart pound.

"Yes. Why, are you thinking about a storefront?"

He moved away a bit and nodded, pulling on some gloves so he could serve the approaching customers.

"I am."

"What does Mr. P say about it?"

He gestured for a pause in our conversation and turned to help the family at the counter. Once they were on their way with a massive boat of donuts, and he'd done his very efficient counter wipe and glove removal routine, he smiled at me.

"He says the business is mine if I want it. He even suggested that a permanent location might be the way to go. Keep the cart for seasonal stuff and special occasions. I'm very seriously considering it."

I couldn't contain my smile. "Well, then. I happen to know someone who can help with that."

"Yeah?" His long fingers stroked the side of my face and I closed my eyes for a few breaths.

"You bet. I'll give my realtor a call. She's been waiting for a firm answer from me for a while."

"Is it too soon to do something like this? Reckless?"

I shrugged and wrapped my arms around his waist. "Probably. Do you care?"

He tilted his head as he considered, eventually shaking it. "No. This is just my next big wave."

A smile spread across his mouth and I couldn't help but join in his happiness.

"Sounds about right. You sure you won't get sick of seeing me?"

"No, but we don't know until we try, right?"

I nodded, and he swooped in for a quick but thorough kiss before turning back to his assembly line.

My gaze trained on him, I watched in admiration as his muscles worked, his every move an efficient dance. Eventually, I pulled my attention away and stepped out of the cart, making some phone calls to get started on the next steps. It was exhilarating and terrifying but nothing about it felt wrong.

My realtor had an opening the following afternoon thanks to a cancellation, so I agreed that we could meet her at the building just as soon as the cart closed down for the day.

My nerves were strung tight, but Neil looked calm as he drove us across town to the potential location. It was just blocks from O'Malley's, deep in a strip mall that had some great anchor stores and a few boutiques.

We parked and waited a moment for my spunky realtor to pull in beside us in her flashy Mercedes. She jumped out with a clipboard and a smile, swinging a large set of keys.

"So good to see you again! You ready?" Her eyes quickly assessed me, then Neil. I felt the first pricks of jealousy as she lingered half a beat longer on him than I would have liked. He must have felt me tense, because he gently shoulder-checked me, his face split wide in a knowing grin.

"Easy, tiger." he teased. I narrowed my eyes into a glare. Neil just laughed. "Come on. Let's go inside."

Once the door was open, I took in a deep breath and started to wander around. It still needed drywalling, and all the wires and plumbing were exposed. I knew it would take some work, but I wasn't afraid of that. My realtor was rambling enthusiastically, gesturing to things that were probably important, but I couldn't hear a word she said.

Neil came up beside me and threaded his fingers through mine, patient, and quiet as I glanced around, inside my mind seeing everything as I wanted it.

Mentally I placed racks of trinkets and wooden signs painted with clever phrases, family names, or fun designs customized to match the customers' decor. A refrigerated case full of flower arrangements. Shannon was going to be so annoyed when I asked her to help and just the thought of my sister fired up at me brought me joy. I could picture wreaths lining the walls and a wide butcher-block-topped workstation.

My newest version of the vision also included a glass-fronted bakery case for Neil's creations and maybe an espresso machine if we felt like getting fancy. I would absolutely *not* be allowed to use it though —too many delicate parts for me to break. I could imagine a handful of tables on the far side of the shop for those that wanted to eat their treats before leaving. I grinned wide picturing one of them with a permanent "Reserved for Pops" sign on it. Neil met my eye and smiled back. I thought he'd like that idea just fine.

I felt content and optimistic. Neil's warm, strong hand holding mine was likely the only thing keeping me from floating up to the ceiling.

It was the future I'd envisioned for most of my adult life, but better.

This version had me falling in love with a man I hadn't even been looking for, and found where I least expected. This version smelled like apples and sparkled like crystallized cider sugar. This version was perfect, just like Neil's newest recipe.

I had set out to get donuts, but managed to get the whole cart and the man who ran it. I wasn't mad about it either. Not even a little bit.

ABOUT THE AUTHOR

Lily is a Colorado native enjoying the fantastic climate of Southern California with her family and cranky cat after surviving more than a decade in hot, humid places where hurricanes get their own season and Winter is a myth.

The written word is her favorite thing. Reading or writing; she doesn't discriminate. Left to her own devices she can read a book a day —a good happily ever after is a powerful drug!

An only child, she grew up inventing elaborate stories for her dolls to act out. She started word processing on a computer around age 10 and never looked back. After suffering the heartbreak of catastrophic drive failure a regrettable number of times, she has finally learned to back things up appropriately and often.

http://www.authorlilyalexander.com/
http://bit.ly/ALANewsletter

AFTER TONIGHT

LAUREN ELIZABETH

Can two botched proposals and a horse with a mind of its own convince an unlikely pair to take a chance on love?

1

HOLLY

"*I* don't know what I was thinking not packing my snow boots in March," Holly said, pulling back the sheer curtain covering her window at the bed-and-breakfast. "If it gets much worse, I'm going to have frozen toes by dinner."

"Stop changing the subject, Hol."

Holly sighed and twisted the cord on the room phone. "Okay, but why else would he have asked me to fly home, Kate? Syracuse is a long way from Nashville."

"Did he ask you, or did you offer?"

Holly's eyes roamed the room as if they were looking for the answer in the roses covering the faded wallpaper. "Both, I think."

The hesitation on the other end of the line knotted Holly's stomach. There were definite drawbacks to being known so well.

"I just want you to go into this with your eyes open," Kate said. "He's let you down before."

Holly pinched the bridge of her nose between her thumb and middle finger. "I can't blame Jeff for leaving. I turned him down."

"You turned down an apartment key, not an engagement ring. And aren't you the one who fussed at me about that very thing? Who told me I deserved a commitment?"

Wedging the phone between her chin and shoulder, Holly hung her garment bag in the armoire. "No fair using my own words against me. But if you had heard his voice when he called, you'd understand why I had to come. I can't explain it, but he sounded different. Expectant."

Holly stood in front of the long mirror and held her dress against her chest. Kate had been right—the emerald color was the perfect complement to her auburn hair.

"If you're sure this is what you want, I'll support you," Kate said, "but don't settle."

Holly couldn't expect Kate to understand anymore—not since she had fallen head-over-heels in love and started holding everything and everyone to that starry-eyed standard. But just because Jeff was familiar didn't mean she was settling, and she was tired of hearing about it. Jeff was handsome, successful, and smart—more than that, he was her first love. And in her gut, she knew that, after tonight, everything would be different.

2

ADAM

*A*dam twisted the empty ring box around in his pocket and watched the restaurant's front door—as much as he could with his glasses perched on the tablecloth in front of him. No way was he going to have Jessica's memory of this night include an image of him with duct tape wrapped around the bridge of his glasses.

No, he wanted everything to be perfect for her—surprises and all. She had made more than a few hints about the lack of spontaneity in their relationship, and it had struck a nerve. It wasn't that he didn't want to be spontaneous, it was just that med school didn't allow for much of it. Plus, he didn't get to the top of his class by being spontaneous. It took hard work. Planning. But if she wanted spontaneity, spontaneity she would get. He could hardly wait to see her expression when she realized this was all for her.

"Mr. Crawford, your champagne."

Adam tore his gaze from the door and smiled at the restaurant manager, who held out the special-order bottle of Dom Pérignon for him to inspect.

"Thank you, Jacques. Is the piano player ready?"

The manager nodded and maneuvered the bottle around the ice in the champagne bucket. "She has the music, and we'll alert her when the waiter is ready to approach with the tray. And I wanted to let you know that the guests have all arrived."

Adam turned his head toward the private room at the back of the restaurant, its smoky glass obscuring his view of the room's occupants. As his eyes tracked the shadowed figures, the glass caught a hazy reflection of the front door.

He turned, and there she was: a blurry vision in a green dress. There was no doubt. After tonight, everything would be different.

3

HOLLY

olly shook the snowflakes from the sleeves of her jacket and handed it to the attendant. One glance around the restaurant confirmed her suspicions—the starched, white tablecloths, the glowing candles, the soft piano music—this was a place to drop to one knee with a promise of forever, not a place to put an apartment key on a sticky table with a shrug and a "Whaddaya say?" Not that she would have turned down a proposal from Jeff at La Hacienda—it was one of their favorite haunts—but a restaurant like La Folie seemed more appropriate for such a momentous occasion.

Smoothing her dress, she took in a deep breath to steady her nerves. *Be confident,* she thought. *Shoulders back, stomach in, big smile, and turn—*

—directly into a man holding a glass of champagne.

The man's broad smile flattened as his eyes squinted and landed on the dark spot spreading across her chest. "Oh my gosh. I'm so sorry."

Holly's hands flew to her chest. "My dress! What did you do?"

"Your elbow hit my hand," he said, his face reddening. "My contacts. My glasses."

"What?!" Holly said, unable to hide her irritation.

The man closed his eyes and gave his head a quick shake. "I'm really sorry. My glasses are on the table. I thought you were someone else." He rubbed his brow with his free hand. "Of course, I'll pay for the dry cleaning."

The guy looked mortified, but Holly couldn't worry about that. "Just . . . never mind," she said as she stormed past him and into the bathroom.

She blinked back hot tears as she dabbed at the darkening spot with a cloth napkin. Useless. Of course, silk would spot. She threw the napkin into a basket and slumped on a tufted bench situated against the wall. This night was supposed to be perfect—a night where she and Jeff admitted their mistakes and agreed to move forward—not a night where she sat defeated in a restaurant bathroom.

As she tried to flap her dress dry, she willed her mood to lift. *It's just a dress. Jeff won't care*, she told herself. And she knew he wouldn't. He had been her best friend for most of her life, and one stained dress wouldn't ruin the rest of it. It would simply become part of the funny story they would tell their kids one day.

Eventually, she found herself smiling as she thought of the guy who had run into her. He was kind of adorable—all flustered apology and abashed smile—and he was undeniably handsome. Whoever was the recipient of those broad shoulders, chiseled jaw, and steely blue eyes was one very lucky girl.

After dinner, she would go over and apologize for yelling at him, but first, she would enjoy her evening with Jeff. After all, one near-sighted guy wasn't going to ruin everything.

4

ADAM

Adam berated himself for not getting his glasses fixed last week, but it's not like he ever wore them. Who would've thought he'd drop his right contact lens into the toilet? And that poor woman. It was clear she had dressed for a romantic evening. If he had had his glasses on, he would've noticed immediately that she wasn't Jessica—her long, red hair, alone, would've told him—but there was no denying he had been off his game lately. Picking out the perfect ring, planning the perfect proposal—the rest of his life hinged on this, and his nerves were getting the best of him.

He grimaced as the "champagne girl" emerged from the bathroom. He put up his hand to get her attention, but her eyes were focused elsewhere. Following her gaze, he found the recipient of her attention. The man looked happy to see her, and Adam smiled as the pair embraced and sat at a table by the front window—at least he hadn't completely ruined the woman's evening. After he and Jessica had had a good laugh over his mistaken-identity gaffe, he would drop some money for dry cleaning by her table and introduce himself.

Turning his attention to the door, he saw Jessica enter the restaurant—or he was pretty sure it was Jessica. Taking no chances, he stood by the table and tried not to squint as she approached. He exhaled when she acknowledged him with a small wave. Her blonde hair was pulled back tight, and her drawn expression said she wasn't too happy to see him, but then again, it had only been two days since their last argument. Just another reason she would never see the proposal coming.

"Jessica, you look beautiful," he said, pulling out her chair.

She turned her cheek to his lips as he leaned in to kiss her.

"La Folie. What's the occasion?" she asked.

His eyes narrowed. "Our anniversary. Next week. Since you have that conference on the weekend, I thought we'd celebrate early."

The corners of her mouth turned down. "Oh. That's right. I forgot about that," she said, her fingers restless on the silverware.

"You forgot about the conference or our anniversary?"

"I've just been so busy," she said, her smile tight as she picked up the menu.

He tried to ignore the fact that she didn't answer his question. "Are you okay? Have some difficult patients today?"

Her eyes were fixed on the menu. "No. Just tired."

Dryness overtook his throat. He had planned to propose after dessert, but there was no way he'd be able to get through dinner with this anxiety pumping through him. He needed to get things back on track and fast. Two carats of princess-cut flawlessness ought to do it.

Adam nodded toward the restaurant manager, who tapped the shoulder of a waiter and disappeared into the kitchen.

"Champagne?" he said, offering a glass to Jessica. "I ordered it especially for tonight."

Her eyes briefly met his. "Okay. Maybe a little."

Holding his glass toward hers, he said, "To you, Jessica. To us. And to many more anniversaries."

As their glasses touched, notes of Billy Joel's "Just the Way You Are" floated across the room. Jessica's eyes darted to the pianist, to Adam, to the approaching waiter, and back to Adam. Her eyes widened, but it wasn't anticipation he saw in them, it was terror. His chest tightened as panic flooded his body. His mind grasped for a way to stop everything and everyone, but it was too late—everything had already been set into motion.

The waiter stood tableside and brandished the tray with a flourish, revealing the Tiffany engagement ring. Blood pounded in Adam's ears as he sensed the buildup of pressure from the happy guests waiting to burst from the private room with their congratulations. Jessica's eyes shimmered, and Adam grabbed the ring from the tray, clenching it in his lap. After a few awkward seconds, the waiter's smile vanished, and he turned, the sound of his rapid retreat echoing through the room.

"Adam," Jessica said, "I don't know what to say."

Her trembling voice hollowed him out. She didn't have to say anything.

5

HOLLY

A loud sound from the back of the restaurant caused Holly to flinch. She turned toward the commotion and saw the man who had spilled champagne on her, his face blotchy and red.

"Yikes," Jeff said, his eyes wide. "That doesn't sound good."

Holly's eyebrows arched. "No, it doesn't. And that was the guy who caused this," she said, pointing to the spot on her dress.

Jeff's eyes went to her chest, and she was immediately glad she had worn her good bra.

"Well, it's hardly noticeable," he said with a smile, his cheeks tinged with pink.

His nervousness was endearing, but five minutes was too long to be spent in awkward small talk about the late snow and the menu. She took a deep breath. Someone had to get the apologies started.

"Jeff, I want you to know how sorry I am for how things were left between us. We've been friends for so long, and the last few months of radio silence have been horrible."

The dimple she knew so well appeared in his cheek. "I know. I feel the same way."

Her shoulders relaxed. "And I want you to know that I didn't say *No* because I don't love you. It's just that I was expecting . . ." She paused.

She didn't want to steal his moment. "Well, I wasn't expecting a key to your apartment."

As he reached across the table and took her hand, a horse-drawn carriage pulled up in front of the restaurant window. Her heart skipped a beat. He had thought of everything.

"I know, Hol. And you're right. You deserve more than that. You deserve someone who can give you that." He squeezed her hand and looked down before returning his gaze to hers. "And that's why it was so important to me that you were here in person. You're so important to me."

Every part of her beamed, and she returned the squeeze of his hand, urging him to continue. They wouldn't just pick up where they had left off this time; finally, they were going to start something new.

"I'm engaged."

A buzzing sound filled her ears, and her hand went limp. She couldn't have heard him right. "You what?"

"I got engaged. To Amy Simmons."

"You what?" she said again, hating the broken sound in her voice. She pulled her hand from his.

"Amy Simmons and I are engaged."

"Amy Sue Simmons?"

He nodded. "Last weekend."

Last weekend? How had she not heard? The Sycamore Valley High School grapevine was relentless. Something inside her collapsed when she realized everyone probably felt too sorry for her to tell her.

"When you turned me down, I came back here broken. I had to ask myself a lot of questions about us, and after I thought about it, I knew you were right. If I really loved you, I would've given you a ring. And I do love you, Hol, but not like you deserve. And you deserve everything."

She was gutted. She wasn't even sure she was still breathing. The last seventeen years of her life had had Jeff Wilkins in it in some way, and now, he was gone. She wasn't even sure who she was without him.

Her eyes searched for his, looking for some sort of clue that this was all a huge misunderstanding, but something else had gotten his attention, something that made his face brighten and his dimple reappear.

Her shoulders stiffened as she heard the click-clack of heels behind her.

No, no, no, no, no, no, no.

6

____

ADAM

*A*dam downed a glass of champagne as the plans for his life sashayed out the restaurant door. Hesitant footsteps crossed the floor and stopped beside him.

"Mr. Crawford."

Adam let out a slow breath. "Jacques, you've just witnessed the worst night of my life. I think you can call me Adam."

The restaurant manager cleared his throat. "Adam, I am so very sorry for what happened."

Adam groaned and put his head in his hands. "Just leave the bill for the champagne."

"Oh. No, sir. It's on us."

A clipped laugh escaped Adam's throat. "That bad, huh?"

The manager was silent.

"Yeah, that's what I was afraid of," Adam said, raking his hands through his hair before putting on his broken glasses.

"We had the guests leave through the back."

"Thanks, Jacques. You're a good man."

"Unfortunately, sir—and I don't know how to tell you this—the carriage you ordered is waiting out front, and he won't leave without payment."

Adam's head dropped. "Okay. I'll take care of it."

As he stood to put on his jacket, he sensed people averting their eyes. And no one said a word as he grabbed a glass, tucked the bottle of champagne under his arm, and walked out of the restaurant. He wondered how many stories this little debacle would be featured in tonight.

The carriage ride had been a last-minute decision. Who could resist the romance of a horse-driven carriage on an unexpectedly snowy night? But now, it might as well have been a kick to the groin. So much for spontaneity.

"Hey, buddy, how much do I owe you?" Adam asked as he walked up to the coachman.

"After the deposit, that'll be another hundred."

The man's voice was as gruff as his appearance—he looked like a grumpy, off-season Santa Claus.

Adam sighed and handed over the money. "Here you go. Have a good night."

"Aren't you getting in?"

"The night didn't exactly go as planned."

The coachman's mouth screwed up as he nodded. "Sorry."

"Yeah. Me, too."

As the carriage pulled away from the sidewalk, a flash of green caught Adam's eye. The champagne girl.

"Hey. Wait up a minute," Adam said as he jogged back to the carriage. "See that woman up there about three or four blocks? Would you catch up to her and give her this?" Adam flashed forty dollars at him.

The coachman's head pulled back. "I don't think so, young man."

Adam shook his head. "No, it's nothing like that. I owe her some money."

"Seems to me the right thing to do, then, would be to give it to her yourself. And you've already paid for the carriage."

Adam scratched at his hairline as the horse's tail flicked lazily in the snow. A single guy in a carriage riding up to a woman on the street? If it weren't so ridiculous, it could almost be gallant.

"Fine," Adam said, placing the glass and the champagne bottle on the seat and hoisting himself into the back of the carriage. He tightened his suit jacket around his torso as the horse continued down the road. "Can you get the horse to go any faster?"

"Hester goes as fast as she goes," the coachman replied. "Use the blanket if you're cold."

Adam glanced at the plaid blanket folded in a tidy square on the seat. "That's okay. I don't plan to be on here that long."

"Suit yourself," the coachman said with a shrug. "But I'm betting you owe this girl an apology more than you owe her money, and that takes a little time."

"Excuse me?"

"The look on your face. You look . . . grumpy."

Adam snorted and rubbed his jaw. "Are you the resident expert?"

"What?"

"Nothing. And don't worry about the look on my face. She has nothing to do with it."

"Ah. Too bad. I saw her walk by earlier. She's beautiful."

Adam rolled his eyes. He had had his fill of beautiful women.

7

———————

HOLLY

olly rubbed her arms and picked up her pace. How she had made it out of the restaurant without crying was a mystery, as was what she had said to get out of dinner, but in her haste to leave, she had left her jacket in the coatroom.

"Hey! Champagne girl!"

She turned to see a large black horse pulling a gleaming red and black carriage—the carriage she had thought she would be riding in with Jeff. Instead, sitting in the back was the guy who had ruined her dress. How had the night become so backward?

"Are you okay?" the guy said as he hopped down from the carriage.

"I'm fine," she said, looking away from his concerned eyes. Pity would surely start the waterworks.

"I forgot to get this to you earlier. It's the money for your dress."

As he held out the bills, one fluttered from his hand and landed at the edge of her open-toe shoes. He stooped to pick it up, then looked her up and down. She rubbed her arms again.

"I'm Adam, by the way. Adam Crawford," he said as he stood.

"Holly Jenkins."

"Where are you walking to, Holly?"

Her eyes narrowed. She did not need some weirdo following her back to the inn. "Why do you want to know?"

A half-smile tugged at his lips. "Because you are clearly not dressed for this weather. I thought old Hester and I could get you to wherever you're going," he said, patting the horse on the rump.

She tried to think of a good reason to say *No*, but she was freezing, and he looked harmless enough. "I'm staying at the Battle Creek Inn."

"That's the bed-and-breakfast on Millersburg, right?"

She nodded.

"That's several blocks off the square. I can't, in good conscience, let you keep walking out here like that. If your arms don't freeze, your toes might. Get in the carriage, and I'll get you to Battle Creek."

"Battle Creek is five blocks off our path," the coachman said over his shoulder.

"I'll cover it," Adam said, rolling his eyes before holding out his hand to her. "Come on. Seriously, you're going to end up with frostbite."

As she took his hand and stepped onto the platform, she noticed the champagne and the warm blanket. If it weren't for the wrong guy stepping into the carriage, it would be perfect.

8

ADAM

After a night of having his ego trounced, Adam was glad to have the opportunity to do at least one thing right. The woman was clearly freezing, and the inn was only a few minutes off the main road.

"You're not from around here, are you?" Adam said, handing Holly the blanket.

She let out a shiver as she wrapped it around herself. "Actually, I grew up not far from here. In Syracuse."

"Really?" he said, eyeing her shoes, which were peeking out from the blanket. "You don't look like you're from around here."

"Yeah, I wasn't prepared," she said, pulling the blanket up to her neck. "For anything."

The sadness in her voice was evident.

"Are you okay?" he said.

Her reaction was half wince, half smile. "Let's just say that the night didn't go as expected."

"That makes two of us," he said after a sharp laugh. "Champagne?" He held out the champagne bottle.

"Champagne? Seriously?" She lowered the blanket and nodded toward the stain on her dress.

His chin dipped. "You have these to blame," he said, pointing to his duct-taped glasses. "I should've known from the start that the night was going to be a disaster."

"Me, too. Who would've thought that that event would be the highlight of my night?"

For the first time that evening, she smiled, and her eyes shone. He hadn't noticed before how blue they were—cornflower blue with sparks of silver.

He cleared his throat. "Well, I bet your night wasn't as bad as mine."

"Are you a betting man?" she said with a smirk.

"Really?" he said, crossing his arms on his chest. "Well, I wouldn't be a gentleman to let you take that bet. There's no way for you to win."

She lowered her chin and looked him straight in the eye. "Try me."

He raised an eyebrow at her, leaned forward, and tapped the coachman's shoulder. "Hey, buddy, do you have a cup hidden in here somewhere?"

"Lift the latch on that storage box," the coachman said with a backward nod of his head. "There are a couple cups and a thermos with hot chocolate, if you want some. And the name's Willy."

Adam grabbed a cup and poured some champagne into it, handing it to Holly before he poured himself a glass.

"Hey, Willy, I think you're taking us off course," Adam said as the horse turned off the main road and onto a side street.

"Hester goes where she goes," Willy said.

Adam rolled his eyes and shrugged. What was one more detour on this horrible night?

"Apparently, Hester runs the show," he said with a whisper. "Anyway, ladies first. Let's hear it."

She shook her head. "Your story will pale in comparison. You go first."

He nodded. "Okay, but what's the wager?"

Putting her chin in her hand, she gazed into the distance. "Hmmm. How about this? If you win, I'll give you your money back; if I win, you go back to that restaurant and get my jacket."

"Back to the scene of my embarrassment. Diabolical." He smiled and nodded his head a few times. "Deal."

He reached in his jacket for the ring and was relieved that it was still there after he had hurriedly jammed it in his pocket earlier. "This was supposed to be on Jessica's finger tonight." He held out the ring and tipped his head toward her. "Jessica, by the way, is who I thought you were when you came into the restaurant." He put the ring back in his pocket. "You can probably guess how well that went."

"Oh no. You proposed?"

"Not exactly. I didn't get the chance. But that's not the worst part."

"It gets worse?" she said, her eyes wide.

"I flew in both sets of parents and invited friends and colleagues for this happy occasion, all of whom were waiting in a back room to file out when she said *Yes*. Instead, Jacques had to sneak them all out through the back."

She grimaced. "Adam, I'm so sorry. That *is* bad."

"But wait. There's more."

Holly's eyebrows hitched.

"She was cheating on me."

Holly's hand flew to her mouth.

"Yeah. A resident at the hospital. Undoubtedly someone I know." Adam pushed his hands through his hair. "I wouldn't be surprised if he was at the restaurant."

"You didn't ask who he was?"

"Of course, I did. She just didn't answer. That's probably why. I bet he was there." He shook his head. "I'm such an idiot."

"I doubt that."

He leaned his head back against the seat cushion. "No, I am. She said things hadn't been good with us for a while, and she was right. They hadn't." He leaned forward and put his elbows on his knees. "I kept arranging and rearranging things, trying to make it work. Somehow, I thought this would do it." He shrugged. "I have no idea why."

"I'm really sorry. How long had you been dating her?"

"A year next weekend."

"Ouch. Had you known her long?"

"We went to med school together."

"You're a doctor?"

He shook his head. "I'm getting ready to start my last year of med school; she's in her first year of residency." He poured himself another glass of champagne. "This whole night has been one failed romantic gesture after another. Including this stupid carriage ride."

The coachman harrumphed.

"Sorry. No offense, Willy. Anyway, she had mentioned once that she thought it looked romantic, so idiot, here, sets it up. Pathetic."

Holly laughed through her nose. "Want to hear something more pathetic?" she said.

"Yes, please."

"I thought this carriage was meant for me."

"No."

She nodded. "But that's not the worst part."

9

———

HOLLY

"She just showed up? At the restaurant?" Adam's eyes practically bugged out of his head, which only confirmed how horrific the whole night had been.

Holly nodded and took a drink of champagne.

"That's horrible," he said.

"Here I am, holding Jeff's hand and beaming from ear to ear, and he tells me he's engaged to Amy Sue Simmons. I mean, her initials say it all."

A loud laugh escaped Adam's mouth.

"Itty bitty blonde thing. Perky. Horrible. We couldn't be more different."

The corners of Adam's mouth tipped up as he pushed his glasses back on his nose.

"She sits down between us and tells me she knows it's going to be awkward, people talk, blah blah blah, and then she says that she hopes we're okay and that I'll come to the freaking wedding because she knows how much I meant to Jeffrey. *Meant to Jeffrey*. Past tense. Not to mention *Jeffrey*." She rolled her eyes. "No one has ever called him Jeffrey. I thought I would vomit."

Adam choked on his champagne.

"I've known him my whole life, everyone expected us to get

married, and then, out of the blue, Amy Sue Freaking Simmons. And in only four months. How does that happen?" She tipped back the rest of her champagne. "My life made sense with him. Now . . . I just feel lost."

Adam refilled her glass. "I get that. When Jessica walked out the door, it was like all my plans walked out with her. It feels strange to be rudderless."

She glanced at him, his cheeks ruddy from the cold and covered in a sexy five-o-clock shadow. She wasn't sure how anyone could let him slip through her fingers.

"You hardly seem rudderless. Maybe it's just a course correction. And I wouldn't worry too much about it. You're a young, handsome, soon-to-be doctor. Unless you're hiding a jerk in there somewhere," she said, her hand gesturing in a circle around his chest, "there'll be more chances."

He sat forward, a mischievous grin stretching across his face. "Handsome, you say?"

She shook her head. "*Handsome* is all you take from that? Don't get a big head. I'm just trying to be nice."

He smirked. "Okay, but I heard it. You think I'm handsome."

Heat rose in her cheeks, but she rolled her eyes dramatically to try to distract him from it. He was handsome, but she had had her fill of handsome men. For the time being, at least.

"Oh my gosh, you guys are all the same," she said.

"Come on. My ego has just been trampled. Cut me some slack."

"Okay, okay. You're very handsome."

"Thank you," he said with an exaggerated huff.

She giggled as he bumped her shoulder with his.

"Here's to us," he said, raising his glass. "To love's losers."

"I'll drink to that," Holly said.

As she took a sip of champagne and sat back, her eyes wandered to the star-spattered sky. This wasn't how she'd imagined the night going, but it could be worse. She could be half-frozen and stumbling stiff-legged back to the inn alone; instead, a complete stranger had pulled up beside her, in a horse-drawn carriage no less, and she wasn't miserable. As a matter of fact, she was surprised to realize she was actually enjoying herself.

10

ADAM

*A*dam put the empty champagne bottle on the floor of the carriage and gazed everywhere but at Holly. She was funny and adorable, but she also was in pain, and he needed to act accordingly. Plus, he had just been dumped. Any attraction to her would be inappropriate. Wouldn't it? He gave his head a shake and focused on the steady clop-clop-clop of Hester's hooves on the street.

"How about sharing some of that blanket?" Adam said.

"Oh. Sorry," she said, an embarrassed smile spreading across her face.

As she lifted the edge of the blanket and offered it to him, the horse whinnied and stopped suddenly, jerking them back and causing Holly's hand to grip his leg. *Inappropriate. Inappropriate*, he thought as a jolt shot through his thigh, the effects lingering long after she had removed her hand.

"Uh, Willy?" Adam said after several seconds of the horse's inactivity.

"Hester stops when she stops," the old man said. "And if I were you, I'd get out and stretch my legs. She might be a while."

Adam sighed and helped Holly to her feet. She wrapped the blanket around her shoulders.

"That horse has a mind of its own, doesn't it?" Holly said as they walked toward a pergola perched in the grass in the middle of the town square.

"Something like that," Adam said, motioning toward a bench.

She sat and offered him some of the blanket. He draped it over his legs, trying to ignore how near she was.

"So, what's next for you, Adam?"

He scratched his head. "I guess I need to figure out where to apply for residency next year. After tonight, my plans have kind of changed on that front."

Holly's lips turned down and inward, the classic look of pity.

"You could still fight for her, you know. Show her that you care and want to try to make it work."

Adam shrugged. Fighting for her hadn't even been a consideration. He decided not to dwell on that realization.

"Maybe," he said. "What's next for you?"

Her shoulders drooped, and her gaze grew distant. "I guess I go back to Nashville and try to figure out what my life looks like without Jeff in it."

"Mm-hmm."

"What?" she said, eyeing him warily.

"Nothing."

She turned toward him, folding her arms over her chest. "What?"

He knew he should keep quiet, but he couldn't help himself. "I was just wondering if your life was going to look all that different."

"What do you mean?"

"Well, he lives here and you live there. How long has that arrangement been going on?"

Her eyes narrowed. "Four years."

"Four years is a long time to be apart."

"We made it work."

He scratched his eyebrow and let that comment slide. "You said you grew up with him. Is it possible that he was just comfortable? Familiar?"

Her eyes widened. "Oh my gosh. You sound like my roommate. Just because Jeff was familiar doesn't mean I was settling."

"I never said you were settling. You did," he said, rubbing his chin. "And I agree, familiarity doesn't necessarily mean settling, but it just sounds like he was your fallback guy. Your safety net." He shook his head. "No guy wants to be a safety net."

She crossed her arms on her chest. "He was safe, not a safety net. Two different things."

He shrugged. "Not that different."

"Is that so? But I guess girls love to be part of a 'plan,'" she said with accompanying air quotes.

His neck bristled. "What?"

"You talked about her like she was part of your plan. No girl wants to just fit into a plan. We want to feel like somebody would work a plan around us, not the other way around."

"Just because she fit my plans doesn't mean the whole relationship was contrived. We worked well together, we had something."

"If she's sleeping with someone else, I don't know that you had that much."

He bolted to his feet. "Whoa, whoa, whoa. I could say the same thing to you."

The tears that sprang to her eyes set him down hard on the bench. Silence crept between them in frozen puffs of quiet breath.

"I'm sorry, Holly," Adam said, pressing the heels of his hands against his brow. "I shouldn't have said that."

She dabbed at her eyes. "No, I'm sorry. I shouldn't have taken a jab at you." She kicked at the snowy grass with the toe of her shoe. "You hit a nerve. And to be honest, I just want to be mad right now."

A quiet huff left his nose. "Yeah. Me, too." He turned to her with a slight smile. "This whole conversation kind of took a bad turn, huh?"

She nodded.

"Truce?" he said, extending his hand.

A hesitant smile tugged at the tight line of her lips. "Truce."

As he looked in her eyes, an ache grew in his chest. A strand of her hair had tumbled across her face, and he had to restrain himself from brushing it back from her cold-flushed cheek. Why did he have to meet her tonight?

11

HOLLY

*H*olly took Adam's hand, and the warmth of it spread up her arm. Why did she have to meet him tonight of all nights? Tomorrow, she would be on a plane back to Nashville, and with the confused way she was feeling, the sooner the better.

"You think the horse is ready?" she said, wrapping her arms tightly around her shoulders.

"Hester is ready when she's ready," Adam said in a perfect imitation of their grumpy coachman.

She chuckled.

"But we should go find out before you freeze to death," Adam said, extending his arm toward her. "That blanket can only do so much."

As she slipped her arm in his, a shiver that had nothing to do with the cold ran through her. Part of her wished they could keep walking. Past the carriage. Past the restaurant. Had they met a month from now, even a week from now, things might have been different, but any feelings she had for Adam couldn't be trusted. She was too vulnerable, too raw. He was just a nice guy, and that's all he ever could be. The timing was simply wrong.

"I wish we had met under different circumstances," Adam said as if he had just read her mind.

She glanced at him, but his gaze was fixed straight ahead. She cleared her burning throat. "Yeah. We both could've been happily engaged. Maybe we'd have had a chance to be friends."

Friends. That should do it, she thought.

He shook his head and stopped, turning toward her. "Can I say something really stupid?"

"I haven't stopped you so far," she said.

Adam barked out a laugh and shook his head. "You're a piece of work, Holly Jenkins."

What was wrong with her? She shouldn't have encouraged him. She gave him a tight smile and averted her gaze, hoping he would let the unspoken remain unspoken.

"There you are!" Willy said, his timely bellow interrupting what was bound to be an uncomfortable moment. "I was wondering when you two were going to come back. Hester's getting antsy."

"You could've said something," Adam said, returning the coachman's gruff tone.

"I didn't want to interrupt your canoodling," Willy said.

"Canoodling?" Adam said with a clipped laugh. "If that word means what I think it means, there was no canoodling."

"Whatever you say," Willy said with one eyebrow quirked. "Hop in. I went ahead and poured some hot chocolate for you. I can't stand the stuff, and I'd hate to throw it out."

The coachman handed them both a steaming mug as they sat on the bench.

"What did you say earlier? To losers in love?" she said, holding her mug out for a toast.

His eyes were soft as they looked into hers. "To love's losers." He touched his mug to hers. "There's a slight difference in meaning."

"Slight," she said as she looked at her feet.

The rest of their ride was quiet, and she found herself both relieved and disappointed that the horse didn't make another unexpected detour.

"Here we are," Willy said as they pulled up to the inn. "I'll wait for you while you escort the lady inside."

Adam laughed through his nose. "Thanks, Willy."

Helping her from the carriage, he walked her to the door and held it open.

"Well, it's been . . . unexpected," Adam said after they had entered the warmth of the inn.

"That's one word for it."

"And for what it's worth, Jeff was an idiot."

She laughed despite the odd sadness she felt. "Thanks. Jessica was, too. I mean, the ring, the restaurant, the carriage ride. The woman clearly doesn't know a good thing when it's standing in front of her." The irony hit her like a punch in the mouth.

He put his hands in his pockets. "Holly—"

"So, I'm headed back to Nashville tomorrow night."

"Holly—"

"I probably need to get some sleep. Things will look better in the morning."

"Holly—"

"I want to thank you for everything. You took a horrible night and somehow made it better."

"Holly—"

She put her hands on her hips and hung her head. "Adam, I'm trying to get you out of here before we make a huge mistake."

"I know what you're trying to do, but would it be such a huge mistake if I kissed you?"

Her head snapped back.

"Of course, it would be. My boyfriend just broke up with me."

"You've been broken up for four months."

"And you just proposed to someone else."

"Technically, that never happened."

"Still. It would just be a Band-Aid for whatever in the world we're feeling." She shook her head. "Or not feeling. None of this is real. The carriage. The snow. The starry night. It's all an impossibly romantic mirage that disappears when we wake up in the morning."

"It feels real."

"But it's not. Real happens in the light of day. Real happens when I take off this push-up bra and put on sweats. Real happens when you go with someone to the grocery store."

"The grocery store?"

"No fancy dinner. No fancy carriage, for Pete's sake. Real life. Not romance. Not fantasy. Jeff was real. This is not."

He took in a deep breath and looked at the ground for a few seconds before taking her hand and pressing it to his lips. "Thank you for a wonderful night, Holly. Best of luck in Nashville."

A lip-shaped tingle pulsed through her hand, and she swallowed the ache in her throat. "Thank you, Adam. For everything."

As he turned, she said, "Oh, the blanket. You'd better return this to Willy. I'd hate for him to charge you extra."

He smiled and took the blanket before heading to the door.

"And Adam?"

He swung around.

"We never decided on the wager. Who lost?"

A sad smile crossed his lips. "I think we both did."

She blinked rapidly. She had a feeling he was right.

12

ADAM

*A*dam pushed against the inn's heavy door, the cold night air smacking him in the face. Willy was standing by Hester, feeding her an apple.

"I wasn't sure you were coming back out," the old man said.

Adam grunted.

"Night didn't end the way you'd hoped?"

"None of this night ended the way I had hoped," Adam replied.

"Yeah, well . . ."

"Yeah, well, what?" Adam said, irritation leaking into his voice.

The coachman shook his head. "Never mind. She seemed like a sweet gal."

Adam sighed. "Just take me back to the restaurant, Willy."

He raked his hands through his hair. None of this made sense. Maybe Holly was right that it was all a mirage. Maybe he was just trying to prolong the pain he was bound to feel over Jessica.

As the carriage pulled up to the restaurant, Willy said, "You could always fight for her, you know."

Adam closed his eyes and nodded as he remembered those same words coming from Holly's mouth. She had been talking about Jessica, but Jessica wasn't the one making his chest hurt.

He climbed down from the carriage. "Thanks, Willy. Thanks,

Hester," he said, patting the horse on the rump. "How much more do I owe you?"

"Don't worry about it," the coachman said, the lines on his face deepening with his frown. "Good luck to you, young man."

As the carriage pulled away from the sidewalk, Adam turned toward the restaurant where it had all begun—or where it had all ended, depending on how you looked at it. His broken glasses, the spilled champagne, the green dress: he shook his head when he realized these were the memories he would take from this place.

For once he hadn't tried. For once, he hadn't planned. And it had almost been perfect.

13

HOLLY

Holly turned her head toward the ringing phone, but she wasn't ready to talk to Kate yet—not until she could shake off some of the gloom from the thoughts that had kept her up half the night. Adam had been right. Jeff was her safety net. She had been trying to force a happily-ever-after into their friendship, and she had been creating a fantasy—the very thing she had fussed to Adam about. Ironically, the most real she had ever felt was riding in the back of a fancy carriage while she bared her soul and sipped champagne with a total stranger.

She stretched her neck and rubbed her eyes. She needed some coffee. As she opened a door of the large armoire to get her sweater, her hanging dress rustled like a curtain in a breeze. The stain was barely noticeable. A shiver passed through her arms. She'd skip the coffee; chamomile tea with honey sounded more comforting.

Crossing the room, she pulled back the curtain, revealing a bright blue sky. The warm sun had left behind puddled memories of the previous day's snow on the sidewalks, and her eyes followed two toddlers who splashed through them as they ran toward a large black horse.

Holly gasped and stepped back from the curtain. She shook her head. It couldn't be him. Returning to the window, she brushed the curtain behind her. It was. It was Adam, feeding Hester a carrot.

The pounding of her heart blocked her ears. She should shower. No, just brush her hair. Put on some lipstick. Maybe some mascara. Her push-up bra? She shook her head and tried not to run to the street.

"It's about time," Adam said, walking toward her. "I've been out here almost two hours, and it's not as warm as it looks."

She bit her lip to restrain her smile. "What are you doing here?"

"A deal's a deal," he said, holding out her jacket.

She stepped toward him. "I thought you said we both lost."

"Well, I was thinking about it, and you definitely had the worst night. Especially after spending most of it in a carriage with an unbearable cad."

She put her hands on her hips. "You or Willy?"

Adam smirked as Willy grumbled. "You're a piece of work, Holly Jenkins. Anyway, there's this new grocery store a couple blocks down the road I've been wanting to try. I hear it's very romantic."

She drew her lips inward, but she knew there was no way it could hide her grin.

"I mean, I know you want real, but I think I can steer you back to romance once you see what I can do with a peach." He raised an eyebrow. "And a strawberry? You don't stand a chance."

She wiped under her eyes as she laughed. He was so annoyingly adorable. She wrapped her arms around herself. "You know, if this is a rebound, we both get hurt."

His expression was soft and his eyes, warm. "Something tells me it might be worth the risk to find out," he said, extending his arm.

Her heart fluttered as she took his arm and stepped toward the carriage.

"Good morning, Willy," she said. He winked.

As she settled herself on the seat, Adam bumped her shoulder with his. "Can I say something really stupid?" he said.

She drew in a breath. "I haven't stopped you before."

His eyes crinkled as he grinned. "Would it be a huge mistake if I kissed you?"

The horse whinnied.

"Stay out of this, Hester," Adam said.

Holly held back a smile and shook her head. "Maybe after I see what you can do with a peach."

Snickering, he said, "Fine. It was just a thought."

Holly's heart thrummed in her chest. "On the other hand, maybe a small kiss wouldn't hurt. Just a little one. If it's bad, we could save ourselves a whole lot of trouble."

His head fell back as he laughed. "Pragmatic. I like it," he said, turning toward her. "But just a little one."

True to his word, he drew her to him and placed one soft, small kiss on her lips. As he pulled away, the tingle in her lips spread through her body, and she was sure that if she were to touch something, it would spark.

She cleared her throat. "Well, maybe just one more."

Cupping her face, he smiled and pulled her in close, his mouth soft, strong, urgent.

"Real or mirage?" he asked as his lips hovered over hers.

She leaned her head against his chest, his heartbeat loud in her ears. She was breathing, but only barely. Lifting her head, she raised her eyes to meet his.

She had never felt anything more real.

EPILOGUE
TWO MONTHS LATER

"You didn't look this nervous walking into Vanderbilt," Holly said as Adam straightened his tie in front of the mirror in the hotel lobby.

"Interviewing with neurosurgeons seemed easy compared to this," Adam said. "Plus, Kate's your best friend. Her approval could have a lot more impact on my future than taking a year off med school to do research."

Holly came up behind him and wrapped her arms around his waist. "I wouldn't go that far, but I promise she's going to love you. Just like I do."

Adam turned around and drew her in close, running his hand along her cheek. "I hope so."

"I know so. But before you kiss me and get me all flustered," Holly said, taking a step away from his embrace, "we need to get going. My car's parked at an expired meter, and I want to pick up some champagne before we head over."

A crooked smile tugged at Adam's mouth. "Champagne? Are you sure about that? It doesn't always make the best first impression."

Holly's head tipped back as she laughed. "Maybe not the best but definitely unforgettable."

"That's one word for it," Adam said, taking her hands in his. "I love you, champagne girl."

And this time, as he pulled her toward him and his lips neared hers, she didn't step away.

ABOUT THE AUTHOR

Lauren Elizabeth is an author of women's fiction and sweet contemporary romance. Before making Tennessee her home, she lived in Indiana, New York, and California, where her careers included journalism, book editing, copywriting, and marketing.

She is the only woman in a houseful of boys, so when she's not on some ballfield or court, she can be found writing books that don't include mentions of bodily functions. (And when she's avoiding writing, she's probably watching reruns of *Parks and Rec*—because Leslie Knope is the cutest.)

Currently, Lauren Elizabeth is writing *Give Me Christmas*, the second book in her new Wildflower Lake sweet-romance series. The first book, *Give Me Always*, is available for purchase here: My Book. And if you want to read more about Holly's roommate, Kate, join Lauren Elizabeth's newsletter here https://BookHip.com/XSKRCM to get *Until Now* (the Wildflower Lake prequel) for free.

A SECOND SHOT AT LOVE

KERRY EVELYN

Lost dog tags bring together a tormented police officer and grieving hockey trainer afraid to love again.

1

———

A guttural cry from Gil Spurgeon, the Townsbury Perfect Storm's burly defenseman, shot straight to Sarah Hutchinson's soul. She halted midway through loosening his laces. "Easy, Gil. I have to get this skate off. Grab onto the bench for support."

He sucked air through his teeth as she made quick work of the laces, carefully maneuvering the boot from his foot. Sarah flung her auburn ponytail over her shoulder, keeping her expression neutral as she peeled off his sock and examined the ankle. He'd taken a ninety-eight-mile-per-hour slapshot at the top edge of his boot just before the buzzer blared. Off balance, he caught his skate blade in a rut. He fell into an opposing player, and his foot twisted out from under him as he went down. Hard.

"Just needs ice, right?" His question was hopeful, but the look in the eyes of the thirty-three-year-old alternate captain bore the truth—the prognosis wasn't good.

She gave a sympathetic half-smile. "Looks like you might be getting some extra quality time with your new baby. You really do believe in taking one for the team, don't you?"

"Just doing my job. It stayed out of our net, didn't it?" He flashed her a toothy grin.

"Oh, yeah. You're done for today, though." *And probably the rest of the season.*

"Yeah, I figured." Gil sat back and looked out over the crowd. "Hey, Sarah, not to freak you out, but there's some dude a few rows back staring at you. I thought he was staring at me at first, but he's definitely checking you out."

Sarah didn't have time or patience for hockey fans—or anyone—trying to get her attention. After her fiancé died two years ago, Gil and some other players had made it a point to look out for her. One of the many challenges that came with being a female trainer in a men's sport. Especially for a twenty-something former model.

She'd hated modeling, but it'd paid for school and led to the job she'd always wanted. For a while, all her plans had fallen into place.

Then Colin had been blown up in the Middle East. The only man she'd ever loved had been ripped away from her, along with the life they'd been building together.

Normally, she'd roll her eyes and ignore the attention. But this time, the hairs on the back of her neck prickled.

Sarah turned her gaze upward. "Holy hell." She locked on the intense, dusky blue eyes staring back at her from a face that haunted her recent dreams.

"I don't think I've ever heard you swear before. You know him?" Gil struggled to sit up. "Sarah? Hey, you okay? You look like you've seen a ghost."

"I—I—" Her ears rang, and her heart thumped painfully in her chest.

"Ow! Uh, Sarah—"

Giving a quick shake of her head, she loosened her grip on Gil's foot. "Oh, shoot, I'm sorry."

When she turned back, the man was gone.

ZACH MILLER SPENT the first two periods alternately watching the game and Sarah, waiting for a chance to talk to her. They'd only met briefly two weeks ago when his station lent support to a manhunt in an area where she'd rented a cabin. They'd shared a moment and a few quiet words of commiseration about the deaths of her fiancé and his brother.

After the FBI cleared her cabin, officers completed a final sweep of the area. Zach found something on the ground he was sure belonged to Sarah and had finally decided to ask a mutual friend for her phone number. Unfortunately, calling her had proven to be more difficult than he expected.

Upon learning her team would be in town to play the Acadia Harbormasters, he'd bought a ticket to the game, a few rows behind the opposing players' bench, and waited for the right time. When the horn sounded the end of the period, the home team's star defenseman hadn't gotten up. Two of his teammates helped him to the bench, where Sarah now tended to him.

When the stretcher rolled in, Zach's sense of urgency grew. He had to talk to her before she left. He shuffled past the spectators in his row, apologizing while keeping Sarah in sight.

She'd consumed his thoughts, and not just because of the charged circumstances of their meeting. No, it'd been much more than that. In the cabin, he'd looked into the blue depths of her sad eyes and recognized the pain hidden there—the same pain he saw every time he looked in the mirror. In that moment, after six years, a long-absent feeling of peace had washed over him.

Had she felt a similar wave of emotion?

Zach was halfway around the arena when Sarah looked up from the injured player and noticed him, her rosy cheeks paling. He'd known he might be an unwelcome reminder of her harrowing experience. The last thing he'd wanted was to cause her alarm, but it was important that he see her.

Never losing sight of her as they loaded the player onto the stretcher, he continued wading through the crowd grabbing concessions and milling about between periods. He yanked his ever-present pocket journal from his jacket, scribbled a note, and ripped the page free.

"Sarah!" The name flew from his lips with a hint of desperation, not how he'd imagined it. He cringed inwardly and squared his shoulders. Now was not the time for his insecurity to rear its ugly head. He was a cop, after all. Hesitation on the job could mean the difference between life and death.

Oddly, in this moment, that was exactly how he felt. *Assert your strength.* He used his command voice when he called her name a second time.

Sarah whirled around, her mouth dropping open. Uncertainty flickered in her eyes.

He leaned over the barrier and held the paper in his outstretched hand. "Take this, please."

Her eyes dropped to the note, then lifted to meet his. He held his breath until, finally, she inched closer, extending a shaking hand to snag the note before heading into the tunnel.

Zach watched her until she cast a questioning glance over her shoulder, then disappeared out of sight. He thought of the small but significant box back at the station and its precious contents, and hoped she'd call him before her team returned to Boston.

2

———

The next day, Sarah sat at her kitchen table, absently pushing the now room-temperature grilled chicken around her plate. The note she'd tossed into the catch-all basket with her keys and miscellaneous mail called to her. She'd awakened that morning certain she'd be in a better headspace to read it. Hours later, it was still in the basket.

To say she'd been surprised to see Zach would be a major understatement. Had he attended the game specifically to speak to her? If so, she wasn't sure how she felt about that. And why did it feel like opening his note would upend her life? It was just words on a piece of paper, from her best friend's husband's cousin's friend. Zach was no one to her, really. But it had been important enough that he'd sought her out at the game.

Unease coursed through her veins and her heart pumped hard as she pictured Zach's face. Classic chiseled cheekbones and jaw. Kind baby blues she could get lost in. There was a vulnerability to him that she didn't see in the hockey players she worked with that made her wish he *was* someone to her.

"You're being ridiculous." Sarah shoved back from the table and stood. Not giving herself a chance to change her mind, she snatched the note up and unfolded it.

Her hand flew to her mouth. The message was short:

Sarah—Dog tags belonging to Colin Charlton were found outside the cabin you stayed in. They aren't related to our case. Are they yours? Please call me. —Zach

Tears pricked the back of her eyes as a heavy weight lifted off her shoulders. She'd thought Colin's tags were lost forever. Sarah unplugged her phone from her charger and dialed the number written below his name.

One ring. Two rings—

"Hello?"

"Zach?" Her voice was a ragged whisper.

"Hey, Sarah. I'm so glad you called. Are you still in Maine?"

He got right to the point. Good. Keeping this strictly business made this much easier for her.

"No, I'm not. I'm ... um ... sorry I didn't call you last night. I was busy with my player, Gil. He had to undergo surgery." Okay, so that was only half true. "How long do I have to pick them up?"

"As long as you need."

His soothing voice took her back to their conversation in the cabin. It helped still her nerves then, and it was helping to calm her now.

"Um." Her calendar was packed the next couple of weeks. "I can't get there until March. And I'd rather not have them mailed to me." She'd never survive losing them again.

"I can bring them to you." His velvety reply caused an involuntary shiver.

"I can't ask you to do that. You live far—"

"I offered, and I have this weekend off. I don't mind. Honest."

Sarah twisted and smoothed her ponytail with her free hand as she considered his offer. Maybe she could squeeze in some time.

She wasn't sure she wanted to be alone with him, though. The feelings he evoked in her were alarming. Feelings she shouldn't be having for another man.

You only get one soul mate.

Right?

But the fact that he'd drive Colin's dog tags to her—five hours each way—touched her deeply. "I've got this thing on Saturday. The Spurgeons are hosting a Sip-and-See to introduce friends to their new baby. Could you meet me there at five o'clock?"

They could do a quick exchange and he could be on his way.

"Sure. Text me the details."

"Okay." She ended the call before he could make small talk. There was no denying part of her wanted to get to know him better. But she needed more time.

～

Zach rang the Spurgeons' bell Saturday afternoon, his conversation with Sarah replaying in his head for the millionth time. She'd seemed in a hurry to get off the phone, and he hadn't pushed, knowing she still struggled with the loss of her fiancé. He hoped the tags would bring her comfort.

The door swung open, revealing a pretty blonde. "Hi, can I help you?"

He cleared his throat. "I'm Zach Miller. Sarah asked me to meet her here?"

"Oh! Yes, hi! I'm Reese Spurgeon. Pleasure to meet you."

"You, too." He shook her hand. "Congratulations on your new baby."

"Thanks. Come inside. It's freezing out." She waved him in and shut the door. "Sarah should be here any minute."

Inside, a handful of couples sat around a spacious living room. At the far end, a broad-shouldered, dark-haired man held court from a massive microfiber sofa-recliner, his cast-encased leg elevated. A small pink bundle sprawled across his chest.

"That's my husband, Gil, and our daughter, Stefani. She's two months old and already has her daddy wrapped around her tiny little finger."

"She's adorable."

"Mmhmm. Even when she's fussing at three a.m." Reese sighed, her smile warm with a mother's love. "Why don't you take my spot next to Gil while I grab you a drink?"

"Um ..." Zach cast a quick glance at the assembled group regarding him curiously.

She leaned close and lowered her voice. "Don't worry, they've all been warned not to grill you."

"It's ... Well, I'm not sure I can stay." Had Sarah intended for him to stick around the party? The last thing he wanted to do was put her on the spot.

"Don't be silly. Meet the baby, have dinner, and stay for the game."

He hesitated. "Okay, thanks."

"Great! Beer?" Reese took his coat.

"Sure." One drink, and if Sarah seemed uncomfortable with him being there, he'd leave.

Zach watched his hostess disappear down a hallway. He turned back toward Gil and the others.

Gil grinned. "You better sit down before my wife comes back."

Zach chuckled, and a small amount of tension left his shoulders as he settled himself on the other side of the armrest.

Gil flattened one big hand over the baby's back and twisted slightly to shake Zach's. "Welcome to our home, Zach."

"Thanks for having me. How's the ankle? I heard you needed surgery."

"Yeah, I'm out for the rest of the season. But that has its perks. I scored precious time with my Stefi girl." He kissed the top of his daughter's head.

Gil introduced him to the other couples, and Zach relaxed a bit more. As Reese started back his way, the doorbell rang. She all but tossed him the beer and hurried to the door.

Zach stood as Sarah entered and removed her coat. She glanced his way and gave him a small wave, but he noticed her lips purse and her throat move up and down. Apparently, he wasn't the only one who was nervous.

"Hi, Zach." She blessed him with a shy smile, and that zingy feeling whooshed through him again. "Thanks for coming."

"My pleasure." She sat next to him and folded her hands in her lap. Her orange and vanilla-scented ponytail invaded his senses as the warmth from her body touched his.

Zach took a long pull from his beer, trying to cool down. *Say something, anything, you idiot.*

Gil's voice cut through the tension. "So, Sarah, how's the planning coming with the Valentine charity gala?"

"Great..." Sarah gave him an odd look as she dragged the word out like a question. "According to Lanie, everything is on track. The committee is set to raise more money this year for the kids." She smiled warmly. "The gala benefits underprivileged athletes in the community, granting money for camps, equipment, things like that."

"Sounds awesome." Zach sometimes volunteered at a youth center working with at-risk kids. He knew all too well how much financial help they needed.

"So, Sarah, you don't have a date yet, right?" Gil tipped his chin up toward Zach. "I bet Zach would love to take you."

3

____

Oh, no. No, he did not. Sarah felt Zach's eyes on her and forced herself not to look at him.

"Yeah, Sarah, you missed last year." Ashton Blanchard looked over at Zach and grinned. "Turned down everyone who asked."

Sarah narrowed her eyes at him. "I was busy."

"Washing your hair?" Team captain Patrik Liška teased, remnants of his Czech accent sneaking into his speech. "C'mon, Sarah. We've got room for two more at our table. If you take him, you won't have to keep saying no to Houlihan." He chuckled.

Sarah rolled her eyes and shook her head. Houlihan, the rookie center, had been trying to charm her all season.

How could she say she didn't want to go without being rude?

"When's the fundraiser?" Zach asked.

"Next Saturday." All the guys answered at once.

Her breath caught in her throat when Zach's warm hand curved over hers. "Sounds fun. I'd love to take you." His eyes held hers, as if forcing her to really *see* him.

She should say no. Right? Or was it time for her to take a leap of faith?

Unable to pull away from his gaze, she drew back her shoulders. "Okay."

~

AS THE NIGHT WORE ON, Zach sensed the battle brewing within Sarah. He didn't want her to feel trapped into attending the gala.

He was having a great time getting to know the group. It was obvious they all cared about Sarah and wanted what was best for her, and he wanted to pass whatever test this was.

The hockey game ended with the Bruins suffering a grueling loss to the Buffalo Sabres.

Sarah leaned toward him. "I need to get going. Walk me to my car?"

"Of course." He stood and offered his hand. After a brief hesitation, she placed her hand in his and held tight. The buzz of conversation in the room faded as they stared at each other. Zach's mind drew a blank as her blue gaze held him captive.

Gil pushed himself off the couch, balancing precariously, and clapped Zach on the shoulder. "Hey, man, where're you crashing tonight?"

Zach dragged his eyes away from Sarah. "I was planning to drive back."

"To Maine? This late?" Reese joined them. "Please, stay in our guest room."

He shot a glance at Sarah. "That's very generous, but—"

"You should." She seemed surprised by her words. "It's late."

He nodded. "Okay. Thanks."

Reese handed them their coats, and they said goodbye. As Zach watched her hug her friends, he reflected on his own support group, or lack thereof. He had friends, sure, but he mostly lived the life of a loner. He'd always been happy hanging out with his brother and his brother's friends. They'd done most of the talking and planning, and Zach tagged along.

When Dylan died, everything changed.

Tonight, he was reminded of what he'd been missing—true friendship.

Out in the biting cold, Sarah's shoulders drew up to her ears, and she wrapped her arms around herself as they hustled toward the vehicles.

Zach opened the passenger door of his truck, snagged a small box from inside the console, and handed it to her.

Her fingers shook as she removed the top. Light flashed off the small metal rectangles. After a moment of simply looking at them, she lifted them from the box, clasped them in her fist and held them to her heart. Her eyes dropped shut, and a tear slid down her cheek.

"Thank you," she whispered.

Zach opened his arms and she stepped into his embrace. Her tremble rocked his soul and sent a spark through him at the same time. Clutching her tighter, he whispered into her hair. "It'll be okay." This evening confirmed Zach's attraction to Sarah, and if her pounding heart was any indication, she felt it too.

"How can you know that?" She raised her head, their faces inches apart. "Today was the best day I've had in two years and twenty-eight days."

4

Taz Houlihan flashed a flirty smile at Sarah from his prone position on the table. She had his leg extended against the front of her shoulder and slowly pressed forward, stretching it as she strategically worked on his hamstring muscles.

"Ow!" The usually-cocky rookie grin gave way to a grimace.

"Too far?" Sarah asked innocently. "Gosh, I'm so sorry. I thought you could handle it."

"Oh, I can handle it." He waggled his eyebrows.

Sarah laughed. The eighteen-year-old was as goofy and as full of himself as one might expect a teenage professional hockey player to be.

"Sarah!" Lanie Saunders called from across the large, airy training room. She skirted around the equipment, phone in hand, a glare on her face.

"Everything okay?" Sarah asked, concerned. Her best friend had had a rough year and was juggling a lot of glass balls.

"When are you done with him?" Lanie asked.

"Gee, Lanie, you make me sound disposable." Taz stuck his bottom lip out in a mock pout.

"Not now, *Travis*." He winced at Lanie's growl. Phone to her ear, she turned to Sarah. "I've got Meemaw on the phone. She wants the scoop."

"The scoop?" Uh-oh. Lanie's husband's grandmother was infamous up and down the east coast for her well-meaning meddling. "Gimme just a minute."

Sarah finished Taz's hamstring and tried to ignore Lanie's tapping foot. "Okay, Taz. Don't move. I'll be right back."

Sarah wiped the sweat from her brow and motioned for Lanie to follow her into her office. "What's up?"

"You're not only going to the gala, but you're bringing a plus-one? Zach isa friend of Matt's cousin. Why am I the last to know?"

She sighed. "I'm sorry, Lanie. I—don't know." Why *hadn't* she mentioned it?

Through the phone, the elderly woman's voice was chatting away.

"She wants to talk to you." Lanie tapped the screen to change to a video call.

"Sarah, dear! How wonderful you've started dating again." Daisy Mae Saunders in all her poofy white-haired glory smiled back at her. "I just wanted to tell you myself I'm so glad you're back in the game."

Sarah chewed her lip, unable to express the doubts about getting involved with Zach that had begun to creep into her battered heart. "Thank you, but I'm probably going to cancel." She darted a glance at Lanie.

"Oh, don't do that! It's time, dear. It's devastating to lose someone you love. But you're remiss if you're trying to live *without* Colin. The love you felt for each other will always be there. You should be trying to live *with* the love he left behind. He wouldn't want you to spend your life alone. Would he?"

Boom. Sarah fought back tears, swallowing past the painful lump in her throat.

"No, ma'am," she whispered. "I ... I have to go." Sarah ended the call and handed the phone back to Lanie.

Lanie tucked it in her pocket and gave her a sad smile. "It's okay to cry, you know. Tension release?"

Sarah pulled her chair out from behind her desk. Lanie positioned herself behind her and began to knead Sarah's shoulders.

"I'm fine," Sarah sighed. "I think. Anyway, I've done enough crying the last two years to last a lifetime."

～

I'm looking forward to Saturday.

Delete.

Hi, Sarah, how was your Monday?

Delete.

Five days to go!

Delete.

Without sending a single text, Zach stepped out of his police SUV and shoved his phone into one of the pockets in his tactical vest. Frozen grass crunched beneath his boots as he approached the familiar headstone. The biting chill of the starlit February night sliced straight to his bones.

Beneath him, six feet down, lay his brother Dylan, who'd died of exposure on a night very much like this one.

"Hey, Dyl." He crouched down and swept dried leaves from the headstone. "I met someone. But you probably already know that, huh?"

Zach pulled off his glove and traced the crossed hockey sticks that were carved into the cold granite. Dylan had been a star player in his teens, turning down an opportunity to play semi-pro when it would take him away from the town and the people he loved so much.

"You'd definitely like her. She's a Bruins fan."

He shoved his hand back into his glove and sat on the ground. Closing his eyes, he embraced the cold swirling around him.

What would today look like if Dylan hadn't died six years ago? His brother and Hollis would be married. Maybe even have a couple of kids who spent weekends with Uncle Zach at his cottage by the sea. Motoring around the harbor in the boat.

The fantastical thoughts whispered away, replaced by the loneliness he felt whenever he thought about his brother.

"I went to see Hollis last week. She still believes if she hadn't canceled on you, you wouldn't have picked up that extra shift. And if I'd listened to you and gone to the police academy after college instead of the military, I would've been here that night." His voice cracked. "Nothing, not even a blizzard, would've stopped me from finding you."

He could almost hear Dylan's voice in his head arguing with him.

"Sarah lost her fiancé a couple of years ago. We connected ... I really like her, and it kills me to think of her living with the same kind of pain

Hollis has since you died. I think ... maybe we can help each other. I want to try, at least."

Zach stood and pulled his phone from the pocket, tugging off his glove again, this time to send a text message to Sarah.

Thinking about Saturday. It's been a long time since I've been on a date. We'll figure this out together?

5

Sarah didn't sleep well with thoughts of Zach invading her mind. Her eyes were gritty and burning when she arrived at work the next morning.

"You doin' all right today, Sar?" Ashton fell into step beside her in the hall. His thick Boston accent blanketed her with a welcome security.

"Yeah, Ash, thanks." She forced a smile. "Didn't sleep well, you know?"

Keeping busy, that was the key to surviving today.

"I do." He averted her eyes and adjusted the strap of his bag.

"Still pining for Zoe, I see." To see Ashton mope was unusual, especially over a woman. "No plans today?"

"Game night. Besides, we're going to the gala together."

"Whatever you say. But it's Valentine's Day, so if it's more than that—and I'm guessing it is by the way you were acting like a lovesick puppy last Saturday—you should call her. Today. Don't wait. You've got several hours between the morning skate and the game. Make it count."

He grunted. "I don't know."

"If I have to convince you, maybe she isn't as important to you as you think." Sarah stopped outside the locker room. "But if she's your lobster, don't mess around."

"My lobster?"

Sarah shrugged. "They mate for life. Time is something you can never get back, Ash. Believe me, I know."

Sarah left him with that heavy thought and headed to her office. Why was it so easy to give advice, but so hard to take it?

All day she'd tried to focus on doing her job, forget the memories, and push aside the guilt she felt over liking Zach. She wanted to see if there was more between them than friendship, but the loss of Colin was still too raw. Everywhere she looked, she was flooded with reminders that today was Valentine's Day, from the team's pink and red jerseys to the sweetheart cam during time-outs.

The Storm had defeated the Albany Hilltoppers at home, but it'd been a physical victory—over a hundred checks. They'd be hurting tomorrow.

As would she, just not physically. But she planned to stay as busy as possible to keep her mind from the memories of the Valentine's Day three years ago, when Colin had proposed.

Later that night, it was all she could do to hold herself together long enough to make it home.

Sarah toed the boxes at her front door to the side as she keyed open the lock. Her guilt magnified, knowing they contained the dresses she'd ordered for the gala.

In her bedroom, she set the boxes side by side on the duvet, stepped back, and stared at them.

Her fingers itched to grab the biggest, boldest black marker she owned and scratch *Return to Sender* all over and leave them outside. But another part of her, the little girl within, wanted to tear open the boxes and play dress-up. Only she wasn't an innocent child—she was a pain-scarred almost-widow who knew emotional upheaval lurked within all that cardboard and tissue paper.

"All right, Gingerlocks, let's see which dress fits just right." Recalling the nickname given to her by player Dane Blanchard, a fellow redhead, lightened her spirit a little.

As she opened the first box, Sarah was bombarded with memories. The last time she'd been dress-shopping, it'd been for her wedding with her sisters and Lanie. She'd found *the* dress, and Colin had video-called from overseas.

That call ended after an explosion on the other side of the screen.

She blinked a few times, stiffened her spine, and slipped the first dress over her head. *Too sexy.*

The next box held a black, long-sleeved number. *Too somber.*

The third, a wispy ivory-blush chiffon, floated around her legs like a cloud, and the silver-ombré sequins shimmered across the fitted bodice. The woman staring back in the mirror looked renewed, beautiful, and *alive.* The easy confidence and proud posture of her modeling days returned in her reflection. *Just right.*

She pictured Zach on her arm and froze. Fresh tears stung and spilled down her cheeks as the clock struck midnight.

Valentine's Day was officially over.

How could she think about moving on when she still felt so much pain? Sarah recalled her conversation with Ashton. Recognizing the mutual exchanges between him and Zoe convinced her they were in love and didn't want to address it. *Lobsters.*

Sarah had thought for sure Colin had been her lobster.

For life.

She lifted the delicate chain hanging from her neck and studied the diamond solitaire on the gold band. A symbol of a promise she'd intended to keep forever.

Until death do us part. They'd never gotten the chance to say those words to each other.

Did forever end with Colin's death? She wasn't sure.

Sarah reached for her phone to text Zach. *I'm so sorry.... I just can't do it.*

ZACH WAS WATCHING sports commentary on his phone when Sarah's text came through. His heart sank like an anchor, a gradual drop until it came to rest with a thud on the ocean floor. Before he could think it through, he called her. After six rings, her voicemail picked up. He understood her grief, more than she probably knew. The understanding didn't negate his disappointment.

He texted her. *It's okay, Sarah. I understand.*

Right now, the important thing was that she knew he was willing to wait as long as it took for her to feel ready to move on.

Zach tossed and turned until he finally gave up on sleep just before six a.m. He showered, dressed in extra layers, and filled a thermos with coffee.

The sun's bright orange-gold rays were just beginning to paint the horizon as he shuffled down the path from his cottage to the private dock. He needed to clear his head, and the fifteen-degree morning weather seemed like a good way to start his day off.

At the end of the dock, Dylan's boat bobbed and gleamed as it caught a ray of morning light. Zach picked up his pace and stepped onto the wooden planks, careful not to slip on the thin layer of icy frost. The boards creaked in protest under his heavy boots. He carefully climbed aboard and took his place behind the wheel.

Zach set his coffee in the cupholder as he felt an urgency to *go*. A few seconds later, the boat rumbled to life, its sound shattering the morning's stillness.

Save for routine maintenance over the years, the boat was as Dylan had left it, from the ratty UMAINE hoodie stashed in the cabin to the framed picture of Hollis on the keychain, even the Zdeno Chara bobblehead on the dash. Zach tapped the plastic likeness of Dylan's favorite player with his finger and set it jiggling. The action elicited a sad smile, bringing back favorite memories of traveling down to Boston every winter to watch a Bruins game or two with their parents.

He'd connected with Sarah watching the game Saturday night. Working for the team's affiliate, she'd shared inside stories he knew his brother would've loved to hear.

When the engine warmed, Zach eased the craft into open water, slowly picking up speed as he exited the no-wake zone. With a flash of determination, he pressed the throttle forward and worked up to top speed.

This was where he felt most alive, out here in the harbor, slicing through the liquid blue, connected to his brother. The simple act of taking the boat out, even briefly, eased his heart and helped him get past the heaviness. Did Sarah have a ritual when her grief became too much to bear?

An hour later, he was walking up to his back door when his phone rang. Zach dug the phone from his pocket, thrilled to see Sarah's name on the screen.

He used his teeth to pull off his glove and answered. "Hey there, Sar—"

"I'm sorry. I mean ... about last night," she cut him off. "I—I wasn't in a good place."

"It's okay, really." Zach sat on the rocker on his back porch, not ready to leave the cool morning air. "I understand."

"You're not disappointed?" Was that a hint of regret in her voice?

"I am, but I get it."

Her voice softened. "Yeah, I guess you do, don't you?"

"I do."

She sighed. "Do I hear birds?"

"Yeah, I live on the harbor. Seagulls year 'round."

"Sounds nice." The sadness in her voice tugged at him. "You're out early."

"Yeah. It's peaceful." His mind jumped to thoughts of taking her out on the boat with him.

What would happen if he and Sarah started dating and became serious? Would she be willing to relocate? Would he? The thought of leaving the cottage—the home he'd shared with his brother—tore him up inside.

No, he could never give it up.

Where did that leave them?

6

———

In the dark living room, backlit by the kitchen light, Sarah snuggled little Stefi Spurgeon to her chest. Her eyes closed and she stroked the baby's downy-soft hair, inhaling the powdery scent.

Due to back-to-back home games, Gil and Reese were celebrating their Valentine's Day a day late. Sarah volunteered to babysit, thinking one chill baby would be a piece of cake compared with caring for her sister's twins.

She'd been wrong. Stefi made her think about what could have been.

For so long, her response was always "I can't." *Nothing can hurt you if you don't take a chance, right?* Somewhere, without realizing it, she'd given up on the "I cans."

Colin died, but that didn't mean her dreams of a family, of motherhood, died with him. She could still have all those things, but only if she allowed herself to.

Was it possible she was moving beyond the pain of Colin's death?

Zach's handsome face filtered through her mind. She wanted to call him and apologize again for canceling. Mostly, she wanted to hear his voice and tell him how much she liked him and couldn't stop thinking about him. Would he want to see her again?

Five ... four ... three ... two ... one. Sarah sucked in a deep breath and snatched up her phone, tapped the video call icon and waited. The countdown technique always pushed her when she was afraid.

"Hey, Sarah." Zach appeared on the screen, looking surprised to hear from her.

"Hey. I ... I just wanted to call to apologize again." Her voice wavered. "I really did want to see you this weekend. But ..."

"No need to explain or apologize." He ran his hand through his wavy golden hair. Butterflies pounded in her gut. His sincere expression was everything to her in that moment.

"I—don't think you quite do. I just now figured it out myself." He opened his mouth to speak, and she said, "Please hear me out?"

"Of course."

Sarah tightened her hold on the sleeping baby. "It's not that I'm not ready to date—I want to, truly...it's—I —I'm afraid, Zach."

There, she said it.

Deep breaths. Keep going.

"I'm afraid of how much I like you. I'm afraid of leaving Colin behind, and—" She choked back a sob. "But, I'm also afraid of what I'll miss if I *don't* leave him behind."

Her chin quivered, and she lowered her cheek to the baby's head, drawing comfort from the warm bundle in her arms.

Zach remained silent, letting her find her way.

She swallowed. "I don't want to grieve forever." Her last word was barely audible.

"I don't want you to grieve forever either, Sarah."

She lifted her gaze to the screen, surprised to see Zach's eyes shimmering, and willed herself to continue. "But how? How do I move forward?"

"One minute, one hour, one day at a time." He appeared to gather himself. "Listen, if you're up for it, I'd still like to see you this weekend. Charity gala or not."

"I'd like that, too."

"Saturday morning?"

"Yes." The front door deadbolt clicked. "Sounds like Gil and Reese are back. Can we talk when I get home?"

"I'll be here."

"Okay."

He'd been there, and picked up on the first ring. They'd talked for hours, and for the first time in over two years, Sarah had no difficulty falling asleep.

Zach's hand shook as he rang Sarah's doorbell Saturday morning.

She flung open the door and greeted him with a shy grin.

"Hey." He held out his arms, and she fell into them. Zach wrapped an arm around her back and used the other to cradle her head to his chest. "I'm so glad you invited me," he whispered. "Ready to go?"

"Yes," she mumbled into his chest.

Zach had no plans of breaking that hug. He was letting Sarah set the boundaries, and if she wanted to hug him for five minutes—or five hours—he'd go with it. Holding her, he felt joy he'd been missing for so long pulse through his veins.

She stepped back and he followed her inside the apartment. "Nice place."

"Thanks. It's small but cozy. I like it."

"My place is small and cozy, too. The limo should be here any minute."

"The limo? But we're not—"

"Gil rented it for the day. I'm staying with the Spurgeons and he wouldn't take no for an answer."

Sarah half-smiled. "Can't be mad at him for meddling. But I feel bad that you guys have gone to all this trouble and—"

"Sarah, relax. It's okay." He took her hand. "And since we have it for the day, I thought maybe you could give me a tour of your town? Show me your favorite places?"

She nodded slowly. "Okay. Yeah. Let's do it."

Twenty minutes later, the limo slowed to a stop in front of The Plex. The driver put the car in park.

Zach leaned forward and addressed him through the open partition. "Don't worry. I've got it."

He opened the door and offered his hand to Sarah. She bit her bottom lip and placed her mittened hand in his. Her light squeeze sent shocks up his arm and straight to his heart.

They scanned the collection of buildings. "This is my home away from home," she said fondly.

"It's impressive. Are they all connected?"

"Yep. Let's go." She tugged him toward the main entrance.

Sarah had a story for every room of the massive sports complex, from the training areas to the ice rink. As she spoke about the Plex, her voice held the same love and appreciation he felt for his cottage.

After the tour, they ate lunch in the café before returning to the limo. Over the next couple hours, they explored the downtown center, drove around her college campus, and cruised by her parents' and older sister's homes.

"One more stop," she said and leaned forward to give the driver directions. A few minutes later, they pulled up to the entrance of Kimford Farm.

He shot her a quizzical look. "A farm?"

"Not just any farm. This one has everything from bumper cars to a country store." She directed the driver down a lane off the main entrance. "The ice cream stand—and pretty much everything else—is closed for winter. The walk-up hot chocolate window is open inside the store, though."

The limo stopped in front of the store and, once again, Zach opened the door. The driver tipped the brim of his hat, pulled away and parked in the small lot to wait for them.

After buying hot chocolate, Sarah took his hand again. "I want to show you something." She led him down a path that led behind the store. "This is the Merrimack River."

An empty bench sat nearby, and she guided him to it. They sat in comfortable silence watching and listening to the water rush past, sipping the steamy beverages in the chilly air.

"The other night when I called you ... I was..." She hesitated. "I wanted to tell you..."

He wrapped his arm around her lightly, hoping the comforting gesture would help her get the words out.

"When I saw Colin at the funeral home ..." she stared across the river, lost in her memories. "It didn't even look like him."

Zach pulled her against him.

"I told myself it wasn't real, that it wasn't him. But I saw the strawberry birthmark where his hair parted and knew it was, and I felt the devastation all over again." She took a deep breath and swallowed. "Then I ... I took out the tiny folded scissors I carry in my purse and cut a lock of his hair." Her eyes scanned the riverbank, then the sky above. "This was Colin's favorite place, so I came here, bought a rose in the store, tucked the hair into the petals, and tossed it into the river."

Zach squeezed her shoulder, and she rested her head against him, the pom-pom on her hat tickling his chin.

"We still don't have any details about what happened to him. It's classified." Sarah's voice became stronger with each word spoken. "I think that makes it even harder. How am I supposed to get closure without an explanation?"

"Faith," Zach whispered. "It's all there is. Faith that his life wasn't for nothing. Faith that he loved you until his last breath."

She nodded. "He did love me. And that's why I think he would understand this. Us." She took a lengthy pause. "Do you think it's too late to go to the gala?"

7

Sarah put the finishing touches on her makeup and looked in the mirror. The image staring back at her looked effervescent and bright.

Earlier, she and Zach stopped by Colin's parent's house. She wanted them to have their son's dog tags and the engagement ring, which had belonged to Colin's grandmother. Returning the items felt right.

It was time for her next chapter.

She'd come home after that to get ready for the gala, and Zach went to Gil's. When the doorbell rang announcing his return, Sarah released a long breath before swinging it open. Zach, handsome and strong, stood on her stoop in a perfectly fitted tuxedo.

Her cheeks heated. "You look amazing."

"Thank you, but you're taking my breath away."

She knew the feeling.

Zach escorted her to the limo, where the rest of their party awaited. Sarah sat pressed to his side, her head on his shoulder. His body warmed her as her friends chatted around them.

"Right, Sarah?" Ashton asked.

She blinked. "Hm?"

Zoe giggled and leaned forward. "Ash told me you lit a fire under him on Wednesday to take me out. Thanks." She placed a hand on either side of Ashton's head and drew his face down. They met halfway in a steamy kiss.

Sarah smiled and cast a sideways glance at Zach. He brought her hand to his lips and kissed her knuckles. Her eyes fell to his mouth, wondering what it would feel like to kiss him.

One thing was for sure. She wanted to.

Tonight.

The limo pulled up to The Plex's conference center. Sarah held tight to Zach's arm as they followed the players down the red carpet. They maneuvered around the reporters and weaved their way through the partygoers to find the coat check.

Sarah scanned the room. Off to the side, Lanie pored over a tablet. She looked up and smiled as Sarah approached with Zach. "You're here!" She rushed over to wrap Sarah in a tight hug.

"Zach, this is my best friend, Lanie, and her husband, Matt."

"It's so wonderful to finally meet you." Lanie hugged Zach. "I'm glad you came."

"Nice to meet you, Zach." Matt offered his hand, and they exchanged small talk about work and their military experiences.

"Okay, you two, enough chitchat. Go have fun!" Lanie commanded.

"We'll see you out there." Sarah took Zach's arm and led him deeper into the room, where conversations and music mingled. She spied the parquet dance floor as they found their table. "Do you dance?"

"I do." One dark brow arched up. His low baritone washed over her like a gentle wave, stilling her nerves and radiating that peace she'd come to rely on in his presence.

She set her purse on the table. Sarah couldn't remember the last time she'd danced, and she didn't want to waste one moment of this night. "Let's not wait 'til after dinner."

Zach returned a smoldering gaze that caused her to shiver. As tall and built as any of her players, he cut an impressive figure. He took her hand and led her to the center of the dance floor.

Sarah's pulse kicked up as she relaxed into his embrace. They were the only ones on the floor, and she didn't care. Swaying in his strong arms, the outside world faded away. To be held by someone again ... No, to be held by *Zach* made her feel safe, cherished.

Who cared if they were the only couple dancing? It felt good to be in the moment. To be held in the arms of someone who made it clear that she mattered. That her future mattered.

One that he wanted to be a part of.

"Kiss him." Sarah jumped when Zoe whispered near her ear. Ashton gave a thumbs-up as they whirled away.

I think I will.

Sarah curled her arms around Zach's neck and smiled shyly at him. In his arms, she felt peace, security, and the familiar fluttering of rare connection. She brushed her fingers over his temple and let her fingers run through his hair, pulling his head down to hers. Realizing her intent, his eyes sparked and his embrace tightened.

When their lips touched, stars burst in a flash of blinding light behind Sarah's eyes, and the walls around her heart crumbled. Misery and grief faded away into the ether, and she knew that with Zach by her side, as he promised, everything would, in fact, be okay.

EPILOGUE
SIX WEEKS LATER

*Z*ach slammed his tailgate closed and glanced back at the cottage. *You're not letting go. You're grabbing hold of something new and moving forward.*

Matt had approached him regarding a job with his company, providing disaster relief services. Zach had been ready for a change, and the move put him closer to Sarah. He'd fallen hard and fast for her over the last two months.

Her boots crunched behind him in the snow, and she wrapped her arms around his waist. "We'll be back soon, and your friends promised to look in on it while you're away." She swept snow from his shoulder. "Try not to worry."

"You're right." He twisted to kiss the top of her head. "I can't wait for you to see this place in the summertime."

"Every time I'm with you it feels like summer. I'm not cold anymore, Zach. And you're the reason why." Her eyes shimmered, no longer darkened by sadness.

Zach's heart melted at the impact of her words. "You're my sunshine, Sarah. No, not just sunshine. You're the flowers and the leaves underfoot and all the things that make life's seasons easier to bear." Zach tightened his hold and spun her around. Sarah's laughter floated in the air, music to his ears.

He slowed to a stop and set her down. His hands cradled her face. "Sarah, I—I know it's fast, but ... is it too soon to tell you I'm in love with you?"

She placed her hands over his and smiled. "It's not too fast. I love you, too, Zach."

He pressed his lips to hers, and their kiss held the promise of a spring filled with love and new beginnings.

ABOUT THE AUTHOR

Kerry Evelyn is the author of the Crane's Cove series, #sweetresortromance set in Coastal Maine, and several short stories that span multiple genres. She's also a Guest Author for the Cat's Paw Cove romance series. A native of the Massachusetts SouthCoast, Kerry changed her latitude in 2002 and now calls the Orlando area home. Fueled on faith, Dunkin' iced coffee, and a love for people, including her amazing family, Kerry loves (in ever-changing order) books, boybands, cats, hockey, sweet drinks, taking selfies, traveling, and the madness of getting the stories in her head onto the page.

https://amazon.com/author/kerryevelyn

https://kerryevelyn.com/newsletter/

HER LAST FIRST KISS

E.J. DEAN

When grief pushes Bonnie to kiss a stranger, and Chuck returns the favor, will they find that love at first sight isn't just for fairytales?

1

"*The least* you could have done was dance."

"Trust me, this thirty-something mom-body does not need to shake any more than necessary." Bonnie Sullivan fumbled with the clasp of her strappy heels to hide a smile, wondering if her best friend would continue this rant up to the eleventh floor. The product of good intentions and far too much champagne. At least they had the elevator to themselves. Bonnie slipped off the shoe and plunged her aching toes into the plush carpet, sighing internally. "And I did dance."

"Pushing Charlotte's grandmother around the dance floor does not count." Mara's finger wagged. "Look, I know you miss Marcus, but you *deserve* to be happy again. It's time to move on."

How could she, when just the mention of his name still brought a twinge of pain? "I have moved on."

"Really?" Mara challenged.

Honesty was the basis of their friendship, and Bonnie appreciated that. Just not right now. So, Bonnie lied. "Yes."

"It sure doesn't seem like it. It's been *years* since you danced or went on a date. I doubt you've even talked to a man other than the guy at KwikLube. God knows how long it's been since you've kissed a guy or—"

The elevator slowed to a halt on the ninth floor, and the doors slid open to reveal a man in a perfectly tailored suit. Or maybe it was just an average suit that happened to stretch across the most perfect shoulders in Houston.

Second-most perfect, after her favorite Texans' defensive end, Bonnie corrected. But this guy was definitely in the running.

He smiled—a very, very nice smile.

Bonnie forced a frown. Any butterflies that suddenly uprooted themselves to frolic in her belly could sit back down. The man settled across from them and focused on his phone.

"So how long has it been?" Mara asked.

"We are *not* continuing this conversation right now." Bonnie glanced at their new companion to make sure he wasn't paying attention. It seemed as though he wasn't.

"How long?" Mara asked louder.

"Mara—" Bonnie warned. Heat crept up her cheeks, and the place where her heart used to be reverberated again, a hollow aching chime.

Mara leaned in and whispered, "Do you even realize *why* you can't admit the truth?"

Bonnie stilled. The interrogation was brutally honest, even for Mara.

"Because you're scared."

It was the worst possible thing Mara could have said.

Bonnie glanced away from the knowing look in Mara's eyes. Hating it and hating the way that look and those words made her feel. Hating worse the way she'd felt all night—every night for the past four years. Alone. Numb.

Hated that the taunt was true.

Without thinking, Bonnie crossed the small space. "Excuse me, sir? Would you mind settling an argument?"

His attention shifted to her, and amusement brought every feature of his face to life. His smile may have been very, very nice, but this grin of his was lethal. "Sure."

"Super," Bonnie whispered, grabbing his tie. She threw an arm behind his neck for balance and planted a kiss. The second first kiss she'd ever given.

Point proved, she let go.

He didn't.

∼

THE KISS WAS UNEXPECTED, given the stern glances the woman had thrown his way, but Chuck Wilkerson didn't want to let her go. The feel of her lithe body in his arms was electric. He held her a moment longer, searching for something witty to say that might earn him her name and maybe her number. But then she opened her eyes. The veil of fiery bravado he'd seen earlier was gone, and beneath it, she looked shattered.

Instinctively, he pulled her closer, wanting only to comfort her. Her skin beneath his fingertips was warm silk. She turned into him, and their lips met again. Nothing like that first rushed peck—this was an unhurried introduction. When her lips parted, he happily accepted the invitation to know more of her.

She jerked away with a gasp, those deep blue eyes of hers rounding with surprise.

"I'm sorry," Chuck said as he stepped back, realizing he wasn't. Not one damn bit.

"Bonnie?" Her friend waited in the hallway, holding the door of the elevator. An amused smile danced at the corners of her lips. "This is our floor."

Bonnie's gaze landed once more on him, and color fanned across her cheeks. Her fingers flew to cover them. "This is my fault. I should never have done that. Believe me when I say it is not like me to go around kissing strangers."

"Me neither." Chuck buried his shaking hands in his pockets to stop himself from reaching for her. "But everyone's a stranger—until they're not."

Bonnie seemed to consider that before she spun away from him, the skirt of her dress, a rustling purple swirl around her legs as she limped away.

The doors closed behind them, and the elevator motor began its soft whir. The moment was gone. When the doors opened again, Chuck had reached the top floor. The penthouse suite of apartments his parents kept for their family's private use when any of them traveled back to Houston.

He should go in. Take a shower. Get some sleep. It had been a long day celebrating his niece's graduation—and an even longer month, moving into an apartment in a new town, beginning rehab on the old house he'd purchased, and training the recruits for the new volunteer fire department.

He didn't need or want a relationship. Didn't have time for one.

But he didn't move. Didn't want to. His mind refused. Instead, he tried to think of a way to connect with the woman he'd kissed that wouldn't come off as totally creepy. There probably wasn't another Bonnie on the eleventh floor. He knew a couple of clicks into the hotel records, and he could have her name, phone number, and room number.

Yeah, Wilkerson, like that's not creepy.

He slipped two fingers behind the knot at his neck and loosened his tie. That was something he'd never do. He could never betray the trust of his parents or any of the Windmere's guests in such an underhanded manner.

The elevator doors started to close again, and he reached for the button to stop them and tripped. A silver shoe glinted up at him. Bonnie must have dropped it when they kissed. He picked it up while an idea formed. He tucked the shoe into his jacket pocket and jabbed the button that would bring him to the main floor.

In the lobby, he spotted Judson, the man who had held the night manager position at the hotel as far back as Chuck could remember. After scribbling a quick note, he instructed the manager to see the shoe returned to the lady on the eleventh floor first thing in the morning.

The manager gave him a nod. "I'll see to it personally, Mr. Wilkerson."

"Thank you, Judson." Halfway to the elevator, Chuck spun on his heel. "One more thing— don't mention—uh, anything about the family and all of this."

Judson looked offended. "Never."

2

———

The kiss played on repeat in Bonnie's dreams. Not the first hit-and-run kiss that she'd intended to give him to get Mara off her back. No. It was that second, steamy, melting-over-you-like-butter kiss that had kept her up all night. That and the memory of the way he smelled of woods and spice and something that delightfully played with her senses.

That was one of the things she'd loved doing for Marcus—going to the department store and picking out a new cologne for him.

Bonnie threw back the covers, desperate to dodge the memory and the feelings it brought up. Traces of dawn peeked around the edges of the drapes, leaking light into the pitch-black room she shared with Mara. Careful not to wake her, Bonnie padded to the open area near the windows. All was quiet except for the hum of the hotel air conditioner. Bonnie forced her mind to focus on the sound, then the empty peacefulness around it as she stretched her neck, her arms, methodically breathing in, then out. Reaching instinctively for the yoga practice that had kept her world sane in the wake of her husband's death, the routine that had helped her salvage what remained of their once-perfect two-parent life for their three kids.

She'd discounted yoga at first as new-age fluff. But she stuck with it because the poses were a challenge, and she'd never been one to back down from a challenge. The poses required less effort on her part now, just like managing life without Marcus had become less complicated. Breath by breath, day by day.

Three-quarters of the way through the routine, she pushed back into downward dog, added the leg lift—hold, deep breath in, exhale, release—stretching her left leg through her arms into a forward lunge. The tail of her braid skimmed across her cheek, much the same way his fingers had brushed over her skin last night in the elevator.

That's when she'd pulled away from him. When she realized a stranger's touch had sent shock-waves of desire through her, waking up limbs that had been asleep for so long. She'd thought she'd buried every ounce of her heart, and all of her desire with Marcus, yet here it was—stone-cold embers stirring back to life and betraying her.

Betraying him.

An unexpected sob caught in the back of her throat, and Bonnie missed the next move, falling to her knees. Mara stirred at the sound and sent Bonnie scrambling to her feet, racing to the bathroom where the spray of the shower could wash away the sound of her tears.

By the time Bonnie emerged, dressed, her clothes packed away, Mara had rolled over. She groaned out a request for two painkillers and water.

Bonnie brought them to her. "Regretting that last glass of champagne?"

"My head hurts so bad I'm regretting the first." Mara sat up, reaching for the water. "Someone left a package for you while you were in the shower. Jenson or Judson? Said he was the night manager of the hotel."

"What is it?"

"I dunno," she mumbled around a mouthful of tablets. She downed them. "The manager said someone left it at the front desk for you."

The white box outside their door had the Windmere logo embossed in the corner. Mara watched as Bonnie broke the seal. Nested in soft tissue paper was the shoe she'd lost last night. Tucked beside it was a note.

"It's from him, isn't it?" Excitement laced Mara's words.

Bonnie laughed, "No duh. He's the one who made me drop it."

"Yeah, he did." Mara giggled. "What's it say?"

Bonnie skimmed the precise lettering to make sure there was nothing that could embarrass her further before reading aloud. *"Good morning, Cinderella. Sorry about the way last night ended, and I would love to make amends today over coffee. There's a great shop across the street. I'll be there until nine, waiting for you."*

The last line of the note made Bonnie chuckle.

Mara bounded across the bed, reaching for the note, her hangover forgotten. "Read the rest. Did he sign his name?"

Once it was safely out of reach, Bonnie said, "No. He just added a P.S." Bonnie read the line a second time. To herself.

Prince Charming was a stranger, and Cinderella still gave him a chance.

"Whatever. I'll find out eventually." After a roll of her eyes, Mara glanced at the clock. "Are you going? If so, you better hurry. It's already after eight."

The feelings from this morning haunted her. "I don't know if I should."

"Go!" Mara stumbled out of bed and grabbed Bonnie's bag from the dresser. She shoved it into Bonnie's hands and pushed her towards the door. "If nothing else, you can chalk it up as practice for flirting with guys again. Plus, you'll get that horrible first date experience out of the way—"

"It's not a date." Bonnie pushed back. "And why do you think it's going to be horrible?"

"I don't. I'm just saying— Ugh! Never mind. Go, get some caffeine. Have a good time. I'll grab a shower and pack everything." Never one to miss a chance, Mara reached one last time for the note. "Let me put that in your suitcase for you."

"Nice try." Bonnie hugged the piece of paper to her chest and walked down the hallway laughing. "I'll put it in my bag for safe-keeping."

3

———————

*O*nce inside Magic Beans, Bonnie stepped out of the way of the group of customers walking in behind her. While her eyes adjusted to the dim light, she paused, breathing in the rich, dark aroma of freshly brewed coffee. Delicious.

The character of the upscale shop was enchanting. Groupings of leather couches and comfortable-looking chairs scattered across an expanse of stained concrete. Deep green ivy climbed the far wall of exposed brick, and above her, small lights glinted against a charcoal ceiling like stars in a night sky.

From the corner of her eye, she saw a man rise from one of the couches. He waved, and she waved back, smiling without thinking. How unlike herself.

He was dressed more casually today, jeans and a gray button-down. His thick dark hair looked more finger-raked this morning, so the curl was visible. Somehow he was even more devastatingly handsome than last night.

"Good morning," he said in a voice much like the ambiance of the room: rich, dark. Deliciously enchanting. "I was beginning to think you weren't coming,"

It suddenly occurred to her; she wasn't, but then she read the rest of his note, and his P.S. changed her mind. "The package arrived while I was in the shower, and Mara forgot to tell me. Thank you for returning my shoe."

"Thank you for giving me a second chance," he said, stretching out his hand. "Chuck Wilkerson."

"Bonnie Sullivan." Her hand felt small in his, but safe and warm, not intimidating. And that dratted tingle traveled along her limbs, just like the first time. "It's good to meet you."

"And now we are strangers no more. Bonnie." His voice softened when he added her name, sending a shiver up her spine. That lethal grin of his flashed again. "We better get in line. It gets a little crazy in here on Sundays."

The line moved quickly, and while they waited, they discussed the menu board, which had dozens of beverage options listed. In the end, Bonnie opted for a double espresso. Chuck ordered the same.

While observing him in small, surreptitious glances, Bonnie noticed the way his eyebrow raised. "You look surprised. Were you expecting me to order some mocha-latte frothy thing dripping with caramel?" She smiled at the way he answered her with a half-shrug and sent him what she hoped was a flirty one of her own. "That's my afternoon order."

He laughed a lovely warm sound that teased her ears in all the right places. She accepted the cup the barista handed her. "What can I say? I'm around kids all day. Caffeine is second only to oxygen."

"Same." Chuck was still smiling as he put away his wallet and thanked the cashier. They said nothing more until they settled at a table tucked away in a quiet corner.

"So, what do you do that requires all that caffeine?" she asked, serving up the inevitable first question.

"I just transferred to a new town so I could help my sister with a project. And act as a fill-in babysitter when she needs me. She's—uh— in a high profile position and is going through a prolonged divorce."

"Ouch." Prolonged translated quickly into messy from the sound of it, and that was never good, especially with children. Bonnie's sympathy went out to her.

"So, what do you do that requires you to be around kids all day?"

"High school English teacher by day. Mom by night."

His expression gave away nothing. "Basic superhero stuff."

"Something like that."

"How many kids do you have?"

Bonnie took a deep breath. If anything would encourage a new guy to cut and run, surely this would. "Three."

~

"Three?"

Her shoulders straightened, and something about the way she met his gaze issued a challenge. "Yes, three. A boy and two girls. Twins."

She probably thought that news alone should scare him. And it did, in a good way. She *was* a freaking superhero. Whatever the circumstances were that led her to be a single mom, she'd been through enough to not put up with any games.

He lifted his cup, sipped, then leaned in. "So, tell me about them. What are they into?"

She looked away, fidgeting with the napkin beside her. "You didn't invite me for coffee to talk about my kids."

Instinct told him she was about to bolt, so he decided to take a chance and covered her hand with his. When her gaze lifted, he smiled. "Bonnie, I invited you because I'd like to get to know you. Your kids are part of you." He squeezed her fingers and let them go. "And if you're like my sisters, you probably find it easier to talk about your kids than yourself. Right?"

That guarded look remained, but her shoulders relaxed a bit. "Sisters? How many do you have?"

"Two, plus three brothers. All older than me."

"So you're the baby of the family? Spoiled rotten, I assume."

"I can't help that I'm everyone's favorite."

The tight line of tension around her eyes eased. *He* was a safe topic. Okay. He pulled out his phone and scrolled through several pictures from the family celebration of his niece's graduation, pointing out all the siblings, their spouses, and children.

At Bonnie's request, Chuck scrolled back to the picture of him surrounded by all his nieces and nephews, most of them in his lap or piled on his back—his favorite image of the night.

"See—favorite uncle."

Her fingers touched his as she took the phone, and he felt that jolt of energy travel through him again. From the way her gaze flew up to meet his, she did, too.

Her focus returned to the phone, her lips moving as she silently counted faces.

"Thirteen, plus one on the way. I come from a big family, Bonnie, so kids don't scare me."

Her full lips curved. "Spoken like a guy who has never run barefoot at two in the morning through a minefield of Legos."

"True. But I did dress up as a clown last year for Layla's birthday, so I do have some experience."

"Oof, that sounds rough." She giggled as she leaned back and crossed her arms.

"Let me tell you—five-year-old girls do *not* like clowns."

"No, not usually. Bethie liked them, but not until she was seven. Grace never did." Her soft smile revealed a dimple. "You don't know what difficult is until you try to plan a birthday party for seven-year-old twins who have suddenly decided they no longer want to dress the same or like the same things. But they still do. It's just some odd phase they go through, searching for independence. The worst part is, even *they* can't keep track of who likes what. They had us running in circles for weeks trying to come up with something."

Her laughter trailed away, and she plucked at her sleeve, fidgeting again. Finally, her fingers stilled as she got lost in the memory.

He gave her space before he asked, "So what did you end up doing?"

"A circus. Marcus suggested it so we would have all the bases covered."

"Marcus is your son?"

"My husband—late husband." Her voice held a thread of tension. She reached for her phone and swiped through an album quickly until she found an image.

Five smiling faces stared back at him. Two girls, one dressed as an acrobat, the other a lion tamer, stood on either side of a boy lifting a fake barbell overhead. The girls hammed up a look of astonishment as they pointed to his padded biceps. Behind them stood Bonnie, dressed as a circus monkey, clinging to the arm of her ringmaster.

"You have a beautiful family. Good looking guy."

"Thanks. He was. I think Justin looks a lot like him." She took the phone and swiped the photo away, showing him another one of the kids. "You'll have to excuse all the crazy faces. We were a bunch of goofballs back then."

"And now?"

"The kids still are. I try, for their sake. It's just . . . different."

"Do you mind me asking what happened?"

This time when she handed him the phone, there was only one face staring up at him. Her husband, looking solemn in his uniform.

"Marcus picked up an extra shift one night, and while he was on patrol, he stopped to help someone changing a flat tire on the side of the highway. They were almost finished when a drunk driver veered into them." Her gaze flickered away. "He was always rushing in."

Those last words knocked the wind from him. If he told her he was a fireman, would she run? "Bonnie, I'm so—"

"Don't. Please." She pushed a strand of dark hair behind her ear with shaky fingers. "I'm only telling you because I want you to understand about last night. My friend, Mara, had way too much champagne —looking back, I think I may have had too much, too, for that matter. Anyway, she's been after me to start dating again because she's afraid I haven't moved on from Marcus."

"Have you?"

"Yes. I mean no, but I wanted Mara to believe I had." Confusion creased her brow. "But I didn't think I had at the time."

He had a hard time following her logic, but the truth was there, in her eyes, and in the fact that she was here with him. Still talking to him long past their last sip of coffee. Hope swelled within him. "You didn't think you were over him until last night?"

She leaned forward and whispered, "It was a silly impulse. A dare, really. Just a quick kiss to get her off my back. That's all this was ever supposed to be."

"But then *I* kissed *you*. And you felt it, too."

"It? No." The firm shake of her head sent her side-swept bangs into her eyes. "I'm still not sure what I felt."

"But you felt something," he insisted.

"It was probably just the buzz of champagne."

"Why don't we experiment?"

"I am not kissing you again." Her eyes widened as she scanned the crowded room. "Regardless of the impression I must have given you last night; I do not usually make out in public."

The thought of a make-out session with her was immensely appealing. "No, not a kiss this time—"

"Well—" she said, shaking her head. "I am not doing anything beyond a kiss just yet, either."

He fought the urge to smile. "I like the way you said *yet*."

Her brow creased. "What?"

"You said yet. Like you're considering more at some point." He sat back with a grin, watching a most delightful shade of pink flush her cheeks. "I was going to suggest something like a trial run."

"Trial run? You sound like a science nerd."

He shrugged, not bothering to deny it because he was one. "It'll be a chance for you to see if you're ready and a chance for us to get to know each other. Ten dates—"

"*Ten*. Definitely not. Two maybe—but only if this counts as one of the dates."

"Oh, so we're bargaining now? Five, final offer." He leaned closer, challenging. "And coffee is neutral. It never counts as a date, which is why I suggested it."

"Well, *this* coffee counts, and three is *my* final offer."

"Done." He held out his hand, and thankfully she shook it before she considered anything that might change her mind. "But, the coffee doesn't count."

4

Two hours before their first date, Chuck's phone rang. It was Bonnie. "Hey, I was about to call you." Through the phone, Chuck heard a metallic crash followed by multiple screams and what sounded like chair legs squealing. "Is everything alright?"

"I won't be able to meet you at the restaurant," Bonnie explained over the clatter of what sounded like a pot lid. "My sitter canceled, Mara's not available for back-up, and, as you can probably hear, the world is coming to an end. Bethie saw a mouse in the kitchen cabinet, so now Grace is on top of the table freaking out."

Another scream sounded, followed by Bonnie telling someone to watch out for the light fixture. "What were you calling me about?"

"Same thing. Rain delays have my sister stuck in Oklahoma. So I still have the boys." He heard another metallic crash. "Are you trying to catch the mouse with a pot?"

"No," she laughed. "I couldn't find any of the traps. Justin thinks he can scare it out into the open where Bethie is waiting with a broom to sweep it out the door."

The sound of her laughter made Chuck's heart thump harder. "I was really looking forward to seeing you tonight."

The chaos in the background settled, and he heard her sigh. "Me, too. But it looks like we're just going to order pizzas and remain on mouse patrol. Rain-check?"

"I've got a better idea."

~

THE PIZZAS and sodas were delivered right as Chuck and his two nephews arrived. Thomas and Nathan climbed out of the truck, a bag of mouse traps in hand, and instantly bonded with Justin over the idea of setting the sticky square booby-traps all over the kitchen.

Bethie and Grace, hearing the warfare that was planned, immediately asked after the welfare of the critter once it was stuck.

Grace gasped. "Mom, no!"

Justin looked at his sister in disbelief. "You were the one who crawled up on the table, screaming your head off."

"He grosses me out, but that doesn't mean I want him dead!"

Grace ran to Bonnie's side, burying her face. Bonnie wrapped her arms around her daughter's small shoulders. It broke her heart the way they trembled.

One of Chuck's nephews snickered, but Chuck ended the reaction with a firm look.

He dropped to a knee beside them. "Hey, Grace? What if we catch the mouse then set him free outside? Would that be okay?"

Grace peeked out at him. "You won't hurt him?"

"Promise."

Once they demolished the pizza and soda, Chuck handed the girls a plastic bottle and told them to rinse it out. Then he asked Justin if there was any scrap lumber in the garage. Bonnie ran to the closet to find the wire hanger he wanted. The design was ingenious. The bottle balanced on the wire like a see-saw. Chuck dropped a piece of bread with peanut butter into the bottle and placed it on the floor behind the stove.

"Once the mouse climbs in, the bottle tips, and he won't be able to escape until we let him out."

"Cool." The boys tipped the bottle, testing the design.

"It is cool." Bethie agreed, lacing her fingers with her twin's. "Plus, he gets a peanut butter sandwich while he waits. He'll be okay with that. Right, Grace?"

Grace nodded, still watching Chuck with eyes filled with uncertainty.

~

THE BOYS HAD PICKED out a spy movie, and as the end credits rolled, Bonnie announced softly, "And they're out."

The three boys were sprawled across the living room floor in sleeping bags while her two girls curled deep into the recliner.

Chuck whispered, "Thanks for letting me bring the boys over."

His smile warmed her to her toes, and the way the light played with the shadowed angles of his face and body did amazing things for her heart rate. Bonnie's mind scrambled, searching for a topic that would be safe. "Justin was ecstatic. This was the first time he didn't feel outnumbered." On her end of the couch, Bonnie shifted to face him. "I'm sorry about canceling on you tonight."

He turned. "Why? This is nice."

"Yeah? You have a thing for rushing into chaos to save the day?"

His gaze slipped, but only for a moment. "I had ulterior motives."

"Let me guess, free pizza?"

He didn't hesitate. "To kiss you again."

She swept the room with a glance. "Fat chance with this crew around."

"Slide on over here so we can find out."

It was tempting. *He* was tempting, with his teasing drawl and the playful lights dancing in his eyes. Eyes that promised kissing him would be a pleasure. Everything with him would be a pleasure. He would be hard to resist if Bonnie let him.

"Chuck—"

A single thunk sounded in the kitchen—the sound of the soda bottle landing on wood. Like two kids, they jumped from the couch and raced to the kitchen to see what they'd caught. Chuck lifted the trap, careful not to tip it. A brown field mouse stared back, nose twitching.

"Looks like mouse-watch has ended," Chuck said.

"I'm glad. I didn't want to say anything, but I hated the idea of a mouse crawling around in here." Bonnie shuddered as the mouse

270

looked for a way out. "He is kind of cute. Grace will be happy he wasn't hurt."

They took a picture of the mouse as proof before Chuck set him free in the field beyond the fence.

Bonnie had just finished loading the dishwasher when he returned to wash his hands. Standing there with him, shoulder to shoulder felt easy. Everything with him tonight had been easy. There was such a simple peace that washed over her in his company.

So when he turned to her and lifted her chin to kiss her, she let him. No, *let* was far too passive. Bonnie wanted to kiss him again. She was ready to feel warm and wanted, alive once more. Her lips met his with eagerness, and she wrapped her arms around his waist, pulling him closer, enjoying the way his lips moved over hers as if he were savoring her as much as she was him.

Once they were both breathless, he rested his forehead against hers. His fingers cupped her face. "I have thought about that ever since you mentioned it in the coffee shop."

The way he molded her to his body while he nibbled her lower lip left her senseless. She tried to focus on what he'd said. "Wh-what did I mention?"

"Making out."

Making out. Bonnie smiled, barely remembering saying the words, but it thrilled her that he remembered. He'd thought about her since the coffee shop, too. "Did I say that?"

"Yeah, you did." That devilish gleam flashed in his eyes, and his arms tightened around her. "Want to do it some more?"

She reached for him, pulling him down to her. "Heck, yeah."

5

———

onnie and Chuck agreed their second date would be a reschedule of their first. They made their reservation for Friday. Mara had agreed to watch the kids, and she arrived early to cook supper and help the kids with their homework while Bonnie got dressed.

Mara's voice sounded from the doorway. "Is that what you're wearing?"

"Yes." Bonnie glanced down at her favorite slacks, blouse, and cardigan. "It's comfortable. It's what I wore to work today."

"Exactly." Mara dug through the closet, finally settling on a fitted black dress stuck way in the back. "This one."

"No. I'd have to shave my legs."

Mara glared, "From what you've told me about the guy and the way the last date went, you might want to shave them anyway."

"Mara!"

"And go above the knee. Just in case."

Bonnie met her gaze in the mirror above the dresser.

Mara tilted her head and shrugged. "If you need me to do a sleepover with the kids, I'm available."

"It's *not* going to go that far." Bonnie slipped on her earring, her fingers fumbled and dropped the back. Last weekend, Bonnie didn't

272

think she'd be standing at her kitchen sink, making out with the guy, either. Didn't know she'd stay up past midnight to talk to him every night this week. And she loved talking to him. They talked about everything, from the little things that happened during the day to solving world problems. Bonnie shook her head. "This is moving too fast."

"No, it's not. Not if you both know what you want," Mara said softly.

What did she want?

She wanted more. More time with him. More kisses from him. More Chuck.

Bonnie's hands stilled. *Crap.* She put her earrings down, jerked the dress from Mara's hands, and headed toward the bathroom.

Mara's laughter echoed down the hallway. "I'll be on standby if you change your mind about me staying the night."

BONNIE TOOK HIS BREATH AWAY. Chuck had a hard time focusing on anything but her from the moment she walked into the restaurant until now, sitting across from him surrounded by flowers and candlelight.

That was a lie. Chuck had a hard time focusing on anything but Bonnie from the moment he saw her in the elevator. His parents raised him and his siblings to believe in love at first sight—their marriage was a product of it. He just never thought it could happen to him.

Chuck ran his thumb over the leather binder that held the check, trying to think of a way to make this moment with her last. "Are you sure you don't want anything else?"

"Appetizers, entree, *and* dessert. Chuck, I couldn't eat another thing if I tried." Her eyes searched his. "Is something wrong?"

He shook his head. "I'm not quite ready for tonight to end."

Her smile was soft and sweet. "I'm not either."

He reached for her hand, and she placed hers in it. His heartbeat drummed in his ears. "I'd like to show you something I'm working on, a project. Would you be willing to go for a drive?"

She smiled. "Sure."

He returned it, remembering their first exchange in the elevator. "Super."

The drive was quiet. Bonnie seemed as lost in thought as he was. A few miles outside of town, he slowed to make a turn.

"Chuck, you can't turn here. It's a private drive."

"I know, but it's mine." Her surprise was easy to see in the dashboard lights.

"The old Marshall place?"

"I bought it a year ago, and when my sister needed me, I decided this would be a great time to start working on it." He drove down the rutted drive far enough so the headlights lit the front of the old farmhouse, and shifted into park. Thoughts raced through his head as he began second-guessing the best way to say what he wanted to tell her.

"Every time I'd come down to visit Sutton, I'd pass this old empty house and think, what a waste. I could see this house was built for a big family. Huge Christmas trees in the front window and big Thanksgiving dinners with kids playing football in the front yard. A bachelor doesn't need all this space, but I hated seeing it go to ruin. So I bought it with the idea that I would flip it.

"Then I met you, and Bonnie, now all I can see is the two of us, old and gray, sitting on that porch swing surrounded by a ton of grandkids." He looked at her and saw the tear roll down her cheek. He wiped it away. "God, I don't want to scare you off, and I know this all sounds crazy. Most people don't believe in love at first sight, and over the last few years, I've doubted it myself. But I believe now."

He forced himself to stop, to let her breathe and take it all in.

BONNIE REACHED FOR HIS HAND. "I don't know what to say."

"You don't have to say anything." Her fingers trembled as he lifted them to his lips, brushing the lightest of kisses over her knuckles. Chuck searched her face. "Just tell me we can renegotiate."

The sob she'd held back broke free with her laughter. The emotions flooding through her left her feeling overwhelmed, but also alive— loved and alive. And as much as it scared her, it felt good, too.

Chuck pulled her across the seat and held her close before he kissed her. "Or tell me that coffee doesn't count, so I'll have at least one more chance to change your mind."

Bonnie laughed again as he nuzzled her ear. She wiped away her tears. "Coffee does count, you big goof—"

Because that's when I started falling for you.

Everything in her stilled. It was true. She was falling and falling fast. Falling, something she'd thought she'd never do again.

And the perfect guy to fall again with was Chuck. He was everything she didn't know she wanted. "I do want to see you again, and I'm not sure what I'm feeling, but I don't want this to end."

"Yeah?"

"Yeah. And I don't want tonight to end either," Bonnie whispered with certainty. She cupped his cheek, tracing her thumb over that lethal grin before she kissed him again. "Not yet."

JUST BEFORE MIDNIGHT, Chuck drove Bonnie to the restaurant to pick up her car, their fingers twined together on the seat between them. The restaurant was closed, the parking lot empty except for their two vehicles.

Beneath his fingertips, her shoulder was warm silk. In the hours before, Chuck had learned that every inch of her was just as smooth— and she was just as warm, and giving. He wanted nothing more than for Bonnie to stay the rest of the night with him, to know what it was like to wake up in the morning with her in his arms and his bed. He kissed a path along her neck to whisper in her ear. "Stay with me."

"I want to," Bonnie sighed with a smile. She pulled back, but not entirely out of his arms. "But I need to be there in the morning. Justin has soccer practice. The girls have recital fittings. I have a stack of papers to grade, grading that I put off because I was on the phone with a very handsome guy every night this week—"

He stopped her with a kiss. "Okay, Cinderella. I get it. Let's get you into your carriage before it turns into a pumpkin."

He circled his truck, opened her door, and helped her down when he heard a car approaching along the highway at a high rate of speed. The vehicle came around the curve in a blur, running through the stop sign before hitting the curb and going airborne. It flipped several times, then landed at the bottom of the embankment.

He heard Bonnie's gasp just as his instinct and training kicked in. He caught her by the shoulders and felt her trembling. "Are you okay? Can you call 9-1-1?" Seeing her nod, he let her go and reached behind the seat for his medic bag, racing for the smoking vehicle.

6

———

"So how long has it been?" Mara asked.

"A little over a month," Bonnie muttered, folding her arms around her middle as if she could somehow hold her life together that way.

"Maybe it's just stress."

"Maybe." Mara was sweet to offer her such encouragement, but there were three white test sticks strewn across Bonnie's bathroom counter with little pink lines that begged to differ.

"Are you going to tell him?"

The question forced Bonnie's eyes closed, and the tears she'd been holding back fell. A month ago, she felt like she was walking on clouds, and in a single moment, she'd watched Chuck race down the embankment and climb into a smoking vehicle and her world had come crashing back to earth.

When she opened her eyes, Mara was still waiting. The truth sat in her gut like a stone. "I don't know if I can live like that again. Watching someone I love so much walk out that door every day, not knowing if he's going to make it back home to me. To us."

"Oh, Bonnie. Do you realize what you just said?" Mara pulled her into a hug. "You love him."

"I do." Bonnie buried her head into her friend's shoulder and wallowed in the comfort. "But how can I put the kids through that again?"

"Those kids are stronger than you think they are. They're strong, like their mom." Mara rubbed her back. "I hate to bring this up, friend, but with three kids already, did it ever cross your mind to use protection?"

"Of course, it did. And we did, but—"

The door to Bonnie's bedroom crashed open, and Bethie's voice called out, "Mom?"

"*Mom?*" Grace's cry was more frantic.

Bonnie tossed a hand towel over the test sticks. "We're in here."

Grace and Bethie's faces both peeked around the door. Grace looked stricken.

Bonnie sank to her knees, pulling Grace into her arms, rubbing warmth back into her hands. "What happened?"

Bethie's eyes were wide. "There was a fire on the news, and he was there—"

Grace shuddered against her, and Bonnie's heartbeat sped. "Who?"

"Chuck." Bethie blinked back tears. "They were spraying water on the fire, and a bunch of guys got too close. Then Chuck ran in—"

Gracie looked up with hollow eyes. "And the building fell."

ONCE THE DOCTORS in the ER had Chuck's vitals stable, they moved him to a room where he could rest. While he slept, a steady stream of visitors came and went. Most of them Chuck's new co-workers stopping by to leave their well-wishes and thanks to Sutton, Chuck's sister. Sutton told her they were the volunteer firemen Chuck had been training when the accident happened. The men he had saved.

The room was finally quiet. Bonnie knew from experience that quiet was such a relative term. The soft cadence of machinery beeping and oxygen hissing reminded her. Signs of life that left Bonnie feeling profoundly grateful. For hours she'd stared at the monitor, counting every heartbeat, listening with her hand upon his chest as it rose and fell with each breath.

He was still with her.

"Hey." Chuck's voice cracked over the word, hoarse and raw. A beautiful sound when earlier that day she wasn't sure if she'd get to hear it again.

"Hey, you." She managed to say past the lump in her throat. She moved to his side, careful of his bandages and all the tubes and wires connecting him to the monitors, and helped him take a sip of water.

"See the lengths I'll go to to get your attention." He settled back against the pillows, and his eyes traveled over her face. "God, I've missed you."

"I've missed you too." Her lips brushed against his forehead and stayed there when his arm circled her neck, and he held her close. She wrapped her arms around him while shudders traveled through his body. Did he realize just how close he'd tempted fate today? It could have been so much worse.

He kissed her cheek. "I thought I'd lost you."

A soft laugh tore through her throat. "I think you've got that backward. We thought we'd lost you."

"No. These last few weeks have been hell. The only thing I could think of was you. When you wouldn't return my calls or my texts, I knew I blew it by not being completely honest with you."

"Well, for future reference, not telling me the truth didn't help your case." Bonnie straightened the blankets over his chest. "I just had to work a few things out."

Chuck caught her fingers, stilling her fidgeting. "Have you?"

"I think so." She met his gaze and knew, without a doubt, the one she had waited for was Chuck. "I didn't think I'd ever fall in love again, and part of me was afraid to."

"And now."

"When we were waiting to hear . . ." Bonnie stopped, forcing herself to breathe deeply, in and out, not wanting to remember what it felt like to wonder if he'd made it out alive, if she'd lost her chance at loving him. Chuck's fingers tightened around hers. "Chuck, the only thing I'm afraid of now is going through life without having loved you." Again, she breathed deep, in and out, focusing on this moment, on life, on him. "I will love you for whatever time God allows, whether that's a day, a year, or a lifetime. I will love you every second that you're by my side."

EPILOGUE

"Where the heck is he?" Bonnie grimaced between hard-fought pants.

"How long has it been?" Mara asked, checking her phone for the twentieth time.

"Long enough to get here since you left that last message." The contraction finally eased, and Bonnie relaxed. "Quit pacing and come rub my back. If he isn't here in the next ten minutes, I'm pushing this thing out, with or without him."

The obstetrician raised a brow, implying without a word that Bonnie's ten-minute estimate was a little generous. "Mrs. Wilkerson, this is your third pregnancy, and your body knows exactly what it's doing this time. You're ready. The baby is ready."

"This is my husband's first pregnancy." Bonnie shifted up to her elbow and gave the man her best glare. Through gritted teeth, she said, "So, we're giving him ten more minutes."

The doctor shrugged. "At this point, I'm just here to catch."

The next contraction was a doozie, and it took everything Bonnie had to breathe through it. Just as it eased, the door opened, and Chuck raced in. "I'm here, I'm here, I'm here."

"You're late," Mara and the doctor said in unison.

Chuck's face fell. "Did I miss it?"

The older nurse who had been a godsend to Bonnie grabbed his arm and shoved him towards a side door. "Not yet, sweetheart. Let's get you gowned up."

The next contraction gripped Bonnie without mercy. "Hurry!"

He made it with two minutes to spare before Gia Rachel Wilkerson made her debut, and the first heart she captured was Chuck's. From the moment she was placed in her father's arms, he was a goner.

Later, after they were placed in a room and all of their family and friends had come and gone, Bonnie woke from her nap. She watched her new husband rock the latest addition to the family to sleep. With the lightest touch, he counted each knuckle of Gia's small fist.

"You really do fall fast, don't you?"

"Love at first sight." His gaze rose to meet hers. "I just know what will make me happy." He stood and placed the baby in the clear bassinet. He crossed the room, then leaned over her, kissing her gently. "And you make me very happy. Thank you for my daughter." He smiled, then kicked off his shoes. "Move over. I'm coming in."

"The nurse won't like it," Bonnie warned, but scooted over with a giggle, loving his impulsiveness, and loving him. She relaxed once she was safely wrapped in his arms. "When did you know?"

"As soon as you kissed me." His voice was a deep rumble in her ear.

"No, that kiss was awful. First kisses usually are." Bonnie looked up to find him staring. "Did you know you were only my second first kiss?"

"No, I didn't." He tucked her hair behind her ear. His fingers followed the curve, then trailed over her cheek. "I only knew I wanted to be your last first kiss."

ABOUT THE AUTHOR

E.J. Dean is the author of the newly released Sparrow Hill series. A life-long reader of romance, she enjoys writing sweet contemporary stories with small-town heart, stories filled with love, healing laughter, and characters you will root for from page one.

When she is not writing, you can find her and her husband of 30+ years, rocking on the front porch and sipping sweet tea, surrounded by the gorgeous pines of East Texas, planning their next big adventure.

https://www.amazon.com/E-J-Dean/e/B078HLXVTZ

https://mailchi.mp/ae3b72b75cb0/ejdml

BLESS YOUR HEART

K. A. GANDY

Thirty and unmarried in the south, can Marlie find her forever wedding date?

1

I tried not to tap my foot impatiently as the cotton-topped little old lady in front of me in the checkout line slowly loaded her groceries on the belt. Apparently *Express Lane* didn't apply to the patrons, just the number of items. Although, on second look, she'd packed more than 15 items on the belt, too.

Pasting on my best smile, I asked her, "Ma'am, can I help you load up your things?"

"Why, yes, dear. How lovely of you to offer!" she said as she ambled towards the front of the line to pay.

"It's no problem, happy to help," I said, and quickly finished loading her very full grocery cart onto the belt. Just then, a handsome stranger joined the line behind me, carrying a bouquet of red roses and a box of chocolates. *Somebody in this town is going to be thrilled tonight.* I took him in from his thick, dark hair and chocolate eyes, to a well-defined chest, fitted jeans, and dark leather shoes. I snapped my gaze back up to see him give me a smile that could melt a popsicle, and a nod before he assessed the reality that this lane would not be moving quickly.

"So dear, are you married?" The lady asked, inspecting my clearly bare left hand. I reached up and tucked a strand of auburn hair behind my ear to remove the offending digit from her scrutiny.

"No ma'am, not yet." I forced a smile, despite my inward loathing of the question. I got it; I was thirty. Most of the women I went to high school with were well past married and on to their second or third child. However, Prince Charming had yet to show himself. So there I was: thirty, unmarried, and no kids in sight—much to my mama's chagrin.

It's not like I wouldn't love to find someone—if not to marry, then at least to have a serious relationship with—but I have always struggled with putting myself out there. Being vulnerable is hard. Plus in this town, once that first blush of your twenties has passed, everyone started treating you like a bug under a microscope, and any hint of romance had the tongues wagging.

"Well, you aren't getting any younger. You look at *least* twenty-five. In my day, you'd be considered a spinster by now!" She pulled out a checkbook and pen, which saved me from being forced to answer.

I turned to the side to check out the magazines, intent on not drawing any more of her attention, only to spot Mr. Handsome with a barely concealed grin, having clearly seen the whole thing. My face colored instantly. *Why must my humiliation be in front of the hottest man I've seen in a month? Just why?*

He leaned in conspiratorially and whispered, "If it makes you feel any better, I'm sure you've got plenty of child-bearing years ahead of you."

"Ha-ha, aren't you hilarious." I shot him a glare. Handsome or not, there's a line.

He stuck his hand out to shake, "Tucker Jones. And, yes, some people say I am," and flashed me a cocky grin.

I reluctantly shook his hand, "Marlie."

"Nice to meet you, Marlie. I know it's forward of me, seeing as we just met and all, but do you have plans tonight?"

I glanced down pointedly at the flowers and chocolates, which were clearly intended for someone, before answering, "Yes, actually, I'm afraid I do have plans tonight." *My baby sister's wedding rehearsal.* Jenny's a girl who's never had an issue putting herself out there. Twenty-three, and she'd already blown through an impressive list of boyfriends before she committed to John.

"Honey, when a man that tall and good-looking asks you out, you say, yes! Bless your heart, I think we found the problem." The little old lady tsked and took her receipt from the cashier and slowly pushed her cart away.

"You have a nice day now, Mrs. Lindy," the cashier said to her retreating form.

Tucker chuckled behind me as I chucked my bottle of nail polish on the belt and shoved a five-dollar bill at the cashier. She took it all in with an amused expression and popped her bubble gum loudly, in no hurry to end my nightmare of shame.

Dear ground, please swallow me now.

"Have a nice day, now," she drawled.

I nodded abruptly and fled out the door, eager to hide my flaming face. Digging in my purse, I pulled out my keys and climbed into my SUV. I started it up and threw it in reverse, only to hear an odd thwump-thwump as I back out of the space. *What in the world is that?*

Tossing it in park, I jumped back out and walked around the car to see if I could find what caused the noise.

"You've got to be kidding me. Really?" I looked up at the sky, as if to question the heavens directly. "Today of all days. Ugh," I groaned.

"Don't tell me the car asked if you're single, too. What is the world coming to?" A now-familiar voice startled me from the side, and I spun on my heels to face none other than Tucker Jones, his gifts now tidily bagged.

"No, thank you very much. My tire is flat." I pointed to the offending piece of rubber, tempted to kick it. *I still might, once he leaves.*

He set the bag down on the pavement and walked over, "It sure is. Let me take a look."

"Oh, no! I can't put you out. I'll call my dad. Really, you should go," I urged him, but he ignored me. Dropping down to one knee, he looked around the flat tire.

After a moment of me watching him tensely, he let out a whistle, "You picked up a screw straight through the sidewall. I'm afraid you're going to need a new tire. Do you have a spare?" He stood, dusting off his hands before he looked to me for an answer.

"Yes, but really, it's fine. I can just wait for my dad to get here!" I tried to wave him off, but he was a man on a mission.

"It's probably in the back." He popped open my hatch, and made quick work of the cover, exposing the spare. He did a quick inventory of the tools, and then pulled out what he needed and went to work.

We stood in silence while he pumped on the miniature jack handle for at least a minute, and I just watched his arm muscles move up and down. The car barely budged despite his efforts. The fact that he dwarfed the tiny thing made him look ridiculous, but he didn't seem fazed in the least. I watched in fascination as a single bead of sweat rolled down his tanned neck, taunting me as it slipped inside his shirt collar. I could see myself kissing that same path, down to what has to be a drool-worthy chest underneath.

I mentally shook myself, and finally thought of something coherent to say. "So, do you just go around changing women's flat tires all the time? Isn't someone expecting you?"

His brow furrowed, but he didn't stop pumping on the jack when he answered, "Why would someone be expecting me, exactly?"

I gestured to the bag, forgotten on the ground, "Well, you bought those for somebody. She's probably expecting you, right?"

Understanding dawned on his tanned face, "Ahh, yes. Great-aunt Celia is in fact expecting me. I've been out of town for a while, and I always bring her a little something when I visit. My uncle died about five years ago now, so she gets lonely when I'm away on business."

Well, it's official. I'm a heel. God, the man had just met me and was changing my tire, meanwhile I was ribbing him about the flowers and chocolates for his widowed great-aunt.

"That is really sweet of you to think of her," I said, contrition in my tone. "Not many people take time to visit their older relatives these days."

The wry grin he gave me sent a flutter through my stomach, which I chose to ignore. "Aunt Celia is a hoot. I enjoy the visits as much as she does." He removed my sad, deflated tire and rolled it to the back of the car where the spare waited.

"Are you sure I can't help you with that? It looks heavy." I watched as he picked it up and settled it in place as if it were in fact, not heavy and awkward to hold. His forearms flexed enticingly as he started tightening the lug nuts and I swallowed, mouth suddenly dry.

"Nah, wouldn't want you to get your hands dirty for your plans this evening." He winked, and a blush engulfed my face.

"I really do have plans that I can't break. I'm sorry, I wasn't trying to blow you off." I said, as guilt hit me for being dismissive before.

"It's all right, maybe another time." He quickly worked the jack back down, and then checked the tightness of my spare. With a self-satisfied nod, he brushed his hands off on his dark jeans before looking back at me. "Ok, you should be good to go. I'll pop this in the back here. That spare isn't full sized, so you'll need to get a new tire as soon as you can. It's not safe to drive on a donut too long."

"Thank you so much, Tucker. I really do appreciate it. Here we just met, and I can't believe you were so kind as to help me out," I said, unsure where to go from here. While I wished we could go back in time to that moment where he'd asked me what I was doing later, that chicken had already flown the coop.

"Don't worry about it. My daddy raised me to always help people out when I can. I hope you and I run into each other again sometime." He picked up his bag, gave me one last nod, and then walked away. I circled around to my driver's-side door and pretended not to watch as he climbed into a jacked-up red pickup truck two rows over.

AFTER A QUICK TRIP to the tire shop, I rushed to get dressed for the rehearsal dinner. I didn't have time to apply my new nail polish, but there was always tomorrow. At least I felt confident in my strapless black dress; it hugged my curves just right, and showed off my porcelain skin. *Not that there will be anyone to impress tonight.* I slipped on my strappy black heels and hurried out the door, knowing I would probably be a few minutes late despite my best efforts. Having a good excuse wouldn't stop my mama from getting after me for holding things up.

I pulled in at the small country church, and the parking lot was so full it looked like Jenny had invited the entire family to the rehearsal dinner. That meant I was probably in for a night full of, "When are you going to catch a man like your baby sister did?" *Great. My favorite way to spend a Friday night.*

Making my way up the steps, I slipped through the back doors of the sanctuary and stopped for a moment to let the blasting AC wash over my already sticky skin. As suspected, most of our extended family and John's were taking up the pews. Jenny and her three other brides-maids stood off to the side and spotted me immediately.

"Marleen Delilah Abernathy! Where have you been? We were supposed to start fifteen minutes ago. You missed all the partner swap-ping!" she scolded, voice rising at the end.

"I'm sorry, Jenny. I got a flat tire and had to get it changed out. I'm here now, and I'll walk with whoever is left," I said, trying to placate her.

"Well," she gave a dainty sniff, "You are my favorite sister, so I have done you a favor, whether or not you'll appreciate it."

I knew I shouldn't ask, because, knowing Jenny, I wouldn't like the answer. But I couldn't stop myself. "What do you mean, 'a favor?'"

"Why, she gave you the *best* groomsman, of course," Joanne pouted.

"Gawd, he is a tall drink of water," Betty agreed, fanning herself.

"Well, who is it?"

"If you'd been on time, I could have introduced you. But now I guess you'll just have to meet him on the way to the altar." Jenny waved to the wedding planner, who then cued the pianist to start playing. Jenny turned on her heel and led us back out into the heat to await our groomsmen.

The groomsmen made their way out in matching t-shirts with 'Grooms Crew' on them. A snort sneaked out of me before I could stop it. John's brother, Tim, led the way. His best friend Adam and my cousin Junior followed behind. And then, to my eternal shock, I caught a glimpse of perfectly waved dark hair. *It can't be him.* I knew every other man in this town, and not a one had a head of hair worth writing home to mama about. He stepped to the side and I got my first full glimpse of Tucker Jones in that tight, black t-shirt. I felt my temperature climb five more degrees, and it wasn't because of the Georgia sun beating down on my bare shoulders.

Betty leaned in to whisper. "You lucky duck, she gave you the only eligible bachelor in this lineup. I've got to walk with Junior, and you've got the hot college friend. Life is just not fair." She openly gawked at him, and I had to squash a surge of jealousy. *One tire change doesn't give me any right to be jealous.*

About that time, Tucker looked over at me and I saw confusion cross his face for a brief moment, but before he had a chance to say anything, Jenny grabbed him by the arm and led him towards me. "Tucker Jones, this is my sister Marlie. Marlie, Tucker Jones. Y'all make nice now, ok? It's time to get this show on the road." With that whirlwind introduction over, she turned and sashayed to the back of the line.

The other pairs had already linked elbows for our practice walk down the aisle. Tucker gave me an affable grin, and stuck his elbow out in my direction. "So, *Marleen*, is it? Jenny really talked up her gorgeous red-headed sister, but I didn't dare dream it would be you."

I groaned. "She's the only one that calls me by my full name. I think at this point she just does it out of habit."

I wrapped my hand around his warm bicep, and it felt like my heart skipped a few beats being this close to him. Why did he have to be tall, handsome, kind, good at changing tires, and built like a god? Was somebody out there trying to kill me? I glared up at the heavens for the second time today, and nearly missed our cue to start down the aisle in the process.

Tucker led me through the doors of the sanctuary, and after the couple ahead of us made it about halfway down, the wedding planner waved us forward.

"So, I guess you really did have plans tonight, huh?" Tucker whispered. I whipped my head around to see if he was kidding but found his serene gaze locked ahead where John waited next to the pastor.

"Of course I had plans," I answered in a heated whisper, "Did you think I lied to you?"

I felt his shrug in response because the bicep where my happy hand was snuggled rose and fell as he did it.

"What kind of women do you usually ask out that they lie to avoid you?"

"Well, I tried to ask you out, but you turned me down. It is nice to know you weren't just blowing me off, though."

"Speaking of, you were asking me out to what, a rehearsal dinner? Isn't that an odd first date? Maybe *that's* why women turn you down." I muttered the last bit under my breath, not intending for him to hear it. We reached the front of the aisle and split off to our respective sides before he had a chance to answer.

Jenny jaunted down the aisle on our dad's arm to the pianist's enthusiastic bridal march, before being handed off to an eager John.

The pastor said a few short words, and they sneaked a kiss before the planner sent us all out to do it over again. Tucker stuck his elbow back out for me to be escorted back out of the church, and I accepted it.

"I'll have you know, women don't *usually* turn me down," he said as we started down the aisle.

I laughed, "Ok, good for you, then."

"I just wouldn't want you to get the wrong impression, seeing as we'll be spending some time together over the course of the next few days," he drawled.

"Uh-huh," I responded noncommittally.

We reached the back door of the church, and he held it open for me to pass through, ever the gentleman. Once we were all lined back up outside, we started the whole shooting match over again.

"Should we be offended they don't seem to think we can all walk a straight line?" I asked no one in particular.

Betty snorted, "Some of us could use a little more practice than others." She gave Junior a pointed look, which he ignored.

"How many more times do we have to do this?" Tim asked the planner.

"One more time, and if y'all get it right we can head on over to supper. So don't screw it up." She said and pointed at him with a no-nonsense look in her eye. She then turned and signaled the pianist to start again as she made her way into the church.

With the first couples leading the way, we waited our turn huddled by the door.

"You know, if you want to talk about making assumptions—if I hadn't wanted to go out with you, I'd have just said so. I didn't need to lie about having plans." I said as we started our slow pace down the aisle.

The planner motioned exaggeratedly for me to pretend I was holding a bouquet, so I snapped my other arm into place. To my surprise, Tucker didn't say anything else for the rest of our trip down the aisle.

There you go again, Marlie. Always scaring off the handsome ones. I thought to myself and tuned out the pastor's pretend sermon. The planner motioned for us to make our exit again, so I met Tucker in front of the altar and took his elbow for our walk out.

About halfway down, he surprised me by asking, "So, does that mean you *do*, in fact, want to go out with me?"

"I'm sorry, how exactly did you come up with that idea?" My throat tightened, and I tried not to let my panic show through my voice.

"Let's call it a hunch that you would have said yes, if you didn't have this rehearsal dinner to attend." He looked over at me, grinning like the cat who just swallowed the canary.

I stayed silent, as I hadn't intended to give myself away like that. *He's not wrong, if not for the embarrassing circumstances, I probably would have said yes. Maybe. What is wrong with me?*

We exited the church yet again, and thankfully the planner was pleased with our two run-throughs and told us to head to the dinner portion of the evening. I let go of his arm and crossed mine across my chest instead. Before either one of us realized what was happening, Joanne swooped in and snagged his other arm.

"Why Tucker, do you think you could escort me over to the dinner? I'd love to hear about your latest business trip. What is it you do, exactly?" She batted her false eyelashes like a pro.

"Uh, well," Tucker looked over at me apologetically, "Sure, I can walk over with you. I think we'll all be walking together, though."

She laughed, and stroked his arm lightly, "Oh, Tucker, if I'm on your arm I don't think I'll notice what everyone else is doing."

Laying it on thick, Joanne. I rolled my eyes at her obvious flirtation and trailed towards the reception hall at the back of the boisterous group.

Dinner turned out to be spaghetti, and I mentally patted myself on the back for wearing black. I made a heaping plate and stacked a few slices of buttery garlic bread on the side for good measure. As I made my way back to the tables, I noticed that the only seat left was directly across from Tucker. The entire extended family made it over here before the wedding party, which wasn't too surprising given how much our family likes to eat.

I set my plate down carefully and managed not to knock any of the bread off onto the tablecloth. Right as I settled a napkin in my lap, Tucker abruptly stood from his seat.

"I'm going to go grab something to drink. You ladies want

anything?" His voice came out even, but his eyes looked a little wild. "No? Ok, I'll be back." He hurried across the room to the drink table.

"Joanne, what are you doing to the poor man? He just about ran away from you. And scaring the men off is usually Marlie's job," Betty asked from her place next to me.

"I don't have the faintest idea what you're talking about," Joanne said innocently. "I just asked him if he had his eye on any of the desserts."

"Well, I'd give it up if I were you. He's clearly not interested in your sweets. You got that man running for cover," Betty said wryly.

Joanne sighed, "You're probably right, but you can't blame a girl for trying. I guess that means it's up to you, Marlie," she said, eyeing my mountain of spaghetti with her eyebrows raised in judgment.

"What are you talking about, up to me?" I asked, fork paused halfway to my mouth.

"We cannot let him out of this wedding without one of us attached to him. Look at that man! He needs a good southern girl in his life. And frankly, he is clearly looking to find someone if he came solo. He could have asked just about any available woman if he didn't want to come alone. Yet here he is, ripe for the picking." She waved her hand around the gathering as if this was all obvious.

My mind went back to the grocery store, where he'd asked a complete stranger to accompany him to this dinner, and I couldn't help but question her logic; it seemed to me he didn't want to be here alone.

"You better snap him up, Marlie!" Betty agreed and snapped her fingers in punctuation as Tucker returned to the table with a glass in hand.

"Did you ladies miss me?" Tucker asked with a smile as he sat back down, and his gaze lingered on me.

"You know it," Betty responded with a wink, but I just looked down at my spaghetti.

∼

THE NEXT MORNING, the bride's room was engulfed in a veritable cloud of perfume and hairspray. Coughing, I tried to back out slowly, but

Jenny spotted me and gestured in my direction, the stress plain on her face.

"Marlie! Thank God! I was worried you were going to be late again." She huffed out a breath towards her bangs, which having been curled and sprayed to within an inch of their lives, didn't budge.

I forced a smile, "No, definitely not. You are my number one focus today, Jenny. What can I help with?"

She worried her bottom lip between her teeth for a moment before answering, "Well, I need you to be honest with me. This is the *most important day of my life.* Do you think I picked the wrong eye shadow? I don't want it to clash with my lipstick."

My instinct was to chuckle at her dramatics, but her eyes were genuinely concerned, and I knew in that moment we'd gone past humor. "You look great, Jenny. When John sees you, he's going to be knocked off his boots with how beautiful you are." I gave her hands a squeeze, and she instantly relaxed.

"Oh Marlie, I love you, you know that? Once me and John are back from the honeymoon and settled, we're going to find someone for you to marry, too."

"Don't worry about me today, Jenny. Let's just get you down the aisle for now." I brushed off her promise of matchmaking. I hoped she'd forget all about it by the time she came home. A loud bang echoed in the room behind me, and I spun to see what caused the noise. Betty and Joanne had opened a bag of celebratory poppers. "Would you knock that off? Somebody's going to take a mascara wand to the eye!"

"Spoil sport!" Joanne said. "We're just keeping busy until it's our turn in the chair."

Betty elbowed her, and then zeroed in on me with a wicked gleam in her eye, "Why don't we talk about your plans with Tucker instead?"

Letting out a groan, I shook my head at her, "Can you two not let it rest? I am not the type to chase a man down; I prefer to let things happen of their own accord."

"How's that working out for you?" Joanne practically oozed sarcasm, "Sometimes you've got to get out there and push the envelope, girl. You are in the prime of your life, it's time to let loose a little."

A small part of me couldn't help but think that maybe she was right. The instant I spotted Tucker in the grocery store, I felt attraction spark between us. If it hadn't been for the peanut gallery roasting me on my age, maybe something would have happened of its own accord. But that ship had already sailed. Did that mean I had to write Tucker off, just because we met in a less-than-ideal way? He hadn't seemed overly put off last night at the rehearsal.

Betty chimed in before I had a chance to respond, "Word on the grape vine is that his ex-girlfriend will be attending the wedding tonight with her new man. I bet he snaps her back up in no time flat. That's what helped my Jackson along in getting back together with me, after all. One well-timed date and he was overcome with jealousy." She looked in my direction with pity before continuing, "Sorry, Marlie. But fine men like Tucker just don't hang around on the market forever."

"Y'all need to stop talking about that poor man like he's a piece of meat. And leave me out of it, too, would you?" I snapped, stung at the thought of Tucker with his ex.

"Marlie, I'm ready for you." The hairdresser gestured to her empty chair, and I hustled over to get away from Betty and Joanne.

Nearly two hours later, we'd all been primped, prepped, and stuffed into bright purple bridesmaids gowns. The color didn't look too horrible, even though I'd have never picked it for myself. I attempted to pat the large fabric flower down away from my face, but it sprang right back up like a perky nightmare for the thousandth time since I'd donned the dress.

The wedding planner arrived at the bride's room door and announced that it was time to start the ceremony. Butterflies took flight in my stomach at the thought of seeing Tucker in a moment, and I tried to shove the feeling down. I wasn't the one getting hitched today, so I had nothing to be nervous about. *Except falling flat on my face in these shoes.* I glanced down at the offending peep-toed purple footwear. They may have been ankle death traps, but they showed off my freshly painted nails to perfection.

I fell into step behind Jenny, holding up the end of her voluminous train as we made our way through the very full parking lot to wait outside the sanctuary door. The gaggle of suited groomsmen gathered there jostled each other, but quieted as we approached, and then separated to find their assigned bridesmaids. The fifteen pounds of pure white satin had my arms burning, and I gratefully sat it down.

Tucker whistled slowly as he approached and took me in, "Why Marlie, you are a vision in purple."

"Stop it. This is not my color!" The blush took over my face with a vengeance, the curse of redheads everywhere.

He proffered his elbow genially, "Beauty is in the eye of the beholder, and I think you'd be gorgeous in a potato sack. So, I guess you'll just have to get used to it," he said and gave me a sly wink.

My hand clutched his jacket sleeve tightly at his words, and I forced it to relax. I looked at him sideways and took in the full picture that is Tucker Jones in a tux. The sight of him was enough to buckle my knees; he's got "tall, dark, and handsome" on lock, and his hair had just the slightest wave to it where he'd styled it back for the occasion. His warm chocolate brown eyes drew me in the minute I saw them. Although, my favorite thing about him so far was that no matter what, he was always smiling.

The door to the church opened, and we could hear the pianist playing as the first pair headed for the aisle. We all slowly made our way forward, and the snail-like pace of the procession gave me plenty of time to feel the warmth radiating off of Tucker. When it was our turn, we paced sedately down the aisle. My eyes flitted over the gathered crowd before coming to an abrupt stop on a curvy blonde in a tight green gown. Her acidic glare stood out in stark contrast to the crowd of well-wishers.

I whispered discretely to Tucker while trying to keep my smile fixed in place, "Do you know that woman? She is glaring at us fit to set us on fire."

He tensed, as he followed my gaze and spotted the woman in question, "Unfortunately I do," was all he had time to say before we arrived at the flower-bedecked altar and had to go our separate ways.

The ceremony passed in a beautiful blur. Jenny and John beamed at each other with all the hope of a new life together. I tried my best not to, but I still teared up a little as they said their vows so sweetly. My tears turned to laughter when after the pastor announced them, John tossed Jenny over his shoulder and carried her down the aisle.

The rest of us quickly made our way out for photos, and then on to the reception.

My mood was light as Tucker held the door for me, and then led me over to the drink selection. He quickly procured two sweet teas for us, and then we turned to take in the happy crowd. "Jenny and John sure are good together, don't you think?"

"I do, they seem really happy together. I'm glad for them," I responded. Across the room, the angry blonde spotted us and headed our way.

"Marlie, I need your help with something."

"Sure, what's up?"

"Just don't slap me, okay?"

"What?" I looked over at him in confusion. Why in the world would I slap him?

Before I could ask, the blonde broke through the crowd with a tall man in tow, and Tucker turned to me, slid both hands around my waist, and planted a kiss directly on my lips. My brain short-circuited, and the warmth of his kiss felt like it rolled over my entire body in an instant. My hands drifted up to the back of his neck seemingly of their own accord, and the rest of me melted into his hard chest.

After a small eternity, he pulled back and took in my glazed expression.

"What was that for?" My hand went to my lips. I was both excited and confused by this turn of events.

"Really, Tucker? Way to be mature about this!" The angry blonde stormed off, dragging the hapless man in her wake.

My mouth dropped open. "Who was that, exactly?"

For the first time, Tucker looked abashed, "My ex. Susan. I'm sorry for the impromptu kiss, but she's been hounding me for nearly a month. She cheated on me with her co-worker."

"Oh," I responded. "Happy to be of service, then." Deflated, I sat my tea glass down and beat a hasty retreat to the hallway. I had nearly made it to the ladies' room when a masculine hand snagged my wrist, stopping me mid-flight.

"Marlie, please wait! I wanted to kiss you." His voice was strained.

I spun angrily, "Really, Tucker, did you? Or was it just a show for your ex?" I said the last bit quietly, hoping to avoid fueling the gossip that I was sure had already started to spread like wildfire through the reception.

"No, Marlie, I wanted to kiss you. I've wanted to kiss you since yesterday when I asked you out the first time." His eyes pleaded with mine for understanding, and he slipped his hand down from my wrist to hold my hand.

"Why me, Tucker? You could have your pick of women in this room. Including your ex, who's over there glaring at your back as we speak," I stated, finally letting my insecurity peek through.

He raked a hand through his perfectly styled hair in agitation, "I'm not interested in giving her another minute of my time, Marlie. I can promise you that." He stilled, and then ever so slowly reached a hand up to brush an escaped strand of hair back behind my ear. "Because, the minute I saw you in that grocery store, I was hooked. You were so kind to Mrs. Lindy, even when she embarrassed you. You kept your head high, and you had this look on your face, like . . . I don't even know," he paused, seeming to run it through in his mind, "You looked like you were going to charge a hungry bear with nothing but a biscuit."

A startled laugh escaped me at his absurd comparison, and he smiled softly in return, running his thumb over my chin.

"I knew in that moment that you were used to taking it on the chin, and making the best of things. You aren't the kind of person that lets life get you down, no matter the hand you're dealt. You're stronger than you give yourself credit for, Marlie. And I'd like the chance to get to know you better. So, it seems I'll have to ask you again, would you please go on a date with me? Because I need a repeat of that kiss."

Could I let myself take a chance with him—really go all in? I took in his earnest expression, and in that moment, I decided to trust him. Sometimes, you have to go out on a limb to get what you want.

"Tucker Jones, I'd like to go on a date with you." I stated matter-of-factly.

His expression morphed into a wide grin at my bold proclamation, "Marlie Abernathy, I'd like to go on a date with you. How does tomorrow night sound?"

"It sounds perfect."

EPILOGUE
ONE YEAR LATER

$\mathcal{B}$etty and Jackson's wedding was a lovely evening. The outdoor ceremony was quaint and festive, with friends and family all around. I glanced over at Tucker as he sipped his sweet tea and chatted with John like the old friends they were. Jenny rubbed her baby bump as she leaned on John's arm contentedly. It'd been nice to have a handsome man to call my own tonight.

The last year, really. Tucker and I had taken that first date, and then another, and another. Before long we were so wrapped up in each other that we decided after six months we'd rather not keep living in different towns. So, Tucker packed up and rented the little house right next door to his Great-aunt Celia, only ten minutes from me. Turns out, life's just better with your other half, no matter when or how you find them. His smile still makes me weak-kneed, just like it did on that first day.

The DJ interrupted my musings, "If I could get all of the single ladies to the dance floor for the bouquet toss, Betty is ready to give it away to one lucky lady!"

I snorted, watching several teenagers elbowing each other for prime positions. Jenny grabbed my arm, "You better get out there!"

"Jenny, I don't know if you know this or not, but I'm happily no longer single. Haven't been single a day in the last year," I protested.

"Until there is a ring on that finger, you are still single. Now get!"

She shoved my shoulders. I rolled my eyes at Tucker, but rather than argue with my pregnant sister I made my way to the dance floor.

Betty made a big show of the countdown, but when it was time to toss the bouquet over her shoulder, she spun around and put it straight into my waiting hands.

"Betty! What are you doing? You're supposed to toss it!" I laughed at her antics. When I turned around to show Jenny, I froze in my tracks. Because there, settled in the middle of the dance floor on one knee with a diamond ring in his hand, was Tucker Jones.

"Tucker, what are you doing?" My voice shook with the question.

"Well, you see, I thought it was high time we made this official. So, I wanted to ask you, Marlie, if you'd do me the honor of becoming my wife," he said, and to my utter surprise, I picked up a hint of tension in his jawline.

"Tucker Jones, there is nothing that would make me happier than to be your wife," I said softly.

He surged to his feet, and in one smooth motion drew me into a blistering kiss. His arms held me tight to his chest, and he gently rested his forehead against mine, his grin ear-to-ear. I threaded a hand into his thick hair, and grinned back. *He wants me, forever.*

"It's about time you locked him down, sugar! You ain't getting any younger!" The shout from the crowd startled me, and we broke apart to see old Mrs. Lindy cheering us on.

At that, we both busted out laughing. Some things will never change. But sometimes, life can surprise you in the best possible ways. I looked into Tucker's shining eyes and I couldn't wait to see what surprises life had in store for us.

ABOUT THE AUTHOR

K. A. Gandy was born and raised in Jacksonville, Florida. She is married with two babies of her own. K. A. has worked as a restaurant hostess, library book shelver, ranch hand, tour guide, Realtor, tech whiz, landlord, and small business consultant, all in addition to pursuing her passion of writing. As a person of many interests, her life has never been boring. She likes to write late in the evenings and thinks drinking hot tea and baking great cookies fuels hopes and dreams. If you would like to find more of her works, you can sign up for her newsletter at https://www.subscribepage.com/e0v1b5.

THE MATCHMAKER'S CATCH

FRIEDA J. DOWNING

Three Dates. Two Players. One Hail Mary.

1

FIRST QUARTER

*N*atalie grits her teeth and waves wildly. I hold up my hand, but her gestures grow more frantic.

"We're the perfect solution for your delicate relationship needs, Ms. Danksbury. Our algorithms limit the uncertainty of romance so you know what to expect. Check out our success stories." I turn the laptop toward the photos of happy couples on my wall. Behind the screen, where no one but Natalie can see me, I make emphatic slicing motions. This client is the chance of a lifetime; the last thing we need is for *him* to show up. Natalie narrows her eyes and points at the door. I scribble on a notepad and hold it up. *Stop him at all costs!*

I smooth my face into a friendly, yet professional demeanor and face the laptop. "Consider us your matchmaking concierge here at The First Three Dates. First, we match you to fitting profiles. Second, you choose your favorite three. Third, we do the planning so you can do the dating. Maybe, when you least expect it, something wonderful will happen."

"If you can match another high profile client, then maybe..." The door to our cozy office slams open hard enough to make the frames behind me rattle. Ms. Danksbury flinches. "What was that?"

I wave dismissively as Noah "Stone" MacCallion barges in, his face ominous. "Construction. It's affecting our connection. I'm...losing you..."

I snap my laptop shut just in time. From the thunderous expression on his face, Mr. MacCallion didn't cooperate, again. I hold up my palms in a calming gesture and stand. After all, he has a good eight inches and at least a hundred pounds of muscle on me. I cringe when I see what he's gripping in his white knuckled fist. "Mr. MacCallion, you could at least try."

"Stop sending these empty headed bimbos, Zoe." He throws the racy black negligee in the trash then leans down, braces his hands on my desk, and scowls. His forest green eyes flash while his spicy cologne invades the space between us. "The last one wrapped her undies around my windshield wiper. I only agreed to this thing because I thought you were flirting with me."

I clear my throat and step back, mostly because it's terribly hard to focus in close proximity to him. The quarterback for the Denver Broncos is handsome, elusive, and my golden ticket to a new bracket of clientele. True, I had been perhaps a tiny bit flirtatious, but then our profiles turned out to be the farthest thing possible from a match, and the profiles are never wrong. "Mr. MacCallion, you agreed to give The First Three Dates just that, three dates. Only you've chased away fourteen candidates, without giving them a chance. We even matched you with our most sophisticated profiles."

"Ever think that maybe your profiles are wrong? Still, I'm a man of my word. I signed that contract, so I'll see it through. This time, however, we're playing it my way." He grabs one of the Belgian chocolates from the glass dish on my desk and lobs it toward me. When I lunge to catch it, he gives me an ominous smile. "You want a raving review from me about these dates? You're going on them with me."

With that proclamation, he strides out. I sink into my chair and drop my head in my hands. It should have been so easy. Noah's profile clearly ranked as Tier Gatsby, which means he should relate most to other Gatsbies. While we've had rare cases of clients needing wide exposure before finding matches, we've never sent someone on fourteen non-dates which still resulted in zero actual meet ups. I can't for the life of me figure out what's going wrong.

Natalie sets a steaming cup of Macadamia coffee beside me. "Zoe, maybe he's too much of a wild card. Why don't you choose another high profile client to break into Danksbury's circle?"

I rub my temples. "There's no time to land someone else of Noah's calibre. Ms. Danksbury's annual Cottage Romance Bash is this weekend. Three fun dates is all that's keeping us from a herd of rich, romantically motivated new clients. No, we're stuck with Noah, for better or worse. We already went public with him. We have to figure out what's going wrong with the profiles."

Natalie perches on my desk. "Seems to me what you need to worry about is how you're going to make sure he has a good time on those dates. Best find your inner Gatsby, Zoe Belle. You have champagne glasses to clink. He's probably choosing bottles as we speak."

I glare at her but she laughs and walks away, leaving me to the knots in my stomach.

I have three dates with Noah "Stone" MacCallion, the exact opposite of my dating profile. This is going to be nothing short of an awkward, painful disaster. Never, in the history of ever, has a Tier Gatsby successfully matched with a Tier Indy. No. The only thing left to do is the one thing I swore I'd never do again. I have to become somebody else.

2

SECOND QUARTER

I've already failed. I had planned to be intelligent, poised, and cultured. I'd intended to establish some trust. Yet here I am, one stiletto on, one off, my arms twisted behind me. My head is tethered at an awkward tilt as I try to extract my hair from my zipper. How can a professional quarterback entrust his love life to a woman who can't manage her own zipper? The doorbell rings, so I thrust those thoughts away and hobble like Quasimodo to the door. At the last second, I remember to smile. "Good evening, Mr..."

Denver's most eligible and enigmatic bachelor stands on my doorstep, clad in jeans, chaps, and a Carhartt coat. Every thought in my head melts at the sight of him. Snow drifts down, dusting his cowboy hat and broad shoulders. He touches the brim of his hat in a charming, surprisingly old fashioned gesture. For a Gatsby, he's looking terribly rugged. In fact, he's looking way too much like what an Indy like me would want. Once again I vow to have my IT guy go back over the software.

"Seems I may be a tad overdressed." I smooth my hands down my blue cocktail dress. The long sleeves sit slightly off my shoulders. From there, the bodice cuts to a vee that bares just enough cleavage. Simple yet elegant, or at least that's what the salesperson said.

Noah's mouth opens and closes twice and a single red rose dangles forgotten in his right hand. He gives his head a bit of a shake and clears his throat. "You, ah, definitely might get a bit chilly. I have a surprise. Do you ski? Natalie said you ski. She said you have boots and everything."

"You asked Natalie about me?" I would tilt my head, but it's already there. "I practically skied before I walked, but the nearest ski slopes are a bit far away, don't you think?"

Mischief lights up his face. "Who said anything about slopes? You gonna change?"

"Please, step inside." From his profile, skiing should be one of the last dates he'd have planned for tonight. A quiet dinner at an upscale restaurant where we would see and be seen should be more his style. Still, I move away from the door and automatically turn my head, or try to. I wince when it feels like a chunk of hair rips out of my scalp. Noah frowns, so I grit out a confession. "I caught my hair in my zipper when I tried to zip my dress while putting on my shoe. I can't straighten my head."

"Multitasking. Not for the faint of heart." His smile warms about a hundred degrees. "Want help?"

I lift my chin the tiny bit I can without creating a new bald spot. "I have the situation completely under control."

He cocks an eyebrow. A swath of hair floats down in front of my nose as if to mock me. I huff it away and unceremoniously present my back to him. "Fine, but I still have it under control."

"I would never think otherwise." His fingers brush my spine as he works my hair free with gentle tugs. For a huge guy who makes big bucks throwing a deformed ball around and slamming into other full grown men, his touch is surprisingly soft and deft. Not that I can really focus with that danged cologne of his wrapping around me and fogging my brain. His rich burgundy voice breaks through. "...since we're supposed to be dating and all."

I snap back to attention as he eases my zipper into place, hair blissfully free of the teeth. "Sorry, Mr. MacCallion, what?"

His fingertips brush my hair away from my collarbone as I face him. He gives me a soft, almost confused smile. "For these three dates, please call me Noah."

I hobble back a step. "Mr. MacCallion, I have a strict 'no dating the clientele rule.' This is a very rare exception. If you don't mind, I'll stick with surnames so we can both remember how temporary this is."

He opens his mouth and frowns, but then smooths his expression. "Anything you'd like, Miss Zoe Belle, along with a warm pair of ski pants, if you please."

I shift my weight up on my stiletto then down on my bare foot as I try to figure out why him addressing me by my full name has me blushing. When no quick answer presents itself, I blurt the first thing that comes to mind. "First you zip my dress then you request snow gear. Funny, I'd heard your goal was to get a woman out of her clothes as quickly as possible."

I'd meant it as a joke, but a dark cloud crosses his face and his smile fades. "Fourteen of your clients will tell you exactly how false that rumor is."

I bite my lip. "I'm sorry. That was rude. I'm nervous. It was a stupid thing to say. Honestly, I've never had a guy ask me to put more clothes on. Maybe I'm losing my touch."

His cognac eyes turn warm and mesmerizing. "Maybe they were all the wrong guys."

I'm not really sure how to take that, so I ham up my retreat to my room with some over the top hip swing added to my hobble. Thankfully, from the sounds of his chuckles, I'm forgiven. Not exactly professional, but at least we're back on friendly footing.

THE SNOW IS FALLING a bit heavier by the time we get to Mile High Stadium, adding to the two feet of snow already blanketing the city. Since the football season ended, the stadium is a ghost town. We park right up front and walk through the gates. The stadium lights illuminate the field. Half a dozen men and a one horse stand around a snowy obstacle course. I count four low jumps, two gates, and even a ring dangling at one end. "What on earth is this?"

Pride sparkles in Noah's eyes. "This, Miss Belle, is skijøring. A certain receptionist birdie told me it's on your bucket list."

My words come out embarrassingly breathy. "I've always wanted to try this. I didn't know the stadium offered skijøring."

He shakes his head. "It doesn't. Tonight's a special night. Besides, a few guys owed me favors."

He introduces me to the men, most of them names I recognize from the Broncos' roster. The final is an older gentleman, the wrinkles in his face deep and plentiful but stamped with humor. His torso has a minor, but distinct sideways bend in it. When he takes my hand and bows over it, though he hides it well, I get the feeling it causes him pain. "Ma'am. Hope this ugly bucket of oats is remembering his manners."

A gust of wind knocks his hat off his head. Before he has the chance to bend down farther, I retrieve it, dust off the snow, and return it to him. "Oooo, if I say he isn't, will he be in trouble? Pleased to meet you, Mr..."

He straightens as much as he's able and accepts his hat with a warm smile. "MacCallion. Henry P. MacCallion, at your service."

Noah grins. "My pop. Best bronc rider on the Front Range."

The elder MacCallion claps his son on the shoulder. "Used to be, back in the day. Enough of that. What do you say, Miss Belle? Shall we see if Noah here can manage to stay on Lothario long enough to give you a fun go of it?"

I glance carefully between Noah and the dark horse. It's not that it's acting aggressive. In fact, he seems rather bored. No, the part that makes me nervous is I've seen Noah on the football field. His aggression combined with that powerful animal doesn't strike me as a beginner experience waiting to happen. "I haven't spent much time around horses."

Noah walks me over. "Lothario's a Colorado Ranger, one of the best ranch and trail horses. His previous owner couldn't handle his spirit so the guy left him in a stable. By the time I found out, Lothario's hooves hadn't been cared for in a year. It was so painful for him to walk he wouldn't even get up for food or water."

I try to picture the magnificent creature in that state. "Why didn't the owner find him another home?"

Noah shrugs. "To prove he was alpha, I guess. Now he can feel like a big man in his tiny cell for the next five years."

He gives a musical whistle and Lothario turns, then bows. "Lothario's a pussycat. Besides, if you don't like the speed or skijøring in general, let go of the rope. You have all the control literally in your hands."

Noah nudges me with his hip and I come face to face with the behemoth. We stare, eye to eye, and while I'm waiting for him to either eat me or whip around and sit on me to establish dominance, he head butts my belly with a gentle shove. It sends me back a few steps, which he covers with a few lazy ambles. As soon as he does, he starts rubbing his head on my side and hip like a giant cat. A laugh burbles out of me. "What on earth is he doing?"

Noah plops a helmet on my head, hands me a rope, and swings into the saddle. "Telling you he likes you. Now if you're ready, remember. You're the quarterback. You call the plays."

I shoot him a dubious grin. "Do you give that pep talk to all your dates? If so, I think I may know what happened with those fourteen matches."

He chuckles, and the full magnetic force of the infamous "Stone" MacCallion hits me. The sight of him on Lothario, head tilted, that smile promising all kinds of forbidden fun nearly buckles my knees. To break the spell, I pop on my skis and grip the rope for dear life. I just manage to shout, "This is insane," when Noah gives the horse a gentle nudge.

Instead of the rocket launch I expected, we start at a walk, an easy cruise for me on the flat snow of the field. My grin widens as the breeze teases the hair around my neck and face. I appreciate Noah's careful approach, but this isn't going to cut it. I raise my voice and call out, "You and Lothario fall asleep?"

Noah winks, gives Lothario another nudge, and they break into a peppy trot. Our speed increases, along with my adrenaline, so I yell again. "That all you got?"

Noah checks over his shoulder. When I wave him on, he gets a feisty glint in his eye, gives a whistle, and we pick up speed. This time, I weave in and out of the gates, then over a few slopes, even catching a tiny bit of air. Noah checks my progress, I nod, and we really pick up speed. The wind whips past me, my skis shush through the snow, and my belly jumps with every slope and curve of the course. The next time Noah glances back, I point at the ring. He nods, hunches down a bit, and gives Lothario a final, speed boosting nudge. I tuck a bit lower and get ready to push off the jump in order to reach the ring. Right at the lip of the miniature jump, however, my helmet slips down over my forehead. In the split second I try to shove it back with my upper arm, the lip of the jump comes and goes, and I find myself flat on my stomach, skis popped off somewhere, completely spreadeagle with my face in the snow.

I feel hands on my shoulders. I'm still spitting snow out of my mouth when Noah asks me if I'm okay. I'd tell him I'm fine except I've already laughed so hard I have no air left in my lungs, so basically I'm quivering and jerking with silent glee. He must think I'm having a seizure because he yells for someone to call an ambulance. I manage to roll to a sitting position where I remove my helmet, toss it in the air, and yell, "Unfreakingbelievable!"

Noah slouches down beside me. "You scared me. I may not be the relationship pro, but even I know you're not supposed to break your date."

I giggle. "I'm a matchmaker, not a relationship pro. Big difference. Also, nothing's broken. I'm fine."

He tilts his head and his forehead creases up a bit. "I'll never get used to that."

I dig some snow out of my coat then unzip it to really shake it out. "Get used to what?"

I'm not looking at him but I still hear the funny catch in his voice. "Your laugh. It does something funny to me every time. It's not terrible."

I freeze up for a minute then carefully go back to shaking out my coat. "Just wait until we find you a real match. I think you'll find that's not too terrible, too."

Out of the corner of my eye I can see his gaze drop. "You didn't have fun tonight?"

I close my eyes and exhale softly. I shouldn't encourage him, but I don't want him utterly defeated, either. "Even with that epic faceplant, this is quite possibly my favorite date ever. Still, let's remember this isn't about us."

He brushes some snow off my scarf. "What is it about, exactly?"

I fidget with my gloves. "It's about helping you find a legitimate match. You and your agent both expressed the desire for someone outside of the professional football circle with whom you could relax and unwind, someone well suited to you. I intend to help you find someone."

He glances off into the empty stands. "What's in it for you?"

"Well..." I stand to dust off my snow pants. "There's a potential client who's holding a party day after tomorrow, sort of a Who's Who of Denver. If I succeed in helping you, Ms. Danksbury has invited me to profile the entire party. Apparently she wants to turn matchmaking into a party favor."

"That could mean new clients for you." He stands and stuffs his hands in his pockets. I notice his face has grown flushed with the cold. "I'll still put my money on people hanging out over computer profiles any day."

I give him a playful nudge with my elbow. "You stacked the odds in your favor tonight. You pumped my coworker for info."

He tries to hide a smug grin. "I'm a quarterback. I orchestrate plays for a living."

I hold my hands out by my sides. "Bingo. Call me the digital quarterback of the dating world."

Right about then I notice lots of people have arrived at the stadium, and many of them have their cell phones out and pointed at us. My stomach clenches. Spotlights aren't my thing. "Looks like we best say cheese."

Noah steps closer, puts his hands on my lower back, and pulls me to him. "I have a better idea."

His lips melt over mine, soft and tentative. They hesitate there for a moment before they brush back and forth one time, then settle back in to blanket mine once again. Rich warmth winds its way from my lips all the way to my curled up toes in my ski boots. He pulls away a fraction and stares at me for what feels like an hour. Then he steps back, takes my hand, and holds it up like we just won something, all the while still holding my gaze. People all around us cheer. Me? I'm trying to remember how to breathe.

Noah "Stone" MacCallion just kissed me, the untouchable bachelor with a rock hard heart. He kissed me, in front of tons of people.

I let go of his hand. He did it for the people, the quarterback giving them a show. I need to stay focused. If these next two dates aren't complete disasters, he's free of his contract and maybe I'll get Ms. Danksbury's party invite.

My focus drifts back to his lips. I remind myself the numbers don't lie. People can sort of change for a while, but over time, the truth will out. Noah and I are no match, nor will we ever be. Still, a quiet part of me, one I haven't listened to in a long time, whispers that maybe, just maybe, this time it could be different.

I shove it away. The numbers are always right. To expect anything different is foolhardy. I'll never make that mistake again.

THIRD QUARTER

By the time I get home and changed into my fluffiest pjs, social media is buzzing about our kiss. While part of me wants to believe the coverage could bring new clients, another part wants to hide. I've never been the focus of such public scrutiny, and not all of the comments are kind. Not only that, but how is Ms. Danksbury going to see this, as success or cheating on my part? No sooner do I think it than my cell phone vibrates. Speak of the diva. "Ms. Danksbury, if you'll let me explain..."

Her ear piercing squeal deafens me momentarily. I pull the phone away. By the time I get it back to my other ear, all I catch is, "...will be the biggest fête of the decade!"

Then she's gone. I guess she's not too concerned with company policy. With that off my mind, I grab some blueberry pie yogurt and settle in to pretend I'm watching The Princess Bride.

Memories of Noah at his first thirteen introductions parade through my mind. I was there for every match, except the last. Thirteen beautiful, sophisticated women vied for his attention. Why did he never show that romantic side of himself to a prospective match? The man could have dated any woman in this city, yet he seemed to delight in driving them away within the first five minutes. The biggest question of all, though, the one that keeps filling my mind every time Wesley says, "as you wish," is this: how did my emotions for a guy completely not my type get this tangled up after one fake date?

I leave Wesley and Buttercup to their Happily Ever After and turn in. Tomorrow will be a full day at the office, I'm sure, with all the calls that are likely going to come from the posts. If we can convert some of those to clients, we could really maximize this momentum. Then, after that, Noah and I have date number two. The thought of it sends nervous tingles through me. I tell myself it's anticipation for the activity. I mean, if Natalie told him about my skijøring wish, what else did she tell him? I fall asleep promising myself that's all it is.

～

THIS TIME, when Noah comes to the door, I'm dressed in my favorite jeans, a dressy-ish emerald blouse, and versatile black boots. I feel ready for anything. With full confidence I swing the door open, only to find Noah in a perfectly tailored three piece suit. I consider slamming the door on him. "You're doing this on purpose."

His grin is unapologetic. "Why yes. Yes, I am."

Once again, he steps inside to wait while I head to my room. I grab the first dress I come to, the off the shoulder blue number I first wore last night. This time, however, I'm careful to move my hair and slide the zipper without issues. I pull on some black platform peep toes, take a calming breath, and start down the hall as if none of the last few minutes happened.

He's made himself comfortable on my couch, but, when he sees me, he shoots to his feet and smooths his jacket like a nervous teenager headed to prom. I lower my chin, add some flirt to my smile, and put a tiny bit of sultry in my sway, because making one of the male species nervous never gets old.

His eyes take in my outfit and, when they meet my gaze again, I'm pretty sure the heat in them is enough to melt the snow outside. "We have...you look...you're really... food."

The surge of pure feminine power I feel is heady. My smile grows teasing. "You forgot to include cannibal on your profile, Mr. MacCallion. I'm afraid that changes things."

His eyes grow cartoonishly wide and he shakes his head. "No. I'm not...beautiful. I mean, you're beautiful, and I'm not French. Of course I'm not French. What I mean is we have food. Do you like reservations? Natalie said..."

I open the door and this time it's me who offers my arm to him. "Easy, Smooth Talker. I do, indeed, enjoy food. Shall we go so we don't miss those reservations?"

I'm all grins as we hit the front walk, right up until the last person I thought I'd see tonight steps in front of us. All the joy and warmth drains right out of me, leaving a dull nausea in its wake. "Hunter. What are you doing here?"

My ex boyfriend puffs out his chest under his fake leather jacket. "This is how you treat me, after everything I've done for you?"

I try to step around him and drag Noah with me. Noah, however, doesn't budge an inch. "I don't have time for this. I have other plans. Good night."

Hunter puts a hand on my arm and I feel Noah stiffen. "Babe, you know how my ex hurt me. That's why I need to know where you are and who you're with, so I can protect you, so I can protect us."

I shake off his hand. "There is no us. My life is no longer your business. You're a manipulator and you need help, but not from me."

Hunter steps closer so he can stare down at me. He grips my arm to that point right before pain. "You don't know what you're saying, babe. Have you forgotten how much I love you? If I was ever a little harsh, it was only because you made me that way. I mean, you're hardly perfect, we both know that. Can't you give me a second chance? I can change."

Noah puts his hand on Hunter's shoulder and squeezes. From the way Hunter flinches and releases me, I'd say Noah's thumb choked off an important nerve bundle or something. "The lady told you to leave, *Hunter*. I suggest you do so, while you can, in one piece."

I lay my hand on Noah's arm. He glances down at me. In that moment, the anger in his tight expression seems to give way to something softer, something like concern. I square my shoulders and face my ex. "I did give you a second chance, and a third, and way too many after that. Somewhere in there I realized I wasn't the problem. Things were never going to change, because, despite what you say, you're not going to change."

Hunter jerks away from Noah. He grabs me by both shoulders and shakes me so hard my head hurts. "You owe me."

I stomp his instep with the heel of my stiletto. As he doubles over, I shove him away. "That's all I owe you. Don't you ever touch me again."

It's a foolhardy move, given that Hunter, although not as big as Noah, is still bigger and stronger than me. The feeling of finally standing up for myself, though, is worth it.

Noah steps forward, a menacing sneer twisting his full lips. "I, for one, would hate for you to feel cheated. Why don't you let me pay up, as well?"

Hunter scrambles back, mutters some whiney threats, and disappears into the night. I close my eyes as if it'll stop the shaking. When Noah's hand wraps around mine, I still don't open my eyes. "He's why I rely on profiles so much. Men like that can make you doubt what you're thinking, even doubt your own name. Data, though, data you can trust."

I take a steadying breath, square my shoulders, and lift my chin. "Someone promised me food."

Heroes Wear Crepes, a tiny bistro in the eclectic part of town, is toasty warm and smells like edible joy. People pack around tiny tables, smiling and chatting away. I've got to admit, after the run-in with Hunter and the awkward, mostly silent drive over, the atmosphere is sort of grating. Still, despite the dull headache still in the back of my head, I paste on a smile. A stout elderly woman in a jaunty chef's hat lights up when she sees us. She claps her hands. "Noah! *Vite, vite!* We need all hands on deck, *mon trésor.*"

"*Oui,* Chef Baudelaire." Noah puts his arm around my waist and wiggles his eyebrows. "Surprise. How do you feel about playing master chef for the evening?"

I glance between him and the kitchen where the chef disappeared. "No way. Bad things happen when I go in kitchens."

He tugs me through the door. "Nice try, but Natalie told me you're an amazing cook."

I pull back a bit. "There's something you should know about Natalie's sense of humor..."

It's too late. Within seconds, someone is strapping me into an apron while someone else is tucking my hair into a hair net. I'm not talking some cute jaunty hat. Nope, I'm talking lunch lady black mesh, on my second date with the most handsome man I've ever met.

Chef Baudelaire trundles up to me, hands me a miniature rake without spikes, and gestures to a round hot plate about the size of a vinyl record. After a string of potentially French and English words, she's gone again. I face Noah with my mini rake. "We should leave...now."

Instead of listening, he squirts a pale mixture from a tube onto my hot plate. "First, crepes. Go ahead; swirl the batter. Show us the legend behind the cuisine."

He demonstrates with gusto. Since my batter is rapidly cooking into a misshapen blob, I half-heartedly start to spin the tool like Noah, but I drop it. Using the edge of my apron, I pull it out of the batter. "I really think we should let the pros handle this."

"Nonsense." Noah, with his perfectly emerging crepe, glances over with a confused frown. Ever so helpful, he scrapes my mess into the trash and squirts another blob of batter on the hot plate for me. "Here you go...fresh start."

I bulldoze the batter back and forth with the stupid tool and feel my throat tighten. "What is it with men and their unwillingness to listen?"

Noah's frown deepens. "Natalie said you adore cooking."

I bulldoze so hard the half cooked crepe slides right off the hotplate. "I guess Natalie thought it would be funny, only I'm not in the mood for practical jokes."

"Forget about Hunter, Zoe." Noah comes toward me with that tube of batter again, faking from side to side like he's holding his danged football. "Get ready to drive that batter, Belle. Blue 42, hut!"

Several snickers draw my attention to the people around us. Three people have their cell phones up, filming. I duck my chin and blink rapidly at the prickling in the backs of my eyes. I don't like attention when I'm at my best; I definitely don't need it when I'm at my worst.

Noah aims for my hotplate again, but I push his arm away. Batter sprays the floor. I jerk the hair net off my head and throw it in the trash.

"Hunter gaslighted me for years. He ignored my wants and tried to coerce me into submitting to the roles he chose for me. He especially had a hang up about me cooking. I will never be a chef. Can we just stop trying to be something we're not?"

Noah sets the batter on the table and reaches for my hand. I pull away. "Zoe, I'm not trying to force you to do anything. I also need to tell you something."

"I'm not really in the mood to hear it." I start wrestling with the knot in my apron, but it doesn't budge.

Noah steps closer. "I lied to you, on my profile. I filled it out the way I thought would score me a date with you. In the interview you were so professional and confident. I figured you'd want to go out with a sophisticated man way more than a ranch hand."

I spin and face him. From the slight step back he takes, the storm of emotions inside has made it to my face. "What is with you manipulators? What makes you think you have the right to decide anything for me? Lying to get what you want isn't okay. My thoughts and feelings matter, just as much yours."

Noah holds his palms up. "I didn't mean it like that. I mean, you presented yourself as sort of an untouchable perfectionist at the first thirteen meet ups. That was you pretending, wasn't it?"

I grab the tube of batter and gesture with it. "It's called being professional. People do that in their careers. If you'd been honest on your profile, we wouldn't be here and I could've already had that invitation."

He takes another step back, but I close the distance. "Exactly. I might not have gotten to see you again."

"That was my choice to make." I wave the tube back and forth. "Why do you even care?"

He wipes his palms down his apron. "You were like this beautiful quarterback there on your dating field. Dating is foreign territory for me, so I was fascinated. I felt I had to find a way around your no fraternizing policy."

When I swing my arms, a thin stream of batter arcs through the air and splatters the three people and their phones. I don't even care. "What are you, then, for real? What kind of man?"

He glances left and right then lowers his voice. "Can we maybe talk about this in private?"

Now he cares about privacy? I hold the batter tube at my mouth like a microphone. "Oh, don't be shy, 'Stone' MacCallion. Give the people what they want!"

He leans in closer. "Will you stop? After all, you only took interest in me as your golden goose to get to Ms. Danksbury's crowd, remember?"

The hurt in his face is unmistakable, but rather than deal with his pain on top of mine, I embrace my anger. "Maybe I did see you as a bit of a catch, but I also actually care about my clients. I care about you. I got into this business because, idiot me, I believed I could help people avoid a bit of awkwardness, a bit of heartache, and a bit of humiliation so they could have a better shot at being happy than I'd had."

A look of wonder spreads across his face. "You care about me?"

Holy crepes, I do. Not only that, I just shouted it at the top of my lungs in a kitchen full of people videoing every word. The humiliation of it all comes crushing down on me, and all I want to do is escape. "Out of everything I just said, you had to catch that. Alright, Mr. Football Star. You catch footballs. You catch humiliating confessions. Let's see if you can catch this."

With that, I aim and fire. Crepe batter sprays him from head to foot. He doesn't even try to dodge. When the tube is empty, I drop it on the table and lift my nose in the air. "Mr. MacCallion, consider yourself released from your contract."

I take a step, intending to march myself right out and find a taxi, but my stiletto lands in a puddle of batter and shoots out from under me. I see my peep toes midair before strong arms catch me. Noah's face, covered in batter, hovers above mine. "Are you alright?"

I glare at him. "Why do all our dates end with that question?"

I shove away from him, then slip and slide my way over to Chef Baudelaire. I pull my emergency twenty from my cleavage and hand it to her. "For the apron, since I can't seem to unknot it. I apologize for the mess. If you'll send me a bill, I'll gladly pay for the cleaning."

The stout woman kisses me on both cheeks. "Oh, *l'amour.*"

I manage to find a taxi quickly, even with, or maybe because of, a dripping, battered Noah hovering nearby. I also manage not to cry the whole way home. Once I close the front door, well, that's another story.

4

———

FOURTH QUARTER: HAIL MARY

*M*s. Danksbury's house looks like an elegant cottage from the English countryside. Stone walls and cobblestone courtyards all whisper old money. Inside, polished mahogany, dripping chandeliers, and ornate flooring exude near nobility. In the middle of the crushing soiree, I've never felt so alone and out of place in my life. I find a corner near a massive carved fireplace in the Great Hall to hide and wait for the inevitable confrontation with Ms. Danksbury. After all, there's no way she missed the clips of my horrific behavior last night. A batter dipped "Stone" MacCallion meme has already gone viral. Mr. Privacy is gonna love that.

Still, Ms. Danksbury texted to remind me of her annual Cottage Romance Bash, so here I am. A professional faces her mistakes, then goes home to lick her wounds. Maybe I can become a ski instructor. It'll be a whopper of a pay cut, but I could use the time outside, in the snow and crisp air. Heck. Maybe I could even bring skijøring to one of the resorts.

I fuss with the skirt of my wine colored dress. The tea length cut is modest but form fitting, and the draped bodice lends it a casual, approachable air. Understated, yet elegant, at least that's what I'm hoping.

The moment finally arrives. Ms. Danksbury winds through the

crush of people. Yet right as she calls out a, "Huhlooo, darling," the imposing front doors swing open.

Noah MacCallion wears a tux like no other man on earth. His muscular physique fills it out perfectly, and he moves with confidence forged by countless battles on the football field. He also walks with the assurance of a man who knows how to handle a horse, who's not afraid to stop abuse, and who treats his aging father with respect and love. He's a man who gets back on his feet after a three hundred pound lineman knocks him down, yet who can detangle hair from a zipper, strand by strand if necessary, so as not to inflict pain. He's the most amazing man I've ever met. If I were in a different place in my life, maybe I could apologize for losing my mind. Maybe he'd give me a second chance. After seeing the memes, though, I know better. I publicly humiliated him, and he's here to confront me about it. I don't blame him a bit.

He stops about three feet away from me. Without breaking eye contact, Noah lifts his voice and addresses the crowd. "As you know, I signed on with The First Three Dates to see if they could help me find a companion, someone I could relax with, who would like me not just as 'Stone' MacCallion, but as Noah. I've only had two of my three dates, but I felt it's time to give you my review."

I straighten my spine, lift my chin, and nod. I dished it out; I can take it. A ghost of a smile flits across Noah's lips. "I got off to a rocky start. You see, I lied on the profile because I noticed this woman, this beautiful matchmaker. She was mesmerizing. I was afraid if I showed her the real me, the boy who grew up mucking out stalls and plowing fields, she wouldn't be interested."

I drop my head for a moment, unsure what to say. He didn't need to admit to any of that. I take a breath and meet his gaze again. "Noah…"

His eyes blaze with an emotion I'm too unsure to name. "You just called me by my first name."

I feel a frown tug at my forehead. I feel like asking, "So what," but he's already addressing the crowd again. "I'm old school. I believe you can't know what's in a person until you see them in a tough spot."

My hands start shaking so I grip them in front of me. I'm not sure where he's going with this or why, but I very much wish it were over so I can start packing. Surely there are ski schools in Alaska.

When he turns back toward me, his eyes seem glassy. "In the space of two dates, I've seen Zoe tangled up, yet she still maintained her composure. I've seen her fall flat on her face, yet rise to laugh it off. She's been threatened and cornered, yet stood her ground. You want to know if my two dates were a success? I'd say so; after all, I fell in love."

I suck in a sharp breath. "Noah, that's impossible. Love doesn't happen like that. You can't have feelings for me, and I don't have feelings for you."

It's a complete and utter lie, and, from the looks of his tender smile, he knows it. "That's the second time you called me Noah, Zoe, and you told me last night you care. Still, maybe I don't love you. You say I don't have feelings for you, but I definitely have something. The way I see it, since you're the pro, it's your job to help me figure out what it is."

He gives a musical whistle and in walks Lothario, wearing a giant bow tie. He ambles over to me and bows. When he stands back up, he nudges my hand with his soft lips and drops an odd bouquet into it. It's a bit wet and gooey, but charming all the same. "Thank you, Lothrario. You look very dapper."

Noah withdraws something from Lothario's saddlebag. "I drove fourteen potential matches away, yet you were always gracious. Not only that, you convinced me I could find someone who would enjoy spending time with me, the real me."

I glance down at the bouquet. Instead of flowers, rolled up pieces of paper fill my hand, our company's logo clearly visible on each. "Noah, what is this?"

He shrugs. "Profiles. Blank ones. I thought we could start over and fill them out together. I'm sorry I lied. I'm sorry I tried to fool you into liking me. I'm asking for a do over. Most people take a lifetime to live as genuinely as you do, if they ever manage it. I don't want to miss a single moment with you."

A wonderful, rich feeling blossoms low in my belly. "I don't date the clientele."

He steps closer to me. "Then it's a good thing you freed me from my contract last night."

I ignore the giggles around us. He holds out his palm to me. Cradled in it is the miniature rake from Heroes Wear Crepes. He drops to one knee, right in front of everyone. "Miss Zoe Belle, will you do me the honor of giving me three more dates, not as your client, but as the man who can't possibly be in love with you?"

I stare down at the tool in his strong hand and choke back a wave of emotions. The most private man in Denver just proclaimed his not love for me in front of every hotshot in the city. Before I can gather myself enough to answer, Noah shoots to his feet. "No pressure, Zoe. What you feel, what you want, that matters completely. That's why I'm giving you this. We'll call it the Scepter of Dating. If at any point you don't like the way it's going, we can fix it, or you can simply let go. All the control is, quite literally, in your hands."

He places it in my hand then moves his hands to cradle my face. "You've upended my life, Zoe Belle, and I never want it to stop. I can't say I regret lying on my profile, because it gave me fourteen chances to be near you. I do regret abusing your trust, but I swear to guard it from here on out, as long as you'll let me."

I lift my chin and give him my best school teacher expression. "Mr. MacCallion, a word of advice? When you have a woman in the palms of your hands, sometimes you should just shut up and kiss her."

His eyelids lower as he closes the distance between us. "You're the pro."

5

———

OVERTIME

"Noah." I sling my arm and give his chest a sleepy smack. He grunts, but keeps snoozing.

"Noah, it's your turn." I dangle one foot out from under the covers for a minute, then slide my chilled skin up the inside of his calf. When he jumps, I nudge him again. "Henry's hungry."

Noah burrows into my shoulder. "My pop can feed himself."

I tousle his hair. "Your infant son can't, though, and this is my shift to sleep."

That actually boosts him into a wobbly, yet upright position. "Daddy to the rescue."

After he runs into the closed door, Noah staggers into the hallway. I follow to make sure he doesn't grab Henry a bottle of soda instead of milk. Noah emerges from the fridge with the correct beverage and sets it in the bottle warmer. He gives me a more alert grin. "I got this. Go sleep. I'm gonna teach Henry all my dating secrets."

I groan. "Don't you dare. Someday I want grandchildren."

He blows me a kiss and silently commands me back to bed. I happily oblige, but only after tossing an "Aye, aye, Cap'n Crepes" over my shoulder. Some things will never get old.

ABOUT THE AUTHOR

Frieda J. Downing lives in the mountains of Colorado with her husband, three kids, four pets, and a family of bears down in the canyon. She loves to mountain bike, loses her coffee cup daily, and never has the laundry caught up. She also writes light hearted romantic adventures because life is surprising, love is complicated, and romance can be terribly funny.

www.friedajdowning.com

FIREFLIES AND WHISKEY

RANDILEIGH KENNEDY

Saying 'yes' could change everything...

1

─────────

$\mathcal{M}$y entire life was on fire – literally. I sat under the streetlight on the hood of my rusted-out Honda, staring across the road as orange and yellow flames swallowed up everything I owned.

I managed to save one box of books, but they weren't even mine. There was also Walter, the black and white cat purring in my lap at the moment...but technically he was just the neighborhood stray.

"That's a shame, isn't it?" The deep voice startled me. I turned to see a man with piercing hazel eyes, thick dark messy hair, and a dangerous amount of stubble around his jawline.

"Yeah, it's terrible." I shook my head. "I think I'm still in shock."

"Me too. They had the best margaritas." He shoved his hands into the pockets of his jeans, preparing to walk away.

"I'm sorry?"

"Los Aces," he clarified, gesturing at the charred taco stand next to my apartment.

"Oh, right. The restaurant. I was referring to my *home*."

"You live here? Oh, wow, I'm so sorry. I heard everyone got out okay. I didn't think anyone would still be lingering around, watching the rest of this. Where's your jacket? It's freezing out here." He took off his soft gray coat, resting it around my shoulders.

331

"I'm from Arizona. I've only been in Michigan for forty-eight hours, so I haven't yet adjusted to your winter climate."

"It gets worse. Wait until February."

He smiled, trying to keep the conversation light, but my emotions were all over the place. I came to Grand Harbor for a fresh start. Instead, this felt like a bad ending.

"I'm heading over to the motel now, but thanks for the warmup." I began pulling the coat off my shoulders, but he stopped me.

"No, keep it. I'm in a bit of a rush, I have to go check on someone. I'll get it back from you later."

"I really appreciate that, thanks. I'm Brooke by the way."

"Johnny Knight. Sorry this isn't the 'Welcome to Grand Harbor' you were expecting...but that means things can only get better from here, right?"

Like meeting an insanely handsome stranger on the same night I become both homeless and poor...

"I hope that's true," I agreed, pulling the gray fabric tighter around me. "You're sure about the coat?"

"I'm not worried about it. I'll find you later."

"What if I'm not at the motel anymore? If I find another place to stay..."

"Grand Harbor's not that big. I'll find you, I promise. It was nice meeting you, Brooke."

I smiled and offered a slight wave and within seconds he was gone. I tucked my hands into the coat pockets to warm up my fingers.

Was that his...*wallet*?

I pulled out a black leather bifold, feeling guilty for opening it. The picture inside matched – light hazel eyes, perfect smile...but something was wrong.

The ID didn't say *Johnny Knight* at all.

It was another name entirely.

2

———

I was being smothered.

I flailed my arms around, woken up by the disorienting feeling of a cat sleeping on my face. Walter spooked and jumped onto the floor, leaving me with remnants of fur in my mouth.

It wasn't the fresh morning start I'd hoped for, but as he purred and rubbed his body against my legs as I brushed my teeth, my mood softened.

I did the walk of shame in last night's clothing down to the front office of the motel, again cursing myself for not grabbing anything practical as soon as the smoke alarm sounded.

"Hi, I'm Brooke Taylor," I said, stepping up to the front desk. "I checked in last night after the fire, but I was still in shock. Is there anything else you need from me? A signature or something?"

"Oh, yes. Gina told me about the fire last night, I can't believe it. Los Aces had the *best* margaritas."

"That's what I've been told," I muttered, still slightly annoyed that everyone seemed to be grieving these margaritas when, oh, I don't know – everything I *owned* was turned into dust. I had an unwavering pit in my stomach just thinking about it.

"I don't need a signature, but I do have a message for you." The fifty-something-year-old bubbly brunette turned her back to me for a moment, grabbing a piece of paper and a bag off the back counter. "Here you go. Some cat food? And a note. It's from Johnny Knight." She was blushing as she said his name.

"You know him?"

"Of course, everyone in Grand Harbor does." Her face was still too smiley for my liking. It made me uncomfortable, like she had old stories about him I would never be privy to – even though she looked to be twice his age.

I wanted to ask her a few questions...did she know he had a different name? She clearly called him *Johnny* just now. If *everyone* knew him, why wasn't anyone calling him *Cade Daniels* – the name on his ID? Or was I mistaken about all of this? Was the ID fake? Oh no... did that mean he was some kind of *criminal*? The questions in my head were spiraling out of control.

I grabbed the items and thanked her, reading the note as soon as I'd returned to my room.

Pancakes at midnight? I'll come grab you at 11:55pm – same time we met last night. ~ Johnny

I stared back at the message, trying to decipher if this guy was charming...or absolutely crazy.

3

————

*H*ot water cascaded down my skin. I hoped a long shower would absolve me from the trauma of last night, but the small motel toiletries were doing little to cleanse my nerves. I had so many things to buy...but a very limited budget. I wanted to crawl back under the covers at the overwhelming thought of it all.

My eye caught Johnny's note, still sitting on the nightstand. There was a phone number at the bottom.

I stared at the handwriting, overthinking *everything* – which was a specialty of mine. It seemed innocent enough. Pancakes weren't exactly a threatening suggestion. But there was something about his phrasing... First off, what was all this midnight nonsense? Isn't that when *normal* people slept? Sure, I was only twenty-four. I *could* stay up that late if I tried. However, I was entering a period in my life when I didn't *want* to anymore. I was in bed by ten most nights.

I analyzed the signature at the bottom. It clearly said *Johnny*. There was no mistake about that. But upon checking his ID again for the umpteenth time, it still didn't match. Johnny wasn't even his middle name.

He said he was going to 'come grab me' later – where, at the motel? He wouldn't know which room I was in.

Scrap that, the woman at the front desk looked so smitten, I bet she'd already told him exactly which room was mine. The bigger issue was agreeing to go out with a complete stranger...in the *middle of the night*. I watched a lot of Dateline episodes with my grandma back in Phoenix and that was a red flag for sure. Strangers at midnight never had good intentions. *Ever.*

It was settled. I would have to call and tell him I couldn't make it. That was the only sensible thing to do. After all the rogue decisions I'd made lately – breaking up with Chris, breaking my apartment lease in Phoenix, breaking my car's heater while driving across the country on an emotional whim... Yes, there were too many broken things already. The last thing I needed was for some small-town handsome stranger to break *me*.

I dialed the number without hesitating any longer. His smooth deep voice responded on the second ring.

"Hey Brooke, you okay?"

"H..uh, how did you know it was me?" A knot formed in my throat. He really *was* a crazy person.

"The Arizona area code..."

I immediately felt embarrassed. "Right, of course. Well, yeah, I'm doing okay. You know, other than the fire. I was going to spend the day unpacking more boxes, but, now... Anyway, the cat food...and I got your note. Thanks, but I can't do that. So it's a no to the pancakes..." My nerves were keeping me from rational, complete sentences.

"Yeah, you're right. Breakfast foods aren't for everyone. We should get tacos. It's not Los Aces-quality, but there's another cantina open until two in the morning..."

"I wasn't saying I don't like pancakes..." I cut him off before he could finish. "I mean, everyone *likes* pancakes. That's a pretty universal food. So many varieties." I squeezed my hand into a fist, hoping I could stop rambling like an idiot. "What I mean is, I can't go out with you in the middle of the night."

"Oh." He laughed. "Now I realize that sounds crazy. I'm not on the same schedule as most people. I get how disturbing that sounds, expecting you to go out with me that late... Sorry, I didn't really think that one through. I totally understand."

My nerves relaxed. I was never good at turning people down. I usually got all sweaty and I couldn't stop talking. This was going well. He didn't even sound upset, which was a relief.

"So no pancakes," he continued. "No midnight rendezvous, that was a misjudgment on my part. I absolutely hear you loud and clear."

"So then..." I began, but he started talking at the same time.

"So I'll pick you up in ten minutes then," he said quickly.

"What? I...Well, I..." I couldn't even finish protesting – the other line was already dead.

Ten minutes? That was all the time I had? This was a disaster.

I scanned the outdated motel room. I was still wearing last night's clothes. Walter was stretched out across my bed, completely helpless and unaware of my pending crisis. All I had was a tiny makeup satchel from the gym bag I'd found in the trunk of my car.

I spent every spare second pulling my short blonde hair into a high ponytail and made my best effort with what little makeup I had. Did I want to smell like motel lotion? *Did I even have a choice?*

There was a knock at my door. I balled my fists again, my telltale sign that I was losing control.

Should I be honest and tell him I wasn't interested? Although that wasn't exactly the truth. Based on what I saw of his face last night, *any* woman would be interested. I could lie and tell him I was busy? Oh wait, my *life* burned down...clearly I had no pressing obligations at the moment other than buying things like soap.

I opened the door and hoped the gasp I heard came from Walter, though I suspected it was from my own throat.

His dark hair stood up high in a messy-cool way, and he was wearing a thick black and white flannel coat and dark jeans. As soon as he smiled, I knew all lies were off the table. His face looked like every bit of truth I wanted.

This was going to be a problem. A man like this...a face like *that*...

I was just a girl in day-old clothes, with a stolen cat, sleeping in a used bed. I didn't deserve this kind of luck.

I thought briefly about why I was here – moving to Grand Harbor on a whim, chasing a dream that wasn't mine... But suddenly, it looked like all my dreams were standing in Levi's and a flannel outside a Motel 6.

I stepped toward him and pulled the door closed behind me.

4

———

"Where are we heading? By the water? You mentioned a cantina?" Dark gray clouds swirled overhead, threatening to drop snow any minute.

"You ask a lot of questions," he said with a laugh. "I know getting in a vehicle with a stranger isn't usually a good idea. We can walk if you'd prefer, if you don't mind the cold. But I swear I'm a decent guy." The hinge of an old blue truck squeaked as he opened the passenger door.

I appreciated his thoughtfulness. I looked over toward the motel lobby where the clerk smiled and waved enthusiastically at me through the front window. She gave me a thumb's up, noting her approval, and it made me giggle.

She did say *everyone* in town knew this guy. That made me feel safe in leaving with him. I thought about the hundreds of times I got into an Uber with an unknown driver. *Meanwhile this guy brought me cat food for heaven's sake.* He seemed like such a genuine person. I nodded and climbed in.

"Nice coat by the way," he added as he slid in the driver's side.

"I'm probably supposed to give it back to you now, but I haven't exactly had time to pick up a new one."

"Honestly it looks better on you. Keep it."

I could feel the heat on my cheeks. "Seriously, where are we going? I feel like I have so many things I *should* be doing, but instead I'm shrugging off responsibility and climbing into a stranger's truck. I feel like that's the exact opposite of everything I've been told my whole life."

His lips curled as he pulled out of the motel's parking lot. "Do you always do everything you're told?"

It was a loaded question. *Yes*, as a matter of fact, I *did*. I always followed the rules. I always tried doing the *right* thing. Yet while following the straight and narrow path – so far everything had gone *wrong*. Maybe losing my impulse control for the day would be just what I needed to get back on track. The logic of it all sounded backwards in my head, but as I stared at him from the passenger seat, I decided logic had no place here.

"I'm still shaken up about last night," I admitted. "I swear I can still smell the smoke. I've never experienced anything like that. The image burning through my mind is like a still photograph, yet the flames are moving while everything else is frozen in place. I can't get it out of my head."

"You probably won't for a while," he said sympathetically. "That was a traumatic experience. I feel like my hands are still shaking a little bit too. I've never been that close to a fire of that magnitude." The truck jostled us down roads I hadn't yet explored. "I saw a box in your room. At least you made it out of your apartment with a few things?"

I shook my head. "Just my phone, which thankfully had my ID and bank card attached to the case. The box you saw belonged to my grandma. It's full of old journals and a few of her favorite books."

"That's pretty cool. Out of everything, *that's* what you saved? They must be significant."

I thought about his words for a minute. They did mean a lot to me, but I also I wished I'd grabbed more practical items. "I would trade at least four of those old books for pants," I said with a laugh. "I'm not sure how poetry and old love letters will help me now."

"What are you doing in Grand Harbor? You said you just moved here? For work or something else?"

"You're full of questions too," I replied playfully.

"We may as well get to the important stuff now. I have to be back before seven tonight. I just figured since you're new to the area, we could grab some food, I can show you around a little bit..."

"That sounds great." I stared out at the massive trees stretching up toward the sky. The snow looked like powdered sugar as it rested delicately on each branch. "I'm here because of my grandma."

"The one with the books?"

"Yeah. She passed some months back. She used to live around here. That's what led me to Grand Harbor. She talked about it all the time. Says she 'found herself' here...whatever that means."

We pulled up to a small restaurant called *Cantina Especial*. "So that's what you're doing here? Finding yourself?"

"That sounds really cliché and stupid, I know," I said uncomfortably, unsure as to why I was even telling him all this.

"I don't think it's stupid at all."

"Why, you've already *found* yourself? What exactly does that look like?" I stared back at him as he parked the truck, leaving the engine running.

"I'm not sure we're ready for all my secrets yet. We can save those for some other time."

I narrowed my gaze. "You have secrets, huh? A lot of them?"

He paused for a minute, then spoke softly. "Yeah, I do. More than I'd like."

5

———————

stayed in the warm truck while he ran in to grab some food. The purr of the old engine rattled in my chest. I couldn't help but think of his wallet still tucked away in my coat pocket. He would notice it when he went to pay, wouldn't he? Should I confess that I had it all along when he came out with no food? Or should I act dumbfounded, unaware it was ever in the coat at all?

Moments later he emerged with two carry-out bags. An older gentleman in an apron waved at him as he left. "See you next time, Johnny!"

This guy really does have secrets. Who has two names? Who walks into a restaurant and comes out with a bunch of food they didn't have to pay for? I wanted to feel more concerned. I wanted a pit to form in my stomach, telling me to run away from this questionable situation. There were so many red flags. But for some reason, one look at his face...and I couldn't run away from him at all. He was like quicksand.

He slid back into the truck, the bags of food scraping across the leather bench seat as he set them down. "Are you ready for an adventure?" There was an excitement in his tone and I had to consciously move my stare away from his mouth.

"I think I'm in too deep to say no to that." *Don't overthink this, Brooke. For once in your whole life, do NOT be sensible.*

We left the cantina, traversing back and forth up a steep snow-covered mountain. He must've told me a hundred facts about Grand Harbor. We finally pulled up to an adorable rustic cabin at the base of a ski area.

"Tell me you live here," I said in awe, looking at the picturesque landscape. When my grandma talked about this town, it was always warm and whimsical. She described the magnificent sunsets, the smooth sandy beaches, the fireflies dancing around the tree-lined paths at dusk... Her stories were never about cute mountain ski cabins. It felt like such a disconnect from the world she sold me on all those years when she described her nights of freedom and wonder back in her early twenties. I imagined her walking down one of the grandiose piers along Lake Michigan, falling in love under starry skies, lying in the sand as smooth rhythmic waves rolled around her legs. I pictured the breeze coming off the lapping water as she danced to music outside of a quaint beachside cafe...but never *this*.

"I don't know what's running through your head right now, but I feel bad for disappointing you. It's not mine. But I have a key and free rein to use it anytime."

I followed him inside and immediately smelled pinecones and cinnamon. The maple floorboards creaked as we stepped over them. There were wood beams across the ceiling, a cozy kitchen, and a table made from a whiskey barrel.

"This place is amazing. Do you live nearby? What do you do for a living?"

"Yeah, we should cover some of the basics. I wasn't even sure what kind of tacos you liked, so I got one of everything." He pulled out the food and it smelled like a homecooked Sunday dinner, which instantly calmed my nerves. "That one's pork, steak, chorizo, potato... I see that look on your face, yes, it's a potato taco. Don't knock it 'til you try it. Have you ever had one?"

I shook my head. "No. But I guess at this point I'm game for anything. Tell me about yourself while we eat. All the good stuff."

"I don't know that we have enough hours today for *all* the good stuff," he joked, "but I'll give you the speed round. We can talk more on the gondola ride."

"A *gondola* what?"

"Yeah, up the mountain. I told you I was going to show you Grand Harbor. It's the best view. You can see the entire town from there." He smiled and took a bite of his taco. His eyes rolled back like it was the best mouthful of food he'd ever had. "My general life story, let's see, I was born a few towns inland but spent a lot of time here. My family eventually migrated this way to be closer to the water. I went away to college, MSU. I had big plans to go into microbiology – genetic engineering, nerd stuff like that. Came back to work here one summer before grad school and, well, never made it back to pursue any higher education. Life got in the way, and I ended up staying here to be closer to my family."

There was a sadness in his voice, but I didn't want to pry any further.

"Once I decided to stay around, I changed course," he continued. "No microbiology. I've been working for Jones Media for a while now, and the schedule allows me to surf all summer and ski all winter. That's why I love this area so much, it has everything. Beautiful summers, breathtaking winters. It's hard to find one place that has it all."

I mulled over his words, probably giving them a deeper meaning than he intended. It *was* hard to find it all in one place...in one *person*.

"Your turn," he said, nudging another taco across the table in my direction. "What's your story?"

"Well, born and raised outside of Phoenix. We had a family cabin up north though, so I'm at least familiar with a little snow. It never felt quite this cold, but still... Anyway, a couple years at college trying to figure out what I wanted to do. I worked as a vet assistant, a photographer's assistant, a brief stint in medical but that didn't go well... Turns out I can't see blood without fainting. I've been struggling to figure out what to do with my life."

"You said you moved out here to find yourself, right?"

"Kind of. I mean, that sounds ridiculous when you say it out loud. I'm just giving it one year. It's more of an experiment." I was embarrassed to be talking about this with a complete stranger, but I also felt like I had nothing to lose. If I sounded crazy, this guy could just drop me back off at the motel and forget about me entirely.

"My grandma is the one who sold me on the idea. She told me all these amazing stories from her time out here. She had these wild adventures. One time she got stranded on the lake in a storm when her boat ran out of gas. She was rescued by some handsome guy from the Coast Guard and they hit it off and had a summer fling until he was relocated. She learned how to make whiskey and moonshine and the best apple butter I've ever had. She started her nursing career here. Everything just fell into place."

"So you're hoping to find all of that while you're here? In a year's time?"

"See, I told you it sounded stupid..."

"It's not stupid at all," he said with a soft laugh. "I think that's actually really cool. You up and moved to a place you've never been before, just to experience something new? I think that's amazing."

"What if the best part of my new life is these tacos?" I shrugged. "What if the fire was just the beginning of new disasters? I have such an unsettled feeling in my stomach. I don't know if that's from losing so much, or just fearing the unknown of what's coming next. I feel so anxious about everything."

"You already made a huge leap, leaving your life behind and coming out here on your own. There's a lot of courage in that. I'm sure you'll find exactly what you're looking for."

"And if I don't?" That was my biggest fear. What if I uprooted my entire life, moved to the middle of nowhere, and ended up further away from whatever it was I was trying to find?

"You're afraid of a little bit of failure?" He let out a low whistle. "You need to hang out with me more. I fail at stuff all the time."

"Maybe it's not necessarily about *failure*," I tried to explain. "I just wonder if this place will live up to my grandma's stories. She made it sound so fun and magical...But honestly so far it's been tragic and cold."

"What's your *real* fear? That you won't *find* yourself out here? I'm not convinced any of us really *find* ourselves at all. I think you just take chances and say 'yes' a little more than you think you should, and then sit back and enjoy the ride. The *journey* is the whole point. Your grandma didn't take the lake back with her, or the Coast Guard dude, or so many other tangible things from this place, right? It was a series of individual experiences that made all the difference."

I nodded. "You're probably on to something... Hey, I stole a cat already. How's that for reckless? Maybe I do need to say 'yes' a little more instead of overthinking every decision I make."

"Great, it's been decided then." He lifted his bottle of water, motioning for me to do the same. He 'clinked' them together, though the plastic made no celebratory sound. "To all the adventures we're going to have. Do you trust me?"

I hesitated for a minute. *Could* I trust him? I wasn't sure I knew enough about him to answer that. Heck, I didn't even know his *name*.

"I'll trust you if you can answer one question honestly."

"Okay. Shoot."

I pulled out his wallet and slid it toward him across the table. "I found this in your coat pocket. Who is *Cade Daniels*?"

6

An amused expression spread across his face. At least he didn't look angry. That proved he wasn't a criminal running from the law, right?

"I was dreading this conversation...Knight at Night?" He raised an eyebrow at me, but I wasn't sure what he was getting at. *"One more smooth love song..."* His voice deepened and softened all at once as he said it. "Have you listened to the radio since you've been in town?"

"What? No, I don't think so. Who still listens to the radio?"

"Mostly women between the ages thirty-four to fifty-eight, according to my radio show's demographics. I run the night program. It's super cheesy, but it pays the bills and I only have to work from seven to midnight, so that's a win. Plus the perks are good. I get free haircuts, free food... People are always gunning for a chance at free advertising. It's crazy."

"I'm sorry, what? So you're, what, like a radio DJ?"

"Yeah, Johnny Knight is my radio name. My real name is Cade."

"Why would you change your name?" I was still confused.

"Just one of radio's many secrets," he continued. "Almost every DJ changes their name. Sometimes you get to pick it yourself, but other times the station picks for you based on what's 'tested' well with audiences. That's just the business."

"Really?"

"Yeah, there's a lot more to it behind the scenes than what people think. They speed up all the songs ever-so-slightly to make time for more ads...and don't even get me started on the whole 'caller number nine' thing."

"The contests are rigged?" I gasped. "You're ruining my childhood right now."

"I don't want to say *rigged*," he clarified. "I'm not trying to murder all the magic. Although if you have a really excitable voice but you're only caller number seven, well...maybe we 'lose count' and make *you* number nine instead... Especially if we're confident you'll scream."

"That sounds horrible and kind of...*illegal*. That's really how it works?"

"It's an interesting industry."

This entire conversation was blowing my mind.

"So does your family call you Johnny? Or Cade? Does *anyone* call you Cade? How do you get by with two completely different names? Don't people screw them up?"

"That's why it's easier to just tell people I'm Johnny Knight," he explained. "Especially in a town like this. You need everyone to call you that, to make it 'real.' Only people I'm close to call me Cade. That way I can stay in 'character.' It makes the job easier."

"Stay in *character*? So you're just playing a role, even now? Who *are* you really?"

"I don't know most days," he said with a sigh. "That's why I was drawn to you, I guess... It's refreshing to meet someone new. I can be anyone I want."

"You don't get to be who you want at work?"

He shook his head. "Definitely not. I have to pretend to love Rod Stewart. I have to tell stupid jokes sometimes, and I have to make every fifty-year-old woman out there think that true love is just one love song away..."

"But you must like it, to stay at a job like that."

"Are you kidding? I love it. I like how it makes me feel. I like the compliments and feeling like 'somebody' when I walk into a bar. I like people thinking I'm always good at saying the right thing. I like the escape of...of not being *me*. I'm not that cool in real life. But Johnny

Knight, he's smooth...cool under pressure...suave. I am none of those things. I literally get paid to pretend I'm something better than I am."

His face looked more serious than it had before this conversation.

"What's so bad about being *you*?"

"Real life isn't always so glamourous." He shrugged. "Most people can't just walk in and get their dry cleaning expedited or have some diner special named after them. I like the illusion of it all. The rest of my life...well, it's more complicated. That's all. Not bad. Just more diffi-cult than swooning sixty-year-old women with another Bryan Adams song. I like the simplicity of it I guess. Maybe that's *my* adventure. You want an escape from your old life, right? Well I guess the radio thing is mine. For a few hours every evening I get to be Johnny Knight, and he's a whole lot more interesting than *me*."

"Maybe you just need more real-life adventures too," I mused.

"I guess we both do. Come on. I have an idea."

He disappeared for a few minutes, returning out of a back bedroom with a pair of snow boots and a thicker coat. "The temp has dropped quite a bit. You'll want these in case the storm starts before we make it back."

"We don't have to go out if you don't wa..."

He cut me off. "Adventures, Brooke. You agreed. We're not going home until we find one."

His hazel eyes were intense. I couldn't protest even if I wanted to. The look on his face mattered a great deal to me. He was pleading in some way for adventures of his own. Maybe we *both* needed this.

"I trust you, by the way."

He raised his brow. "What?"

"You asked me earlier if I trusted you. Now that I know your real name, my answer is yes. But I don't want to call you Johnny. I don't want your 'fake' persona, even if he really is significantly more charming. If we're going to do this, then I want the *real* you. Even if you suck some-times. And in return you get the real me – homeless and unsure of everything."

He laughed. "Fair enough. Let's start over then. I'm Cade. I hope you like heights and hot chocolate."

"I only like one of those, but yes. I'm in."

I slid on the boots and the winter coat. A few minutes later we boarded the gondola, heading up the steepest mountainside I'd ever seen in person.

I clung on to the metal pole nearest to the door. The gondola was half-full, mostly with skiers and snowboarders, but there were a few others like us without that kind of gear. The skies looked melancholy, but not overly threatening.

Out of nowhere the gondola came to a swinging stop, and I thought I was going to re-live those tacos. Cade put his arm around me.

"Why are we stopping?"

"They're just loading and unloading other lifts, it's fine," he said with a comforting tone. "You can release your death grip on that pole. Hold onto me if you want. It'll feel more steady."

I slid my arms around his torso, now hoping the ride would last a solid six more hours given the way we were interlocked together. He smelled like soap and cedar. My daydreams were halted, however, as we stopped to unload just a minute later.

We headed to a lookout point on the ridge. Lake Michigan looked infinite, more like the ocean rather than just a lake.

"That's the whole town?" I said in disbelief, pointing down at the specks beneath us.

"Yeah, most of it. Pretty incredible view, huh?"

"It's breathtaking. Where's the cabin?"

He leaned forward, pointing down below, and I could feel the warmth of his face on my exposed cheek.

As promised, we ordered hot chocolate from a cute mountaintop chalet and watched ice skaters spin around a colorful rink. The scenery looked like a postcard. Light snowflakes began falling around us and I would forever have this image in my head. It felt like a scene from a movie.

Winter. Hot guy in a flannel coat. Ice skaters holding hands, dancing around us as we sipped hot cocoa and laughed together as snowflakes clung to our gloved hands.

"Now for the adventure." He pointed toward a steeper part of the mountain where people were sliding down the snow on innertubes.

"Oooh, I don't know about…"

"We say yes to adventures, Brooke," he teased. "All of them."

Without another word he grabbed my hand and before I knew it, we were standing at the top of the peak.

"I don't know if we should..."

He scooped me up and put me on the tube, sliding in right behind me. "Say *yes*, Brooke. Just say it."

My nerves were in my throat. I wrapped my hands tight around the handles, and finally squealed, "Yes!"

It was the most exhilarating ten seconds of my life. We flew down the hillside even faster than I anticipated, gliding and bumping over the snowy ground. I laughed the whole way down. The wind whipped at our faces and I felt completely *free*. As soon as we reached the bottom, I quickly stood up from the tube and almost fell over. Cade laughed and reached out to steady me.

"That was amazing," I gushed. "Let's do it again."

A second later, an attendant called out through a bullhorn that they were going to shut the ride down due to weather.

Cade checked his phone, and sure enough the storm was moving in quicker than expected. "We should probably head back now, before the gondolas get too packed."

"After that rush, my motel room is going to feel awfully boring tonight," I replied, tucking my arm in his as we walked around the chalet shops.

"Maybe we shouldn't go back." He looked at me with a flirtatious smile. "Where's the adventure in doing what we're supposed to?"

"Don't you have to work tonight?"

He completely dismissed my question. "Would you stay if I asked you to?"

"What? I mean, I like the idea of it, but I hardly know you. I just found out your real name, like, an hour ago. Maybe we should..." I immediately stopped talking as Cade stared down at me, his eyes searching mine.

He moved his lips closer until they were only a whisper away. "Stay."

7

_I_ moved my lips closer to his, closing the space between us. Kissing Cade felt like a dream I hadn't had yet. I couldn't foresee the end. Heck, I couldn't even see far enough into the future to see the middle – but I knew this was a good beginning.

Was it reckless? Absolutely. But hadn't I just agreed to say 'yes' more often? I felt like this was the universe pushing me to give my best, most confident, most authoritative _yes_ of my whole life.

Yet I couldn't say _anything_.

Instead I just stared back at him, unable to hide my smitten eyes, and I'm pretty sure he could read the answer all over my face.

We rode the gondola back down, his arms wrapped around me once again. The snow had picked up and the flakes were bigger now, covering everything around us.

Cade leaned down and kissed me again as we descended, and I was as nervous as I was excited. He was handsome. Charming. Unexpected. We'd just scratched the surface in getting to know each other, and I knew I needed more time with him.

"I'll start a fire," he offered as we walked back into the cabin, peeling off our coats. "There's some soup in the pantry we can heat up later once we're settled."

We shed the rest of our winter gear and sat on the couch in front of the crackling fire, taking in its warmth. The snow was falling heavily now, and Cade's truck was already completely covered. We played some board games and laughed until our faces hurt. We told old stories and the evening felt *perfect*.

The aroma of Italian soup filled the kitchen while Cade promised to teach me how to snowboard and ski. As he talked about all the things we were going to do together, I finally felt part of something here in Grand Harbor. It felt good for my soul.

"I'm going to grab some more firewood," he said, sliding on his boots. "The snow doesn't look like it's going to stop any time soon."

"It's only supposed to be four inches..."

"Oh no, out here we have this thing called 'lake effect snow' – which is a fancy way for weathermen to say they have *no* idea how much we're getting. Sometimes four inches turns into four feet. We're definitely trapped here tonight. You sure you're okay with that?"

I was definitely okay with that. I smiled and nodded.

He stepped out to get the firewood and I heard multiple chimes from his phone. Someone was trying repeatedly to get a hold of him.

I took our soup bowls to the sink to wash them out, glancing at his phone on the counter as I turned on the water. Against my better judgement, I read the text thread illuminated on the screen.

I know you blame yourself for the fire, Cade.

We need to talk about this.

They will likely press charges.

I dropped a bowl in the sink and it shattered.

8

———————

A lump formed in my throat. The fire? *What* fire? The one that burned down my apartment?

Cade had something to do with that?

My hands started shaking as I turned off the water, unsure of what to do. This was bad. Everything felt *bad*.

Is that why he invited me out today? Because he felt *guilty*?

The door opened and Cade appeared with an armful of wood, completely unaware of what I knew.

He set the wood down by the fireplace, noticing my demeanor had changed. "What's wrong? You look different. Is everything okay?"

"I...I looked at your screen..." I was stammering now. "I mean, I didn't mean to, I was just washing the bowls, and..."

He walked over to me, picking up his phone – reading the same messages I had just read.

He threw his head back, looking completely frustrated. "It's not what you think, Brooke. I can explain."

"The fire at my apartment...was it your fault? Just answer that, Cade. Did you have something to do with that?"

He stared back at me with defeated eyes. "Yes," he said quietly. "But..."

"I feel so stupid." I wiped off my wet hands and headed toward the front door. I slid back on the gym shoes I came with.

"Where are you going? It's too cold out there, Brooke. Just talk to me. Let me explain."

"I knew you were too good to be true." I couldn't hide the hurt in my voice. "I shouldn't have moved to Grand Harbor. I shouldn't have said *yes* to you...I shouldn't be *here*."

"Brooke, I..."

"No, this is on me. You told me you had secrets. You told me you weren't who you pretended to be. I should've known. You *literally* warned me. But because of your stupid face, I didn't listen."

"My face? What are you..."

"I'll find my own ride back, Johnny." I purposefully used that name instead of calling him Cade because that's all he felt like to me now. Like a character. Like a role he was playing in the destruction of any glimmer of happiness I thought I'd found here.

"Don't call me Johnny. We're past that, you already know my real name is Cade. Look, you can't go. It's dangerous out there."

"More dangerous than it is with you?" My tone was scathing.

"I'll take you back myself. Right now. But you have to hear me out. Just listen to me for three minutes, and then I swear I'll take you back and you never have to talk to me again."

His eyes were full of emotion and he looked gutted. I wanted to walk out the door and never look back, but his face pulled me back in. He looked sad. Hurt. *Broken.*

"It's my brother," he began, slowly walking toward me. "He had a TBI last year from a car accident."

"A what?"

"Sorry, a traumatic brain injury. It's bad. He's...he's changed. Completely. That's why I ended up staying in Grand Harbor – to help take care of him."

"Why didn't you tell me about him?"

His expression saddened and his voice got choked up. "I don't know how to explain it to people, Brooke. I *lost* my brother – but yet I see him *every damn day.* He was my favorite person in the whole world, my *entire* life, but there are days when he doesn't even know me. Sometimes I have to wipe food off his face. My family has to take care of him like he's a child. Everyone around me keeps reminding me to be thankful that he survived the crash at all, but yet *every* day my heart breaks for him and I wonder if it would've been better if he didn't survive. You wanted some truth? How about that?"

Tears slowly slid down his face and I felt frozen. I wanted to console his heartbreak, but it wasn't just sadness on his face. He also looked angry.

"So forgive me for liking the illusion that I have a different life," he said quietly. "Half the day I get to pretend like I'm someone else, without my own reality, and honestly those hours are the only thing getting me through. Because then I go home and I'm reminded every single second of the greatest loss I've ever experienced. And instead of getting to just *grieve*, I am greeted by it every morning and sometimes I just *can't* do it."

I had tears streaming down my own face now. Losing my grandma was hard on me, but I could also smile about it because I had so many beautiful, happy memories of her. She inspired me on this journey and it warmed my core to think of the impact she'd made when she left this earth. Seeing Cade swimming in this kind of daily heartbreak – losing someone he hadn't completely lost – I could hear the pain is his voice.

"Last night his caretaker called me while I was working," he continued. "She'd had a family emergency and asked if she could leave a little early. My brother Dean was sleeping and I knew I'd be home within a half hour so I told her it'd be all right. But obviously it wasn't all right."

"He left the house?"

"I believe so, yes. I think he went looking for me, knowing how much I loved Los Aces, and, I don't know... Maybe when he realized I wasn't there and didn't know where to find me, maybe he panicked..."

"I'm so sorry, Cade," I said sympathetically, "I can't imagine. But it's not your fault."

"Of course it is," he replied, shaking his head. "It was my bad judgement. I didn't even know it at the time. Can you imagine how stupid I feel now, stopping by your car all nonchalant, having *no* idea he was involved? I came home and my brother was belligerent. My parents rushed him to the hospital and they sedated him. He kept saying 'fire,' that's all we could understand. We were told he was seen on an outdoor surveillance camera. I'm trying to convince myself it was a grease fire or something. I truly don't know. But if that fire was Dean's fault, in *any* way...then it's my fault too."

"Oh, Cade." I wrapped my arms around him. He buried his face in my hair and I could feel his tears on my neck. "You should've told me. No more secrets," I said softly. "Okay? We can get through this but you have to tell me the truth – about everything."

"You really want the truth?" He pulled his head back from me, searching my eyes with his, brushing a piece of hair back from my face. "The truth is, I can't help but wish I was in the car that night instead of him."

9

I pulled Cade into my arms and his tensed muscles relaxed. Daylight slipped away as easily as the bottle of red wine we found in the pantry. We spent the rest of the night by the glowing fire, talking about our pasts. Cade told me stories about growing up with Dean and all the mischief they got themselves into. Once Dean had stolen the school's coveted football trophy and led the principal on a wild scavenger hunt to find it – which led to a two-week suspension. Another time he and Dean crashed a sled through their patio door. His stories and memories about his brother warmed my heart.

I told him more tales about my grandmother and her love for fire-flies, whiskey, and an endless sandy beach. It wasn't long before the early morning sun filtered in between the curtains. We were still curled up on the couch together, reluctant to leave the solitude of the cabin.

We finally packed up and drove through the fresh snow back into town. Cade wanted me to meet his family. He wanted me to see his *real* life, with a promise from me that it wouldn't change anything between us.

"Everyone, this is Brooke," Cade introduced me as we walked through the front door of his parents' house.

"We've been trying to call you all morning, why weren't you answering your phone?" His mom Kate looked worried.

"Sorry, neither of us had a charger. We were up at the cabin," Cade explained. "How's Dean?"

"We're on our way to pick him up," his dad replied. "He's doing great, now that the story broke about the fire. That's why we were trying to reach you. It had nothing to do with him."

"It didn't?" Cade's eyes glanced back and forth between his parents in disbelief.

"No," his dad continued. "He *was* there that night, looking for you. That's why he's on the surveillance feed, but it was just bad timing. He was leaving as it happened. It was actually someone else's fault. A *cat*... can you believe that? Some old stray snuck into the restaurant and got spooked. It jumped up onto the counter and knocked over the grease container, and somehow one of the kids smoking by the back door on his break, he threw his cig down and boom, the place went up in flames."

"Walter?" Now it was my turn to be stunned. "Was the cat black and white?"

"I think so, yeah," Kate chimed in. "That's the story from the Los Aces employees anyway."

I turned to Cade. "Oh my goodness, I'm harboring a criminal," I said quietly. "Walter is in my motel room!"

"What's this about a cat?" A gray-haired gentleman climbed out of a nearby recliner and made his way over to us in the kitchen.

"Brooke, this is my grandpa, Paul," Cade said, gesturing toward the old man.

Paul was staring me down. I started to wonder if something was wrong.

"It's nice to meet you, Paul," I said, extending a hand to shake his. He didn't reciprocate.

"Grandpa, stop staring. Hello." Cade moved his arm up and down in front of Paul's face to break his concentration.

"Sorry...you look like someone I used to know," Paul said, shaking his head. "It's the darndest thing. You just took me back fifty years."

"No Coast Guard stories today, Dad. Let's go." Kate put a hand on her father's back, ushering him out of the house.

"Best whiskey I ever had," Paul muttered, slipping into his coat.

My eyes widened. *The Coast Guard*? People often told me I looked just like my grandmother back in her youth... Was it possible that this man was...

"Come with us to get Dean," Cade's dad said warmly, motioning for us to head out with them. "We'll stop for pancakes on our way back."

Cade smiled. "Everyone likes pancakes," he said with an animated shrug. "They're so universal. So many varieties."

I playfully punched his chest, realizing he was mocking me for our prior conversation when I was trying to get out of going on a date with him.

"Pancakes would be great, thank you," I said with a sincere smile.

Cade grabbed my hand. "Here's to many more adventures."

I thought of my grandma in that moment. There were no fireflies now in the dead of winter. No fancy pier stretched out into the water. None of the warmth and magic she talked about here, dancing under starlit skies.

Instead the snowflakes began to fall again. They were big, beautiful, and unique...each with their own story of what they were when they started, and what they'd become when they landed.

Here I was with Cade – our stories now intertwining – and I finally started to feel like I was changing too.

ABOUT THE AUTHOR

Randileigh Kennedy lives in the Midwest with her insanely handsome husband and two average children. She's been a world traveler, a pig farmer, a radio DJ...and now she spends her time writing love stories (between soccer practice, basketball practice, track practice...) She is obsessed with theme parties and fun food and would be much more productive if she learned how to say no...but where's the fun in that? She loves online friends (go find her on Facebook!) and she has a serious shoe problem. For more book info check out her Amazon page, and for a more personal experience (including pictures of her beloved themed party food) check out her website.

www.amazon.com/Randileigh-Kennedy/e/B00JH0FMQQ
www.randileighkennedy.com

LOVE AT ASPEN LODGE

DANIELLE KEIL

A surprise guest, an injury on the slopes, and unexpected love.

1

————

he first guests of the morning were due to arrive any moment, and I needed to be prepared. Setting my steaming coffee mug on a coaster, I opened the reservation book.

Welcome to the Aspen Lodge stared back at me. A sense of pride filled my chest, a smile stretching across my face.

The chime over the front door rang before I got to the page with the names of the guests for today.

I threw on my manager smile and greeted the guest regardless. "Hello and welcome to—" I stopped, my jaw dropping as Chris Hemsworth's brunette twin strolled through the door. I swear I caught a sparkle flash off his toothpaste-commercial white teeth.

"—Aspen Lodge. I'm Tasha—" I cut myself off again, embarrassed that I didn't know his name. I prided myself on a high level of customer service, yet here I was, struggling to even speak.

"James," he said, peeling off his glove and reaching over the granite counter to shake my hand.

The second I shook it, everything went haywire. Electric sparks ping-ponged along every nerve ending in my body.

"Right, Mr.—"

He shook his head, the shaggy chestnut curls brushing his forehead. "Not Mister. Just James."

"Right." I took a deep breath to collect myself before glancing at the book and reaching for his room key. "Well, James, you'll be in room six. Welcome to the Aspen Lodge!"

He took the key and moved aside, as if he were waiting for something else. I started his check in paperwork to file later when bell chimed again.

"Welcome to Aspen Lodge, I'm Tasha, how—"

For the second time this morning, I was left speechless. But not because of a handsome gentleman.

But because of the vibrant cobalt blue eyes I locked onto.

Eyes that matched mine almost identically.

"Tommy?" I shrieked, practically leaping over the side of the counter as I threw myself at my twin brother. "What in the world are you doing here? When did you get here? Why—"

Tommy wrapped me in a massive bear hug, chuckling at my rapid-fire line of questions. "One thing at a time, Tash. First, give me a hug. I missed you so much!"

I rested my cheek on his shoulder, pulling him in close. It had been over four years since he moved to Australia for a new job. We talked on the phone only two days ago, and yet he never mentioned he was coming home.

Pulling away, I swatted his chest with the back of my hand. "Now answer the questions, jerk!"

His laugh sent a sharp pang through my heart. "First, I'd like you to meet my friend, James."

My gaze became a tennis ball, bouncing between my new guest and my brother, my brain attempting to understand what was happening.

My brother, back on U.S. soil for the first time in four years.

The charming, handsome man standing to my right, the one I didn't realize had a deeply rooted Australian accent.

How did I not notice that?

Oh, right. The dimples in his cheeks. The over six-foot stature. The muscles growing on top of muscles, each intricately defined under his tight Henley shirt. The rumpled hair from the beanie he swiped off after our short, embarrassing conversation.

"This... is your friend?" I sputtered, my eyes growing as wide.

"Sorry to spring that on you. I assumed you knew Tommy boy here was coming back in town?" The words coming out of James' mouth made me practically melt to the floor now that I was of sound mind to recognize his accent.

"I... I... I had no idea. Him. You. Anybody—"

Saved by the bell, again. Thank goodness. I jumped into manager mode instantly.

"Hello and welcome to the Aspen Lodge! I'm Tasha. You must be Mr. and Mrs. Altridge?" I pushed Tommy out of the way, opening a path for the new guests to approach the desk.

After I checked them in, I turned back towards my brother. My emotions also checked in, and now I was pissed off. My eyes narrowed; my lips pulled into a tight line.

"Uh oh, mate. You have a mad one on your hands here. I'm going to take my things to the room. Meet you in a bit, yeah?" James said, slapping Tommy on the back with a sympathetic grin.

My heart leapt out of my chest, following him up the stairs and down the hall to the right, straight to room six. It was one of the more masculine rooms and would fit James perfectly. Slate gray walls, minimal artwork, clean lines, a massive king-sized bed, and the shower with the jets that sprayed out of the walls.

Tommy, who didn't reserve a room, but thankfully we had a few spares, would get the floral room. Purely out of spite for not telling me he was coming.

I snapped out of it, collected my heart, and turned to my twin. "What in the world, Tommy? I just spoke to you two days ago! Why didn't you mention you were coming home? And with a hot friend too?" I socked him in the shoulder playfully, but with purpose.

"Man, that's my friend. Don't say he's hot." Tommy pretend shuddered, pushing the blonde locks that matched mine out of his face. His hair had grown out since he last lived here, hanging down in waves almost to his ears. The girls from the other lodges would be all over him in a second.

Where Tommy had always been handsome, I had taken some time to grow into myself. My mom always said my personality was the best part of me, but at least now I felt like my looks caught up to that.

With our identical blonde hair, dark blue eyes, and one dimple each, Tommy and I were the same in every way except height and personality.

Me, the introvert bookworm, and him, the extrovert sports God. We were both walking clichés.

"Whatever. Have you seen him? Is he related to a Hemsworth? I swear, Tom, if you brought a Hemsworth to Aspen Lodge, I'll owe you big time. Bigger than the time you covered for me when I went to that awful concert junior year of high school."

I glanced at the reservation book, noting the Altridge's arrival before heading to the kitchen, dragging my brother behind me.

Dimitri, our chef, slid another mug of coffee at me when he saw us barge through the swinging double doors. He knew how to read every one of my moods without me even speaking a word. Dimitri had been here when I started working at Aspen Lodge four years ago, when it was falling apart from disrepair and had next to no guests. Yet he showed up day in and day out, ready to cook for whoever wanted to grace the halls, no matter what.

Needless to say, we got along famously now that we were the number one lodge on the mountain and he was busier than ever.

"Dimi, meet Tommy, my brother," I said, heading to the far counter to grab a blueberry scone off the platter before the crew brought it out to the dining room. I tossed it to Tommy after he shook hands with our chef.

"Your brother in Australia? He looks mighty close up," Dimi joked, turning his attention back to the stove and stirring an unknown liquid. I trusted him with everything in the kitchen, not asking any questions. Lord knew I couldn't cook, so whatever Dimi wanted, he got.

"The one and only. The one who failed to mention he would be here. And bringing a guest. Have you ever met an Australian man, Dimi?" I asked, biting into a scone for myself. He made a dozen blueberry every morning, knowing they were my favorite.

"Can't say I have, sweetheart. Have you?"

"I have now. His name is James, and he looks like a fitness model." That got his attention. For someone who was interested in the same gender, he hid it well. Until you mentioned massively attractive men.

"What room is this new mystery man in?" Dimitri stopped stirring and stared at me with mischief in his eyes. "I should bring him a welcome basket of pastries..."

I threw him a look over my shoulder as I dragged Tommy out of the kitchen as quickly as I dragged him in. We had some catching up to do, including intel on the man he flew halfway around the world with. "In your dreams, Dimitri!"

"Oh, trust me, he will be!" he shouted after me with a chuckle.

2

____

I twirled my spaghetti around my fork, watching the long, limp noodles wrap around each other to join as one giant lump.

Like the one forming in my throat. This was *not* how I expected things to go. The three of us spent the whole day together. I showed them all around the Lodge, explored the town, and brought them to the coolest arcade a half hour outside Aspen Falls.

Then Tommy said he wanted dinner with me. Alone.

That should have been my first cue that something was wrong.

"Tasha, it'll be fine. We'll still talk and everything, just like we were doing before. And I'm here for an entire month. Plus, now that this place is up and running, maybe you could take some time off and visit me instead?"

It had been a major issue between us after Tommy moved. The fact that the Lodge was in such disrepair, I couldn't possibly imagine leaving for weeks at a time. And to fly all the way to Australia, I would need more than a few days.

He and James worked a well-known international design firm that had offices all around the globe, including multiple in the United States. They worked in four-year contracts. Once that was up, you could put in your request for another office.

Tommy put in for the Colorado office, which would make him within an hour of the Lodge. He wouldn't know if he got it until he returned to Australia and sorted things out.

Deep within my heart, I felt the pain of losing him all over again. Sure, there was a chance he could get it, but with thousands of applicants across the globe putting in their requests all the time, there was also a chance he wouldn't and have to stay in Australia another four years.

Which meant another four years alone for me. Right when I built up hope of having him home.

"I can tell this is stressing you out. Let's talk about something else, huh?" he said, reaching for another piece of garlic bread.

Dimitri set us up in my office, spreading a tablecloth over the conference table I used when meeting with vendors, and making my absolute favorite meal even though it wasn't on the Lodge's menu tonight. That man was too good to me, and I thanked him every moment I got. I also made sure he got paid extremely well.

"Sure. Are you going to hit the slopes tomorrow? See if you still know anyone out there?" I reached for my water glass, eyeing Tommy for any non-verbal cues he would throw off.

He shook his head, the blonde curls swishing across his forehead. "Nah, I doubt anyone I know will be out there. I'll go out if you do, but not expecting much. Maybe over the weekend I can surprise some people like I surprised you."

I smirked, remembering the heart attack his surprise gave me earlier. "Or maybe you could tell people you're back in town for only one month, and they would rearrange their schedules to come see you. Like I would have done."

I planned on getting as many of my shifts covered as I could, so I could spend more time with Tommy while he was here.

And James.

It would fly by in the blink of an eye, but at least I would be able to enjoy it without having to worry about the Lodge.

"That's not what I wanted to talk about," Tommy mentioned as he bit into a meatball. "I want to talk about James."

I coughed, sending water sputtering and dripping down my mouth. Tommy chucked his napkin at me, laughing.

"Well, that gave me the answer I wasn't actually asking for," he said.

"Excuse me? What answer? What question?" I feigned innocence.

"You have the hots for James."

"Do not," I lied.

"Do too."

"Do not."

"Do not."

"Do too!" I spat out before slapping a hand over my mouth. "Ugh, dang it, Tommy. You always do that!" I threw the napkin back at him, which he caught and put on the table before it hit him.

"I only do that when I know you're lying. I saw you flirting with him all day," he answered.

I stayed quiet, pushing my spaghetti around my plate once more.

"I get it, Tash. He's a handsome guy. And a good guy at that. He's not a player. He's serious about his job. He even keeps his apartment clean. Couldn't pick someone better for you. But…"

I glanced up, finding a worried look on Tommy's face. He switched into his glasses before dinner, the black rims outlining his deep blue eyes.

I wiped my face with my own napkin and settled my hands in my lap. Here it was. The big reason why James would be off limits. He had a girlfriend. He recently broke up with a girlfriend and Tommy didn't want me to be a rebound. There had to be something.

"He's leaving, Tash."

Bomb dropped. Of course he was leaving. The man lived in Australia, for goodness sakes. Didn't Tommy think I knew that?

"I understand that."

"Do you?" Tommy questioned, cocking his head to the side and staring at me again. I didn't need to say what I thought, as he already knew.

I had a track record of falling for guys and getting my heart broken over scenarios exactly like this. The French exchange student in high school, the guy from Florida in college.

I fell, and fell hard, only for them to eventually leave. Just like James would eventually leave.

And I would be on my own again.

"I don't want to see you get your heart broken again, Tasha. He's a great guy, but just know in a month, he heads back to Australia. He came with me because he had never been to the U.S. before. The chance of him staying in Australia is probably high though, being his hometown and all." The frown on Tommy's face seemed out of place and made my heart drop just that much more.

I took a deep breath, holding it for a moment before letting it all out. "Got it. Keep my heart in check."

3

Ski day.

The one day of the month I personally took guests out of the Lodge and onto the mountain.

I found it fun to help people find which trails they were the most comfortable with, to teach them how to use a chair lift for the first time, or even how to complete the challenge course on the South side of the mountain. Sometimes they needed me and stayed close by, sometimes they just wanted someone to show them what trails to take and left on their own.

I surveyed the line of people in front of me. A family with two teenage kids who looked like they would rather be anywhere else but here, Mr. and Mrs. Altridge, a young girl about my age with her boyfriend, and my brother.

My rather lonely brother without a friend by his—

"Sorry I'm late!" a voice shouted from behind me. I followed the gaze of the teenage girl in front of me, turning around slowly

James headed toward the group, his navy-blue coat and charcoal ski pants covering the muscles I so desperately wanted to see again.

"Glad you could make it! We were just about to head over to the slopes," I said with a grin while willing my heart to stop doing gymnastics in my chest.

I could practically feel the worried look on my brother's face without even seeing it, so I purposely avoided looking his direction. I had everything under control. It had been three days since he warned me to lock my heart up while around James.

Clapping my hands together, I announced, "Okay friends, we're off! Snap your boots into the bindings on the skis. We're going to take the trail to the main mountain. It should only be a minute or two, and it's an easy Green, so everyone should be comfortable. Follow me!"

I pushed off, gliding on the snow down the path between the trees. I took this route multiple times a week, either to get to other Lodges or to the main street of town.

In Aspen Falls, skis were the fastest mode of transportation.

"You're still pretty good on those," Tommy stated as he slid up next to me. Ever the show-off, he pushed hard, widening the gap between us by a good fifteen feet before turning around and heading down the small decline backwards.

I rolled my eyes. Typical Tommy, always getting into some sort of trouble.

I got the crew to the base of the mountain safely, then handed out chair lift tickets. Showing everyone how to attach the sticker to their wire and looping it onto their ski jackets, I sent them into the line for the lift.

"You're last. Does that mean I get to ride with you, Teach?" The deep rumble of James' voice sent shivers down my spine.

"Looks like it. Ever been on one of these?" I questioned. He told me yesterday that he had never been skiing before, which made me wonder why Tommy would have brought him here, to Colorado, in the winter.

"Can't say that I have. Will you hold my hand and walk me through it?" A smile stretched ear to ear.

I was thankful it was only thirty degrees out, or I would have melted into a puddle right there in line.

"Unfortunately, if we hold hands, we'll most likely fall off the chair. But place your feet here," I pushed him forward slightly so he was in position to get on the lift, "and one, two, three!" The chair swept us off our feet and into the air.

"It's pretty up here," he mentioned, his head swivelling to check the scenery. I hit the slopes almost every day starting from the first snow-fall, so it was nothing new to me.

But seeing the awe on his face as he took in the mountains, the snow-capped tops, the people whizzing around down below gave me a new appreciation for the place I called home.

"It's definitely something. I'm so used to it now that I don't always take time to appreciate the wonder of it."

"I would be out here admiring it every day. In Australia, we have hot, warm, and hot again. The best scenery we get is at the beach."

I sighed, thinking about a nice warm beach. As much as I loved the mountains, watching the sun dip below the horizon seemed like a wonderful dream. I mentioned my thoughts to James.

"Well, you'll have to come visit sometime and see it for yourself. It's a beautiful experience, watching the reds and oranges change to pink and purples, watching the sun extinguish itself in the infinite amount of water. All while digging your toes into the warm, white sand..."

"Okay, now you're just being mean."

He lifted the corner of his lip in a slight smile, as I sighed again, lost in his smile.

I gave him quick instructions on how to get off the lift before we got to the top, which he followed flawlessly.

"Alright everyone, here are the trails. The green circles are to the left, the black diamonds to the right. If you've never been around before, stick to the bowls. They'll be the nicest to your knees." I shot a glance at James, knowing he shouldn't push it, no matter how athletic he said he was.

"And the doubles with moguls are where?" Tommy shouted from the back of the pack. I rolled my eyes.

"The sign for death is behind me. Hope you have good life insur-ance." It had been years since he had skied. However, if that's what he wanted, who was I to interfere with destiny?

James laughed and slapped his friend on the back. "I'm with you!" The mischievous grin on Tommy's face now scared me. A newbie could absolutely *not* handle a double black diamond, moguls or not.

"No!" I shouted, shaking my head. "James will stick with me."

"Even better. I get the good lookin' twin," he replied, shuffling his way over to me. I could have sworn he winked, but it was hard to tell with his sunglasses on.

Tommy shook his head and took off, shouting something inaudible behind him.

I gathered the rest of the crew, finding the family with the teenage kids more than capable of exploring on their own, and Mr. and Mrs. Altridge eager to get to their favorite green bowl runs. The girl and her boyfriend took off right after they disembarked the chairlift.

That left me and James. Alone. My heart fluttered, then sank as Tommy's warning played in the back of my mind.

"How I became the only person out of this group who still needs a teacher is slightly embarrassing," he muttered, shuffling his skis back and forth with his gaze down.

"No worries. I've done this a lot. As long as your balance is steady, and you can do this," I showed him how to make a wedge shape with his skis, "then you should be good to go."

"If I can balance on a surfboard, I can balance on these things, right?" he said with a hopeful grin.

That smile could melt all the snow off this mountain.

I pointed to the trail we would take and jammed my poles into the ground. "A surfboard is more like a snowboard, but we'll take it slow. Ready?"

I had to admit, for someone who had never been on skis before, he didn't do half bad. We made it down the mountain at a decent pace, with James listening to every one of my directions. He even got himself onto the chairlift again without hesitation.

"You get to see this view every day?" he asked as our legs swung over the bright snow below.

"Pretty much. It's easier to ski to the nearby lodges, or into town, than it is to drive. Especially at peak tourist season, like now. There are only two main roads around here, and they get congested quickly. The trails, though, they're always open."

He shook his head in amazement. "I never knew snow was so... sparkly."

I laughed, his description of snow accurate, yet quite funny when it was said with his deep, masculine voice.

After we got off, James pointed to a different trail. "Can we try that one?"

I grimaced. "It won't be as easy as the last one. It's still a green, but it's mostly downhill, not curved and no bowls."

James puffed out his chest, and I half expected him to beat on it with his fists. "I can do it. Last one was too easy. I was just letting you feel like a good teacher."

This time he slid his sunglasses down his nose and showed me his wink.

I rolled my eyes, but couldn't help smiling. His accent mixed with his confidence and pride were a killer combination.

That, and his devilishly handsome looks. I noticed quite a few ladies staring at him everywhere we went. Heck, there may have been a few times I let him go ahead of me just so I could watch him from behind.

It had been some time since I had a nice-looking man by my side. When I got hired at the Lodge, I threw myself into work, avoiding other distracting life choices like dating.

I was proud of the reputation I built with the Lodge, but loneliness had settled in. Sure, I saw a few of the girls now and then, and the managers of lodges nearby had become friends. But it wasn't the same.

"You ready?" James asked, nudging my shoulder with his.

I shook my head, clearing out my thoughts. My long blonde hair tucked safely in a braid swished across the back of my pale pink ski coat.

"Sorry. Yes, totally ready."

4

"Okay, okay, sit here. Yup. Lean back. And leg up," I directed, sliding the gray tufted ottoman under James' foot.

I snatched the ice pack from the side table, laying it gently over his ankle.

"Well if this isn't the most mortifying thing ever," James murmured, avoiding eye contact with me.

"You aren't the first and you won't be the last," I tried to assure him.

A sprained ankle wasn't something to mess around with on the mountain, but now that we were back at the Lodge, I wasn't too worried. He may have had to be put on the sled of the Ski Patrol snowmobile, but I wasn't one to laugh about it.

I settled on the couch next to him, bending my left leg to face him.

"You don't have to babysit me."

I swept my arms out to the side, showing the emptiness of the lobby. I had been on schedule to work the trails today, so I wasn't even needed inside. This place ran like clockwork due to my over-attention to schedules and details.

"Not like I have anything else to do right now. You're stuck with me." I grinned. My smile wavered for a second as he hesitated.

"Unless you'd rather be alone. Or I can try to find Tommy…"

His head snapped up, his hazel eyes staring straight at me. "No!" he practically shouted. Lowering his voice, he continued, "I mean, no. It's fine. Please stay." He reached out, placing one massive hand over my knee.

Electric sparks returned, shooting through every nerve in my body, my heart pounding in my chest.

"Well... okay then."

We sat in an awkward silence for a beat, watching the roaring fire crackle and pop. I didn't know what to say. Tommy had mentioned James a handful of times in the past four years, so I knew they worked together, but didn't know much past that.

James shifted, trying to keep his foot elevated while facing me better. He grimaced, and I knew he had to be in pain, no matter how many times he turned down medicine.

"Did you know I was the one to train Tommy when he first came to Australia? I felt bad for the guy after the first week, so I took him out to the pub for a coldie. He was such a dag, sorry, a nerd," he revised when he saw the confusion written on my face, "All he did was work. Came in early, left late, made the rest of us look bad. Your American work ethic is slightly different than the Aussie one."

I laughed, brushing an escaped curl behind my ear. "Typical Tommy. He was such a slacker in high school, but once he found his groove in graphic design, the lightbulb went off. He loves work more than he loves me sometimes."

James' expression turned serious. "That's not true."

"I know. But he loves it more than most people love their jobs."

"He talks about you all the time, Tasha. Always telling us about your accomplishments here at the Aspen Lodge, how proud of you he is. I knew it was you the second I walked in— I've seen your picture so many times over the past four years."

My cheeks got warm as I looked away. They practically blazed with heat as I felt his finger curl around my chin, forcing me to face him again.

"Don't think for a second that just because he was on the other side of the globe that you weren't on his mind all the time."

I tucked in my bottom lip, wondering just how James knew what had been weighing on my heart so heavily.

When Tommy took the job in Australia, my heart broke. We were twins; we spent all our time attached at the hip, from birth through college. Within one month after graduation, Tommy applied, got accepted, and moved Down Under.

And I was left here, alone. Struggling to revive a lodge that most people had given up on. Before I came on board, a developer had been in verbal negotiations to buy it and knock it down, wanting to replace it with a luxury boutique hotel.

I took the job a week before Tommy left. He said I was crazy, that the place lost its potential years prior. But the second I walked into Aspen Lodge, I felt it.

There was a vibe about this place. Something magical resided in its walls. All it took was one Aspen Falls native to tell me the story of the original owners falling in love while they built this place, and I knew I was meant to be here.

"He mentioned something about your parents?" James whispered after letting me sit alone with my thoughts for a moment.

I nodded. "They both died while we were in college. Tommy is all the family I have left."

James' hand curled around my own hand. "I'm sorry to hear that. It must have been so hard when Tommy left then."

I blinked back a tear, remembering the day I brought him to the airport. I felt like my heart ripped out of my chest. The hole had only grown since then.

"Tasha..." I turned to look at James, finding his eyes softened, his brow furrowed. "You're amazing, you know that? Your brother was halfway around the world, you had no other family support system here, and still... you built all of this from the ground up. It's nothing short of spectacular."

I stopped breathing then. Besides Tommy and Dimi, there weren't many people in my life to tell me they were proud of me. It felt... strange.

"Anyway." I shook my head, attempting to shake off my quickly darkening mood. "Let me go make some hot chocolate. Keep that ice on the ankle for a bit longer, okay? I'll be right back."

I bolted out of the lobby before James could say another word.

Despite Tommy's warnings, I was beginning to feel something for

James. Not only was he more handsome than any man I had laid eyes on before, but seeing his face when I talked about my family? It almost broke me. It wasn't pity. It was pure empathy.

And it scared the crap out of me.

5

"You flew? Like superhero flew in the air?"

I heard Tommy's voice before I saw him. A small smile grew as I rounded the corner back to the lobby, two steaming mugs of hot chocolate in my hands.

Dimitri saw my saddened expression immediately as I burst through the kitchen doors. In four years, he had seen me go through every emotion possible. The bad days when I missed my parents and my brother so much I could barely work. The frustrated days when I wanted to give up and quit, thinking the Lodge would never see another guest again. The uplifting days too, like the day we cut the red ribbon, proclaiming the Aspen Lodge open for business once more.

And the happiest day, of course, a year ago when we were proclaimed the number one rated Lodge on the mountain. At twenty-five, I was the youngest manager on the mountain *and* had the top rated one at that.

Before he sent me back out with the drinks, Dimi poured us both a small mug and shared a bit of silence together. He, too, lost a lot when he moved to the States in his early twenties, after his family practically disowned and shunned him. He ran away to an entirely different country, where he didn't know a single person and his only skills were in the kitchen.

We understood each other.

I placed a mug in front of each of both Tommy and James. James hadn't moved, but Tommy slid into the spot I had occupied, which forced me into the armchair on the other side of the wooden coffee table.

"Thanks, Tash." Tommy's eyes lit up at the sight of the mug piled high with whipped cream and marshmallows, just the way we both liked it. "I heard about the great flying leap James took, and had to come back and make sure he was all right."

One glance at me told me that wasn't the only reason he came back. I frowned, trying to telepathically tell him to mind his own business, but he didn't care.

Tommy's eyes sparkled as he looked at his friend mischievously. Once he knew James was fine, he poked fun. That was Tommy's way of showing affection. If you weren't actually hurt, it was fair game to roast you.

I had been on the butt end of that more times than I could count.

"Thanks, mate. You bring me all the way out here, to a place so cold I can't feel my toes, throw me on a pair of wooden planks and then leave me. I crash, I sprain an ankle, and you're here takin the mack outta me?" He pretended to look hurt, but the small wrinkles in the corner of his eyes said otherwise.

"I left you in the most capable hands I could have, James. Tasha has won more medals and awards for skiing than I have. If there is anyone to blame here, it's her!"

I jumped up, holding my hands up in front of me. "Oh no—" I started, but James cut me off.

"It's not her fault at all!" he exclaimed.

My eyes shot open at the harshness of his tone. While it really wasn't my fault—James tried a jump on the side of the hill that I warned him against—him rushing to protect me was a surprise.

Tommy shot me a glare before turning his attention back to James.

I could keep my heart in check, just like he told me to. His and James' impending departure weighed on my heart every moment.

The three of us sat in silence, them drinking their hot chocolates and me staring at the fireplace. The dancing orange and yellow flames always seemed to comfort me.

"Well, let me help you to your room, James," Tommy said, standing up and gathering both mugs in one hand.

I took them from him, narrowing my eyes and cocking my head. I wasn't working, and the three of us had the rest of the day to hang out. Why he was kicking James out didn't make—

Oh, wait. Sure it did. Tommy wanted to send me a message by keeping James far away from me.

"Sure, mate, thanks. Tasha, hope to see you soon. Sorry about dragging you back here today. I hope I didn't get you in any trouble."

I waved him off. "Not at all. I'm so sorry about your ankle. I should have—"

"No. All my fault, really."

I tucked a lock of blonde hair behind my ear and gave him a small wave as I went to return the coffee mugs to the kitchen.

Watching Tommy and James hobble upstairs together was a sight. James had a good four inches on Tommy, which didn't make him much help to James at all. But James kept his arm around Tommy's shoulders, still leaning on him in the slightest way.

I turned and called out for Dimitri, needing to tell him of a change in dinner plans. My brother and I would be dining in private again tonight.

6

———

*D*espite Tommy's attempts at keeping us apart, I failed at keeping my heart in check. No matter what I did in life, I gave it my all. And that included falling head over heels for a hot Australian man.

James, Tommy, and I spent a lot of time together over the last two weeks. Once James' ankle healed, we cautiously got him back on skis, only allowing him slightly past the bunny hill under strict instructions to stay far away from any jumps.

He and I also spent a lot of time in front of the fireplace, talking until way past the last guest went up to bed, until after Dimi closed the kitchen for the night, and long after Tommy went to his room.

I had a room at the back of the Lodge, as a manager perk, and used it often.

The countdown had begun. Tommy and James had a week left in the States until they returned to Australia.

Tommy heard some chatter about openings in the Colorado office, so he was hopeful he would be relocated. There would be no official word until he returned. As much as I tried to stop, I kept getting my hopes up every time he talked about it.

James had yet to say where he optioned. It drove me crazy, but I also didn't feel it was my right to ask.

That morning, I came into the dining room to find only James at his regular table, surrounded by Dimitri's famous cider donuts and a vat of coffee.

"Where's Tommy?" I asked, sliding into the chair next to him and grabbing a mug.

"He went to go visit some friends. Said he may be gone until tomorrow."

My heart sank. With little time left, I was trying to cram as much bonding time in as possible.

"He told me to keep an eye on you, though," James continued.

I raised an eyebrow, waiting to see what he would say next. The two of us were in that awkward stage, where we knew we liked each other, but didn't push any boundaries. The amount of flirting had jumped to an insane level, however.

While I was ready to give in, James was more reserved. Whether he held back because he was protecting his heart, or because of his inevitable departure, I wasn't sure.

James licked his lips, staring straight at me. "Want to hit the slopes today? I think I can graduate from the bowls," he said, sliding his hand across the table to reach mine.

My body lit up as soon as his fingers touched mine. He intertwined them, holding on as if he were keeping me from floating away.

Which was a real possibility.

"I have a better idea. Instead of going downhill, how about we go cross country?" James agreed before he even understood what the difference was.

～

"Why didn't you show me this before now?" James asked in a hushed voice, as if speaking would disturb the silent wonder of nature.

We stopped near what was a waterfall in the spring and summer, but now a frozen lake surrounded by snow covered cliffs.

It was my personal recharging spot. I didn't take any guests out here, nor did I tell any employees about it. Anyone could find it, but most didn't bother trekking this far off the regular path.

"I come here when I need to think," I said, sliding up next to him.

He looked down at me, lifting his arm and resting it around my shoulders, pulling me into him. A warmth spread through my body, setting me at ease.

"This is almost as gorgeous as you are, Tasha."

I gasped, surprised at his outburst of emotion. Sure, we flirted like mad, but he never gave the impression of moving past that, as much as I wanted to.

I looked up at him just as a light snow began to fall.

"Tasha..." he began, turning so we were face to face.

"You're leaving soon," I whispered, my breath coming out in a puff in the crisp air. I tried to put a lasso on my heart, to remind it of why we couldn't do what it seemed we were about to do.

"I know. But if I leave without kissing you at least once, I'll regret it."

He leaned down, touching his forehead to mine and hesitating, waiting for my permission.

I didn't bother responding. Instead, I reached up and wrapped my arms around his neck, tipping my chin to let my lips meet his.

He kissed me. Deeply and with a passion only someone who felt such a longing in their soul could kiss.

I felt a tingle from my head to my toes as our lips touched, his soft, plump lips taking mine tenderly and with care.

All too soon, he broke away, breathing heavily. "I'll never regret that, Tasha."

"Feel free to do it again," I answered him with a smile. He grinned and tucked me back under his arm as he admired the beauty of nature in front of us.

Instead of admiring it with him, all I could think about was the little clock in my head, counting down the days until he left for good.

7

"I'll call you as soon as we land, Tash. Or text you, depending on the time change." Tommy wrapped me in a hug, smooshing me against his chest. My tears soaked into his sweater, but I didn't care.

"Call me anyway." I hugged him tightly, never wanting to let him go.

We still didn't know if he would be gone for a few weeks or potentially four more years. The anticipation stressed me out.

"Love you, Tashabean. Be good." Tommy winked as he headed towards the security line, leaving me to say goodbye to James.

We snuck away every chance we had since that kiss by the frozen lake, going skiing together, having dinner in town, or just snuggling up in his room and watching movies.

We never went any further than making out, however. Giving up that part of me would have made this moment even harder.

"I'll call you too?" James said like he was asking permission.

I gave him a sad smile. "I'd love that," I answered. I wasn't lying, but knew after a short period, things would fizzle. They always did.

James cupped my chin, lifting it so he could look me directly in the eyes. "I'll miss you, Tasha. Thank you for an amazing State-side experience I'll never forget. Ever."

Leaning down, he captured my mouth in his again, sending shock waves through me. Kissing James was like drinking three energy drinks at once— it awakened me, sending jolts of electricity through my body.

"Bye, Tasha," James muttered against my lips before heading to meet Tommy.

"Bye, James," I whispered to his back.

I left the airport then, my soul shattered. It was back to life as normal now. Alone again.

~

IN THE MONTH after Tommy and James left, I threw myself into work. I felt guilty taking time off while they were here, so I overbooked my schedule, taking any extra shifts people needed.

What I really was doing was distracting myself from the pain of losing them both.

I thought it would be easier this time, since there was a slight hope of getting Tommy back, but it wasn't.

My heart broke doubly hard. At first, James and I kept up constantly with text messages and the occasional phone call. The time difference, plus our work schedules made it difficult to stay in communication.

I knew it wouldn't work out, but somehow James had hope. At first.

It had been two days since I talked to either Tommy or James, and the loneliness had set in once again. Not even going out with my girlfriends to the arcade helped.

As I rearranged the reservation desk for the sixth time in the past two weeks, my phone chirped with a message.

Tommy: Hey! I heard back about the job...

My heart sunk. My mind raced between hopefulness and devastation, unable to focus on a single emotion.

I couldn't even answer him. My palms sweated as chirp came through.

Tommy: Sorry, Tash.

I collapsed behind the desk in a heap. Thankfully there were no guests on the main floor, so I was able to make my way to the kitchen unseen, in the mess of a state I was in.

Dimi would cheer me up. Somehow.

8

———————

$\mathcal{A}$nother lonely week later, I poked at the logs, rotating them in the fireplace to get an even flame when I heard a car door close outside.

My back was turned to the front door, but I called out my usual greeting when I heard the bell chime. "Hello and welcome to the Aspen Lodge! My name is Tasha and if you give me just one moment, I'll be right with you!"

I put a cheery smile on my face, hoping it would be believable.

Turning around, my smile, and the poker, dropped.

James.

My heart pounded in my chest, but I couldn't move. I was obviously hallucinating, as James was currently across the globe in Australia.

"Hi, Tash," he said with the same sparkling grin as the first day I met him.

A wicked case of déjà vu hit me, and I looked around his shoulder for my brother to walk in any moment.

"Am I not good enough? You need more?" James joked. All it took was him to spread his arms, and I ran straight into them.

"How are you here?" I asked, my voice muffled against his winter coat.

"Change of plans," Tommy's voice answered from behind me.

I squealed and launched myself at him. "What? Who? How? I thought you—"

Tommy shook his head and gave me a hug. "Always with the questions, this one. Doesn't even care that we're back to stay."

My eyes grew wide and my jaw dropped. "What?" My gaze bounced between James and Tommy, completely lost.

The dimple on James' cheek grew. "You heard him, gorgeous. We're back. Sorry we had to lie, but both Tommy and I here got the Colorado transfer. He thought it would be funny to surprise you again. You ready to have us stick around for at least the next four years?"

I didn't know who to throw myself at first, so I flung an arm around each of them, pulling them both toward me.

"Am I ever!"

"Okay, Tasha. Give me a room and I'll leave you two to it," Tommy replied with a cough, pretending I was choking him.

"Go take mine for now," I answered, not bothering to watch him walk away.

"You're here," I said as I turned towards James.

"For as long as you'll have me."

I threw my arms around his neck and crashed my lips onto his. The bell over the door chimed again, but I didn't dare pull away.

My heart soared at the realization that I finally wasn't alone anymore.

ABOUT THE AUTHOR

Danielle Keil grew up in the Chicagoland area. A recent transplant, she is enjoying the Mississippi life, especially the pool in her backyard.

Danielle has been happily married for over 10 years, and has two young children, a daughter and a son, who are exact replicas of her and her husband.

She also is a fur mom to their Corgi, Cozmo, who loves barking, mud, and peanut butter.

Danielle's love language is gifts, her Enneagram is a 9w1, and she loves everything purple.

The way to her heart is through coffee, chocolate and tacos (extra guac).

Website: authordaniellekeil.com

Newsletter: bit.ly/newsletterdaniellekeil

STUCK IN LOVE

CARINA TAYLOR

Sawyer, the new flight paramedic, always finds Rhian stuck in awkward situations—now if only he could find a way to get her stuck on him.

1

RHIAN

"Unbelievable..." With a grunt, I reluctantly admitted I was stuck in a bathroom window.

Climbing onto the back of the toilet had been easy. Even the pull up to reach the window ledge hadn't been so bad.

Unfortunately, I'd misjudged the width of the window. Or maybe I'd misjudged the width of my hips.

I wiggled one more time, hoping it would be enough to free me. Below me on the outside of the building sat the recycling bin, which was full of cardboard. Falling out of the window wouldn't hurt nearly as much as staying with my date would.

I'd never ditched a date before, but there was no time like the present to try.

My blind date, Nevin, had claimed to be an aspiring food critic.

Immediately after being seated, he'd swiped his finger on the table-cloth, checking for dust. Then he'd demanded a fresh glass of spring water—because he could 'taste the difference.' He even sniffed the silverware. I tried to be understanding. But when he started to yell at the restaurant staff and demand to speak with the chef, I excused myself for the women's bathroom.

It was okay to have your quirks—it wasn't acceptable to be rude.

Which led me to frantically trying to escape from the bathroom window. The window that I would now grow old with.

The bathroom door opened. A scraping sound echoed through the room, and I hoped whoever it was didn't look up.

I planted my elbows against the side of the building and squeezed an inch forward.

My hand slipped, and my elbow hit against the brick wall.

"Fudge nugget," I gasped as the pain shot up my arm.

"Do you need help?" a deep, baritone voice asked—from behind me, I might add. Which led me to the ultimate conclusion, that I had not made my sorry escape attempt through the *women's* bathroom.

"I'm not sure there's anything that could fix this."

"I'm willing to catch you," he offered helpfully, his voice slightly muffled.

"I'm sure you are," I muttered.

"Or I could go ask the restaurant staff if they have a stepladder you could use to climb down." There was a note of laughter in his voice.

I twisted and turned, wiggling my way backward. At least I was wearing jeans—a skirt would have been much worse.

Stretching my toes downward, my Converse finally reached the back of the toilet. I held on to the window ledge as I carefully turned around to face my would-be rescuer.

I coughed when I saw the handsome face in front of me—a face I recognized. "Corn nuts."

He leaned against the stall doorway, grinning. His dark hair brushed against his tan forehead. A small dimple on his chin drew my attention.

With a huff, I stepped down—straight into the open toilet bowl. The splash was deafening.

"You really stepped in it this time," he said, his chuckle dying when he saw my glare.

With a frustrated snort, I pulled my drenched, germ-ridden foot from the toilet. I brushed past him, though he didn't bother to step out of my way.

He smelled good. His soft cologne or shaving cream was like an oasis in a stinky bathroom. All I'd wanted was to finally feel like a woman tonight.

To dress up, (casually of course) go on a date, and be appreciated for the fact that I was a woman. Instead, I'd just cemented the fact that I was just one of the guys in front of any man I found attractive. Always up to some mischief.

I pulled a pile of paper towels from the dispenser. Trying not to think about what I was touching, I did my best to mop up the excess water from the bottom of my skinny jeans and tennis shoe. It wasn't easy. The paper towels disintegrated as I scrubbed at my pants. Why couldn't I be cool and collected like other women? Why did I have to be the one to step in the toilet?

"Erm, do you need any help?"

I glanced up at the man standing there, in glorious clean apparel. Sawyer. The new flight paramedic. The one who'd gotten the job I'd wanted. I wished I could be mad at him, but unfortunately, he was qualified. I would have had to complete more training, and he was eligible with a few years of experience already. I tried to hold it against him. Unfortunately, Sawyer was too nice to hate and too good at his job for me to hold any bitterness against him. He was also extremely good looking.

Black hair, a ready smile, sparkling eyes. His face alone had already inspired several proposals from the patients. He was a magnetic personality that drew people toward him—me included.

I'd met him briefly and had witnessed him in action multiple times. Our interactions had been minimal up until this point. Until the stuck-hips-in-the-window incident.

Unfortunately, I'd had enough time to see what a great guy he was... and I may have developed something of a crush—the kind where I fantasized about catching his attention.

I, of course, would be in the middle of saving someone's life when he showed up at the scene. He would be wowed by my skill at stopping a bleeding femoral artery. He would load up the injured individual (I'd never bothered to envision *who* the victim was) into the helicopter, demand that I ride along with him because I was as qualified a flight paramedic as he was. We, of course, would then share long, meaningful looks across our patient. After delivering him to the ER doctors, he would ask for my number, and we would be inseparable from there on out.

Nowhere in my dreaming of impressing him did I ever picture myself stuck in a bathroom window.

I started to reach for more paper towels, but a large hand popped up in front of my face, handing me another handful.

"Thanks," I mumbled as I tried to soak the last of the dirty toilet water out.

"I know you, don't I?"

He hadn't recognized me. At least not entirely. This was good. This meant I could run out of here and have a chance at a great first impression later. With that thought in mind, I stood up, shoved the filthy paper towels into the garbage, and took a determined step toward the exit.

Only wet shoes on a slick bathroom floor weren't a good combination. My foot slipped from under me and I flailed, trying to not meet the floor.

Sawyer caught both my arms and steadied me. His eyes sparkled. "Rhian. EMT?"

I should deny it, but he was smiling at me now and I couldn't think straight. "Paramedic, but yeah, that's me."

"I thought I recognized you when I walked in."

I frowned, thinking about the view I would have presented when he walked into the restroom.

He must have read my mind because he blushed in the most adorable way. "I meant when I walked into the restaurant. I saw you with your..." He paused and arched a brow. "Cousin?"

I tried not to laugh. "Luckily I don't have to claim him by blood. He was my blind date."

He smiled again, did he ever really stop? He said, "I saw you run out of the room."

"And you're here... with your cousin?"

He shook his head solemnly. "No, not my cousin."

"I didn't think so." I glanced down at the strong hands that still had a firm grip on my arms. Not hurting me, merely holding me.

"Yes, I'm not the type to take my cousin to dinner."

"Girlfriend?" I chanced asking. I didn't want my attention too noticeable, but I had to know.

"My grandma."

I laughed. "You're not serious."

"Don't let my grandma hear you say that. Come on, you're probably ready to get out of that wet shoe."

I hummed as we both stared at the offensive wet shoe.

"What are you thinking?" he asked as I clicked my tongue.

"I'm wondering if I should soak the thing in a vat of bleach or just throw it in the garbage."

"That is the question," he agreed in mock seriousness. "The other question is, why were you stuck in the window?"

I reached up and brushed a lock of hair out of my face—I could salvage this. "I just needed some air."

"Okay." He shrugged, as if he liked to climb on the back of the toilet for some fresh air from time to time. "Want me to help you get out of the restaurant unseen?"

2

SAWYER

Rhian's face broke into a beautiful smile, her dimples showing. She was beautiful, vibrant, and she'd had full command of my attention ever since I'd first laid eyes on her.

"If you do that, you'll be my favorite person in the world," she answered.

Sign me up.

"All right, come on. We'll walk around the edge of the main seating area. I'll block you. But..." I paused for dramatic effect. "You'll have to meet my grandma though. She's going to wonder why I'm leaving the restaurant with another woman."

"Point me to her. I'll scout first." She straightened her shoulders and marched to the bathroom door. She pulled it open enough to stick her head outside.

Silent laughter shook my shoulders. Her sense of humor was what had caught my attention originally. Anyone who worked as a paramedic was required to have a warped sense of humor. It was practically a requirement. It was also a coping mechanism. The trauma we saw on a nearly daily basis was enough to cause most people a mental breakdown. Which was where inappropriate humor came in. Most people didn't understand it, but it was the only way we could sleep at night. Rhian had that humor in spades.

"I don't see a grandma anywhere," she reported when she pulled her head back inside the bathroom.

I opened the door wide, grasped her hand and tugged her after me. Her blind date was still busy railing at the poor waiter and now the restaurant manager. I maneuvered us around the lines of tables until we reached a corner table where my grandma was sitting.

Rhian kept glancing frantically over her shoulder, keeping an eye on her date. "I don't see your grandma anywhere."

"Right here," I told her. I pulled her to a stop next to our table.

Grandma smiled at her.

"Is this a joke? Why don't you just say this is your date?"

I chuckled. "Grandma, I'd like you to meet Rhian. We sometimes work together."

"Aren't you going to sit down?" Grandma patted the seat next to her.

Rhian still stood there gaping at my grandmother. Her glossy black hair and tan skin made her look decades younger. She'd often been mistaken as my sister since we looked alike. My grandma was one of those elusive, ageless people.

"This is your sister, because there's no way."

And there it was. But I knew it would make Grandma's night to hear it again.

Grandma laughed. "I like her."

Rhian smiled.

A loud yell erupted and we turned to see the chef had finally come out to talk to Rhian's blind date. It didn't look like the date was going to make it out unscathed. The chef was holding a rolling pin, although I don't know why since he wasn't running a bakery; he was holding it on his shoulder as though he were about to use it on something—or someone.

"Grandma, I'm going to walk Rhian out to her car then be back."

Rhian shook her head and smiled. "No, don't worry about it. I think he's so absorbed with being a jerk to everyone he's not even going to notice."

She was so low maintenance it was like a dream come true. Never asking anyone for anything. It made me like her even more. "Ah, come on, you're not going to ruin my rescuing-a-damsel-in-distress moment, are you?"

"You're going to put me in distress," Rhian muttered under her breath.

I fought off a laugh.

"It was nice to meet you," she said to Grandma as she turned to go.

"You too." Then to me, Grandma said, "Take your time, honey." With a not-so-subtle wink.

"I'll be back in a minute," I reiterated before Rhian could melt into a puddle of embarrassment.

I gently grabbed her elbow and steered her around the outskirts of the main dining area, intent on avoiding her date.

I leaned forward and whispered, "I've got to ask, how did you get set up on a date with *him*?"

"My best friend Tori. Who's married and thinks everyone should be as blissfully happy as her and her husband."

"And she's friends with that?" I glanced meaningfully at the man, who was now sitting by himself in a full pout.

"They met in her yoga class."

"Maybe he should look into a relaxation class. Seems like he could use it."

Her laughter filtered back toward me as we stepped outside into the parking lot. It was a nice laugh. Not a soft fake laugh. It was a hearty, contagious laugh that made you think she actually thought you were funny.

"Imagine him sitting there trying to relax." She chuckled and snorted at the same time.

"He'd probably critique their method."

That set her off again. I followed her to her car.

She paused to thank me. "Thank you for walking me out—and hiding me from Nevin."

Nevin. What kind of a name was that? But since I didn't want to keep talking about her blind date, I left that topic alone. "Hey, anytime. Next time you need to escape a bad date, just let me know. I'm probably a safer option than the bathroom window."

She lifted her eyebrows and fixed a glare on me. "The bathroom window will not be mentioned again."

I mimed zipping my lips... but I would *definitely* be mentioning the bathroom window again.

"Thank you again," she said as she fished around her small clutch for her keys.

She kept looking. And looking. It wasn't that big of a purse.

She glanced at me nervously before she peered into the car—and groaned. I stepped closer and looked over her shoulder. Her keys were sitting on the front seat. I tried the door handle. Locked.

I looked at Rhian. Her cheeks were bright red, so I didn't have the heart to chuckle. "Don't worry, we'll call and get a—" I stopped talking when she bent down and reached beneath her car. She fumbled around for a minute before she stood up triumphantly with a slim-jim in her hands.

She slipped it in between the window and the door, popping the lock on the car.

I leaned an elbow on the roof of the car as I watched her. "You're very good at this. Do you moonlight as a thief?"

"I like to keep my options open." She shrugged and climbed into the car. "I'll see you around!"

With that, she started her car, slammed the door and drove away, leaving me in a stupefied mess.

3

____

RHIAN

Three days had passed since the most mortifying experience of my life. Now that I looked like a perfectly incompetent idiot, I was sure Sawyer would avoid me at all costs. Maybe even suggest to management that I wasn't competent enough to be a paramedic.

When looking at the evidence stacked against me, it didn't look good. It didn't scream dating material. My plans of impressing him were smashed to smithereens.

Stuck in a window? Check.

Stepped in a toilet? Check.

Embarrassed myself talking to his grandma? Check.

Locked my keys in my car and peeled out of the parking lot in sheer embarrassment? Definitely check.

Hopefully I'd never have to look in his face again. As a matter of fact, I was counting on it. If I had to look him in the eye again, I'd probably have to run away to the Caribbean. Although that did have potential...

I stretched my shoulders as I rode in the ambulance to the scene of a wreck.

We didn't know how bad it was yet. No one did. The ambulance would be the first on the scene.

"So. I was thinking of renovating my bathroom."

I glanced up sharply at my partner, Dave. He was in his early fifties and had been my partner ever since I started five years ago.

"I was wondering if you'd want to come check the height of the window for me." Dave's gray mustache twitched suspiciously.

The newest trainee sitting next to him snickered, and I glared. "I'm going to kill him."

Apparently, Sawyer was not the tight-lipped individual I had hoped he was.

After responding to the accident and transporting our not-too-terribly-hurt patient to the hospital, we went to grab some lunch at the hospital cafeteria. It wasn't the average cafeteria. We had choices like Café Yumm or Panera, which was why we didn't mind hanging around the hospital when it was close to lunchtime and we were waiting for the next call.

I had just gotten my sandwich and had set it down on a table in a corner before I went to find a water fountain to refill my bottle.

I finished refilling my water bottle as a lab tech came rushing out of a side room, carrying a box of supplies.

I stepped to the side of the hall. Trying to get out of the way, I moved directly in front of a door—that swung open.

The door handle slammed into my lower back, and I stumbled forward as it pushed me.

A nurse stepped through the door. "Oh, I'm so sorry! Are you all right?"

I smiled and nodded, and she went on her way, letting go of the door that automatically closed, pulling me with it. With a grunt, I reached behind me to discover that the metal lever handle had caught the back of my shirt, and I was now entangled on it.

Not wanting to rip my shirt, I craned my head around, trying to figure out how my shirt was stuck on there. The water bottle in my hand made it difficult, but I couldn't bend down to set it on the ground... because I was still stuck on said door.

"Running from a bad date again?" a cheerful voice asked.

The heat started in my chest and spread to my cheeks. I was glad for my messy hair that hopefully hid my expression from Sawyer, who was standing in the middle of the hall.

"What are you doing here?" I asked.

"We did a medical transport today; I stopped in to grab some lunch. I see you're just hanging around here too?" He didn't smile, and I gave him credit for delivering that line with a straight face.

"I'm trying not to rip my shirt…"

"In that case, mind if I help?" he asked.

With a heavy sigh, I nodded.

He stepped close to me, and instead of leaning around me to help untangle it, he reached both arms around me. His smile was barely contained as he untangled the shirt from the door handle.

He didn't wear cologne but I could smell a faint hint of laundry detergent. I glanced up at his chin, where a hint of stubble was starting to show.

"How in the world did you do this?" he asked with a laugh as he finally loosened my shirt from the handle. He dropped his hands to his sides but didn't step back.

I reached behind me and tucked my shirt into my pants. Hopefully, I'd avoid getting stuck on anything else. "Erm, thanks for the assist."

"My pleasure." His deep voice practically shook the air between us.

"How's your grandma?"

"She's great, thanks for asking. She's training for a marathon coming up this spring."

I blinked rapidly, trying not to let my surprise show. "Is this a Benjamin Button case?"

Sawyer tipped that handsome chin up and laughed. "Oh, I'm going to have to tell her that, that would make her day."

"Has she been recorded as a Guinness record? Best preserved grandma?"

He shook his head and grinned. "She had my mom when she was seventeen. My mom had me when she was eighteen. And now they're horrified that I'm ruining their chances of being great-great grandmas."

"No babies on the horizon?"

"Maybe someday. If I can convince someone to put up with me."

I nodded, not sure if this was a conversation I should be having with him. "Did you grab lunch?"

"I just came from the EMS room."

Room was being generous. It was more like a coat closet with water bottles and dry as dust granola.

"That doesn't count as lunch. There are a lot of better options around the corner."

"Are you eating here?"

"Yes..." Was this the part where I invited him to lunch? Or would he think I was a clinger?

"Mind if I join you?"

Thank you, Sawyer, for reading my mind. "Sure! I've been rehearsing my lecture about not spreading stories about finding women stuck in a bathroom window." I raised both eyebrows.

Sawyer groaned. "I told one guy. Actually, I think it was your partner. I was asking after you, and he wanted to know why."

My lecture brain froze on the point where he said, "I was asking after me." Was it in a way he wanted to know more—or avoid me entirely? Because I would definitely ask after Nevin simply to avoid him. But I would ask after Sawyer because I'd want to be with him.

There was a big distance between the spectrum.

I waved for him to follow me, and I led the way back to my table where I'd stashed the food.

He sat down after I did.

"Aren't you going to get something to eat?" I asked as I began unwrapping my sandwich.

"In just a minute. I want to hear your lecture first. I'm afraid the food won't settle well if you try to tell me while I eat."

I laughed and took a bite of my sandwich. A pickle slice fell and slid down my chin to land on my lap. There was now a yellow mustard stain on my blue pants.

"I promise I'm not this klutzy all the time."

"When are you this klutzy?" he asked with a straight face. Too bad, I could see his eyes twitching, fighting a smile.

"Only when you're around," I muttered as I tried to mop up the mustard with a thin napkin. I seemed to be constantly cleaning myself up when he was around.

"Did you save them?"

"Save what?" I glanced up to see him leaning forward, resting his forearms on the table. The muscles bunched and rolled every time he shifted.

"Your shoes."

I shook my head. "No. I didn't have the heart."

"The jeans?"

"I cut off the bottom half and made shorts."

"Aren't you just the smarty?" he teased with a chuckle.

"You shouldn't flatter a girl that way—she might get ideas!"

His laughter stopped, but his smile stayed in place. "I hope you—"

He was interrupted when his pager went off. He mumbled as he stood up. "I guess I'll catch you later."

"Here." I shoved the untouched half of my sandwich toward him. "You didn't have time for lunch."

"Thanks," he said as he snatched it out of my hand without hesitation. "I owe you one." With that, he jogged off, eating the sandwich as he went.

I didn't mind the view.

4

SAWYER

I was about to ask Rhian out on a date when my pager went off. Of all the luck. It didn't seem to be on our side. I kept wanting to ask her out; she kept getting stuck places. There was a pretty good-sized chance she'd turn me down. I'd heard from one of the EMTs that Rhian had wanted my spot as a flight paramedic before I came along.

I still wasn't sure how she felt about it. She hadn't lashed out at me at all, but that didn't mean she didn't harbor some type of resentment. It would be easy to do. I knew how competitive it was to become a flight paramedic. And I would feel guilty about snatching the job out from under her, but if I hadn't taken the position, I never would have met her.

After I'd finished the last call, I was off for four days.

I'd immediately gone home and caught up on some much-needed sleep, but when I woke up I was faced with trying to decide how to spend my time off. Time off, which unfortunately meant I didn't stand a chance of seeing Rhian.

The restaurant had been a chance in a million. We'd probably never run into each other, which was why I jumped in my car and drove to the fire station.

I needed to come up with an excuse to go there on my day off. I was sure I owed someone something. Maybe I'd borrowed a movie. Did people still do that?

Oh well, at this point, I was willing to do anything to get Rhian's attention.

Hopefully, she wasn't out on a call.

I pulled into the station and headed inside. I needed to find her before I lost the guts to ask her out.

Dave was standing in the front room. "Oh ho, look who it is. The bathroom fixer."

I smiled as I shook his hand. "Say, uh, is Rhian around?"

Dave's bushy eyebrows practically climbed up his forehead. "You want to see Rhian? Is this work related?"

I smiled guiltily. "Definitely not."

"But it's Rhian!" an EMT piped up as he walked into the room. I didn't recall his name.

"So?"

"She's one of the guys," the EMT went on to explain. "People aren't interested in her outside of work."

I gritted my teeth as another guy walked into the room. "What's that supposed to mean?"

"She hasn't been on a date in years!" the other guy chortled.

No wonder she had seemed a little wary of me if this was the treatment she was used to.

"She was on a date this week."

"What?" A collective gasp filled the room, and I was beginning to wonder if I was at a knitting club where they shared all the tidbits and gossip.

I nodded solemnly.

"She was not."

I grinned, liking seeing them shocked that Rhian had people who were interested in her. "She was. So maybe since she's one of the guys, you can tell me where she is."

A door slammed and Rhian walked through the room. She was out of her uniform, wearing jeans and a sweater. She hurried past me and out the door.

I glared at the guys and followed her out.

5
____

RHIAN

Just one of the guys. It's just Rhian. Just. Just. Just.

How many times had I heard that from the crew I worked with? How many times had I heard that from my cousins?

I shouldn't be hurt by it. It was my own sensitivity, and I needed to get over it.

But I couldn't. I wanted someone to look at me as more than a *just*. I'd hoped Sawyer would be different, but it turns out I was wrong. He was exactly the same. He would never view me as something more. In fact, he'd seen me at my worst, so I couldn't imagine why he would ever view me differently.

I unlocked the car—with my keys this time—and tossed my bag in. I slammed the door, but the dangling handle of my purse got caught on the corner. With a frustrated groan, I opened the door and yanked the purse out. I slammed it again. It banged off the seat belt that fell out of the car.

Wrenching the door open again, I pulled the seat belt back into place. This time the door shut completely.

"You're not one of the guys to me." The deep voice behind me made me jump.

I spun around to face Sawyer. He wasn't smiling. I tried to recall a time when he wasn't smiling, but I couldn't.

I gulped and took a step back, bumping against my car.

"You're not just another paramedic to me," he continued.

I cleared my throat. "Um, where exactly are you going with this?"

"On a date." This time his boyish smile was back in place.

"With your grandma?"

"No, with you."

Now I was grateful that I'd been leaning against my car. It was holding me up—all of me except my jaw that was resting on the pavement. Sawyer asked me out on a date. Or told me we were going on a date, maybe? I wasn't exactly sure. But I did know that I would happily go.

"I promise to do everything in my power to not ruin dinner by yelling at the waiter."

Good ol' Nevin.

"And I promise if you want to ditch our date in the middle of it, I'll help you."

I cleared my throat again. "Well, who could turn down that kind of an offer?"

He rocked forward and backward on his heels. "No more bathrooms though."

I grimaced. "No, none of those. So gross."

"So, Rhian... will you go to dinner with me? Tonight?" he asked with a serious face.

"Only if you bring your grandma."

"I'm not bringing my grandma."

I rested a hand on my hip and sighed. "Well, I guess you'll do."

He grinned and took a step forward, closing the distance between us. "Thanks for giving me a chance." He leaned down and surprised me by kissing my cheek. "I'll pick you up at six!"

His grin was contagious, and I couldn't help the smile that stretched across my face.

I watched as he started jogging toward his car. I wondered how long it would take him to realize...

"Hey! I forgot to get your number!" And there it was. He jogged back toward me. Did the guy ever walk? Maybe if I took a lesson from how much energy he expended, I'd start fitting through bathroom windows.

He pulled his phone from his pocket and I told him my number. With another quick kiss to my cheek—that I didn't mind at all—he darted back to his car.

I was going to wear a dress. Sawyer was the kind of guy I didn't mind putting in a little extra work for.

And I knew exactly what I'd be doing all afternoon... shaving my legs.

6

SAWYER

On the way to Rhian's townhouse, I tried to tell myself to play it cool. I only got pulled over once on the way.

I'd worried that bringing her flowers was too cliché, but if I was understanding the guys at the station, then no one seemed to show Rhian any type of attention outside work relationships. Maybe it was high time someone actually did bring her flowers. Of course she might throw them in her trash...

When I finally knocked on her door, the flowers were starting to wilt from how many times I'd tossed them in the back seat, then picked them up again.

Ultimately, I decided to risk being original and bringing her a bouquet of flowers on our first date.

I knocked on her door and waited impatiently.

It felt like years before the oak door opened. Rhian stood there wearing a blue dress with a flared skirt. She wore sandals and had curled her hair. When her eyes landed on the sad excuse for a bouquet, she smiled so big that both dimples showed.

I was going to keep her forever—if she'd let me. Who knew simple flowers could make someone so happy?

"Do you want to come in for a minute? I need to put the dog away."

I followed her inside and stared at the biggest Great Pyrenees I'd ever seen. "Did he eat the neighbor's dog for breakfast?"

Rhian laughed. "Not quite, but he does eat a lot. This is Mumford. He's not actually my dog, but he comes and hangs out here anytime Ian and Tori leave town."

Mumford ambled toward me and rubbed his head against my dark jeans, leaving a patch of white hair there.

"No Mumford!" Rhian cried as she snatched his collar, pulling him away from me. She tiptoed backward, trying to save her dress from the same fate. "Kennel, Mumford, kennel!"

Now the dog was focused on giving her all the love and attention. She ran down the hall, the dog chasing after her, "Mumford, nooooo!"

I set the flowers on the counter and followed after her. The two of them were having a standoff in a bedroom with a large dog kennel beside the bed. I picked up a squeaker toy off the ground and tossed it in the kennel. He darted in after it, and Rhian hurried and shut the door.

"Good boy, I'll be back in a little while."

She was breathing heavy and when she turned around, I saw that she hadn't escaped a big glob of slobber that was smeared across her dress.

"Why am I always such a mess when I'm around you?" she wailed. "Why can't I be put together for once?"

Fighting a chuckle, I reached out and grabbed her hand, tugging her toward me. "You know, I think you're just perfect the way you are."

"Stop being nice! We both know I'm a hot mess." She scowled and I laughed.

"You can say that again," I teased as I pulled her into my arms. "Rhian, I don't want to go out with someone who's always put together. I want to go out with someone who thought climbing out of the bathroom window was a good idea. I want to spend time with the woman who laughed off stepping in a toilet and made my grandma's night by calling her my sister. I want to get to know the beautiful woman who gave me half her sandwich when I know you've been out on calls for almost twenty-four hours."

Rhian rested her hands on my chest—she could probably feel my rapid heartbeat. Her eyes were wide as she stared up at me.

"You're kind, funny, brilliant, and I don't know why you can't see how amazing you are. You're exactly the kind of woman I want to be with."

She smiled tentatively.

"I hope you know, I've never thought of you as just one of the guys. You caught my attention the first moment I saw you."

She chuckled. "Well, that makes two of us. I never thought you would see me as a person though, and not just a paramedic."

"You're a darn good paramedic, but you're an amazing woman as well. I kind of like to think I get the double package when I'm with you."

Her eyes sparkled as she looked up at me. "In that case, I am quite the catch, aren't I?"

I grinned and pulled her closer, only a few inches separated us now. "I don't think I'll be letting this catch get away."

"Do you know that I wanted to hate you for getting the flight paramedic position I wanted?" she asked as she tapped a finger against my chest.

I nodded, I'd suspected as much.

"I wanted to not like you, but you horrible man, you made it impossible to hold a grudge against you."

"I'll have to keep working at it then." I leaned down, resting my forehead against hers. "Is it bad to kiss you before we even go on our first date?"

"I'd rather call it original. Which we know we both are."

I groaned and tugged her even closer. "Good. Close your eyes, Mumford," I told the dog.

And then I kissed my perfect date. Her arms wrapped around behind my neck, and I traced a perfectly soft curl that draped down her shoulder. She was beautiful. Soft. Someone I never wanted to let go of. Someone who was constantly stuck in trouble. Someone who always made me laugh. And I knew—without a shadow of a doubt—that I would be happily stuck in love with her.

EPILOGUE
RHIAN

I had five minutes before Sawyer showed up to take me on a date. He had told me we were going somewhere special and that I should dress accordingly. After carefully curling my hair and putting on a maroon sweater dress, I'd glanced around my house to realize a slob lived there.

With a mad dash, I cleaned up the clutter around my house, shoving everything into the spare room and then grabbing the garbage bag to run it outside into the backyard, hoping to be back inside before Sawyer arrived.

I opened the gate into my fenced off garbage cans. I tossed the bag into the can then slammed and bolted the gate.

"Ouch!" I shrieked. My finger was firmly wedged between the bolt and the wood.

With a furious yell, I tried to pull it out. It felt like it was going to break—if it hadn't already.

I took a deep breath, trying not to panic.

"Rhian?" Sawyer's voice drifted over the fence.

"I'm back here!" I wailed. I didn't even care about being stuck in front of him anymore. We'd been dating for almost a year, and he was well used to these types of things.

He stepped through the backyard gate and stopped when he saw me. "Oh no, what happened now?"

"I'm stuck," I said pitifully.

He jogged over to me and examined the bolt on the gate. "You poor thing. I'll replace this."

Before I had a chance to think about what that meant, he ripped the bolt from the wood, freeing my finger.

"Okaaay, I hadn't realized I was dating a superhero."

He grinned as he gently grabbed my left hand and examined my ring finger. He gently felt up and down the swollen digit.

"I don't think you have a break, but you'll probably have a nasty bruise for a few days."

I leaned up on my tiptoes and kissed his cheek. "Thanks for getting me unstuck, again. You're the best."

He frowned as he continued to stare at my finger. "Well, this is definitely going to put a damper on what I had planned for tonight."

He pulled me close, and I stepped into his arms. He still held my left hand out, as though we were dancing.

I glanced at my hand. The finger was quickly swelling to twice its normal size. I looked back at his face. He was trying to frown, but as per usual his signature grin was trying to sneak out. "What?" I demanded.

"Oh, nothing. I was only wondering how we were going to fit this ring on there tonight." He let go of my waist to pull something from his pocket. A small, velvet red box.

"No." I gasped.

"Yes."

"Really?"

"Yes." He grinned and popped it open to the most perfect, beautiful ring. There was a large diamond set down in the band, with a small diamond on either side.

"This is the prettiest thing I've ever seen." My eyes were getting dangerously watery.

"I had it specially made for you. I had the diamond set low, so that it won't get caught on anything."

"That's the most thoughtful thing anyone's ever done for me," I admitted as I stared at the ring. And that also meant he knew me better than anyone else.

Sawyer took a step back and knelt down on one knee. The soft light cast from my patio lanterns reflected off the white gold of the ring.

"Rhian, I love you more than anything. Will you do me the honor of being my wife?" he asked. His expression was uncharacteristically serious as he asked me.

"Yes! Yes! I think I've loved you ever since you found me in that bathroom." I smiled and held out my hand as he pulled the ring from the box and attempted to slide it on my finger.

It didn't fit, so he grabbed my right hand and slid it on there. "When the swelling goes down, we'll make sure it fits just right."

My face was starting to hurt from the amount of smiling I was doing.

Sawyer smirked, "Of course, I wouldn't mind if that ring is stuck on you for the rest of your life."

I reached down and grabbed the lapels of his black shirt, pulling him to his feet.

"Shut up and let me kiss my fiancé."

He scooped me off my feet, lifting me against his chest. "Gladly."

And I kissed those gorgeous lips that were going to be mine to kiss for the rest of our lives.

ABOUT THE AUTHOR

Carina Taylor writes zany romantic comedies to make you ugly laugh. When she's not writing, you can find Carina chasing after three little boys, ignoring her laundry pile, pretending to work out, drinking large amounts of coffee, and dreaming up the next story.

Stay up to date on new books and stories from Carina Taylor by signing up for her newsletter. She promises not to blast you with point-less emails. https://sendfox.com/cjtaylorauthor

FRENCH TOAST WITH A SIDE OF LOVE

D.E. MALONE

Despite her don't-date-the-clientele rule, waitress Janie Wendell wonders if longtime customer Mark Christie will give her another chance after she turned him down for a date a year ago.

1

The first and only time the guy at Table 13 asked Janie Wendell for a date, she turned him down without missing a beat. That was eighteen months ago, but Mark Christie still came around Daisy Gap Cafe every Friday. Her heart always did that little flapjack thingy when she saw him, like Monte did with his spatula and the hotcakes back in the kitchen. She'd been mentally kicking herself for saying "no" ever since.

She looked up when the sound of the door chimes drowned out the cafe's breakfast time murmur. Mark was ten minutes later than usual, but his arrival was no less monumental. Her pen continued totaling Table Nine's meals on the order pad, then jogged onto the countertop while she watched him make his way to his usual table. Mark lifted his finger for his first cup of coffee, his laptop case swinging from the other hand. If she was busy serving other tables, he'd wait. She was the only waitress he wanted to see.

He settled in at his single red booth near the door. When he saw her coming with the carafe and an empty mug, Mark's one-sided grin made the dining room a little brighter. And it never failed; he turned those light green eyes her way and her heart melted like butter on a griddle.

"Hey, Mark. How's my favorite customer today?" If only he knew how true it was.

"Good. Even better now that you're here to properly caffeinate me." His voice was smooth and soft. Sometimes she had to ask him to repeat himself.

She laughed. "What can I get you? The usual, or is it time to move on?"

His go-to breakfast for the last two months was three eggs over easy, hash browns, and toast. Before that it was pancakes, bacon—"fried to a crisp"—and fresh strawberries on the side. Her regulars usually had a favorite meal or two they'd alternate between. Mark changed to something new every two months like clockwork.

The skin between his brows pinched as he looked down at the menu. He had that McConaughey hair going and a Hemsworth barely-there beard, and somehow he pulled off being more heartbreaking than the sum of those two swoony guys put together. Today his look wasn't as polished though. The beard had grown out some, patchy in spots. Underneath the canvas coat, his collared shirt begged for an iron. She knew him well enough to guess something was off.

Mark pushed the menu away. "Tell you what: surprise me."

This was a twist.

"You're living a little dangerously today. What's up?"

He turned his dreamy eyes her way again and she swallowed a sigh.

"I'm working on a project. It's wearing me down," he said thoughtfully, turning to look out the window. "Guess I'm just tired of being so single-mindedly consumed by it."

"I'm sorry to hear that." Janie cocked her head, studying him for a moment. "I think you've been through everything."

Mark glanced at her sharply. "I have?"

She laughed. "No, I meant the menu. Not...not in life."

The tension in his face softened.

Janie stepped to the side so she could see the menu. She tapped it with her finger. "Except for the French toast. You haven't tried it yet. Monte makes it with pecans and almond flavoring and it's—"

He flipped over the menu. The corner of his mouth ticked down.

"Wanna try it?" She shifted her weight. "Then you'll have the dubious honor of being one of my menu masters. Actually, the only one. You'll be the charter member."

"No French toast."

His tone took her aback. A little brusque, almost snappy.

"Okay, forget that. How about the farmer's skillet?"

"Perfect."

"Ham or sausage?"

"Sausage, please." He picked up his phone, frowned, and set it upside down on the table.

"You got it."

She poured his coffee and noticed his hand shook as he poured cream from the diminutive silver pitcher into his mug. If she didn't have another table, she'd sit down and let him unload for five minutes. Monte was easygoing like that. It was good for business, her boss said. Treat them like family and they'll always come home, he liked to say.

Besides, Monte and Mark were close. One reason why coming to Daisy Gap Cafe was included in Mark's Friday routine was because the restaurant was on his list of ad accounts. He and Monte pored over the ad proofs and set the schedule for the coming week in the River Cities Tribune and its five smaller newspapers. She liked to fantasize the other reason was to see her.

"About that project." She paused, watching him sip. "Talking it through sometimes helps. Helps me anyway. Maybe you need someone's ear to hash it out?" Being so close to him was almost too much.

He gave her a quick smile. "I'll keep that in mind."

Janie walked back his order, pushing it across the back counter to the kitchen where Monte promptly tacked it above his head.

"Mark's here." She lowered her voice. "Something's not quite right with him either."

Monte gave her a long look and lifted his chin. He was a man of few words when he cooked.

Since that day she turned down the date, Mark maintained a friendly yet cool distance. Maybe he took rejection to heart. Or maybe he had so many other options for female companionship that she was but one little fish in his vast dating pool. If Mark had asked again she would have said "yes." Jumped on it actually. She'd been seeing Tate at the time—nothing too serious—but dating more than one guy at a time wasn't her style. Her no-dating-the-customers rule would be kicked to the curb in a heartbeat for Mark. Yet he never asked again.

She told herself if the day ever came that she left the cafe for another job, she'd ask him out. But deep down she knew there was a slim chance she'd follow through with it. Janie was an old-fashioned girl at heart. She liked guys to do the asking, even when she'd missed her chance the first time.

The door chimes rang in quick succession. Three groups came in, and suddenly the quiet cafe was alive again. With two more of her tables filled up, Janie kicked it into high gear. Orders for coffee were taken, menus shared.

Monte poked the bell to let her know an order was ready. Across the dining room, Mark watched her while she came toward him to serve the table on the other side of the door. She flashed him a smile. He blinked and looked down at his phone again. Janie's heart sank. Maybe she'd overstepped, hinting that he might confide in her. It wouldn't be the first time she talked too much. Sometimes he responded to it, other times he shut down.

While she set two tables with new silverware rolls and brought out pitchers of cream, Janie snuck looks at Mark. His phone monopolized his attention, but he glanced her way now and again, lingering a second too long before she caught him. Monte's bell rang again for Mark's order and once she delivered it, she spent the next twenty minutes taking care of the other tables. And thinking about striking up her next conversation with him. Her time came after she delivered food to her remaining tables.

Janie stopped next to him to top off his coffee.

"I have to ask: what's the deal with no French toast?"

Mark sniffed and looked across the dining room. She could almost hear his wheels turning as he sorted out his answer.

"Old girlfriend dumped me over French toast."

Oh. Here she was trying to get him to ask her out again and she's suggesting trigger foods for breakfast. Well done, Janie.

"That's rotten," she offered.

"Tell me about it. She buttered me up with a good meal before she dropped the bomb."

"Sorry she broke your heart."

He set down his phone and cupped his mug between both hands, looking down. "I wouldn't go that far."

"No?"

"There was trouble from the start." He glanced at her before he looked out the window again. A city truck rolled by, laden with brush, branches with gold and crimson leaves waving over the sides. "In hindsight, it was good riddance. But it soured my taste for French toast."

Janie could relate to relationships not starting on the right foot. She and Tate had met at River Blues Fest last summer in the concession stand line where he'd dismissed the entire blues genre as "just sad." That red flag should have stopped her, yet she'd agreed to a date because Tate was funny in a geeky, quick-witted way. Janie wasted all of August and September on him. She'd even turned down Mark. Foolish on so many levels.

"Did you know French toast didn't originate in France?" she blurted, steering the talk away from breakups. She sat down across from him.

He turned those hypnotic eyes on her again and his forehead crinkled. "You don't say."

"It's true. An early recipe was written in Latin in, like, the fifth century."

"Fascinating." A little smile quirked his lips.

"And French toast in France is actually called pain perdu. That means "lost bread." She shrugged. "You know, since it was made from stale bread. Get it? Lost bread."

"I do. How do you know so much about French toast?"

"I don't know." She waved her hand dismissively, now a little embarrassed about the weird tangent. "It's one of those things that drives me a little crazy. Like Canadian bacon didn't come from Canada and Denver omelets didn't start out as a Colorado thing."

"And I suppose Belgium waffles—"

"Actually, they came from Brussels. But nice try." She patted his arm excitedly, holding on to it for a few seconds too long.

The reaction was electric. Their eyes locked. The skin on Mark's throat rippled. He'd felt it too.

"Well, thank you for the mini lesson on breakfast food misnomers," he said quietly. His gaze caught on something over her shoulder. "Here comes Monte."

"He'll probably scold me for spending an inordinate amount of time with you." She slid out of the booth. While gathering his empty plate and silverware, she paused. "I would never do that, by the way."

He looked at her over the top of his mug. "What's that?"

"Break up after cooking you French toast. Or anything for that matter." She nodded toward his mug, trying not to smile. Mark's complexion had taken on the hue of a pink grapefruit, despite his late-summer tan. "I'll top that off again in a minute."

Janie passed Monte, who grumbled about waitresses prioritizing socializing over serving. But he fought that crooked smile while he said it. He'd sit with Mark and go over a half hour's worth of business while Carla took over the grill. Mark and Monte would mostly sit and laugh, then grow quiet when she came by with the carafe. It was all very secretive, this male bonding thing they did every Friday.

Either she'd had one too many coffees that morning or the sudden urge to run a lap around the block came from her really focused conversation with Mark. It was the most they'd talked in a long time.

Maybe ever.

EVERY NERVE TINGLED as he watched Janie walk back to the kitchen. He looked down at his sleeve and stared at the indentation her hand had made in the material, wanting to replay that moment. And prolong it too.

He let the air out of his cheeks in a slow, steady exhale as Monte sat down in front of him. The file was ready and waiting. Mark pushed it across the table toward him.

Monte shifted the papers in his hands while his unwavering gaze rested on him.

"A little bird tweeted in my ear that you're off your game today," he said. "That true?"

Mark leaned back against the booth. "She said that, did she?"

"I wouldn't kid about such things. You know I've been pulling for you two to drop the pretense and just go out."

"I already tried that. She wasn't interested."

Monte gave him an exasperated look. "Please."

While Monte studied the papers, Mark settled back to watch Janie.

Janie poured coffee for the table of three guys up front. While she filled his mug, one of the guys gazed up at her. Mark recognized that look. He was charmed by her, but he could hardly fault the guy. Janie played her customers like a Vegas card shark.

She laid a hand on the guy's shoulder while she pointed out something on his menu. The twinge in Mark's gut wasn't the skillet disagreeing with him. Janie had a gift for making a person feel like the center of her universe. It was the laser-sharp focus. The little touches and sharp-witted banter. He loved it. And so did everyone else. After visiting the Daisy Gap Cafe every Friday for the better part of two years, he'd come to know Janie pretty well. She was an expert flirt with a heart as big as the moon. Sharp too.

"You are so not here with me, are you?"

Monte's voice snapped him back to earth. "What?

"I said this is ready to go." He patted the papers in front of him.

"Perfect. Thank you."

Monte narrowed his eyes like he had something more to say.

"We tease her all the time, man," he said. "She does this thing with her face"—Monte puckered his lips and squinted—"when she looks at her reflection in the microwave before she comes out to greet you. Never fails."

Mark laughed, but all the hairs on his head stood on high alert. "Seriously?"

"Not kidding you. She watches you leave like she'll never see you again. Almost brings tears to my eyes." Monte liked to embellish.

"But she turned me down."

"I don't know what to tell you, man. Women are one of those world wonders."

Mark tapped his finger on the table, his thoughts swirling. "She doesn't know I'm not in ads anymore."

"Why are you hiding it?"

"I'm not hiding it. It just hasn't come up in conversation."

"What does she think we talk about every Friday?"

Mark shrugged. "I have no idea. Ads probably."

A few seconds later, the other waitress named Helen came to tell Monte he had a call. At the cash register, Janie's attention drifted toward him as it always did until Mark noticed.

Monte rose. "Maybe it's time to take it a step further since she won't. You can start by telling her about the job."

"I don't know."

"It's nothing to be ashamed of." He lifted his chin toward Mark's file. "And good luck on this one. They'd be fools not to snap it up."

"I hope the editor agrees with you."

As soon as Monte returned to the kitchen, Janie didn't waste any time coming back with the carafe in hand and a syrup dispenser in the other.

Time to take it a step further.

Mark took a deep breath as she stopped in front of him for the refill with a bright-eyed smirk wrinkling the skin around her eyes. After all these months, the prospect of asking her out again was even more daunting than the first time. He'd been full of bravado that day he'd first visited Daisy Gap Cafe. It was one of his new accounts, one of a handful his boss had divvied up among the reps after someone left the ad staff. Her warmth and humor hit him like a comet to the chest when she pointed to her name tag and spoke to him for the first time:

Rhymes with "rainy." You?

He'd chuckled. *Mine rhymes with "dark," "spark," and "bark."*

Her eyes had lit up. *Ooo, I like those. They tell me a lot.*

Like what?

She'd looked toward the ceiling, squinting as she thought. She was pretty in a wholesome way. Very little makeup. A complexion as smooth as buttermilk.

You have a skeleton or two in your closet. You're outgoing, confident. You have a dog.

She was wrong on all accounts, but they'd kept up the banter for a few more minutes until he blurted he wanted to take her out. Totally out of character, but he was feeling on top of his game that day. Janie gave him a quick "no" without batting an eye and went on gabbing about her cat.

It'd be a lie if he told himself it wasn't a big deal she'd turned him down. On the contrary, he'd thought of little else. But Mark wasn't sure if now was the right time to try again, if ever.

～

"You two had a lot to talk about this time."

The dark ribbon of coffee filled his mug, steam curling upward. Janie took the towel from her waistband and wiped away the dribble dotting the table. "The ad business must be booming. Getting ready for the holidays already?"

"Not quite," Mark answered.

She caught the derisiveness in his tone. Mark's eyes were downcast as he studied the papers before him. A glance told her he wasn't working on ad copy. It looked like a manuscript with cross-outs and erasures decorating the paragraphs.

"It looks like you're busy so...let me know if you need anything else." She choked on the last word, the dryness in her throat catching the word as it happened whenever he was near. Mark looked up sharply. His forehead creased.

Janie smiled, embarrassed. Behind her, a voice interrupted.

"Miss? Our syrup."

The three older women sitting behind Mark were regulars too. They were impatient and condescending, but they tipped well. She should have delivered the syrup first, but her priority was always Mark.

Mark's focus was again on the manuscript. It gave her another chance to sneak a look. One sentence popped right out:

Calhoun's glorious boneless chicken wings, lacquered with a sublime honey-lime sauce, and smothered in enough chilis to make you wish you'd ordered milk...

"Oh, I love Calhoun's." She didn't mean to say it aloud. It was barely a whisper.

"Huh?"

Mark shifted in his seat like he was surprised she still stood there, until his attention was drawn to his sleeve. He grimaced.

"What is this?" He touched the wet spot still growing larger on the material. His finger came away sticky with dark fluid.

She looked dumbly at the syrup pitcher she'd accidentally tilted while she read over Mark's shoulder. A little thread of liquid continued to drip.

Janie jumped back. "*Oh!* I'm so sorry!"

Her attempt to stop the flow by jerking the dispenser upright sent a thin arc of syrup through the air and onto the tabletop behind her. Janie winced. She hadn't meant to deliver the woman's syrup that way.

While Mark dunked his napkin into the water glass and dabbed his sleeve, Janie leaned over him for the napkin holder. Napkins spilled onto the table. A few fluttered onto his lap. Her elbow brushed his mug as she straightened, coffee sloshing onto the table again.

"I should freeze right now. I'm making everything worse." She laughed nervously. Being this close to Mark made her feel like a cotton ball, soft and airy, light on her feet.

Mark swept the file folder off the table before the papers soaked up coffee. He tucked the manuscript into his leather case, a grin stretching across his face. It was so good to see him smile.

"I think you've managed to cover all the bases," he said. "Nothing else could go wrong."

She gave a short laugh. "Oh, watch me."

He stopped dabbing and stared at her. Goosebumps crawled up Janie's spine. *Those eyes.*

She cleared her throat while she collected the napkins. "I'm known for my clumsiness."

"And your breakfast trivia."

"Right."

Mark picked at his sleeve. He sniffed it and wrinkled his nose. "I've always wondered if maple would make a good aftershave. Now's my chance to own it."

Behind her, the woman slid out of the booth and took the syrup dispenser from Janie, fixing her with a withering look.

"I'm so sorry," Janie said to her, but the woman was already seated again, talking in sharp undertones to the other two ladies.

She sighed. Tending tables when he occupied one of them proved impossible every time. Mark was a sweet distraction. Janie turned back to him, gritting her teeth, but he was already focused on the manuscript again. She leaned in closer to get a better look. What *was* he working on? Definitely not one of his ads.

"Maybe you'd like to sit down and ask about what I'm working on?" he said with a hint of humor in his tone.

Her only table left to close out was the one behind her. They didn't look like they were in a hurry. Janie slid into the booth again and folded her hands, waiting.

Mark chuckled. "I'm writing again."

This was news. She hadn't known this about him.

"You're writing about Calhoun's?"

"Yes, among other things. A review for the *Tribune*. It's not much, but I'll take anything at this point."

"I didn't know you're a writer." She rested her chin on her hand. "There's something so intriguing about writers."

His lips held a one-sided smirk. "I don't know about that, but it feels good to be creating again."

"I know what you mean. I love making furniture when I have spare time. It's my way of unwinding." She picked at her nails, embarrassed about turning the conversation to herself.

Mark's eyes widened with wonder. "I had no idea."

Janie felt herself flush. "Nothing too complicated. Side tables, bookshelves, knickknacky things. My dream is to travel to weekend events year-round and sell stuff."

"Then you should."

She looked down at her lap. "Listen to us. We're two imposters in our chosen fields."

"Yeah?"

"Sure." She pointed to her herself. "An artist disguised as a waitress. And you're a successful ad rep moonlighting as a writer."

"I've always been a writer. Just not one who earns a living from it."

"Your time has come. I feel it."

Mark fiddled with the salt dispenser. "I hope so. I'm waiting to hear about a big assignment," he said. "It'd be huge if I got it."

"You'll get it."

He pushed the shaker aside, crumpled his napkin, and set it on his plate. "I hope you're right." He looked around like he should have escaped a while ago.

Janie collected his mug and saucer as he slipped on his jacket, casting a glance at his face. He looked tense. The muscles in his jaw rippled. Was he upset about something she'd said or just nervous about the project?

"I'll be right back with your bill."

Janie met Monte at the counter. He was sifting through the meal tickets at the register.

"Is this Mark's?" he asked.

She glanced at it. "Yes."

"I'll take care of him."

Janie hooked her thumb toward the dining room. "But I'm heading his way again. I have to clear Eleven anyway. "

"No problem. I've got it." He lifted the receipt from the pin and left her watching his back.

Is he discreetly not charging Mark?

It was a quick exchange: Monte pushing Mark's card away when it was offered. Mark slipping the card into his wallet. No receipt. It wasn't the first time she'd noticed Monte give him a *pro bono* breakfast.

Across the cafe, Mark's gaze burned into her. His hands, resting on the table, were balled into fists. The leather briefcase sat in his lap. A second later, he got up and left the cafe.

Monte avoided her gaze when he came back to the register.

She let out a soft sigh. "Did you get a chance to find out what's wrong with Mark?"

"Somewhat," he said nonchalantly, walking back to the kitchen.

Janie followed him, annoyed. Like Mark, Monte was sometimes a man of few words. Other times he could talk your ear off. She waited for him to offer more, but he was infuriatingly quiet.

Monte greased the griddle, casting furtive glances at her. She caught him shaking his head, mumbling something while he worked. Finally, he set the spatula down with a metallic *clang*.

"Tell you what. Why don't you clock out?"

Confused, she looked at the clock on the wall. "I've still got twenty minutes left in my shift."

"If you wait until then, you won't be able to catch him."

"Catch him?"

Monte waved the question away. "Don't pretend you don't know what I'm talking about. I've watched you two circle around each other like Chilean flamingos for over a year now."

Janie snorted. "You're exaggerating as usual. I don't date—"

"—the customers." His hand flipped again, dismissing it. "I know, I know. He's more than a customer though. Admit it."

She let out her breath, surprised she'd been holding it.

Monte bugged his eyes at her. He picked up the spatula again and scraped the blackened batter spots on the griddle. "Tell me I'm right."

There was no denying it. Mark was so much more. In the make-believe life she'd created for her and Mark, he was her confidant, her dashing hero. The scrambled eggs to her bacon.

Her best friend.

Embarrassed, she shrugged. "You're right."

"Then what are you waiting for? *Go.*"

"But what makes you think he wants me running after him?"

Monte gave her one of his loaded looks. "I *know.*"

Those two words sent every nerve ending in her body into a mad dance. This was it. Her chance.

Janie untied the apron, shucking it onto the counter with one hand while she pulled her hair tie out with the other.

Monte was back to mumbling as she hurried out of the kitchen.

"And don't come back in here until you two have stopped all the pretense," he called.

She threw him a smile over her shoulder. "Promise."

Outside, the midday sun cast a golden light on Main Street. Leaves skittered down the sidewalk, catching on her shoes as she looked for Mark. Under the green-striped awning next door, an eddy of leaves turned in a mesmerizing dance. Her insides seemed to mirror the motion. Hand on her stomach, she watched the leaves catch another breeze and float upward until movement farther down the sidewalk caught her eye.

Mark.

He leaned against the wall between Harold's Flower Shoppe and the ice cream parlor, one foot braced against the bricks. His eyes were downcast, staring at the sidewalk like he was deep in thought. Thank goodness he hadn't disappeared.

Janie approached him. He looked up when her heard the scuff of her shoes on the sidewalk.

"What are you doing?"

He gave her a winsome smile. "Getting up the nerve," he said finally.

She shook her head. "You're overthinking this. Don't worry about the manuscript. They'll love it."

"It's not that."

She searched his face. "Then what?"

"I lost my job three months ago when they downsized the ad department. Monte has been letting me crash in his spare bedroom after I had to sublet my flat."

"Oh, Mark. I'm so sorry. I had no idea."

"I didn't expect you would. I've kept it under wraps to everyone."

"But...but you come in here every Friday to see him. Like you've always done."

Mark shrugged. "He's been reading my restaurant reviews."

"I hate that you're going through this." Janie slumped as she searched his face. "I wish I'd known."

"Why?"

Good question. What could she possibly do to make his situation better?

"Maybe because I'm good at commiserating."

He gave her a soft smile but grew serious again. "There's something else too," he added.

What could it be? She said a silent prayer what he was about to tell her wasn't something horrible. Like he was moving away. Or worse, he was sick.

"I have this *affliction*, and..."

No.

"...it's something more serious than infatuation but not quite, well..." He glanced away and shook his head, like he struggled with finding the right words. Mark gave a short laugh. When he looked at her again, his eyes were soft, full of longing. "I'm a little crazy about you, Janie, and I'm not sure what to do about it."

Her heart had dropped somewhere in the vicinity of her knees when he mentioned an affliction. But now it soared. Janie chewed on her lip, trying to keep the smile from overtaking her face. He wasn't finished, and she didn't want to miss a word.

"You said 'no' the first time," he said, pausing again. "But even after you turned me down, I couldn't get you out of my head."

She sighed. All this time he'd felt the same way. He was so hard to read. Janie took a step closer. She kissed her finger and pressed it against his temple. "Because maybe I'm supposed to be there."

The look on his face was everything. All the bad stuff melted away —the doubt, frustration, even the three worry lines crisscrossing his forehead. He closed what little space was between them and slid an arm around her waist.

Janie trembled. It might have been from the crisp September breeze lifting the hair away from her neck. But it was a safer bet to attribute her sudden chill to the weight of his arm against her back and the words he'd said.

Mark rested his forehead against hers as he looked into her eyes. He smelled of cedar and leather. A little syrup too.

His words came out in a whisper. "You have no idea how much that means—"

Janie tilted her head, meeting his lips before he finished. Her months-long curiosity about how it might feel to kiss him was too much. Mark froze. His eyes closed. It was as if they were caught in the eye of a storm, leaves swirling around them while time stood still. Then his kiss deepened as he pulled her closer.

"Oh, yes I do," she said, breathing the words against his lips.

The kiss, his revelation, all of it could be summed up in one word.

Heaven.

THE MORNING SUNLIGHT threw stripes across the table as Janie opened the menu and zeroed in on the list of specialty scones. For such an obscure little diner, the selections were pretty eclectic.

Ham, feta and spinach.

Lemon raspberry.

Honey pear with cheddar.

There were a dozen more on the list. Her mouth watered.

Across the table, Mark studied his own menu. His brow furrowed.

Janie chuckled. "Breakfast shouldn't be that serious."

His face softened when he looked up. "No, you're right. But there are Danish on the menu, and I'm wondering if they originated in Denmark."

She laughed again. "Sorry. That's my fault, isn't it?"

"Your knowledge about the origins of breakfast foods is one of your most endearing traits." He'd taken on a serious look again, but she could see him struggling to keep a straight face.

"I'd call it a quirk."

Mark set the menu aside and took her hand. "I love your quirks."

Janie squeezed his hand. "I'd love to hear what else you love about me after we decide what we're ordering. The waitress will be back any minute."

Since their first date two months ago, Mark had taken her to more places for breakfast than she'd visited in all her thirty-one years combined. They'd sampled the sumptuous buffet at the Carlisle Hotel in Burlington along the river and local diners from Rock Island to Galena. These morning adventures were a perk of Mark's new project: a new travel guide for a small publisher in the Quad Cities. She loved these road trips through the river towns along the Mississippi. She marveled at the different ways to make a skillet, how the taste of a standard cup of coffee varied from one diner to the next, and the nuances of restaurant decor. And being with Mark added a delightful layer of magic to every experience.

The waitress returned then and Mark nodded to Janie.

"You first," he said.

It was a hard decision, but Janie settled on the ham, feta and spinach scone.

"And for you, sir?" the waitress asked with her pen poised above the order pad.

"French toast." He handed her the menus.

Janie waited for the woman to leave before she leaned forward.

"I thought you hated French toast."

"Did I say that?" Behind his puzzled look, a hint of merriment was still evident.

Janie huffed. "'An old girlfriend dumped me over French toast.'"

His grin broadened at her poor attempt to mimic him.

She bugged her eyes at him. "Isn't that what you said?"

He nodded slowly, still smiling. "It's about time I change the narrative on French toast."

"What does that even mean?"

"What I mean," he said slowly in that husky voice Janie loved so much, "is that I'd eat French toast with you every day if you wanted me to. I'm saying...I love you."

She took his hand, intertwining her fingers with his. They were supple, sturdy, and warm. She didn't want to let go. Ever.

"I love you too."

Mark leaned back against the booth, holding her gaze. She sensed that he'd wanted to say it for a while now. Janie caught him staring at her during the lulls in their conversations the past few weeks. But she'd learned that he weighed his words carefully, and giving her his heart was not something he took lightly. Maybe that was why her vision clouded. She wasn't the weepy type, so it took her by surprise.

He noticed and squeezed her hand. "What's wrong?"

Janie dabbed at her eye with the corner of her napkin.

"I'm just really...happy I can finally make you French toast," she answered, her voice an octave higher with emotion.

It took him a few seconds to sort through the juxtaposition of her tears and the offer to make him breakfast. When he did, he chuckled. It was so good to see him laughing more.

Mark had scored that big assignment he'd wrangled over the day they finally broke down and admitted their feelings for each other. He was able to get out of Monte's basement and back into his own place with the help of his freelance gigs and the advance from the travel guide project. In a month's time, she'd seen a change in him. His confidence was back. He'd found his swagger again.

Janie floated her napkin into her lap.

"You laugh now, but wait until you taste it. Monte taught me all his secrets."

Mark gave her a skeptical look, propping his elbow on the table. He rested his cheek against his hand. "Oh really?"

She nodded. "It'll become a breakfast staple, because you'll want it every day. Like coffee." Janie clinked her mug on his before she sipped.

"Do you know what I want every day?" he asked.

She set down the mug and met his gaze again. "Not French toast?"

"Only if it's synonymous with your love."

Janie smiled as her heart swelled.

"It's yours."

ABOUT THE AUTHOR

D.E. Malone writes sweet contemporary romance and is the author of the Hearts in Hendricks and Blueberry Point Romance series. A former newspaper reporter, she finds creating fictional worlds rather than writing about the real one more enjoyable. She loves traveling to places off the beaten path which inspire the small-town settings in her stories. When she's not writing, she enjoys reading, hiking, cultivating the weed patches and continuing her quest for the holy grail of bakeries. She lives in central Illinois with her husband and their Catahoula hound rescue dog.

Find her on Facebook, Pinterest and Instagram as *dmalonebooks* and visit www.demalone.com to subscribe to her newsletter for the latest book news and a free novella.

SECOND CHANCE RUN

MEREDITH DEICHLER

Arriving in the nation's capital to run a marathon, Ellie starts her weekend with an unexpected twist when she is picked up from the airport by her ex-husband.

1

———

Ellie pressed her phone against her ear again only to shake her head in frustration a half minute later. Nope, the third time was not the charm. Even standing against a wall, away from the foot traffic in the airport terminal, the only part of the voice message she could decipher was that her sister was not waiting out beyond security to pick her up. With a sigh she shoved her phone back into her purse. Reagan International Airport offered several public options to make her way to Trish's apartment. The Navy Yard stop on the Metro system was a five-minute walk from her sister's building, and even with a lighter crowd at this evening hour, there would be taxis waiting outside. It was just that after a full day of work and then traveling, Ellie had looked forward to the easy chatter of sisters catching up, not navigating polite cab conversation or Metro lines.

Past the security checkpoint and its bored guard monitoring the one-way movement of exiting passengers, she scanned the wide corridor, her eyes searching for the ground transportation signs. Her gaze stuttered on an unexpected sight, and her stomach flipped. Ellie blinked, but her ex-husband still stood fifteen feet away, a white placard with her name on it in his hands.

"I would ask what you're doing here," she said, approaching him.

"But you'd just raise an eyebrow and nod to the sign for the obvious response that you're picking me up."

Logan chuckled and closed the distance between them for a quick hug. "Trish said she'd leave you a message."

"She did, but all I could hear was that she couldn't get to the airport." Ellie stepped back from his strong embrace. Their marriage may have ended seven years ago, but his touch still sent tingles down her spine. She chalked it up to the amicable nature of their divorce and the rebuilding of their friendship over the last two years. No chance these sparks hinted at a deeper simmering of emotions between the two of them.

"That explains your surprised, uncertain look." Logan's smile had her stomach flipping again. "Her best friend from work who's eight months pregnant-"

"Alejandra." Ellie had met the woman during her visit to D.C. that summer.

"Yep." Logan nodded. "She started feeling contractions, but her husband is on a business trip in Japan. Trish asked me to pick you up while she stepped in to rush her to the hospital."

"Living only two floors apart makes that convenient for you to do," Ellie replied. It was a strange twist of fate that her sister and ex-husband had moved into the same apartment building on the same day.

"So now that I've answered your question, how about you answer me one?" A hint of hurt crossed Logan's eyes before shifting to an intense focus that made her heart rate speed up a notch. "We message each other at least every other day. We just talked on the phone last weekend. How come you never told me you were flying into town to run a marathon?"

"I haven't really talked about it with many people, maybe a handful or so." Ellie shrugged. "I'm trying not to make a big deal about it."

"Twenty-six point two miles sounds like a big deal to me. I know how winded I am after charging around the soccer field for a half hour, and a marathon is a lot longer than that."

"My last one was a little over four hours."

"Right. Wouldn't having more people cheering you on be better?"

"The course goes right through the heart of our nation's capital. There are going to be a lot of spectators making noise."

"Spectators that know you?"

"Trish will be out there."

"Huh." The slight narrowing of his eyes and closer press of his lips was a look she recognized. Logan had more to say on her marathon-running secret, but having picked up on the vague edge to her answers--her dodge of getting too personal--he was letting the topic go, at least for now. "I'm parked out this way. You can tell me about your flight on the drive."

As the elevator doors from the parking level closed, Ellie caught herself yawning in the reflection. "I really hope Trish has some healthy microwaveable dinners in her freezer."

"I haven't had dinner yet myself," Logan said. "How about I cook us up some pasta? Two nights before your big race is a good time for loading up on carbs."

Logan's suggestion caught her mid-yawn number two, her jaw left hanging at his unexpected words. She blamed it on the tiredness from her day. Why else would the thought of him cooking for her leave her fumbling for words?

He chuckled. "Come on, I know I wasn't the greatest cook when we were married, but you haven't forgotten that I could handle making pasta, right?"

"I didn't realize you knew about nutrition for runners."

The edge of Logan's mouth quirked just as the elevator dinged to announce their arrival at the lobby level. "I'm going to continue on up to my floor and get dinner started while you grab the key to your sister's apartment and then go ahead and drop your bags off there. Give me a text when you're ready to come on over, and I'll give you the number of my place. That work?"

"Sounds good." Ellie gave a nod before walking away from the elevator bay. She and her sister had done this exchange a couple of times. Trish would leave the key in a labeled envelope with the front desk. Then when Ellie arrived while her sister was out, she would ask for the envelope with her name on it. Like each time before, the exchange with the concierge went smoothly, and Ellie breathed a short, grateful prayer as she rode up to the ninth floor.

A turn to the right, past a few doors sporting a variety of welcome mats, and Ellie was in her sister's studio apartment. The dim lighting and cooler temperature cocooned her in a sense of cultivated calm. Walking past the pristine kitchen counter and its two clear barstools, she dropped her bags on the other side of the dark wood dresser that doubled as a TV stand. Three more steps and she stood flush against the glass sliding door to the tiny balcony, the white obelisk of the Washington Monument breaking the skyline in the distance. She had loved this view since that first evening in her sister's apartment two years ago.

"I know it's a great view, but how long are you planning on staring out over my balcony?" Trish's voice came from behind her. Ellie bit back her sigh even as she kept her eyes on the skyline.

"It's soothing."

The sound of shuffling feet approached, and then Trish's arm curled around her shoulders. "Wondered how long before you'd want to talk about running into Logan."

"I haven't seen him in years, and today when you're starting a new chapter of your life, the elevator doors open, and boom, there he is, his own moving box in his hands."

"He looked as shocked as you did if that makes you feel any better," Trish replied. "I knew he was moving somewhere different in the city, but I had no idea it was into my building."

Ellie ignored the strange pang of jealousy at Trish's casual comment. She wasn't proud of her divorce, but she was proud of how calm and non-divisive it had been. She and Logan still texted birthday wishes, and each year she sent him a Christmas card, care of his parents. Their families were on even friendlier terms; their mothers were in the same online book club while Trish and Logan followed each other on social media. Ninety-nine percent of the time Ellie was grateful that the divorce had split only their already-failed relationship, but this was one of those moments when she almost wished that everyone else had not moved along so easily. She shoved the selfish feeling down. "Well, good thing that it's your building he's moved into and not mine. Imagine how awkward that would be."

A buzz sounded from the floor where her purse had landed, and Ellie broke away from the view and her memories.

"You said for me to text when I was ready," she murmured, but her half-smile turned into a guilty grimace when she realized the message was not from Logan but from her parents back home in South Carolina. She had forgotten to call them when reaching Trish's apartment as promised just before going through security at the airport.

She quickly punched back a reply: "Flight was good. I'm at Trish's. Having dinner soon!" Then she turned to unpack a few items, refusing to consider why she had felt disappointed that her ex-husband hadn't been the one to text her.

～

716. The number was clearly marked and yet Ellie hesitated before knocking. It had hit her in the elevator that this was the first time in years that she and Logan had been alone together. Even though they had hung out over her last several visits to D.C., Trish had always also been with them whether it was a casual dinner in her apartment or sightseeing in the city. The group setting made it easy for Ellie to claim that the ease and enjoyment she felt around Logan was from Trish's presence, not a deeper bond forming as she got to know the man her ex-husband had become over the years since their divorce. This meal though didn't come with a cozy buffer, and she took a deep breath before finally knocking.

"Hey!" Logan's smile filled his face as he opened the door for her. "Come on in. I just put the garlic bread in the oven, so we're about five minutes out from eating."

Ellie stepped into the short entrance hall, savory scents wafting to her nose. "Need me to help with setting the table or anything?"

"Nope. I've already got everything ready." He waved towards the kitchen bar with its two wooden barstools where two place settings waited. "You can go ahead and sit or wander around, check the place out."

"Not giving me the grand tour on my first visit?"

Logan smirked as he opened the refrigerator door. "My apartment is five hundred square feet. I can give you a running commentary from here."

"I'll let you know if I have any questions," Ellie replied, matching his hint of sarcasm. Logan was facing the stove, his focus on the food, and giving her the perfect opportunity to admire his broad shoulders and-

"Stop that!" she chided herself. Turning to the right, away from the kitchen and her ex-husband, Ellie scanned Logan's living room. While Trish's apartment style could be described as modern and minimalist, Logan's conveyed a more lived-in, rustic atmosphere. Warm espresso walls complemented the deep mahogany floor and earth-toned area rug. Books of varying heights and colors shared shelf space with various sentimental memorabilia. A desk over by the door to the balcony had a project in progress scattered across its surface. In the center of the room, an old chest doubled as a coffee table.

A collection of framed photographs above Logan's couch caught her attention, and she wandered closer. "You've got some great scenery shots here."

"Thanks. That wall was bare the first year I lived here, and then I got the brilliant idea to use some of my travel photos."

"You always were a good photographer. This waterfall is breathtaking."

"Gullfoss. It's in Iceland."

"Wow." Ellie's eyes traced the series of cascades. "I almost had a layover in Iceland when Trish and I flew to Europe last summer, but we went with a different flight."

"It had amazing landscapes. I'd love to go back sometime when there's more than eight hours of daylight."

"When did you go?" Ellie half-laughed, turning towards Logan.

He looked over his shoulder, his eyes meeting hers. "Thanksgiving several years ago."

"Thanksgiving is family time."

The frown disappeared as quickly as it appeared, but Ellie saw it. "That was the first year after our divorce. I didn't feel "family-ish" that holiday."

"Oh." Her eyebrows creased in compassion. "I get that. Yeah, that first set of holidays wasn't the easiest."

"So when one of my college buddies suggested heading out for a long weekend, I jumped on it," Logan replied, his eyes dropping to the pasta as he transferred it to a large bowl.

"Iceland in November though? Wasn't that freezing?"

Logan shrugged. "Not that bad really. I mean a beach baby like you might have frozen but-"

"I do go on vacation to places other than the beach now." She pursed her lips at him, and Logan's grin turned sly.

"I know even though I'm still surprised that your friend managed to get you to stay in a hostel."

"We were able to stay right in the middle of Madrid, and it was a private room with its own bathroom. It felt like a regular hotel."

"Exactly what I tried telling you a decade ago." Logan rolled his eyes but then winked.

"Did you stay in hostels in Iceland?" she asked. Asking questions seemed like the best bet to distract from the fluttering in her stomach his wink set off.

"Nah, with four guys it wasn't that bad to split up the cost of an actual hotel room. Hey, I forgot to get out glasses. Do you mind grabbing them from the cupboard while I finish adding the sauce to the pasta?"

"Got it." Ellie came around the kitchen island. "Which cupboard?"

"Right side."

"Should have known."

"We had a good kitchen organizational system going when we were married. No need to change it," Logan replied.

"At least we did some things right," Ellie laughed as she reached into the cupboard for two clear glasses.

She almost jumped when she went to close the cupboard door and Logan was staring at her. "I can think of a few more things we did right beyond organizing the kitchen."

Logan's eyes glinted, and Ellie just managed not to bite her lip. "Like being courteous divorcees?"

He snorted. "You make that sound so clinical. I think we're doing better than courteous. Courteous was two years ago when I texted you that embarrassing message about locking myself out of the building and wondering if your sister was home and could come down to let me back in."

Ellie giggled. "More embarrassing was me almost falling off the treadmill at the gym when your message came through. I was so surprised to see a text from you that I forgot to keep moving."

"You never told me that." Logan turned to pull the garlic bread out of the oven.

"Because it was embarrassing."

"But funny."

"Okay, your turn. Embarrassing gym story."

"Don't have any."

Ellie raised an eyebrow and shot him her best disbelieving teacher look although granted not one that she used much. Preschoolers didn't respond well to it.

"Well, maybe there's one..."

~

"Thank you for dinner," Ellie said, picking her plate up and following Logan over to the small kitchen nook. After Logan's story about complaining to the gym manager about the lock on his locker not working only to find out he had been trying to get into the wrong one, their conversation had bounced around in an easy-going manner.

"Dessert?"

"Thanks but no. It's getting late."

"I've got ice cream." Logan stepped towards the stainless steel refrigerator, his movement drawing him close. He shifted, resting a hand on the edge of the sink, the distance between them just inches. "Sure I can't tempt you?"

Ellie drew in a breath, her eyes locking on Logan's. There had been a slight tease in his voice, but his expression held only intensity. His gaze flickered to her lips, and Ellie swallowed, a tumble of emotions pouring through her. She missed that intimate touch, the closeness that came from being in his arms, but she was wary. Their easy connection over dinner didn't erase all the hard moments at the end of their marriage. Her focus this weekend needed to be on her race, not indulging her desire to curl up in her ex-husband's embrace.

"You can tempt me to help wash up the dishes," Ellie offered, dropping her eyes over to the sink.

"I've got them," Logan replied, his voice a bit more reserved. She glanced up, but Logan was reaching for a dish towel.

"Hey, you okay?" She reached a hand out and laid it on his lower arm. Even through the flannel shirt, warmth radiated.

"Yeah. Maybe a little disappointed that the evening is ending already, but you're right. It is getting late."

"Uh huh," Ellie squeaked out the neutral response.

"Let me walk you to the door." Logan dropped the dish towel on the counter and motioned towards the entrance. Ellie walked ahead of him and then waited while he undid the locks.

"I really did enjoy dinner tonight," she said.

"I did too." Logan smiled, affection glimmering in his eyes.

"Sorry I can't stay for the ice cream."

"You might have been disappointed in it anyway."

Ellie tilted her head at him. "It's chocolate, isn't it?"

"Do you even have to ask?"

Ellie shook her head. "I don't understand how your favorite ice cream flavor hasn't changed since you were five."

"Haven't found anything better. Sometimes that happens." Logan held her gaze, and electricity shot through the casual atmosphere. Ellie felt her earlier resolve to keep things platonic melting. Logan lifted an arm towards her just as they both heard a faint buzz from the phone in her hand.

"I should check that," she murmured, her voice catching.

"You could wait a minute." Logan shifted forward, leaning his right hand on the wall next to her, his body very much in her personal space. A thrill buzzed through her only to dim when her phone vibrated again.

"It's probably Trish." The words were an apologetic whisper as she twisted away from him and glanced at the phone's lit up screen. "Yeah, she's back."

"So heading out then?" There was a weight behind the question that Ellie wasn't ready to deal with.

"Yep, thanks again for dinner." She reached behind her for the door handle and tugged, grateful that Logan had already undone the locks. "I'll see you again this weekend sometime before I go."

"Okay." Logan drew the word out, a slight crease of confusion crossing his forehead.

"Bye then!" Ellie gave a quick wave and slid out the door. As she pulled it shut, she got one more glimpse of Logan, and her stomach flipped at his perplexed expression.

"Not right now," she muttered, trying to shove away thoughts of this unexpected potential romance in favor of focusing on her upcoming race. However, by the time the elevator arrived on Trish's floor, she had to admit defeat in the face of the roller coaster her emotions were riding. Contentment. Uncertain nervousness. Anticipation. Worry. Excitement. Hope.

Ellie stopped in front of Trish's door, groaned, and spun around to stalk back down the hallway. No way was she going into her sister's apartment feeling this wired.

"You should have expected something like this." Her feelings for Logan had run strong since they had started dating in high school. She had attributed this depth of emotion as the bond that had kept their relationship together even when he went away to the University of Maryland and she stayed at home and commuted to the local community college. At least until he had spent half his summer away on an internship, and she had started feeling that Logan was slipping away. That insecurity had played into her push to get married between their junior and senior years of college, on the four-year anniversary of their first date.

Ellie completed one circuit of the hallway, but her emotions still roiled, the memories clear.

The romance of that sunny summer day had faded, and Ellie had faced the reality of marrying more out of fear of losing than a desire to build and grow together. In the end it had not come as a surprise when following yet another fight on continuing to rent versus buying their first house that she had seen clearly that her marriage was over and not for an earth-shattering reason such as an extramarital affair or abuse. She and Logan simply no longer fit, and it made more sense to let go before they resented or even hated each other. He could follow his desire to live in a city and work on his career before starting a family.

She could stay in a small town near her parents, meet a nice guy, and have two babies before thirty.

Except of course post-divorce hadn't turned out as planned, and now when she least expected it, Ellie found herself reconsidering her feelings for her ex-husband.

"Our evening went so well-"

"No," she said out loud, breaking the thought off. "Be grateful for the new connection between you and Logan, but don't push. That didn't work before. This weekend is not about a second chance at romance but a second chance at meeting your race goals."

The spoken words bolstered her. Ellie took another deep breath and made her way back along the hallway to Trish's door.

THE NEXT AFTERNOON Ellie and Trish stepped out of the building lobby and onto the sidewalk next to South Capitol Street. The morning rain had given way to a slightly chilly but dry October afternoon. Ellie had gone to the marathon expo that morning to pick up her race shirt along with the numbered bib and its electronic tag that would track her during the race. Trish had stayed in her apartment to catch up on some work but now was accompanying Ellie for her final training run before the big race.

They jogged to a streetlight and then across the street to follow the sidewalk alongside the Nationals baseball stadium. Trish gave Ellie an update on Alejandra, and Ellie described the throng of runners picking up race packets and browsing various booths with running gear for sale over at the Gaylord Convention Center.

"After navigating that crowd, I can definitely believe that there will be twenty thousand participants in the race tomorrow. Oh, the race booklet has guidance for spectators. We'll want to look at that when we get back to the building."

"That's awesome," Trish replied. "Logan wants to cheer for you too tomorrow."

"He said that?" Ellie's breath caught in a way that had nothing to do with their exercise.

"Sent me a text this morning. I told him I'd fill him in on the plan once we had one."

"Okay." There was a slight shake in her voice, and Trish's next comment squashed any hope Ellie had that her sister wouldn't notice.

"You haven't talked about dinner last night at all. Everything go okay?"

"I think Logan wanted to kiss me."

"Yes!" Trish's shout bounced out over the water of the Anacostia River.

"What's with the strong reaction?" Ellie forgot to watch where she was running and almost bumped into the railing separating their path from the water.

"I knew there was still something between the two of you!"

"Trish, our divorce didn't happen because we stopped caring for each other. We separated because we could see that we were very different people that didn't fit and wanted better for each other."

"And that was true then, but now I think the two of you fit better than you did when you got married. You've both grown and changed over the years since your divorce. Honestly, I kind of wonder if you two aren't more suited to each other now than on your wedding day."

If it weren't for the instincts of picking up her feet honed over dozens of miles the last few months, Ellie would have tripped, Trish's statement catching her off-guard. "We're divorced! How can you think we're more compatible now?"

"Because you're both in the same stage again. Listen." Trish popped a hand up, forestalling whatever protest Ellie had opened her mouth to deliver. "Yes, I know you both were in college when you got married, but Logan was excited about his future career and discovering a world bigger than where we grew up. You didn't have that same enthusiasm for your future job. You wanted a family and took a position in a daycare to use your degree not because you felt called to it. So you two struggled for a few years and then separated. Both of you had to figure out what you really wanted your lives to look like on your own. Ellie, moving to South Carolina was the best thing you could've done."

"Didn't you just contradict yourself? Did you forget that when I moved to South Carolina I lived with Mom and Dad? That's not being on my own."

"Pfft." Trish dismissed Ellie's comment. Either that or a bug flew into her mouth. "You only lived with them for what, the first three, four, six months?"

"Seven."

"Right. You were getting your footing under you as you adjusted to your new job."

"Also thanks to our parents."

"All Dad did was tell you about the job!" Ellie could feel Trish's glare. "You're the one who made the decision to interview with the school and then move. You're the one who took the chance on teaching in a preschool that was attached to an elementary school and found your fit. You know, I loved those phone calls from you that fall when you talked about your day with the kids. Your voice overflowed with joy."

"I was so tired every day after work that first year, but I had never felt so fulfilled. It's a big change when you want to go to work and feel like you're actively helping build towards the future."

"And being content in your job is only part of your growth in the years since your divorce. Logan always had his recreational soccer league. You've developed a passion for running. I know the both of you are involved in volunteer opportunities in your churches and out in the community," Trish laughed. "Even in that you two are on the same wavelength. Remember how both of you were volunteer Santa elves at a Christmas giveaway last year?"

"That was not planned."

"So maybe a coincidence or maybe something more."

"Trish, I think you're stretching for a happy ending."

"Most exes don't text each other multiple times a week."

"Logan and I have moved past our divorce and get along well."

"If he wanted to kiss you, then I'd say you get along better than well." Trish replied drily.

"Even if he did, that doesn't mean anything."

"Or maybe I'm right and there is something deep and significant between you and Logan."

Ellie's chest tightened to hear her own thoughts spoken out loud by someone else, but she stayed silent for several feet as they jogged.

"Ellie?"

"You're right." Her response wasn't much louder than the sound of their feet pounding on the wooden boardwalk that ran alongside the fenced Navy Yard. "At least on how I feel."

"You do care for Logan as more than a good friend."

"Totally not expected when we started talking again. Then he called me on my birthday in May. A month later we were having bi-weekly phone conversations. Usually just fun chatting about what was going on in our lives, but the more serious moments like when I could hear the sincerity in his voice about looking forward to having his own kids soon brought us closer. I've done a good job keeping those thoughts in the back of my head, and then last night brought me face-to-face with those feelings."

"But?"

"I didn't come to D.C. for Logan. I came for me, for my race, and that's where I need to keep my focus."

They made a U-turn to start working their way back. A seagull squawked, but Ellie still heard Trish's sigh. "Well, not the full confession I was hoping for, but it's a start."

"Trish."

"I'm done," her sister replied. "What movie do you think we should watch this evening?"

~

ELLIE WAS PUTTING her dinner dishes in the dishwasher when there was a knock at the door. "Expecting company, Trish?"

"No." Her sister peeked through the peephole. "It's Logan."

"Logan?" Ellie's heart rate sped up. She was still processing her afternoon conversation with Trish. Facing Logan was not on her evening to-do list, but she could already hear the door opening.

"Hey, hope I'm not interrupting."

"Not at all," was Trish's breezy answer. "We were just cleaning up after dinner and are thinking of watching a movie. Want to join us?"

Ellie gulped but had to turn her semi-murderous glare at Trish into a welcoming grin as Logan appeared. He returned her smile despite the tenseness she noticed in his shoulders.

"I was actually hoping Ellie would go for a walk with me."

"Oh, that sounds nice, but I'm trying to limit a lot of movement tonight."

"Good thing I planned to walk on the rooftop terrace. It's not that big."

The elevator ride was short, tension sparking between the two of them in the confined space. Out on the roof beneath the dark sky, it wasn't much better. Ellie wandered around to the left, and a light breeze followed her as she walked along the concrete terrace. The Capitol building glowed ahead of her in the distance, Logan a step behind on her right.

"I've been thinking about last night." He broke the silence.

"Dinner was good."

"I thought so too. But," Logan paused and Ellie's nerves heightened. "I'm not sure if I misread things at the end and overstepped."

"Overstepped?"

"Everything between us was clicking last night like when we were together. I'd almost say it felt even easier than when we were married. I wanted to kiss you goodnight."

Ellie bit her lip and kept her eyes focused on the Capitol building.

"Except you kept things casual and polite, so I've been asking myself if I've read too much into our interactions over the last year. Ellie, tell me the truth. Why didn't you want me to know you were coming to D.C.?"

"I told you when you picked me up at the airport. I didn't want to make a big deal out of this race."

"Okay." Logan bit the word out and stared ahead, his jaw tight. "That still doesn't sound like the whole story to me."

Ellie turned back towards the Capitol building and took a deep breath. "I don't want to have to tell people that I failed again."

"What?"

"Last year I ran my second marathon with the same goal that I'm going for tomorrow. Breaking the four-hour mark. I put in the long runs, ran in the rain, did cross-training. Told everyone-"

"Not everyone."

Ellie paused and raised an eyebrow at Logan before continuing. "Paid careful attention to what I ate that last week. Then the day of the race I just didn't have it. I finished in four hours, six minutes, and twenty-nine seconds."

"Was that faster than your first one?"

"By about two minutes."

"That's good."

Ellie rolled her eyes. "Not when it misses my goal. I failed. I'm afraid that's going to happen again, and I don't want to have to tell people that I didn't make my goal."

"Telling someone you failed isn't the worst thing in the world."

"That first Thanksgiving, the one you spent over in Iceland? I was with my extended family. We're talking all the aunts and uncles and cousins and their spouses and their kids. I can't even tell you how many people I had to explain that no, my husband wasn't coming and that he was actually my ex-husband. It was a good warm-up for all the Christmas events I guess." She gave a sharp laugh. "So no, a marathon is a lot less important in the big scheme than a marriage, but I don't want to deal with any of that again."

"So you're just going to play it safe? Not set big goals?"

"I've done that before, and it didn't work out so well," Ellie snapped, realizing she was talking about more than only running now.

Logan leveled a look at her. "It didn't work out for either of us, but I haven't given up on fighting for what's important to me."

Anger flared up, edged close to rolling over. This weekend was supposed to be about her race not bringing up the past. "You don't get to decide whether I'm a fighter or not. I decide how I approach what's important to me. What I choose to fight for."

"I'm not deciding. I'm observing."

"And your observations are flawed. Sure, we've been getting to know each other again a lot over the last several months, but you don't know what I'm thinking."

"So have you considered the possibility of us again?" Logan looked squarely at her.

Ellie opened her mouth and paused, trying to collect her thoughts. She only managed to grab one of the thoughts tumbling through her head. "My race is my priority this weekend."

He chuckled, but it wasn't a happy laugh. "Ironic, isn't it? We're getting along better than we have in years, but we're still in two different places."

A chill ran through Ellie that had nothing to do with the breeze. The openness between them at dinner the night before, that had been growing over the last two years and especially the last several months, was gone from Logan's voice.

"Anyway," he continued pushing away from the railing, "I might have misread us being on the same page with our lives, with the idea of us, but I don't want to make your race tomorrow any harder by keeping you out."

Logan turned to walk back to the entrance into the building, and Ellie followed, keeping quiet until they stepped into the elevator.

"You really think we're in two completely different places?"

He kept his eyes on the door. "Maybe not completely different but enough that attempting something more than this friendship we've rebuilt would probably end painfully."

"Rebuilding our friendship took time. Moving into something more would take time too."

Logan drew in a long breath. "And for that to be successful, it wouldn't be something you could hide like you're doing with your marathon."

The elevator dinged as it stopped on Trish's floor. Ellie reached over and held the "Doors Open" button.

"Not being vocal about running a marathon isn't the same thing as hiding it."

"But you said you have kept it and your goal mostly to yourself."

Ellie bit her lip, unable to deny the truth of his words. She blinked, a tear forming. She didn't want Logan to be right, but his point was undeniable.

"Hey, it's okay. Come here." Logan stepped out of the elevator and held his arms open for a hug. Ellie moved into his embrace, her head tucking against his shoulder. "How many divorced couples even make it back to a friendship like we have? We're in a good place."

Ellie squeezed, and Logan tightened his arms around her. Closing her eyes, she relaxed into the closeness and ignored the finality underlying Logan's voice.

"I'm heading back to my apartment. Enjoy the movie with Trish and good luck tomorrow," Logan loosened his hold and moved to press the elevator button, the doors sliding open again.

"Thanks." Ellie replied, managing to keep the thread of sadness out of her voice.

"No problem," Logan smiled, but as the doors slid shut, Ellie noticed that his eyes reflected the disappointment in her own.

❧

SHE WASN'T GOING to find her pacing group before the race started. Trish had dropped her off in the morning darkness with plenty of time, but a misjudgment on the length of the Porta Potty lines now had Ellie jumping up into the grassy median and jogging past runners aiming for a slower marathon. Nerves jangling, her heart leaped at one of the small signs signifying a pacing group and then dropped as she read "4:15." She needed the four-hour pacer or else her marathon plan was shot. Thanks to the electronic tag in her bib, her official race time started when she crossed over the starting line timing mats, but her race strategy was based on running with the four-hour pacing group and letting someone else do the hard work of not going too fast or too slow.

She didn't make it. The noise rose, cheers filled the air, and the crowd of runners flowed forward. Frustration welled up. This, this was exactly why she hadn't wanted to talk about her goals. She was facing failure even before completing the first quarter mile of the race.

"Keep it together." Ellie turned her attention to the crowd around her, still scanning for her pacer. Her watch buzzed at the one-mile mark, and she bit back a growl. Nine minutes and twenty-three seconds. She needed to be hitting nine-minute miles. Technically nine minutes and nine seconds would work, but the turns and curves of a marathon meant she would probably run a third or half mile longer than official race distance. Mile two took them between the tall buildings of Rosslyn, but Ellie noticed few details. Her attention turned to her watch as she counted off the quarter miles and did the math in her head to try to stay on pace.

"Shoot." Her watch blinked the second mile time at her, 9:15. Closer but not quite enough. She was nearly a minute behind where she

460

needed to be. "See, Logan, I was right not putting my goal out there for everyone to know."

Ellie blinked, startled by her words. Why was she talking to an imaginary Logan? He had nothing to do with her race. She had been doing a commendable job of compartmentalizing, thoughts of last night's fight and Logan only crossing her mind two or three times since waking up that morning. Her mind flittered back to her words, and a phrase jumped out.

"You don't get to decide whether I'm a fighter or not."

She had said the words in frustration, more on the defensive than anything else. Now she realized she had a choice. If finishing this marathon in under four hours mattered to her, then it was up to her to fight for it. She knew what time she needed to hit for each mile and even what the quarter mile splits should be. The cool breeze sliding around her shoulders combined with the clear sky hinted that the weather would be in her favor. The city setting equaled thousands of spectators to boost her energy, and the crowd of runners around her had thinned enough for her to ease into her stride instead of needing to focus on weaving around other competitors.

"Just focus on this mile. Fight for this mile." Ellie centered herself and stretched her legs. When her watch buzzed, she breathed in relief. Nine minutes on the nose. Although she figured the downhill slope on the second half of that mile had been a factor, she was encouraged even more when the next three miles all clocked in under nine minutes with one super fast mile at only eight minutes and fifteen seconds. By Mile 10 when they passed by the Lincoln Memorial, she was securely in her running zone and waved excitedly at Trish staked out shortly before the Mile 11 marker as planned the night before.

Continuing along Ohio Drive and nearing the Jefferson Memorial, Ellie was startled to hear her name.

"Looking great, Ellie! Keep it up!" Logan stood over in the grass, his legs on both sides of a bicycle. She waved, a warmth spreading through her at his support. Her mood sobered at Mile 12, the Blue Mile lined with photos of fallen servicemen and women, but the strength stayed. Another glimpse of Logan at Mile 15 and then Trish near Mile 16. Mile 17 curved around the Washington Monument and Ellie's heart lifted as the course raced up along the tree-lined Mall past the museums of the

Smithsonian Institute. She was feeling good, taking in the sights of the Capitol Building, National Botanic Garden, and Air and Space Museum.

"Awesome job! You've got this!" The cheer echoed, and Ellie grinned as she realized why. Trish and Logan were both on the side of 14th Street, their voices climbing over other cheers as she headed into the final quarter of the race.

It was in Mile 23, running between the tall buildings of Crystal City, that Ellie felt the first twinge from her calves. She grabbed a cup from the next water station, but the truth stared at her when her watch tallied the next mile. Her heart dropped. She was still under nine minutes, but she was slowing down.

The cramping increased, the pain seizing her with every step. She whimpered as her stride shortened to a walk.

"You are so close. You're less than two miles from the finish line. Choose to fight for this." The words were more than a pep talk. They were a command. Pressing her foot up against the curb, Ellie stretched one leg and then the other before starting out again. The tightness wasn't gone, forcing her to stop and repeat the stretching two more times before her watch notified her that she had taken almost ten minutes to run a mile.

Ellie batted down the wave of panic and whispers of failure. "You decided to fight for this race, and that's what you are going to do. You made up the first slow miles and have been banking seconds ever since. Keep moving."

Her lower legs aching, she pushed one foot out in front of the other. Arlington Cemetery sprawled to her left now, but Ellie's eyes focused straight ahead. Drawing in one deep breath after another, she kept picking spots ahead of her as her next micro-goal.

Then they were turning to the left and starting the final hill. She had trained specifically for this ending and powered up the incline, the cramping fading amongst the cheers of the crowd. She surged across the finish line, and her fingers fumbled to stop her watch.

"Congratulations," the Marine beamed as he draped a red medal over her neck.

"Thank you," Ellie breathed out. A few more unsteady steps and she glanced down at her watch. Her face split into a smile at the number: 3:59.

~

ELLIE STEPPED out of the shower. Well, more maneuvered out of the shower, one hand planted firmly on the wall as she gingerly lifted first one leg up and over the tub's side and then the other. Her toes relishing the soft bath mat, she reached for a towel.

"Ellie?" Trish called from the other side of the bathroom door.

"Yeah?"

A slight pause and then, "There's someone here to see you."

"Logan?" Her heart pounded as if she was in the final mile of her race again.

"I can tell him to come back later."

"No!" She blurted the word out. "No, I just need a couple minutes."

She had to lean against the sink for balance to pull on her yoga pants, and then her arms screamed in protest when she raised them to slide into her comfy long-sleeved shirt. She gritted her teeth as she peeked in the fogged mirror to pull her wet hair up into a messy bun, the original plan of borrowing Trish's hair dryer forgone for now. She took a breath to try to calm her heart rate and opened the bathroom door.

"I wanted to say congratulations." Logan stood in her sister's kitchen space. "You made your goal."

"Thank you." Ellie glanced around. "Where's Trish?"

"She wanted to give us some privacy."

"Oh." Ellie shuffled out of the bathroom and over to the couch. Even through the fuzz of marathon brain, she could tell that Logan wasn't here just to say good job.

"How are you feeling?"

"Exhausted and exhilarated." The smile came from deep within.

"I'm proud of you. You were amazing out there."

"You got a workout too this morning. I saw you a couple times."

He chuckled. "Riding my bike around doesn't equal what you did."

"Well, thanks for the support."

"It's what I should have offered last night instead of accusing you of not being a fighter." Logan slid down onto the couch next to her. "That wasn't fair of me, asking you to prove that you could fight on your own when at the same time I was asking you to consider building a life with me."

"It's a fair question though. Am I going to fight for a relationship? Or shy away from putting a real effort in? Tell myself that if it doesn't work out, it's not as big a deal?"

"But a relationship doesn't mean doing it by yourself. It means the two of us pushing forward through the hard parts together. I was wrong last night to demand that you prove a willingness to fight. I'm sorry." Logan's eyes held a mix of regret and hope.

Ellie reached over for his hand. "You know, my race did not get off to a good start."

"It didn't?"

"Nope." She shook her head. "I didn't find the pacing group before the race started. Then the course was really crowded at the beginning which is normal, but my first two miles came in slow. I wanted to give up on my four-hour goal."

"But you didn't."

"Okay, I realize I'm bouncing around here a bit, but last night's conversation, it hurt."

"I am sorry." Logan squeezed her hand and she squeezed back.

"But you weren't entirely wrong. Last night I didn't know what I was capable of fighting for. If someone had told me how the race would start this morning, I would have decided so much for my goal and not pushed." Ellie paused, her lips curving into a gentle smile. "Sure, a race isn't the same thing as a relationship, but I proved to myself this morning that I am strong enough. Running, working, dating, I'm ready to fight for what I want."

"And what do you want?" Logan's voice was husky.

"My marathon today was a second chance at my goal time." Ellie's eyes locked onto his. "Even though this was the last outcome I ever expected when we started talking again, I want that second chance with you."

Logan's eyes glowed, a slow grin spreading across his face, and he scooted closer to her. He wrapped an arm around Ellie's shoulder. "I want that too."

"It won't be easy."

"Few things worth having are."

"We have some big things to figure out."

"Later." Logan leaned in close, and his voice dropped. "Today we're celebrating, and I have the perfect idea."

"Really?" Ellie tingled, her lips already feeling his touch.

"There's a container of ice cream on the counter. Your favorite: mint chocolate chip."

"Oh." Ellie blinked, confused at the tangent. She started to shift back, but Logan chuckled and pulled her closer.

"But this first." He bent towards her, and her confusion gone, Ellie lifted her face towards his, their kiss the promise of a true second chance.

ABOUT THE AUTHOR

Meredith Deichler has been writing since preschool when her stories apparently featured bunny rabbits that climbed trees. While characters and settings have changed over the years, her desire to create with words has not. Through her writing she enjoys showing readers new places on the way to a happy ending.

Ms. Deichler resides in Ohio where she teaches Spanish. She is also active in a local running club and has participated in several shows at the community theater. Additional passions include photography and travel.

To learn more, please check out her author profile: https://www.amazon.com/~/e/B07B467QSN.

LITTLE SHOP OF GEEKDOM

RACHEL RADNER

She's finally found the man of her dreams. Problem is — she might've just caught him stealing from her gaming shop.

1

———

*G*lass shatters against a back wall the moment I'm about to win big.

I jerk away from my gaming app.

Peering over the edges of the phone, ignoring that it's my turn to make a move against the player I'm sparring, I glare across rows of merchandise on shelves. Strategy games, comics, and unpainted miniature figurines are stacked neatly in proper placement.

All in order, nothing in disarray.

I search for the source of the crash, eyes darting around, keen like a fox. Under my ownership, Geekdom Games has always been completely organized, so this abrupt noise brings an extra sense of panic racing through me. I glance past patrons seated at cherrywood tables with games laid out on the surface. Their ears collectively perk. Even the table with the heated campaign of *Dungeons & Dragons* pauses. A disturbance of this kind is unprecedented.

On the far side, furthest from the exit, a body dashes between shelves so quickly I'm unable to discern any physical features. One thing's clear: that person's rushing to leave the scene of what might be a crime.

"Oh, no, you don't," I mutter, jumping up from my seat by the register.

Instinct guides me. I disregard every piece of advice I've ever read about not chasing after shoplifters—or whatever this person is.

Without a second thought, I bolt toward the exit doors, French braids whipping across my neck. Though I'm short, I force elongated strides in hope of reaching the stranger before he or she can make it to the exit. I don't know what happened, or what this person has broken or possibly stolen, but the abrupt movement tells me everything I need to know.

The individual whisks past the final shelf, male body moving into view in the clearing en route to the front door. Shaggy, mid-length dark hair bounces as he runs. He's wearing an olive cargo jacket with flare from various fandoms, predominantly anime. A messenger bag is slung over his shoulder, and I catch what appears to be a *Darkness Rising* patch stitched to the side of it. Shaking my head, I run faster now, ashamed someone representing my favorite anime would not only commit a crime but also attempt to flee the scene.

He thrusts his body into the doors, pushing through to the outside right as I near him. With every ounce of strength available to me, I barrel into the stranger, knocking him down. Together, we tumble outside, rolling on the hard concrete until I stop myself and pin him to the ground.

I plant a strong palm against his chest which heaves up and down with erratic movement. His eyes press together in a tight line, thick brows knit in either anger or defeat; I'm not sure which. My jittering nerves begin to settle, and I take in his physical attributes. He's the super attractive, geeky gamer type—my *only* type, my kryptonite. Roundish nose, square jaw, tanned skin. His boyishly mature face suggests he's around my age, potentially in his late twenties or early thirties.

All at once, he looks familiar. I recognize him. I just don't know how.

"What the hell do you think you're doing?" I grit out, jerking my hand into his solar plexus once more to remind him I have the high ground.

Slowly, he unclenches his eyelids. Caramel irises helplessly gaze up at me, and he lifts his arms in surrender.

"Okay," he says with relenting hands. "You win."

"You *bet* I win." A thick layer of irritation fills my throat cavity. The hand not holding him down balls into a fist, and I realize how angry I am. Furious. I'm too heated to care that he could sue me for lack of probable cause, and I've chased someone down without actually seeing them committing a crime. But right now, none of that matters to me.

Geekdom Games is all I have, and some punk isn't going to pull one over on me.

"What happened in my shop? Why were you running? What did you take?"

Accusations fly from my mouth, and I regret none of them.

"Whoa, whoa, whoa. I'm not a thief." His expression clouds with guilt. Against reason, his puppy dog eyes disarm me, those warm features softening my resolve. A part of me wants to believe this is all some kind of misunderstanding, to forget this whole thing and let him go. But I'm a female in a male-dominated industry, and I've been messed with too many times. Experience warns me to beware.

"Oh, yeah, you're not a thief?" I ask. "Innocent people don't run like you did."

"They do when they break something valuable. I'm sorry. I panicked."

My palm continues to dig into his chest. His focus slides down to my hand, like he's trying to assess how he might get out of this. But then his eyes meet mine, and he's searching me for what seems like forgiveness.

"Whatever you broke smashed into the wall," I say with a locked jaw. "Like you threw it. Am I missing something here?"

He turns away, lips slanted downward.

Using my free hand, I reach for the phone in my pocket. "Exactly what I thought. Let's see what the cops think, huh?" Of course, I wonder if calling the cops might not work in my favor considering how I've handled this, but he did just verbally admit to breaking a product. I let go of the worry and assume his admission will help my case.

"No. Wait." One of his arms snakes up, and he gently rests his fingers over my hand holding the cell. For someone who's a complete stranger, his touch doesn't feel so strange at all. "Please don't do that. Can't we work out a deal?"

Yanking back, I dial the local police department, a number I've committed to memory in case of emergency. Before I connect the call, he slides up onto his haunches, linking his fingers together. He's holding out his hands, pleading.

"*Please.*" His voice comes out as hardly more than a whisper.

I glance between him and the phone. There's a second *Darkness Rising* patch by the breast pocket of his olive cargo jacket. The design is of my favorite character, Vanya, a woman who takes crap from nobody and strives to fight corruption. She's one of the few honest characters in the show—a fact that makes his choice in flare ironic.

"Vanya would be disappointed," I say.

His nose crinkles, as if I've confused him, but I point to his jacket. His eyes color with understanding. Dipping his chin, he once again gazes away, his shame so thick it rubs off on me and something tight gnaws at my stomach. All at once, I feel bad for him, like I've been a real jerk, even though *he's* the one in the wrong.

Ignoring my better judgement, I lower my phone.

"What happened?" I demand.

He opens his mouth but another voice answers from behind.

"Looks like he completely destroyed our crystal Yoda bust," Travis says in his familiar baritone. I turn. Behind us, my assistant manager, Travis, stands at the helm of a throng of customers all crowded around us by the side of the building. Every eye is trained on me and the stranger. One young girl with glasses uses her phone to film the scene, and I wonder how much of this she's caught on camera.

Great.

Travis steps between the two of us, glancing at me protectively before casting hardened eyes on the unknown man. Travis's Geekdom Games T-shirt, frayed at the edges along his biceps and triceps, shows off burly, stacked muscles. It's an unspoken understanding that, if I need him to, he'll *take care of* this man.

In Travis's arms, he cradles the head of the Yoda bust—what's left of it, anyway. The collector's item, busted in half and jagged where once polished, has a million cracks shooting down its split core, reflecting light in many different directions. Yoda's remaining ear has been clipped off at the top, leaving his expression with an even grimmer appearance.

Broken, Yoda very much is.

"What the hell did you do to Yoda?" I ask the man, glaring. "This crystal bust was one of our rarest items."

Travis flashes a tiny, white piece of paper with an inked number on it. "You damaged a bust worth close to two grand, guy."

"*Two grand*?" the stranger asks, caramel eyes wide. "For that?"

"Excuse me?" I cross my arms, chest lifted, words so loud they've carried through the entire crowd. He's just set off my fuse. If it wasn't lit before, it is now on fire, and he's burned every single one of my cookies. Without looking, I sense my customers taking a step back. "You walk in, vandalize my shop, and then insult the quality of my product?"

"I didn't vandal—" he begins to say.

"Uh, yeah, you did," I interrupt, pointing to the busted Yoda head. All at once, the weight of this causes my insides to tense. Unbeknownst to anyone, save me and Travis, bills have been piling up. Keeping Geekdom Games afloat since I inherited the business two years ago has proven to be a challenge. One broken bust may not sink us, but it certainly doesn't help our rocky financial situation. "To come in here, break something, and rush off so recklessly and irresponsibly, you clearly don't understand how difficult it is to run an independent gaming shop."

"I'm not going to argue," the stranger says with a thick voice, studying me with those soft eyes. "You're right. I shouldn't have run, but..." He pauses, peering over at the young woman with the phone who's still recording this. Lowering his voice so only Travis and I can hear, he continues. "I've got reasons, okay? Can we please just go somewhere private and discuss this? Work out some kind of arrangement?"

"Fine," I hear myself say like a reflex I'm not in control of. Though I doubt the stranger's ability to pay for the damages, and I don't know what he can do to rectify this mess, his plan sounds more logical than anything else I've got. Besides, like him, I'd rather discuss this without an audience. "We'll go to my back office."

Travis and I exchange a nod. As usual, we're on the same page, and I can count on him to have my back, unlike most people in my life. I intuit from Travis's less-than-stellar background that he, too, would prefer to handle this without the police present. Less anxiety that way, he'd probably say if we were speaking alone.

Travis backs into the crowd, excusing himself as he steps inside Geekdom Games with broken Yoda.

I wait, stern eyes tracking the stranger, expecting him to head in before me for obvious reasons. Thankfully, he reads my pause for exactly what it is. Lowering his gaze in defeat, he shamefully clumps after Travis, hanging his head the entire way to the back room.

I don't know what bothers me more—that this is happening, or that for the life of me I can't think where I've seen this stranger before.

Biting my lip, I follow after the two of them, mentally preparing myself for what I'm sure will be the most uncomfortable conversation I've ever had.

2

———

"Name and ID, please," I start, voice stern like the cop I most definitely am not.

Travis waits by the door, arms crossed over his chest. He's cradling Yoda, standing like a statue in a way I imagine is reminiscent of when he worked as the doorman at a bar. I see him channeling his former role as he glares at the stranger sitting across from me at my desk.

Our resident vandal appears gigantic in my cramped office, legs spread wide apart on the folding chair I've given him to use, much too long to fit in the space. He's hunched over the messenger bag in his lap, eyes cast down at the tile floor. Dark tresses of hair somehow fall in neat, tousled waves around his head. Truthfully, he's quite pleasing on the eyes with his smooth, clear skin, and athletic build. In another circumstance, he might have caught my eye.

Except troublemakers are not my type.

Raising a brow, the stranger's eyes slowly pan up to meet mine. "Did you bring me back here to interrogate me, or so we could work something out?"

I clasp my hands on the table. Unsteady aluminum legs tilt with the weight of my fingers.

"You're not in a position to negotiate," I say.

The stranger's lips curl into a stifled grin. For whatever reason, he's fighting not to laugh—which is both frustrating *and* frustratingly cute.

"Who the hell do you think you are, anyway?" I ask. "This isn't a joke."

His mouth drops into a neutral line. "Oh! No. Of course not. It's just—"

"What?"

"*Darkness Rising*." He points to his breast pocket, indicating the patch of Vanya with her dark, wavy locks and formfitting elastic suit. "Vanya's favorite expression. 'You're not in a position to negotiate.' Sorry, I thought you did that on purpose."

"Oh." I blink, instantly recognizing the truth in his words and not surprised that it took me a second. I have a tendency to compartmentalize my life and be so stuck in my own head that I don't immediately pick up connections like that. Now that he's pointed it out, I can't help but hear Vanya and her popular catchphrase. Under my breath, I instinctively mutter her words in Japanese.

The stranger's eyes widen, and he responds in kind, like an impulse, with the appropriate Japanese—another Vanya thing.

"I guess you're not a fan of dubs either, huh?" I ask, referring to the dubbed English version of *Darkness Rising*.

"Nah," he says, waving a hand in the air. "I always watch anime with subtitles. I can't stand some of those English dub translations."

"Yeah!" I agree. "You lose enough meaning with the subtitles as it is."

"Right." He smiles and a visceral level of tension slips away. All it took was one simple conversational exchange. Some of my guard slips, and I find myself smiling back at him, cheeks flush with excitement over this shared connection. It isn't every day I run into a *Darkness Rising* fan, especially not one who knows some of the Japanese phrases. Even in my gaming shop that isn't common.

Swallowing, I force myself to remember why I'm here with him. We're getting too comfortable. I don't do comfortable with troublemakers.

I groan loudly, cutting through the pleasant mood. "Ugh. Stop, okay? This isn't supposed to be a lighthearted conversation. You damaged something, and we need to get down to business."

"Sorry," he says. "I wasn't trying to cause any issues."

"Clearly." My voice stings of sarcasm.

He brushes a hand through his hair, and those caramel irises study me. Despite our circumstances, and the way I've just reprimanded both of us for being so casual, he regards me like I'm familiar, like he might recognize my face.

I don't dare pursue that avenue to find out why.

"The piece is $2099," I say matter-of-factly, "and we have a 'you break it, you buy it' policy."

"You're expecting me to pay full price?" he asks.

"Yeeuuup." I click my tongue for emphasis.

He flashes an incredulous look, but his next words betray his facial expression. "Fine. You have a Venmo account? I can pay half now and half next week, so long as you agree to let me take the pieces of the bust."

I don't see what he could do with a broken Yoda bust, but his request seems reasonable enough. For the first time since we've been in the office, I glance over at Travis to gauge his reaction to this. He shrugs his shoulders.

"That sounds like a fair deal," Travis says. "What say you, Kora?"

The stranger's ears perk at Travis's use of my name, and a crease forms between his brows. "*Kora*? Your name is *Kora*?"

"Uh, yeah?" I ask, fully expecting the stranger to make some *Legend of Korra* reference—a show that rocketed to popularity around my junior year of high school. Classmates teased me so much over *Kora* versus *Korra* that it's become a natural reflex for me to get defensive. "That's my name. What about it?"

"Nothing about it," the stranger says, though his brows knit together further. "It's, umm, pretty... that's all."

"Uh huh." The response leaves my lips automatically, because I don't believe him. The stranger inspects me, and I sense there's something else he's not saying. Something along the lines of, he recognizes my face *and* my name. But I couldn't even begin to guess why or how that would be.

He whips out his phone and types on the screen, averting his eyes. "So, Venmo then?"

"Yeah," I say, finishing the conversation from earlier. "Venmo's fine.

Half up front, also fine. We'll hold the broken pieces here until you pay in full. If you're okay with that, we have a deal."

"Sounds like a plan." He passes me the phone, and I see that he's waiting for me to type my info into Venmo for the funds.

Quickly, I enter in my personal email, the handle I use for all my gaming accounts and everything else under the sun. I realize too late I should've used the Geekdom Games work account. My gaze lifts, and I catch the stranger smiling gleefully, like I've just given him the key to something wonderful.

My phone dings with a notification from Venmo, telling me I've received money from one *Knight Raider King*. So, even in Venmo the stranger keeps his anonymity. In the process of swiping the message away, I accidentally click on *Outlaws of the Night*, my roleplaying game I had up in my app before this fiasco went down.

The one I was about to win.

Not surprisingly, my absence cost me the game. I've not only lost against my competitor, but the rest of the players have beaten me by a landslide. I've been docked some major points and merits for ghosting. I've never ghosted before, but the other players might be too circumspect to invite me back into their next campaign.

No one likes a flake.

Flashing the phone to the stranger, I frown and make a face. "Here's the worst part of today. Do you see this?"

"*Outlaws of the Night*," the stranger says with a suave tone. "Roleplaying game with combat for money, right?"

"Uh, yeah," I say, "and *you* cost me a major win."

"Is that the real reason you're making me pay for the bust?" he asks. "Because I cost you some game?"

Glaring, I lower the phone and slip it back into my pocket. "*Outlaws of the Night* is not just some game. And, no, I'm making you pay for the bust because it's the right thing to do."

Plus, the price of half the Yoda bust is only a little bit shy of the $1200 I would've made if I'd won the last round of my game.

"Yeah. Guess so." The stranger taps the table twice, as if signaling an imminent farewell, and rises from his chair. He's smirking as he pads over to Travis and snatches the bust. The first half, anyway. The rest I'm sure is in a million pieces on the floor—where Travis and I will be heading after this.

"Hey!" I cry. "You're not supposed to get any of the bust until you make the second payment."

"I paid half, I should get half," the stranger says, reneging on our deal from earlier. "I'll come back next week, so I can collect the rest of the bust, and we can do another Venmo transfer."

"Your ID, please," I press. "For accountability."

"I don't think that's a good idea." The stranger shrugs his shoulders. "Don't worry, though. I'll be back."

Gliding around Travis, Knight Raider King does a spin of sorts, and Travis shoots a warning look his way. With one word, I could have Travis stop him, but we've already gotten more than I expected, and I'm still a little worried that the law may not work in my favor considering I placed my hands on this stranger. So, I say nothing. The man and I lock eyes one final time, his glowing as they meet mine, a dazzling smile crossing his lips. Then, he's through the door and out of sight, leaving me flustered in his wake.

I never even learned his first name.

Expecting I'll be screwed out of the other half of the money, and that he's gone for good, an unsettling pang nestles in my stomach.

Not because of the money, though. At least, that's not the number one reason.

What eats away at me now is I *want* to see him again.

And I gravely dislike myself for it.

3

I play *Outlaws of the Night* to keep my store from going under.

This truth hits me harder as I settle into my next duel, legs draped over my couch, virtually rolling my D20 die to see how much impact my strike will leave. The gentle heat from the fireplace across the den laps over my body, warming me, but a shrill chill works its way down my spine. I have a lot of work to do to make up for earlier.

While I wait for the die, I scan the battlefield, which looks no different than the setting of a Wild West shootout town from the movies. Then the die lands on a nineteen—a fatal blow. My bounty hunter peers through the slit eyes of his royal blue mask. He uses his fire blaster to roast the cowboy on the other side of the dirt road. The hit point indicator drops to nil, cowboy clutching his throat as he reels and topples to the ground. Four thousand points deposit into my account, and my lips curl into a grin. I've just beaten a character at level 250 and pulled $452 from the pool of money the campaign members bet into this round.

Virtual celebratory confetti dances across the screen, and a big banner announcing I've won reminds me why I play this game. The money. The rush. And I'm good at it.

Not a second after the confetti fades, gameplay resumes. This is the roleplaying portion of the round where character development occurs.

In *Outlaws of the Night*, it's a balancing act between combat and story that drives the campaign forward. That's why ghosting a game annoys the rest of the team—it halts action from moving forward and prevents the other members of a team from leveling up.

I go to join in, but a chime from the internal messenger portion of the app pops up. Taking this as an opportunity for an acceptable break that no one will get upset over, I excuse myself and exit the active gameplay, sliding over to respond to the person I figure this is from.

"Great job, Kora," the message reads.

Like I guessed, the text is from my greatest competitor, Wyatt, who plays in my campaign. He's the one I came close to beating earlier today before that random vandal with the cute eyes threw a Yoda bust at my wall. I've never beaten Wyatt before, and that would've been my greatest victory. Alas, it wasn't in the cards. Today, anyway.

"Level 1,001 speaks," I type back, referencing his character. Like me, he plays with a bounty hunter, though his avatar wears a purple-colored mask. "I figured you'd be too ashamed to show your digital face after I nearly beat you earlier."

I see a few dots appear in the chat box. He stops. The dots appear once more. And stop.

"Well, thank you for the congrats," I say, surprised he hasn't said more. That isn't like him.

"Hopefully we get a rematch soon," I add when Wyatt still hasn't responded.

In *Outlaws of the Night*, players don't pick their sparring partners. That happens organically through the roleplaying. So, I have no way of knowing when we'll get to duel each other again.

Wyatt starts typing, and my eyes glue to his profile picture. Since almost the beginning of our gameplay history, it's been the same photo: a guy with dark hair wearing a balaclava mask in what's clearly *Outlaws of the Night* cosplay. Once, in the beginning, he used a profile picture that actually showed his entire face, but he's long since taken it down. With how small the photo was, I truthfully don't remember what he looked like under that mask, and sometimes I wonder if the anonymity has been what's helped me open up more to him.

The dots in our chat appear for a solid thirty seconds, and I chew on my lip waiting to read what he has to say. Wyatt and I have been exchanging messages for years, ever since the algorithm placed ten of us together in our campaign. Our team meshed so well that we all elected to stick together.

Despite my heated moments with Wyatt in the game, I'm fond of our chats, even if the most we know of one another is our first names and gaming handles. That doesn't mean we haven't gotten extremely personal. I share things with Wyatt that I could never tell someone offline, such as about my deadbeat dad and why I work so hard to be different.

"You okay over there?" I ask once we reach a full minute with dots jumping in the chat box. "You know we have to get back to a game, right?"

The dots stop. A second later, he shoots back an emoji sticking out its tongue.

"Sorry," he writes. "Today's just been... jarring."

"Yeah, tell me about it," I say. "You wouldn't believe the day I've had."

"Oh, yeah? Try me."

"You first."

He's typing now, and I wait to hear some juicy story. Though Wyatt and I have never gotten specifically personal, he always entertains me with generalized anecdotes.

One time, for example, Wyatt spent a night in Paris with the Gypsies. They roasted food over a fire near Notre Dame, and he talked with them until the crack of dawn, learning about their lifestyle in the streets.

"They treated me like family," Wyatt said once. "They fed me their food and gave me their blankets. Frankly, they amazed me. And from this experience, I realized how much most of us take for granted."

Like this story, I see Wyatt's humanitarian beliefs in so many of our conversations. He champions for human rights to the point that I'm sure a percentage of his game money goes toward helping out the less fortunate.

I've never met anyone else like him.

He's still typing after a minute, so I shoot back a quick message.

"Must've been some day," I say.

"Yeah lol," he says. "I, uh, got laid off at work two days ago."

"Oh, snap. That's awful!" Once I've sent this message, a knot forms in my stomach. I don't know what else to say that'll comfort him. I'm not the sort of person who gives someone false hope or who claims everything will magically be okay. And I wouldn't want to hurt him with my realistic nature. Fortunately, he's typing again.

"It'll be okay," he says. "I've got something else lined up, I *think*. I'm just a little on edge with all the uncertainty and did something else pretty stupid today because of it."

"I'm sure whatever you did wasn't a big deal," I say, confident in every word I've just typed. In one sense, Wyatt's a stranger. But I've talked to him for so many years online that, in another sense, he feels like my closest friend, and I know his character. Sure, during the game in battle mode, there are many instances that I get so angry at him I swear he's my greatest foe. But behind the scenes, in our own little chat bubble, our metal shields slide away, and we're two lonely people talking in a digital sphere.

Wyatt sends me one of those emojis making crazy eyes.

"It was a huge deal that sprung from one massive miscommunication," he writes. "I could've explained it all, but I got scared and didn't. I made the worst impression with this woman who I really respect, who I *really* like, and I don't think I'll ever be able to fix it."

A woman? Oh.

I try not to let that get to me, but a stab of jealousy pings inside my chest. We've never discussed our dating situations, and a part of me hoped that was because neither of us had someone, as irrational as it sounds to want someone I know through a video game. But now, I blanche at his mention of there being another woman, and all my insecurities from being hurt by men in the past rise up.

He's entitled to date anyone he pleases. Of course, he is.

So then why can't I stop the unsettling swirl of emotions pulling at me?

He's typing again.

"Enough about me," he says. "I want to hear about you. Tell me about your crazy day."

Swallowing, I push away the uneasiness in my gut from the bomb he's unknowingly dropped.

I consider telling him about what happened at my shop today. But

I'd have to first explain what I do for a living since we've never talked about our specific careers, and I really do need to get back to the RPG before the team kicks me out for ghosting. I also need some space to process what he's just told me.

"Let's just say I had to deal with some troublemaker at work today," I write, "and it was a real pain in the butt."

He may not know I own a gaming shop or what I do, but he knows the abstracts of my life. Wyatt understands enough about my childhood, and about my dad, to understand that my use of the word troublemaker means I've been triggered.

My dad is a convict. He's currently in jail. I inherited Geekdom Games from him—it was once Dad's façade to deal drugs in a central location.

This is why I severely dislike anyone who causes issues or disrupts my calm, orderly space.

I've been trying to atone for Dad's wrongdoings by cleaning up after his mess my entire life.

Geekdom Games is no different.

"Whoever that guy was," Wyatt says, "he couldn't be as bad as your dad."

I shrug my shoulders like Wyatt can see me. "No one's as bad as my dad. It's just... the circumstance made me feel like I had no control. Like everything I'm doing at work, all my efforts to keep things running smoothly and free of any issues—it's all been for nothing."

Wyatt sends an upside-down smiley face.

"Nothing is for nothing," he writes.

"I guess you're right."

"Besides, for what it's worth, you seem like the kind of person who would be amazing at anything you do."

I can't help the smile that tugs at my face, and I try to pretend I don't know he's interested in some other woman as I stare at his message a little bit too long. I feel an urge to say something else, though I don't know what. Wyatt and I have almost crossed that line many times. But something, probably fear, stops us both. Maybe it's better he's into someone else. I wouldn't want to accidentally damage what we have by getting too emotionally invested. I'm safe in this little bubble with

Wyatt, in a game where we're all cloaked by virtual identities, and I love that I have this space.

"Thank you," I say, feeling our conversation naturally draw to a close. "I really appreciate you listening. Especially in a world where not many understand."

He hearts my last message, and I can't help the way my actual heart leaps in my chest.

Without waiting for another response, I click back over to the live game, and I jump in just in time to watch another set of players dueling in town.

A few rounds pass, and the hurt from what I've learned about Wyatt being interested in someone else rests in my chest.

I excuse myself from the game, hop back into our chat, and proceed to compose a lengthy message that goes into details about how I feel and why.

Once I finish, I sit with my words for a solid ten minutes, debating if I should hit send.

Eventually, I resolve it's all been for naught and that sending this will only cause problems. I close out of the app, leaving the message sitting in my drafts.

4

———

The next day, I'm reorganizing one of the shelves at the shop when the stranger with the messenger bag bolts through the doors. I'm instantly immobilized, dangling an unpainted, miniature Warhammer figurine in a box.

He doesn't see me, and his eyes dart around the store while he passes from one shelf to the next. For a moment, I'm frozen in place as I admire the way his puppy dog eyes helplessly search for something they can't find.

Deciding to make myself known, I slide the miniatures into their proper place next to the others, and then I'm marching after him, hands clutched by my side. I'm not sure yet whether this unexpected meeting will go well, so I head into it on the defense, expecting a tense exchange, at best.

I follow Knight Raider King to the center of the shop, where patrons continue active tabletop roleplaying campaigns. They carry on, engrossed in their respective games, not at all aware that the Yoda vandal has returned.

And he's returned so soon, too.

Once I'm near enough, I tap the stranger on the back.

He spins around. His expression brightens with recognition, and I see his lips curl into a broad smile. Waves of dark hair fall around his face, and he's gripping the messenger bag across his chest. Today, I notice a few extra *Darkness Rising* pins that weren't there before.

His caramel eyes study mine, and I can't look away. I should be mad at him, but I'm not. In place of any sort of anger, I'm overcome with excitement that he's here again, as if we're old friends who haven't seen each other in years. A part of me feels guilty, like I'm a hypocrite for being so upset with Wyatt over finding someone while I'm insta-falling for a stranger. But I can't help it.

An electric jitter works its way down my body, and I wonder how someone I don't even know can affect me like this.

Unless, of course, I do know him.

"I didn't think I'd ever see you again," I admit, hardly containing the electricity in my voice.

Light glints in his eyes as he scans my face. "I said I'd come back."

I steady my jittering nerves and clear my throat, attempting to play this cool. "All right, well, you're here to pay the other half, then, or what?"

He rubs a hand over his back. "No, unfortunately I don't have the money yet. But I promise you I will pay it like we agreed."

"Then why are you here right now?"

"I wanted to clear up a few things," he says. "I know I came off like some guy causing trouble yesterday, but I can explain if we just talk for a few minutes."

"Hmm," I say, placing a finger to my lips. Part of me wants to tell him there's nothing he can tell me that will change how I view him, that once I've made my judgement it's set.

But deep down I know that this isn't the truth and, if I said that, it would be because of my brain's natural defensiveness.

"I've got a few minutes," I say, gesturing toward the back of the shop. "We can speak in my office."

With a smile on his face, he steps ahead of me. As we walk, he turns around and steps backwards, an inquisitive look plastered across his face, and I wonder if I've made the wrong choice to agree to this.

He's smiling even wider now, and I suddenly feel as if I've missed some inside joke.

"What?" I ask.

"Huh? Oh, nothing." His nose crinkles, and I know it isn't nothing.

But he's doing it again. Looking at me like he knows me.

"Why are you doing that?" I ask.

"Doing what?"

"Looking at me like that."

"Like what?"

"Like you know me."

"Oh, that?" His mouth spreads into a mischievous smirk. "No reason."

"You're lying."

"What if I am?"

We cross into my office, and I flick on the light before shutting the office door. The bulb in the ceiling lamp pops for a second, as if it's about to die, but then it makes a comeback and shines brightly.

The folding chair is on the other side of my desk from the last time he was here, but instead of sitting he simply inches a little closer and pulls out his phone. He's so close I feel his breath.

"Well, if you're lying, I graciously request the truth," I say. "Especially given you requested this meeting to clear your name."

We stand side by side, and his arm brushes against mine. Instead of my normal Spidey senses working on overdrive, demanding that I flee, warmth washes over me.

"Who *are* you?" I ask, exasperated by the level of comfort I'm feeling.

He dips his chin, rubbing a hand over the stubble around his mouth. His lips part, but before he answers his phone dings from his pocket. As he's switching it to silent mode, I catch a notification from the *Darkness Rising* forums app. The most popular forums of the fandom.

"Oh, I see," I say. "You know me from the forums, huh? It all makes sense now. Is Knight Raider King your username? Funny, I've never seen you on there."

He lifts his eyes to meet mine, and I can feel my heart beating a little more wildly in my chest.

"You're active on the DR forums?" he asks with a shocked tone, placing the phone back into his pocket. "I mean, Knight Raider King *is* the name I use for all my DR stuff, but I'm more of a lurker there than an active participant."

"Then that can't be how I know you."

"Right, it isn't."

My brows furrow. "So, how?"

The lightbulb flickers once more before popping. A crackling noise sparks through the air. In an instant, we are in darkness. The energy between us thickens, and there's something romantic about being alone with this stranger in a dark space.

"Ugh, sorry about that," I whisper. "I can go and—"

He gently places a hand over mine. "You don't have to. Maybe it'll be easier this way?"

"Somehow I think you might be right."

As my eyes adjust, I barely make out his figure. We're so close his lips nearly graze my nose. His hand remains on my fingers, and I don't push him away.

I'm scanning my brain to think of all the online places where I interact with people. But, really, *Outlaws of the Night* is it, and when *OftN* came up the last time, this stranger acted like he'd only barely heard of it.

"Listen," I say, breath heavy as my chest rises and falls. "I don't understand what's happening here. I'm a very guarded person but not with you."

He fingers linger on top of mine. There's a safety about his touch, like a weighted blanket. I don't want him to move, especially while we're in the dark. As if he senses my very thoughts, he doesn't sway an inch.

"Do you think sometimes we're simply drawn to people?" he murmurs.

"I'm a realist," I spit out, a defensive edge to my tone. "I don't believe in anything I can't see."

"I know you don't," he says, and I hear the hurt in his voice while simultaneously wondering how he would presume to know something about who I am. "I guess that was more of a rhetorical question."

"Sorry," I say. "I've just been burned by too many people. Outside of a few close friends, I don't trust anyone or anything. Least of all concepts like cosmic force and being drawn to someone inexplicably. Do you really believe that's what's happening here?"

He heaves a big sigh. "Why don't I tell you the truth about the Yoda bust, and then we can discuss, or debate, fate and serendipitous meeting. You okay with that?"

"Fine by me."

"Kora, I'm—"

Now my phone dings, and I recognize my designated sound for *Outlaws of the Night* notifications. Without thinking, I slip out my phone to shut off the volume, but it automatically opens to my *OftN* app. My unsent message to Wyatt pops up in drafts at the bottom of our conversation, the last thing I viewed before closing out last night.

The stranger raises a brow, face lit up by my phone screen.

"Unsent midnight confessions?" he asks.

"You could say that," I breathe.

"Boyfriend, huh?" He smirks once again like he's in on some secret.

I shake my head, shifting in place and lowering my head. "No. I mean, maybe in a different circumstance. But not in this one."

"What different circumstance would that be?"

"One where we knew each other offline, for starters. Besides, he's interested in someone else." The words fall especially heavily as they land, and a lump forms in my throat.

Figuring I've blown it with some new guy over a person who wants someone else, I slide my hand away.

"Why not send him the message?" he asks.

I shrug. "For the same reason I've never said anything, I guess. What if it scares him away, and I lose him?"

He cocks his head to the side. "I'm no psychic, but my intuition tells me he wouldn't do that to you."

"What if your intuition is wrong?"

"Then I'll make it up to you by taking you out."

"What makes you think I'd want that?" I ask, words so obviously betraying my emotions.

Once again, his caramel eyes latch onto mine, and I know he sees right through me. A magnetic pull keeps us connected. He's searching me, and deep in those eyes I see someone I've known for years. My brain is screaming, telling me to be cautious, but every other part of me wants to give in and fall into his arms.

Averting my eyes, I focus on the phone in my hands. My message, my intimate confession, sits there. I hover a finger over the send button as my chest tightens.

I can't send this message. I can't tell Wyatt the truth.

Shaking my head, I lower my device.

"I can't do this," I say, looking directly into Knight Raider King's eyes. "I can't do any of this. You need to just tell me what happened with Yoda, okay? Let's start with that like we discussed."

"Okay. I can do that."

His mouth remains open, and I expect him to start telling me something, but instead he reaches for his phone. Facing the screen away from me, he begins to type.

"What're you doing?" I ask.

"Giving you the entire story, Kora," he says aloud as he's writing, my name leaving his lips as if he's said it a million times. "Because I know how this came off. And I promise you, I wanted to tell you that day, but I knew what it looked like, and I didn't want you to think differently of me when you found out who I was."

"Wait..." I'm glued to my phone, gripping the device so hard I'm sure my knuckles have turned white. Suddenly, I'm realizing why his face looks so familiar.

Knight Raider King types feverishly, fingers moving swiftly, gliding over those keys. Finally, he finishes, and his eyes flick back to mine.

A few moments later, my phone lights up. When I look down, I see something new has popped into my chat with Wyatt.

"I have an explanation for everything," Wyatt's written. "I had no idea this was your shop, or that we even lived near each other. And when I started to lose against you, I threw my hands up in the air and turned away from the game so fast that my clumsy self barreled right into that Yoda bust. I never threw the bust. I don't even know how I managed to smash it so badly, but it was completely by accident. I'm so, *so* sorry."

"Wyatt?" My voice squeaks as I place down my phone.

"Hi, Kora." He breathes my name from his lips, and the soft way he says it sends a welcome chill down my spine. "Do you hate me now that you know?"

"No," I say. "Of course not. But why didn't you just tell me?"

"How could I?" he asks. "By the time I realized who you were, you already thought I was some criminal."

"Well, I thought you were some criminal." I stop, realizing how our bodies have organically entwined. His hands gently cradle the small of my back, and I've slid my arms around his waist. I sigh, letting out all the anxiety that was swirling around in my stomach.

"So, the other woman, the miscommunication..." I begin to say.

Wyatt nods his head, finishing my statement without a single word. Our mouths hover dangerously close, and with one movement we could break a barrier I've kept up a long time.

He murmurs something in Japanese. Another reference to *Darkness Rising*. This time, he's quoting one of the most famous lines of the season one finale.

Out of the confusion, something new and magnificent grows.

"I know you're a realist," he adds in a soft voice. "But this, all of this serendipity? There's something magical here, Kora. And I want you to know I've felt the magic between us from the very beginning when we started talking through the game. Our meeting in person, and the attraction I instantly felt for you the moment we met—it only solidifies everything I already knew."

With his final words, he leans in and gently kisses my forehead. Once, then twice. He plants a series of soft kisses that begin to fall around the side of my face. Every cell in my body glows, and there's a fire inside of me burning, raging, beating with life.

"I feel it, too. This magical connection," I murmur. "And I'm not scared, because I feel it with *you*."

Tilting my face, my lips brush against his. We take a beat, heart steadying in my chest. My hands rest on the back of his belt, and I clutch him a little more tightly.

Then, his soft lips meld into mine, and I don't fight him. We're finding one another in the dark, two strangers discovering each other for the very first time

But none of this feels strange. Everything with Wyatt feels familiar.

And we fall away together in the dark, though I've never been closer to the light.

ABOUT THE AUTHOR

Rachel Radner is a former Pennsylvanian who will always miss Wawa.

She's been writing since the first grade when her teacher handed her a journal and instructed her to write about her day. From then on, she was always writing down the stories in her head.

After she graduated from Penn State in 2010, she spent time in NYC doing improv, acting for film, and performing on the stage in musical theatre.

She participated in NaNoWriMo for the first time in 2012 and started what would become her first romance novel. Since then, she's written a total of fifteen novels.

When she isn't writing and drinking coffee, Rachel can be found geeking out about Star Wars or SNL, watching something from the Marvel universe, reading, or studying Latin and German.

She currently lives in Los Angeles, CA where she's also pursuing her dream of acting and filmmaking.

Major thanks to Jacob Marquez who introduced her to the phrase, "That really burns my cookies!" :)

www.rachelradner.com

Newsletter Signup: https://mailchi.mp/e6e3b7ed625f/rachelradner

SARAH'S BUCKET LIST

RONNIE ROBERTS

The satisfaction that comes from scratching items off your To Do List...

1

———————

*A*gain, Sarah glanced at Sushi Heaven's entrance. How long was she willing to wait for her blind date? The waiter had asked for her order twice. Now he sent her fleeting, periodic looks of pity.

To appear busy, she picked up her phone and added a fourth goal, "Live in a seaside cottage" to her bucket list after "Do work I love", "Spa Day—*all* the stuff—no guilt", and "Wear a red bikini in public".

Why was she still here? She caught herself chewing on her thumbnail and added, "Stop biting my nails", before texting her roommate, *Mr. Perfect-for-me is a no show.*

Chrissy texted back, *I'm so sorry! I thought he was a good guy.*

Not your fault. I'm ordering sushi and coming home. Interested?

Spicy California rolls?

Sarah smiled. *So predictable. Sushi, wine, and finish our bucket lists.*

Mine's done. Added "Kiss a hot stranger." You should too.

You're crazy. Laughing quietly, Sarah added, "Kiss a hot stranger" to her list then stood up, blind date over. She approached the takeout counter, moving past a customer waiting for his order, made her request and paid. When she was done, she noticed the waiting customer was smiling at her. He had crazy nice eyes. Did she know him? He was severely cute. But so apparently was Mr. No Show.

He remarked, "You're tall."

How original.

He nodded toward her table. "Someone stand you up?"

Now I'm being judged? Perfect. She called up her bucket list and to the "Live in a seaside cottage" entry, added "alone—with a cat".

"Cause if he did, his loss."

Why was he still talking to her? She pretended to study the posted menu.

"Seriously. Not cool."

She gave up and looked straight at him. Tall, built, mocha skin, light blue eyes, stubble on his jaw, dark hair. All the things she liked—in her previous, willing-to-date life. When he didn't look away, *she* did.

The woman reappeared with two paper bags. Reaching for her order, Sarah dropped her phone. Blue Eyes jumped to retrieve it, stopping to read the screen.

"What are you doing?" she demanded, grabbing for it.

Grinning, he dodged away, still reading, then handed it back. "Bucket list, huh?"

"Seriously?" She snatched it from him, her face flushing.

"A red bikini?"

"None of your business."

"Can't help it—I'm a fast reader."

"You're rude. You're *all* rude!" She stalked to the door, then stopped, turned and approached him, her eyes narrowed. When he didn't look away, she reached out, gripped his Henley shirt in her fist, drew up on her toes and kissed him.

For a long time.

Which was very nice.

She released him with a surprised gasp, blinked up at his astonished face, then turn and fled the restaurant. By the time she reached her car, she was laughing.

She could cross "Kiss a hot stranger" from her list.

Taylor caught the latest save-the-cat callout at the fire station. This one was along Beachside Road which amounted to an overgrown goat trail. He was about to turn around when a worn roof appeared in the distance among the thick trees and scruffy brush. As he drew nearer, he could see the building in its not-so-great splendor. The warm summer sunshine and fresh sea breeze didn't help it. He knew this was what the locals optimistically referred to as "a charming rustic seaside cottage". Whoever believed that was a fool. It would surely collapse upon itself with one little puff from the nearest big bad wolf.

He pulled alongside the cottage and was met by—he sat back in shock—the same woman who had kissed him at Sushi Heaven three weeks ago! She came charging around from her dilapidated front porch, her sandy hair half-pulled from a scraggly braid, one knee bloodied, her face smudged, her blue eyes frantic.

"You, again!" he declared heartily as he climbed from the truck, abruptly happy he'd caught this save-the-cat callout. He'd had no luck identifying his mysterious "Kiss a hot stranger" woman, and man, had he tried. Turns out Sushi Heaven wasn't big on revealing contact information from customers' credit cards, even when he admitted why he needed it. Not romantics, those Sushi Heaven owners...

Naturally, the guys back at the fire station thought he'd lied about the whole thing.

When she pulled up for a fleeting moment, he witnessed first her startled recognition then effort to shove aside their strange encounter in favor of saving her cat. She gasped, "Thank you!" He followed her past two overflowing dumpsters to a stand of trees. She pointed up. "There. Around fifty feet high. A stray dog chased her up there last night. She's been crying for help ever since." The woman's voice caught. "Honestly, I don't know how she even got up there." She turned pleading eyes to his. "I tried a ladder..." She waved at an old ladder laying in the deep, unmowed grass. He shuddered at the thought of anyone climbing the rickety old thing let alone this pretty girl. "Now she's too weak to even cry for help." She blinked rapidly, her gaze boring through the foliage overhead.

He strained to see what she was seeing. "What's her name?"

"Pumpkin. She's orange. The shelter named her."

He searched the branches to no avail. Not an orange speck to be seen. Was the cat still up there? "She's a rescue?"

"Yes. I've only had her four days."

"You can see her?"

"Yes. Can't you?"

"I'll get the ladder, you get a can of tuna, open it and have it ready for me to take up. Pumpkin's hunger just might outweigh her fear." He stopped. "I'm sorry. What's your name? As long as we're rescuing your cat together and all."

"Sarah Meyers," she gasped as she sped by.

"I'm Taylor..." he called after her fleeing form, trailing off with, "Taylor Theron... In case you're curious."

They met back at the tree. Taylor quickly lashed the extending ladder to the trunk, and with the can of tuna in hand he ascended, calling, "Pumpkin?" Sure enough, fifty feet up he found the cat clinging to the bark, her golden eyes large and following his every move. Murmuring soothingly, he positioned himself close and extended the tuna. The cat remained frozen in place, her eyes never leaving his face. The offered tuna was of no interest to her. Okay. Plan B. He stuffed the can into his pocket with a shrug—he'd returned from callouts smelling of worse things than tuna.

"That's okay. I'll carry you down." Leaning against the tree trunk, he slowly unhooked Pumpkin's claws from the bark, shifting them to himself, hissing as her claws buried themselves into his vest and shirt, clean down to his chest. "We're going down, little lady."

She yowled plaintively, her nails digging further into his skin. Yikes, that stung! He moved down the ladder quickly to end her terror and his pain. Back in the overgrown yard, he attempted to disengage the cat from his chest with no success. Pumpkin was plastered against him, well and truly dug in.

"Oh, Pumpkin, you poor girl!" Sarah looked from the rigid cat to Taylor. "Come inside, maybe, let her relax, feel safe?"

Through clenched teeth he answered, "Pumpkin relaxed sounds good to me."

Sarah led the way into her cottage, stepping first onto the creaking porch, past a huge hole. Pointing out the boards he shouldn't step on she brought him into a small living room. It was furnished with a neatly made up futon, two kitchen chairs and a TV table. She shrugged her shoulders. "Sorry. New wiring takes precedence over furniture."

"You're not living here, are you?"

"No! I don't have an occupancy permit yet."

Was that true? Should he be worried?

Still holding the cat, he let his gaze drink in the disaster surrounding them. He could name a dozen fire and safety hazards without another step inside. The walls were in disarray, mostly stripped back to the studs, the insulation gone or on its way out. There was evidence of new wiring, plus new framing where he supposed rotten wood had once been, plus evidence the exterior studs were being built out from two-by-fours to two-by-sixes. That meant better insulation. If this were his, that's what he'd do. He glanced at Sarah who was stroking Pumpkin's head gently, cooing encouragements. He looked again at the cottage's interior. She'd taken on a huge project, one many would never consider. Sarah was a go getter. He liked that.

"You bought this? On purpose?" he asked lightly, hoping for a smile.

It worked. She smiled up at him. "Sure did." She eased the suddenly limp, exhausted cat from his grasp. "Thank you for saving Pumpkin. Her life's been hard. I'm hoping this will be a safe place for her." Her gaze dropped to his chest. "Oh no! You're bleeding."

He ran his palm across his chest gingerly. "The hazardous life of a firefighter."

"I have antiseptic and antibiotic cream if you like."

"I'm good. I should get back."

"Okay." She sounded disappointed, which made him very happy. Maybe she was remembering her "Kiss a hot stranger" goal as much as he was? He watched her cuddle the purring cat now tucked under her chin.

"You're doing this all yourself?"

"Not the wiring or plumbing. That's for the professionals. I'm doing the demo and replacing the studs and windows. Once the wiring and plumbing is done, I'll insulate, drywall, mud and paint. I'm hoping to be done before the cold weather sets in. I'll think about a kitchen in the winter." She smiled brightly, though her eyes looked tired. "Microwaves are wonderful things, don't you think?"

He smiled and nodded. This was a classic Taylor situation—he heard a hard luck story and he wanted to step in and help. Looking at Sarah, he knew she would not welcome his help. Catching sight of her knee, he said, "You could use some first-aid yourself."

She laughed ruefully. "Forgot which board I was supposed to walk on."

He raised his eyebrows and whistled. "That hole in the porch?"

"Yup."

Why wasn't he leaving? He looked around again, then up. "How's the roof?"

She rolled her eyes. "One thing at a time, my friend."

His gaze returned to hers and locked. "Friends, huh?" He smiled.

She blushed a deep pink. "I... I owe you an apology. For the restaurant."

"Not complaining."

She shifted toward the door as if to see him out. He followed her to the porch. She said, "I'm so embarrassed. I was... upset that night. My friend set me up on a date and I..."

"You had reasons. I'm sorry you were stood up. Forget about the kiss. I know you didn't mean it. I forgot about it, actually." *Liar.*

When she didn't answer, he added. "*I'd* never stand you up."

She bit her lip. "I've given up dating. This cottage will get all my attention for the foreseeable future. I have plans."

"Here's a thought—if you went out with me, you'd never have to wear flats again."

She burst out in surprised laughter. "Now there's an offer! But no, thanks."

Okay. He could be a patient guy. He changed to a safer subject. "How much land do you have?"

"Eight acres."

"No kidding? You could do good things here."

She shrugged again. "Don't forget your ladder."

"Did I see a spare piece of plywood out by the dumpsters?"

She frowned. "Why?"

"It's a good thing. Wait here."

He went around the cottage, found the plywood and brought it back to the front. Here, he laid the plywood across the portion of the porch leading into the cottage, effectively covering the hole and suspect planks. "Until you get to building a new porch."

She smiled ruefully. "So simple. I should have thought of it myself."

"You're busy. Can't be all things to everybody."

There was a beat of uncomfortable silence.

Sarah said, "Ah... Your ladder?" She seriously wanted him to leave.

Together they walked around the cottage. While she waited, he moved past the dumpsters piled high with discarded cottage parts and retrieved the firehouse ladder. Back at the truck Sarah and Pumpkin watched him secure it to his truck. She told him, "There's an old orchard out back with dozens of fruit trees. I'm hoping to bring it back to life."

"That's amazing. This *place* will be amazing."

"You didn't think that when you first got here. I saw your expression."

"Ouch!"

"You know I'm right."

He laughed, jumped back into his truck and started it. As he drove away, he called out the open window, "Good luck, Sarah. You're doing great."

All the way down the bumpy driveway, he watched her in the rear-view mirror watching him. Did she think about their Sushi Heaven kiss like he did?

❧

Chrissy and Sarah were laughing when they came into Sweet Spot, here for copious, bad-for-you calories in the form of French Slices and Death By Chocolate cream puffs. They'd hit Starbucks on the way home for two chai tea lattes. Sugar rush.

Gwen was out front chatting with her fiancée Sig from the firehall and here was Taylor, standing with the pair. They knew each other? Sarah experienced a flash of happiness at finding Pumpkin's rescuer. He'd often popped up in her thoughts over the last few weeks. His number had also popped up on her cellphone—twice—asking her out. She'd declined. Taylor was a complication she had no time for. Yet she was secretly delighted to see him. "Sarah, Sarah, Sarah," she chided under her breath.

"What?" Chrissy asked.

"Nothing. Act natural."

"Act natural? How do you think I'd—" Chrissy's gaze followed hers

503

to Taylor and back, her eyes growing big. "*This* is the guy? The stranger, right?"

"Don't embarrass me, I beg you."

Taylor was walking toward her, a big smile on his face and she found she had an answering one just like it on her own face. Chrissy disappeared, everyone disappeared, and it was only her and Taylor in their own shiny bubble.

"You look great."

She blushed. "Thanks. I had a spa day with my friend…" She looked around. Chrissy, Gwen and Sig were in a tight huddle, all grinning at her and Taylor. She sent them a death-ray warning glance before returning her attention to Taylor.

He said, "You cut your hair."

"I did. Killer highlights, a blowout." She wiggled her sparkling nails. "Mani." Pointed to her sandaled feet. "Pedi."

His eyes dimmed a bit, but he nodded gamely. "Nice."

She laughed. "It's all lost on you, right?"

He grinned. "Yup. How's Pumpkin?"

"Fully recovered. Thanks again. This your day off?"

"Me and Sig have the next couple of days off. We're trying to rustle up some action."

"In a bakery?"

"Camping up on Eagle Mountain—if Gwen agrees. If she doesn't, no plans. The guy's a goner."

"So is Gwen. The wedding's in ten days."

"You going?"

"I'm a bridesmaid. Try and stop me."

"How goes the reno?"

"Wiring and plumbing are done and inspected. Roof's built. I'm tarpapering and shingling starting tomorrow."

He frowned. "After the nail thing?"

"These are tough. I got them to protect my fingers, believe it or not. Looking pretty is a bonus." And to force her to stop biting them.

"You've been shopping." He was looking at her tiny *Nailed It* bag. "New jewellery for the roof shingling?"

"Ha ha. Funny."

"You'd impress the seagulls. They love shiny things."

She whispered, "The red bikini. Katie found me the perfect one. That woman's a genius."

"Can I see?"

"No!" she blurted in laughter, heat again returning to her face. "Why would I show you my new bikini?"

"Quality control?"

"What do you know about bikinis?"

"Try me?"

She pushed against his torso, playfully shoving him away. Ooh—rock-hard abs. He pretended to stagger. She said, "You're impossible."

"And a fast learner."

She moved to the dessert display labeled *Sinners*. "I'm here for fattening food. You're in my way."

He followed her. "Not a good look when combined with a new red bikini," he warned, jumping to avoid another shove.

"I'll sweat it off tomorrow up on my new roof." She bobbed her eyebrows at him. "Maybe while wearing my new red bikini."

Taylor's face dropped in surprise. Was he picturing it? Ha ha. Nice she could stop him in his tracks.

Sig appeared beside them. "Gotta go, buddy. Tux fitting."

"Right."

Sarah asked, "You're the best man?"

"You're surprised? I think I'm insulted."

Sig pushed Taylor out the door ahead of him. "Everyone else turned me down. This guy didn't have a quick enough excuse."

"I was trapped!" Taylor called out just before the door closed behind the pair.

Chrissy was at her side. "No fair! Your stranger was Taylor Theron?"

"I didn't even know his name, remember?"

"Until he rescued Pumpkin!"

"I guess I forgot."

"No sane woman forgets Taylor Theron, Sarah Meyers. Nobody."

⁓

SARAH WOKE UP WITH A START. What was that sound? She sat bolt upright on the futon, her heart pounding in alarm. Why had she delayed getting the security system set up?

There it was again. A thump on her roof, followed by a man's laughter.

Someone was on her roof? She bolted from her bed, darted out the door and off the porch, turning on her scrubby "lawn" to squint against the bright morning sunrise to the roof.

"Hey, sleepyhead," Taylor greeted. He was wearing a worn t-shirt that clung to his body like a second skin, and faded, low slung denims along with a loaded tool belt.

"What are you doing up on my roof?" she demanded in a sleep-croaky voice that failed to convey just how alarmed she was at seeing him there, so completely the vision of a man's man, surrounded by early-morning sunrays like some kind of apparition. A man a woman might find herself daydreaming about when she was alone. Like last night on the cottage's front step, sipping on a cold cup of tea after hours of taping the vapor barrier, dreaming of what her future might look like here in this place, with maybe a family one day...

"Waiting on my first coffee." His gaze shifted to behind her. "Ah, there it is."

Sarah twisted around and saw Gwen holding two travel mugs. "In case they drop them," she explained. Behind Gwen two bright yellow tents had been set up with evidence breakfast had been had right here in Sarah's front yard—an optimistic label that: front yard—while she'd slept inside.

"They?" Sarah croaked again.

"Sig and Taylor. They're doing your roof today."

"They're..." Sarah twisted back to peer up at the roof again. Sig was kicking the roll of tarpaper across the width of the roof ahead of him.

"Where's my coffee, woman?" he demanded cheerfully.

Sarah looked back at Gwen who shook her head and rolled her eyes. "You want to bring these up? You know I'm afraid of heights."

"I... I guess so."

"Ah, Sarah?" This from Taylor overhead.

She turned again to the roof, her neck protesting the constant swiveling.

Taylor looked over the edge with concern. "You maybe should think about getting dressed first?"

"Ack!" she yelled, pulling down the scant edge of her nightshirt and running inside. "This can't be happening!"

Gwen followed her. "It's okay. They're too far away to see anything."

"I saw plenty!" Taylor yelled out cheerfully. "And I'm fine with that. Only mentioned it 'cause you probably—"

"Shut up!" Sarah yelled out the open door before slamming it closed. Hastily she yanked a t-shirt over her head and pulled on her raggedy cut-off denims. To Gwen, she whispered, "How long were you out there?"

"We showed up at five. The guys wanted to get as much done as they could before the heat of the day."

Sarah stilled. "Oh. When did you decide all this?"

"Yesterday, after their tux fitting. Those two need something to do—badly. You have to keep them busy and out of my hair till the wedding. I kid you not. They're driving me crazy. Your roof is a Godsend." Gwen closed her eyes and let her head drop back with fatigue and moaned, "Anything you can do to keep them busy. Please, Sarah."

Sarah winked. "Well, I do have a ton of stuff to do around here."

"This is why you are one of my bridesmaids. I can make you do me favors."

She gave Gwen a quick hug and took the two coffee mugs. "Thanks."

The day went fast once Taylor and Sig stopped joking around and settled into work. Sarah climbed onto the roof and worked along with them, splitting bundles of shingles apart and sliding them in place as fast as she could ahead of the guys' swinging hammers. Sig and Taylor took turns bringing the bundles up the ladder on their shoulders, something she could never do. Sarah had taken a whole week off to shingle. At this rate, the guys would be done in a day.

The good news—this gave her six extra days to work on her cottage. It was a gift.

Gwen supplied them with water and food, content to putter around the yard with Sarah's brand-new weed eater between cuddle sessions with Pumpkin. At seven, they were finished, and back on terra firma.

"Time for a dip in the ocean to wash off," Taylor announced, dropping his tool belt beside his tent with a jangly thud. He glanced over at Sarah who was draped across a camp chair holding a cool bottle of soda to her hot face. "Time to test out your new red bikini, maybe?"

"Give it a rest," she moaned. "Every muscle in my body just went on strike."

"Okay—your choice."

"My choi—"

Taylor lunged for her.

She screeched when he picked her up, threw her over his shoulder, and headed for the water. "Don't you dare!"

Sig and Gwen made no move to rescue her.

"Don't you even think about it, Taylor Theron. I promise I'll—"

He hit the water running. Slowing at waist deep, he plunged in, taking her with him. The shock of the cold water took her breath away. Free of his grip, she rose splashing in the water with a wail of protest. "It's freaking freezing!" She pushed away her hair to glare at him. He was still up to his neck in the water. "Why are you grinning like an idiot?"

"Cause I'm smart. I stayed in the water. It feels fantastic."

She pouted then reluctantly lowered herself back in. It *did* feel good. Refreshing. Grudgingly she admitted, "It's okay."

"Okay? It's *better* than okay!"

She laughed and splashed water at him. "It *is* better than okay." Her gaze shifted to her cottage. "I can't believe my roof's done already."

He bobbed to her side. "Me and Sig are at loose ends for the next few days. Pick something you need done and we'll tackle it. I have it on good authority Gwen will be relieved to see the last of us."

Sarah giggled. "She told me. She didn't actually utter the word incorrigible, but it was implied."

"No way—me and Sig? No way." He considered the cottage with her. "So, what'll it be?"

Extremely aware of his proximity, she pretended to muse. "Ummm... Paint the outside? The clapboard siding is in surprisingly good shape."

"And since it's worn to bare wood, no scraping, though I suspect that wood will suck up paint like a dry sponge. I hope you bought a lot."

"I did. The guy at the store told me all about my 'thirsty wood'."

He gazed at the cottage. "If you're talking a sprayer, we could give it two coats in one day, two the next, if the weather holds out." He smiled at her, his face only inches away, beads of water clinging to his dark skin and hair. Her heart picked up its pace. "We'll talk it out over hamburgers at the campsite."

"Wow. That... that would be awesome. Truly, it would." She just might have the cottage ready to live in by fall after all. She laughed, using the action to put distance between them. With these suddenly wobbly emotions, Taylor this close could be dangerous. She'd die of embarrassment if he even guessed. Remembering the tents waiting for them by the cottage, where Taylor would sleep overnight, would wake up tomorrow morning, still here in her life, her heart tripped with excitement.

She liked it and was afraid she liked it.

She scrambled for something not-lame to say. "So, my front yard is a campsite?" Her words came out in a stutter, a surprise. Why was she suddenly shaking?

He frowned. "You cold?"

She nodded. "Y-yes." Her teeth were chattering, not with cold but with nerves. What was wrong with her? She never behaved like this.

She was over-tired and feeling grateful was all.

He rose up from the water, reaching out his hand for hers. "Let's get out of these wet clothes and make a fire in that firepit Gwen discovered."

Hand in hand they waded back to shore. She felt both shaky and happy at the same time. This thing between her and Taylor, and there was definitely something happening between them, was happening fast and at the same time, was sweet and welcome and comfortable. Her heart did a full-on flop at recognizing these new feelings.

He looked down at her. "Admit it, until Gwen cleared around the tents with the weed eater, you had no idea you had a firepit."

"That's true. Nice perk."

"Who knows what else we'll find when we clear the whole yard?"

"The two filled dumpsters will be picked up tomorrow and they'll leave me an empty one for yard waste. I'm thinking it'll be the last I'll need." She felt a little breathless telling him this. She was talking about a dumpster, for heaven sake!

"If you tape off the exterior windows ahead of us, maybe between coats we could take a stab at getting some of your drywall up inside? It would clear out some space in there if we did. You and Pumpkin would have room to move. You know—since you're *not* living there yet."

"Hey! Only some nights, when I'm too tired to drive home."

"Did I say you were living there?"

She pulled back on his hand to make him stop. "You are being so kind and you hardly know me. You... you don't have to do this, you know."

"I *do* know." He drew close and murmured, "But I want to."

This time she didn't move away. Their eyes locked and Sarah found herself falling into the depth of his blue eyes, like sinking into a safe, warm hug. She couldn't shift her tongue to say a word in reply.

His eyes crinkling in a smile, he pulled her up the path into the yard. "Let's warm you up and talk out our next few days with Sig and Gwen."

FOUR DAYS LATER, after spraying the cottage with two coats of white primer followed by two coats of light blue, then spraying the shutters a darker blue, Taylor finally got to read the rest of Sarah's bucket list. It was by accident this time, better than when he'd actually stolen her phone to read it, and yet, this time it felt more invasive. At Sushi Heaven, he'd been playing around, trying to cheer up a random pretty girl who'd just been stood up by some jerk. Here at Sarah's cottage, he'd been snooping into the private thoughts of a girl he'd come to like. She was smart, and funny, and hard-working, and so appealing he had a hard time even taking his eyes off her.

Okay—so Sig was right. Taylor was hooked on Sarah Meyers—she was the whole enchilada. Brains, beauty, and brawn—kinda—in a super cute way. Yeah, he had some very interesting feelings milling inside his chest when he was with Sarah. Well, maybe interesting wasn't the right word. More appropriate words might be—unsettled, welcome, scary, happy, energized. Let's just say the world was looking pretty good to him these days and leave it like that.

But back to the bucket list. Sig and Gwen had folded up their tent early this morning and returned to the real world. It was crunch time for the wedding. That left Taylor and Sarah alone at last as they say, at the cottage. She'd just gone into town to pick up supplies when he spied her phone on the step by the front door, picked it up to flag her down, but... The bucket list popped up as her screen saver and Sarah was long gone.

He tried not to read the list, truly he did.

Instead he sat on the step and studied it.

Already crossed out were "Do work I love". That was easy. She was half owner of Twice Loved, a successful consignment shop in downtown Poet. According to Gwen, Twice Loved had somehow helped the new Sweet Spot Bakery's launched after the fire last year. That was a story he'd be interested in learning more about.

"Spa day—*all* the stuff—no guilt" was also crossed out. They'd met at Sweet Spot after her spa day. Her skin had glowed, her thick hair had shone, her expression was light and happy, the opposite of the night they'd met. Now he knew her better, he knew she'd been hurt and embarrassed by the no-show guy. *His loss, my gain.*

In Sweet Spot, she'd flirted with him, showing off her Mani and Pedi—yes, sadly he now knew what that meant—and he'd been caught somehow inside her orbit with no urge to escape. He couldn't remember another week he'd enjoyed as much as he'd enjoyed this week with Sarah. He'd learned so much about her, watching her, working with her. She worked hard, was willing to tackle anything, always with good cheer. And she was smart, recognizing something in this scruffy acreage he would have dismissed. Another point for Sarah.

"Wear a red bikini in public." Huh. She'd forgotten to cross this one off, but it *had* finally come to fruition last night and what a vision she'd been as she'd approached him, wrapped in a beach cover-up across the sand, her face unreadable as she watched his expression. After three straight days of painting—the paint guy had been right, the clapboard cottage had been mighty thirsty—the cottage looked awesome.

They'd all shed their paint-stained clothes and escaped onto the beach, heading for the beckoning cool water that lapped gently along the stretch of sand that lay before Sarah's little piece of heaven. Sig and Gwen were already in the water on sea-doos they'd rented, whooshing across the water here and there, pretending they weren't about to tie the knot in front of three hundred people in only a couple of days.

Stopping before him, Sarah untied her cover up, let it fall to the sand, exposing her creamy skin and perfectly fitted crimson bikini. Wow. Just wow. She'd taken his breath away. She'd murmured, "You approve?", totally surprising him. Did what he think matter?

He'd stood up from his beach chair and placed his hands on her shoulders, a little tongued-tied and unsure how to express the jumble of thoughts and feelings that red bikini, her thick sun-streaked hair, and hopeful blue eyes set to coursing through his veins. Sarah Meyers was the gorgeous, confusing time bomb that had been ticking inside him for weeks and was about to go off.

Finally, he'd said, "I am absolutely certain I'll never forget this moment."

She'd smiled then with satisfaction. "Then it was absolutely worth the search. Let's go in and cool off. Sig and Gwen can't have all the fun." She'd reached out to take his hand and together they'd walked into the sea. That's when Taylor knew his life had just changed course forever.

That was yesterday. He would have Sarah all to himself for the next three days.

"Live in a seaside cottage—alone—with a cat." This made him smile. She'd been annoyed by him and had added "with a cat" at Sushi Heaven. He *had* been obnoxious, and man was he glad he had. That chance meeting had led to this week of revelation. Sarah Meyers was his future; he was certain of it. Now to convince Sarah. They'd met a month ago, she'd turned down two date requests, no, three, then they'd spent every waking hour together this last week. Pretty fast to have these feelings by anyone's standards. But that could count as dozens of dates, right? He laughed softly at himself. Yes, when pressed, I *can* rationalize anything.

But it was the truth. He began to do the math then gave it up. Moot point. He wasn't going anywhere.

Living in a seaside cottage was also not crossed off. Why not? She was, for all intents and purposes living here. She spent more nights here than at home with her roomy Chrissy. He smiled. Maybe because she wasn't here living alone. He liked to think this was the reason it wasn't crossed off—it wasn't quite true. *He* was here with her.

"Kiss a hot stranger". Now this entry gave him hope. It was crossed off, for obvious reasons. She'd kissed him and considered him a hot stranger. Good to know.

She'd crossed off and added, "Yay!" to "Stop biting my nails". He hadn't seen her bite her nails even once. She *did* have the fancy nails from the salon, which had held up surprisingly well all week. She was right. They were tough.

"Ride in a hot air balloon." That would be fun. He knew a guy who was a member of a local club. He'd get in touch and see what he could set up.

The final item was different from all the rest. "Don't make the same mistake Mom made." What mistake had her mother made? He realized he knew nothing of her family, her background. A big gap in what he knew of Sarah.

But then, he hadn't talked a ton about his own family back east. Not that they were a secret. They were just... back east, living their lives. He'd still head back for Thanksgiving. This year he'd bring Sarah with him. His mother would love Sarah. So would Dad and his two brothers. There would be no lonely bachelor jokes this year.

He froze. What was he considering here?

"What are you doing!" Sarah darted up the steps and seized her phone from his hand. "I turn my back and you dive right into my personal space?"

"I... I found it and was going to run after you, but you were gone—"

"So, you elected instead to violate my privacy by scrolling through my phone? Find anything interesting?"

"I... I guess it looks that way. I was only looking at the bucket list. You were adding to it at Sushi Heaven—"

"I know exactly what I was doing at Sushi Heaven. You don't have to remind me how stupid I was. First the blind date, then you!"

Her words were a blow square to the center of his chest. He stood. "That's not how it was. I felt bad about your blind date."

"Oh, so feeling sorry for me excuses this?" She shook her phone at him. "Good thing I came back for my phone. Otherwise, I might have spent entirely too much time learning who you really are. This was my short cut. You've even got Sig and Gwen fooled. Your first chance, you're in my business like a dirty shirt."

Taylor laughed despite himself. "Dirty Shirt?"

She narrowed her eyes at him. "That's your defense? My dismay at your invasion of my privacy is funny to you? I didn't articulate myself to your liking? Get out, get off my property. Now; right now. Take your stupid tent with you."

She whirled around and ran back to her car, jumped in and was gone before he could come up with even one acceptable reason he'd done what he'd done.

Sarah's joy in her cottage had lost its glow. After hiring a crew to finish up the drywall, she'd gotten a conditional occupancy permit for the cottage and had semi-permanently moved in with Pumpkin, but the magic was gone. Her half-completed cottage, once filled with hundreds of exciting projects to make it her own now looked flat, everything reminding her of Taylor Theron. His devilish smile, his easy strength, his get 'er done attitude, his teasing manner. Oh, how she'd been taken in.

Last night's rehearsal had been torture. She'd gone through the steps with the rest of the wedding party, then made her excuses to skip the dinner. She purposefully avoided Gwen's questioning looks. This was not Gwen's problem. As for Taylor—she only glanced at him when he wasn't looking her way—he wasn't Mr. Cheerful either. He'd made no move to speak to her, or to stop her from leaving. It was as if he didn't even know her. What should have been a relief had felt like a betrayal. Had she held on to the hope he'd come after her, apologize, explain himself, patch up their misunderstanding? Yes, she guessed she had. Obviously, their time working together at the cottage meant much more to her than it did to Taylor.

He *was* just burning up time till the wedding, after all.

And it was her own fault. Who keeps a bucket list as their phone screen saver and expects it to remain a secret? Would she have done the same in his place? Probably.

She looked at her reflection in the full-length mirror she'd propped against the wall in her not-yet painted bedroom and sighed. The bridesmaid dress was pretty, and her hair was perfect, complete with fresh flowers. It was her expression that was the problem. She looked as if someone had died. That's how she felt. Not someone, *something* had died. She should be thrilled she was in the cottage so quickly, that this much was already done. She wasn't, not even a little bit. The cottage was just a wooden structure now, an endless, lonely construction project. She was heartsick.

And today she had to face Taylor, not just for a quick run through, but for hours, in front of hundreds of people. How was she going to pull off this wedding and not have everyone guess the ridiculously hand-some best man and the too-tall bridesmaid were on the outs? She took a big breath. "I'll act my tail off. Right, Pumpkin? Fake it till you make it?"

Pumpkin, who had obviously met up with a rascal or two in her life-time looked back at her with understanding. Sarah grabbed her clutch. "Wish me luck, Pumpkin. I'm gonna need it."

Sarah had promised herself she would not cry at this wedding. But it was so beautiful, and the way Sig and Gwen looked at one another as they said their vows, she simply could not hold back her tears. Her surroundings—the grand lawns and curated gardens, the huge canopied buffet lunch, the band, the polished, portable dance floor—the brightly coloured, tethered hot air balloon, waiting to take guests up into the clear blue skies throughout the afternoon and into the evening—all blurred. To make it a thousand times worse, after she surreptitiously dabbed at her eyes, she made the mistake of looking at Taylor—who was looking steadily back at her.

And there was no looking away.

His expression was not indifferent, not that of a stranger. His eyes were warm and kind and full of promise. He mouthed, "I'm sorry."

She blinked rapidly, swaying in place for a second before deliber-ately shifting her eyes to watch Gwen's glowing expression as any good bridesmaid should do, shocked at where her thoughts had abruptly taken her.

Self-knowledge so often came at the most inopportune times.

Keeping her gaze on the happy couple, she schooled her face to a gentle smile. Inside she was reeling. *Reeling!* She was in love with the best man—hopelessly, completely and irrevocably—in love with Taylor Theron. A man she'd known for a total of thirty-one days.

She bit her lip and adjusted her bouquet of sweet peas and baby's breath with damp hands. The minister pronounced Sig and Gwen husband and wife and introduced the couple to the guests, who all jumped from their insanely expensive country club lawn chairs, cheered in celebration and rushed to encircle the couple.

Sarah reached blindly out to a garden rail for support. Instead of the smooth metal, her hand was enclosed by a familiar warm hand. She took in a ragged breath and turned her face away from the surging crowd. How embarrassing!

Taylor's arm came around her and led her away from where the crowd of well-wishers were taking the wedding party. "Over here," he murmured. "Just till you get yourself together."

Did he know? Had he guessed? Was he just being the good guy she knew he was? What a mess. How could she extract herself from this with some kind of dignity?

In a quiet garden, she and Taylor sat on a bench. Taylor laughed softly and handed her the decorative handkerchief from his tux pocket. "Weddings and funerals, right? You never know how they'll hit you."

Not trusting herself to speak, she simply nodded.

He motioned toward the balloon. "Want to go first, test it out? I know it's on your bucket list."

"Don't be so nice to me. I was awful to you about the phone, about the list."

His eyebrows shot up. "I'm forgiven?"

"You did what anyone would do. You picked up a forgotten phone, you read a list. I'm apologizing to you. I was horrible. Please forgive me?" Her eyes were still leaking stupid tears.

"My mother's just like you. All happy occasions—she's a crier. Can't help herself. We all come prepared with hankies for Mom—me and my two brothers and my dad."

Sarah laughed despite herself. "A cavalry of hankies to the rescue?"

"Something like that. You're going to love her. I know she'll love you; they all will."

"I'm meeting them?"

"We'll take a road trip. Thanksgiving."

When she sent him a tremulous smile and softly answered, "I'd like that," and a curiously vulnerable grin crossed Taylor's face, she knew his heart was in this the same as hers was.

He said, "Let's hit that balloon before the others come to their senses and ditch schmoozing for ballooning. It wasn't easy getting this set up at the last minute."

"You did this?"

"I read your list. I pulled some strings; called in some favors. I was hoping this would make you happy."

She laughed, mopping her face for the last time. "I'm in."

Holding hands, they raced to the balloon and scrambled inside.

The balloon rose, carrying them above the beautiful grounds. The happy sounds of the wedding swiftly faded. The entire Oregon coastline came into view—sandy beaches, rocky cliffs, thousands of frothing waves rolling inland.

"Beautiful," Sarah breathed.

"*You're* beautiful." Taylor snugged his arm around her. "One question?"

"Shoot."

"What mistake did your mother make you won't?"

"That's easy—she never let her heart lead, never took a chance. She died two years ago, and she was so disappointed in the end. She made me promise I'd follow my heart, no matter what." She looked up at him. "I want an *extraordinary* life."

"And that's why I love you, Sarah Meyers—your adventurous spirit." Tenderly he stroked her face.

She gripped his lapel, whispered, "I love you, Taylor Theron", and thoroughly kissed the hot stranger—no longer a stranger—who'd captured her heart.

For long time.

Which was *very* nice.

EPILOGUE

*B*lind-folded, laughing, Sarah let Taylor walk her through to the cottage kitchen. He'd made her stay with Chrissy for two weeks in order to surprise her and tonight—Christmas Eve—was the big reveal. This was her Christmas gift.

She wasn't complaining. Life with Taylor was never a dull moment.

He stopped. "You ready?"

"I'm ready."

His lips pressed against hers, soft and warm and all thoughts of a new custom kitchen flew out the window.

"Hey, you two! Get a room!"

Sarah pulled off her blindfold and blurted, "Steve?" then gasped at seeing the kitchen, all white, with live edge oak counters, a sleek laptop, and a beach glass backsplash. "Taylor!" she squealed, jumping up and down. "This is gorgeous! More than gorgeous! This is—" She threw herself into his arms. "This is perfect! *You're* perfect!"

Ryan complained, "Alright, that's where we draw the line, Sarah. My brother's head's big enough!"

With her arms still around Taylor's neck she looked at the laptop. The faces of his entire family—his brothers Steve and Ryan, his dad Geoff and mom Carol were all there on a Zoom call to share the kitchen reveal, which was also perfect. She and Taylor had been back to visit them three times already and she loved them all. "Hey! Merry Christmas!" she greeted, then frowned. "Where *are* you guys?"

Carol answered, "We're in the car, on our way to a party. We wouldn't miss this for the world."

Sarah hugged Taylor and grinned from Taylor to the faces beaming on the laptop. "He did good, huh? I think I'll keep him."

"I'm counting on that." Taylor kissed her nose and released her. "Have a look around. Get acquainted with your new digs."

She did a little happy dance then grabbed the laptop and walked the family around the kitchen, Carol and Geoff expressing their admiration for the job Taylor had done while his brothers poked fun, as usual.

When she was done touring everyone around the kitchen, she noticed she was alone. "Taylor?"

She went into the living room. Taylor had lit several candles and the Christmas tree lights were on. Pumpkin was curled up in the rocker, sleek and happy. It looked so cozy—but empty? "Taylor?"

She screamed and cleared the floor when the cottage door burst open and Carol, Geoff, Ryan and Steve poured into the living room. Carol, of course was crying. "Surprise! Merry Christmas sweet Sarah!" They handed her around for the usual bear hugs, shedding their coats, bringing in covered trays of food and boxes of wrapped gifts.

"What's going on?" she asked, delighted they were here and mystified why it was a secret. She'd have prepared. They were always so welcoming to her.

They were suddenly all quiet, beaming at her. Carol's eyes flooded. Wordlessly Geoff handed his wife a tissue which she pressed to her cheeks. When her gaze shifted to behind Sarah in anticipation, Sarah turned to look.

Taylor was down on one knee, looking up at her, his expression unlike any she'd seen before.

"Oh... my..."

He reached for her hand. "Sarah. I love you and I know you love me. We're good together. Let's spend the rest of our lives together." He laughed. "With Pumpkin, of course." He produced a ring box, opened it for her to see the sparkler inside. "Marry me. Make me the happiest man in Poet."

Tears poured from her eyes, blurring her vision. Taylor handed her a tissue. She turned and looked at his family—her family now—their expressions silently imploring. They wanted this. *She* wanted this.

She looked back at Taylor, and choked out, "Yes! Yes! Absolutely yes!"

Naturally, the cheering and crying that followed went on to become Theron family lore.

ABOUT THE AUTHOR

Ronnie Roberts lives in northern Canada in an off-grid cabin for half the year, and sadly, in a proper house the other half. She writes wholesome small-town romance because she loves to catch up with fun, recurring characters, and time travel sci fi because she can't help wondering what would happen if we had to suddenly stand up and be counted in a time of crisis.

Why such diverse genres? Because love, humor, adventure and heroics in any story is a ton of fun to write! (*This bio is approved by Ronnie's in-house editor cat, Stevie King.*)

Visit Ronnie at RonnieRobertsBooks.com

ACCIDENTALLY INTO YOU

JO NOELLE

When sparks fly on a trip to Edinburgh, Meg and Scott find love is closer than they imagine.

1
———

$\mathcal{M}$egan Nichols sank into the overstuffed sofa, leaving her travel bags in the middle of the living room. She'd been in Panama for a three-week shoot. Beautiful. Exotic. Fascinating. But not home. She wiggled down more, stretching her legs out. She'd be home for a month before touring Romanian castles. A groan slipped out. She wasn't tired of taking pictures, just the ones someone else assigned to her. Tired of going to amazing places and missing a chance to feel the spirit of them.

She closed her eyes and took a deep breath. *It will pass.*

A clatter in the room jolted her attention. Her luggage had fallen over and tipped her purse onto the side, a few items spilling out. She rolled off the couch and began stuffing it all back in.

Her hand hit the envelope that had traveled to Panama and back. She fished it out. Megan didn't have to open it to know who was getting married. It was the topic of every phone call she'd had with her mother lately. Her mom bugged her to invite a date—specifically Vic. Tricky since Megan had broken it off with him but hadn't told her family. The groom was her best friend Scott's little brother, making her feel ancient.

The heavy paper gave way as Megan wiggled her finger down the envelope's spine. She removed the invitation and studied the photo of the couple in a relaxed pose—good balance, vivid color, nice lighting, and oozing with love. Models couldn't fake what real couples had. She felt as if she were witnessing a personal moment between them. She studied their faces, their eyes, and smiles. Her chest tightened, and a hole in her heart pulsed open. Would someone ever look at her like that?

Megan scanned the RSVP card. It was due today. She read the dreaded questions at the bottom: *Accepts with joy, Declines with regret,* and *Number of guests.* A nice way of asking if you'll sit in the very back at the singles' table—again.

Megan tapped the card on the floor as she made the decision. She set the card aside, opened email, then typed, starting with a winky face, "Accepts with regret. Party of one. Can't wait to see you! Love, Meg."

She leaned against the couch. A selfie of Scott was at the top of her Instagram feed. The caption said, "Anyone want to be my fake girlfriend for my little brother's wedding? Tired of the disapproving looks."

Seventy-three comments. Megan hearted his picture, then sat back to enjoy the comments.

"Can't help you. I've got a date."

"Me too, and I'm twice your age. Haha."

"Just send regrets. Your brother already knows, and your mom will forgive you, eventually."

A DM alert from Scott popped up on Megan's screen. "Come on; go with me to the wedding."

The only person she talked to more than her mom was Scott. How had someone not snatched him up yet? Oh, wait—workaholic. His CGI company was killing it if the credits in the blockbuster flicks gave an indication.

Megan popped a frozen lasagna into the microwave, then pulled out her computer to back up the pictures from her last trip. She had another message from Scott. "It's a pity date, but I'm okay with that. Is this working?"

She typed back. "You're making it sound so wonderful. I'll think about it." She added a laughing emoji before sending. Scott didn't have to know, but there was no pity in her decision. In fact, she couldn't think of anyone else she'd rather be with.

When her work pictures were safely stored, Megan opened a folder on her desktop and stored her personal ones. She took pictures in those exotic locations that her company wouldn't own, and she could post to her travel blog.

Her phone screen lit up again. "I'll sweeten the deal with excursions, adventures, and romantic public displays of affection. Or any two of those—your choice."

She typed back quickly, "If I only choose one, which would you want?"

"PDA, definitely. Just to get my family off my back."

Megan leaned back on the couch and laughed. A little piece of her heart wished that were true. Anyway, the wedding would unquestionably be a lot of fun with him and more than without him. Just as she was typing yes, another message popped up.

"I'll pay for everything. It's my birthday present to you."

He remembered. The wedding was actually on her birthday. It wasn't like she would have had special plans, so going to a wedding was fine. "You win. I'll be your date." She pulled out the lasagna and sat at the table, then checked her phone.

"I owe you. I'll let my mom know."

"I already sent her an RSVP, but you can't back out now. It's a very long date, and you're paying. I'll send you my flight info."

"I'm so relieved; I don't even care that you played me. Besides, now I can be there for you as you turn the big thirty-five. In case it's traumatic."

"Thanks, Snot, for reminding me of my age. You're only a month younger than me so you're an old man too."

"Your auto-correct did a funky thing there."

She sent an eye-rolling emoji. "See you soon, Snot."

2

Edinburgh was Scott Curtis's favorite city. It was compact and sat like yin and yang with the old town and new town separate but pushing together; there was an ancient church on every block, and the castle stood guard over it like a medieval knight. The ocean breeze and damp air was like having a swamp cooler always blowing on you.

Scott stood outside the airport near the H of the tall concrete letters spelling out Edinburgh. He'd arrived the night before and was anxious for Meg to join him. Guilt trembled in his gut. He hadn't been completely honest. Although they'd been friends for their whole lives, over the past few months, his feelings for her had changed. He'd have three days to convince Meg that he was the guy she wanted. Even thinking about it made his stomach feel like a mosh pit for bees. Their friendship had turned to love—for him. Could she feel the same way?

He checked the time. Her flight should have landed. He unfolded a large sign that he'd made, saying *Welcome home from prison* to hold over his head when he saw her.

She came out the closest door but walked toward the covered side-walk. He hadn't seen her face yet, but he knew it was her by the copper highlights in her brown hair and the way she walked—fast.

He held the sign up. "Hey, Meg. Over here. Welcome home!" He whistled as he used to when they were kids, and her face turned toward

528

him. He waved the sign and continued calling her name. He knew the moment she read the sign as a mischievous grin overtook her face. Other passengers read the sign, then stopped to see who would approach Scott.

A few steps away, Meg dropped her carry-on bag and ran toward him. He put the sign down just in time to catch her as she hurled herself into his arms, and onlookers clapped. He turned her in a circle, and as he set her down, her eyes turned up toward his. Scott was taken aback by the sparkle. She was always stunning, but he hadn't expected her to look beautiful this early in the morning after an all-night flight.

"Thanks for the welcome," she said, turning to retrieve her carry-on.

"That's it?" he asked, pointing at the small bag as she rejoined him.

"Yeah, my parents brought the rest."

"What's in these bags?"

"My camera's in my cross-body bag, and I have some clothes and toiletries in my carry-on." She winked at him. "It's not my first rodeo."

Scott offered Meg his hand to lead her to the car park tower. He'd been holding her hand since before they were in kindergarten, but at that moment it felt like a new experience—one he really enjoyed.

He stopped beside a pink Hummer limo. "What if we don't go right to Primrose Manor?" The driver hopped out and opened the door for them.

"Pink? Love it." She gave Scott a crooked smile. "You have my attention."

"I might have made some plans, and you'll get some great photos. Are you in?" When she didn't answer right away, he added, "Unless you're tired."

"I'm not tired at all. First class is comfy. I'm spoiled now. I had my own little bed. So, thank you." The dimple in her cheek deepened with her smile, and Scott had to force his eyes away from it. "I've photographed Scotland several times—old buildings and older castles."

"I don't think you've photographed the Scotland where I'm taking you." He climbed in beside her. "I've read your blog for years and haven't seen this."

"I'm in!" she said, reaching across the seat. She squeezed Scott's hand, and his heart took off like a bullet bike. They drove a few minutes and parked. Meg squealed. "We're going on a helicopter?"

Meg was out of the Hummer before the driver could open her door. Scott grabbed her carry-on and followed.

After a quick safety lesson, they buckled up, and the helicopter lifted. They got a fifteen-minute tour of Edinburgh, and then of Glasgow. All the while, Scott enjoyed the delight on Meg's face as she clicked photos. He even took the camera from her to capture her in the helicopter. He pulled out his phone and took some selfies of them together. The helicopter continued west until landing in Renfrewshire.

"That was amazing," she said as they approached a waiting car.

"There's more." He loved surprising her. She'd always been the kind of girl who sought adventure and anything spontaneous. Apparently, she still was.

The car took them to another business outside of town where a green military tank sat.

A little furrow formed between Meg's eyebrows, and she gave him an incredulous look.

"You're going to drive it," Scott said. He could see the confusion turn to excitement in her expression.

"There's not much to it," the owner said. "Up you go, and we'll get started."

Scott took pictures while Meg scrambled over the metal skirt covering the track, up to the turret, then dropped down through the hatch. She stood back up, her eyes bright. "I thought it would have a steering wheel, but it's more like an airplane with the little bars to hold onto," she called down to Scott.

The owner sat to the side of her, explaining what to do. He motioned to Scott. "Come on up and sit on the other side." He pointed to the side of the tank where tiny seats with hand-holds were welded on. "She'll want pictures to remember this. Slide closer to her, and I'll take some of you both on the tank."

Meg stood up through the hatch, and Scott leaned across the copula next to her. "Best date ever." Meg threw her arm around his shoulders and kissed his cheek.

There's more. When Scott planned the excursions, he'd hoped to impress her, but now, he wanted to watch her surprise and hear the laughter in her voice. This was definitely his best date ever also.

Moments later, Meg maneuvered the tank along the road and through mud holes. She squealed and laughed with each new obstacle. His chest burned with pleasure that this made her so happy. The beast powered over steep ridges, the gun barrel pointing way above the horizon.

"Hang on!" the owner yelled, then the balance flopped the tank forward, and it rumbled down the slope. When they returned, Scott took a turn and followed much the same route while Meg rode behind him and took pictures.

After the adventure, they buckled into their seats in the helicopter. "Ready for more?" Scott asked her.

"Yes!"

"We have options." Scott made his eyebrows bounce, and Meg rewarded him with a giggle. "We can take the helicopter to Mallaig over by Skye or take it back to Edinburgh."

"What would we do in Mallaig?"

"We'd have lunch on the beach, then we'd board a steam train and take it back to Edinburgh, enjoying the scenery along the way."

"Ooh, I like how your mind works. I'm strongly leaning toward that option. But what if we go right to Edinburgh?"

"We'll have lunch with our parents and be there in time to go to the bachelor and bachelorette parties this evening."

Meg wrinkled her nose—that was exactly what Scott expected. "I've always wanted to ride an old-fashioned train," she said.

3

————

Megan watched out her window as the helicopter landed near Morar. A car took them to Silver Sands Beach near the end of the bay. The colors were intense with dense green shrubs and gray rock, giving way to stark white sand, and stripes of blue and green water painted the loch. Megan laced her fingers with Scott's. She felt completely at home with him though they were thousands of miles away. A table sat near the water's edge with a pink tablecloth whose edge fluttered on the sand and beautiful pink flowers decorated the center. As they approached, servers jumped up and made final preparations.

"I'm seeing a pink theme today. Any special reason?"

"It's your favorite color." Scott shrugged like it wasn't a big deal, but Megan's chest exploded with warmth. When was the last time someone had gone out of their way to please her? More than that—to make a whole day special for her.

Oh, she'd missed him. She hadn't realized how much. Texts and phone calls just weren't the same. He centered her, and she felt more real around him than anyone she'd ever known. Being with him was worth coming to the wedding. "What's for lunch?" she asked.

"If I were to choose your favorite food, what would it be?" Scott smiled broadly but didn't look right at her when he said it, seeming suddenly shy.

"Lobster?"

His gaze met hers. "And mine?"

"Scallops." She tipped her head to prove she knew she was right. "You gave me a choice. How did you know I'd choose the train?"

"I know you, Meg." Scott held out his hands as if weighing a balance scale. "Attend a party with strangers or go on a spontaneous adventure." He chuckled—Megan loved the sound. "I'm glad you chose this," Scott winked at her, "or the servers over there would have had a great lunch if I was wrong."

Two chairs faced each other. Scott helped her sit, then pulled his chair to moved it across the corner from her. Before he could reach for his plate, a server had rearranged it in front of him. Another server delivered a platter with two enormous lobsters. Some large seashells with seared scallops and black pudding, and salads were added to the table.

Megan couldn't help but laugh. "There's no way we can eat all this."

"You'll have to prioritize," Scott suggested, picking up a lobster so large it hung over her plate. "Bon appétit."

They ate in companionable silence for several minutes. "Why did you plan all of this?" Megan asked. "Don't get me wrong, I'm loving it. But why?"

Scott's eyes looked worried for a moment. He brushed his mouth with his napkin and replied, "I wanted you to have the best birthday imaginable. I want to make you happy."

Megan looked into his face. "You have." Every nerve in her body seemed to reach toward him. She wondered if, not for the first time, Scott was the reason she'd never found someone to spend her life with. She measured every man against her best friend, and they all fell short—including the recent ex-boyfriend. Vic had been pushing hard for their relationship to go to the next level, but she didn't feel a strong emotional connection with him. He wasn't *the one,* which meant dating him was pointless.

Maybe she and Scott . . . Megan stopped. She didn't want to lose him. Romance didn't work out for her, and she'd ruin their friendship when being a couple soured.

Half an hour later, Meg threw both of her hands up. "I gave it an effort, but I'm done. It was amazing, but I swear, I won't be able to eat at all tomorrow."

"I ordered currant tarts for dessert." A grin slowly grew on Scott's face, and Meg knew he knew he had her.

"Bring them with us. I might want a midnight snack."

A hired car took them to the rail station in Mallaig, and they boarded a full train, settling in to a table for four. When the train chugged out of the station, Meg pointed to the empty seats across from them. "This looks a little suspicious. Did you buy the other two seats too?"

"Yeah. I thought it might make it easier for you to drop the window and take pictures if no one else was with us."

"You thought of everything." Megan immediately opened the window and began taking pictures. She captured brilliantly green gorges, mountains, and an incredible arched viaduct bridge she remembered from the Harry Potter movies. Now and again, Scott shot some selfies with her.

They changed trains at Fort William, taking a faster train through Glasgow to Edinburgh. Scott rested his arm on the back of the sofa, and Meg settled beside him.

It felt right with Scott—always. "I didn't think this trip was going to be enjoyable at all. I'm glad you asked me out." Scott chuckled as Megan tipped her head against his shoulder. He was a perfect fit for her. She wasn't going to jinx this—she'd just wait and see what happened. A yawn pulled a breath deep into her chest. "Sorry. I'm more tired than I thought."

Scott motioned for her to stand. He scooted into the corner and spread his arms wide. "Have a nap. I'll let you know when we get there."

Megan took a good look at his broad muscled chest. How hadn't she noticed that before? His shoulders were wide, and his shirt strained against the fabric. The short sleeves rode up to reveal chiseled biceps. *Good heavens! I will never unsee that. Mmm.* She slid back onto the seat and snuggled close.

He wrapped his arms around her. "Close your eyes. I've got you."

Megan wondered if she could sleep with the shocking awareness of how hot her best friend was. She was definitely seeing Scott in a new way, and she liked what she saw. She relaxed to the gentle movement against his chest, and the soothing rattle of the train muted as sleep overcame her.

"Megan. Megan, we're almost at the station."

She thought she felt Scott's lips on her hair.

"You awake?"

Megan stretched and looked up over her shoulder at him. Her head stopped spinning as the train pulled into Edinburgh, then they got out to meet their car. "The pink Hummer again?"

"It could make several more appearances." They watched the lights pass them by as they traveled north of town to Primrose Manor.

Megan was thrilled—they'd have two more days together.

"The wedding party starts early. My brother said that there's some kind of surprise that will take us most of the day to complete."

"Oh, no. A big group-type activity?" She took his hand. If she could choose, it would just be the two of them.

Scott nodded seriously. "You never know when we'll need a quick escape. I figure the only thing I'm obligated to show up for is the ceremony. The rest of the time, I'm celebrating your birthday." He lifted her hand and kissed it lightly.

Warmth combusted in her chest, and she held back a sigh. She'd never again say a man kissing a woman's hand was corny.

The driver let them out near the manor house entrance.

"I couldn't imagine a better birthday or any day," Megan said. She watched Scott's expression turn from happy to smoldering. His eyes darkened. Her heart banged against her ribs as the moment stretched.

The manor house's door flew open, flooding the driveway with obtrusive light. Megan's mother came striding out, waving. "I have a big surprise for you, Megan. Vic's here." Right behind her was Megan's ex with a smirk on his face. "It was so hard to keep this secret. Isn't it great?"

Yes, it's a surprise. And no, it's not great.

Scott leaned close to her ear and whispered. "See you in the morning. Good night, Meg." His voice was soft but resonated, sending chills down her neck.

4

———

The next morning, Scott joined the guests gathered in a very barren dining room, and whispered to Megan, "No breakfast?"

"Not even a whiff of bacon."

He watched as a little crease deepened between her eyebrows and turned to see where she was looking. Vic was walking their way. He stepped up close to Meg and slipped his arm behind her back.

Scott thought she stiffened, and Vic's challenging gaze slid toward Scott momentarily. Meg looked just as displeased with Vic's attendance as Scott was. After all, if she had wanted him there, she would have invited him. Scott didn't like the possessive grasp of Vic's fingers at Meg's waist.

"Oops." Meg's purse hit the floor. Instead of just leaning down to pick it up, she squatted, removing herself from his grasp. When she stood back up, she took a step behind and away from him. Her glance shot toward Scott, and he thought he saw an apology or regret.

A foghorn blared at the front of the room where Ryan and his fiancée held their phones in the air, the screens flashing between red and yellow. Ryan smiled at Calista, and she returned an adoring expression. It was the same look he thought he saw on Meg's face yesterday.

"Welcome everyone to our wedding. We hope you enjoy the fun

today." Calista smiled and added with her lilting Scottish accent, "Ryan created a special app just for us, called *Looting the Scavenger Hunt*."

Ryan was quickly typing on his phone. "I sent you all a link to download."

Scott nodded toward his brother. He was so proud of Ryan and his success as an app developer.

"I hope you all elected to get the UK phone service. Otherwise, you'll be slow." There were a few chuckles and a few moans. "You might want to pair up with someone who did," Calista suggested.

Panic shot through Scott. They were going to work in pairs—twos. While everyone else was still downloading, Vic leaned across Meg. "You'll need to find a partner, Scott."

"Okay," he answered brightly. "Meg's my partner." He loved the shocked expression on Vic's face.

"I don't think so," Vic replied. "She's my girlfriend."

"Yeah? She's my date." Both men looked toward her. Scott didn't like putting her in that position, but he wasn't going to give up being with her today.

Meg smiled and took them both by the hand. "We'll be a trio."

It was obvious when the app had loaded across the room as a foghorn sounded from each phone, and lights flashed around them.

Ryan raised his hand. "Here's how we'll play. Teams need to locate five objects around Edinburgh. The app will give you a clue for each location. You'll get points for time, the loot you collect, and how precise you are in the required destinations. Yes, my app just connected with your GPS signal. Thanks for accepting the terms and conditions without reading them."

Calista clapped her hands. "The grand prize is a three-day vacation in London."

Scott couldn't help notice how Ryan and his fiancée were so in sync. He'd found someone who fit him well. Scott wondered if he'd found that long ago and hadn't realized it.

Calista raised her finger in the air. "That's not all. The app will notify you of winning possible add-on prizes. So, pay attention."

Ryan continued, "Enter a team name for your group. We need to know who's winning, but that will preserve the surprise until we hand out prizes."

Scott typed quickly. *Three's a Crowd.*

"Great name," Vic mumbled.

"It just came to me," Scott replied.

Ryan looked at Calista and both of their smiles grew as they clasped hands and raised them above their heads. Together they shouted, "Ready. Set. Go!"

Dozens of foghorns sounded, and Scott tapped the clue button on his screen, reading, "Find almond croissants. Upload a picture of your team eating them."

"There's a quaint patisserie on North Bridge," Meg said. "Everything I've eaten there is amazing. Let's go."

"Is that the closest one?" Vic asked, following as Meg and Scott jogged out the door.

"No," they both replied, running toward the stretch Hummer. This would be a great way to wander around Edinburgh with Meg. Vic was in the way, but Scott could ignore him—maybe. Scott decided to take as many selfies as he could with just him and Meg. Challenge accepted.

He snapped pictures in the limo and the bakery. After their picture was uploaded, a listing of the teams and their place flashed on their phone screens.

"We're in second place," Vic said. While Meg and Scott cheered with a high-five, Vic added, "We could do better if we make better choices."

A new button appeared for the next item for their scavenger hunt list. "Upload a panoramic video from the Edinburgh Castle. Point out Calton Hill in your video."

"Across town." Meg laughed. "I'll bet Ryan and Calista are enjoying watching our little dots rush all over town."

They entered the castle and ran to the top level, then chose a spot near the rock battery. Scott handed Vic his phone. "Start filming the city from over there." He pointed to the other side. "We'll be ready to point out Calton Hill when you turn the camera this way."

Vic panned slowly around the city.

"Hold my hands," Meg said.

"Yes, ma'am."

Meg's smile widened. "We'll make a frame around the hill."

After uploading their video, the next clue popped up. "Visit the National Scottish Gallery and stand near the olive trees."

"Hey, Meg, your parents are here." Scott pointed over the edge to where they were walking up the path from the gatehouse. Although he whistled, they didn't look up. "Let's get a picture of you by Mons Meg before we leave."

"What's that?" Vic asked.

"A huge cannon that shares Meg's name."

"Another stupid choice. That team could pass us."

Scott ignored him, and led Meg past St. Margaret's Chapel. They veered toward the massive cannon. "Sit by the sign." He took several pictures around the cannon while Meg made faces, tried to look sultry, or appeared contemplative. "Let's come back when we have more time."

Meg nodded. They rejoined Vic, hurried down the path, and out of the castle grounds. Dodging the people exiting tour buses or walking up the steep hill, they ran down Castle Terrace, to where the limo waited.

"Where to?" the driver asked.

A foghorn blared on their phones and the screens showed a pot of gold and a rainbow with more gold coins dropping into it. *Sweeten the Pot* was scrawled across the picture. A dialogue box popped up. "First team to stand on the Heart of Midlothian wins iPads."

"Heart of Midlothian," Vic yelled toward the driver and plopped into the seat.

"It's back up where we just came from, and no cars are allowed," Meg replied.

"I can drop you off near Deacon Brodies Tavern. It's fairly close," the driver offered.

"Thanks."

They were half a block away when Scott watched his cousin and her husband lift their phone over the heart mosaic on the sidewalk in front of Saint Giles cathedral. They were nearly there when his group's phones started to flash with a picture of confetti. *Congratulations to the Funny Bunnies for winning the iPad.*

Vic turned away from Meg and headed back the direction they had come from. "What a waste."

"Wait," Meg called. "Let's take a picture by the heart. We're this close, anyway."

Scott wished Vic would just keep going, but Vic turned around and said, "Have you seen the heart before?"

"Of course," Meg replied. "The history is fabulous. The legend is that if you spit on it, you'll have good luck. You can't come to Edinburgh without visiting it."

"I can." Vic pulled up his phone and turned it toward them. "We're in third place now because of that side trip. We need to make up ground."

Scott could see what Meg was trying not to show as she pressed her lips together.

"Go get a cab," Scott called toward Vic, hoping to rid themselves of the killjoy. "We'll get a quick picture and meet you at the next location. The museum's not far away—just at the bottom of the mound." Scott pointed the direction. "We'll hurry." *Or not.*

Without waiting for Vic to respond, Scott took Meg's hand, and they jogged toward the heart. "Are you hungry?" Scott asked.

"I will be," Meg answered.

"I'll order something for us to pick up on the way." Scott began typing on his phone as they waited for a large family to finish taking pictures. He completed their carry-out order and offered to take the family's picture. Before the family left, everyone spit on the heart.

Meg and Scott turned toward each other at the same time. "There's no way I'm stepping on that," she said with a chuckle.

"Maybe we should spit on it," Scott suggested. They stepped behind the heart. Meg put her arm around Scott's waist and pulled him tighter. He slipped his arm around her shoulder and did the same as the father took pictures for them. He didn't care what Vic thought—the Heart of Midlothian was definitely lucky.

5

—————

*M*egan knew she had to talk with Vic. She would. Before the rehearsal dinner tonight. She shook her head—what part of we're not dating anymore did he not get? She wouldn't let that spoil her enjoyment now. Seeing the men together today made it obvious why she wanted to come to Edinburgh with Scott and not Vic. "What did you order?"

"Mashers. Go that way." Scott pointed to an alley. "We'll cut through Lady Stair's Close. After we eat, we can run down the mound and meet Rrr—go to the museum."

Megan laughed. "You couldn't even say his name." She continued to chuckle.

"I admit it. I'm jealous. I had you to myself all day yesterday and thought I would for the entire weekend." Scott winked as they continued to walk. "I wish I could say I'm just disappointed, but I'm not that big of a man—I'm jealous."

Meg's heart thumped louder with each sentence. She could blame that on the uphill climb, but she knew it was because she liked what she was hearing. Her chest tingled with hope—maybe there was love.

The alley opened to a cobblestone-paved courtyard enclosed between the buildings. The Author's Museum was tucked at the side. "I want to go there, but not during the game."

"We'll have to come back," Scott said.

Megan nodded. "Yeah." *When it's just us.*

At the other side of Lady Stair's Close, they hurried down the broad rock steps to Bank Street and turned right toward the restaurant to pick up their mash plates.

"One is chicken with mustard sauce and the other is a haggis entrée. Which do you want?"

Megan sniffed near the boxes and rolled her eyes. "Mmm! Both. Let's share."

They ate quietly for several minutes, dipping out of each box. It was so easy to be with Scott. There was nothing fake. They didn't have to try hard. They could just be.

Megan realized that she was staring into Scott's face.

His eyes were fixed on hers, as well. Slowly, he reached up and caught a wisp of hair the breeze blew across her cheek. "Thank you for having lunch with me."

Tingles raced below his fingers as they pushed the hair across her skin. Delicious chills ran down her neck when he tucked the hair behind her ear. Megan's head leaned against Scott's palm. "Anytime." She closed her eyes and savored the feeling. Scott was in every good memory of her life. No doubt, she'd file this one with all of those.

His forehead lightly touched Megan's. The moment stretched, and she could hardly breathe in anticipation. Megan wished she were sitting close enough to be in his arms. She thought she heard a faint growl, then Scott moved away. "I guess we should get going." His voice was rough.

"You're right." But she wished he wasn't. The wall she thought was between love and friendship with him was very thin, and Scott was chipping big holes in it. Soon the wall would collapse, and they'd have to decide what to do about that.

By the time they made it to the museum, Megan was out of breath and Scott looked it too. They clipped up the flat steps, between the massive, Greek columns, and through the doors. Vic was standing just inside when they entered.

"There are no olive trees in any of the paintings. Now what?" Vic's voice was flat, but his eyes flicked over to Scott and back to Megan with some fire in them.

That was too much drama for the moment. Megan wasn't going to deal with him now, and she turned toward the interior of the museum. He and Scott followed as Megan walked toward the back. "Let's check again."

The first room had amazing, ancient altar pieces that she'd love to study again, but they had to find the olive tree first, then two more challenges. "Did you check upstairs?" There was no answer but when she looked at Vic, he shook his head.

She passed through the second room, feeling the eyes in the portraits daring her to come study them. Ooh. She'd love to. That was her favorite part of photography, the eyes of the people she met. There was so much to see in them. It was also why she didn't love her job— she shot pictures of places. The history of each was interesting, but she always liked the stories of the people more.

Megan tried to ignore the jewel-toned walls dotted with dozens of gilt-framed paintings. She started up the stairs and continued climbing until they came to a cozy display room. The carpet was a sea of tan and the walls were brilliant blue, dotted with impressive works of art—one of them *Olive Trees* by Vincent Van Gogh. The GPS on their phones kicked in, and they all dinged. *Location Achieved* flashed on their screens, unlocking the next clue.

"Finally," Vic said with a rough sigh, then read the clue. "Although you won't find a house elf in this café, one was penned here."

"The Elephant House," Megan and Scott said in unison. Vic looked confused. Apparently, he didn't know J.K. Rowling wrote some of the Harry Potter books there.

"Jinx," they said again, then laughed as they followed Vic down the stairs.

"Which way, Megan?" Vic asked once outside.

"The other side of Old Town."

"Seriously? How many times are we going to crisscross that place?"

Megan could hear the irritation in his voice. She doubted any other teams considered it a burden to walk around a medieval city, or considered running straight through the way Vic wanted to. She looked up the hill they had to climb. It was hard not to chuckle—anywhere you went in Edinburgh was up or downhill.

She clicked on her phone to search for a public toilet that might be close. Nope. It's not like she could come to Scotland and not have their national soda, but she regretted having the second bottle of Irn-Bru. "I need to stop by the bathrooms near the castle before we can go to The Elephant House."

Vic huffed at her comment. "We're in a contest." He threw his arms wide. "A race—we're trying to win! Can't you hold it?"

Megan decided to ignore him—for now. Why would he come after they'd broken up? That's why she didn't invite him. He wasn't for her. It was a relief to be so positive of it.

She went into the restroom, leaving the men outside. Her phone flashed and the pot of gold and rainbow filled the screen. *Named for an apostle, and also the first official green—can you make the links? Be the first and join a four-some."* She washed her hands, combed her hair, and put on some lip gloss.

Scott was leaning against the rock wall when she came out. "So, should we go for the next clue or for the pot of gold prize?" she asked. His smile broadened slowly. Oh, he was handsome. She was glad she took the time to fix her hair.

Scott was obviously holding back a laugh.

"What?"

"Vic left. He said he was going to the St. Andrews Links to claim the golf prize and when you got out, you should join him."

He ditched me while I was in a toilet? "I'm not interested in helping him win. In fact, I'd like him to lose. If he's waiting for us in Fife, he's going to rot there."

Scott laughed out loud and pushed off the wall.

Megan loved the sound and laughed with him. "I wonder when he'll figure it out?" She laced her fingers with his.

"What would you like to do?"

"First, I'd like to go to Primrose Manor. Then I'd like to get rid of Vic's stuff. Then we'll play your brother's game."

It didn't take long to move Vic from the wedding location to a room at the Balmoral. Nor to check off the last two locations of the game— The Elephant House and Greyfriars's Kirkyard. When they returned to Primrose Manor, Vic was sitting on a bench.

"I'll see you at the dinner," Megan told Scott, and he squeezed her hand. She approached Vic, sitting beside him. They sat quietly for a minute—maybe he was trying to put his ideas together as she was.

"I'm sorry, Vic, but—"

His hand went up to pause her. "I need to say this." He rested his forearms on his knees. "We broke up. I get it. I came because I thought we would get back together." He shook his head. "Your mom told me to keep it a secret, and we'd surprise you." He laughed ruefully. "We sure did." He sat up and took a deep breath. "Sorry."

"I want to be with someone who takes the journey with me, not who only wants to reach a destination. The right girl for you is one who wants what you want—that's not me."

"I put you in a bad spot."

Megan patted his arm. "Yeah. I'm sorry I moved your clothes without telling you."

"That was probably not as cruel as it could have been. Sorry, I left you in the bathroom."

Megan nodded, then her eyebrows arched. "We're done, right?"

"We were done a while ago." A car pulled into the circular drive where they sat, and Vic stood. "Here's my ride."

"Bye, Vic." Megan hugged him quickly and turned toward the manor.

THAT EVENING, Megan entered the room for the rehearsal dinner and looked toward the back table.

Scott approached her from the other side. "We have seats in the front." Although his voice sounded happy, his eyes told her that he was uncertain about where their relationship was now.

Her heart thumped with fear, but it would burst if she didn't tell him. Once the words were out, there would be no taking them back. The risk of change was ice in her veins—she had to do it. Instead of taking his extended arm, Megan grabbed his hands, leaned forward, and kissed his cheek. "I'm glad you asked me to be your plus-one." She smiled brightly and watched Scott's smile grow.

After the meal, Ryan and Calista stood up with a microphone between them. She leaned in. "We have prizes to give away!"

Although Megan knew they hadn't been in the running to win, she had won, in a way. She could finally see what was in front of her the whole time. With Vic gone, she just had to tell Scott how she felt about him, and risk their friendship and losing him. She scooted her chair closer to his. She'd find a way.

"Betsy and Paul won the iPads. Mark and David won the round of golf at St. Andrew's Links. And our grand prize winners are Gigi and Papa," Ryan announced. When the prizes were handed out and the applause died down, he said, "Calista and I have decided to give an impromptu prize for the most random team who only sort of played our game. To let you know what I mean, please watch this video."

Megan sucked in a gasp at a picture of her and Scott standing in line at the patisserie making faces with their eyes crossed. A caption popped up. *They started off on the right track.* Then a string of photos followed them on the first few stops. One showed them hugging at the Heart of Midlothian, followed by a close up of the spittle-covered heart. The next few were of their lunch, then the museum.

"This is incredible." Meg scooted her chair close to Scott, and he placed his arm over her shoulders. Then she saw it—awe flooded her. In every picture, she and Scott had the look of forever love. You can't fake it. It flashed brightly from every photo of them together. Loving someone deeply made every picture into personal moments anyone could witness. Scott was her *one.* Her voice was clogged with emotion, and she cleared her throat. "Were you sneaking photos to Ryan all day?"

"No. I made the video while you were talking to Vic."

Megan lay her head on his shoulder and reminisced about how they'd combed through the ancient city together, zigzagging off course when something interesting caught their eye. "I want a copy of this. I love it." She wanted more moments of him to fill her future. She wanted Scott.

"So, here's your prize, big brother." Ryan dropped a canvas bag on the table in front of him, and Scott pulled out the tissue and looked inside. "It's empty."

"That's because you lost."

6

———————

fter the wedding, Ryan and Calista had a Scottish céilidh complete with Gaelic music and dance instructors. Scott wasn't sure if he could be comfortable in the kilt Calista's family had arranged for the men, but it was growing on him. After dancing a jig, a reel, and a march, Scott grabbed a pastry box from their table and led Meg outside into the cool air.

Contrary to the locals' belief, Edinburgh was never hot. Right now, Scott felt like his chest was filled with Las Vegas in July. He could hardly breathe around his anxiety or maybe from his effort to restrain himself from kissing Meg senseless.

"Have I told you how great you look in the kilt," Meg said.

"A few times." He chuckled and tried to play it off, but his chest roared with heat. "Let's sit in the garden."

A coy smile tipped up the corner of her lips before they settled on a concrete bench.

Meg's perfume, like the first blooms of spring, enveloped him. "Happy birthday, Meg," he said, handing her the box and adding, "Wait." He fumbled around in his pocket to find the candle and lighter. "Ready now."

She laughed when she looked inside. Six colorful macarons sat at the bottom.

"You don't like cake." Scott pushed the candle into the center cookie, then lit the wick.

Meg looked at the candle. Her eyes closed in thought. She set the box aside and turned to face him, so close that her nose brushed the side of his.

Scott was overwhelmed with the desire to kiss her. *Just wait.* He repeated it again.

"I wish—"

His hand lifted of its own will and cupped her jaw. "Your wish won't come true if you tell it," Scott reminded her. His fingertips lightly caressed her earlobe.

"This one might." She closed her eyes and placed her hand over his. "I wish that being with you would last longer."

Her words whispered across his face. He locked his muscles and willed himself to listen and not act.

"I wish that we didn't live on opposite sides of the country. That I could see you whenever I want to." She took both of his hands and stood. They gazed at each other—the moon and stars the only witnesses.

Scott stood with her, looking into her upturned face. He could see every Meg he'd ever known within the woman before him. His heart beat against his chest as each of her ages called to him, clear to the moment they stood in now.

Her gaze roved from his eyes to his mouth. "I love you, Scott. I wish you would kiss me." Her lips parted, and he was lost to her.

He pulled her hands around his neck as his hands glided down her shoulders and back, then his arms tightened around her waist. Her soft body fit perfectly with his. "I love you, Meg." His lips immediately found hers, slanting and turning with hunger. Time stopped as life rushed faster than minutes or hours could track.

Scott sat on the bench and pulled her onto his lap, assaulting her lips, drowning in the passion she returned. When the kiss broke, she sighed his name and desire roared through him again—a dizzying pleasure enveloping them. He knew that he'd never stop loving, or stop wanting, every moment with Meg.

Her head bent to the side, and Scott trailed kisses down her neck. This was the woman he'd searched for and hadn't realized it was Meg.

But it always had been. Wherever they'd gone in the world, whatever joy or sorrow they'd had, they'd shared it with each other and would in the future.

Meg hugged him, her fingers roaming through his hair as Scott caught his breath. At the end of the bench, faint light danced in the white box. He glanced over as Meg did. The small candle had burned down to just a nub and a puddle of wax, the yellow flame guttering in the breeze.

"We're backwards, Meg. For us, the deep love came before we even knew the simple, flirtatious kind. I've loved you in ponytails and your track uniform, in emails and phone calls. I've rooted for your success and worried for you too." He kissed her temple and her cheek, then took a deep breath of her scent. "I fell in love with you accidentally, and a long time ago."

She kissed him quickly, and he nearly lost all thought.

"You don't have to answer now, but I have to ask. Meg, marry me?"

Meg cupped his face. "You're all my best memories. I thought it was friendship until, when I least expected it, love engulfed my heart and soul. I don't need time to think about it. I've been deciding every day of my life that I want you in it. Yes, I'll marry you." Then her mouth was on his.

Her kiss was life to him, and his future flared open with her in his arms.

ABOUT THE AUTHOR

Jo Noelle is a USA Today Bestselling Author.

She's a Colorado native but lived in several other mountain states—Idaho, Utah, and California. She has two adult children and three small kids. She teaches teachers, grows freakishly large tomatoes, enjoys cooking, builds furniture, sews beautiful dresses, and hikes in the nearby mountains.

Oh, and by the way, she's two people—a mother/daughter writing team. Jo loves romance and stories about first kisses, how we met, and finding love. They write contemporary, historical, time travel, wild west, and YA —all with sweet, swoony ever-afters.

Join their newsletter and download an epilogue of celebration vignettes for Scott and Megan at the BookFunnel link below.

http://JoNoelle.com

https://dl.bookfunnel.com/ey2ltvin7o

LOVE REKINDLED

LYZ KELLEY

A chance meeting proves it's never too late to fall in love again.

1

────────

 $\mathcal{G}$ loria bumped up the volume to the beat of the Rolling Stones and peeked at the electronic track on the treadmill. Almost three miles. She increased her pace to hit the twenty-four minute mark.

She loved the gym at the Silver Fox Resort. Besides it being the only workout room near the California coastal town, the blues and grays were welcoming, the ocean view exceptional, and the "Be stronger than your excuses" mural on the wall suited her philosophy.

Three months ago she hired a trainer to get her ready for the cruise of a lifetime. She was all set to sail to Australia until Jean, her travel buddy, bailed. Her granddaughter was having her first child, and while Gloria understood, she still struggled with a deep-seated disappointment. With two weeks to go, she was left with a non-refundable ticket and the challenge of finding someone willing to take a monthlong vacation.

She hit the stop button and allowed the belt to slow. Just as she turned, a stability ball careened across the gym floor, bouncing off the treadmill, hitting the bench press machine, and then lodging in between two elliptical trainer machines.

"Sorry. So sorry," an older gentleman called out as he trotted after the ball.

She admired the rear view of the silver hottie while he leaned over. He was around her age, late sixties, but unlike others, he'd kept up with the times. Gone were the dorky calf-high white socks. Nor did he have his navy shorts hiked up near his armpits. Plus he received bonus points for having hair.

She glanced down at her tank top. Thank goodness she was wearing her good bra, the one that heaved the saggy bits back into place.

"Hello," he offered with a tentative smile, flashing his white implants.

She popped out an ear bud, stepped off the treadmill and looked up at him. And up. My, he was tall. "You look familiar." She patted a tissue over her sweaty forehead, careful not to disturb her makeup. "Are you staying at the resort?"

"Just for a few days while a work crew renovates my home on the lower bluff, down by Sea Glass Cove. I was about to leave for breakfast. Would you like to join me?"

"Love to. Chef Nate makes the best omelets." The way he was giving her the once-over was promising. Wouldn't it be fun if he were single and loved cruises? With a house renovation going on, he was a definite possibility.

"I should introduce myself. I'm Walter Douglas."

She looked a little closer at Walter's crooked nose, and the small scar on his chin. "Oh, dear." What were the odds? "Yesterday, I heard activity next door, but I assumed it was maintenance workers. I had no idea it was you," she said as her heart flipped back the pages of hurt and reality kicked in. She just agreed to go out with a man she promised to hate for all eternity.

Forty-nine years ago she'd put on her cheerleading uniform with the sole purpose of cheering Walter Douglas over the touchdown line. They had plans to attend college together in California. Then he broke her heart when he accepted a football scholarship from Southern Methodist in Texas, and again when he didn't return home for summer vacation. And no amount of time would heal that hurt.

The room spun like a Tilt-A-Whirl carnival ride. She took a step backward, bumped into the treadmill, and landed on her butt.

Owww. Pain shot through her hip, and she grabbed onto the first steady object to end the topsy-turvy spinning. When her vision cleared, she discovered her fingers anchored to Walter's arm.

She snatched her hand back. Of all the days to droop like a wilted flower. Her cheeks heated. The last thing she needed right now was to fall at Walter Douglas's feet.

She peeked at him. Yep. He looked adorable and concerned, and his sweet vanilla and spicy cedar aftershave reminded her of the carefree times they used to spend on the beach—her suntanning and him surfing—oh, what a hunk he was then, and still was.

"Are you okay?" he asked, looking at her closely. "Should I call the paramedics?"

"Heavens no," she waved him off. "If someone called the paramedics every time I got dizzy, I'd need to clear out my sewing room so the EMTs would have a place to stay. The trainer warned me to triple my water intake and lay off early morning caffeine to avoid dehydration. Give me two minutes and a chug from my water bottle, and I should be good to run a marathon."

He grunted, knowing she was kidding about the marathon, but he apparently didn't believe the water bottle swig would cure her dizzy spell, either. He'd always been a smart guy.

"Here," Walter extended his hand. "Let me help you up."

She didn't want to touch him. Really, she didn't, but her body and brain got their connections mixed up and her hand slid into his. She blamed the intimate gesture on him taking her breath away, causing the lack of oxygen in her brain.

Then again, she was a sucker for gentlemanly gestures. Walter's concern increased when she didn't let go.

Stepping back to a socially appropriate distance would have been the proper thing to do, but standing there holding onto his arm gave her a level of comfort she hadn't felt in years.

"Ready to go eat breakfast?" he asked.

Oh, those glorious blue eyes were dangerous. "I had better get on home. I've got... a... um... I've got chores to do."

His eyes narrowed with concern. "If you're dizzy, you shouldn't be driving. Let's go have a quick bite to eat. I bet eating will help you feel better."

Darn him for being so logical and nice and gorgeous. "I don't think so. Breakfast with you is not a good idea. You must not recognize me. I'm your next-door neighbor, Gloria Stein. The best friend you traded in for a football scholarship. You broke my heart forty-nine years ago, and I've never forgiven you."

He looked like someone handed him a hundred-pack of free lottery tickets. "Gloria Stein, my goodness. I haven't seen you in... Wait!" His excitement deflated. "Did you just say I broke your heart?"

Why did he look confused? Maybe all those years of playing football gave him one too many concussions. Time and age allowed some people to forget, but this hurt she remembered like it was yesterday.

"You broke your promise." She punched out the fact. "We made plans to attend university together. We both got accepted, but then you decided football was more important."

He plopped his hands on his hips. "The scholarship was a full-ride, and Southern Cal only offered me a partial." His eyes narrowed. "Is that why you never returned my phone call?"

"You called?" she searched his face.

"You weren't home, so I asked your sister to have you call. I walked to the administration building every day for two weeks to see if I'd gotten a letter or you left a message."

If the clock rewound, she'd be plotting some sisterly revenge. "I never got your message. I wrote several times, but I never mailed the letters. I was angry and hurt, and you wouldn't have wanted to read what I wrote." Gloria's frustration dulled to a soft roar. "If I had called, what were you going to say?"

Walter tugged on his ear. "I'm not sure I had a plan. I just wanted to hear a friendly voice. Coach was threatening to cut me from the team, the university classes were much harder than I expected, and I didn't like being away from home. No, that's not it. I hated being away from *you*. I didn't realize how much I depended on your advice and support until you weren't there anymore. Talk about hurt. I was hurt when you didn't call or write. I felt like I was getting pulled out to sea with no way to make it back to the shore."

Gloria sighed. "I was planning to tell you how much I liked you once we got to college. We couldn't be more than friends growing up, because if I let on I liked you, our parents would have been planning our wedding before we had our first kiss."

"True," he chuckled, "Mom always went on about how we were womb buddies."

"It was just like you to pop out two days early because you wanted to see the world."

"And you were born twelve minutes later screaming because I beat you."

And like that, the clock rolled back to those adolescent years when they played together all the time, squabbled over the smallest things, and defended each other when needed.

His gaze softened. "We have some catching up to do. Shall we go have breakfast?"

"Fine. But I'm buying my meal. I wouldn't want you to think this is a date."

"What happened to the idea that a gentleman pays for the meal?"

"That idea got tossed out at the same time bras and girdles were burned."

He chuckled, and his eyes met hers. "I'm old-fashioned, but I'll admit, I liked when they invented the string bikini."

"You would," she laughed.

❧

"Good morning, Gloria, Mr. Douglas," Zoey, the owner of Silver Fox Resort, greeted. "Are you two going to dine with us this morning?"

"You betcha. Table for two. And tell that gorgeous husband of yours we will have two of his specials. Check that." She glanced at Walter. "Got any allergies?"

"Nope."

"Do you trust me?"

"I always have," he winked.

She held up two fingers. "Make that a double, two coffees, and a mini-mimosa to celebrate old friends. Oh, and keep the coffee coming."

Zoey took a step back. "You two know each other?"

"Our mothers were best friends, and we were born a few minutes apart." Gloria leaned in and whispered, "He was the one who got away."

"Ohhh. Then today *is* a special day." Zoey glanced between them and smiled. "Pick any seat, and I'll go give Nate your order."

Gloria looked around the 24-table dining area. The intimate lighting, soft cream and butternut squash colors, and modern light fixtures set a cozy mood, and she chose a two-topper by the windows looking out over the water. The sun made the water shimmer, and the visual matched the way she felt inside.

Walter held her chair out for her and waited until she settled to push it in for her. Lordy, lordy, but she loved a man who had manners.

She set her napkin aside. "So, what brought you back to California?" she asked Walter as Zoey set cream and sugar on the table and poured two cups of coffee.

Walt waited until Zoey moved away before returning his gaze to her. "The simple answer is I came to find a purpose." He shrugged. "My Anne died two years ago after a long battle with cancer, and she was the core of the family, while I enjoyed being the backbone, working quietly behind the scenes. The problem is, none of the kids think I'm able to take care of myself. If I receive one more phone call asking me how I'm feeling or if I've had enough to eat, I swear I'm going to block calls. I'm perfectly capable of heating a can of soup."

"Thank goodness for the invention of microwaves." She took a sip of her coffee and closed her eyes to enjoy the bitter, nutty taste.

"I especially like delivered food box kits. They are easy to prepare and come in single-serving sizes." He smoothed the white tablecloth. "Last month, after the anniversary of Anne's passing, I decided a change of scene and a new focus might do me some good."

"I am sorry about Anne. I heard she was a lovely woman. And, before you ask, yes, I kept up-to-date on your whereabouts." Gloria stirred cream and sugar into her coffee. "Renovating your family's summer home is quite a project. After John died, I did the same. I was tired of living in San Francisco, plus my two girls had settled across country, one in Chicago, and one in New York, and I was not about to move east. My sister wanted nothing to do with our old summer home, so I bought her out and spent the next three years upgrading the kitchen, baths, landscaping...you name it, it got upgraded," she chuckled, but inside she cringed, remembering how much those renovations cost. "If you need the name of a contractor, just ask. I have business cards for most of the contract workers in town.”

“Good to know.” He sat back. “I loved spending the summers here. Those days were the best. Surfing, listening to music, bonfires on the beach. There are so many splendid memories.”

“I don’t know how our moms kept track of us five kids. I can remember some of the shenanigans we got up to, and I swear we were never still.

“It relieved them to have a break when our dads came up on the weekends. Remember how we started a savings fund, a nickel for every time one of our moms said, ‘Wait until your dad gets here’?”

“I wonder whatever happened to that jar?” Gloria chuckled, then took another sip of coffee. “Come to think of it, my sister had a crush on you. That’s most likely why she never told me about your call.”

“Sarah, wow. I never knew.”

“No, you wouldn’t have. You were too busy learning to surf or working out for football. It’s like you always looked toward the future, never around you to see what was going on at the moment.”

Zoey deliver the mimosas and paused before leaving. “Gloria, before I forget, I heard Mrs. Landry might be available to take that cruise with you.”

“That’s kind you thought of me, Zoey.” Gloria forced a smile. “Someone just this week suggested Mrs. Landry, but I checked and she doesn’t want to be away from her grandchildren that long.”

Zoey shrugged. “It was an idea.”

“Thanks, Zoey, and please keep them coming.”

Gloria unrolled her silverware and placed her napkin in her lap as Zoey walked away.

“What was that all about?” Walter set his water glass aside and leaned in.

She studied his face and liked the keen interest. Having a man tag along meant she would have an on-board dance partner. She dearly loved to wiggle.

“A friend of mine can’t go on a cruise and land tour we had planned. Wanna come along?” she joked.

“When is it?”

“I’m supposed to leave in two weeks. It’s a twelve-day Australia and

New Zealand cruise with a post fourteen-day land tour going to Kangaroo Island, the Barossa Valley, and the Great Barrier Reef. The problem is, I can't find anyone who wants to travel that far or be gone that long."

"I'll go," he said, as if being gone a month was no big deal.

"You'll go? Really?" She sat up straighter. "Jean, my friend, said she'll sell her tickets cheap."

"I'll pay cost. I don't want anyone to be out money."

"Jean will be relieved." And so would she.

The details of the cruise and land tour spilled out over breakfast. He told her about his prior travels to Australia and New Zealand, provided insider tips, and made the museums and city streets come alive through his vivid descriptions.

The way he talked with his hands and his facial expressions when he mentioned his newest great-grandchild made her remember why she fell for him all those years ago. He described his life with his wife and kids and left her with the impression he was proud of his family. Their mutual conversation continued to ebb and flow, and by the time she checked her watch, hours had passed.

She took the last sip of her refreshed coffee. "You are a talented storyteller."

"I am?" He looked surprised.

"You are. I was thinking—"

He held up a finger to pause her and tugged his ringing phone out of his shorts pocket, his cheerful, easygoing expression erased like a blackboard at the end of the school day.

"Is something wrong?" she asked.

"It's my oldest son, Brad. He's trying to Facetime me." He held up the phone.

"So, answer. It would be fun to meet him."

His expression darkened.

Then she got it. *Anne.* His children's mother. They wouldn't approve of a new woman in his life. All his comments about his kids added up. He didn't know how to set healthy boundaries, which meant he could never live the life he wanted, or the life she wanted for him.

She dipped her head, closed her eyes, took a deep breath, and then set her cloth napkin on the table. "Take your call." She slid her chair back and patted his wrist "It's been nice seeing you, Walter. If you need any help with your renovations, let me know. Breakfast is on me. It's been good catching up." She didn't wait for a response, only headed for the door.

At her age, she didn't need the drama.

Her life was marching onward toward the finish line, and she didn't want to waste one minute.

THE NEXT MORNING, Walter stopped by the resort's gift boutique, the local bakery, and then headed toward Sea Glass Cove. The Douglas and Stein families built identical summer homes side by side on a bluff overlooking the ocean. The homes were exactly the same, only his dad added another bedroom after his youngest sister was born. In between the three-bedroom cottages, a sandy path led down to the beach. Gloria had replaced the cedar shingle roof and paved her driveway. Neither house looked like much on the outside, but the scenery was what made a person sigh at the splendor. The one-hundred-and-eighty degree view couldn't be beat.

He reached for the bundle of sunflowers and a tray of coffees and pushed the car door open with his shoulder. His heart picked up tempo as he reached Gloria's front steps. Nervous energy pushed its beat up to the point where he was out of breath. He clutched the bouquet and stood like an idiot looking at the buzzer, not sure whether to push it.

"This was a bad idea," he grumbled as the front door swung open.

"I figured I'd better come rescue you so you won't stand out here all day, or worse, leave." Her eyes filled with laughter.

She found his discomfort funny.

He'd been an ass, and she was conveying he deserved it.

"I am sorry for the way I acted yesterday. I made you uncomfortable, and I was insensitive." He handed her the flowers and raised the gray carton with two coffees and a brown danish bag stuffed between two white paper cups. "French roast, soy milk, extra hot cream, and two sweeteners."

"You remembered." She stepped back and let him in.

He liked the way her smile enhanced her lovely, red-painted lips.

"I remember a lot more than the coffee you like. Remember that yellow swimsuit you wore the summer of our junior year or those short-shorts you had on for our Disneyland trip? Yowsa!"

"You mean the cut-off jeans shorts my mother insisted I exchange for a more decent pair? My parents grounded me for three weeks for destroying a good pair of jeans."

He walked into a kitchen graced with rich cherrywood cabinets, granite countertops, and hardwood floors. Brightly colored pots overflowing with flowers and plants were scattered around the room, making the space feel alive.

He chuckled over the kitchen towel that read, "Takeout is the only dish I serve." The sentiment was so Gloria. And more his style. Anne had always insisted on family meals, and that meant the more the merrier. Since his wife passed, the house had become far too quiet.

"You always did like coffee." He handed her the paper cup and the bag. "If I remember correctly, you like warm pumpkin bread too."

He laughed when she grabbed the bag, shoved her nose inside, and took a deep whiff. The bliss on her face made joy seep into his heart, an easy feat whenever he was around her.

"This smells so yummy." She gave him another smile, the kind that made her eyes blossom like a flower on a spring day. "You might remember what I like to eat, but you seem to have missed a few important things, like my feelings about you."

"It might have helped if you'd ever explained how you felt." He lowered into a stool at the island while she grabbed a vase out of one of the many cupboards lining the walls. "I had feelings for you, too. I just didn't know what to do about them. When I'm not sure what course to take, I usually don't take any action until I have something solid to go on."

"You make relationships sound like a computer program." She shuddered and turned on the water to test the temperature before filling the glass container. "Music, magazines, sports were easy distractions. I had to work hard to get your attention. I even tried out for cheerleading."

"I always wondered why you became a cheerleader." He eased back into the chair. "You looked mighty fine in your uniform."

"Not fine enough to get you to stay in California and go to college here."

"Southern Cal might have been a better choice. I hated Texas when I first arrived. The heat. No ocean. Weird food. But then once football season started, things settled in. Which reminds me…" He waited to get her attention. "Before I forget, who do I pay for the cruise?"

"You still want to go?" Her open expression shuttered. "What would your kids think?"

Oh, boy. The look on her face reminded him of Keegan, his old lab, the one who'd stand in the kitchen staring at him until the dog guilted him into giving him a treat. He crossed and uncrossed his arms, unsure what to say.

Her chest rose slowly with a deep inhale, and then she let it out slowly. "You haven't told them."

"Not yet, but I plan to."

Gloria set the vase on the counter, settling a hard gaze on his face. "Do you think it's wise to put it off?"

"I'll tell them. I will. I just need to figure out what to say first."

"Let me ask you a question." Gloria leaned back against the counter with a frown. "What happened to all the dreams you had as a kid? You wanted to ski in Japan, surf in Australia, check out the Northern Lights. When have you ever gotten to do those things?

He opened his mouth and then closed it again. He'd never been able to visit for the summers. There wasn't enough room at the house to fit all the kids and grandkids, and Anne would never think of leaving out anyone. Besides, the grandkids were young and travel difficult. The kids had stuff going on. Anne had three or more volunteer meetings per week. Something always came up. The harsh truth made him look away.

"Thought so." She reached for her coffee and took a long swig from the paper cup. "Our kids pulled the same stunt on me and John. As soon as we planned a vacation, just the two of us, one girl would call with an emergency. We'd drop everything and rush to the airport only to find when we landed that the dilemma had been resolved. After the third time, we started setting boundaries."

She wanted him to go with her on this trip, and rightly so. He understood the loneliness after losing a spouse. Nothing felt the same.

He wanted so badly to go, but he'd never been good at saying no to his children. More accurately, Anne had never said no. Not to the kids, grandkids, or the neighbors. Gloria had a point. Seventy was around the corner, and he'd yet to do what he wanted. Renovating the summer home was an excellent step in the right direction, but he wanted to go a lot further.

"Did saying no work?" he asked.

Gloria chuckled. "Not at first. The girls threw a hissy fit, and my oldest didn't talk to me for three months."

"But they came around." He made the assumption because of how many pictures of Gloria and her happy family were plastered to her refrigerator door.

"They both did eventually. Family is hard." Her voice softened as if she was taking a trip back down a path leading to some unhappier times.

"Yes, it is." He picked up the coffee cup to savor the warm robust flavors and to study the woman on the other side of the counter. She'd always been the smart one, and years ahead of her time. She liked certain bands before they were a thing, and her style of dressing was always her own. The picture of her on the back of a camel suggested she hadn't changed. She wore confidence like a sexy designer dress.

"So, who do I make that check out to?"

Gloria sighed, as if she didn't believe he'd actually go through with it. "Your kids are going to come up with some reason you shouldn't be going on the cruise. You know that, right?"

"Yeah, you're probably right. For all of my married life, I've put my wife and children first. This cruise is important to me. It will be the first time in years that I've done something for myself. It's time I find my footing and stand my ground."

"You say that now, but it's harder when faced with the choice."

He tapped his fingers on the granite counter. "I think I'll manage. I've been in business a long time. I've learned to say no."

"But saying no to a client and saying no to your kid is different."

"I'm going on that cruise with you. Nothing is going to stop me."

"Fair enough." She slipped a pad and pen out of the drawer and provided Jean's information. "Here you go."

"Great." He tucked the information in his pocket, patted it for good measure, and let the satisfaction fill him. "Now, how about we go build sand castles on the beach?"

Gloria's jaw dropped. "You want to build sand castles? Today?"

"Why not? The sun is shining, the tide is low, I had Nate pack us a lunch. What do you say?"

"I say yes! It sounds like a glorious way to spend an afternoon." Gloria scooted around the end of the kitchen island. "Let me go change my shoes. I'll be right back."

A smile stretched across his face, and an easiness that he hadn't felt in years lingered. He didn't get to play much. Anne never liked the kids getting dirty. So camping, hiking, sailing, all the things he loved were off the list. Over the years, he learned instead to play golf and fit in at the country clubs.

He couldn't wait to free his inner child again. With Gloria, he knew he could just be. She'd never required him to be anything other than himself. Possibly that is why he hadn't fully appreciated her all those years ago.

A big mistake on his part.

He wanted to get to know Gloria again.

He'd told Brad, his son, he wouldn't be returning for his grandson's baseball game because he had to stay and work with the contractors, but Gloria was the real reason he wanted to stay. Brad was angry, but Walter was going to stick to the plan. He was going to pay for the cruise and get on that boat.

Fingers crossed.

THE SUN'S rays passed through Gloria's stained-glass window, casting colored patterns on her kitchen floor. The reds and purples fit her feisty mood as she shuffled her dancing feet to Queen, squirted disinfectant on the counter, and scrubbed away the invisible germs with her microfiber cloth. Four more days and she'd be cruising with a wonderful man. No housecleaning or laundry. A new daring adventure each day. Excitement spiraled up her arms and over her shoulders.

"Dear me, look at the time." She stowed the cleaner and downed the dregs of her first cup of coffee.

Today she and Walter were going to bicycle over to the farmers' market and then have lunch down at the cove. A few days ago they lounged on the beach taking turns reading to each other. A few days before that, they indulged in a movie day, complete with popcorn and snuggles on the couch. Each day had been romantic and perfect, with a promised whisper of what was to come.

A knock at the door sent her scurrying across the room. She opened the door with excitement dancing through her.

"Good morning," Walter said, handing her a new bunch of sunflowers and a carrier with a single cup of coffee and a sole pastry bag.

Her heart knew before her brain that something was off. "You're not dressed for riding."

"No," he said. The word was so simple, yet contained so much weight. "I need to return to Texas for a few days. May I come in?"

She didn't want to let him in. Slamming the door would have been easier, but when had she done easy? She opened the door and let him in, then followed him back to the kitchen.

"You're not going on the cruise, are you?" She stated her fear, putting the question out there, hoping she was wrong.

He reached for her hand. "I am going on the cruise."

"But..."

"No buts. I'm going to be there. It's just that my grandson got in a fight at school and is in the hospital."

Guilt made her push her selfish demands aside. "What are you standing here for? Go."

He tugged a key from his key chain. "Would you mind going over all the details with our house sitter? She's going to be there tomorrow, and I can't get in touch with her today. The renovation crew has all my info, and there's a lockbox on the house."

"Of course. When does your flight leave?"

"I need to leave now if I'm going to make it on time."

She pulled her hand away. "You should go. Let me know how your grandson is doing."

He reached out again, but she didn't want to be touched. History was repeating. He was going to leave her again. He had already promised once to stay in touch, come back home over the summer, but the promises weren't kept and life moved on.

"Speedy, look at me."

Her heart ached. She hadn't heard the nickname in years. Her eyes stung, and tears were threatening to spill over. She didn't want to look at him, but she did anyway.

"I will make sure the house sitter gets your key," Gloria said, choking off the pain.

"I'm not worried about the house; I'm worried about you. I *will* be on that cruise. I've already looked at flights. Once I land in Dallas, I'll change my flight to Sydney, and I *will* meet you at the ship."

"You need to take care of your family."

"And I will. But I will also be on that ship. You need to trust me."

That was the kicker right there. She had trusted him, right up until he shattered her eighteen-year-old heart into little pieces, and she vowed never again. Even with John, she'd held back a piece of herself, never falling in love unconditionally.

"You are a good man, Walter, and you will do what's right for your family. You always have. You played football because your dad wanted you to. You went to Methodist college because your mom wanted you to. You're getting on that plane because your son wants you to.

"I wonder when you'll get to live the life you want to live. Remember, our clock is ticking, and there isn't much time left." She opened the utility drawer to get a spare keychain and place his key on the hook. "I'm too old to not speak my mind. So please forgive me if I've overstepped." She set the key down so her shaking hands wouldn't drop it.

"I like never having to guess what you're thinking." He tucked a strand of hair behind her ear. "I'll see you in four days." He kissed her on the forehead like it was no big deal. He had never kissed her before, so this was their first sort-of kiss, and she was disappointed.

He was halfway to the door when he stopped and turned. "No, that won't do." He walked back to her and cupped her face. "I'm going to kiss you. I've wanted to do it for days, but I don't want to leave without you knowing how I feel."

He lowered his head and paused. His mouth hovered over her lips, asking her permission.

She could have turned her head or said no. She *should* have said no, but after so long, she wanted that intimate connection. Even if it was their first and last kiss, she wanted to store the memory in her mental keepsake box.

She lifted onto her toes and pressed her lips to his. She expected a brief peck, but when he slid a warm hand around the nape of her neck and deepened the kiss, she rose a little higher to match his need. The kiss was more than exceptional. It held a promise. He was telling her he'd be on that cruise.

She hoped this time he would keep his word.

Gloria rolled her travel case into the ship's cabin and then sank down on the twin mattress. The room was eight hundred square feet with a balcony, but the space felt more like a closet with the walls closing in.

The sixteen-hour flight, customs, embarking queues, paperwork, all the many steps had worn her to the bone. The worst part was she had to do it all alone.

Walter tried to match her flight, flying from Dallas to San Francisco and then on to Sydney, but the only last-minute flight he could get was through Los Angeles. He was supposed to meet her at the Sydney airport, but the arrival monitor indicated his flight had been delayed. The shuttle driver had other passengers and suggested she meet her other party at the terminal. She stalled boarding until the last minute, hoping to catch Walter at check-in, but no luck. There were so many people that she could have easily missed him. Hoping he was on board, she checked in.

The roar of the boat's horn signaled their departure, and she quickly put a safety harness around her heart. Walter not making the trip was going to hurt. A lot.

She should find the hostess and explain she'd changed her mind about taking the cruise. It wouldn't be much fun without someone to share the adventure. Maybe she could find a boutique hotel and go shopping. The challenge was getting her muscles to cooperate.

In the middle of coming up with a contingency plan, the door opened.

Her hand flew to her chest and tears of exhaustion trickled down her cheeks. "You're here."

"Sorry I'm late. I was talking to the captain." Walter pushed a roll-on through the door. "Where are the flowers, strawberries, and champagne I ordered?"

He looked around the space, then noticed the tears. "Whoa, are you okay? Did something happen?"

"You're here," she whispered, not sure her voice would hold.

He dropped the papers and key in his hand on the dresser and then sat beside her, draping an arm around her shoulder and squeezing. "I told you I would come."

"Yes, but when I couldn't find you at the airport or terminal, I thought..."

"You thought because I abandoned you all these years ago, I would do it again."

She rubbed at a ketchup stain on her khaki travel pants. "You not showing crossed my mind a time or two."

He nudged her shoulder, then sat patiently while he waited for her to tell the truth.

"Okay, I didn't think you would come. Jean said I should trust you, and I did. I got on the plane, but when I couldn't find you anywhere, I thought the worst."

"Thought so. I took an earlier flight to make sure I would get here on time. But I shouldn't have gone to see the captain. I should have waited here to meet you."

"What was so important you had to see the captain first?"

He pushed up from the bed and grabbed a piece of paper, placed it in her hand, before again settling beside her.

"What's this?" She glanced over the list of registry offices in Australia and New Zealand, but her mind couldn't triangulate the information.

"Turns out the ship's captain does not have the authority to marry people on board," he fought to keep the agitation silent, but failed. "However, if we want to get married in New Zealand or when we get back to Sydney, we just need to coordinate everything through the shore excursion desk."

"Wait." She placed a hand on his knee. Her heart ripped off its security blanket. "Did you say married?"

His face softened. "Yeah, I did. After I landed in Dallas, I realized I had let my kids again manipulate my life. My grandson was fine. A broken nose and a few cracked ribs. He got in a tangle protecting one of his classmates from a bully. While it was serious, I didn't need to be there, and it led to a serious conversation with my kids. The truth came out that the real reason my kids dragged me home was to question me about the cruise and you. I was furious. I didn't want to say anything until we were together, and I could explain."

"Oh," she encouraged him to continue, unable to anticipate what was to come next.

"You had a point when you reminded me I've never done the things I wanted to do in life." He held out a hand to stop her from saying anything. "Don't get me wrong. I adored my wife and love my kids and grandkids. I don't have regrets, but I've worked hard to provide for my family. If now isn't my time, I don't know when that will be."

A new round of hope trickled in. "So, what's on your bucket list?"

"Besides having the time of my life on this cruise, marrying you, and moving to California—not much. You like spontaneity. I was thinking we should see where life takes us. I've always wanted to go to Thailand."

"I'd like to go to Germany—oh! And Iceland." She grabbed a pad and pen. "Should we make a list?"

"Nope. No list." He got up, unzipped the top of his roller bag, and pulled out a small box. "Not until you answer one question."

He settled on the bed beside her. "Speedy, my womb buddy, the one person who laughed at me when all my front teeth were missing, who helped me with my English assignments when I couldn't figure out how to put words on the page, and who kicked my butt every time at cards, will you agree to become my wife for as long as we both shall live?"

"If I say yes, will you promise never to tell me to turn the music down, or tell me I'm too old to skinny dip, or tell me that two blue cheese martinis are too many on a day when three martinis aren't enough?"

He drew a cross on his chest. "I promise never to put you in a box with a label."

Her breath hitched. The sting of tears turned joyous. "You remembered. That day on the beach, you remember what I had said."

When he opened the box, she gasped. "I remember a lot of things about us."

The blue sapphire-and-diamond band tucked into a white silk cushion was perfect. He knew she'd never want fancy, even if she could afford designer labels. She'd rather have a ring she could wear lifting weights or splashing around at the beach.

"I would like to get married," she said, not sure whether to trust her heart, "but I would rather wait until I've met your kids and grandkids. I think it's important to get their support. And I'd like you to meet my girls. Besides, a piece of paper isn't going to change the way I feel about you. I want to be with you. We're going to have such a great time together."

His eyes filled with a warmth that provided a forever promise. "You can take as long as you want. We don't even have to get married. I've been married and raised my family. Now I want to be with you—today, tomorrow, and always. I don't want to waste any more time."

"I don't either. You're a special man and I feel luck about our chance meeting. So what do you say? Ready to go find some champagne and celebrate?"

"You betcha, Speedy."

And just like that, her energy returned, and she was ready to be off again.

Funny how life can take a turn when you least expect it.

ABOUT THE AUTHOR

Lyz Kelley is a total disaster in the kitchen, a tea snob, plant lover, and an all-around creative who lives in Arizona with her husband and four-legged fur babies. She's also an award-winning author who loves to tell stories about amazing women who have faced extraordinary challenges and then pair them with men who have an enormous capacity to love, even if they may not know it. Exploring these wounded and strong characters—discovering what drives them, frightens them, heals them, makes them laugh—takes Lyz on an incredible and sometimes unexpected journey.

If you enjoyed reading Lyz's over forty short romance story find more sweet books in her Silver Fox Resort series click here https://geni.us/SilverFoxSeries and enjoy falling in love all over again.

THE WRITE TIME FOR LOVE

CALLIE TIMMINS

Her exclusive might just be his comeback.

1
___

GABBY

$\mathcal{B}$anoffee pie. Two words I won't easily forget. It doesn't help that I'm gullible, possess a penchant for useless information, and have an innate desire to have the last word. Traits that my brother, Liam, and cousin, Derek, are keen to exploit any chance they can. Which they – much to my detriment, and their amusement – have been doing since we were old enough to ride bicycles to the creek on our own when they convinced me that fireflies were sand fairies that lived in the creek bed.

Mom says I should've been a lawyer. I chose to be a journalist, which suits two of those traits perfectly. Gullibility – not so much.

The desire to make my life miserable is something my brother and cousin haven't grown out of, and at twenty-six, I'm not much better. You'd think I'd be able to ignore their taunts that banoffee pie was something I made up to win the round of Scattegories. Banana split was the obvious choice for a dessert, starting with B. But being a wordsmith, I knew better. Ha!

You'd also think I'd graciously prove to them, using technology that's been around for decades, what a banoffee pie was. But no, I had to go all out by making one. At ten o'clock on a Sunday night. I didn't take into consideration the half-hour I would need trying to find bananas from a store that was open that late. Nor the fact that I would

575

burn the dulce de leche before I achieved the right consistency. By the time I finally took the pie to their place at ridiculous o'clock, they informed me they knew what one was all along.

But thanks for the pie, Gullible Gabby Glasman. Ugh.

And that is why said pie will be stuck with me forever. Because I'm now driving to the middle of nowhere to do a feature article for *The Monument Hills Times*. An article on the small town of Castella Creek. And it just so happens that there's a ten-year reunion for the champion high school football team on at the same time. They won a ton of awards, or competitions – or whatever it is footballers win – back in the day. And my boss wants me to feature the reunion as an aside.

"It will be a great interest article, Gabby. Two birds with one stone," Jefferson Linscott, the editor of *The Monument*, informed me when I slipped into the staff meeting on Monday morning. I wanted to throw a stone at *him* for nominating me for the assignment. Ten minutes late, thanks to sleeping through my alarm, thanks to late-night banoffee pie making, I'd hoped to sneak in unnoticed and catch up on the latest news from my colleague, Alice Mulford. But eagle-eye Jeff, with a penchant for spotting the tiniest of errors in an article, was also very good at noticing tardiness among his staff.

I'd missed the more appealing assignments, and out of the two reporters remaining, Jefferson assigned me the road trip to Castella Creek purely because I was single and had no other family commitments.

And here I am. On my way to goodness knows where to write an article about a town no one's heard of, and a football team that will undoubtedly comprise of washed-up has-beens trying to relive their glory days.

2

***

GABBY

"Nice place." I couldn't keep the surprise from my voice as I stepped up to the counter of Main Street Diner to peruse the menu. My stomach growled in appreciation at the blend of aromas wafting from the kitchen. I don't think my jaw had left my chest from the moment I entered the outer limits of Castella Creek, nestled in the shadow of the Blue Ridge Mountains, just over three hours northwest of Monument Hills.

Castella Creek, population of about six thousand, was cute and quaint in every way imaginable, and screamed, '*Welcome Home*' from the moment I drove into town in my silver Prius. Which was a silly notion, given that home was Monument Hills. Always had been. Always would be.

Colorful banners swayed from every lamppost, heralding the ten-year reunion game of the champion football team. Tubs of colorful flowers lined the sidewalks. And blue and white bunting filled almost every shop front. I almost expected a marching band to appear, complete with baton twirlers and marching girls.

"You here for the reunion?" A curvy middle-aged woman with gray curls and kind silver eyes slid my order onto the table in front of me. *Patty* was embroidered in white on her black collared shirt.

"Er ... kind of." Habitually, I patted my neck, making sure I wasn't

577

wearing the lanyard containing my credentials. When people discovered I was a journalist, they did one of two things - turned ice cold and clammed up as though I was their worst enemy, or they suddenly wanted to be my best friend, eager to share – or learn – any tidbits of gossip.

"Well, I hope you enjoy your stay. Everyone's lookin' forward to the big game. To see if the boys still have it after all these years."

I nodded politely, as if I completely understood what was going on. As if I *cared* about what was going on. My area of expertise was lifestyle, not sport. Our regular sports reporter, Dave Farrington was on stress leave, and my brief from Jefferson was that the has-been Crushers (my nickname for them), were playing their rivals, the Savages, in a reunion match before the current high school team took the field. He had given me a pass for the game and reiterated more than once that I needed to have an exclusive with Cash Amberry, the star quarterback.

My research into the team revealed that the star quarterback played pro after college, but retired in a cloud of controversy several years ago. Since his retirement, there were very few articles, and it seemed he had disappeared off the grid. Although frustrated by the lack of information, I spent some time drooling over images of Cash in his glory days. With sandy-brown hair that fell over sky-blue eyes, I was captivated by his chiseled jaw and cheekbones that would rival Michaelangelo's handiwork. Researching a football game suddenly became a lot more appealing.

Seated at a table by the front window with a bowl of minestrone, a plate of salad, and half a grilled turkey sandwich, I jotted down some notes.

Community spirit was tangible, and anticipation for the upcoming game buzzed like electricity through the air. Most people in the diner were wearing various shades of blue, in support of their hometown heroes, while I stood out like a sore thumb in my red sweater and jeans.

An hour later, with a full stomach, and my notes tucked away, I gathered my belongings and stood. Before I knew what was happening, my chair slammed into the back of my knees, and I flew forward, sprawling across the table covered in my lunch dishes.

"Oof!" My hand darted out, sending cutlery clattering to the floor and upending my glass of water. Inhaling sharply as iced water seeped through my sweater, I slowly pushed up, glancing down at the remnants of soup, lettuce, and breadcrumbs clinging to my chest. Heat fanned my face as all eyes in the diner turned toward the commotion. As if I didn't stand out before, I certainly did now.

"Are you okay?" A deep voice rumbled from somewhere to my left.

"Yes, I'm fine." Annoyed, but fine. *Maybe look behind you next time, mister.*

Busy brushing food scraps off my sweater and straightening the dishes on the table, I didn't take any notice of the stranger until impossibly enormous hands, that looked like they should be wielding an ax somewhere in the mountains, pushed mine aside and straightened the glass, grabbed some napkins and began dabbing at the mess.

"I'm so sorry."

My gaze followed tree trunk forearms, skimmed over the broadest chest I'd ever seen before reaching a chiseled jaw covered in a dark brown beard that had my fingers itching to see how soft it was. Light brown curls poked out from underneath a blue cap.

"Th ... thank you," I stammered, forgetting food scraps adorned my sweater. My gaze slammed into blue eyes, framed by black rimmed glasses, that reminded me of the Caribbean sea, or a cloudless summer sky.

"No problem." His lips curved upward in a half-smile as Patty bustled over.

"I've got this, Alex," she said, shooing both of us away. "Off you go."

"You here for the reunion?"

"Gosh, no!" Laughing, I shook my head as the mountain man held the door for me. "I don't understand the first thing about football. Can't you tell?" I gestured over my stained sweater and then to the sea of blue and white blanketing the main street.

"Well, you're wearing red, so I assumed you were supporting the opposition. Which would be a pretty brave move. I'm Alex, by the way."

"I'm Gabby. As I said, football's not my thing. What about you?" I asked. "Kind of hard to tell with your neutral gray sweater there. Are you visiting for the game?"

"I live here."

"So, this must be pretty annoying, huh? Such a sweet town being invaded so people can watch a bunch of grown men reliving their glory days.”

Laughter rumbled in his chest sending a flurry of goosebumps over my skin. At that moment, Patty called out, halting us on the sidewalk outside *La Chocolat Shoppe* where a mouth-watering display of hand-made chocolates filled the window. I made a mental note to purchase some before leaving town. Patty shuffled toward us, handing me a white box with *Main Street Diner* embellished on the lid.

“A welcome to town gift.” Smiling, she patted me on the hand before bustling back to the diner.

I glanced at the box, then up at Alex. “Does this happen in all small towns? Or is this a once off?” Because hospitable was going to go right at the top of my article on Castella Creek. Along with mention of gorgeous men with oceanic blue eyes and sandy-brown hair that made my knees weak.

“Patty likes to make people feel welcome.” Alex glanced at his watch. “Well, it’s been nice to meet you, Gabby. I apologize for messing up your sweater.”

I waved his comment away. “Gives me a reason to change into some-thing inconspicuous and avoid the masses.”

He grinned, ducked his head, and walked away. Only when his broad shoulders disappeared into a shop further down the street did I remember to breathe. And see what was inside the box. Opening the lid, I peered inside to where a delicious-looking slice of banoffee pie lay on a paper napkin.

You’ve got to be kidding me.

3

ALEX

I'd been dreading the reunion and the influx of tourists descending on the town. Mayor Brimble's idea to increase tourism hadn't sat well with me when he announced a reunion game between the Crushers and the Savages. The boys at school were keen for the rival game. As were most of the residents in town. Me? Not so much.

"Good publicity," Mayor Brimble said when he fronted up to my office back in April. "And a wonderful opportunity to bring in some tourism."

I'd hung up my professional gear three years ago and returned home hoping for a life of obscurity, teaching high school maths, and being an assistant coach to the football team. Mayor's unspoken words about positive publicity lingered between us, silently urging me that it was an opportunity to put to rest all the rumors that had surrounded my early retirement.

The media had followed my every move since my full college scholarship. The highs and lows. The relationships and break-ups. But I didn't care for the circus. The constant hounding from the press had been part of what had driven me away from the game. Along with the endless gossip and expectations that allowed no room for mistakes. Ultimately, it was my mother's illness and subsequent passing that made me return home for good. Since being home, I'd set down some good roots and didn't want my peace disturbed for some stupid reunion.

From my front porch, I watched the endless procession of news vans and media trucks wind through the valley and into town. Anxiety coiled in my gut like a loaded spring. Soon, the reporters would descend on the town looking for a scoop to twist the truth.

My fridge was stocked and I had enough food to keep me out of the grocery store until the reunion game was over. I wanted to avoid going into town if I could. Avoid the press. I knew some of my old teammates would be in their element. A couple of them still played pro and lapped up every media opportunity they could, while I tried to avoid it at all costs. I'd been burned before when my ex sold lies about our relation-ship to the media, and I was wary about anyone representing a news outlet.

As I turned in for the night, I couldn't help but think of the gorgeous brunette from the diner. *Gabby.* With emerald eyes that sparked with delight, and a cute dimple in her right cheek, her complete disinterest in the game I once played made me wonder why she was in town if not for the reunion.

I'd been thinking about her for the past few days. Thankfully she hadn't recognized me. It would have to be one of the few occasions when a tourist didn't do a double-take and harass me for my autograph. And for that, I was thankful. I'd already embarrassed her enough when I sent her sprawling across the table, so to have her recognize me as *Cash the Crusher* would have been mortifying. For both of us. I'd ditched that nickname years ago, and it was refreshing to talk to a stranger without them looking at me with stars in their eyes, or like they only wanted to be with me for my fame.

Gabby's expression when Aunt Patty handed her the box containing the pie was priceless. An interesting mix of embarrassment, curiosity, and disbelief. I wondered what that was about. Even more so, I wondered what Aunt Patty was trying to do. She never handed out boxes of pie to just anyone.

4

GABBY

Imagine a town surrounded by mountains with clear blue skies and lush green grass. Where people are friendly, the food is divine and the scenery is breathtaking. Imagine no further. Such a place exists. Even the men here are dreamy ....

I hit the backspace, deleting my errant thoughts. The cursor blinked on the screen as an incoming message pinged on my phone. Jefferson, asking how my trip was going and if I'd scored an interview with Cash.

Not yet. Still early days. I'd had no luck in trying to track this guy down. Every time I asked where I might find him, people avoided eye contact and shook their heads.

J: *Make sure you get the scoop, okay?*

Yes, boss.

Taking a glass of sweet tea to the outdoor balcony, I sighed. The Blue Ridge mountains created a picturesque background for the undulating green landscape surrounding the town.

Jefferson had put me up at The Lister Hotel so I would be front and center for any interviews. As a feature article writer, I didn't know the ins and outs of interviewing sports stars. But I couldn't go wrong with the basic who, what, when, where, why, and how of Journalism 101.

I decided to write the article on the town first, before giving more time to this mysterious Cash fellow and doing my best to make it sound like I knew what I was talking about for the football reunion.

Leaving my car in the basement parking lot, I set out on foot to explore. First stop, the diner for some coffee.

"Thank you for that delicious piece of pie the other day," I called out to Patty working behind the counter.

"I can't offer you the same today, love, but I have coconut cream pie." Her head popped up above the glass display cabinet. "Did you know coconut became popular when a shipment was sent to a flour miller as payment for debt?"

Chuckling, I shook my head. "Huh. No, I did not know that. I must add that to my repertoire of interesting facts."

After explaining my purpose in town, Patty spent a few moments telling me the best places to go and sights to see. I asked if she knew Cash Amberry and where I could go to meet him.

"Hmm ... Cash was a wonderful boy. To this day, he was the best quarterback this town has seen. We were all so proud of him when he went on to play pro. Really put Castella Creek on the map." She disappeared behind the coffee machine and twiddled some dials. "Coffee's up, love. By the way, the information center is a great resource for all things history about the town."

I thanked her and stepped outside with my coffee in hand and my trusty satchel over my shoulder. A day of sightseeing suited me perfectly. Given that the town was delightful, it wasn't the hardest of assignments I'd been given.

As I headed toward the information center, I realized Patty had given me a ton of information about Cash's playing days but not the answer I wanted.

5
____

ALEX

"Cheers!" My old teammates raised their glasses. We'd taken up four tables in the middle of The Lister Hotel's restaurant. With rock music blasting from the speakers, and raucous laughter and spirited conversation filling the room, it seemed the guys had no trouble slipping back into old habits.

Coach Earnshaw had made the trip down from Nags Head. After a cancer scare made him reprioritize his life, he'd retired from coaching and now spent his days by the water. While it was great to see all the guys again, I was content sitting at the end of the table, nursing my soda water as I observed the goings-on. It was hard to imagine we'd been a champion football team. Instead of the young, buff stags we'd once been, our team now comprised of dad bods, bald patches or saggy jowls concealed by beards.

Only three guys from the high school team had made pro. Myself, Jackson Bontoft and Seth Holfman. Some of the other guys had gone to college, completed their degrees, and were now living the great American dream – wife, kids, and house with the white picket fence - while others worked at management level in construction, running hire companies or some other elite job. Me? I was a high school maths teacher and felt like the under-achiever of the group.

"Not partying tonight, Cash?" A sharp elbow in my ribs drew my attention to the Cheshire cat grin of Justin Sambrook, the team's notorious jokester. He'd pulled many a prank during our high school years, and rumor was he hadn't outgrown his ways.

"Nah. Gave it up a long time ago." I chuckled.

"Too bad. Could be a fun night letting our hair down."

Even if I wanted to, I wouldn't. My home was here now, and I had a reputation to uphold, especially among the kids I mentored at school. Besides, Aunt Patty would have my hide if any unsavory rumors spread around.

Talk was loud and decade-old memories flew around the room, along with rowdy laughter and plenty of back-slapping. Keen for a chance to escape the noise, I slipped away to the bar and ordered another soda. As I eyed the room, a flash of brown hair caught my eye.

Gabby. She sat alone at a nearby table, so I grabbed my glass and strode over.

"Is this seat taken?" *Of all the clichéd lines to use.*

Her eyes widened in surprise, then morphed into something I could only hope was a delight to see me.

"It's all yours," she said, her lips breaking into a gentle smile, and I wondered if they were as soft as they looked.

"Good to see you're not wearing the opposition's colors tonight." I grinned, eyeing her black sweater, accentuated with an emerald green silk scarf that matched the color of her eyes. Her skin was luminous and I wanted to trail my finger over her cheek to see if it was as smooth as it appeared.

A shout from my teammates drew me out of my trance. Clearing my throat, I nodded toward the notepad and pen next to her place setting. I couldn't quite make out the words scrawled on the page.

"Working?"

"Unfortunately, yes. Not that it's a hard gig. This town's great."

Quirking an eyebrow, I waited for her to elaborate.

"I write for *The Monument Hills Times.* My boss sent me to write a feature article on the town."

"You didn't get a choice?"

"Long story. Anyway, it's not so bad. I've seen the winery, spoken to a few locals, and eaten my fill at the local restaurants. Now I just have to write about the football game." With that, she sighed heavily and rolled her eyes.

I rubbed a hand over my face, trying to hide my smirk. "Not a fan?"

"Heck, no! I can't see the point of grown men wearing shoulder pads and knickerbockers and slamming into each other. Where's the attraction in that?" She took a sip of water and I couldn't help the laughter rolling through my chest. Nor the flutter in my stomach when her eyes met mine. They sparkled like jewels in the glow from the pendant lights above the table.

"My boss wants me to interview Cash Amberry. Rumor has it he'll be here for the reunion."

I swallowed hard. She was supposed to interview *me*?

"Want to go for a walk?" With my heart hammering against my chest, I changed the trajectory of the conversation. Previous experience with the media had left me with a bitter taste. Although Gabby seemed different to other journalists, friendlier and more approachable, I wasn't going to risk my teammates exposing me as the reclusive Cash Amberry. "Maybe I can help a little with your article about the town."

As we left the restaurant, I sent a message to Coach letting him know I'd be at training bright and early. I only hoped he wouldn't put us through suicide drills or endless sit-ups. I was fit but none of us were at the same level of fitness we'd once had.

Spinning around on the sidewalk with arms outstretched, Gabby looked like a child on Christmas morning. "This place is just so ..." she sighed, falling into step beside me. "Exquisite."

My heart pounded as I eyed the sheer delight on her face. Entranced by her beauty, I was lost for words. We stopped at the fountain in the town square where the three tiers were lit up in blue and white. I'd seen it a thousand times before, but seeing it through Gabby's eyes stole my breath. *She* stole my breath.

"It's stunning," she gasped.

"Yeah, it is." My voice was a little gruffer than I'd intended. But *she* was stunning, and she affected me in ways no one else had. Perhaps it was the thrill of anticipation. The electrifying atmosphere around town that was sparking something else in me. But then Aunt Patty's words from years before swept through, knocking the wind out of me – '*When you know, you know. And it'll be when you least expect it.*'

I'd had my share of flings during my short career, but I'd never been lured by the celebrity lifestyle, thanks to my mom and Aunt Patty who kept me grounded, encouraging me to enjoy my fleeting minutes of fame but to think about life beyond the bright lights. And they'd been right. Except I'd never met anyone who'd made me dream of a future beyond football. Until now.

"Did you know that three thousand Euros end up in the Trevi Fountain each day?"

"Really? That's crazy." I shook my head.

"And, you're meant to throw a coin with your right hand over your left shoulder. Like this." Gabby fumbled in her purse for a coin and turned to face me. Raising her eyebrows, her tongue darted out as she flipped the coin over her shoulder. A faint plop sounded as it landed in the water and sank to the bottom.

"Did you make a wish?" I teased.

"Only that I wouldn't have to go to the football game. I'd rather spend my afternoon at the winery or exploring more of the town than sitting in a high school stadium watching old men toss a pigskin around."

I coughed to cover my surprise. She *really* detested football. Not wanting to dampen the mood, or bring up Cash, I fumbled in my pocket and produced a quarter. "My turn."

Turning my back, I flipped it over my shoulder before watching it arc in the air and land with a small splash.

"Throwing a coin into the Trevi Fountain means you'll return to Rome." There she went again, spouting off information like she was some kind of living encyclopedia. How she remembered such facts was beyond me. The extent of my knowledge comprised of high school algebra and sport, and given her intense dislike for football, I'd bore her to tears.

"Have you always lived here?" she asked with her gaze fixed on the water spouting into the air.

Woah. What? My instincts went on high alert. Was this some kind of slick journalistic trick? Lead with a fact then straight shoot with a hard question? Or, was she simply being friendly?

"Does that mean you're going to come back here?" I deflected, holding my breath as I anticipated her answer. A man could dream.

Despite her credentials, part of me wanted her to return to Castella Creek after her assignment finished.

Her fingers toyed with the ends of her scarf while her mouth twisted in thought.

"It's a nice place. But home is in Monument Hills."

Of course it was. I don't know why I'd allowed myself to get caught up in silly romantic notions of Gabby turning to me saying, '*Of course I'll come back*.' It had to be the atmosphere that was affecting me and messing with my head. Turning me into a romantic sap.

That's what I told myself when I cupped her elbow and turned her toward me. Her skin was luminous with only the slightest hue of rose coloring her cheeks. Long dark lashes framed her emerald eyes. I saw the moment they darkened before dropping to my lips. My thumb brushed over her cheek as I lowered my head and feathered my lips across hers. They were as soft as I imagined and sent a wave of desire coursing through my veins. Her fingers curled around my arms as she leaned into me, and I threaded my fingers through the soft locks of her hair. She was divine. Closing my eyes, I savored the intoxicating scent of her lemon shampoo, and the hint of cinnamon on her lips, before a catcall and shout of '*Way to go, Cash*', drew me back to reality.

Resting my forehead on hers, I willed my heart to slow. I'd forgotten we were in a public place, and the town would be swarming with journalists. Heck, I'd just been kissing one! What had I been thinking?

6

GABBY

y fingers feathered over my lips as I tried to work on my article. I could still feel the imprint from Alex's kiss two nights ago. Could still smell his delicious sandalwood cologne. Feel his warm breath on my skin.

He'd walked me back to the hotel and kissed me on the cheek, promising to meet up again. And we had. A late breakfast. A picnic lunch by the lake. A twilight walk. And all the while I blabbered about my job and my friends, and spouted useless facts about presidents, black bears, and mating habits of seahorses. I even told him about my late-night banoffee pie making, and how I'd ended up with this assignment.

He'd laughed and said he was glad for the banoffee pie saga, before sharing some of his own tidbits about his work as his fingers entwined with mine. Which was all very distracting when it came time to write, because all I could think about was him.

Jeff had been pestering for a preview of my article. "Time is ticking, Gabby," he'd said the previous evening.

I was well aware of just how fast time was ticking, and how soon I would be leaving Castella Creek and Alex. And all too soon I would need to write about the football game and find the elusive Cash Amberry. My only lead was from the current Crusher's coach who had, like everyone else I'd asked, been vague about Cash's appearance at the reunion game. Who was this guy? Did he even exist?

Carrying my laptop inside, I closed the balcony door and grabbed my purse. It was a gorgeous day. Perhaps some fresh air and small-town exploration would be the inspiration I'd need to make some progress.

With my camera around my neck, I strolled through town, stopping in a park to admire the colorful gardens before finding myself at the cemetery. Graves and tombstones weren't normally my thing, so I don't know what lured me there other than the lush green lawn and bright flower arrangements dotted among the plots. I paused, reading some of the names. Some I'd read about at the tourist information center. I loved history. Which was why I was so profound at remembering interesting facts.

A few other people milled about paying their respects to departed loved ones. A gardener tended to some rose bushes by a pavilion. And then my gaze landed on sandy-brown hair a couple of rows over. Alex. His shoulders were hunched, and his hands tucked into his pockets. The plot was one of the newer ones where the plaque was flush with the grass. I didn't want to disturb his moment of reverence, and so I continued walking. When I glanced over several minutes later, he'd already gone. Curiosity got the better of me, and I soon stood in front of the plot where Alex had been.

Diana Amberry, read the inscription on the marble plaque.

Amberry? As in ... Something tugged on my memory. '*Way to go, Cash.*' Our kiss by the fountain. Cash Amberry? My inquisitive brain kicked into overdrive. Had Cash been in the town center that night? I'd been so caught up in the moment and being lip-locked with a gorgeous man, that I'd taken no notice.

Why didn't Alex say something? And what did he have to do with this gravesite? With more questions than answers, I needed to do some more digging. And although I wasn't a fan of football, I couldn't put off writing the article any longer.

7

———————

ALEX

*P*laying with my old alumni was surprisingly more fun than I expected. We shared plenty of laughs about our fitness, or lack of, and our ailments, and reminisced about the mischief we got up to in our youth. The bleachers were always full during our training sessions with school kids, townsfolk, tourists, and of course, the media all keen to witness the old guys in action.

Pulling off my helmet at the end of our last training session, I swigged down some water.

"Ready to win, men?" Coach Earnshaw barked.

We all grunted in acknowledgment. The Savages would be tough. A few of them had played professionally, but mostly, we were all there to have fun and draw in the crowds just like Mayor Brimble wanted.

"Coach Amberry," a kid from the high school team called out as I untied my cleats.

"Hey, Sam. What's up?"

"You know you could probably still play pro, right? You've got the accuracy and the speed. Dad still calls you Cash the Crusher."

I scoffed at the kid's praise. "Thanks, bud. But I'm getting a little old for it all now."

"Yeah, probably."

I chuckled as he walked away.

"Coach Amberry, is it?"

I stilled at the familiar voice. Raising my head, my gaze slammed into emerald eyes that contained a conflicting mix of surprise and hurt.

"Coach *Cash* Amberry, by any chance?" Gabby stood with her arms folded, one eyebrow quirked and her lips pressed into a firm line.

Guilt squeezed my chest as I lowered my gaze and pulled at the strapping tape on my knee.

"It's Alex Amberry," I murmured.

"Right."

She sat at the end of the row, far enough away to form a canyon between us.

With one leg crossed over the other, she toyed with the blue lanyard around her neck. Her media pass. Of course. She wasn't here as Gabby, the woman I'd been enjoying getting to know. She was here for a scoop. For the gossip. I needed to remember that first and foremost. She was here for work, and I was her assignment.

My skin burned beneath her gaze as I gathered my belongings. "Look, Gabby," I started.

"Are you looking forward to the game?" she interrupted.

"It should be good." Simple answers. I could do this.

"Can the crowd expect to see some of Cash the Crusher's signature moves?"

I shot her a glare. So she knew a little about football? So much for pretending she couldn't stand the game.

"What about future games? Will we see a return of the great Cash?" Hurt laced her voice. "What about Cash the Casanova? Are those stories true?"

Ignoring her questions, I grabbed my bag and strode toward my pickup.

"Cash, wait!"

Tossing my bag in the back, I whirled to face her. "The name's Alex."

"But you're Cash, right?" she queried, stopping near the hood.

"Was." *Cassius Alexander Amberry.* Cash was just a nickname from boyhood when the kids couldn't pronounce my first name.

"Will you be Cash at the game, or Alex? Why the name change?"

With one hand on the door, I huffed out a sigh. I wasn't about to divulge my reasons for the sake of her name on a byline. She'd played me. And she'd played me well. I should've known that someone would try to dig up my past.

"The only game I'm playing is the one on Saturday afternoon. I'm not interested in this game," I gestured between us, "or anything else."

With that, I slammed the door. The tires kicked up gravel as I sped out of the parking lot. Regret lodged in my chest as I dared a glance in the rearview mirror to find Gabby wiping her eyes looking as hurt as I felt. I should've been honest from the start, but I coveted my anonymity and she was a threat to the life I'd created.

8

———

GABBY

"I'll send through the article on Castella Creek soon," I informed Jefferson on Friday. I'd spent the past few days interviewing a few players and Coach Earnshaw, sneaking in a few questions about Cash, and curiously discovering that the media had painted the star quarterback all wrong.

"But I will not be interviewing Cash. I've had no luck." Which was true. He'd been ignoring my calls and messages. Admittedly, I was hurt. Why hadn't he been upfront with me? I had no idea he was *the* Cash Amberry until I saw him at training. Why had he hidden that from me?

My emotions oscillated between feeling hurt that he'd lied by omission, while part of me dreamed of something beyond the sweet moments we'd shared.

"Gabby, Gabby, Gabby." I rolled my eyes at Jeff's condescending tone. I could imagine him lounged in his leather chair, feet up on his desk, squeezing the life out of the stress ball he kept in the top drawer.

"I'll be heading home Sunday. If I get to interview Cash, great. But don't bet on it."

"Your article needs to be on my desk first thing Monday morning."

I gave a silent salute and closed my eyes as Jeff ended the call. My spirits sank knowing Sunday would be my last day in this beautiful town. I'd messed up with Cash. Alex. Whatever his name was. We'd shared some glorious moments during my time here. Moments I'd treasure and remember on nights when I was lonely. But he'd lied, even if by omission, and I wouldn't stand for dishonesty.

I was a fool for thinking what we shared could be anything beyond a holiday fling. Castella Creek was a fantasy that didn't exist in the real world. I'd been lured in by its charming small-town feel – and an extremely gorgeous ex-footballer who did something to my insides whenever he was near.

"Snap out of it, Gabby," I chided. "Focus. What's done is done. You'll be out of here soon enough."

9

ALEX

The harsh afternoon sun streamed across the field. Huddled on the sideline, we talked strategy before chanting the Crusher's anthem. The words came easily, as though it had only been yesterday we'd stood here and not a decade before. A sea of blue and white covered the bleachers, and the aroma of popcorn and hot dogs filled the air. A roar erupted from the crowd as we jogged onto the field and took our positions.

Twisting my torso back and forth, I ran on the spot as per my pre-game ritual. Adrenalin coursed through my veins as the familiar rush of game day came flooding back, and I realized how much I missed it. The chanting crowd. The tension. The rivalry. The lively atmosphere that burrowed into my core lifting my mood.

I scanned the bleachers. Flanked by blue and white, the opposition's support occupied one portion of the stands. I took one last look at the crowd, noticing the media section with cameras aimed on the field. Shimmering chestnut hair caught my eye.

Gabby.

Guilt and longing tugged in my chest at the sight of her sitting away from the other journalists. What would she write about me? Would she be kind? Or would she drag up my past? I didn't have time to think because the whistle blew and the crowd roared as I called the play, grabbed the snap, and threw the ball to our running back. A few moments later we scored the first touchdown and Gabby was soon forgotten as I slipped back into the rhythm of the game.

When the final whistle sounded, I yanked off my helmet and jogged over to my teammates. We'd lost by one point, but the atmosphere – the pounding on the bleachers, the roar of the crowd and the waving of banners, was electric. It didn't matter that we'd lost. We'd provided an afternoon of superb entertainment, and I'd resurrected my love for the game.

After spending some time mingling with the crowd, the high school guys prepared for their game. I eyed the crowd once more, but couldn't find Gabby. She'd come for what she needed and disappeared without a goodbye. She'd played me well, pretending she didn't know the first thing about football, and I'd been stupid enough to fall for her cute, quirky ways. Well, good riddance. I didn't need that betrayal in my life.

Except I couldn't forget her. Even as the boys won their game. Even during the celebrations with my old teammates afterward. I couldn't enjoy anything because I kept thinking about Gabby. The fun conversations. The kisses we'd shared. Foolishly I believed it had all meant something. But she knew how to dig, and I was a sucker for falling for her ways.

❧

I SPENT all night vacillating between feeling hurt and feeling hopeful there had been something between us. Had I imagined our connection? Or was it because I hadn't had a relationship in a long time that I was desperate to fall for the first woman who sparked my interest?

Perhaps it was the residual adrenalin in my system that made me barge into the diner early Sunday morning needing some of Aunt Patty's corn beef hash and eggs with a side of her wisdom.

"I thought you'd be sleeping in after all the celebrations last night." Aunt Patty glanced up as she exited the kitchen carrying a breakfast casserole.

"I didn't stay." Perched on a stool at the counter, I watched her bustle about preparing for the day. The aroma of sausages and eggs wafted from the kitchen as she poured me a coffee.

"Oh?" Her raised eyebrows let me know she had an inclination of my woes.

"I came home to get away from all the hype, but I can't hide anywhere. That woman ..."

"Gabby?"

Cradling my coffee, I nodded. "She took me for a ride. Can't believe I fell for it." *For her.*

Aunt Patty tossed the dishtowel over her shoulder and folded her arms, giving me an incredulous look that bordered on pity.

"What?" I asked as she shook her head and muttered something under her breath that sounded like, '*You're a fool.*' Without another word, she pulled an envelope from her apron pocket and slid it across the counter.

"I'll leave you to it." She returned to the kitchen while I pulled a folded piece of paper from the envelope.

Dear Alex ...

By the time I finished reading the words, a lump the size of Texas was lodged in my throat and my eyes burned with something unfamiliar.

10

―――――

GABBY

Stirring my bowl of noodles, I tugged a leg underneath me and mindlessly watched images flicker across the television screen. My drive home had been harrowing as I wrestled with my seesawing emotions.

Patty had been so sweet and encouraging, patting my cheek as tears pooled in my eyes. I hadn't meant to hurt Alex, but I couldn't get past the fact that he'd lied to me. Because I always believed the best in people, I'd been so gullible to fall for his charming ways.

Moping over my time in Castella Creek, Patty had slid a slice of banoffee pie in front of me before squeezing into the opposite seat in the booth.

"He didn't mean to hurt you," she'd said, as though she knew my inner thoughts. "He just carries a lot of pain from the past, and journalists bring out the worst in him."

"I didn't mean to hurt him," I'd blurted. And I hadn't. I only wanted to know why he'd kept his identity hidden from me. Yes, I may have used a bit of sass to taunt him, and for that, I was regretful.

"I know that. And I think deep down, he does too. He came home to start again, and this reunion has dredged up a lot of memories." The older woman's silver eyes crinkled in the corners as she offered a soft

600

smile. "You're a lovely woman, Gabby. And I know you'll do the right thing."

Her words puzzled me. The right thing? I had a deadline to meet and I needed to return to Monument Hills. I didn't have time to see Alex before I left. More to the point, I was too chicken to do so in case he was furious with me. And while I was usually one to have the last word, I never did it out of spite. Instead, I wrote him a letter of apology, entrusting it to Patty to pass on to him.

The long drive home had given me the inspiration for what I needed to do. And with a sense of satisfaction, I submitted my completed article to Jefferson at one minute past midnight. Although I was saddened things had ended with Alex, I also had some wonderful memories from my time in the town that had captured my heart.

11
―――――

GABBY

"Can I help you?" Alice's voice carried down the hall.

My morning had been busy with meetings and planning new assignments, and I was also thrilled to discover my article on Castella Creek had been nominated for an award. Lost in the world of my email inbox, someone knocked on my door.

"Come ... in."

Alex.

My breath hitched and something tightened in my chest as he took a few steps forward. Clutching a white paper bag in one hand, and a newspaper in the other, he wore a black sweater and jeans. His beard had been trimmed, and his hair was neatly combed. His glasses were gone, giving me a clear view of his ocean eyes which drew me in, as though an invisible thread connected us and tugged on my heart.

"I ..." I cleared my throat. "You can leave, Alice." I nodded to my friend and colleague. Part of me wanted her to stay, but I was also curious why Alex was standing in my office.

"You wrote the article." He placed the newspaper on my desk, tapping the headline, *The Truth About Cash.*

"You read it?"

"Yep."

My cheeks warmed as I trailed my fingers over the black and white image of him I'd captured after the game. His hair was scruffy, and flecks of grass clung to his sweaty skin, but it was his smile and the sheer joy sparkling in his eyes that had captured my attention and burrowed into my heart.

"I hope you didn't mind."

He shrugged. "Aunt Patty put me straight. I can recite the article word for word." The corner of his mouth tipped up into a grin that unfurled a tsunami of butterflies in my stomach.

"I'm sorry," I whispered. I'd wanted to dispel the rumors about addiction and rehab that had plagued him for years. I'd wanted to present the truth – that he had been supporting his mom through her cancer treatment. My article had been tasteful and empathetic, but perhaps I'd overstepped a line.

"No, Gabby. I'm sorry." He stepped around the desk, and my pulse kicked up a notch. "I let you believe I was someone else. I've been burnt before, and I never know if people are interested in me for who I am, or for my fame. It felt good to be known as someone other than Cash, and I loved that you didn't recognize me."

"Yet, I treated you bad when I found out your identity," I said, lifting my gaze to his.

"So, let's call it even. Let's not even keep score. We both made mistakes."

I nodded. "I was going to call the article, *Cash's Comeback*. I wanted people to know the real you."

"The only thing I'm coming back from is the past I left behind." Placing the paper bag on the desk, he pulled me to standing and brushed the pads of his thumbs over my cheeks. Happiness spread like wildfire through my chest, and I clung to him as the depths of his ocean blues pulled me under.

"Oh, I brought you something." Releasing me, he gestured to the bag.

I shot a curious glance his way before peeking inside.

"I should've known," I groaned. "Banoffee pie. If this isn't a sign, I don't know what is."

"Aunt Patty couldn't help herself after I told her your story."

"Nor can I." Scooping some onto the spoon, I held it to his mouth.

"It's just like you," he murmured, darting his tongue out to lick a blob of cream off his lips.

"How so?" I spooned some pie into my mouth and savored the delectable flavors as they hit my tongue.

"A delicious combination of textures and flavors. Sweet. Comforting. Fun. And anyone who tries it is instantly hooked."

"I could say the same for you, mister. Except you're much better for my waistline and ..."

He tasted like caramel and cream as his lips moved over mine. My heart felt like it would burst through my ribcage as we kissed in a dance of forgiveness with a promise of tomorrows.

Smiling against Alex's lips, I chuckled about the remnants of pie on my desk. Who knew my penchant to have the last word, and subsequent banoffee pie baking, would lead me into this wonderful man's arms?

ABOUT THE AUTHOR

Callie Timmins lives with her husband and four children in beautiful Queensland, Australia. She fills her time sorting odd socks, being the family's Uber driver, and drinking copious amounts of coffee. In spare moments, she writes sweet, contemporary romance with loveable characters. Heartwarming without the hot & heavy. Clean without the cringe. Sweet, swoonworthy reads with a guaranteed happily-ever-after.

Amazon https://www.amazon.com/Callie-Timmins/e/B07VD72143

Newsletter http://eepurl.com/gCWc2z

CALLING HIS SHOT

CHELLE HONIKER

Jeremy has loved Shelby since the fourth grade. It took Shelby a little longer to fall for the small town boy just before she goes off to college and he leaves for Afghanistan as a Marine. They're torn apart just before they're reunited. Will their second chance at a happily ever after come at their ten-year class reunion?

1
———

JEREMY

"That's cheating, Jeremy Rivers! I'm telling your mama!"

Heads whipped around on the Pioneer Elementary playground to stare in shock at that audacious threat. Shelby Wingate pulled no punches. Invoking telling one's mama was the most terrifying thing an almost-fourth grader could do to another kid.

"You know you can't hit for Tara and let her run!" Shelby continued. "No way, buddy."

Game rules and regulations dominated the brains of all forty-two kids at Pioneer Elementary. They were the very cornerstone of playground balance and order.

Jeremy knew he couldn't hit for Tara. It was sneaky on his part. But his aim wasn't to cheat.

He knew it would make Shelby real mad. And that was his goal. He really liked seeing her hands on her hips and her thick wavy reddish-blonde hair somehow puff up the angrier she got. When her almond-shaped green eyes flashed with ten-year-old fury, it did funny things to his insides. Sometimes he couldn't concentrate on math because he was paying attention to her pouty lips. He didn't even mind that she smacked her gum, which also broke the rules -- but since they all did it, the kids kept quiet about that infraction.

Of all the things he liked about her, he especially liked that she was using his full name.

The more attention Shelby gave him, the better. Even if it was hollering as the opposing team captain.

Jeremy didn't play to win.

He played to irritate Shelby.

RIIIIIIIING. The recess bell had interrupted his evil master plan, signaling the time to line up and head back to class.

"This isn't over, cheater cheater pumpkin eater," taunted Shelby.

"Not by a long shot, Shelby Leanne," replied Jeremy smoothly, lining up behind her, smelling the vanilla in her hair. "Not by a long shot.

2

———

JEREMY

*J*eremy stopped short when he finally found the girl he loved and her British bestie lounging in the bleachers, listening to their conversation.

"Are you bloody kidding me right now Shelby Leanne?! Because I will BLOODY END YOU if you're kidding me. They will never find your body, I promise. I am British. We know how to hide a body."

"I could not be kidding you less," Shelby replied at a considerably lower decibel level, "My mom said I could drive us to Reno this weekend for the concert and stay with Uncle Dan afterward, so we don't have to make the drive back so late."

Bree asked, "Is she tied up somewhere? How did you force her into this? I won't judge, but it might give me some ideas on how to ask for the car next time I need it."

"You know if I admit to anything that makes you an accessory after the fact. Just start planning your outfit already."

Jeremy grinned and walked around the corner to join the girls.

"Bree, you're gonna fly right off the bleachers. What the actual heck? Did the Queen announce she's coming for a spot of tea?"

Shelby finally opened her eyes, squinting into the sun at the towering boy above her. "Har har, Jeremy Rivers. Don't you ever tire of making British jokes?"

Bree ignored Jeremy and slung her backpack over one tiny shoulder, stepping sideways down the bleachers like a surefooted mountain goat until she reached the cement steps. She hopped the last foot to the grass and jogged to where the other band geeks waited.

"Don't you have to play catch with your big sweaty friends now?" Shelby remarked. Jeremy's smile widened. "No afternoon practice today, as a matter of fact. Coach is working on defense. Mr. Harlan wants to see us both now and asked me to fetch your peppy booty from tumble club."

Shelby jumped to her feet, and with her hands on her hips, fixed him with 'the look'. "Jeremy Rivers, we have a real shot at taking the first-place trophy this year in Orlando!"

Jeremy still loved it when Shelby used his full name. Somewhere around late eighth grade, he realized he loved it so much he wanted to hear her holler it every day for the rest of his life. He just didn't know how to tell her that, and it worried him that time was running out.

He fixed her with a bored stare, although he was anything but, and replied in a flat monotone, "Yes, I know, cupcake. You're a winner. Rah. Rah. Now, can we go see what Harlan wants? I've got party logistics to figure out for this weekend. You coming to the campground?"

Jeremy's casual question wasn't so innocent. He planned to make a move this weekend after the fall fling game and finally let Shelby see that his feelings for her went deeper than he let on.

Shelby snorted. "Of course. You and your friends need me and my friends to make any party worth having. You have zero skills as DJ, let's be honest. Your parties are tragic without my playlist." Shelby shoved her book in her backpack, ready to join him in the short walk to Harlan's office, and nervously smoothed down her skirt.

Jeremy reached down to grab her backpack. "I'll give you that one. Although you have to admit the polka mixtape I made you in seventh grade was pretty amazing."

Shelby laughed at the memory.

"Can't wait to see you slay this weekend, Jeremy!" Called out one brunette-haired volleyball player. "And definitely can't wait for the after-party you promised me."

Shelby rolled her eyes as they passed, whispering, "Gross. Get a room."

"Jealous? You know you can have this anytime you want." Jeremy turned and walked backward in front of Shelby, flexing his arm.

Shelby mimicked the southern damsel-in-distress accent, "Oh, can I? Be still my heart. You're such a catch, Jeremy Rivers. How did I not see it before now? You're so big and strong, and you'd make such a fine husband. Come away with me now, and let's go speak with my Pa!"

Jeremy met her eyes with intensity, his face suddenly serious.

"I'll marry you in a hot second, Shelby Leanne." Jeremy replied steadily "Name the date and time."

Shelby's eyes locked on Jeremy. She blushed and opened her mouth to say something sassy, but she quickly closed her mouth. Jeremy could see that she couldn't form words. She tried again, opening her mouth to retort, and again closed it when nothing came out.

An arm slipped around Shelby's shoulders. "You look like that singing mounted fish my dad has on his wall, Shelbs." Todd Lorenzo chimed in, mimicking her opening and closing her mouth. "What did you say, Rivers? She never shut up when we were dating."

Jeremy kept his eyes locked on Shelby's. "I asked her to marry me. I'm waiting for her to answer."

Todd looked between them. "I'm guessing her silence should be enough of an answer, Dude. Shelbs, wanna marry me instead? You'll be barefoot and pregnant by prom."

Shelby broke eye contact and replied, "Haha, Todd. You're hilarious. Now get off. We're late for a meeting with Harlan."

Todd didn't see Jeremy's fist coming until the split second before it connected with his face. Jeremy put the full weight of his upper body behind it, dropping Todd like a fishing lure in the local lake. Shelby wasn't sure if the crunching sound she heard was Todd's face or Jeremy's hand. She desperately hoped it wasn't his hand.

3

JEREMY

*J*eremy sat on the exam table in the nurse's office, watching through the large bay window as the nurse and Coach spoke. Shelby sat next to Jeremy on the long table, holding his arm by the elbow to make sure he kept it elevated. His hand was purple and mottled with an ice pack strapped to his wrist. He shifted uncomfortably every minute to escape the pain from the cold.

He was more concerned with Shelby's temper than the pain. "You're an idiot. You know that? Todd says stupid stuff all the time. Why would you risk your entire future by going and getting yourself hurt?"

Jeremy's voice strained as he replied, "I was done listening to him talk nasty about you, Shelby. I couldn't take it anymore."

Whatever football career he'd planned was over. In his gut, he knew this injury differed from other hits.

But he'd do it again for her. Always for her.

Jeremy lifted his chin, turning slightly to look at Shelby. He'd been serious when he told her he'd marry her in a heartbeat. When they were nine years old, Jeremy decided Shelby was his soulmate.

He'd called his shot.

Despite the pain, his voice was clear and strong. "Shelby Leanne, I'd just asked you to marry me."

Shelby's breath hitched in surprise, followed by the barest smile.

"Well, as proposals go, that one was pretty weak, Jeremy Rivers. You haven't even taken me on a first date."

Jeremy's grin lit up the room. At night when he lay in bed thinking of her auburn curls and the way she smelled like a vanilla sugar cookie, he cataloged and filed every memory.

"I have so. I've taken you on a hundred dates, Miss Bossy Pants. Remember the field trip in the fourth grade. We read by Spanish Creek? I brought an old horse blanket and kicked Trevor off it so you could sit by me. You kicked off your shoes, squished your toes in the grass, and read The Hobbit for nearly two hours. That was our first date. Seriously, Shelby. I've been dating you for a while now."

The nurse opened the door and breezed into the room. "We need to get you over to the District Hospital for an MRI, but as I told Coach Howe out there, I'm pretty sure it's not broken. I'm concerned about that ligament, though."

Shelby slid from the exam table gingerly and bent to pick up his backpack. "I've got this."

Jeremy had dreamed often of having Shelby's fiercest instincts work on his behalf. He'd never imagined how good it would feel. She hustled around the room gathering everything in her arms and asked, "Why aren't you moving? We've got a hospital to get to. Move it, buddy."

Jeremy slid off the table and threw a glance at the nurse. "I guess we're going to the hospital. Shelbs, do you think we can run through the Polka Dot real quick? I'm starving." He ignored his pain and concentrated on having an extra few minutes with Shelby before he heard what he expected would be bad news.

"I would love a caramel shake, but aren't you in a lot of pain? Shouldn't we get you there as soon as possible?"

"I'll be okay for a few minutes, and I really want to be sure you understand we're officially a couple. It seems like you're still fuzzy on the details."

Shelby's smile assured Jeremy she wasn't fuzzy anymore.

4

JEREMY

*J*eremy winced.

Mark Benson was the best physical therapist in three counties. He told Jeremy the way he manipulated the fingers would hurt, but his job was to get Jeremy's range of motion back, and pain was part of it. "Play through it. I need you to touch your thumb to every finger faster than that."

Jeremy sucked in a sharp breath, "Ow, dude. That still hurts."

"Do you want to start Basic Training prep in January or not? It'll hurt now, or it'll hurt while your girl here goes off to college and finds a new guy." Mark nodded at Shelby sitting with her feet tucked under her, reading a magazine. She waited for Jeremy to finish physical therapy so they could spend the rest of the day together.

"Fine. I get it. You're torturing me for my own good in cahoots with my girl."

Shelby called over without looking up from her magazine. "I'm not the one that made a sad choice. Violence is never the answer."

Jeremy ignored her teasing. Surgery to repair the ligament had ended his football career had changed the trajectory of their lives, but he'd made it all work. He enlisted in the Marines and planned to serve for four years. If all went according to plan, Shelby would graduate with her degree at about the same time they discharged him, and then he could go to law school as planned on his G.I. Bill.

"What are you doing over there anyway?"

"I'm trying to 'find the scent to keep your long-distance relationship from fizzling out'. I have to find my signature scent."

"The only scent I love more than yours is a Polka Dot hamburger. Can you bottle that when I'm deployed? And you smell like vanilla. I fell in love with it in the fourth grade."

Shelby looked up with a smile Jeremy knew was just for him.

Since the day Jeremy finally told Shelby how he felt about her, theirs had been the most natural relationship in the world. Shelby joked that they were like when her mom Elaine would lose her glasses to remember they were on her head and say, "Oh, there you are!"

They'd been together their whole lives until Jeremy finally made Shelby look at him and say, "Oh, there you are."

Six weeks later, it was still perfect.

Jeremy finished physical therapy and they spent the rest of the day Christmas shopping, popping into the small shops around Feather River Falls and visiting with the shopkeepers they'd known their entire lives. After shopping, they searched for a Christmas tree to chop for his mother. Shelby had been on a mission to find one that had 'perfect symmetry'.

"New rule. When you reject a tree, I get to kiss you."

She rejected many trees, and when they kissed she tasted like peppermint and cocoa.

"Shelbs. The perfect tree doesn't exist --"

The pop of a snowball cut him off, and Shelby ran away laughing. He chased her until he gently tackled her and kissed her icy lips until they were warm again. Lying side by side in the snow, Jeremy stared into Shelby's eyes. "Yep. Sugar cookies."

Shelby pressed her frozen glove to his face and looked up.

"Oh, here it is. It's the perfect tree."

Jeremy had to pry his eyes from Shelby's face to look up at the tree she'd proclaimed was perfect.

"You're absolutely right, Shelby. This is perfect. My mom will love it."

That night they made sure it was straight as an arrow and spent the evening hanging ornaments and horrible stringy tinsel. Jeremy loved Shelby's horrified face when he sprinkled tinsel on her head.

"You know, you still haven't answered me. It's been six whole weeks. Are you really going to leave me out here twisting like this?"

"Who gets engaged when they're still in high school? It feels like a jinx. We're together and we're happy, right?"

"Right. Yes, of course."

"Then trust that we'll both know the moment will come when I'll say what you want to hear. For now, just be happy. I am."

Jeremy felt some inexplicable anxiety that she hadn't said yes, but the rational part of his brain knew she was probably right. They were young. They had time.

5

BREE

*W*hatever the speed limit was didn't matter. Bree raced down the California coast from San Francisco to San Diego, with just two thoughts in her head.

1. Get to San Diego and be there for Shelby's breakdown.

2. Kill Jeremy Rivers in the most excruciating way possible.

Those thoughts overrode any others, including speed limits.

She arrived without incident, and Bree let herself in and to find her best friend wrapped like a burrito in a comforter in the middle of her bed. Her stringy hair was half in and half out of a bun piled on her head. Mascara trailed on either cheek from her tears.

Shelby was listening to her favorite Irish band, which played sad ballads of lost love and tragedy.

Bree recognized this situation instantly. Shelby was wallowing. She'd seen it in the ninth grade when Shelby's cheer squad didn't qualify for Nationals in Orlando. She'd seen it in the eleventh grade when she didn't make what she thought was a high enough score on the practice SAT test.

And she saw it when Jeremy left for his first tour of duty in Afghanistan.

Bree had seen Shelby wallow, and she'd been there for her every time with tissues, chocolate, and pumpkin spice lattes. Bree had developed a finely tuned system for Shelby's wallows.

Bree was finishing a staff meeting at her office in San Francisco when Shelby called her barely coherent. "Please... I need you. Jeremy's gone..." and then she had hung up.

Bree didn't waste time trying to call Shelby back. She had called Shelby's mother, Elaine. Jeremy wasn't dead or injured. Shelby wouldn't tell her mother the details, but they had broken up via email and according to Shelby it was absolutely final.

"Talk to me, Shelbs. Your mum says it's a breakup, and it's final and that it happened over email."

Shelby's eyes were glassy, but she focused on Bree and drew out a breath.

"He broke me, Bree. I've known him my entire life. I've loved him my entire life, even when I didn't know that's what love was. I thought he was the best person I knew, but it turns out I didn't know him at all." Her voice trailed off in a wail and fat tears rolled down her face.

"Sweetie, what's happened? What's so final about this?"

Shelby dissolved into a new flood of tears alternating with hiccups, and Bree waited it out. Finally, Shelby composed herself and whispered, "I will tell you and then we will never speak of this again. Deal?"

"Of course."

Shelby's voice was flat. "He emailed me. It said he hadn't had the courage to face me and tell me. He's met someone there. And... and... she's pregnant. He didn't mean for it to happen, but he hoped I could eventually forgive him. He feels honor-bound to marry her."

Bree squished onto the bed next to her burrito-friend and rubbed her arm soothingly. "I won't lie. I'm surprised, Shelby. Have you spoken with him?"

Shelby replied flatly, "I have nothing to say to him. Nothing. We had been misconnecting for weeks. He wouldn't show up for our video chats. I could see he had read my texts, but wasn't replying. I called, and she answered the phone once and hung up on me. I thought it was just the pressure and stress of his deployment ending. I thought we would be okay once he was back, and we were together again."

Bree nodded, and Shelby continued.

"But this was a complete shock. And he told me by email. Email!

Now he's calling and calling, but I can't forgive this, Bree. I can't. It's a betrayal of everything we are. He's going to be a father. This isn't something we could put behind us and move on with time... there will forever be a reminder I wasn't enough for him."

"Oh, no. None of that. This isn't in any way your fault, Shelby. Plenty of people go into the military and stay faithful to their partners. This lands on him. I won't have any of that nonsense." Bree took Shelby's face between her hands. "Listen to me. You are the single greatest person I know. You're generous and loving and funny and beautiful. You simply don't deserve this, and I'm sorry this happened, but you're strong and we'll get through this. It's his loss. I'm betting he's already kicking himself that he's lost you."

Shelby fought with her cocoon to sit up. Bree tried not to laugh. "Oh, my sweet burrito-friend, allow me to help you." When Shelby was upright, Bree dug into her bag and pulled out the provisions. "I come bearing practical gifts, and something more." She poured a shot of tequila and snapped off some chocolate. "Okay. That's the practical things handled. Now for the unconventional. I need you to hear me all the way out. Deal?"

"Deal."

Bree fixed Shelby with a stare Shelby called 'her very serious attempt to be British'.

"You're about to graduate with honors with a degree in communications, right?"

"Right."

"I hired a new director of communications today. Guess who?"

Shelby thought quickly about her friendship with Bree. The laps they ran in grade school for talking too much in class. Their sixth grade talent show act. The sleepover that left them both sick for a week from eating godawful Swedish fish and staying up talking about boys.

There were too many memories to catalog, but the one constant was that Bree had been there for her, unfailingly for the better part of two decades. And despite Shelby's crushing disappointment with Jeremy, she still trusted her best friend.

"I'll take it. Bree. I love you. We'll be back together in San Francisco, and I will be nearly two thousand miles away from Jeremy Rivers."

Bree beamed and hugged her partially cocooned friend. "Now, let's toast our bright futures."

6

JEREMY

Stop calling. I've moved on with Todd. Everything is as it should be.
Jeremy read the text again for the fiftieth time. Each time he got angrier and more murderous. He was mad enough to go AWOL. How the hell had he been so wrong about Shelby? To break up with him over text. He read it again.

When she didn't show up for their weekly video call, Jeremy became irritated. Their weekly video chats sustained him over the years. It was their time to plan their lives and dream of their futures. His G.I. Bill would cover the cost of law school, so they planned to move to Boston. They looked online at apartments together. For three years they planned and dreamed.

From the time he deployed until about three months ago, she'd never missed one of their dates. In the last three months, however, they kept misconnecting. At first, they both chalked it up to scheduling conflicts or technology issues. His birthday gift hadn't arrived, and she thought he had forgotten her birthday.

As if.

He hadn't forgotten a birthday since she was nine years old.

They bickered over silly things. Shelby said she sent him emails that bounced back. When she called, she said his phone rolled straight to voicemail. One time, she said a woman answered and hung up on her.

Jeremy tried to reassure her. They were riding out a rough patch and would be together soon. He knew it frustrated Shelby but felt confident. Once they were together again, it would be better than ever.

But now, in a text, she broke up with him, moving on with the worst guy he could imagine. His high school rival. The one responsible for losing the scholarship to USC.

Jeremy had never felt bitter about losing the scholarship. He had told Shelby he might not have mustered the courage to make his move if Todd hadn't baited him that day. He told her, "everything is as it should be, Shelbs."

She used that phrase to describe her relationship with Todd.

Now he was bitter.

"Hey, Rivers. You've got your killer face on. You alright?" Lucia Dawson asked.

Jeremy looked up from the text to find he'd absentmindedly walked across base to the office he shared with Lucia. They were assigned to the support team for Damon South, the Judge Advocate assigned to their base.

"Hey, Dawson. I'm not alright, actually. I think I just got dumped for good."

"What? Didn't you just sign the lease on your new place in Boston?"

"I did. Student housing. I guess I need to figure out how to swing that now."

"I'm sorry to hear that. Anything I can do?" Lucia offered.

He considered her offer. "Not a thing, Dawson. Thanks anyway."

They settled in to work on the case, researching details for their client. Work distracted him, and Jeremy was grateful that Lucia was an easy partner to work with. She managed most of the technology for the team, and she was as smart as a whip.

"Hey, would you mind looking at my email again? I'm still getting those weird error messages, and I can't figure out what the issue is. I ran the anti-viral software. Everything I sent to Shelby bounced back."

"Sure. I'll look... I hate to mention it, but do you think she might have blocked you?" Lucia asked.

"I didn't even think of that." Jeremy groaned. "That's probably it. She's cut me off everywhere else."

"Sorry I brought that up. Hey, wanna grab a beer after work? I'm a good listener."

Jeremy knew Lucia had a crush on him, but he had been clear from the beginning. His heart belonged only to Shelby. He still hoped that once he arrived stateside, he could see Shelby in person and they could work it out. Todd or no Todd, he loved her and would not give up so easily.

"Hey, thanks, but I'm going to try to video chat back home and hopefully figure some things out."

"Sure, whatever you need. You know I'm here for you." Lucia replied.

7

LUCIA

*L*ucia knew it was only a matter of time.

She had started with little things. Deleting Shelby's emails. Adding her phone number to Jeremy's blocked list every few days and then unblocking it so it looked like Jeremy was avoiding her. Just enough to look like he was making excuses for the missed calls.

"It's for his own good," she rationalized. "I'm the one that's had his back the last three years. Not her."

Lucia's obsession with Shelby had reached its tipping point three months prior, when she realized her time with Jeremy was growing short. The subtle hints weren't working, so she kicked it into high gear and started taking active measures. Her discharge was a few weeks before his, and her plan wasn't paying off fast enough.

Since she was the team's technical support it was easy. The calendar invites were the first she sabotaged. She was in and out of his computer often enough to do those with little effort. She blamed it on a software upgrade one time, and a server glitch another.

Canceling Shelby's birthday present was a little more challenging, but she could guess his shopping password.

IShelbyLove4Ever? Gross, Rivers. You're a Marine, for Pete's sake.

Lucia ticked off that task from her "Operation Breakup" list and moved on to the next task. Arranging a call from Shelby to Jeremy's phone when he was in court and she was in charge of the team's electronics.

She answered the call, breathless and giggling. When Shelby asked to speak to Jeremy, she disguised her voice and said, "Baby, someone's asking for you. I think you're in trouble," and then disconnected the line.

The things I do for you, Rivers.

Lucia was certain that would have been the final straw, but somehow Jeremy had convinced Shelby she'd called a wrong number or that wires had gotten crossed between America and Afghanistan.

Time to take it up a notch. A direct breakup letter. But something final. Something she won't forgive.

For the briefest moment, Lucia had a crisis of conscience. Writing the email to Shelby as if it was from Jeremy breaking up with her was risky. She would have to send it and delete all traces of it from his computer. But then she had to take it one more step and add Shelby to the base blacklist severing their electronic tie completely.

She wasn't concerned about whether she should send it and break them up.

She was concerned about being disciplined if she got caught.

But now it looked like her plan had worked even better than she'd hoped.

Lucia had one last step in her plan.

She would use her head start back in America to get settled in Boston before contacting Jeremy with a sob story about losing her apartment. She knew he was a stand-up guy and would offer to room with her, especially now that he needed help financially.

With Shelby out of the way, she could make herself indispensable to Jeremy as he finished law school. They made a perfect team, and she saw no reason they wouldn't make a lovely life together.

She smiled at how the day turned out.

8

SHELBY

"I can't believe I let you drag me to this," Shelby complained.

Bree peered over her glasses at Shelby from the passenger seat. "I didn't drag you anywhere. This is your victory lap for every one of our classmates that has ever said nasty things. Look at you now. You're the CEO of your own company. You work with movers and shakers. You're still my best friend. Girl, you're killing it."

Shelby loved working with Bree. After four years she had started her own company and worked with some major political figures in California. She loved being her own boss and the feeling that she finally had her feet underneath her again.

"I appreciate you not mentioning you-know-who this trip. I'm fine and wish him and his family well."

"That's impressive. You're so good at public relations that I almost believed you."

"I mean it."

"Of course you do," Bree cooed.

"You're the worst." Shelby said, exasperated, whipping into a parking space and putting the car in gear. "Let's get this over with. Ten years is a lifetime. I bet I won't even recognize anyone here."

"Who do you think you're fooling? You might not have been home over five times in ten years and banned all news of anyone within six degrees of separation of whats-his-face, but trust me, you'll know every-one... and they'll know you."

Shelby groaned.

"Now. Victory lap. Start your engines."

Three minutes later they stood in front of the check-in desk looking at the name badges for their names. Bree found hers quickly and clipped it on her chest. "Would you look at that brace-face and those coke-bottle glasses? Thank goodness for orthodontia and laser eye surgery. I am hot."

"Still as loud as ever, tiny British girl," came a familiar voice from behind them.

Shelby stood completely still, as if frozen by a sudden ice storm. She knew it was possible—probable, even— that she would see Jeremy. She was just hoping for a few minutes to acclimate to the terror of being back before she did.

"Yes, some things never change. I am still loud. And you're still a jerk." Bree retorted.

"Whoa. Ouch. Fine, I get it. I thought we could have kept it civil, since it's been six years."

Shelby turned around to face the man she once believed she would love forever and the woman standing next to him. Her heart sank. She recognized Lucia from the photos Jeremy sent of his team in Afghanistan.

"Hello, Jeremy Rivers. I wish you and your family nothing but the very best life has to offer." And then she walked past him, badge in hand, to join the reunion inside the gym.

I wish you and your family the... Dear Lord Shelby, get yourself together.

Bree caught up to her. "Okay, so maybe that was more of a pit stop than a victory lap. But that's out of the way, so let's not dwell. How are you feeling?"

"Like I really want to kill you and stuff you in the band room closet."

Bree quipped, "Well, that wouldn't be the first time you've expressed that emotion out loud. I say we focus on finding a couple of drinks."

"Good idea." Shelby replied. She knew it would be difficult, but she hadn't expected to have her heart shattered into a million pieces all over again. This hurt was as fresh as the day he had emailed.

I can do this. I deserve to be happy and see my old friends, too. I laughed and cried with these people. We grew up together. He wasn't the only person I cared about. I don't have to leave this all behind because of him.

They made their way into the gym and old friends immediately surrounded Shelby. Despite her genuine hurt at seeing Jeremy and Lucia, she enjoyed catching up with her old classmates. She and Bree found a table conveniently near the bar, but on the opposite side of the room from where Jeremy sat.

A pair of rough hands slid over her eyes.

"Guess who!" A deep voice asked.

"Hello, Todd."

"Hey! How did you know it was me?" He slid into the seat next to her, grinning from ear to ear. "It's fantastic to see you."

"It's good to see you, too." Shelby patted Todd's shoulder, "How's your family?"

"Aww, they're good. My boy is six and a half, and my wife is due next month. She wasn't feeling well, so I can't stay long. I wish you could meet her. Maybe before you leave town?"

"Your son is the same age as Jeremy's kid. Sure. I'd like that. I'll come by tomorrow if she's up for it."

Todd stood to leave. "Rivers has a six-year-old, huh? He must have met her right after you broke up then."

Shelby whispered numbly "Before. Before we broke up. He met her over there, he said it in his email, when he ended it with me."

Shelby didn't care who knew anymore. She wasn't ashamed. It was time to let it go and allow time to heal the wound. That started with the truth.

"Rivers is a lot of things, but I never figured him for a cheater. Especially on you." Todd replied.

Shelby straightened in her chair. "It's done.. Its ancient history. I'm over it." She used her convincing tone of voice.

"Are you really? I promised my wife I wouldn't brawl, but if you want him to take a beating, then he'll get a beating, Feather River style."

Shelby smiled at Todd. Small towns were the best, and she mused things came full circle, if you gave them enough time. Todd had been a sweet boy in elementary school, then her freshman crush, then a jerk, and now he was a sweet guy.

"Nah. Let it go. I have. I'll call you tomorrow and see if your wife is up for a visit, okay?"

Polo cologne engulfed Shelby as he leaned down and kissed the top of her head. "You've always been cool, Shelbs. See you tomorrow."

Todd walked toward Jeremy's table and headed out the main doors. Shelby breathed a sigh of relief and turned back to chat with her friends.

"Todd's not so bad now, and he was a convenient excuse to keep you-know-who away when he came home." Bree mused.

"What do you mean?" Shelby asked. "How was Todd an excuse?"

Bree fixed Shelby with her confessional stare. "Okay, don't get mad. When Jeremy came back from Afghanistan, he came looking for you at our apartment."

"He what? Why didn't you tell me?"

"Because everything was so fresh and you were so raw. I didn't think you could handle his excuses. He said it was a big misunderstanding, which is total garbage. I was protecting you, Shelbs. I told him you and Todd had gone away for the weekend."

"You did NOT." Shelby exclaimed, horrified.

"I did. You had already sent him that text... telling him you were back together with Todd."

"Which was awful, and I regret that. It wasn't right to bring someone else into my mess," Shelby countered.

"True, but I was just, you know, playing off that. It worked. He left you alone."

Shelby couldn't argue, and a clean break was better. She focused on her work, and he focused on his pretty wife and child.

"I don't even know if he has a boy or a girl," Shelby mumbled, her eyes glazed over with unshed tears.

"I'm sorry, Shelby." Bree hugged her friend from the side. "Ready to get out of here? I think we did a good lap. Let's get something fattening from the Polka Dot and go wallow."

They gathered their things and made their way to the main doors. Shelby looked toward Jeremy's table one last time, disappointed to see that he wasn't there.

9

____

JEREMY

*J*eremy was as furious as he was the day Shelby broke up with him by text. He sat sullenly across the room, wishing he had the nerve to get up and walk over to the table and talk with her.

Then Todd arrived and the dam of hurt and anger burst. He watched their exchange, coiled as tight as a spring, clenching his fists as Todd kissed the top of Shelby's head before leaving.

"It looks like she's done well for herself," Lucia said. "That's what you said you wanted to see, right?"

"Yeah. It's what I wanted. I wanted her to be happy. And I guess she is."

"It's been six years. Are you ready to let her go now?" Lucia whispered.

Jeremy turned to face his friend. He knew she hoped somehow he could love her the way he had loved Shelby. They'd been roommates for a couple of years while he went to law school, but after one drunken make-out session, he moved out, saying he wasn't ready for a relation-ship. Lucia played it casual, but Jeremy sensed she was looking for an opportunity. She offered to come with him tonight, and he should have said no. He didn't love her.

Jeremy's heart hadn't been his to give away since he'd given it to the feisty, beautiful girl across the room.

Todd walked by the table and out the main doors turning right toward the men's room.

It's go time.

Jeremy shot out of his seat like a rocket ignoring Lucia's protests. Todd might have been bigger, but Jeremy was a Marine. This time he wasn't defending Shelby's honor. This time was personal.

Todd was drying his hands when Jeremy threw the doors open, a murderous look on his face.

"Hey, Dude. Been a long time. You good?" Todd offered.

Jeremy stopped short. He hadn't been expecting pleasantries, and it threw him off his game. "Are you kidding me? You steal my girl and think we're good?"

"What are you talking about? The way I hear it, you broke up with her like a coward over email." Todd's eyebrows scrunched together like they had in high school when he had a math problem he couldn't figure out.

"You heard wrong, dude," Jeremy replied. "She broke up with me by text. A text. " Jeremy's voice cracked with emotion.

"I just know what I heard. You met a girl over there, and you chickened out and emailed Shelby." Todd stepped toward to leave. "Look, man, you seem to do alright. You've got that pretty wife, and I hear you've got a kid about my kid's age. Sounds like you don't have beef with me."

It puzzled Jeremy. "Who told you this? She's not my wife. I don't have a kid. There's no one. There's been no one. It's her. It's always been Shelby."

"She told me herself. Just now. She's not a liar, man. Don't make me give you a Feather River beating. I promised my wife." Todd growled.

"Wait -- you're married? You're not with her? You have a kid?" Jeremy's head was spinning. He barely heard Todd's description of his little ginger-haired son and his wife he met at community college.

Jeremy interrupted him. "I gotta go." He stuck his hand out to shake Todd's. "I'm really glad we talked. I wish you and your family nothing but the very best that this life has to offer." Jeremy stepped around Todd and left the men's room, bumping into Lucia.

"Oh, hey. You alright?" He asked, steadying her.

"I'm a Marine. Of course, I am." Lucia replied smoothly. "Hey, she's gone. Can we get out of here?"

Jeremy looked down the hall past her. "Gone? How long ago? What am I saying? I can find her in under ten minutes in this town."

Lucia met his eyes, and he saw her barely contained fury, "What do you mean find her? Isn't that her husband in there? You saw her. She's fine. We're fine. Let's go home and be done with her. For once and for all, I can't take it anymore. I've waited for years for you to get over her."

"Luce. It's her. It's always been her. It's some kind of misunderstanding. She thinks we're married. She thinks we have a kid. I don't know where she got that, but if I can just find her and explain -- "

"She thinks that because it's what should have happened. That's what I planned. That is supposed to be our life right now. God, Jeremy, are you really so blind? I did so much for you -- to make you see she would move on as soon as she had the chance -- and she did, didn't she? With him!" Lucia pointed to Todd as he exited the men's room.

Jeremy asked her quietly, "What do you mean, 'you did so much for me to make me see her move on?' What did you do?"

Todd stepped around the couple. "I gotta get home to my wife. She's gonna be mad that she missed this. Just like in High School! Later, dude."

Jeremy waited for Lucia's answer. "Fine. You want the truth. Here's the truth. I've loved you for seven years. I spent every day with you over there. We built something. I had your back, and you're supposed to have mine. She didn't understand that. She didn't understand you. I did. I do."

"What did you do, Lucia?" Jeremy pressed quietly.

"I did what I needed to do. Yes, I lied. Yes, I sent her the email. But I did it so you would see that I was the right one. The one for you!"

Jeremy exhaled as everything clicked into place. He ran his hand through his hair. Lucia's piteous crying in his old high school hallway just made Jeremy tremendously sad. Sad for her, sad for Shelby, and sad for himself.

"Lucia. Please, hear me. Leave. We're done. We aren't friends. I don't want to see you ever again."

She gasped, "You don't mean that. I know you don't. Shelby's not--"

"Take her name out of your mouth. Forever. She's my heart. She's my home. Look around. Even without her the last six years —years you cost us — it's still only her. It will always only be her. She's endgame."

"But..."

"No buts. I've known since I was nine years old Shelby was it for me, and nothing from that day to this has changed. Go. Go wherever you're going to go, but make it as far away from me and Shelby as possible."

Jeremy turned and sprinted out of the school to his car. This time he wouldn't be a coward. This time he would make her listen. Even if she didn't want to be with him, she needed to know he never betrayed her. He never stopped loving her.

10

SHELBY

*B*ree sat in a swing on their old elementary school playground, twisting around and letting the swing spin back as she enjoyed her caramel sundae. "Do you think they put something illegal in the caramel? Why is it that this small town has the best ice cream place in all of California?"

"Dunno. They used to put cocaine in soda though, so who knows what secrets they're keeping." Shelby coordinated her swing to spin in tandem with Bree's. "The place has been there for a million years. My mom and dad had their first date there." She frowned. "I guess technically Jeremy and I did too."

"We did not. I told you when our first date was. It was right over there by the creek in the fourth grade. "

Jeremy stepped from around the building and came into view, and Shelby brought her swing to a stop, taking in the full view of him. She'd run away earlier without looking closely at him. He was harder and sharper, but it was the same face that haunted her nightmares, and before that, inhabited her dreams.

"Seriously, Jeremy? Don't you have somewhere else to be right now? With your wife? Your kid?" Bree said.

"Actually, tiny British Girl, I do not. In fact..." He stepped directly in front of Shelby, "I have never been married, and I don't have a child."

Shelby examined the brown eyes of the boy she had loved her complete life and saw his truth there.

"I don't understand," she whispered softly. "Your email...?"

"Someone I thought was a friend sent that pack of lies. I found out..." he glanced down at his watch, "exactly eleven minutes ago. She made it all up to keep us apart, Shelby Leanne. All of this time. I thought you were with Todd." He glared at Bree.

Bree bent to pick up her purse, "Anyhoo, that's my cue to leave. I'm British, and I love a good drama, but I think this caramel is making me dizzy."

"I would have been here five minutes ago, but I stopped for these." Jeremy pulled a dozen roses from behind his back and held them out for Shelby. "This girl makes me dizzy too."

Shelby gasped, and tears welled in her eyes as she whispered, "It was all a lie?"

Jeremy nodded. "All of it."

Shelby thought of the last six years. She'd made the best of it by starting her own company and made a name for herself, but she couldn't deny she was heartsick over the loss of her happily ever after with the only boy she'd ever imagined her life with.

"It's too late. It's just too late, Jeremy. We're different people."

"Shelby Leanne. I've loved you since I was nine years old. Was that too early?" He held a finger to her lips when she tried to answer. "No. No, it was not. I'm the same boy you played on this playground with. I'm the same boy that kissed you breathless under a Christmas tree. And I want to be the same boy that you grow old with, just like we planned."

Tears fell from Shelby's eyes freely, "I don't even know how to start with this."

"We start here, at the beginning. This playground is where we started and this is where we get to start again."

"How do we start over? Where do we live? How--"

Jeremy cut her off. "Shelbs, there's no starting over because for me, it wasn't ever over. I asked you to marry me and I'm still waiting on an answer. You said we would know when the time is right. It's been right for me every day from that day to this. I'm waiting on you."

A million objections raced through Shelby's head. Too many to count.

But she rose from the swing and took the hand of the boy that called his shot with her on this very playground all those years ago.

She stood on her tiptoes and kissed him with all the love and longing she'd denied the last six years.

He broke the kiss. "Vanilla sugar cookies," he murmured and looked at her breathlessly for his answer.

"Yes," she whispered. "Yes. I'll marry you."

Jeremy lifted her up and spun her around. From far away, she heard Bree hoot in excitement.

He looked at her solemnly. "Shelby Leanne, I love you so much. I'll make you so happy."

She stepped out of their embrace and pretended to pout. "You better. Don't make me tell your Mama on you."

ABOUT THE AUTHOR

Caffeinated - Writer - Mama - Founder - Aspiring Foo Fighter - Speaker - Trainer - Traveler

Chelle Honiker took her empty nest on the road in 2019 only to find herself grounded in 2020. She doesn't mind. Her imaginary friends travel with her.

She writes sassy characters in sweet romance and paranormal fantasy.

Her big audacious dream is to live in her ancestral home of Oban, Scotland, in a home big enough for her writer friends to come to visit anytime they want. She would, of course, wear the tartan of the Clan MacDougall to the Oban Chocolate Factory every afternoon for coffee until someone makes her stop

https://929press.com/chelle-honiker/.

SAFE LANDINGS

ELLE BOTZ

An unexpected flight delay opens the door to a new life and an old flame.

1
———

ALLISON

"**W**hy do they call it a puddle jumper?" Allison asked. She was on the phone with her best friend, Tabitha, while she waited for her plane to board.

"You haven't seen it yet, have you?" Tabitha laughed.

Allison was standing near the giant windows, looking out at the darkening sky. When the taxi dropped her off just two hours earlier, the sky was clear. But, by the time she made it through security, there were several disconcerting grey clouds hanging over the world outside.

She paced back and forth, silently willing the snow to hold off until she made it to her destination.

"I don't think it's here yet," Allison said.

"Oh, I'm betting it is," Tabitha said, sounding certain.

"Tab, how could I miss an entire airplane?" she asked.

"Just do yourself a favor and go ask someone."

"Fine," Allison sighed.

She walked over to the check-in counter, where she found an airline employee clacking away at her keyboard.

"Excuse me," Allison said, pulling the phone away from her face. "Has the plane to Cherry Creek arrived yet?"

"Yes," the woman said. Without looking up, she pointed a long, manicured fingernail toward the tarmac.

"I'm sorry," Allison said, "where?"

The woman met her eyes and pointed again. Allison once more followed the line the woman's finger made out onto the tarmac. She squinted in that general direction, scanning for a moment before registering that she was staring almost directly at a microscopic plane. It was parked away from all the other planes and not connected to the tunnel that sat outside of her gate. Instead, there was a small staircase leading up to the plane's door. Worry pulled at her stomach. She put the phone back to her ear.

"Tab," she whispered into the phone, "what the heck is that?"

"That," her friend replied, "is a puddle jumper."

"I have to go," Allison said before hanging up.

She sat down and began digging through her carry-on bag. Somewhere in there, she'd stashed a bottle of medicine for motion sickness. Her stomach lurched as she examined the bite-sized plane out in the distance. She popped a pill into her mouth and chased it with a gulp of water.

A tall, dark-haired guy strolled over and took one of the empty seats across from her. He gave her a polite smile—which she returned.

She glanced at him again, the familiarity of his face pulling her out of herself. She knew him. Her brain was so fogged from stress and lack of sleep that it wasn't putting the pieces together fast enough, but she knew him.

"Have they said how long the flight is delayed?" he asked.

"No," Allison said. She caught herself staring at his gorgeous blue-grey eyes. She tilted her head, still trying to make the connection. Then she processed what he'd said.

"Wait, did you say delayed?"

"Yeah," he said, pointing to the row of screens behind him. Sure enough, it displayed the word *delayed* in red next to her destination.

"No," she groaned. "Why?"

The man pointed behind her.

She looked outside to find the first puffy, troublesome snowflakes falling from the sky.

Allison swore under her breath. This was the last thing she needed. Her stomach turned over at the thought of having to call her boss and tell him about the flight. Almost more than it had turned at the sight of the small plane. Her heartbeat quickened. She took a measured breath.

"Wait," the man said. "Allison?"

She looked at him again. It clicked. She saw dark hair cropped close, not the black waves that now fell over his forehead. She imagined a smooth face instead of the very attractive stubble now covering his cheeks and chin. And in an instant, the anxiety the plane was causing her was joined by a wave of humiliation.

"No, no. Oh, god, no," she whispered to herself.

"Davis," she breathed. "I thought that was you." She showed her teeth in what she hoped resembled a smile.

About six months ago, Allison met Davis at a training class. They got along well, and he'd asked her to dinner—which also went well. It wasn't until the second date that everything had gone wrong.

Allison's cheeks warmed at the memory. She averted her eyes.

"How have you been?" he asked.

"Uh, okay," she said. "Just, you know… I'm good, I guess. You?"

"Same," Davis said, nodding more than the one-word response required.

"Are you headed to… uh… to there?" she asked, pointing up to the words *Cherry Creek* on the display.

A sly smile spread across his face. "Yeah," he said. "That's why I was asking you about it… remember?"

"Oh. Right. Yeah," she said. She briefly contemplated jumping out of a window.

"I'll just go ask that woman," he said, pointing a thumb toward the same employee Allison spoke to moments earlier.

"Sure," she said, unable to stop herself from nodding once again.

As he walked away, Allison let out a breath and swore quietly. This day could not possibly get worse.

Her boss told her to fly out yesterday. He'd insisted. And why did she refuse? Why did she choose this time to take a stand against his micromanaging and overt aggression? She didn't even know for sure. All she knew was that lately, things with her boss and her job bothered her in a way they never had before. She felt more frustrated, less appreciated, less fulfilled, and thus, less interested in continuing to invest her life and all of her energy into a company that still made her fetch the coffee after nearly a decade.

She had a master's degree. And in the years since she started at the company, she'd more than proven herself. She was dependable, hardworking, and tried her best. But as far as advancement and opportunities to do the aspects of the job she felt most passionate about, she only ever seemed to get the crumbs that her more aggressive co-workers left for her. Case in point: an unknown, gourmet chocolate company in a town she'd never even heard of until earlier this week.

Before leaving for her trip, she'd heard from one of the administrative assistants that her boss was letting someone go at the end of the year because they'd lost several big clients. She didn't need to ask for confirmation that she was on the shortlist. The way her boss acted around her told her all she needed to know. And she knew that messing up this meeting would seal her fate.

"So, what brings you to Cherry Creek?" Davis asked when he returned. Why had he come back to sit with her? Just to prolong the awkwardness? It was probably punishment for not returning his calls. There'd been a few of them before she blocked him. She grimaced. She should have handled the whole thing differently. She knew that. She'd just been mortified and panicked.

"A client meeting," she said. "Well, a pitch meeting. Hoping to convince a chocolate company there to sign with us."

"Oh. Right. So, you're still with The Milton Agency?" he asked.

"Yep," she put as much enthusiasm as she could into the word. "For now, at least." She tried to laugh.

"Still thinking of leaving?" he asked.

"No, not really," she lied. "This is just a big meeting. There's a rumor about staff cuts... so... you know how it is."

"Oh." He winced. "Yeah... I do. That sucks. Hopefully, your meeting goes well." There was an earnestness in his tone that felt comforting.

"Thanks," she said. "Let's hope I make it in time." She gestured to the large windows, where the huge flakes were still falling.

2

____

ALLISON

"Have you told the old grouch about your flight delay yet?" Tab asked.

"Oh my god, no," Allison said. "I'm dreading it, and I have no plans to tell him until I know when we'll be taking off. Perhaps not at all. Do I have to tell him?"

"He probably has Becky giving him flight updates on you."

"Ugh. You're right." He always had his assistant check on travel progress when associates traveled.

"Tell me again why you didn't go yesterday?" Tabitha asked her.

"I don't have a reason," Allison sighed. "I'm just so tired of it lately. Nothing I say seems to matter. When he told me I was leaving yesterday morning without even asking me if I could, something just snapped. I told him no. It was so stupid. And then Becky tells me he's going to get rid of someone—" Allison trailed off.

"Would that honestly be the worst thing?" Tab asked her. "You hate it there."

"I don't hate it," Allison said.

"You do, too. You can sugar coat it with other people all you want, but I know you. You hate that job."

Allison let out a sigh. "Still, what would I do without it?"

647

"Anything," Tab said. "That's the point. The possibilities are endless."

"Right." Allison laughed. "I don't know about that."

"I do," Tab insisted. "Now, call the grump. Tell him about the delay. Then try to enjoy your time stuck at the airport. Go get a drink. Watch the snow fall. Read a book. Do something that makes you feel better."

"Okay, so here's the thing," Allison said, looking around to make sure Davis wasn't in earshot. "Do you remember the guy I had a couple dates with a while ago? Davis?"

"The food poisoning guy?" Tab asked. Although Allison was the one who got food poisoning, it was Davis her friend graced with the title.

"Yes," Allison said.

"You puked on a server in front of him. I'm literally never going to forget that. Or him."

"Well, apparently you and the Universe are in cahoots because he is here."

"He's there? Like, you saw him at the airport somewhere?" Tab asked.

"No. Like, he is standing ten feet away from me and traveling to the same destination."

Tabitha let out something between a screech and a cackle.

"I'm so glad one of us finds this funny," Allison said.

"He's probably just glad to see that you made it out of the bathroom," Tab said, laughing. It took her a second, but she gained her composure enough to ask, "Why is he even there?"

"Same reason as me, I'm assuming."

"Oh. I didn't realize it was like a competitive thing. Does that make you nervous?"

"This whole thing makes me nervous, Tab. I'm not surprised they're shopping around. It's smart. But why did it have to be this guy? Of all the people to be stuck in an airport with—"

"Wait a minute," Tab said. "You liked him, though. Aside from the whole embarrassment thing, you guys hit it off, didn't you?"

"Yeah," Allison said. "That was before I threw up on the waiter, hid in the bathroom, and blocked his number the next day. I'd say the thrill is gone."

"Well, maybe you can avoid him," Tab said. She didn't sound very optimistic.

"I can try," Allison said without enthusiasm. She flicked her eyes toward Davis. He tilted his chin and smirked. She had to admit, it was nice to see him again. If she didn't think about the awful way things had ended, she could almost be glad for his company.

A WHILE LATER, Allison glanced up to see Davis walking toward her again.

"So, I'm guessing by the look on your face that your day isn't going well," he said.

"You would be correct," she replied.

"Sorry." His mouth turned downward.

"Any word on the flight?" Allison asked him.

He shook his head, wrinkling his nose as he did.

Allison looked back out the window and bit her lip. She pulled out her phone to type a quick text to Becky.

Was there any wiggle room at all in the meeting schedule tomorrow? Flight Delayed.

She sent the text and tucked the phone into her pocket.

"So, hey," Davis started. He knelt next to her. She assumed this was so they could speak eye to eye—since she hadn't been polite enough to move any of her stuff from the seats next to her.

Their eyes locked, and she couldn't help but smile. She didn't remember him being so tall. She didn't remember him being so handsome either. She could see the outline of muscles just under the snug-fitting t-shirt he was wearing. It took a concerted effort to bring her gaze back to his face.

He was smirking. How long had she been staring? Heat rushed to her face.

"I was just about to make a run for some coffee. Can I grab you one? Or maybe a whiskey?"

She laughed and shook her head. "That's nice of you, but you don't have to do that."

"Before you say no, you should know those two are treating," he said as he pointed toward the older couple he'd been chatting with earlier. "They're also insisting. And the one in the sweater is bossy."

Allison looked at the couple again. "They're both in sweaters," she said.

"Exactly." He stood, holding out a hand to help her up.

"Why do they want to buy me coffee?" she asked, eyeing his outstretched hand.

"They're bizarrely friendly people," he said. "And also, very nosey people... but mostly friendly."

"Well, okay," she agreed with a laugh. "A cocoa actually sounds nice."

"Great," he said. His full lips turned up in a smile. "Want to take a walk?" His eyes sparkled mischievously.

Her phone buzzed in her pocket. She resisted the urge to check. It could stay there a while longer.

"Sure," Allison said. She took his hand and felt her heartbeat quicken.

3

ALLISON

"So, is Cherry Creek the little hometown you told me about?" she asked as they waited in line.

"Yep," he blurted.

She planned to pry more, but the buzzing in her pocket interrupted her.

"Better check that," she said, pulling her phone out to find two texts from Becky.

The first said, *no room for error. Sorry, Al. How long is your delay?*

The second read, *Boss man wants you to call him ASAP.*

Allison groaned and put the phone back in her pocket without responding.

"More good news?" Davis joked.

"I'm an adult," she said—more to herself than to Davis. "I have an advanced degree. I'm good at my job. But every time I have to interact with my boss, I feel stupid. I shrink away."

"Then why did you stop looking for something else?" Davis asked.

"I looked. But nothing really fit," she said. Everything she found was either more stressful or less pay. Or both. So, she'd stayed where she was, hoping things would get better. They didn't.

Before she could elaborate, it was their turn to order. She asked for a small cocoa, but Davis stopped her.

"I'm not trying to mansplain anything to you. But that's the wrong drink."

"What do you mean? It's cocoa. What's wrong with cocoa?"

Davis lifted one eyebrow and shook his head.

"Nothing is *wrong* with cocoa," he said, "but we've already established that you're having a bad day."

"Yes, to put it mildly," she said.

"So, a small cocoa is not a *bad day* kind of drink. You need something.... more," he said.

"What do you suggest?" she asked with a chuckle.

"May I?" he asked, gesturing toward the woman behind the counter. "We haven't talked in a while, but I think I remember enough to get this right."

"Be my guest," Allison said. She saw his eyes dart to her phone when he mentioned them not speaking, and she felt a twinge of guilt.

"Two Chocolate-Covered Cherries. And Two Candy Cane Cocoas, please. All large. And four brownies."

He turned to grin at her, lifting both eyebrows. "How did I do?" he asked.

"Perfect," she said.

WHEN THE TWO of them returned, Davis introduced Allison to Tess and Marcus. Tess was a tall, lean woman with bright blue eyes and fair skin. She wore a thick sweater, skinny jeans, and glittery ballet flats that made her seem younger than her long grey hair might have suggested. She also had an enormous grin that she aimed right at Allison.

"Thank you for the cocoa," Allison said as she handed Tess a drink.

"Of course," Tess said. She brought the paper cup close to her face and inhaled deeply. "Oh, peppermint. Yum."

Allison handed another cup to Marcus, who then told her she *had* to visit The Cozy Cup while she was in Cherry Creek.

Marcus was shorter than his wife, and though he also wore a thick sweater, its outline suggested he was a little softer around the middle. His salt and pepper curls were short, and he wore a pair of classic, black-framed glasses.

Allison looked around at them all, smiling awkwardly. Should she go back to where she'd been sitting? Should she keep standing there?

Tess cleared some items from the seat next to her.

"Why don't you join us, Allison?"

"Umm, sure," Allison said. "That would be great." A little distraction might be good.

4

DAVIS

*D*avis watched as Allison checked her phone again. Why did he keep watching her? Maybe because he was so surprised to see her—or because she was even more gorgeous than the last time they'd been together. Her enormous hazel eyes, even when filled with worry, were still as easy to get lost in as they'd been six months ago. And much like when he'd taken her to dinner the first time, he couldn't stop thinking about kissing her on those plump, soft lips.

He shook his head, hoping to disengage himself from that dangerous train of thought. She'd blocked his number. She wasn't interested. Even if she was, she wouldn't be if she found out about his meeting with the Williams Chocolate Company.

He tried to remember some of their conversations about work. The training where they met was for client management software, but they rarely took deep conversational dives into their jobs. He learned a little about hers, and how much it stressed her out, but wasn't sure how much they talked about his job, or if Allison would even remember where he worked.

With any luck, they might avoid the topic altogether. He didn't want to increase the already awkward atmosphere if Allison realized they were competing for the same client. His meeting was Friday, not tomorrow. So, it wasn't like they were going to run into each other in the building. He was vague with Tess and Marcus about why he was in town. Mostly because he didn't want to get their hopes up. So, it was possible that his plan might work.

His eyes went to Tess and Marcus then. It amazed him that it took no time at all for the three of them to fall back into their peaceful rhythm. He was only 18 when he lost his mom and dad. There hadn't been a line of people waiting to take in a near-adult. But Tess and Marcus were there with open arms. They'd become his second parents, offering him a place in their home, and even helping him with college.

Seeing the two of them sitting together at the gate was a pleasant surprise. It made him realize just how right his decision to get back home to Cherry Creek was. If his meeting this week was a success, he could argue his case for moving back to his hometown to work from there. The chocolate company was small but growing. As a client, it would take up enough of his workload to justify being closer to the site.

The idea of coming home brought made his heart swell. But the thought of Allison and her situation caused a gnawing, guilty feeling to take root in his gut. Why did it have to be Allison he was up against? Getting what he wanted was only going to make things worse for her.

Two hours passed without an update about their flight. Davis sprawled on the floor in front of a row of chairs, examining the cards in his hand, listening to Allison and Tess chat. It was nice to see Allison free from the weight of her career worries for a little while.

But when Tess brought up the subject of work, it was as if Davis could see a dark cloud move over Allison. Her soft, sunny expression closed in on itself. Her tone became quieter, and she deflated.

"It's not an easy job," Allison said, "but there are parts of it I absolutely love. Though, I don't get to do those parts often. That's why I'm hoping this meeting tomorrow goes well," she explained. "This will be the first client I get to take the lead on. Instead of getting all the work no one wants to do, I can do the delegating for a change. I have some really great ideas. It could be a chance for me to impress my boss. Or —" she trailed off for a second and took a deep breath, "if I don't get to the meeting in the morning, I could lose my job altogether." Allison laughed, but the sound wasn't happy.

Judging by what Davis knew of The Milton Agency, he wasn't surprised to hear her say any of that. Before he ever met Allison, Davis heard the rumors about the agency she worked for. They had a horrible reputation for how they treated employees—female employees especially. It explained her work-related anxiety. What he didn't understand was why she was still there. She was too bright and too motivated to be stuck somewhere like that.

"Surely they wouldn't fire you because of a weather delay," Tess said, looking back and forth from Davis to Allison.

Davis didn't want to interject himself into this conversation, so he lifted his shoulders in a shrug. That didn't stop Tess.

"Can't you just reschedule?" Tess went on.

Davis looked toward the beeping sound that came from Allison's direction. She was checking her phone again. The furrow in her brows returned almost the instant her eyes locked onto the screen. She jabbed at it and turned the phone face-down on the chair next to her.

"Everything okay?" he asked.

She let out a breath and blinked. "That was the office," she said. "Mr. Williams is not interested in rescheduling." Her big eyes became suddenly shiny. "If I don't get to Cherry Creek in time for my meeting, that's that, I guess."

Davis looked at Tess, whose face mirrored his own worry.

"That's silly," Tess said. "I can't believe he'd be so stubborn."

Marcus put his cards down. "I can," he chimed in. "Harold Williams has been an uptight stick in the mud for as long as I've known him."

Davis laughed as he watched Tess swat at her husband's arm. Marcus was right. Davis tried to reschedule his own meeting with Mr. Williams and had received a lengthy and unnecessary lecture from the man himself.

"You never know, though," Davis said, turning to Allison. "There's still time. The snow could stop any minute." He tried his best to sound convincing. He hated seeing her so sad.

Allison nodded. "It's true. Still lots of time. I'm probably freaking out about nothing," she said.

Just a few minutes later when her phone rang, he watched her face fall once again. She offered them a quick apology and hurried away from them. The rhythm of her walk reminded him of the slow dance they shared on their first date.

"And what are you grinning about?" Tess asked him.

"What? Nothing," Davis said, looking away from Allison.

"Little crush?" Tess asked with both eyebrows raised.

"No," he said. He was trying to keep his voice low. "We had a date once. Well, two dates. It didn't end well."

"What did you do?" Tess asked him.

"Why do you assume I did something?" he asked, eyes wide.

Tess narrowed her own eyes in response. "Well, what happened?" she asked.

"I don't know," he said, knowing that answer would not be sufficient.

"Okay, well, she got sick on our second date. And I wasn't as compassionate as I should have been." He was trying to decide how much to say. It was embarrassing for Allison. He didn't want to add to that. He looked over at her to make sure she wasn't walking back.

"What if this is fate?" Tess asked. Her eyes lit up. "This could be your opportunity to ask her out again."

"No," Davis said. "This is not fate. She's probably dating someone else anyway. So, let's not bring it up, okay?"

It was clear Tess didn't want to agree to this, but he pled with his eyes until she relented. Allison was making her way back over, so he lifted both eyebrows in question.

"Okay," Tess agreed.

"Thank you," he said. "I just don't want to make her day any worse."

5

DAVIS

*D*avis had to give Tess credit. She waited almost an entire seven minutes after Allison returned to the group before beginning her interrogation.

"Was that your safe landing person on the phone?" Tess asked, à propos of nothing.

"Huh?" Allison asked, sounding confused.

"You know. The person who tells you to call when you land safely. Like, a boyfriend or husband... or parent," Tess said. She winked at Davis, as if to emphasize how subtle she was. Davis rolled his eyes. Thankfully, Allison seemed too distracted to notice.

Tess nudged Marcus with her elbow. "This one here's been my safe landing person for a very long time."

Marcus smiled. "I usually know when you land safely because I'm almost always right there with you," he joked.

Tess gave him a peck on the cheek. "True," she said. "And I wouldn't have it any other way."

Davis caught Allison staring at the two of them with a look of appreciation. He couldn't blame her. If there was ever such a thing as an ideal relationship, it was Tess and Marcus.

"It was my boss," Allison said. "So... kind of." She gave a small laugh. "He mostly just wanted to remind me about my meeting time again."

"Oh," Tess said.

"Tess and Marcus are the closest thing I have to safe landing people," Davis blurted. His cheeks warmed. It had sounded smoother in his head.

Allison nodded. She was quiet for a second before she rescued him from his own embarrassment—more than he'd done for her on their date.

She turned to Tess and Marcus. "What do you two do back in Cherry Creek?" she asked.

Tess perked up at this, and Davis gave silent thanks to the Universe. Tess loved talking about The Book Nook—the little bookshop Tess and Marcus opened after their retirement attempts. One shop quickly turned into three locations, and the two of them seemed thrilled with their new lives.

Davis felt safe with the current topic of conversation. He let out a breath and dealt the cards while Tess and Allison talked shop.

≈

"WE'RE DOING OKAY," Tess said to Allison a little while later. They'd been all over the place on the topic of the bookstore, and Davis was glad to see the subject stay off his love life, and onto something Allison and Tess seemed able to chat about endlessly.

"It's just hard to compete with the online retailers sometimes."

"It's hard, but it's not impossible," Allison said as she sifted through her cards. "You just have to see it as more than selling books. People don't go to bookstores to buy books."

"They don't?" Tess eyed her skeptically.

"No. If people just wanted books, they'd go online. They want the experience of the bookstore. The nostalgia, the smell, the joy of being surrounded by more books than they know what to do with—even in the smallest of bookstores."

"Plus, you can bring in other products," Davis suggested.

"True," Allison agreed. "Especially in small towns. Collaborate with other small businesses around you. And there are always events. Get local authors involved in signings. You said that you guys have multiple locations, so it's nothing to set up mini author tours at all of your stores. Then those local authors get invested and ask their community to come support them. That gets their community invested. People like to be a part of something. Use that in your marketing. It's not exploiting. It's about community connection." The words were just rolling off her tongue without the anxiety or overthinking he'd seen from her the last couple of hours.

Tess nudged Marcus with her elbow. "These are great ideas," she said.

"I imagine these things take a lot of time to organize, though," she said to Allison.

"Yeah." Allison nodded. "But the time investment is worth it. You could always hire someone to manage that part. Possibly even a marketing firm."

"We can't afford a firm like the ones you two work for, I'm sure. That would eat up a lot of budget," Tess said.

"No," Allison agreed. She didn't react to the part about him working in marketing, too. Maybe she hadn't heard it.

"That's not what you need," Allison said to Tess. "Your own in-house person would be best. Or a small agency. Nothing like the one I'm with. Something more niche."

Davis watched Tess and Marcus nodding at one another. Before Tess could say anything else, the announcement came over the loudspeaker. They were all officially on standby for the next flight to Cherry Creek—tomorrow morning.

Allison swore quietly and started collecting her things. Her eyes were full of tears, but there was a determined set to her jaw.

"Where are you going?" he asked her.

"I'll be right back," she said. She didn't give any of them time to reply before she was racing away from the gate.

6
____

ALLISON

"You must have a car," Allison pleaded with the woman at the counter. "You're a rental car company. How is it even possible for you to be out of cars? It doesn't need to be big or fancy. It only needs wheels. And doors. An engine, maybe. I need anything that runs to get me to Wyoming."

"Wyoming?" The woman laughed. "Honey, where do you think all that snow outside came from? It wasn't Arizona, I'll tell you that. It's been snowing up there all day. It won't matter what kind of car I've got. You're not getting to Wyoming tonight unless you plan to teleport."

Allison's heart sank. The rental car was her last idea for saving her job. She thanked the woman and began her walk back to the gate where she'd left Marcus, Tess, and Davis.

A few gates down from them, she stopped at a charging alcove to call her boss again.

"The Milton Agency," a woman's voice said. Allison pulled the phone away to see the screen. She'd dialed the office, not Mr. Milton.

"Becky?" Allison asked. "What are you still doing at the office?"

"Hi, Al. Oh, you know. Living the dream," Becky said.

Allison laughed. "Yeah, me, too," she said.

"I didn't mean to dial you, but I'm glad to talk to you instead of Mr. Milton at the moment."

"Is that because your flight was canceled and you won't make your meeting?" Becky asked.

"Bingo," Allison said. "I'm screwed, aren't I?" she asked. Becky was always straightforward with her. Allison spent many lunch breaks in her early days at the agency crying to the woman. Becky was one of the few empowering and positive people left at the company after the decade that Allison had been there.

"What am I going to do, Becky? Can you shoot straight with me? He's going to fire me for this, isn't he?"

"It's not fully decided," the woman said. Allison didn't exactly take comfort in that.

"You don't need to make me feel better this time," Allison said. "I can take it."

Becky was quiet for a moment.

"Al, I don't think there is anything you could do to change it. Even if you landed this client. And it's not going to happen tomorrow or anything. But I think it's coming. I'm sorry."

"That's kind of what I thought," Allison said. Her lip quivered.

"What am I doing here? Why am I trying so hard to be good at a job I hate?" she asked.

"I've been asking you that for years, Al," Becky breathed. "You deserve better than the boys' club they've got going on here. You're amazing. And capable. You can do better than this place."

"Thanks, Becky," Allison said with a sniffle. She wiped a tear off of her cheek. "I guess I'm about to find out if that's true."

She ended the call and sat staring at the phone in her hands. What now? She needed a new plan—not for the meeting, but for her life.

"I told myself that I was going to butt out," Allison heard someone say.

She looked up to find Tess standing in front of the bench. Allison wasn't sure how long she'd been sitting there staring off into space, or how long Tess had been standing there in front of her.

"What do you mean?" she asked the woman.

"When you were talking earlier about the bookstore—you had such great ideas. I realize this isn't any of my business, but you don't seem thrilled with your current job. And from what Davis told me about them, I don't see how you could be."

Allison stared at Tess. She wanted to say something, but she didn't know where Tess was headed with this.

"How would you feel about an interview?" Tess asked.

"For..." Allison trailed off, hoping Tess would elaborate.

"Well, I don't have official titles. You just gave me the idea a little while ago. But, while you're in Cherry Creek, you could come see our store and then meet with us about what sort of marketing you might do for The Book Nook."

"Like, as your employee?"

"Hopefully. But you wouldn't need to move if you didn't want to. You would be able to work from Boulder, or move closer to one of the other shops. We can be flexible if it looks like you're going to be a fit."

Allison blinked at Tess for a few seconds. "You want me to come interview with you and Marcus?"

Tess nodded. "And our business partners. You'd have to meet with them, too," she said. "But no pressure. If this doesn't seem like something you'd be interested in—"

"Are you kidding me?" Allison laughed. "It sounds wonderful." Was this real? Or had the work-related stress finally caused something to break in her brain?

"I'm not sure what to say," she added.

"Well, you don't have to say anything until we get to Cherry Creek. You can see the shop, and we'll talk through all of it. Assuming you're still coming," Tess said.

With the meeting being canceled, her boss expected her to hurry back to Boulder. But her tickets to and from Cherry Creek were already purchased. It wouldn't take much maneuvering to switch her return ticket, so she had some time to check things out. And going back to Boulder without at least looking into this opportunity would be insane. She knew what was waiting for her at home, but she had no idea what might be possible in this new place.

She felt her heart race again. She wanted to squeal.

"I'm coming," she said. "I need to make some calls, but I'm definitely coming."

"Great," Tess said, beaming. "Wonderful. I'll leave you to your calls. But let's all grab some dinner together. We're going to be here a while."

"I'd like that," Allison said.

Tess got up and walked back toward the gate.

"Tess?" Allison called after her. The woman turned around.

"Thank you," Allison said. "Even if this doesn't work out. I just really appreciate the opportunity."

"You're welcome," Tess said. "But I have a good feeling about this."

The tightness in Allison's stomach eased, and for the first time in ages, she felt hopeful.

7

———

DAVIS

*S*itting alone, wondering whether Allison was coming back, was becoming a trend in Davis's life. She said she would be right back over two hours ago. And not long after Allison disappeared, Tess left, too.

Did Allison find out about the meeting? Was she angry and avoiding him? He probably shouldn't care so much. But there was something special about her. He felt that the moment he met her. Even after their disastrous second date, not seeing her anymore was like having the wind knocked out of him. The few hours in the airport gave him hope that Tess was right. Maybe this was a second chance for them. But somehow, he'd blown it again.

He even called his boss to see if there was any way he could share his meeting time with Allison since the storm ruined hers. His boss laughed entirely too hard at this notion.

"I can appreciate that you're a nice guy, Davis," the older man chuckled, "but it's not great business sense to make it easier for a larger firm to go after the client you want. The Milton Agency losing their spot is a godsend. Capitalize on it."

His boss was right. But he wanted to help her. Not that it seemed to matter much now. She was probably off finding a way back to Boulder.

He let out a breath.

"You alright?" Marcus asked without looking up from his book.

"I'm fine," Davis told him. "It was a weird day."

Marcus nodded.

"It's just—she could have said goodbye this time. We didn't even have time to clear the air about how we left things six months ago, and she took off again."

"Well, there aren't a lot of flights going anywhere tonight," Marcus said. "I'm sure you'll see her again."

"She hid from me in a restaurant that had a 50-person seating capacity. She'll have no issue hiding from me in an international airport," Davis countered. "Why do I even care? She doesn't."

Marcus shrugged. "She could surprise you," he said.

"I'm not holding my breath," Davis said.

Davis was slouched in one of the uncomfortable seats, legs sprawled in the aisle, and eyes closed as he listened to music in his headphones. It wasn't meant to be. She found out about his lie of omission, or she was never that interested in the first place. Either way, he needed to stop obsessing over it. He needed to go to Cherry Creek, sign this client, and get back to life as usual.

"I should have told Allison," he mumbled.

"Told Allison what?" he heard a voice say over his music. His eyes shot open, and there she was, sitting in the seat across from him. Davis sat up and pulled the headphones off.

"Allison," he said, "I thought you left."

"I said I'd be right back," she chuckled.

"I figured you changed your mind," he said as he rubbed at the back of his neck.

"I changed my mind about a lot of other things," she said. Allison stood up and crossed the small space. She took the seat right next to him, not breaking eye contact.

"I need to tell you something," he said. "And I'm sorry I didn't tell you this before. I'm also meeting with Williams Chocolate Company. I'm pitching to them on Friday."

Allison's face was blank as she stared at him. "Yeah," she finally said. "I kind of figured."

"I'm sorry—" Davis started before her words registered. "Wait, what?"

"Davis, I remember who you work for. It wasn't a hard case to crack. Did you think you were keeping it a secret?" she asked. Her eyes were twinkling with poorly concealed amusement.

"Well, yeah," he said, sounding more defensive than he wanted to. "You didn't say anything."

"Neither did you. I figured you didn't want to talk about it."

"I'm an idiot. But I'm glad I could at least cheer you up," he said.

"Can we call it even now?" she asked. "I was an idiot, too," she said. "You know—before."

"You don't need to apologize for before," he said, turning to face her. His breath caught in his throat when he looked at those enormous hazel eyes. "You were probably mortified. I wasn't sure how to react, so I waited. And then I called and called, but—"

Allison made a face. "I didn't have my phone with me. When I finally came out to face the humiliation, you were gone."

"I didn't leave," Davis said. The words poured out louder than he meant them to. He noticed people around him staring and lowered his voice. "I was looking for you outside."

"I was so embarrassed. By the time I saw all of your missed calls, I thought you must hate me. So, I blocked you." She covered her face with her hands.

They both shook their heads.

"So, the whole thing was a misunderstanding?" Davis asked.

"I did embarrass myself in front of you and the entire restaurant," she said. "I wish that part was a misunderstanding."

"But we'd probably still be—" Davis started. "I mean, we might be —" He didn't want to assume anything. Maybe she was only being nice.

"Man, I blew that," she said. "I'm doing that a lot lately."

"I actually tried to help with your meeting," Davis said. "But my boss wasn't keen on me sharing my meeting time with you."

She touched his arm. He bit both lips to stop the smile that tried to form.

"Oh, Davis, you didn't," she said.

"I did," he wrinkled his nose. "I wanted to help."

"That was so sweet of you," she said. "I can't believe you tried to do that for me."

"It didn't work, so it hardly seems impressive."

"It is," she said. She gave his arm a small squeeze. "Trust me."

"How did your boss take the news?" he asked.

"Oh, terribly," she said. "He was even angrier when I told him I wasn't going to be back in the office until next week." She widened her eyes in mock horror.

Davis pointed out the window.

"I don't think they expect the storm to go quite that long," he said with a chuckle.

Tess walked over to them then—a tray of more paper cups in her hands.

"I got us all some teas," she said as she handed one to each of them.

"Did you tell him yet?" Tess asked Allison. An excited grin was plastered across the older woman's face.

Allison shook her head and sipped her drink.

"Oh, good," Tess said, dancing back to her seat.

"Tell me what?" Davis asked, turning back to Allison.

"She's interviewing at The Book Nook," Tess interjected before Allison could answer him. Allison gestured toward Tess.

"What?" Davis's eyes darted between the two women. "Seriously? I didn't know you guys were hiring."

"We didn't either," Tess said. "Not until Allison started talking about all her ideas earlier. After that, Marcus and I talked," she said as she nudged her husband.

"We asked her to come interview with us and our business partners," Marcus added, looking up from his book and joining the conversation.

"Wow," Davis said. He could see it. In fact, that seemed like a perfect fit.

"Would you be moving?" he asked Allison.

"Possibly," she said with a shrug. "I'm not sure yet. My options are kind of open in that regard," she said. She nodded to Tess before adding, "Assuming it all pans out, of course." Tess was still beaming.

"So, you're stuck here waiting out the delay with us?" Davis asked.

"Yep," Allison said.

They sat for a while, watching mother nature cover the runways in a thick blanket of snow while the plows worked to keep up. At this rate, they'd be lucky if the morning flight departed on time.

"How long will you be in town?" he asked.

"I fly back on Sunday," she said.

"Me, too," he said. He bit his lower lip as a fluttery feeling took hold of his chest. "If you want a tour guide, I know a guy. I'll give you his number."

"I already unblocked it," she said, bumping her shoulder into his.

"Does this mean I might be able to take you to dinner while you're in town?" he asked.

"I'd like that," she said.

"It's a date." A bolt of excited energy surged through him.

THE NEXT DAY, when the small plane finally taxied the runway, Allison was next to him. Her breathing was slow, but the furrow in her brow gave her away. He laid his hand on the armrest between them, his palm facing up in offering. She intertwined her fingers in his without hesitating.

"Thank-you," she mouthed.

He winked at her, and a shy smile pulled at her lips. Tess and Marcus were right about having your safe landing person by your side. It was better. Allison gave his hand a small squeeze, and he squeezed back. He hoped that this would be the first of many safe landings he would share with her.

EPILOGUE
ALLISON

llison's breath fogged the window as she watched the huge white flakes falling onto the tarmac outside.

"We could be here a while," Davis said, walking up behind her. His arms enveloped her, and she leaned back, breathing in his smell. His warm, scruffy cheek tickled the side of her face, but she didn't move.

"That's okay," she said. A happy sound escaped her. "I'm in no hurry."

"Me either," he said, nuzzling in to kiss her neck.

They were on their way home to Cherry Creek after spending the last few days at a ski resort—an anniversary surprise from Davis.

"Can you believe it was almost a year ago that I found you at this very airport?" he asked.

It seemed like yesterday and like a million years ago. So much had changed.

"I'm glad you did," she said, turning to face him. He moved his head but kept his arms around her. His eyes were locked onto hers, but she couldn't decipher his expression.

"What's that face for?" she asked him.

"Just thinking," he said. "If not for that flight delay, everything could have been different." He pulled away from her and took her hands into his. He brought them up to his mouth and planted a soft kiss on each.

"It's true," she said, shaking her head. "I'd have missed all of this."

"Just think how different everything could be a year from now," he said. He let go of her hands and knelt down in front of her.

"I love you, Allison," he said. He pulled a small black box from his jacket's pocket. "I want to spend the rest of my life with you. I want to keep growing with you. Laughing with you. Traveling with you. Loving you. Forever."

He held the box up, popping the top open to reveal a diamond snowflake resting on top of a simple gold band. Allison gasped. She gazed around to see the eyes of everyone at their gate on the two of them, but quickly put her own eyes back on Davis.

"Will you marry me?" he asked. His face was pleading. As if there was any question.

Thoughts of the future swirled through Allison's mind like snowflakes in the wind, and every single one of them revolved around a single answer.

"Yes," she breathed. She nodded as tears began to flood her eyes. "Absolutely, yes."

ABOUT THE AUTHOR

Elle is a coffee fiend, baker, and storyteller. She lives in Wyoming—a place where the beautiful landscapes and warm people have inspired the best parts of her writing.

She writes Sweet Romance and Women's Fiction, and she loves being able to give her readers enjoyable escapes and stories where the good guys win and/or fall in love.

http://amazon.com/author/ellebotz

https://sendfox.com/elle-botz

LOST AND FOUND IN BILLIONAIRE BAY

MAGGIE DALLEN

When a gruff sheriff meets a shy librarian in need of a fresh start, it's an explosive new beginning for them both. Literally. There are cannons involved. But they'll soon discover that Billionaire Bay isn't just a tourist destination for the rich, or a close-knit home to the eccentric locals. It's a place where hearts are lost and love is found. Welcome to Billionaire Bay...

1

SHERIFF JAKE TUCKER

*S*taring at the structure before me, I was hard pressed to say if this place was a junkyard or some sort of antique store. It definitely wasn't a fort, no matter what the flag waving above it said.

Fort Lobo was spelled out in big red letters against the bright yellow flag. Call me crazy, but when I'd heard the word 'fort' I'd thought I'd be heading to some relic from the revolutionary war, or maybe a remnant of the Native American population in this part of the Northeast. I had not expected a beaten and battered old log cabin that looked more like a unabomber hideout than a historic landmark.

I shut my car door behind me and took in the serene, sunny setting. Aside from the collection of old crap that was scattered all over the lawn, the little clearing in the woods was downright idyllic. I glanced around for any sign of squatters or kids up to no good.

Nothing. Just this quiet, peaceful little hut with its proud, if inexplicable flag.

Not for the first time since pulling up to the property, I had to wonder if this was the dispatcher's idea of a joke. As the new sheriff in town, some pranks and hazing were to be expected.

I took a few steps toward the log cabin with its wraparound porch, my hand hovering over my holster just in case. You know what they say, you could take the cop out of the city, and blah blah blah.

The serene silence seemed to be taunting me, and I had half a mind to look back and see if one of the deputies was waiting to jump out from behind one of these towering pine trees that lined the clearing, laughing at the gullible city cop.

A disturbance at the old fort, the dispatcher had said. *Shots fired.*

My hand dropped to my side and I shook off the paranoia that had kept me from being shot more often than I cared to count. I had to remind myself of where I was. Two weeks in and I was still adjusting to my new town and to a drastically different pace of life. 'Shots fired' in this county meant kids shooting up old cans or hunters who'd strayed off the sanctioned hunting grounds.

But even so, my heart was pounding in my chest as I approached the front door slowly, eyeing the tabby cat that rounded the corner of the porch with the same suspicious glare it was aiming at me.

From the quilts hanging over the rocking chair beside the door, my gut said that the owner of this bizarre establishment was some little old lady. The tabby cat purred as it rubbed against me. Correction. A little old *cat* lady.

"Hey there, cat," I murmured. A smile tugged at my lips as I reached out a hand to knock. There must have been some mistake. The only disturbance here was a hungry kitty.

The moment of peace ended with a bang.

Literally.

A booming sound cut through the silence and sent my heart into my throat. At the same time, the screen door flew open and a woman came bounding out, moving so quickly she ran right into my chest.

A woman? Yes. A little old lady?

Definitely not.

She bounced back off my chest and my instincts had me reaching out to grab her by her arms before she could land flat on her butt. Those same instincts had my hands tugging her close as her head tipped back and her blue eyes widened in surprise.

I had just enough time to register a click—a sensation that the world had just shifted on its axis. Like the world as I'd known it would never be the same. At the same time, I took in the thick auburn hair, the sweet, wide-eyed beauty of the girl next door...

The woman who'd just stolen my heart.

I shook off the crazy thought as she tugged out of my grip, an apologetic smile curving her lips as she took a step back, her gaze darting toward the back yard of this small cabin. "I should really—"

Boom!

We both jumped and the woman started to race toward the back. "Grandma, cut it out! The police are here."

I wasn't the police. Not technically. But now didn't seem to be the time to point that out. "Ma'am, what is going on here?"

She turned back to me with a wince, not slowing her steps as we reached the back of the cabin. "Please, don't call me ma'am."

Another boom and I stopped short, my mind refusing to believe what my eyes were telling it. "Is that a *cannon*?"

"Yes, sir." Her gaze dropped to my badge and her eyes widened. "Er, yes, Sheriff."

"What is that—" I pointed to a little old white-haired lady who was dressed in a robe and fluffy slippers, dancing gleefully around the antique weaponry with undisguised glee. "What is she doing?"

My voice was impressively even, my tone calm—bored even, considering the cannon fire.

"They're blanks," the redhead was quick to say. As if I might have missed the fact that the woods of coastal Maine hadn't exploded around me.

I met her gaze evenly. "It's illegal."

She stopped mid-stride, her nose crinkling up in confusion. "Is it?"

Was it? How the heck was I supposed to know? Cannon fire was not exactly high on the priority list at the New York police academy. I kept my expression blank and ignored the question. "It's a disturbance of the peace."

Probably. If it wasn't, it ought to be.

She winced and a pleading look entered her eyes. "She's not hurting anybody."

We both looked around at that and the serene peace of the neighboring woods seemed to make her point for her. I just barely held back a weary sigh. "She has to stop, Mrs.—"

"It's miss," she said, a pink tint coloring her cheeks and making me forget entirely about the cannon to my left. "I'm not married."

I was rendered temporarily speechless by that admission.

I blinked in dismay. It might have been a while since I'd been attracted to a woman since my wife left me—us. She'd left our daughter Daisy just as surely as she'd left me. But I couldn't recall ever being so distracted, so disarmed, so...so *overwhelmed* by the sight of a woman that I could forget about a three thousand-pound piece of artillery.

There was distracted and then there was bewitched. This was definitely the latter.

Her lips curved into a sweet, welcoming smile as she lifted a hand to her forehead in a salute. "Ms. Eleanor Perkins, head librarian, at your service."

Her cheeks turned a deeper shade of red as she closed her eyes and gave her head a shake, muttering, "Gah! That was too weird" under her breath. By the time she'd opened her eyes again, her grin had turned to a grimace. "Most people just call me Ellie."

"Ellie." I repeated the name, not sure what I intended to say next.

Luckily another explosion interrupted the silence. We both looked to the old woman who was whooping with delight as she danced around like she was performing her own pagan ritual right there in broad daylight.

"Ms. Perkins—" I started.

"Ellie. And this is my grandmother, Norah."

"Ellie, Norah is a danger—"

"She's eccentric," she said quickly, her eyes wide and pleading. She grimaced. "And it's possible she forgot to take her medication." Once more she muttered under her breath, "Again."

I heaved a sigh. This *was* all part of the hazing I'd expected; I'd bet my life on it. No doubt everyone in this town knew about Norah and her cannon.

Ellie's lips curved up and her smile seemed to say she was thinking the same thing. "You're new around here, huh?"

I gave her a rueful smile in return. "What gave it away?"

She laughed and the sound... Oh, that sound.

I had to stop myself from clapping a hand over my heart. The sound of her laughter—it was like something from my best dreams. A reminder of all that was good and sweet and kind in the world. Her laugh reminded me of why I'd dragged Daisy out of her old school in Brooklyn and brought her to this small town.

"I heard there was a new sheriff in town," she said.

I puffed out my chest. "You're lookin' at him."

She laughed again and I was as good as dead. Stick a fork in me, I was done. *You're lookin' at him?* Lame. So lame. I could practically hear Daisy's voice mocking me.

"Good," she said with a little bob of her head.

"Good that I'm new?"

Her cheeks turned pink as she shrugged. "Good that you're here."

I had a feeling that the only word to describe the grin that spread across my face was 'goofy.' I was grinning like a fool and there was nothing I could do to stop it.

Another boom interrupted one of the more awkward exchanges I'd had in my entire adult life. This was definitely the most nervous I'd been since adolescence. In fact... Holy crap. Were my palms sweating?

She turned to face her grandmother and then back to me. "I'll take care of this. I promise."

"See that you do." I glanced over at the exuberant dancing. "Do you, uh...do you need a hand?"

She shook her head with another sweet little smile that tugged at my heart. "No, but thank you. She'll calm down soon enough."

"All right, in that case..." I made no move to leave. I should. The threat had been assessed and neutralized. There was nothing more to do here. Except... "Ms. Perkins—"

"Ellie," she corrected.

I had to swallow past a nervous sensation I hadn't felt in ages. "Would you have dinner with me tonight?"

She stared. She stared long and hard, until I was so wracked with nerves I couldn't think straight.

"I can't." It came out abruptly and her cheeks turned a brilliant shade of red.

"You can't," I repeated slowly, as if repeating it might help decipher what she meant.

"I mean, I *can*," she said. "But I...I can't."

"Uh huh." I started backing away, feeling more like a fool with every inch of ground I put between us as I headed back to my car.

She could. But she didn't want to. It didn't take a genius to understand that. And, of course, Ellie was too nice to just say 'get lost.'

"I-what I meant to say was—" She took a step forward and then stopped, clasping her hands together in front of her and twisting them together. "I just...can't."

"It's fine." I forced a smile. "I'll see you around, Ms. Perkins." I went to climb into my car, turning back to see her standing right where I left her.

Still blushing. Still wringing her hands.

And still the most beautiful sight I'd ever seen.

2

ELLIE

I didn't move from my spot, not even when the inn's bartender Bailey set a glass down on the bar next to my head with a loud thud. "It couldn't have been that bad," she said.

Even without lifting my head I groaned at the memory. Grandma had tired herself out and fallen fast asleep after dinner, which meant that I was free to get out of that house before I went stark raving mad with regret.

Bailey patted my back. "It was a nasty divorce, hon. Don't kick yourself for not being ready."

I lifted my head, my arms still folded on the bar before me. "But I *am* ready. I want to be ready."

Bailey's long blonde hair was pulled back in a low ponytail, her pointed chin set as she eyed me far too seriously. "Maybe you are ready," she finally declared.

I let out a little sigh of relief at that verdict.

She lifted her hand to point at me and the bar rag she'd been using to wipe down some glasses went sailing in one smooth motion over her shoulder. "You might be ready to move on, but I'm guessing you're ready for a rebound, not the real deal."

The real deal. My mind conjured up an image of the handsome hottie with the five o'clock shadow, the kind dark eyes, and the epic jawline. Another pathetic whimper escaped. He was the real deal, all right. Then the rest of her words hit and I flinched. "I don't want a rebound."

"Sure you do." Bailey ignored any further protests as she headed toward the other end of the bar, where two guys I'd gone to high school with were nursing their beers.

Even for a Tuesday night it was slow in here, and I hated that. For Bailey, but for Mina, too. On cue, the back door of the pub was kicked open and Mina came in juggling two boxes. Short as she was, Mina temporarily disappeared behind those boxes as she set them down on the end of the bar, only her dark curls in view. "What did I miss?"

Bailey grinned at me. "Ellie here just met our fine new sheriff."

"Oh yeah? What's he like?" she asked as she opened the first box and started to unpack cocktail napkins and empty salt shakers. The owner of this inn, and one of the last Billinghams left in Billingham Bay, Mina was almost always in motion. Small but fiery, she had a seemingly endless supply of energy.

"He seems nice," I started.

Bailey leaned over the bar, resting on her elbows. "And hot."

"And hot," I confirmed with a sad sigh that had Mina's brows hitching up in question, her hands stilling for once as realization dawned.

"You like a guy," she breathed, her eyes wide. She and Bailey exchanged a look that made my stomach twist all over again.

"I didn't say that."

"You didn't have to," Mina said. She'd been teasing me since kindergarten that I was easier to read than a picture book. "So, what happened?"

Bailey answered first, her smile wide and gleeful as she hissed, "He asked her out."

"No way."

"Way," Bailey said with a laugh. "He asked her out to dinner like a proper gentleman. Isn't that right, Ellie?"

They both turned to me. "What did you say?" Mina asked.

"I, um, I..." I groaned and let my head fall back down on my arms. "I said I can't."

Their silence had me tensing. I readied myself for words of comfort or sympathy. These two had been through it all with me during the divorce and if anyone knew how much it had wrecked me, it was these two.

"Well, I for one think it's for the best," Bailey said.

I lifted my head to see her crossing her arms, her mind made up. "Like I said, you need to ease into dating again, and the sheriff is not your rebound guy."

"How do you know?" Mina asked.

Bailey rolled her eyes. "Because he's a local." She looked from me to Mina and back again. "I've told y'all my rules. They exist for a reason."

Despite the fact that Bailey had been living here in Billingham Bay for years now, her voice still held a hint of that Southern twang from growing up in the South. Mina and I exchanged a look. Bailey and her rules. I supposed as a drop-dead gorgeous bartender she had to play by these rules of hers to keep the lines from being blurred. But for me...? Well, I wasn't exactly swatting men away with a stick, and as the town's head librarian I wasn't drowning in a sea of dating opportunities, either.

"Look," Bailey said, all no-nonsense as she leaned over the bar. "I am all for you moving on from Tad the Toad, but if you're going to have a rebound you're best sticking with the rich tourists over at the club, not a townie who'll be sticking around for the long haul and who you'll have to face every dang day at the post office and the grocery store, or when you're heading home from work or—"

"I think she gets the point," Mina said. Then she sighed. "And Bailey, could you please not send customers to our competition?"

Bailey's nose crinkled up. "Those bigshot snots who run the yacht club are not our competition, Mina. They're the enemy."

I let out a quiet laugh at her disgust, but it was the truth. Mina was the latest in a long line of Billinghams to run the Inn at Billingham Bay. Her ancestors were the ones to build this town way back when and this inn, with its stately columns and its dark, wood-paneled pub, was the bedrock of this town.

But awesome history or no, the town took off in a whole new direction decades ago when the yacht club was built on the other side of the bay.

The yacht club and the crowd it drew were what had tourists nicknaming this little town Billionaire Bay. It had turned what was once a small fishing community with a small, quaint downtown into a booming tourist town.

These days our little hamlet was split down the middle between the rich and powerful and...well, us. People like me, like Mina and Bailey. Like Ernie and Troy down at the end of the bar. Normal people.

Us normal people loved the inn, but the yacht club had definitely stolen its thunder and as it grew over the years to include a fancypants spa and a five-star hotel and Michelin-rated restaurants, the more it drew the type of people who wanted high class, not quaint and charming. Poor Mina's inn was definitely overshadowed.

"You know Ellie wouldn't actually become a regular at the club," Bailey said. "I just meant if she wants a fling, that's her best bet."

Mina let it drop, turning to me instead with her eyes arched high. "Is that what you want? A fling?"

I opened my mouth to say 'no' but the truth was... "I don't know."

That was the sad state of things. I truly didn't know what I wanted. It had been a year since the divorce was finalized. It was time to move on. But I had no idea how. I had no clue what a normal relationship looked like anymore, not after years of living in a toxic marriage with the guy who'd seemed so perfect when I met him in college and then...

Well, I'd already spent way too much time trying to figure out what had gone wrong. If he'd been the one to change so drastically or if I'd just been blinded by my infatuation that I hadn't seen the selfish, manipulative toad beneath the Prince Charming façade.

I sighed as I leaned back on the barstool. "It doesn't matter anyway," I said. "I blew it." In a few quick and efficient sentences, I told Mina what had happened, ending in my complete and utter fail.

Mina's cute little pixie features crinkled up in sympathy. "You... can't?" she repeated.

I nodded. "That's what I said."

That was *all* I'd said. I slapped a hand over my eyes and just barely held back another groan. *I can't.* No explanations, no excuses.

"Just out of curiosity," Bailey said. "Why can't you?"

I dropped my hand, my gaze baleful. "I don't know. I panicked."

"Because you liked him," Mina confirmed.

I fidgeted in my seat, my cheeks growing warm even though I knew my friends weren't judging me. "I don't know him well enough to know if I *like* him-like him, but..."

"But you were attracted," Bailey said.

I nodded. "That's an understatement." But that was the gist of it. The grown woman that I am went into full-blown panic because I was attracted to a guy.

Nope, no baggage here.

"I've seen him and his daughter around town," Bailey said with an approving nod. "He's definitely hot in that tall, dark, and rugged kind of way."

"I've seen him around, too," Mina said. "They stayed at the inn for a few days while they were waiting for the rental house near Main Street to be ready."

Daughter. Interesting. And he was renting a house downtown? I filed away these facts. It was a testament to what a homebody I was that I hadn't already heard every bit of gossip about the town's newest resident.

"He seems...*nice*," Bailey said, a hint of confusion tinting that one word. Even after my disaster of a marriage and the bitter divorce that followed, my level of jadedness couldn't hold a candle to Bailey's.

"He did seem nice," Mina added. They were both watching me, waiting for me to speak.

"Yup. Nice," I agreed.

Mina rolled her eyes and Bailey laughed as she reached out to nudge me. "So? If he's so handsome and nice, what's your holdup?"

I shook my head. "I wish I knew. I just panicked at the thought of a date. I haven't dated since..." I didn't finish that sentence. They both knew how long it had been since I'd dated, and saying it aloud just felt too pathetic. Let's just say, I was what people called 'a late bloomer.' My ex-husband had also been my one and only boyfriend. "I don't know how to date."

"So..." Mina's expression turned too innocent as she toyed with the straws she'd just unboxed. "Are you just never going to date again then?"

"I didn't say that," I hedged.

Bailey's gaze was filled with sympathy. "I hate to tell you this, El, but unless you want to be alone for the rest of your life, you're gonna have to get past this fear you have."

I frowned. "I don't have a fear." It was lie and we all knew it. I blew out a long breath. "Okay, fine. Maybe men scare me."

"Not all men," Mina pointed out.

"No, just the handsome ones who...look at me." There was some truth there. I'd always been awkward and shy around men who made my pulse race. But honestly, no one had ever looked at me the way the sheriff had. Just thinking about it made my breath catch and my chest ache. It hadn't just been a look, because you couldn't feel a look. But I'd *felt* his eyes on me. Just as surely as if he'd reached out and touched me, I'd felt his gaze and it had made me feel like my world was upside down, like I was toppling head over feet.

It was disorienting, to say the least.

"Okay, so you panicked. No big deal," Mina said, her tone so matter of fact.

"No big deal?" I widened my eyes. "He lives here. In Billingham Bay. Like Bailey said, I'm going to have to see him on a regular basis."

"Exactly," Mina said with a little smile. "Which means you'll have plenty of chances to try again."

Bailey was nodding enthusiastically. "Clearly he was into you if he asked you out. All you have to do is explain that you want a do-over."

I found myself nodding along with Bailey even as my insides withered and died at the thought of having to explain that I could in fact date, but that I'd said no out of panic.

That should be a fun conversation.

My mind called up a warm smile and crinkled-up eyes.

It would be worth it. I took a deep breath and flattened my hands on the bar as the door to the pub opened behind me. "Okay, yes. That is what I'll do. Next time I see him I'll explain that I misspoke and that I would actually very much like to go on a date with him."

They were both smiling at me now with pride and...something else. Something mischievous that set me on edge.

"Excellent," Mina said, her gaze shifting to whoever it was that had walked in. "Then you can start right now."

Bailey's grin was nothing short of wicked in the face of my wide-eyed horror. "Go for it, champ. Now's your chance."

I turned slowly, warily. Surely fate wouldn't be so cruel as to force two run-ins in one day. My heart started thudding against my ribcage.

I wasn't ready. I couldn't do it.

But there he was. Tall, dark, and rugged, just like Bailey had said. And he was looking right at me.

"Hey there, Sheriff. Take any table you like," Bailey called out, already reaching for the menus as I sat there. Frozen.

Crap. Not again. *I will not panic. I will not panic.* I repeated the words as a mantra as my pulse raced and my palms grew clammy. But I did manage to slide off my barstool without falling over so...that was something.

The teenaged brunette beside him was eyeing me with open curiosity as I drew close, her gaze friendly. She had her dad's eyes—warm and welcoming as I reached them. "Hi, Sheriff," I said.

It came out like an airy whisper. I'd gone from being the town librarian to its very own Marilyn Monroe impersonator.

His smile was slow and crooked, tilting up a little higher on the left. He had a dimple on that side, too. Well, now...that was just too much. My mouth was too dry and I realized that I was blocking the way between him and the booths that lined the back of the century-old pub.

"Ellie, meet my daughter, Daisy. Daisy, this is the—"

"Lady with the cannon," Daisy finished, her face lighting up with amusement.

"That's me," I managed. The lady with the cannon.

"That's so cool," she said with a grin.

I looked from her to her father, but he just shrugged. Was it cool to have a crazy grandmother who regularly liked to reenact the revolutionary war in her backyard? Not in my humble opinion, but then again, I wasn't sixteen. "She's eccentric," I said.

"Not senile," I added quickly, though no one had asked. "Everyone always assumes she's senile. She's not. She's always been like that." And I'd always loved her for her eccentricities. But judging by their matching looks of surprise, I was pretty sure I was looking just as crazy. "I'm babbling," I said, shuffling back a step to get out of their way.

They didn't move. Daisy looked to her father, her brows arched high as some unspoken communication passed between them. I took another step back, keenly aware of my friends watching me, of Jake's eyes on me, but what he was thinking I couldn't say. "Okay, well, I'll just..." *Die of humiliation. Bury my head in the bar for another hour or so. Or maybe I'll just—*

"Have dinner with us," he said quickly. He cleared his throat and glanced down at his daughter who was grinning and nodding at me enthusiastically.

"Oh, I-I—" *I can't.* I swallowed down the words and heard Bailey hissing behind me.

"Do it. Do it—*oof.*" I didn't have to look to know that Mina had thrown something at her to make her quit.

The silence that followed was crushing.

Daisy lowered her voice to a near-whisper. "Awkward, party of three, your table is waiting."

We all ignored her, I couldn't have looked away from the sheriff's eyes if I'd tried. He looked so earnest, so understanding, so...hopeful.

I took a deep breath and forced a smile. "I'd love to."

3

JAKE

It didn't take a genius to see that this wasn't going to be the best date of all time. First, my teenage daughter was acting as our chaperone, sliding her gaze between me and Ellie as she sipped on her soda, looking for all the world like an audience member at some interactive live theater experiment.

Then there was the fact that her friends weren't even pretending to do anything but eavesdrop as they hung out quietly at the end of the bar closest to us. Even the two guys at the other end of the bar had stopped talking about sports to watch the first date going on behind them.

Not that this could really even be called a date...what with Ellie refusing to speak and all.

"Have you lived here long?" I asked, the latest in a litany of conversation starters that went nowhere.

She nodded.

"Your whole life?"

She nodded again, her eyes were still wide as saucers. I really needed to stop asking yes-or-no questions.

"Dad, stop already."

I turned to Daisy, who was hissing at me from her side of the booth, as if Ellie might not be able to hear with the foot of table between them. "What?"

She rolled her eyes and I was reminded once again that my daughter was definitely a teenager. And sadly enough, right now I needed her help. I was doing something wrong, that much was obvious, but I had no idea how to make this awkward interaction less...awkward.

Daisy flashed Ellie a smile before muttering to me, "You're using your cop voice. Cut it out."

I glanced across at Ellie and saw her duck her head, clearly trying to smother a smile as a blush snuck into her cheeks.

I rubbed the back of my neck. "I have a cop voice?"

Daisy snickered. "You sound like you're investigating Ellie for murder."

"Oh." I looked from Daisy to Ellie with a rueful grimace. "Sorry, I..." I cleared my throat. Ah heck, this was embarrassing. "I haven't done this in a while."

"Talked to another human being?" Daisy asked sweetly.

Ellie tipped her head down farther and I could have sworn I saw her shoulders shake with a stifled laugh. I arched my brows in Daisy's direction. "You're hilarious."

"And you have no game," she said.

I'd just started to let out an exasperated sigh at being called out by my own daughter on my first date in years when Ellie broke the silence with a laugh that made my heart do funny things.

I couldn't even remember to give my daughter a warning glare. In fact, if Daisy had asked me right this minute I might have even caved on letting her drive my truck, which she'd been pestering me about for a month.

She'd gotten Ellie to laugh, and for that I was forever in her debt.

"So," Daisy said, her tone way too casual. "If you two are gonna be here for a while, can I go meet up with a friend over at the club?"

I whipped my head around to face her. "The yacht club?"

She held my gaze evenly, not giving an inch just the way I'd taught her.

"How do you have a friend who hangs out at the billionaire's club?" I demanded, forgetting for a second about my date who was watching us closely, and not without a good deal of amusement. "Since when do you even have friends? We just moved here."

"Yeah, well, unlike you I know how to talk to people." Her smile softened the words and made Ellie snicker into her hand. "These guys aren't from around here, but until school starts they're the only—"

"No. No way." I held up a hand before she could start again. "If these guys are just passing through town on their parents' yacht, do you really think they're the kind of company you should keep?"

She held my gaze evenly, months' worth of conversations and lectures passing between us in the silence that followed.

"We have a chance for a fresh start here, kiddo," I added softly.

Daisy relented with a sigh. "Okay, fine. Then how about I go back to the house and start unpacking the stuff in the garage." She was already shifting toward the edge of the booth.

"You haven't even eaten."

"I'll heat something up at home."

Ellie leaned forward, her eyes wide as she addressed Daisy. "You don't have to go. I didn't mean to intrude."

Daisy's smile was sweeter than I was used to seeing these days. She liked Ellie, I could tell. The fact that she didn't come back with her typical snarky sass only confirmed it. "You're not intruding," she said, leaning forward as if about to let Ellie in on a secret. "Trust me, I have more than enough quality time with my father."

She took a step back, clapping her hands together as she raised her voice so everyone could hear. "This right here?" She waved a hand between us. "This is just too awkward for life. Seriously. It's hard to watch. So, if you'll excuse me..."

She was out the door and we were alone. At least now Ellie was smiling, though, and the sight of that smile had my chest tightening in a way that would be alarming if I'd already eaten the bacon cheeseburger I'd ordered from the bartender. But as it was...

I had a hunch this sensation had nothing to do with cholesterol and everything to do with the fact that for the first time in my life, I felt like a nervous schoolboy. I hadn't even felt this way with Daisy's mom, and we'd been married.

"I'm sorry," Ellie said abruptly.

I arched my brows. "For what?"

"For being so awkward." She gestured toward the door where Daisy had disappeared. "She's right. I just..." She wet her lips and I tried to keep my eyes on hers or risk looking like a creeper staring at her mouth. She drew in a deep breath and let it out in one long rush of words. "I got divorced recently. Well, a year ago. This is the first date since then and I'm really nervous." She drew in another breath but before I could say anything, she continued, "Unless I'm wrong and this isn't a date. Maybe you're just being nice and I read too much into it and—"

"Ellie." I stopped her with a hand over hers.

Her eyes were ludicrously large as she stared back at me. "Yes?"

"This is a date."

"Oh." She let out another long exhale but she didn't try to pull her hand away and I took that as a good sign.

"And it's been a long time since I've been on a date, too," I said. "Between my job and taking care of Daisy on my own...there hasn't been much room for a personal life."

She nodded. "I can't imagine being a single parent."

I lifted a shoulder. "I'm lucky I got a great kid."

"I never had kids." Her expression didn't alter but I saw the sadness in her eyes. I had this urge to tell her it wasn't too late, that she still had her whole life ahead of her but...who was I to tell her that? I was still basically a stranger, or the closest thing to one.

So instead I changed the topic. "So, are you staying with your grandmother then?"

She nodded quickly, her eyes brightening. "Yes, just for the time being. Until I get back on my feet." She pursed her lips. "Which, I probably should be back on my feet by now, right? I mean, it's been a year."

I found myself fighting a smile, even though my heart went out to her. Still, she was downright adorable when she pursed her lips like that. Almost as cute as when she was nervous and babbling, or smiling and laughing, or... Let's face it. I was smitten with each and every facet of this lovely, unique woman. "I don't think there's a time limit on that sort of thing," I finally said.

She gave me a grateful smile as if that was the answer she'd been hoping to hear and I just barely refrained beaming with pride.

"But anyway..." she said, trailing off and smiling up at the bartender who dropped off the burgers and fries we'd ordered with a wink I didn't miss. "Um, anyway, I've been staying at Fort Lobo for the past year while I save up for a house of my own."

"Fort Lobo," I said, remembering that flag that had flown overhead as the cannon blasts echoed off the hillside. "Where'd that name come from?"

Ellie grinned as she chewed, her eyes dancing with laughter and memories. "It was supposed to be Fort Lo-*Fo*, but my grandmother had a bit of a mishap with the embroidery." She mimed taking a swig from a bottle as she said it and a laugh escaped that I hadn't heard come out of my mouth in months. *Years.*

I let myself slide back in the seat, some of that nervous tension morphing into something lighter, sweeter, and filled with more promise than I could bear. "Okay, I'll bite," I said as I crossed my arms and watched her smile widen into an outright grin. "What did Fort Lo-*Fo* stand for?"

"Fort Lost and Found," she said, pride clear in her voice. "My family has been in these parts since forever and there's a bit of a legend about this bay and the woods that surround it."

"What's that?" I leaned forward like she was doing so we were both resting on our elbows, the space between us growing more intimate with every breath.

"Well, according to Grandma, if a stranger is drawn to Billingham Bay, it's because there's something here they need to find." She leaned back with a wry smile. "Of course, she said that before Billingham Bay became a tourist destination."

I laughed as I picked up a fry. "Well, I definitely didn't come here as a tourist. And I'm certainly not one of those billionaires who gave this town its new nickname. So, I guess your grandmother would say I was one of those strangers who was drawn here."

"She probably would," Ellie agreed with a slow nod. "She'd say you came here to find something."

"A rocking chair?" My brows hitched up as I thought back to the yard filled with old furniture and relics from the past.

Her laughter touched on some part of myself I'd forgotten about, or maybe I'd thought it was long since gone. The romantic in me, the optimist I'd been before I'd married too young to the wrong woman and my youthful notions of what it was to be a cop destroyed by reality.

Her laughter made me feel younger and lighter than I had in ages.

She tipped her head from side to side as though considering the question, her smile teasing. "Maybe not the rocking chair. But there was a nice afghan at the shop with your name written all over it."

"I see," I said, unable to keep the laughter from my voice. "So, according to your grandmother, while I thought I'd just come here to escape the big city and give my daughter a different kind of life, I was actually missing something vital and had to come to Billionaire Bay to find it."

"That's what Grandma would say." She leaned forward and dropped her voice to a whisper. "But don't let the locals hear you call it Billionaire Bay. It's kind of a sore subject."

"So I've gathered." My grin faded as her gaze met mine and held. Time seemed to stop. My world felt like it was being realigned as I sat here, the ground beneath my feet shifting to make way for this new world that lay ahead. "Would your grandmother have some insight on what exactly I came here to find?"

"Well, according to Grandma..." Her smile was slow and sweet. "This is a place where hearts are lost and love is found."

He chuckled at the way she said it, with a sing-song tone that said it was a phrase she'd heard a million times. "So I came here to find my soul, huh?"

She shrugged. "Or lose your heart."

I smiled but I couldn't quite bring myself to join her in laughing. Was that what happened when I'd gone to the old cabin in the woods?

My heart pounded in my chest as her gaze met mine. I'd found something, all right. And as for losing my heart?

I reached across the table and took her hand in mine.

I thought it was safe to say that my heart was officially lost.

4

ELLIE

I stared down my Grandma with my hands on my hips. "Repeat after me." I held up a hand to tick off the list she already knew by heart. "I will not embarrass Ellie. I will not tell her date any humiliating stories from Ellie's childhood. I will not bring out a photo album to illustrate said humiliating stories from Ellie's childhood. I will not—"

"Good grief, girl, I already promised I'd be on my best behavior," Grandma said, rolling her eyes as she rocked in her chair which was still on the lawn, since it was technically for sale, though we rarely got any real customers out this way.

"Okay," I said, smoothing my skirt with clammy palms as I took a deep breath. "Okay." I could do this. I could do this. I could—

"Am I allowed to tell him how you threw up all over your wedding dress because that story—" She was laughing too hard to finish.

I tilted my head to the side, my sigh filled with exasperation. "Grandma, please."

She held her hands up, still laughing. "Ellie, you know I would never do anything to hurt you—"

My snort of disbelief was loud and unladylike and it made Grandma laugh all over again. "Oh please," I said. "You used to love to tell Tad every embarrassing story in the book."

"That's because I didn't like Tad, honey. I never did." Her wrinkles creased even farther with her unapologetic grin. "The only good thing he brought to the table was being fun to torment. Goodness, how that boy could blush."

I shook my head in exasperation. I shouldn't laugh. It would only encourage her. And yet...

I burst out laughing at the memory of Tad's toad-like face whenever my grandmother taunted him with inappropriate anecdotes and jokes. "Fair enough," I finally managed. "But please don't do that to Jake, he's...different."

My grandmother's expression gentled, the creases softening. "Well, of course he is. He came all this way just to find you. I like him already."

I opened my mouth to protest, or at the very least plead with her not to say stuff like that in front of Jake, but the sound of a car pulling up the long winding drive distracted me. I turned to watch his car pull up.

It was bad enough that I'd babbled about all that legend nonsense over our first unofficial date. It would be a disaster if Grandma started in on her theories about love and fate.

Two days had passed since our dinner at the inn and Grandma had spent every minute since waxing poetic about my destiny and his. Our fate, which Grandma believed was already written in the stars.

"Good evening, Ellie," Jake said as he climbed out of his truck. Gone was the sheriff's uniform, but he looked just as dashing in jeans and a buttoned-down shirt. He nodded politely to Grandma. "Ma'am."

"Don't you 'ma'am' me," she said. But she was grinning—she always had been amused by good manners. "You can call me Norah."

He nodded again but his gaze was once more back on me and the admiration and appreciation I saw there transformed everything around me. Or maybe I was transformed. The woods had never felt more magical and even the scattered junk and treasures on the lawn seemed to be laced with romance.

"You look beautiful," he said softly.

"And that's my cue," Grandma muttered, rising from the rocking chair. "You take care of my granddaughter, you hear?"

"Yes, ma'am. And if you could steer clear of any cannons and artillery for the remainder of the evening I would greatly appreciate it."

Her cackling laughter followed her into the cabin as she shut the screen door behind her.

That left us alone.

"I'm so nervous," I admitted on a long exhale as he climbed the steps to meet me.

"Me too." His smile was so sweet it made my toes curl.

"What are you nervous about?" I asked when he was so close I could reach out and touch him.

"I'm afraid that this is too good to be true," he said quietly. "I'm afraid that I'll ruin it, or I'll drive you away with these crazy emotions you've brought to life in me." He took a deep breath. "I'm afraid of losing what I've only just found."

The wind and the stars and the trees behind him seemed to be working in harmony around us to weave a spell of magic. It made me want to speak nothing but the truth, to get past these nerves and these fears to find all the happiness that I deserved.

I reached for his hand and the heat of his skin burned me. It warmed me, from the inside out. When he tugged me closer and I was in his arms, it felt as natural as sliding under the covers on a cold night or wading into the bay on a bright summer day.

"What are *you* nervous about?" he asked.

I swallowed thickly as each fear came to the surface and I did my best to untangle them. "I guess I'm nervous that I'll repeat old mistakes." Saying it aloud made it disappear like smoke drifting into the night air. "I need to learn how to trust myself again, how to trust my heart."

He nodded, his gaze serious now, but no less tender. "We can take this slow," he said. "As slow as you need."

I smiled because...he would. I knew that about him. In fact, being here in his arms, I felt like I knew *him*. And the way I felt right now, this wasn't a mistake, and it surely wasn't a repeat of anything.

This was a first, in every way possible.

"I don't know that I *can* take it slow," I said. I went up on tiptoe, loving the way his arms wrapped around me so gently. I loved the way it felt like home. "I think I may have already lost my heart."

He leaned down and pressed his lips to mine, the touch so perfect, so tender, so sweet. He pulled back just far enough to meet my gaze and cup my cheek in the palm of his hand. "Well, that is good news, because I'm positive I've found mine."

ABOUT THE AUTHOR

Maggie Dallen is the author of more than fifty sweet and lighthearted romance novels. She writes in a variety of romance subgenres, including small-town contemporary, regency historical, and young adult. For a free sweet romance novella, sign up for her monthly newsletter at http://eepurl.com/bFEVsL

THE CAY TO MY HEART

LYNETTE PAUL

Ocean kayaking guide Camila Maas may find more than she bargained for when treasure hunter Max Walker hires her to guide him to the white sand beaches of Treasure Cay.

1

———

I whipped my Wrangler into the half-circle drive of the historic Golden Mangrove hotel. I hated being late, especially to pick up crotchety old treasure hunters. They never appreciated young kayaking guides like me wasting a precious moment of their retirement.

As I hopped out, I scanned the tourists heading into the bright Florida morning. Mr. Walker should be easy to spot. We'd only exchanged emails, but I knew his type—wide-brimmed hat, khaki shorts pulled over the waist, enormous metal detector in hand. My dad had been one of those. He'd wasted all his life and half of mine, dragging me around the Keys hunting for treasure. It's why I knew these islands better than anyone, but I preferred eco-tourism to treasure hunting. I rarely guided clients like Mr. Walker. He'd gotten my name from an old family friend. Someone who'd known Dad well enough to call me Cammie instead of Camila. I'd left that nickname behind long ago, along with a lot of other things I'd rather forget.

Relieved that I didn't see Mr. Walker impatiently waiting for me, I texted to let him know I was the ponytailed blonde next to the red Jeep with oversized tires and two kayaks strapped on top. Then I leaned against the passenger door, careful not to get any mud on my shorts, and watched for him. The usual valet gave me a nod as the early morning golfers headed to their tee times, and the families with kids too little to sleep in made their way to the nearest coffee shop.

The only person who stood out in the crowd was a ruggedly handsome guy leaning against the stone entryway. Sipping from a stainless canteen with a well-worn backpack at his boots, he gave off an experienced adventurer vibe that was out of place in the tourist district. He pushed his sunglasses on top of his tousled dark hair to check his phone, and I got a glimpse of his piercing, gray eyes. *I wouldn't mind taking him on a private tour.*

He squinted up into the morning light and caught me staring. I quickly looked away, but too late. We'd made eye contact, and he took that as an opening. He strode confidently toward me. Any other morning, I'd gladly give this guy directions, but today I didn't want Mr. Walker showing up and thinking he didn't have my full attention. He'd pre-paid a premium price to be guided on an overnight to Treasure Cay.

I greeted the stranger with a polite but brusque, "Can I help you?"

"Are you Camila?" His deep voice matched his brawny build.

"Yeah." My mind spun, trying to place him from a previous kayak tour. I definitely should remember someone like him.

He stuck out his hand to shake. "Max Walker."

Oh no. Treasure hunters my age might be rarer than the old cantankerous ones, but they were far more arrogant—sure that fortune and glory waited for them just around the next sandy cove. If I'd known he was one of those, I probably wouldn't have agreed to take him out. But here we were, shaking hands while the Florida sun beat down on us and roasted the asphalt under my sandals. The only way to make today better was to get out on the water.

THE PUT-IN BEACH wasn't far down the highway, and the wind blowing through the open-top Jeep saved me from having to make small talk till we got there. But once we'd parked and started unloading gear, it was time to play the part of friendly guide.

"Are you enjoying Florida so far?" I asked as I released the ratchet straps that locked down the kayaks. It was the same question I asked every out-of-state client. The answer told me a lot about whether they were set on soaking up some fun in the sun or they were more the to-do list kind of vacationer.

"It's a little more humid than Colorado, but I can't complain about the sunshine." Max reached up for one of the ocean kayaks, pulled it easily off the roof rack, and set it down gently on the sand in front of the Jeep.

"Thanks." I wasn't used to clients lugging their own gear. Of course, I didn't often get tourists that looked capable of climbing a mountain on a moment's notice. "Are you staying long?"

"I wish I could, but I can't take much time off. I'm headed back Sunday."

A career guy. I wouldn't have pegged him for that. "What do you do?"

"I'm a fly-fishing guide."

That explained the whole strapping outdoorsman thing he had going. It did not explain why he'd taken a weekend off in the middle of the summer. It was my busiest season. It must be his too. "Isn't this a pretty busy time of year for you?"

"Yeah," he said with a sigh. "But this is important."

Right. Because whatever treasure he thought he'd find on Treasure Cay would be worth way more than a weekend's worth of guiding fees and tips. That's the same false hope my dad had chased for years, and the only things he'd ended up with were a broken marriage, an estranged daughter, and a pile of debt, and that was all before the cancer took him. But I was professional enough not to lay any of that on Max. I stopped myself from muttering *good luck with that* and reached for the other kayak.

Max grabbed the opposite end and helped me guide it down onto the sand. I thanked him again and started unloading our dry bags and other gear from the back seat. Without any instruction from me, he double-checked that the dry bags were folded over and sealed. Then he strapped them onto the back of each kayak like he was the one who'd done this a thousand times before.

"You said in your emails that you had some kayaking experience?" I phrased it as a question. A lot of guys lied about that when they were making their reservations, either because they wanted to impress their fellow kayaking companions or were trying to impress me, but Max obviously hadn't been making that up.

"Paddling, yes. I've done my share of whitewater in the Rockies, but ocean kayaking, never. That's why I needed a guide. I don't know my way around here," he said with a sheepish grin.

Clearly, he found it a little embarrassing that he would need a guide, but at least he was smart enough to admit it. Whitewater experience meant he knew how to paddle hard and steer well, but ocean currents acted totally different than rivers. Where we were going, you could get lost and potentially swept out to sea if you were overconfident and failed to read the ocean right.

I warned him about that in my abbreviated safety briefing. He obviously knew a thing or two about kayaking. I wasn't going to bore him with how to tighten his life vest, but I wanted to emphasize that I was the expert here—that's what he was paying me for. The way he'd unloaded the kayaks and strapped down his gear, I could tell he was used to being the guy in charge. I didn't want him to forget that I was the guide today.

He nodded along with all my advice, and once we'd launched the boats, he stayed close and followed my lead in the water. The arrogant pushback I'd expected from him was nowhere to be found, but we also hadn't started looking for treasure yet. That would likely bring out the brash traits I'd come to know and despise in all treasure hunters.

Until then, we might as well enjoy a peaceful paddle out to the cay. Max was a natural. With his strong arms, he could have powered through his strokes, but he didn't. He braced his bare feet on the footrests, so his legs were at the best low angle for a long, relaxed stroke. Then he used the leverage of his full body to glide the paddle smoothly through the water. He had no problem keeping up with me, so I set my preferred pace instead of the leisurely tempo I used to corral tour groups.

We'd make Treasure Cay before lunch. I'd insisted on an early meetup because I'd assumed I'd be plodding through the water with an old man for most of the day. Max and I practically sailed over the waves. I even took him the direct route instead of winding through the maze of calmer waters around the other islands on the way. The open ocean was more challenging, but judging by his broad smile, Max didn't mind at all. With the morning sun on our faces, the ocean breeze in our hair, and the occasional splash of cool water across our legs, we paddled toward our destination without the usual chitchat I felt obliged to carry on with other clients.

When Treasure Cay came into view, a twinge of disappointment tempered the exhilaration of the last couple of hours. Once we beached our boats, the treasure hunting would begin for Max, and the fun would end for me. Unless I could convince him to try other, more remote islands. If he enjoyed the ocean kayaking as much as it looked like he did, there were plenty of places we could reach today that would keep us on the water longer.

"Are you sure you want Treasure Cay?" I asked as I slowed my kayak in the shallows. "Despite the promising name, I don't know that there's any treasure left here. It's been pretty picked over through the years. You're a strong paddler. We could venture on to less explored places."

He looked at the white-sand beach in front of us and then on to the string of islands beyond like the idea tempted him, but when he turned back to me, I saw the answer already on his face. "I can't. Today, it has to be Treasure Cay."

I shrugged. "Your choice." Of course he didn't want to explore further. For some reason he was convinced there would be treasure waiting for him on this island. Just another deluded treasure seeker.

We swung our legs over the side of the kayaks and jumped into the water to pull our boats past the high-tide line on the beach. Loaded down with gear, the kayaks were heavy, but Max slid his across the sand as easily as if he were still gliding it through the water. As we brought them to rest out of reach of the waves, I unstrapped the small cooler I'd packed with food and held it up. "Hungry?"

"Definitely," he said as he unclipped his vest and slung it over the front of his kayak. "That worked up an appetite."

Before I could tell him to grab his kayak seat, he was already unhooking it to use as a beach chair. I did the same, and we leaned back in the shade of the palm trees to eat our turkey sandwiches. Nothing gourmet. I wasn't that kind of guide, but Max didn't seem to mind the simplicity. He was even genuinely excited when I offered him trail mix for dessert. He might be a misguided treasure hunter, but at least he was a low maintenance client so far.

"Where do we set up camp?" he asked as he washed his lunch down with a long drink from his canteen.

I pointed to a flat spot not far behind us in the shade. "Tents under the protection of the trees, and I'll stack some wood I brought for a small fire on the beach later."

"Does it get that cold?"

"Not at all. It's just for ambience," I admitted. Then, realizing that might sound like I was trying to set a mood for him, I quickly added, "Most clients expect that kind of thing. You know, stereotypical bonfire on the beach."

He glanced up to the blue sky like he could already imagine the magnificent field of stars that would appear overhead later. "Fire under the stars. That's one of my favorite things."

"Mine too." As I watched him and wondered how much we might actually have in common, he turned his captivating gray eyes toward mine and held my gaze long enough to quicken my heart.

I bounced out of my chair and cleared my throat. "Well, if you want to get started looking for treasure, I'll set up camp."

"I'll help." He jumped up and followed me toward the kayaks.

"No need. I've got it." I did this all the time. I didn't need help. And I certainly didn't need to be attracted to a treasure-obsessed client. I had a rule about treasure hunters, not to mention clients, and I was not about to break promises to myself just because this guy was enticingly handsome and adventurous.

Max shook his head. "Blame it on my day job, but I've spent too many years as a guide to feel right about letting someone else set up camp alone. It'll go faster together anyway."

I couldn't really argue with that. I would have felt the same if our roles were reversed, and he was right—with two of us, setting up camp went quickly. Usually on overnights, I sent the clients swimming or lounging on the beach to get them out of my way while I popped the tents and organized everything, because I'd learned the hard way that "help" from clients meant everything took longer. Not with Max, though. He knew what he was doing. Except he'd never used sandbags to anchor a tent before.

"Useful trick," he said as he filled the last of the empty bags with sand. "If we only had more sand in the mountains, I wouldn't have to hike around with tent stakes."

I couldn't imagine a couple pounds of metal in his pack would slow a guy with Max's build down, but I said, "Island living has its benefits."

"So I'm learning." He flashed a smile as he handed me the full bag to tie the tent down.

I pretended to ignore the flirtation in that look and focused on securing the last tent strap. Then I stood up and dusted the sand off my hands. "That does it. You can treasure hunt free of guilt now."

"Great. Time to find the good stuff." He reached for his boots and backpack.

I wanted to tell him there was no "good stuff" to find on this island, but he would discover that soon enough. I'd planned to leave him to it, but as he laced up his weathered boots to go tramping through the trees, curiosity got the better of me. I wondered what tale could have convinced this otherwise seemingly levelheaded fly-fishing guide to travel all the way to the Keys to spend the night digging through the sand on this particular island.

"Do you have a plan?" I asked.

"Nope," he said as he hefted his pack onto one shoulder. "But I have a map."

I laughed in disbelief. "You have a treasure map?"

"Drawn by hand." He pulled a small paper napkin out of a side pocket of his pack and offered it to me.

I eyed him skeptically, but I took the napkin. On it were some nearly indecipherable pen scratches—some hardly visible squiggles and some that had poked through the flimsy material. In the center of the drawing, a mess of curved arcs topped two parallel lines. "Hand drawn all right. Is that supposed to be a tree?"

"Yep," he sounded surprised. "You must be a treasure map expert."

He had no idea. My dad's trailer had been wallpapered with old maps and lost treasure research. None of them had ever led to the promised chests of gold and jewels, though.

"There's supposed to be a tree carved with G+H inside a heart." He pointed to a crudely drawn heart on the napkin with two letters that could have been G and H marked beside it.

This wasn't a big island, but palms and other trees covered its untamed interior, not to mention the mangroves clustered on the far side. He could spend a week staring at the trunks here and not find one with a heart carved into it, assuming it was ever there at all. "And there's a treasure buried under this tree?"

"Fifty paces out." He indicated a 50 marked at the edge of the napkin next to an X.

I bit my lip, not sure how to tactfully tell him how unlikely that was.

"I know," he said, reading the hesitation written on my face. "Following a map scribbled on a hospital napkin sounds crazy, but I have to try."

I'd seen a lot of far-fetched bids for riches buried in the sand, but this was the first hospital-napkin map I'd ever held. That didn't change his odds of finding anything, though. Deathbed "revelations" rarely led to anything but wasted time and empty pockets. I handed the map back to him. "It doesn't sound promising. That's for sure."

"Promises to at least be an interesting afternoon." He tucked the napkin back into his pack and took a few steps toward the trees before he turned to me. "Want to come along? See if there's anything to find?"

I hadn't been out looking for buried treasure since the last time I'd gone with Dad. That had been a long time ago, and it had not ended well. But something about Max's invitation intrigued me. There was a hint of skepticism in his hope. I'd never met a treasure hunter with a healthy sense of doubt.

With our camp set up for the night, I had nothing else to do and no real excuse to stay behind. Besides, he'd proved to be easygoing company so far. I could hang out with him while he failed to find his treasure. I grabbed my water bottle and said, "Lead the way."

～

As we spent the afternoon surveying the trees of the island for any sign of a carving, Max ran his hands almost reverentially over the trunk of each one we passed. I'd never met anyone else who did that. I'd picked up the habit as a kid exploring these islands. Dad used to say you can get to know a place if you listen to the trees. I'd sat for hours, nestled in the sand, listening to the palms sway in the wind. They were my constant, along with the ever-present chirping of Dad's metal detector. I preferred the quiet companionship of the trees.

So did Max, it seemed. He wasn't a typical treasure hunter. He seemed more interested in exploring the island than actually locating the X on his map. No serious treasure hunter I'd ever known would have taken the time to eat a leisurely lunch and help me set up camp when we'd gotten here or spent the hours since asking me about the ecology of the place and how I'd gotten into kayak guiding.

Then it occurred to me—this was his first time. Max lacked the typical irritating qualities of a die-hard treasure hunter because he hadn't yet found that first trinket that would give him the addictive rush to seek more and more. It made me sad for him. I wanted to tell him to stop looking now, get back in the kayak, and enjoy the rest of his time in Florida. Quick, before obsession could take hold.

"Whoa." Max stopped ahead of me.

I'd been too deep in thought to notice what he had, but now I followed his gaze up one of the twisting branches of a gumbo limbo tree. Just above his head, the curves of a heart carved into the bark met around the initials G+H.

"I don't believe it," I said.

"Me either." Max chuckled. "I mean, I wanted to, but—"

"X never marks the spot," I finished for him.

"I guess that remains to be seen." He pulled the napkin map out again and lined the top up with north, where we could see the waters in the largest cove of Treasure Cay dipping into the island. Then he pointed off toward the denser vegetation in the east where the X on the map indicated 50 paces out. "According to our precise map here, we start looking over there."

I'd been sure we'd never find the carved tree in the first place. Maybe beginner's luck was on Max's side today. Although, when we counted fifty paces farther inland to the east, we ended up near a thicket of jumping cactus, so maybe he didn't have all the luck. I warned him against brushing too close to the plants. They were notoriously hard to pry off once they latched on.

Max eyed the cactus carefully and kept his distance as he reached into his pack for a small hand-held metal detector. He pressed the power button, and the familiar piercing whine followed by intermittent mechanical chirps interrupted the rhythmic swish of the wind through the palms.

Max winced at the unpleasant noise.

"There should be a silent mode," I offered. "Then it only beeps when it detects something."

"I think I saw that in the manual." He dug into his pack for the instructions.

"May I?" I asked with an outstretched hand.

"Please, be my guest."

I took the small orange wand in hand and recognized the brand immediately. My dad had always carried one of these in his pocket— just in case. I tapped the power button twice, and the chirping stopped.

Max breathed a sigh of relief. "Much better."

I handed the detector back to him, and he knelt down to run it over the sand. The poor guy would spend all day hunched over or walking on his knees to keep that small detector close enough to the ground to find anything. If he'd been the egotistical treasure hunter I'd expected, I would have gladly left him to it, but he had been too nice up to this point to relish his discomfort.

"I'll be right back," I told him and headed for the kayaks.

I came back a few minutes later with one of the paddles and a bungee cord. Max had dug his first hole with the foldable entrenching tool he'd brought along and unearthed his first old can.

"Treasure already." He laughed as he proudly held up the rusty hunk of metal.

"Congratulations."

"Uh, do I want to ask what those are for?" He nodded to the paddle and bungee in my hands.

"Lend me your metal detector for a minute, and I'll show you."

He handed the wand over without question and watched me with curiosity as I pressed the release to split the paddle in two. Then I strapped the wand onto the pole end of the paddle with the bungee and handed the makeshift contraption back to him.

"You're a genius," he said as he waved the wand over the sand without having to kneel.

"Hardly. Just something I picked up over the years." Dad and I hadn't always had the best equipment to work with. I'd learned to improvise early.

"I didn't think you were the treasure hunting type."

"I'm not. That was my dad."

"Did he have any luck?"

"You've ridden in my Jeep. What do you think?"

"That you love your job." He gave me a knowing grin and went back to sweeping the detector over the sand.

The handle I'd rigged up for him wasn't perfect. He had to stop every five minutes and press the button to turn the wand back on, but it beat crawling around in the sand all afternoon.

He found his share of cans and bottle caps as he searched in a wide circle around the tree. At first, each new find amused him. His eyes lit up when the metal detector let out its distinctive whine, and he'd stop and dig down. Then he'd pull a piece of rusted junk out of the earth, and we'd toss it in the trash bag I'd brought along for collecting them. I'd drop it at the recycling center when I got back to town.

"If nothing else, I'm cleaning up the island," he joked.

His good humor about finding absolutely nothing was refreshing. We passed the time between metal detector hits exchanging stories about our respective guiding adventures. He even offered to take me fly-fishing if I ever found myself in Colorado. I was horrible at any kind of fishing, but for a minute, I let myself imagine getting tangled up in fishing line with Max, and that didn't seem like such a bad thing.

As the afternoon wore on and the blue sky faded to dark twilight, Max's enthusiasm waned. With no sign of any treasure, he grew less entertained by the whole adventure and more discouraged with every shovelful of empty sand.

I convinced him to take a break for the bread and cheese I'd brought for dinner. We ate perched among the roots of the heart-carved tree. The sound of the waves on the shore and the hum of the evening insects filled the silence instead of our conversation. I doubted he'd run out of funny guiding stories, but the light-hearted mood from the afternoon had turned somber as we finished our meal by the light of our headlamps.

My strong suspicion that he'd caught treasure fever was confirmed when I tried to get him to take a nighttime kayak through the mangroves.

"It's beautiful under the stars," I said. "This time of year, the water lights up with an amazing bioluminescent show. It's really something to see."

He shook his head and picked up his shovel without looking at me. "Another time. I should keep going tonight."

There it was. The misplaced drive I'd seen ruin men my whole life. I don't know why I'd expected any different from him. I guess the way we'd made each other laugh all afternoon had convinced me that he was something more than the usual treasure seeker.

"Suit yourself," I said as I packed up the remains of our picnic. Before I left, I added, "I'll be on the beach if you need anything." I was still his guide after all, but that didn't mean I had to sit up and watch him dig pointless holes all night.

~

WHEN I GOT BACK to the beach, I lit a small fire. I'd hauled the wood all the way here. I might as well enjoy a crackling fire before I turned in for the night. I left my kayak chair under the trees and sat down in the sand like I used to do as a kid. The soft, cool sand under my legs always calmed me. I shouldn't need that tonight, but I was more agitated than I should have been about Max choosing to keep hunting in the dark.

It wasn't any of my business. My business was guiding him here and back safely. What he wanted to do with his time on the island was totally up to him. Even if it was something as completely foolish as thinking he was about to strike it rich if he just dug one more hole.

I watched the fire slowly burn down to embers, thinking about all the nights I'd spent like this with Dad. When I was younger, I'd lain on these beaches, staring up at the stars wishing that I could be anywhere else. But as I'd gotten older, these islands had kept me. There was something about being out here that settled me. Maybe it was because it's all I'd really known, but nothing ever felt as right as being on the water and the sand.

"This is nice," Max said from the edge of the trees.

I jumped at his unexpected voice and turned to see him walking toward the fire. His steps were slow now, much less confident than when we'd met in front of the hotel. He was covered with sand and disappointment.

He collapsed cross-legged next to me by the fire and let a moment of silence draw out between us before he said, "Sorry I didn't take you up on the night kayak."

"It's no big deal. Most people get excited about it."

"It does sound pretty awesome. I just got caught up in the hunt."

I murmured another "yeah." I wasn't sure what he wanted me to say to that.

"Anyway, I wanted to thank you for bringing me out here."

I tried to wave off the gratitude. "It's my job."

"You didn't have to, though. Alan told me I was taking a chance asking you to guide me. He said you never take treasure hunters out, but he also said you were the best."

"Alan is prone to exaggeration." But the thought of him bragging about me to Max made me smile. Alan had known me since I was a kid. He'd been one of Dad's closest friends. They'd hunted treasure together for years, but I hadn't spoken to him since Dad's funeral. That's when he told me he was giving it all up and retiring to the mountains.

"I've heard some of his tall tales," Max said. "But you live up to his descriptions."

I knew well the stories that Alan could tell about me, but I hoped the ones that had reached Max's ears had been the flattering variety. Then, thinking about Alan, a rush of concern flooded through me. Had he been the one in the hospital bed drawing the map? He'd always been like a favorite uncle to me. I'd never forgive myself if he died like Dad, without a goodbye. I swallowed the lump in my throat and asked, "Is he the one who drew you the map?"

"No," Max said. "He's still as feisty as ever. He moved into a cabin by mine a couple years back and never misses a day fishing on the river. He was probably out there today all by himself."

"Sounds like Alan." I relaxed as the panic subsided. I'd make a point to call him this week. It was past time to reconnect.

"My grandma drew the map," Max volunteered. "She raised me, and well, it's important to her, so it's important to me. I told her I'd give it my best shot. She doesn't have much longer."

"That's why you had to come now." That's why he'd taken a long weekend in the middle of his busy season—for her.

He nodded as he stared into the embers.

"I'm sorry," I said. I knew the acute pain of losing someone who had meant so much. At least he could do this one thing for her. If Dad had reached out and asked me for one last thing before he passed, I would have done it without question. But neither of us had been brave enough to take that chance.

"Before I left, she told me that hope might be all I found here, but that alone would be worth the journey."

I remembered the hope he'd had this afternoon with each new ding from the metal detector. Maybe that's all his grandma had wanted to give him—a weekend away in the Florida sun, not worrying at her bedside. "If that's true, then maybe you already found your treasure, Max."

He lifted his eyes to mine then, and I saw something more than hope there. Longing filled his gaze, and I didn't know how to read that. Was it the unfulfillable wish for her health, the desire to find her buried treasure, or was it for me?

My eyes flicked almost involuntarily to his lips, and I knew what I wanted against all my better judgment.

He leaned toward me, and my heart skipped as my mind raced. Was I really going to kiss my treasure-hunting client?

A chirp sounded on the sand between us and answered that question for me.

Startled, we both looked down to see that the metal detector had fallen from his pocket onto his steel canteen. He must have taken it off the paddle after I'd left and tucked it into the pocket of his board shorts for safekeeping.

I picked it up, pressed the power off, and handed it back to him. "You might want to save your battery. And we should probably get some rest."

"Yeah. Rest." He ran a flustered hand through his hair.

I told him goodnight and retreated into my tent.

He was still sitting by the dying fire, staring out at the ocean, when I zipped my tent flap shut and went to sleep.

A HIDEOUS ELECTRONIC whine woke me the next morning. I opened one eye. Pink light crept over my tent, and it was like I was ten years old again, waking to the sound of Dad's metal detector. I knew better than to get involved with anyone who would get up before dawn to look for treasure, however good their reason might be. I was glad I hadn't made the mistake of kissing Max last night.

As I crawled out of my tent, he called me over to the shore. "Hey, check out what I found."

He was crouched net to the water, rinsing something in the waves. When I walked over, he placed a shiny, wet piece of eight in my palm. The telltale cross was still visible on the coin's worn surface.

"Are you kidding me? Where did you find this?"

"In one of the many holes I've dug."

I flipped the coin over in my hands. I couldn't believe he'd found something. But that's how it always started. One small find led to a lifetime of needing to find more, and that was the trap.

"You okay?" Max asked.

I handed the coin back to him. "Yeah, just... I need coffee."

"I made some. Hope you don't mind. You've got the same setup I have back home." He nodded toward the fire he'd stoked and the kettle sitting next to it.

I thanked him yet again, made my way back to the fire, and poured myself a cup. I couldn't believe he'd found a piece of eight on this island. At least he wouldn't leave empty-handed. Now he had some actual pirate treasure to take back to his grandma. I liked imagining that would give them a moment of cheer in what had to be a hard time for both of them.

I dug a couple of blueberry muffins out of my stash and offered him one. "Nourishment?"

"Coffee doesn't count?" He grinned as he pocketed the coin and joined me by the fire for breakfast.

I shook my head. "Personally, coffee is the base of my food pyramid, but I can't have hangry tourists on my trips."

"I'm not used to being the tourist. I could get used to this." He unwrapped the muffin and breathed in deep as he surveyed the beautiful morning around us. The brilliant pink-orange sunrise glistened on the waves lapping at the beach.

Lulled by the tranquility of the moment, I said, "You'll have to book a longer trip next time." Then I inwardly winced at myself. That sounded too much like I was inviting him back.

"I'd like that," he said.

I would too, but I wasn't about to say that out loud. I did not want to admit how much I was drawn to this particular treasure hunter. I took another sip of coffee and cleared my throat. "No rush this morning, but I'll get us packed up so we can make your flight later."

"Okay," he said with a hint of confusion in his voice. "Do you want help, or do you mind if I keep at it?"

"You go find some more treasure. I've got this." I managed not to sound let down that treasure fever had already replaced his insistent chivalry from yesterday.

He disappeared into the trees with his shovel and metal detector as I started disassembling the tents and repacking the kayaks. I'd done it so many times before. My hands made quick work of it while my mind replayed the last day with him.

I'd loved racing through the water with him on the way to the island and listening to his guiding stories and answering his many questions about living on the coast, but that was all a distraction. I was doing the right thing, keeping him at arm's length. He lived halfway across the country, and he'd only come here for treasure, which he'd now found. I could send him back to his life without complicating things for either of us. That's the way it should be.

Once I'd given myself that mental pep talk and finished packing up camp, I went to find him. Despite my reservations about treasure hunting, I was curious to see if he'd unearth anything else before we left.

Max had picked up right where he'd left off last night, completing his survey of a large circle around the marked tree about 50 paces out. This morning, he scanned the ground and dug into it with renewed enthusiasm. His excitement at finding the piece of eight had obviously overcome the disappointment of finding nothing yesterday.

As I watched him dig up another old can, I heard my dad's voice in my head, "That's a piece of history, right there." In hindsight, maybe Dad wanted the same things for me that Max's grandma wanted for him—a little hope, a little appreciation for the islands. That's what Dad had actually given me. That's why I was still here. I couldn't believe it'd taken me this long to see it.

"Think we have time for one more?" Max asked as he tossed the can toward his backpack to carry out with us. "It'll at least make me feel like I completed the circle."

I didn't even check the time. I'd paddle as hard as we needed and drive him to the airport myself if I had to. I'd give Max and his grandma the time I'd refused to give my dad at the end. "Of course. One more."

He walked a couple feet farther until the metal detector gave off another high-pitched whine. I knew it was likely another piece of trash, but my heart beat a little faster as Max laid the detector to the side and started to dig again. I wanted him to find another coin to take back to his grandma.

After removing a few scoops of sand, his shovel hit something solid. The shock on his face echoed my own. He knelt down and dug around the object with his hands. I peeped over his shoulder just in time to see the top of a metal box revealed. I dropped to my knees to help clear out around it. I hadn't been this excited since I'd found my first Spanish pillar dollar as a kid.

With some effort, Max managed to free the box from the sand, and we could see it was an old mid-century ammo canister, firmly latched shut against the ages.

Max stared at it in awe as he sat back in the sand. "I didn't think it would actually be here."

"I don't think the Spanish had those in the eighteenth century. Are you sure that's the treasure you wanted?" Curiosity pulsed through me. What kind of treasure had his grandma drawn him a map to?

Max carefully pried the latch open and peered inside. He pulled out a stack of yellowed envelopes, a brittle dried red rose, a couple of old photos, and a small velvet jewelry box. "It's more than I could have asked for."

I didn't understand. This was not at all the treasure I'd thought he was after. "What is all this?"

"A whole life lived and buried." He passed me a photograph.

In the black-and-white picture stood a striking young man in uniform. He bore an uncanny resemblance to Max, and on his arm was a beautiful woman with Max's same bright smile and dark hair.

"My grandparents," he said. "After she lost him in the war, she didn't have anything to bury, so she came to their favorite cay to bury what she had of him."

That brought tears to my eyes. "That might be the most beautiful, tragic love story I've ever heard about buried treasure."

"Theirs was a love story for the ages," Max said with admiration. "From the moment they happened across each other on this beach, they knew they were destined to be together. They used to sneak back out to Treasure Cay to steal time for themselves away from the world. This was their place, but without him, it hurt too much to be here. She moved away soon after his death. But now, all these years later, she can't stand the thought of leaving the memories of their life together lost in the sand after she's gone. So, I promised that I would do my best to find this treasure for her."

"You came all this way for that." He wasn't treasure obsessed at all. He had to be the sweetest man I'd ever met. He'd traveled across the country during his busiest season and paid me to guide him out to this island so he could stay up most of the night digging holes in the sand for the chance to bring her these lost memories. "Max, that's... I'm speechless."

He cradled the dried rose in his palm and then placed it gently back in the box. "She deserves nothing less."

I laid my hand on his arm as I handed the photo back. "She's lucky to have you."

"I'm the lucky one," he said. "She taught me everything I know about how to live. How to love."

He looked up from the mementos as he said the last, and this time I knew the longing in his eyes was for me. He drew my lips to his with a warm, sandy hand at the nape of my neck. I had no hesitation now about leaning into this treasure hunter's tender kiss. Like his grandparents before us, our love story began on Treasure Cay.

EPILOGUE

Max and I pushed our kayaks into the dark waters under the canopy of stars. Last year, he'd said, "another time," when I'd offered to take him night kayaking. It turned out he was a man of his word. Tonight, I would get to show him one of the best treasures in the Keys.

Our headlamps bounced over the waves on the moonless night as we moved through the rolling waters at a leisurely pace. When we were together, there was no cause for hurry. The whole world could rush by. We had everything we could want already. We'd spent the last year exploring the love we'd fallen into that first weekend on Treasure Cay.

I'd visited Colorado a couple of times, and I'd gotten to meet his grandma before she passed. She was a lovely woman who had embraced me as though I were her own granddaughter. Max had taken me fly-fishing where I'd gotten so tangled in my line that we'd nearly fallen into the river in fits of laughter and settled for cuddling up by the fire under the blanket of twinkling stars in the mountain sky.

Max had helped me reconnect with Alan, and we'd stayed up long into the night telling stories about my dad. It was the closest I could come to introducing Max to Dad, but Alan's hearty approval of Max made me feel like Dad would have given his as well.

Every time Max visited the Keys, which was as often as he could get away from his guiding business for a few days, we paddled out to Treasure Cay together. But tonight was the first time the conditions were right to see the bioluminescent light show among the waves.

Toward the back of the island, we switched our headlamps off and floated in the star-filled darkness. Then, as we rounded the growth of mangroves, the water lit up underneath us. With each stroke of our paddles, the glow rippled through the waves.

Max watched quietly in amazement for a few minutes before he spoke. "This was worth the wait."

I loved seeing him so taken with the natural beauty that had always enchanted me. "I'm so glad you could make the trip to see it."

"I've been thinking about making it a longer trip."

My heart leapt at that. I'd give anything for even one more day together. "How much longer?"

"Well, I've been asking around, and there's plenty of opportunity for fishing guides in Florida."

I almost dropped my paddle. "You're thinking of moving here?"

"That depends on your answer to my next question."

Max tucked his paddle under the tie-downs on his boat. Then he opened the dry storage console at his knees and removed a small velvet jewelry box. I'd seen it before. The ring box we'd found with his grandma's buried treasure. It had contained her engagement ring, a beautiful princess cut ruby set in a delicate gold band.

Max reached for my paddle to pull my kayak over to his. My heart pounded in my chest as our boats bumped together on the waves. When we were sitting side by side, he clasped one hand over mine on the paddle. Then he opened the box to reveal his grandma's ring.

"Will you spend the rest of your life in these islands with me?" he asked.

"I'll spend the rest of our lives anywhere with you." The Keys might be the only home I'd ever known, but now I knew that anywhere with Max would feel like home.

He carefully took the ring from the box and slipped it onto my finger. Then I pulled him in for a long kiss as the waves gently rocked us. Together, we'd found our treasure.

ABOUT THE AUTHOR

Lynette Paul is the author the Cherish Cruises Sweet Romances series and the forthcoming Cherish Adventures Sweet Romances series. She loves the romance and adventure of exploring new places and meeting interesting new people. Inspired by her travels, she nestles into her book-filled study with a cup of coffee and three cuddling cats and writes about love stories at sea. Come along to find your heart's desire in a warm ocean breeze.

www.lynettepaul.com

RISKY COWBOY

ELANA JOHNSON

She's tired of making cheese and ice cream on her family's dairy farm, but when the cowboy hired to replace her turns out to be an ex-boyfriend, Clarissa suddenly isn't so sure about leaving town...

Will Spencer risk it all to convince Clarissa to stay and give him a second chance?

1
___

Clarissa Cooper could only stare as she stood at the window that looked out onto the farm. "This can't be happening," she said, but she'd know that gait, that cowboy hat, and that pair of broad shoulders anywhere.

Just because she hadn't seen Spencer Rust face-to-face in a while didn't mean her memory had been wiped clean. The real question was: What in the name of everything buttery was he doing here?

"This has disaster written all over it." Just like that time she'd tried to make black licorice, cream, and sugar play nicely together. Clarissa could usually get any flavor to marry well with the ice cream base she'd perfected at her family's dairy farm, but that concoction had been her one great failure.

At least in the kitchen.

She'd failed plenty of other times, in plenty of other ways. She had a half-finished business degree, a culinary certificate she hadn't used yet, and four long gashes on her heart that proved her failure with men, almost like a tiger had taken a swipe at her for not mixing catnip into a delicious frozen treat.

Spencer Rust had almost been the cause of one of those gashes, and she wasn't going to let him have another chance to derail her future.

Her father opened the barn door across the parking lot from the

Cooper & Company Shoppe, which Clarissa had been running for the past eight years. He and Spencer went inside, and at that moment, Clarissa's heart started beating again.

Stupid thing didn't realize it was supposed to do that all the time, and that it couldn't stall at the sight of every tall, dark, and delicious cowboy.

She turned away from the window and picked up the clipboard she'd dropped at the sight of Spencer. The store was closing in ten minutes, and she needed to do the inventory. Then she'd know what cheeses to make in the morning and which products she needed to put on sale before they expired.

Cooper & Co. didn't use any antibiotics or hormones, and that meant their completely organic milk and other dairy-based products couldn't sit in coolers forever.

She checked the refrigeration units and made checkmarks on her clipboard, finishing just as the tinkling bell on the door sounded. She put a smile on her face, because if Clarissa knew anything, it was that the customer was always right.

They didn't care if it was closing time, or if she'd just lost a boyfriend, or that yet another chef hadn't returned her inquiry for a job at their restaurant.

"Afternoon," she drawled before she could turn to see who it was. "Oh, hey, Daddy."

The smile faltered as her dad stepped aside and Spencer Rust himself filled the doorway. Those dark eyes had not changed, and they devoured her as easily as they ever had.

"Afternoon, Clarissa," he said, touching the brim of that stunning cowboy hat. "What's the flavor of the day?"

Dark, dreamy cowboy, she thought. She turned toward the menu board, which she hand-lettered every morning with that day's specials. "Looks like it's Rocky Road."

She turned back to Spencer and found he hadn't taken his eyes from her. "Sounds amazing," he said, and Clarissa found herself agreeing with him.

Wait. She didn't agree with Spencer Rust, and the argumentative side of her almost said the ice cream would certainly be disgusting.

Then she remembered she'd made it. "Waffle cone?" she asked, and it sounded like she'd gargled with one.

"Yes, please," he drawled in that sweet-as-honey Texas accent, making her heart kick out extra beats, the idiotic organ.

"Daddy?" she asked.

"I want the butter pecan, baby."

"In a cup," they said together. Clarissa smiled at her father and got busy scooping the treats.

As she rounded the case to deliver the ice cream to the two tough cowboys, she asked, "What are you doin' here, Spencer?" She shot a quick look at Daddy but didn't let it linger for long, because the floor was uneven in the shop.

"He's your replacement," Daddy said.

A strangled noise came from her mouth, and Clarissa's feet caught on the uneven tiles. She yelped as she stumbled forward, managing to lift the cup with the butter pecan high enough, but the motion required her to smash the waffle cone with all that delectable chocolate ice cream right into Spencer Rust's baby blue shirt.

He grunted as he kept her from falling with his body and then steadied her with his hands on her waist. Pure horror mingled with humiliation inside her, making her pulse positively panicked now.

"I'm sorry," she said as Daddy took his unscathed cup of ice cream as if she hadn't just thrown herself into Spencer's arms and ruined his shirt. "I thought you said he was my replacement."

"I did." Daddy licked his spoon, too much enjoyment in his eyes for what had just happened.

In complete disbelief, Clarissa managed to step back, and Spencer's hands dropped from her body. She stared at the horrible chocolate stain on his chest. He did too, finally lifting those glittering eyes to hers.

Then he started laughing.

2

---

*S*pencer Rust accepted the invitation to clean up in the kitchen sink. As he scrubbed at his shirt, he listened to Clarissa talk in rapid-fire words to her daddy about the tiles in this shop and how they needed to be replaced.

He finally tossed the rag into the sink. The shirt was ruined anyway. He sighed as he looked up to the ceiling. "What am I doin' here?"

He didn't have a good answer, other than he didn't want to be at Hope Eternal Ranch anymore. His hope *had* been eternal, and he still hadn't found someone to spend his life with.

He had healed, though, to the point where he actually wanted a relationship that lasted longer than a few months. The problem was, every time he tried, he ended up left in the dust.

Women always chose someone else over him. Always.

So he'd put out some interest in a new job at a new ranch. He'd been working at Hope Eternal for thirteen years, and he had the chops to handle almost anything.

He left the kitchen and came face-to-face with Clarissa Cooper. *Almost* anything.

He wasn't prepared for this woman, and he should've been. He knew he might see her here, but he'd heard through the grapevine that she'd taken a job in San Antonio.

"I'm really sorry about your shirt," she said through nearly clenched teeth. "Please do send the cleaning bill to the farm."

"It's fine," he said. "I'll just throw it away."

"All right," Clarissa's father, Wayne, said from the door. He opened it, setting the bell to dinging. "You two have fun tonight."

"What?" Spencer and Clarissa asked at the same time. She spun toward her father, and Wayne simply grinned.

"I thought you were going to show me around," Spencer said. He'd come for the weekend to learn the ropes, and come Monday, he was moving into a small house here that he still hadn't seen.

"I said you'd get shown around," Wayne said. "You're going to be taking Rissa's place, and she's the expert. She'll get you up to speed by Monday." With that, he tipped his hat and walked out.

"Daddy," Clarissa said, running across the shop after him. She yanked the door open. "I'm busy tonight."

Wayne called something back to her, and her shoulders drooped. She hung onto the door for another few seconds, and then she closed it and pressed her forehead against the red-painted wood.

Spencer wanted to tell her she didn't have to show him around. It was a dairy farm. How hard could it be? "Listen," he said. "I'm starving, and I'll just go grab something and get out of your hair."

She drew in a breath and turned back to him, displeasure sparking in those dark green eyes that he'd once seen drift closed just before he kissed her.

Ten years ago, he told himself.

"Do you know how to make cheese, Spencer?"

"No, ma'am."

"Ice cream?"

"No, ma'am." Discomfort started to seep into him. He'd thought he'd be working with the cows or in the milking parlor or the milk house. He knew Cooper & Co. did all of their own processing, but he'd had no idea they had a retail store complete with refrigeration units filled with cheese, cream, butter, and milk. All organic, of course.

"Then we have a lot to do in just three days," she said. "Here's how this is going to go." Those eyes flashed dangerously. She reached up and slid the elastic out of her strawberry blonde hair, the long locks falling over her shoulders in waves he wanted to touch. "You're going to *take* me to dinner, and we're going to go over all of your duties here on the farm."

His eyebrows drove toward the sky. "You're going to teach me?"

"I'm going to try to talk some sense into my father." She sighed and shook her head. "But in the meantime, yes. I'm going to teach you."

Spencer narrowed his eyes at her. She didn't want him here, that much was obvious. "Aren't you leaving Cooper and Co.?"

Clarissa raised her chin, almost defying him. "Yes."

"Where are you going?"

"San Antonio."

"Some big wig job at a restaurant, I heard." He cocked his right eyebrow, the question clear.

But Clarissa's façade and bluster fell, and she looked at the ground. "I'm still working on the 'big wig job' part of that."

"I'm sorry, could you repeat that?"

She lifted her eyes to his, and he grinned at her. Slowly, a smile crawled across her face too. "Stop it," she said.

"Stop what?"

"Looking at me."

"So we're going to go to dinner, but I can't look at you?"

"Yes," she said, but she didn't stop looking at—or smiling at—him. She even took a step toward him, and Spencer felt the temperature in the store raise a few degrees. Dozens of memories ran through his mind, all of them with her delicate hand in his, her laugh filling his ears, the touch of her lips against his.

They'd had a good summer together, once.

"Why are you leaving the farm?" he asked.

"Oh, you know," she said, stepping past him and going around to the other side of the counter. "First lesson, the store has to be cleaned and left precisely how you want it the following day. You won't have time to do it before you open."

"I *don't* know," he said, putting his elbows on top of the ice cream case and leaning into them. "Tell me."

Clarissa looked up from the chore of wiping the counter where she scooped. Her eyes held fear and hope at the same time, and it sent Spencer's male side into overdrive.

"I'm leaving," she said slowly. "Because it feels like I'm never going to get what I want here."

"Mm," Spencer said, connecting to her in a whole new way. "I know what that feels like."

"Do you?"

"Yep." He smiled at her, and a blush crept into her cheeks, accentuating her beauty and making a few freckles stand out. "What is it that you want, Clarissa?"

3

———————

Clarissa couldn't believe the audacity of the man standing in front of her. At the same time, Spencer had always been a sweet guy. He'd encouraged her to apply to culinary school, claiming they could continue their relationship from a distance easily.

When she'd been accepted, she'd fully intended to do that—until he'd said, *I never expected you to get in.*

In all honesty, she'd used that single sentence to spur her on during difficult semesters. She was going to show Spencer Rust—she was going to show the world—that she'd not only gotten into the best culinary institute in the country, she was the best one in her class.

"What I've always wanted," she said quietly. "I told you once." Her pulse pounded, because the things she hadn't gotten yet made her anxious and upset.

"Husband," he said, holding up one finger. A second one popped up beside it. "Family."

It was amazing how two words could hold so much information and be so devastating.

She nodded, swallowing. "I can't keep doing the same things I've always done and expect different results. So I'm going to San Antonio. I have résumés out with several restaurants, and I have enough money to live there for a month or two before I must have a job."

Spencer nodded. "That's why I left Hope Eternal too."

"To do something different?"

He shrugged one shoulder. "I want something different. So yes."

"What do you want?" she asked.

He held up that one finger again. "Wife." Another finger. "Family."

Clarissa dang near swooned on the spot. She swallowed and picked up her washcloth again. "You didn't want those things last time." It had been a wedge between them, actually.

"I'm not the same person I was ten years ago," he said.

No, he wasn't. He was more confident. Better-looking. Sporting bigger muscles. His eyes still glinted with desire when he looked at her, and the electric zing he'd always produced in her zipped through her bloodstream.

"Let's go over the cleaning procedures," she said. Cleaning always kept her mind busy, and she couldn't be thinking about Spencer...electrically right now. "Then inventory, and then care of the kitchen. Then we can go to dinner."

He nodded and said, "Okay," but he stayed on the opposite side of the case.

"Over here, cowboy," she said with what she hoped was a flirty smile. "You're about to get a crash course in how to run the entire Cooper and Co. retail operation."

LATER THAT NIGHT, Clarissa sat on her front steps with the binder she'd thrown together laying open on her lap. The sound of tires crunching over gravel met her ears, and she looked up to find Spencer pulling up in a white truck that had seen better days.

She closed the binder and got to her feet. She'd given him a firehose of information this afternoon, and he'd taken it all like a champ.

He slid from the truck, now wearing a dark blue shirt with tiny white boxes to make a tight plaid pattern, a pair of jeans, and those sexy cowboy boots. He scanned her from head to toe as she stepped onto the sidewalk in front of her house. "You look amazing," he said, still approaching.

"Thanks. You don't look too bad yourself."

He chuckled and paused a few feet from her, his expression open, that hint of heat in his eyes screaming at her to allow herself to get burned. "Do you mean that?"

When she realized she'd used the words that had been part of their past, her face warmed. In their previous relationship, when one of them said the other didn't "look bad," it really meant they looked absolutely amazing.

"Yes," she said, the word nearly choking her. She thrust the binder toward him. "I made this for you."

He held her gaze, that sexy eyebrow cocking again. "I thought you were going to spend the last hour trying to talk your daddy out of hiring me."

"I decided it was too much work," she said, keeping her voice casual. "Daddy does what he wants anyway."

Spencer burst out laughing. "Must be a family trait," he said as he flipped open the binder.

"It's a lot," she said, suddenly nervous for him to look at what she'd put inside.

"Did you do this tonight?" He looked at her, surprise in those coffee-colored eyes.

"No," she said with a scoff. "I can't believe you've forgotten about my affinity for checklists." She was flirting openly now, and if he didn't know it, when Clarissa linked her arm through his, he surely did.

He snapped the binder closed and bent that cowboy-hatted head toward her. "I haven't forgotten anything about you."

"Is that a pick-up line?" Clarissa giggled, mildly horrified at the sound. She wasn't the twenty-something she'd been when she'd first met Spencer.

"Depends on how well it worked," he said.

"It was pretty smooth," she said, grinning up at him. She'd been prepared to keep her distance from him, spend the weekend arguing with Daddy, and then packing her car on Monday morning for the drive to the city.

But that charge between her and Spencer couldn't be denied, and Clarissa really had no say in what her father did at the dairy farm. Her opinion didn't come second, third, fourth, or even fifth. Those spots belonged to her older brothers. Even Cherry, the oldest Cooper heir, would have more say than Clarissa, the youngest. While no one wanted her to leave Cooper & Co., Clarissa had spoken the truth earlier.

She needed a change.

Maybe Spencer is the change you need, she thought. *Maybe the chance you need to take isn't in San Antonio, but right here in Sweet Water Falls.*

"Tell me what else you remember," she said. "Then I'll know if you were lying or not."

He walked with her toward his truck. "I remember you love deep-dish pepperoni pizza."

"Guilty," she said with a laugh.

"I remember you looking up into the night sky and making a wish on all the pricks of light, even the planets."

Clarissa smiled, that memory as clear in her mind as if it had happened last night. "I love the stars and planets and heavens."

"I remember the conversation that night being real serious," he added, the moment turning just as sober. "I remember how sad you were that your grandmother had died, and I remember you saying now she was up in the stars, watching over you."

He reached past her to open the passenger door, but he slid his hand into hers as she lowered her arm from the crook of his elbow. The strength in his grip made her pause, and she looked up at him.

Mistake, her mind screamed at her. In a tender moment like this, with his eyes sparking with attraction like that...

Clarissa was in serious trouble.

"I remember you being an amazing kisser," he whispered, lowering his head toward hers. He paused only a few inches away, giving her a chance to deny him.

She didn't.

In fact, she reached up with her free hand and ran her fingers along the side of his face, guiding his mouth straight to hers. Her heartbeat stayed in a nice, steady rhythm, because kissing Spencer Rust had always felt like the most natural thing in the world. It felt like coming home.

It felt like exactly the risk she needed to take to get what she'd always wanted.

4

———————

Spencer couldn't believe what he was doing, but an old flame had been reignited the moment he'd entered the same space as Clarissa. He pulled away first, his heart booming in his chest, and his fingers tingling slightly from the chemistry in that kiss.

Clarissa ducked her head so he couldn't see her face, and when she asked, "How was the cottage?" all the tension between them broke.

"Good," he said. "Real nice." Nice enough, at least. He shared a house with three other men right now, so having a place all to himself actually felt a little like heaven. "Clean. I laid on the bed. It was comfortable."

"Good." Clarissa looked up then, a smile on her face and reflecting in her eyes. "You're not going to be seeing much of that bed, I'm afraid. We have *so* much to do before you take over."

They did, but Spencer wasn't worried about it. He was a quick study, and with the pretty blonde at his side, even a long day wouldn't feel like it.

When they arrived at the restaurant, he got out and walked around to get Clarissa, who held the binder in her hands. "This is a working dinner, Spence."

"Mm," he said, not overly thrilled that they couldn't even share a meal together without talking about Cooper & Co. In the end, he didn't mind, because Clarissa had a melodic voice he really liked listening to.

"You won't have to do much with the milk production," she told him over dessert—which they'd ordered first. Clarissa always wanted dessert first, and he *had* forgotten that about her.

He spooned warm apple pie and vanilla ice cream into his mouth while she detailed how the parlor boss would bring the milk to the store. They'd bring the butter too, and the cream, and the cheese curds.

If the farm wanted to keep offering specialty cheeses, Spencer would have to make those. Same with the ice cream.

He started to panic until she flipped to the recipe section and pointed.

Spencer could admit to not tasting much of his dinner, and he was so overwhelmed that when he dropped Clarissa off at her house, he walked away without kissing her.

"Wait," he said, jogging back up her steps. "Tomorrow. Me and you in the kitchen. We're going over cheese and ice cream?"

"Yes." She patted his chest. "After the farm chores."

"And I'm meeting you by the chicken coops at seven."

"Yep."

Spencer took a deep breath, getting some fresh Texas air that was somehow different here than on the ranch he'd come from, though they only sat ten miles apart. He also smelled a hint of orange and a bit of vanilla, and he knew those came from Clarissa.

"Okay," he said, leaning down and touching his mouth to hers again. This kiss sent a rumble through his veins, and he grinned the whole way back to his new cabin-slash-cottage.

The next morning, he went through Clarissa's farm chores with her. These he could do in his sleep, and he was able to ask her where Cherry, her sister, had ended up.

"She's a counselor over veterinarian technicians at SATC."

"Wow," Spencer said. "So she'll be in the city."

"Yes," Clarissa said in a tone that told him she really didn't want to talk about her sister. He switched the topic to something else, and they ended up in the kitchen an hour earlier than she'd said they would, thanks to his help with her chores.

"Okay," she said like they were about to go into battle. "Homemade pimento cheese." She set a huge bowl on the counter in front of them, another binder with all the cheese recipes nearby. "It's not as hard as you might think. You just need to—oh." She cut off as her phone rang. Her eyes widened, and she reached for it quickly, a squeal coming from her mouth.

"Oh, stars above," she said, looking from the phone to him. Her excitement rode on the air, making his pulse quicken. "It's Marco Holmbrook."

"Should I know who that is?"

Clarissa squealed again and swiped on the call, her voice much calmer and at least half an octave lower as she said, "This is Clarissa Cooper." She turned her back on Spencer and hurried out of the kitchen.

"No big deal," he said, looking at the swinging plastic door. "She's just super excited to talk to another man...in private." A sigh accompanied the words, and he wasn't sure how he'd fallen right down the rabbit hole with Clarissa all over again, and oh-so-fast too.

She felt like part of his system—a part that had been missing and he hadn't known it. He pushed against those feelings, because they were dangerous, and they'd only open his chest for her to rip his heart out piece by brutal piece.

He focused on the binder, trying to find the thing he "just needed" to do to make delicious pimento cheese. She'd said she was going to show him how to make spreadable cheese loaves as one skill, and then she was also literally going to take milk and make it into cheese as a second task he'd need to master.

She said if he could learn both, he could make the cheese the store at Cooper & Co. had been selling for years.

The words in the binder read like Greek though, and when Clarissa came crashing through the door a moment later, his concentration broke.

"You're not going to believe what just happened." She danced over to him, her entire being lit from within. "That was Marco Holmbrook, and he owns the best Italian eatery in San Antonio." She giggled, the sound morphing into a full laugh a moment later. He also couldn't help the smile that stretched across his face. Her joy was just so palpable, and he was glad to be near it.

"Guess who has an interview with him on Thursday?"

Spencer's heart fell all the way to the tips of his boots. He somehow cemented his smile in place though. "You do," he said, his voice only sounding slightly froggy.

"Yes!" She threw herself into his arms, and Spencer caught her around the waist. They laughed together, though he definitely saw the door closing on their relationship about as fast as it had reopened.

After all, she was leaving town.

Honestly, he thought. *You knew she was leaving. What did you think would happen?*

5

"Then you just pour it into the machine." Clarissa supervised as Spencer picked up the huge bowl and began pouring it into the industrial ice cream machine. They'd had an amazing day in the kitchen together, and Spencer was just as smart as he'd been in the past.

The spreadable cheeses were easy, and once he'd watched her do the first one, he'd whipped up everything they'd sell in the next couple of days while she ducked out to run up to her house to see if she had anything to wear for a job interview at a high-end restaurant.

While she'd laid outfits out on her bed, Spencer had texted her flirty things like, *Just think you're really grate*, and *You're the macaroni to my cheese.*

Clarissa couldn't stop smiling, but a war had started inside her. She'd been planning her exodus from the Coastal Bend of Texas for months. She couldn't stomach the thought of making flavored, spreadable cheeses for the rest of her life. The Hot Italian was *the* premiere restaurant in San Antonio's river district.

But with Spencer's texts on her mind, she'd turned away from her bed without picking an interview outfit.

"All right," Spencer said, setting the big bowl in the even bigger sink as Clarissa turned toward him. "How long does that go?" He peered at the binder. "Twelve minutes." Meeting her eyes, he asked, "It only takes twelve minutes?"

"Then it takes six hours in the freezer," she said. "So if you're out of mint brownie in the morning, you're not serving it that day."

He moved his focus back to the binder and studied it. Things hadn't been the same once she'd returned to the kitchen, and she couldn't put her finger on exactly what had shifted.

"Looks like you make ice cream two or three times a week."

"Yes," she said in a bored voice. Clinical. Things had turned *clinical* between them. "Cheese almost every day, and ice cream a few times a week."

"And they bring everything else over from the milk parlor."

"Most things," she said, pushing her hair off her forehead. "We'll do the hard cheese tomorrow."

"Hard cheese," he said, flipping a page. "You do that every day?"

"I usually only make cheese on the days the store is closed," she said. "We could try to squeeze it in tomorrow morning, but Saturdays are usually busy."

Spencer looked up from the binder. "You developed all of these recipes," he said, no question mark in sight.

"Yes."

He looked at her with sparks of interest. "Why are you—?"

"I can't make cheese forever," she said, already hearing his unspoken question. *Why are you leaving the farm? Why isn't running this shop good enough for you?* The questions bounced around in her ears, vibrating from one drum to the other.

"It's *spreadable cheese*, Spencer. I have a culinary degree from the best institute in the country." She looked around the industrial kitchen that glinted with too much silver and always smelled a little too much like warm milk about to go sour. "Do you remember what you said to me when I got accepted to the Culinary Institute of America?"

He hung his head. "How could I forget? You ended everything with me because of what I said." He looked up again, his dark eyes so bright. "I apologize for saying I didn't think you'd get in. Really, Clarissa." He tapped the binder but kept his gaze on her. "*You* came up with all of these recipes. *You* are an amazing chef."

"Thank you," she said, but the unrest in her soul rose within her.

"I'm better than this. I want to do more than make cheese and ice cream on a dairy farm in a Texas town no one's heard of."

Spencer studied her for another moment before resignation and understanding entered his expression. "All right," he drawled, though she suspected he didn't truly understand her need to be more than Sweet Water Falls and Cooper & Co. would ever allow.

She didn't really understand it either.

"Should we try for a cheese-making session in the morning?" he asked, consulting the binder again.

"Yes." With that, the bell on the door out front rang, and Clarissa put her the-customer-is-always-right smile on her face. "Let's go see what we can sell today."

Clarissa's patience literally had two millimeters left before it would snap. She and Spencer had been hard at work for what felt like weeks. She couldn't believe it had only been two days.

She employed every ounce of willpower she had while Spencer finished helping her brother and father with a broken gate. They left, and Spencer dusted his gloved hands together and said, "I'm too old to lift gates like that," with a grin.

She smiled back, and he reached for her hand. Fireworks popped through her bloodstream at his touch, and she sighed up at the summer morning sky.

A storm had rolled through town last night, and the remnants of those clouds hung on the horizon. Mud puddles dotted parts of the path ahead of them, but he steered the two of them around them easily.

"What's on your mind?" she finally asked.

He ducked his head, a slight smile on his face. "You still know when something's bothering me."

"Apparently," she said.

"I think that says something."

"What does it say?"

Spencer lifted his head and slowed his step. "This is going to sound crazy, but..." He dropped her hand and continued over to a fence that separated the path from an empty pasture. "I don't want you to go to San Antonio."

Clarissa's chest turned cold, and surely every beat of her heart would crack her now frozen and brittle ribs. "I—"

What was an appropriate answer to a statement like that?

He turned back to face her, his dark eyes as stormy as the sky had been last night. Clarissa watched the unrest move through his expression, feeling it fill her soul too.

"Maybe we need to take a chance," he said. "A leap of faith." Desperate hope filled his face now. "Maybe this is our second chance to find what we both want."

Clarissa didn't know what to say, but "It's been two days," came out of her mouth.

The thunder struck, and all of Spencer's features hardened. "Okay, got it." He started back the way they'd been walking, his stride much longer and faster now.

"Spencer," she called after him.

"Go," he said over his shoulder. "It's fine. Go home and pack. I've got the shop today."

Clarissa wanted to argue, but he *was* supposed to run the shop solo for a little while that day. She watched him walk away from her, the indecision inside her holding her right where she stood.

"What should I do?" she asked the fenceposts, the blue sky, and the Lord above.

None of them answered her.

6

———————

oolishness and Spencer Rust were great friends. They spent so much time together that he knew instantly when he'd done or said something he shouldn't have.

"Shouldn't have said anything about her leaving town," he muttered to himself as he stared at the ceiling on Monday morning. The sun hadn't quite started to light the day, and his alarm hadn't gone off. "Just like you shouldn't have kissed her. Shouldn't have taken her to dinner. Shouldn't have started talking to her and flirting with her and thinking you might have a future with Clarissa Cooper."

His alarm rang, and he reached over to silence it. With a sigh, he swung his legs over the edge of the bed, wishing he had a dog to keep him company in this new, strange house. It wasn't quite a cabin, but it wasn't the cottage Clarissa had called it either.

They'd had a few great days together. That didn't mean they'd fallen in love, though Spencer had a good feeling about Clarissa this time. He'd spent a lot of time over the past three days thinking about their last attempt at a relationship.

He'd been far younger then and completely incapable of having a real, committed relationship with a woman. He was ready now. He thought she was too. He wanted them to at least *try*, and if he hadn't said anything, maybe they could've at least had a long-distance relationship where they flirted over chats and texts and he got to see her on weekends when she came back to the farm.

Foolishness accompanied him through his shower, through getting dressed, drinking coffee, and making the ten-minute walk from his house to the two-story farmhouse that stood tall and proud in the middle of the Coopers' property.

Clarissa bent over the trunk of her car, with at least half a dozen boxes on the ground next to her. "There's no way you're getting all of that in your car," he said, and foolishness flooded him again.

Clarissa gasped and spun toward him, her eyes wide. "Oh...Spencer."

"Sorry," he said, still walking toward her. He saw the full back seat and the depth of the trunk, and he'd definitely spoken true.

"Daddy's going to bring some stuff," she said. "I'm just deciding what I have to have right now and what I can leave."

Spencer looked toward the house, but he didn't see her father or any of her brothers. His heart pounded, but he had to take the risk. He'd never gotten anywhere by sitting quietly on the sidelines.

"Some of this is going back inside," she said, toeing the nearest box. "Maybe you could use some of those pretty muscles to haul it away?" She grinned at him in a flirty way that fed Spencer's bravery.

Instead of bending to pick up a box, he closed the distance between him and Clarissa, took her face in his hands, and kissed her. He poured absolutely everything into each stroke, almost desperate for her to feel what he'd felt these past few days.

"Don't go," he whispered, his lips catching against hers he lingered so close. He pulled away fully and met her eye. "Give us a chance. Let's just take a chance."

Clarissa at least had the decency to wear an apologetic look, and Spencer backed up fast. She didn't even have to say a word for him to know what was on her mind, and he dropped his chin to his chest so he could use his cowboy hat to hide his humiliation.

Without another word, he bent, picked up one of her boxes, and went inside the farmhouse.

Thirty minutes later, she clung to her father while Spencer watched from the corner of the farmhouse. He didn't need to say good-bye—that kiss had said everything.

And it still wasn't good enough. *He* still wasn't good enough to get a woman to choose him over something else. He'd never lost to a job, though. He'd reached a new low in his life.

A dairy farm didn't care about his personal life, and he still had chickens to feed and stalls to shovel out. He needed to make all the spreadable cheeses that morning too, and as he went about his tasks, he could hear Clarissa's sweet voice accompanying him every step of the way.

Women had affected him like this at Hope Eternal Ranch too, and he really just wanted to get in his truck and drive until he crossed the Texas state line.

Instead, he finished his chores and stepped into the Cooper & Co. Shoppe—which screamed Clarissa to him, right down to the hand-lettered menu board behind the ice cream counter.

"You tried," he said to the empty shop. He was proud of himself for that, and he wasn't going to hang his head because a three-day second chance hadn't turned out to be as much as he'd hoped it would be. He just wished his heart wouldn't hurt quite so much and that the negative voices in his head weren't quite so loud.

7
—————

Clarissa packed her bag, her heart thumping heavily in her chest. The time for her interview drew ever closer, but she couldn't stay in this hotel for another night. It cost far too much, and she really needed to find an apartment or a house. Heck, she'd take a private bedroom in someone's basement.

Daddy had asked her for her address last night, and Clarissa had put him off by bringing up Spencer. Daddy gushed and gushed about the man, and Clarissa had laid on the bed with her phone on speaker as it sat on her chest.

She still didn't know if she'd made a mistake or not. She knew Spencer had awakened something inside her that had been missing all these years.

As she stuffed her hair dryer into her suitcase, she frowned. "Why couldn't he have shown up a year ago?" Why did everything seem to happen when she least expected it?

With everything finally zipped up, she headed out the door. She didn't have another hotel for that night, but she could only tackle one problem at a time.

"Interview first," she muttered to herself as she got on the elevator. "Hotel second."

And Spencer? The voice in her head had been plaguing her for four days now, and all it seemed to be able to say was *Spencer, Spencer, Spencer. When are you going to deal with Spencer?*

She didn't know how to deal with him. So she'd felt the earth move when he'd kissed her on Monday morning. It didn't mean she should change her plans to see if they could make a real relationship work this time around.

Take a chance, he'd said. Wasn't that what she was doing right here in San Antonio?

Frustration filled her as she towed her rolling suitcase behind her and out to the valet. She *was* taking a chance right now, but it was on her career. Not on getting the two things she'd once told Spencer mattered more to her than anything else.

A job at a restaurant wouldn't make her a wife or a mother.

As she drove over to The Hot Italian for her interview, another battle began in her brain. "Focus," she told herself as she got out of her car and tugged on the bottom of her crisp, white blouse. She put that fake smile on her face and squared her shoulders. This job was as good as hers.

~

A WEEK LATER, Clarissa was still living out of a half-packed suitcase, in a seedy motel on the outer ring of downtown San Antonio. She hadn't heard back from Marco yet, and at this point, she knew she wouldn't.

She'd put out at least fifteen more applications at various restaurants all over the city, and it seemed no one wanted to hire a woman with dark green eyes and strawberry blonde hair, whose only culinary experience was making spreadable cheese and ice cream for their family farm. She didn't want to call her father and admit defeat, but he'd asked again where he should bring her boxes. He wanted to come see where she lived and where she worked, and her desperation had reached a new high.

In moments like these, she thought about calling Cherry and asking if she could sleep on her sister's couch for a night or two. A week, tops.

If she did that, though, Cherry would call Daddy, and the cat would be out of the bag. Clarissa would have to admit to things she didn't want to acknowledge, and she gritted her teeth to prevent herself from calling her sister.

"Is this your way of saying I should just go home?" she asked, folding her legs underneath her body as she curled into the tiny armchair in the corner of her hotel room and looking up toward heaven. The space held the slight tang of chlorine, as her room sat right next to the pool, but it had provided her with a place to sleep with a door that locked.

She sighed and looked at the TV she'd turned on, some cooking show flickering on the screen. "We're back with Gray Bell, and he's here to show us how to make his momma's Southern pimento cheese."

Clarissa found herself getting to her feet, her eyes stuck to the TV now. A tall man wearing a cowboy hat filled the screen, and everyone in Texas knew Gray Bell, the country music star.

And he was making a flavored, spreadable cheese like it was the greatest thing that had ever happened to him. A family recipe, no less.

"I've made a huge mistake," she said as the heavens opened above her, flooding her mind and heart with light. "I have to get back to Sweet Water Falls."

She had to return to Sweet Water Falls *right now*.

THREE HOURS LATER, Clarissa had cried, stopped to fix up her face and buy a soda with a lot of caffeine, and practiced her speech at least a dozen times.

Her sedan bumped over the dirt road that led to the cottage on the dairy farm. Spencer's truck sat in the driveway, and Clarissa's pulse went wild.

She drew in a deep breath and pressed her palms together. She only needed to do one thing at a time, and the first item was to get out of the car. After managing that, she looked toward the porch only to find Spencer already standing there.

She froze as their eyes met across the distance. With her pulse booming in her ears, she practically yelled, "I made a mistake. I want to take the leap of faith."

He came down the steps, his cowboy boots making plenty of noise on the wood. "You don't have to yell, sweetheart. I'm right here." He smiled at her, and that only caused tears to prick her eyes.

He was so sweet, and so good. "I'm sorry," she said, still unable to move toward him. "Maybe it's too late. Maybe you've already found someone else to take to dinner and send cheese puns to. I don't know." She swallowed, her throat so dry. "I just know that there's no shame in making spreadable cheeses and ice cream."

"No, there is not," he said, still coming toward her, that perfect cowboy hat perched on his head.

"I also know that I'm not supposed to be in San Antonio," she said. "And while I'm kind of mad at the Lord for re-introducing you into my life at a most inconvenient time, maybe it's those times when you least expect to find your soulmate that you find them."

"Soulmate?" Spencer asked, his voice half the volume of hers as he reached her and slid his hands up her arms.

"Potentially," she whispered. "That's what I want, Spencer. Not just a husband. A soulmate. Maybe it's you, and I don't want to throw away this chance without knowing."

"Then let's find out," he said, leaning down and pausing only a breath away from her. "Just so I'm clear, you're choosing to come back here, right? Permanently?"

She grinned and wrapped her hands around the back of his neck. "That's right, cowboy. See, I saw Gray Bell making pimento cheese on TV, and it was his momma's recipe. And I thought, oh my word, I'm not above making spreadable cheeses. What if one of my sons is a famous country music star, and he's on TV one day, making one of my recipes?"

Spencer's eyes softened. "Can't have a famous country music star son without a hot cowboy husband."

Clarissa wondered how he always knew exactly what to say to heal her heart. She laughed with him and then pressed her forehead to his. "I'm sorry, Spencer. Can we try again?"

"I'm not sure if I just lost my job or got myself a girlfriend," he said, and he closed the gap between them. He kissed her like he'd gladly be unemployed as long as he got to see her and kiss her every day.

He pulled away too soon, and she pressed her cheek against his. "You're choosing *me*, right, Clarissa?"

"Yes, Spencer. I'm choosing you."

He smiled, the movement in his mouth subtle against her face. "I'm choosing you too," he whispered, and then he kissed her again.

EPILOGUE

TWO MONTHS LATER

Spencer whipped the cream while Clarissa poured the sugar into the pot he'd set over low heat. Watching it dissolve brought him such satisfaction, much like watching his girlfriend lean over her notes for a new recipe.

"Last time," she mused, studying the page. "We put in two teaspoons of maple extract, and it was far too much."

"We should try syrup."

"I'm worried it'll turn back into a congealed mess." She straightened and looked at him. He smiled at her and shrugged, because he was just the sounding board. He'd mentioned syrup before, and she'd noted it.

"Let's try it," she said, lifting a bottle of amber liquid from beneath the counter, a teasing glint in her pretty eyes.

He left the whisk in the pot and took her into his arms. "You're sneaky." He swayed with her, a sense of love and peace enveloping them.

"You're smart," she said. "And sexy stirring that ice cream base."

"You should see yourself bending over that binder." He leaned down and kissed her, thinking about the diamond he'd hidden in the drawer next to the sink. Maybe he could be sneaky too. He knew for certain he was happier now than he'd ever been, all because he'd taken a risk and embraced this unexpected relationship.

"Talk about smart and sexy." He grinned at her and went back to the ice cream, the diamond engagement ring on his mind. She'd just pulled out that syrup bottle, her message clear. She listened to him. His opinion mattered to her.

He walked over to the sink and turned on the water, his heart pounding. He opened the drawer and took out the black box. He cracked it open, turning toward the woman he loved, his voice suddenly on vacation.

"I think if we—" Clarissa stopped talking as she lifted her widening eyes to Spencer and that ring.

"I love you," he said. "Will you do me the great honor of becoming my wife?"

Clarissa blinked, her smile slow as it filled her face. She nodded, her eyes glassy. "Yes," she finally said, squealing immediately afterward. "Yes, I'll marry you."

He laughed as she threw herself into his arms. "I love you too, Spence," Clarissa said, and Spencer let his fiancée kiss him.

THE END

ABOUT THE AUTHOR

Three-time USA Today bestselling author Elana Johnson writes clean and sweet contemporary romance and romantic suspense. She is the author of more than 130 books across three names, and she believes there's nothing better than sun, sand, and swoon-worthy kisses. Unless it's a sweet-and-sexy cowboy—read those under her pen name of Liz Isaacson, who is a Top 20 Kindle Unlimited All-Star. Or an emotional, heartfelt women's fiction novel—read those under her pen name of Jessie Newton. Find out more and get Clarissa's inspired recipe for her homemade pimento cheese at www.elanajohnson.com/risky!

www.ingramcontent.com/pod-product-compliance
Lightning Source LLC
Chambersburg PA
CBHW070808190726
48292CB00006B/1927